The Bells of Scotland Road

Ruth Hamilton is the bestselling author of twenty-five novels, including *Mulligan's Yard*, *Dorothy's War*, *The Judge's Daughter*, *The Reading Room*, *Mersey View* and *That Liverpool Girl*. She has become one of the northwest of England's most popular writers. She was born in Bolton, which is the setting for many of her novels. She now lives in Liverpool.

Also by Ruth Hamilton

A Whisper to the Living
With Love from Ma Maguire
Nest of Sorrows
Billy London's Girls
Spinning Jenny
The September Starlings
A Crooked Mile
Paradise Lane
The Dream Sellers
The Corner House
Miss Honoria West
Mulligan's Yard
Saturday's Child
Matthew & Son
Chandlers Green
The Bell House
Dorothy's War
The Judge's Daughter
The Reading Room
A Parallel Life
Mersey View
Sugar and Spice
That Liverpool Girl
Lights of Liverpool

Ruth Hamilton

The Bells of Scotland Road

PAN BOOKS

First published in Great Britain 1997 by Bantam Press,
a division of Transworld Publishers

This edition published 2012 by Pan Books
an imprint of Pan Macmillan, a division of Macmillan Publishers Limited
Pan Macmillan, 20 New Wharf Road, London N1 9RR
Basingstoke and Oxford
Associated companies throughout the world
www.panmacmillan.com

ISBN 978-1-4472-0946-1

Typeset by SetSystems Ltd, Saffron Walden, Essex
Printed and bound by CPI Group (UK) Ltd, Croydon, CR0 4YY

Visit **www.panmacmillan.com** to read more about all our books
and to buy them. You will also find features, author interviews and
news of any author events, and you can sign up for e-newsletters
so that you're always first to hear about our new releases.

For Maureen Buckels

ACKNOWLEDGEMENTS

For their help, cups of tea and many kindnesses, I thank the following:

Mr Billy Holden of Kirkby
Mr Don Carroll of Bootle
Ms Sue Bose of Lydiate
Mr M. Moran of Bootle
Mrs Elizabeth Bamber of Retford, Nottinghamshire
Mr Charles Rouane of Walton
Mrs Terri Nairn of Runcorn
Mrs Anne Burton of Bootle
Mrs Veronica Coppin of Runcorn
Mrs M. Kirkland of Halewood
Mrs Eillen Airnsworth of West Derby
Mrs Dora McClelland of Kirkby
Mr Terry 'Mac' of Croxteth Park
Mr F. J. Till of Freshfield
Mrs Julia Banks of Norris Green
Mr and Mrs George of Runcorn
Mr Billy Furlong of Liverpool 11
Mrs Josie Murray of Huyton
Mr and Mrs Adlam of Croxteth
Mr and Mrs Tom Atherton of Toxteth
Mr and Mrs John Nelson of Melling
Mrs Bella Moran, address unknown, of Liverpool

Mr Terence Baines of Kirkby, whose story 'Me Poor Mam' and rentbooks from 1908 to the 1950s (Kennedy and Baines families, Dryden Street) have been in my possession for twelve months. It was a pleasure and a privilege to read his work and to handle these special documents.

A very special thankyou to Eileen Weir of Crosby, who visited many of the above on my particularly agoraphobic days.

Many thanks to my cousin, Cavan Sexton and his wife, Hazel, of Abbots Ann, Andover, Hampshire. Their very professional knowledge and understanding of horse racing proved extremely valuable.

I must apologize to T. Walls, owner and trainer, also to F. Lane, jockey. These two people were involved with the actual winner of the 1932 Derby. I beg pardon, too, of April the Fifth, the grand horse who did all the really hard work.

AUTHOR'S NOTE

Scotland Road is a real place. A few buildings remain, widely spaced like remnants in a lower jaw after brutal dentistry. There are not many houses, yet the pubs were packed on the afternoons when I visited the road. I wondered where all those people had come from. Do they make a daily pilgrimage back to the old neighbourhood?

Although I have adhered to some street names, the parish of St Aloysius Gonzaga is a figment of my imagination. I decided not to use actual churches as I wished not to offend members of existing religious communities. St Aloysius was the patron of my house at school, so I chose him as a good man who would not mind if I pinched his name.

After attending mass at St Anthony's on Scotland Road, I have to say that I have never seen a more beautiful church. Like a miniature cathedral, it is perfectly maintained by a proud congregation whose friendliness and openness were much appreciated.

As a result of my advertisement in the *Liverpool Echo*, I met many ex-residents of Scotland Road. Eileen Weir (my researcher – thanks, Eileen) and I were privileged to meet a number of people whose roots were torn up by the clearances. We talked to teachers, tradespeople, men from the Merchant and Royal Navies, soldiers, social workers and many more. All of these had received their education in the excellent schools around Scotland Road.

These days, we hear and read much about deprivation. Socio-economic factors are cited repeatedly as the guilty parties when people take a wrong turning in life. Scotland Road suffered a poverty that has been stamped out, thank God. Yet out of that happy squalor emerged successful and law-abiding citizens whose standard of education is superb. Their eyes light up, sometimes with pleasure and often with tears, when they talk about their beginnings.

I am not a Scouser, though I have lived in and around Liverpool for more than half my life. This, my ninth book, is the first based in the city I have come to love. It has been a pleasure to meet and correspond with such wonderful, vibrant men and women, to hear about the wash-houses, Scouse Alley, Paddy's Market, the Scaldy where children swam, the Mary Ellens with their baskets of fruit, the penny dip, cherry-wobs, molasses taken from a moving cart, Lascars balancing six bowlers on their heads while carrying a fireplace and several wind-up gramophones back to their ship.

While writing *The Bells*, I have laughed and cried. As a 'foreigner', I can only do my best to depict an area in which I never lived. Forgive my mistakes as I try to portray a way of life in which family was all.

Ruth Hamilton, Crosby, Liverpool

May 1941

She passed the church of St Aloysius Gonzaga and moved north along Scotland Road, heart beating like a sledgehammer, feet weighted by fear, her whole body slowed as if she had entered a nightmare.

This was no dream, though. This was not the work of the eventide goblins whose task seemed to be to trigger a tormented mind into further terrors. Liverpool was burning. Cables from a barrage balloon had claimed an already crippled and falling Heinkel, had sent it crashing and roaring into the Mersey. Other invaders were taking advantage of the doomed craft's colourful death throes. Using light provided by the exploded bomber, a huge force homed in on the port of Liverpool and vomited weighty loads onto cranes, ships, trains and buildings. While the bombers did the biggest damage, cheeky fighters dived to strafe the biggest port in England. Tonight, Liverpool might die. To the woman's left, the docklands breathed fire into a heaving sky, long tongues of orange flame whose exhalations plumed before disappearing into dense, oily smoke.

She stopped to ease a stitch in her side, raised her eyes, saw the parachute. At its base, a landmine floated almost gracefully towards the ground. 'Jesus, Mary and Joseph,' she muttered. 'I'll give him up, I will, I will. Let my innocent daughter survive this night, then I'll see him no more.' How many times had she promised God and herself that she would put an end to her relationship? The Almighty had probably covered His ears against all Bridie Bell's lies.

Bombs crashed into warehouses; incendiaries landed on roofs and in the middle of the road. Somewhere, a gas main exploded and shook the foundations of every structure in the neighbourhood. Beneath her feet, the ground trembled, sending its ague right through to her soul. She wept, not only for herself and for her endangered child. She cried also for the city she had hated and grown to love, for the community in whose robust heart she had been sheltered for more than ten years.

The parachute mine landed in a side street, blew wide open and threw her against a wall. The draught created by its blast stretched the skin of her face until she felt it would surely burst at any second. Heat seared her lungs, forbade her to breathe. Was this to be her punishment, then? Oh yes, yes, she would go gladly into the next world if only Shauna could survive. Aunt Edith might relent, might take pity on a motherless child. But Aunt Edith disliked Shauna with a passion and ... and ...

Tainted air invaded her chest at last, and she coughed until the contents of her stomach were evacuated. She was going to live. The only other punishment that fitted her crime was ... no! The good Lord would surely leave Shauna off His list tonight? He would not take a fourteen-year-old child just because her mother was worthless ...

A warden grabbed her arm. 'Mrs Bell? What the hell are you doing stood out here? This isn't a bloody fireworks show.'

She stared at him, past him and into a crater between two rows of shattered houses in what used to be a street. 'Diddy was right, you know,' she managed. 'This place will disappear altogether, no houses, no shops. And the Germans are helping the corporation and the government, aren't they?'

He scratched his head and tutted impatiently. 'We've no

time for hanging round here jangling about politics, love. There's a war on, you know.'

She turned and looked at the steel-helmeted man. His face changed colour as various lights danced across his skin. 'They want rid of Scotland Road. Big Diddy has always said that. By fair means or foul, the community will be broken up.'

The warden's tongue clicked again. 'They've not started a war just to knock your houses down, girl. There's a bit more to it than that. London's getting it as well as us.'

'All the same, it's another excuse for the government to . . .' Bridie Bell pulled herself together. 'Ah well,' she sighed. 'I'll get back to the shop.'

The man pondered for a moment. 'Have you been injured?' he asked. Perhaps something had hit her on the head . . . No. She had always been a great ponderer, this one. She was usually worrying about something or other. 'You all right now?' he asked.

'Yes.' She would not tell him about the figure that lurked around the corner. Wardens had enough to do without chasing a shadow, a spectre that had reappeared as if by magic after an absence that spanned a decade.

'Come on, then. Let's get you in a shelter. The buggers up there mean business this time.'

She shook her head, felt grit pouring from her hair and down her face. 'I'll go with Shauna. She's in the Morrison under my table.'

The man frowned. 'There's a few been flattened in them indoor contraptions.'

'And a few in the public shelters, too,' she reminded him. 'Did you pass our shop?'

He nodded, lifted his voice against a new wave of bombers. 'Bell's Pledges is still there. Come on, let's have you home, queen.'

3

She allowed herself to be dragged along until she reached the place in which she had lived for eleven years.

As she stretched out beneath the kitchen table between Tildy and Shauna, Bridie mouthed a few words to God. 'This house is no more important than any other,' she advised her Maker. 'But thank You all the same for saving us so far.' She would try to be good.

During a short, dream-ravaged sleep, the man stood before her, long arms outstretched to receive her, laughter lines curling from his eyes until they almost touched that shock of dark, unruly hair. 'Hello,' he whispered. 'Did you miss me, Bridie?'

She would not go to him. Fiercely, she clung to her younger daughter. Shauna must come first. Cathy was fine, she told herself. Cathy was living the life of Riley on a farm in Lancashire. Where Cathy stayed, there were no bombs, no incendiaries, no warehouses to attract the wrath of Germany's airborne armada.

He called to her softly. 'Come here,' he mouthed.

'No. I promised God. For Shauna's sake, I cannot be with you, because we are not married. And we cannot marry. I told God, I told Him that I—'

'Don't bargain with God, Bridget,' the man snapped.

He had changed, yet he remained the same. The eyes were still brown and the hair was black, but laughter lines had shifted to the forehead, had become a deep, accusing frown. 'Go away,' she screamed. 'Go and tend your business.'

'You are my business,' roared the dark-clad enemy.

Bridie woke, heard Shauna weeping. 'You held me too tight, Mammy,' sobbed the girl. 'And the noise is loud. When will it stop? When will the war finish?'

'Ah, there's no-one but God has the answer to that question, my love.' Bridget Bell smoothed her daughter's hair and listened to Tildy Costigan's quiet snores. Tildy-Anne always slept, however bad the raids. When Shauna settled, Bridie

4

plucked at a rosary, counted the decades and begged to be relieved of the terrible weight of her sins. She would see him no more, would love him no more. And poor old Liverpool continued to burn.

One

Bridget O'Brien stepped off an alarmingly unsteady gang-plank and planted grateful feet on firm ground. At last, it was over. Never again would she go willingly within a mile of choppy waters. Even now, the angry waves could be heard among the sounds of a hundred voices, some alien, others as Irish as her own.

For many years, Bridie's compatriots had left home to settle here. The exodus was supposed to be abating, yet the boat had been crammed with emigrants sailing hopefully into the start of a new decade. Hopeful? she wondered. What on earth would she find here in this grim, dark place? No fields, that was certain. No fresh air, no cold, clear water gathered from a sweet mountain stream. This was 1930, and England's northern counties continued to embody the glory and the gloom of industrial revolution.

She inhaled through her mouth to settle the queasiness, wrapped the shawl more firmly round the sleeping Shauna, then gripped the hand of her older daughter. 'We're there, Cathy. And thanks be to God for that, too.' The three-year-old in her arms moaned, sneezed, settled again to sleep. Cathy, her eyes rounded in shock and wonder, clung to her mother's side. This was England. It was dark, smelly and very noisy.

Thomas Murphy was not far behind his daughter and

grandchildren. The trip had been a bad one, even for a seasoned traveller like himself. Two or three times a year he made this voyage in the company of well-bred horse-flesh. The animals, he thought now, were easier company than his daughter had been. She had begun to moan and vomit long before the coast of Ireland had slipped away behind grey curtains of November sleet. 'Come, now, Bridie,' he ordered, pulling her away from the water and across a square of cobbles. 'Sit yourself down on the case till I find the rest of your belongings.' He strode away in search of luggage.

Bridget lowered herself onto the case and took in the sights. Dusk had fallen heavily, was weighted down by black clouds that promised to spill their tears at any moment. Groups of travellers huddled together for comfort, the children crying, the women white-faced with exhaustion. Sailors passed by, canvas bags slung across broad shoulders, skins browned and roughened by sun and saline. Across the rough-hewn surface of New Quay, revellers spilled from a dockside public house to watch two men who fought over some imagined slight. Befuddled by drink, this pair of heroes fell into an untidy and comatose embrace while the audience, deprived of a spectacle, drifted back into the pub. 'This is a terrible town,' Bridget mumbled to herself. 'And I can never go home, for I could not bear the journey. As for putting space between myself and boats – well – we're stuck here, almost on top of the docks.'

Cathy touched her mother's knee. 'Liverpool?' she asked.

Bridget nodded. 'Aye, 'tis Liverpool, child. We shall be living right next door to all these boats and ships, though I'd dearly love to put many an acre between us and them. Still. We must make the best we can of life, Caitlin.'

8

Caitlin, usually Cathy, was too young to understand her mother's words. The crossing had terrified the child to the point of numbness. Mammy had been too ill to speak, while Granda's temperament had not been improved by the boat's lurchings. Granda Murphy was not fond of children. During her seven years on earth, Cathy had learned to be quiet when Granda Murphy was about. 'Will we stay here, Mammy?' the little girl managed, the short sentence forced between ice-cold lips. It was a frightening place, the child thought. People were running back and forth, many of them boys of eight or nine, some bare-footed, others in heavy, iron-tipped boots. Newspapers, hot potatoes and chestnuts were being advertised by folk whose voices seemed to cut a swathe through the air, so shrill and piercing were the tones. The river was quieter, appearing to concede defeat in the face of humankind's cacophonies. 'Will we stay here, Mammy?' repeated Cathy.

'Aye, we must,' sighed Bridget.

'Why?'

'Your stepfather lives in Liverpool.'

Cathy crept closer to her mother and resented Shauna yet again. Since the supposedly frail child's arrival, Cathy had been denied some of the maternal attention she had learned to expect. Her three-year-old sister was not thriving and she needed everything doing for her. Mammy was always saying, 'Cathy, you have to be the big girl, for I've all to do for Shauna.' Cathy didn't feel big. Seven was a grand age according to Mammy, yet the little girl knew she needed her one remaining parent more than ever. 'Why did Daddy die?'

'Not again,' replied Bridget. 'Please don't be starting all of that, Cathy. Didn't we explain to you about the accident?' She shivered all the more, a new ice in her bones owing something to the weather, much to the fact that she had not been allowed time to grieve. Eugene was only six months buried, yet here she was among foreigners and on her way to an English altar.

Cathy bit her lip, felt no pain because of the merciless cold. Daddy was a great man who had gone to stay in another place called heaven. Why hadn't he come to Liverpool instead of going off with Jesus like that? He would have held her, comforted her. He would have played games like cat's cradle and guess which hand is the sweetie in. But he'd gone away and he wouldn't be coming back and Cathy's stomach was empty.

'And poor Shauna misses her daddy, too. At least you knew him for a long time, child,' said Bridget quietly.

'Poor Shauna' was warm and as cosy as a newborn against Mammy's shoulder. Cathy shuddered again, wished that she, too, could be wrapped in a plaid shawl and held close to the body of her mother.

Granda returned, his brow still furrowed by ill-temper. 'Boy?' he yelled at a passing urchin.

The lad ground to a halt, drew a wrist across his nose to dislodge a dewdrop. 'Yes, sir?'

Mollified slightly by the child's respectful tone, Thomas Murphy drew himself to full height before placing a hand in his pocket. 'A threepence for you if you find a cart to carry us and our trunks and cases, lad. No fancy vehicles, mind.' He sniffed and glowered at the boy. 'If you're quick, there'll be a further payment when we reach Scotland Road. Do you know Bell's?'

The barefoot child nodded eagerly. 'Bell's Pledges? We live near there, mister. I can get a lend of a cart for a few pennies if you hang on here a minute. Will there be a name on your things?'

''Tis Murphy. Thomas James Murphy. Can you remember that?'

'I can, sir.' The boy nodded so vigorously that his rain-damped hair sent forth droplets that landed on Cathy's face. 'Sorry,' he muttered. 'It was an accident, girl.' The 'girl' came out as 'gairl'. 'See you after, then,' he added before running off towards the ship.

Cathy watched the lad, saw him wending his way past passengers, sailors, a crate containing live hens. His feet were filthy and bare, yet he ran as easily as the wind across ground that must have proved painful.

'Come away with you, now, Bridie,' chided Thomas Murphy. 'We've a wedding in half an hour.'

Bridget O'Brien swallowed a foul-tasting liquid that had settled in her throat. Her stomach groaned cavernously, yet she could not have eaten to save her life. Oh, what was she doing here? She was a grown woman of twenty-seven years, the mother of two daughters. She had organized the running of a sizeable farm since Eugene's death, had kept books, paid wages, bought and sold stock. Yet here she stood, a lamb prepared for slaughter, a displaced person in a strange land . . .

'Bridget?' The two syllables were coated with steel.

'Yes, Father.' She rose, lifted the dozing Shauna, dragged Cathy to stand alongside the grandfather who had wrenched them all out of Galway. 'I still think there was no need for this,' she mumbled. There was need, an inner voice told her. Da was older and even more cantankerous than he had been during her own childhood. Twice, he had raised his strap to Cathy. Twice, Bridie had intervened, had placed herself between the man and his granddaughter. But she couldn't be in the house all the time. He might slap Cathy when Bridie was out shopping or seeing to the horses. On the one hand, she was being forced to leave home. But, at the same time, Bridie needed space between her father and her little family. She should have run away, she told herself for the umpteenth time. She should have fled from the county and into wherever. Wherever – Thomas Murphy would have found her.

Thomas Murphy glowered. He was a tall man with thick, iron-grey hair and bushy eyebrows that seemed to bristle with anger above clear blue eyes. Even when he wasn't annoyed, he looked dangerous, thought Bridie. Now, with his temper rising, he had pulled those eyebrows south until they overhung his features like the edge of an untidy thatched roof. 'It had to be done,' he snapped.

'Eugene's parents were quite resigned to the–'

'Nonsense,' he roared. 'They bided their time and no more, that's the truth. Do you think I wanted my grandchildren whisked away to the Church of Ireland as soon as my back was turned? Heaven forbid that such a thing would ever happen.'

Bridie sat on her temper. For how many years had she kept herself damped down? she wondered. Oh, such a lovely girl, she was. She had been a model daughter, a diligent worker on the farm, a loving and sensible spouse, a good mother. At what price, though? Since babyhood, she had feared the man who had frightened her mother. Thomas Murphy had never lashed out in earlier days, had never beaten his wife. The long-ago cruelties had been verbal and, it had seemed, eternal. Philomena Murphy had produced just one live child, and that child had been a sore disappointment. A girl? What use was a girl? 'You're not even half a woman,' Thomas had screamed at his fading spouse.

Bridie stared into her father's steely eyes. Just once, she had defied him. She had got herself pregnant and had married 'out', had taken a non-Catholic husband whose family had cut him off for mating with a Roman. Now, with Eugene dead and the farm newly tenanted, Bridie was left with few choices. She and her daughters could have moved in with Thomas Murphy or with the O'Briens. The only other prospect might have been to take a cottage and trust to luck where money was concerned. Instead of opting for any of those unpalatable possibilities, Bridie had agreed to a fresh start well away from her da and her in-laws. 'Where is he?' she asked.

'Who would that be, now?'

Bridie counted to ten. 'The bridegroom, of course.'

He arched an eyebrow, curled his lip. 'He is preparing for your arrival, no doubt. We shall go now. The service cannot begin without you.' In Thomas Murphy's book, a priest should not be kept waiting, particularly when the church was being used for a specially arranged evening service. 'Will you move?' he bellowed. 'Or will you get back on that boat and live with me in my house? We can go home when the tide turns. But if you do return, you will keep my grandchildren away from the O'Briens and their God-forsaken excuse for a religion.'

Bridie inclined her head. The 'you wills' and the 'you will nots' formed a litany that tripped loudly and often from her father's acerbic tongue. Even the landing stage had become a quieter place during Thomas Murphy's rantings. People stood and stared at the wild-looking man who raved at his quiet daughter.

Bridget heaved Shauna into a more manageable position and followed her father, noticing that a knot of men simply melted away to make a path for her furious parent. Sailors, dock workers, sellers of hot cocoa and tea backed off when they saw the towering figure.

On the cobbled square, Thomas Murphy stopped and grabbed his daughter's arm so tightly that she flinched. 'When I'm dead, who's to save these two mites from Protestantism and perdition?' he asked.

'I am,' she replied, her face twisted with pain.

'You? You're just a woman, a woman who was too weak

and stupid to wait and marry a man of her own kind. Oh no, you had to have it all your own way, Bridget. Your mother must have spun in her grave the day you gave yourself before marriage to that heathen. May God have mercy on that good lady's soul.'

Bridie, who remembered only too well how her mammy had suffered at the whim of Thomas Murphy, merely sighed with relief when her arm was freed. She would be rid of him, at least. No matter what kind of a creature Sam Bell turned out to be, he could not possibly be as wicked as this man she called Father.

There were ponies and traps ready for passengers, but the tall Irishman strode past them. 'We'll wait here for the boy,' he told his daughter. 'No point in paying out good money for a fancy carriage when there's a cart we can use.'

Cathy stood on the cobbles, her face lifted upward. 'Look, Mammy,' she cried. 'A train in the sky.'

Bridie glanced at the overhead engine, listened to the noise of it. A tram rattled past, then a ship's horn blared into the heavy clouds of winter. She had never heard such a racket. The lowing of cattle, the frantic snortings of an unbroken horse, the boom when quarry-men mined the Galway stone – all those things were nothing compared to the hellish din of Liverpool's docks. Home? Should she go back now? Should she take Shauna and Cathy back to sweet pastures and soft, kindly voices?

'Move, woman!' roared Thomas Murphy. 'See, the boy's coming just now with the cart. Or is this where you want to stay, in the middle of a busy road, while a priest waits on your whim for the starting of a wedding?'

Bridie put her head on one side and looked quizzically at the man who had fathered her. For a moment or two, she felt a stab of terror, but it passed over as quickly as the overhead carriages. 'I was thinking just now, Father, of the lovely people in Ballinasloe. I was conjuring up the sound of their voices at mass, remembering how gentle they are.' She straightened, shook her head. 'But you roar like a bull. I cannot raise my children near a man who screams all the time.' A corner of her mouth twitched when she saw his astonishment. 'I will not come back, Father. We shall stay here and make the best we can, so. If I never see you again, I'm sure I won't care.'

The tall man closed his mouth with an audible snap. This bold upstart of a daughter was daring to upbraid him in a public place. He opened his mouth again, found no words. The expression on her face reflected no anger, no emotion of any kind. He looked around, wondered if anyone had heard Bridie's speech. But his daughter's words had been spoken so softly. It was the softness that made the brief soliloquy all the more meaningful.

Bridie pulled at Cathy's hand, guided her towards a slow-moving cart on which the boy sat with a grim-faced driver and the luggage. 'Right, Cathy,' said Bridie, a deter- mined edge to her tone, 'let's go and find out what the future holds, shall we?'

Cathy's shorter legs worked double time to keep up with her mother's pace. When her hand slipped out of her mother's grasp, she howled piteously, panic almost chok- ing her as she imagined being lost in such a noisy town. Children ran about in the gloom, dresses, coats and shawls hanging from slender shoulders, trousers torn, bare feet slapping wet cobblestones. Cathy remembered bare feet, remembered the feel of grass against her toes, the smell of new-cut hay drying in the sun. She breathed deeply, sent forth another howl.

'That is enough, now,' said Thomas Murphy. He placed the case on the ground, bent over the child. 'Look, I've had to come back for you. Mammy is tired. See – she's leaning on the cart over there waiting for you. You must behave yourself, Caitlin O'Brien.'

She sniffed, stared at him. 'Don't want to be here,' she announced.

A few children stopped running, watched the scene with undisguised interest.

'You will do exactly as I say,' spat the impatient man. 'Now, come along while your mother gets married.'

Cathy wasn't completely sure about what 'married' was, but she had a vague idea that it might be connected to somebody called Sam who had a shop in Liverpool. Sam was supposed to be her new daddy. 'Don't want to,' she whimpered. This wasn't her place. Her place was on a farm on the outskirts of town. Her place was the market and the castle overlooking the river Suck and the quarrymen walking home at night and waving to her. 'I don't want to,' she repeated angrily.

'She doesn't want to,' echoed a girl in a filthy dress. 'She wants to stop here and play alley-o.'

Thomas, whose dignity was important, ignored the dirt-spattered urchin. 'Come along,' he urged his granddaughter. 'Or you'll have everybody late.'

No-one spoke, yet Cathy could feel the support of those around her, as if they were reaching out to give her strength. They understood. Without knowing her, these comrades sensed her trouble. 'I want to go home,' she told her grandfather.

Thomas glared at the small gathering. 'This is home.'

'Don't want here,' she answered boldly. 'Want my garden and Chucky and Bob.' And she did miss the chicken she had helped to rear from a ball of yellow fluff into a big, brave producer of eggs. 'Want Bob,' she declared, her feet planted apart. Bob was a sheepdog who could speak. His language was difficult to decode, but he had a special

16

word for dinner, a guttural howl that announced his hunger. And Bob had always guarded her, had always—
The smack sent her reeling into the arms of a girl.

'You shouldn't do that, mister,' advised the nearest young stranger, placing her thin body between the large man and the dumbstruck Cathy. 'My dad'll kill you if he sees you hitting her like that.'

Thomas froze, his hand stopping mid-air. 'And who asked you the time of day, miss? Shouldn't you be inside the house cleaning the dirt off your face? Isn't it past your bedtime?'

The streetwise waif gave Thomas Murphy the once-over. She wasn't afraid of him. He was big and ugly, but her dad was bigger and uglier than anybody the length and breadth of Liverpool's docks. 'Me ma shouts me when she's ready,' she replied smartly. 'I'm going back to Scottie now, and I'll hear me ma shouting.'

'And what does she shout?' There was a mocking edge to the Irishman's words.

'She shouts me name, and me name's Tildy Costigan.'

'Then mind your business, Tildy Costigan.'

Tildy placed a dirt-streaked hand on Cathy's shoulder. 'If you ever need me, girl, just send somebody for Tildy Costigan. Everybody knows me, even the Mary Ellens. I'll be there in a flash,' she added. 'With me brothers, me dad and half our street.' She stuck out her tongue, satisfied that the little girl's grandfather had seen the full length of it. It was nice and black, too, as the result of two spanishes for a halfpenny from Dolly Hanson's shop.

After an uncomfortable second, Thomas grabbed the case, then pulled Cathy along behind him. 'Such foolishness,' he told his daughter. 'Did you see the cut of that? The only clean bits were where the child had been rained on. You must be careful, Bridie. Keep Cathy away from these ragamuffins.'

Bridie, who felt that she might as well hang for the full sheep, allowed a few raw words to slip from her tongue. 'She would have been as well at home in Ballinasloe,' she informed her father. 'As I told you before, I could have rented a cottage and found some work.' She raised her chin. 'Also, I allow no-one to smack my daughters. They will not be hit. Ever.'

Thomas's patience was wearing to a state of transparency. 'We shall not stand here and discuss family business in the open,' he snarled. 'And you're here for a reason, Bridie. There's not many a man would take on a young widow with two daughters. We were fortunate to find a good Catholic widower to step into the shoes of their Protestant father.'

Bridie heaved the sleeping Shauna into a more comfortable position. 'Aye,' she replied, amazed at her own continued audacity, 'and I've never even seen the man. Why didn't he come to meet us? Could he not have made an effort to pick us up from the boat? What sort of a creature leaves small girls out in wind and weather?' She bit her tongue, told herself to hush. It was panic that had forced her to speak up. She had a reputation for forbearance, but she was scared out of her wits. This was a strange city in a strange country and she was going to marry a stranger this very evening.

Thomas gritted his teeth, wished that Cathy would stop snivelling. He yanked at the child's hand, felt the resistance in her fingers. 'Sam Bell is a busy man,' he pronounced. 'He's a business to run. In this day and age, shop hours are long. He'll have been up and about since day-break, at the beck and call of customers. There's no time for meeting boats, not when there's a community wants serving.'

'He could have sent someone in his place,' breathed the fatigued woman.

18

'Huh,' spat her father. 'He's not a man to waste hard-earned money on foolishness. Come away now,' he insisted. 'We're expected at St Aloysius Gonzaga's. You must be married before you spend the night in Sam's house. We have not come all this way to start a scandal.'

Bridie bit her lip. Her father was a man beyond reproach, a pillar of the Church and of the community. He was also a disgrace, though few at home in Galway would ever know his secrets. The cold and subtle cruelties of Thomas Murphy had always been discreet, hidden behind the door of his house. 'As you wish, Father,' she replied before passing Shauna to the boy on the cart. She turned, helped Cathy to climb aboard. 'We'll be on the pig's back,' she whispered to the hysterical girl. 'And, as well you know, there's plenty of meat on the back of a pig.' For a split second, Bridie heard her own mother's voice. 'We'll be great, Bridget. We'll be on the pig's back when himself sells a couple of horses.' Bridie glanced at 'himself', then gave her attention to Cathy. 'We shall have a grand house and plenty to eat.'

Cathy placed herself next to the boy. Sobs continued to rack her body, but they slowed when the lad started to talk. 'That was me sister,' he announced, jerking a thumb in the direction of Tildy Costigan's angry face. 'I'm Cozzer. The whole family gets called the Cozzers, like, only I'm the real Cozzer. Our Charlie's older than me, so he should be Cozzer, only he's special – different, like. Clever in his own way, but still different. Me ma's called Big Diddy. She's the boss of our street, me ma. She does all the laying-outs and brings babies. Me dad's a docker.' The words were spat out like rapid gunfire, no pause for thought or breath.

Cathy sniffed back the last of her tears, tried to make sense of her first encounter with this new language. 'We're going to live with Mr Bell,' she ventured.

Cozzer shook his head. 'Could be worse,' he informed her. 'Me ma says he's a miserable bugger, but he's not much of a drinker. He's tight with his money, like. Still, you'll be all right,' he added by way of comfort. 'Come and meet our ma. She'll look after yous all.'

The cart stank of mouldy vegetables and fish. Under different circumstances, Bridget O'Brien might have worried about going to church in a smelly, travel-creased dress, but she was beyond such trivial concerns. She listened numbly while the boy pointed out St Nicholas's 'Proddy' church, Exchange Station, shops, public houses. There were more people on Chapel Street than in the whole of her home town.

Bridie held onto her younger child, heard Cathy's diminishing sobs, tried not to notice Thomas Murphy's curled lip. Fish scales and vegetable matter would not sit well on da's best clothes. Still, he should have paid for proper transport, should have insisted on Sam Bell's attendance at the landing stage.

'This is Scotland Road,' the boy announced proudly.

Bridie allowed her eyes to wander past horses and carts until they rested on a larger than average corner shop in the near distance. BELL'S PLEDGES was emblazoned in a curling script above three brass orbs. Lights inside the shop announced that trade continued in spite of the imminent wedding. Resolutely, Bridie attempted to concentrate on the building, but the distractions proved too much for her. 'What kind of a place is this?' she muttered to herself.

''Tis a city,' replied her father. 'With all kinds of creatures in it. No place for weaklings.' His mouth widened into a mocking grin. 'Still, you'll make the best you can, so – isn't that what you said earlier?'

Cathy clung to her mother's arm. 'Will it kill us?' she

20

asked, her eyes glued to a monster that clattered along beside their hired cart.

'It's just a tram,' said Bridie. She watched while children cavorted along in front of the menacing vehicle. 'Give us a penny,' shouted a boy after walking on his hands just inches from death. A girl ran out into the road and began to play leapfrog with several more daredevils. Each time a child bent over in the foolish game, the tram got nearer.

'They'll be flattened,' breathed Bridie.

Cozzer Costigan laughed. 'No, they won't.' He pointed to the open upper deck. 'See them up there? They're posh men from Seaforth Sands and Waterloo. They'll throw some money in a minute. Nobody gets hurt, missus.'

A barrel organ groaned, its owner red-faced as he stirred the ageing mechanism to some semblance of life. On his shoulder, a monkey yawned and picked at his master's thinning hair. Women scuttered along with shopping baskets, babies, older children in their wake. A youth emerged at speed from a side street, the tails of his ragged coat flapping behind him as a gang of ruffians chased him.

Bridie shuddered. Perhaps they should have stayed with Da after all. She didn't want to be married, least of all to a total stranger. And this place was so wild, so alien. She clenched her teeth, hung on to her resolve. In Ireland, Thomas Murphy would have made their lives a misery. And although Eugene's parents had paid lip-service, she feared that they might have stepped into the arena at some later date to quarrel with their daughter-in-law on the subject of religion. There were no choices, Bridie told herself. None at all. She was here and she must just get on with it.

A gypsy caravan idled past, its wooden frame painted gaudily in yellow, blue and red, the horse almost comatose between the shafts. Romany infants danced along the pavement, sun-browned hands reaching out to beg for money. Two policemen raced after the gang of lads who had disappeared into a picture house, while some men scuffled and cursed outside a public house called the Throstle's Nest.

'I want to go home,' wailed Cathy.

'Shush now.' Bridie's heart heaved as if trying to escape from her body in order to find a separate and more acceptable way of life. 'You'll be used to it in no time at all,' she told her daughter. Really, Bridie herself needed reassurance. Children, she thought, adapted more easily than adults. Then Shauna began to wail. Dear God, would this filthy English city be a fit place in which to rear a sickly three-year-old?

The shabby vehicle stopped opposite Bell's Pledges. Cozzer jumped down and began to remove luggage from the cart. Shauna, fully awake now, screamed piteously.

'Now or never,' spat Thomas Murphy. 'Will you stay or come home?'

Bridie listened to her sobbing children, looked into the devilish eyes of her father. 'We stay,' she said. Anything, anything at all would surely be better than living in the same country as himself?

'Right.' He strode across the road and threw open the door of Sam Bell's pawnshop.

Bridie stepped onto the cobbles, lifted her children down and took their hands. For better or worse, they were here to stay.

Elizabeth Costigan, commonly known as Big Diddy, stood arms akimbo and with her back to the fire. 'You look like the dog's dinner after next door's cat's been at it,' she informed her victim. 'Stand up straight. It's supposed to be a wedding, not a bloody wake.'

Sam Bell sighed, shrugged narrow shoulders. The huge woman seemed to fill the room – and not just physically. There was so much energy about her person that it almost shone around her like a colourful aura. 'It's not as if this is my first,' he told her. 'I have been married before.'

Big Diddy Costigan fixed a gimlet eye on Sam Bell. He was about as much use as a rubber penknife when it came to the niceties of life. The Costigans might be poor, but they knew about dressing up for an occasion, even if all the clothes had to be borrowed or bought on the club card. She'd washed and ironed many frocks and shirts to be returned to the shops as unworn and unsuitable. 'You could have got a suit with a cheque,' she informed him. 'I'd have sponged it to send back.'

'I don't buy from clubs,' he answered.

Big Diddy bristled slightly. He didn't need cheques. He had enough money salted away to retire and live off the interest for several hundred years. 'Scrooge,' she muttered, though there was little malice in her tone. Sam Bell was a mild-mannered fellow who elicited no strong emotion from anyone in the district. He was fair, uncaring and honest. He was also the most boring chap Diddy had ever encountered in all her thirty-eight years. 'You could have bought a new suit, Sam. And some proper shoes.'

Sam glanced down at his mirror-finished boots. 'They're clean,' he ventured.

'So's your shirt. The collar's frayed, though.'

The man heaved another sigh. 'I'm too busy for all this panic,' he grumbled. 'There's a lot of customers for your Charlie to see to. I should be round at the shop to give him a hand.'

Did glowered at him. 'Our Charlie could run Bell's with both arms in plaster and his legs broke. He's been with you six years. Every time you go fishing, he takes over. Stand straight while I brush your jacket.'

The man shrugged and gave himself to the untender mercies of Elizabeth Costigan. He didn't want to get married, didn't relish the idea of young children poking about all over his shop, getting under his feet, asking for pennies. But a bargain was a bargain, and Thomas Murphy was not a man to be trifled with.

'Did you shave?' asked Diddy.

'Yes.'

'What with? A bloody butter knife? You look like a flaming hedgehog, Sam. Still, too late to worry now, I suppose.'

Sam Bell glanced round the Costigans' spanking clean front parlour. This was a fortunate family. Their luck lay in the fact that both parents were energetic workers who refused to lie down in the face of that grim thief called poverty. 'Is Billy coming?' he enquired of his hostess.

'Course he is. I got him ready and shoved him in the Holy House. One pint's his ration, and one pint's what he'll have.'

The pawnbroker jangled some coins in a pocket, pulled out a wedding band. He wasn't a great drinker, but he wished with all his heart that he could get out of here and anaesthetize himself at the Holy House bar. The ring was dull, so he rubbed it on his sleeve to brighten it up a bit.

Diddy gasped. 'You're never getting wed with a second-hand ring?'

Sam stopped polishing. 'It's twenty-two carat, only one previous owner. I'll have you know this was Eileen Heslop's.'

'And she's dead.'

He shook his head in disbelief. 'I know she's dead. Tom Heslop sold me the ring after the funeral. How else do you think I got hold of it?' He waved the yellow band under Diddy's rather large nose. 'She only pawned this twice, you know. Once to pay for her mam's headstone and then when she put the spread on for her daughter's wedding.'

Diddy scowled. 'A new one would have been better,' she insisted. 'Even a nine carat ring or a cheap silver one like the nuns have.'

'This one's got history,' he announced.

'And scratches. It's served its time at the wash-house scrubbing boards, that ring.' Diddy rammed an unbecoming hat onto her over-tight brown curls, then stabbed a nine-inch hatpin through her felt and hair. Gripping a missal, she stalked off towards the door. 'Stop here,' she ordered. 'Till I send your best man.'

Sam peered through the window and watched Diddy stamping off in the direction of a pub near St Aloysius's church. The hostelry's original name was seldom used since its re-baptism as the Holy House. After masses, funerals, benedictions and confessions, the Holy House was a favourite meeting place for many among the church's congregation.

The shopkeeper glanced at his watch, hoped that Charlie Costigan was doing a good job. The oldest of the Costigan brood was an odd lad, stiffened down one side of his body by birth damage, not much to say for himself, a wizard with numbers. Yes, Charlie would no doubt be coping. Nicky Costigan was at the shop, too. Diddy had briefed her daughter carefully. 'Make sure there's plenty of hot water for Mrs O'Brien. You help her with the two little girls.'

Two little girls. Sam paced, stopped in front of the fire, studied a sepia picture of Diddy and Billy on their wedding day. Above the photograph hung the papal blessing and a dried cross from last Palm Sunday. Two little girls. All that noise and running about. They would need clothes, shoes, food, playthings. Still.

Sam examined the wedding ring once more before stuffing it into his pocket to jangle against pennies and sixpences. Oh well, he had made a pact and, as Big Diddy had said earlier, it was a bit late to start worrying now. Bridie, she was called. Bridget, really. She'd been married to some Protestant over in Ireland, a big chap called Eugene. The kiddies were Caitlin and Shauna. He wondered what Muth would make of that lot—

'Sam?'

'Oh. Hello, Billy.'

Billy Costigan was a big man, tall, hefty and prematurely bald. His weather-reddened face was almost split in two by a wide grin. 'Ready for it, are you?'

To his amazement, Sam felt his own cheeks heating up. 'I'm too old for all this,' he grumbled. 'And I hope she's not counting on a big legacy when I'm gone. I'm leaving a lot to Liam.'

'And what about your ma? She'll see us all out, I bet.' Billy knew better than to enquire about Liam's twin. Although there had been no overt arguments of late, everyone knew that Liam and Anthony didn't get on.

Sam thought about Muth, a saint of a woman, who had been bedridden since 1926. The new Mrs Bell would save a few coppers by looking after the ageing Theresa Bell. There'd be no need for minders, no need for folk to carry washing to and fro. 'She can't go on for ever,' he said finally. 'Come on, Billy. Let's get it over with.'

Bridie had managed to change during five stolen minutes. She wore a dove-grey coat and skirt with a matching hat, dark blue shoes and some smart gloves of navy kid. The house was terrible. She didn't want to live here, couldn't bear the thought of spending her life in such a desperate place. There had been no time to go upstairs. She stood in the luggage-cluttered kitchen-cum-living room and righted her hat in a dirty, pock-marked mirror. 'Come on, Cathy,' she said softly. 'We must go to church now.'

Cathy fixed an eye on Nicky Costigan. Nicky Costigan had scrubbed Cathy's neck with a rough cloth and smelly red soap. 'I don't like you,' announced the child.

Nicky grinned, displaying gappy teeth and a bright red tongue.

'Don't be rude, Cathy,' chided Bridie absently. Would that slopstone in the tiny scullery ever come clean? Would any number of scrubbings get through to the actual surface of Sam Bell's kitchen table?

Nicky wagged a finger at Cathy. 'You'd better behave in St Aloysius's. Father Bell's coming down from Blackburn specially. He'll be your big brother. How do you fancy having a priest in the family?'

The girl's words cut through Bridie's rambling thoughts. 'Is he ... is he Mr Bell's son?'

Nicky nodded vigorously. 'There's Liam and Anthony. Twins. Anthony's nice, but Father Liam, well ...' She wet a forefinger and drew it across her throat. 'All hell's flames and misery, me mam says.'

Bridie swallowed. How old was this Sam Bell? Da had informed her that the bridegroom was 'slightly older' than Bridie, but priests? Surely priests went to college for ever and a day? Weren't they well into their twenties before being qualified? 'How old are Anthony and Liam?' she managed finally.

The eldest of Big Diddy's daughters sucked her teeth for a second. 'About thirty, I think. Me mam says they were born the year the queen died.'

So Sam Bell, the father of these two, must be at least fifty. She was going to the altar to fasten herself to an old man. No wonder Da had been grinning like a clown these past weeks. Several times, Bridie had caught him smiling secretly to himself. She took a deep breath, tried to wipe from her mind those pictures of home. Mammy's sewing basket sitting in the hearth, peat glowing beneath a hanging kettle, soft snow clinging to a window-sill. Her mother's home was Da's house now. She would not go back, could never go back.

'Are you ready, then, missus?'

Bridie stared hard at Nicky Costigan, thought she saw something akin to mockery in those pale grey-blue eyes. Could a girl of this age see straight into the soul of a grown woman? Surely not.

'You'd better go and see Mrs Bell first,' advised Nicky, pausing for a few seconds when she saw Bridie's confusion. Had this bride been told about the old woman? 'She's Mr Bell's mam and she lives in the back bedroom.'

Bridie's left hand climbed of its own accord to her throat.

'She's in bed. She's always in bed. Mr Bell's had to pay to get her looked after. I suppose you'll be doing it now.'

Bridget O'Brien swallowed bile and temper. She would not go upstairs. She would not do anything that might persuade her to run back to Galway in the company of Thomas Murphy. 'Time enough for me to meet Mrs Bell later,' she told the girl. 'After all, we must not keep the gentlemen waiting.'

The children followed their mother through the shop. Cathy stared at the strange young man behind the counter. He had a large head, a twisted arm and very strange eyes.

'That's our Charlie,' volunteered Nicky. 'He's a cripple, but a clever one. Aren't you a clever boy, Charlie?'

Bridie shuddered. The mischievous young woman might have been talking to a colourful member of the feathered kingdom. 'Hello, Charlie,' said Bridie. 'I'm pleased to meet you.'

Charlie's mouth spread itself into a huge grin.

'He likes you,' pronounced Nicky. 'Well, you must be all right, 'cos our Charlie only smiles at nice people.' She rubbed a hand on her apron and touched Bridie's shoulder. 'I hope you'll be happy, missus,' she mumbled. 'And our Charlie hopes so too.'

Bridie strode forth into the din of Scotland Road with a child on each side of her and a lead weight in her heart. Da was outside the shop talking to a man in a black coat. 'Here she comes,' shouted Thomas Murphy. 'Bridie, come away now and meet your stepson.'

The man turned and looked at his father's bride-to-be. Such a little thing, she was, no more than five feet two, blonde and quite beautiful. His heart leapt about in his chest, because he understood what it was to lose someone who was meant to be a partner for life. This girl had lost a husband, while Anthony had been deprived suddenly, cruelly, of the woman he had loved. And Bridie was so young, so lovely. 'I'm Anthony,' he told her. Could he go into that church? Could he? There was fear in her face. Yes, he must attend the wedding. His stepmother-to-be would be needing friends, he felt sure.

She could scarcely meet his gaze. What on earth must he think of her? Here she was, a usurper from another country trying to fill his mother's shoes. Perhaps this young man thought she was after Sam Bell's money. 'I'm Bridget – usually Bridie.' In, out, said her inner voice. Just breathe slowly, don't panic, don't let the fear spill out into the street.

Thomas Murphy cleared his throat. 'Anthony's brother will officiate at the wedding.'

Bridie gave her father a brilliant smile. 'I know,' she said. 'Isn't it great to have a priest in the family?'

An expression of shock and disappointment paid a brief visit to Thomas Murphy's face. She ought to have been perplexed, should have been unhappy to realize that her husband-to-be had a grown-up family. But she was so cool, as if she had known all along that Sam Bell was middle-aged. 'Right,' he mumbled. 'Off we go, then.'

Bridie took her father's arm, suppressed a shudder that tried to invade her body. This wedding would be done properly, right down to the last tiny detail. Fiercely, she clung to the words she had read some weeks earlier. Only once had Sam Bell communicated with his intended bride. 'I will not trouble you much except to have you help in the business . . .' He had made no mention of a bedridden mother and twin sons of thirty years.

For a split second, she lent the false smile to Anthony. 'Would you bring the children, please?' she asked the young man.

Anthony took the hands of Cathy and Shauna. 'Off we go,' he told them, 'into the prettiest church in Liverpool.'

Two

It was a beautiful church. Despite her misery and bewilderment, Bridie noticed how lovely it was. Perhaps the interest in her surroundings was a defence mechanism, a way of ignoring the panic beating in her breast.

Narrow windows in stained glass alternated with stations of the cross along the walls. The pews were old, some with little doors leading in from the middle aisle, every piece of moulding polished to perfection. Three altars were spread with fine linen, the central and main table displaying the purple of Advent. There would be no high mass, as this arranged marriage was taking place with special permission during a forbidden time. Bridie shivered slightly as she stood on the threshold of a new life and in the doorway of an unfamiliar place of worship. Lent and Advent weddings brought bad luck, didn't they?

The organ struck a dissonant chord the second she appeared on her father's arm. Bridie had not expected music, partly because of the church calendar and partly because music needed paying for. But the celebrant priest was the bridegroom's son, so the organist was probably playing for free. The hymns would not be joyful, not during Advent, but perhaps the music would serve to muffle the loud beating of the bride's heart.

Anthony Bell and his two young charges sat yards ahead on her side of the church, while everyone else was positioned to the right. A large man rose as soon as the organist played the first bar of 'Faith of our Fathers'. Bridie removed her gaze from a particularly ornate carving of Veronica wiping the face of Jesus, and gave a corner of her attention to the occasion in hand. No wedding march, of course, not during Advent. The chunky fellow seemed to be best man; a smaller figure rose and stood with him. The short man coughed noisily and fiddled with a handkerchief. Sam Bell, she supposed.

'Are you ready for this?' whispered Thomas Murphy.

Bridie stopped mid-stride and wondered whether she had heard correctly. 'What?' she murmured.

'Are you sure?'

'Is this the right time for such a question? They're ready to start the second verse.' She could feel the heat of embarrassment settling in her cheeks. Heads were swivelling in the direction of bride and bride's father, and the singing was beginning to straggle somewhat.

The small congregation of St Aloysius Gonzaga looked quizzically at the grey-haired Irishman and his petite daughter, then were brought to book by the priest's loud singing. Everyone faced the front and attacked anew the famous hymn of battle that curdled Orange blood on Catholic walking days. 'We will be true to thee 'til death,' they droned.

'He's old for you.'

'You already knew that.'

'Yes, but—'

Bridie clicked her tongue. 'We can't stand here talking. Weren't you the one with the brilliant idea? Weren't you the one who shifted us here away from the O'Briens?' She lifted her head and dragged her father the rest of the distance. There was no going back, she told herself doggedly. Here in Liverpool there would be filth and noise, but there would be no animosity between the O'Briens and this tyrannical patriarch.

Sam Bell positioned himself next to Billy Costigan. He pulled the ring from his pocket, tried not to cringe as two halfpennies tumbled and clattered their way across the floor. She was so young. Determinedly, he faced the front and pushed the deceased Mrs Heslop's ring into the sweaty palm of Billy Costigan, his best man. The children were very young, too. One of them was beginning to cry ... Another cough bubbled in his chest, and he squashed it determinedly. The little girl was making enough noise without Sam adding to it.

Bridie stopped alongside the pew that contained Anthony Bell, Cathy and Shauna. 'Shush, now,' she told the mewling three-year-old. 'See – play with my rosary.' She thrust the beads into Anthony Bell's hands. This was her mother's rosary. But she would not think about her mother or about Ireland; she would not even look at the man to whom she must shortly be joined in this celebration of holy wedlock. Holy?

She returned to her father and stared at him full in the face. Although she feared the future, Bridie O'Brien smiled sweetly before giving her consideration to the altar. Father could go home now. He could look after himself, because no-one would cook or clean or sew for him. Perhaps one of the local girls might come in for an hour or two, but an arrangement of that sort would involve money. Whatever, with his wife long dead and his daughter in England, Thomas Murphy was about to find himself without unpaid servants. Even during her marriage, Bridie had given one full day each week to her father. So. Himself was alone now. The grim prospect of total isolation had given birth to Father's sudden dismay – of that Bridie felt certain.

'*Deus Israeli conjungat vos . . .*' intoned the priest.

Bridie found herself gazing at the celebrant. At twenty-seven years of age, Bridie was about to become stepmother to a man of God whose facial expression reflected precious little inner charity. Thirty, if a day, she thought. The features matched those of the other fellow ... the man who was minding the girls. Now, what was his name? Anthony. So this was Liam, then. These were identical twins, yet ... Furtively, she cast a quick glance over her shoulder, saw Shauna playing prettily with Anthony.

The priest cleared his throat, waited until the bride got her mind on the sacrament of marriage. 'Brethren,' he said, 'let wives be subject to their husbands.'

Bridie bit her lip. Though she had avoided looking to her right, she knew that the person standing next to her was Sam Bell. He was not big, but he was real. He was flesh and blood and she could hear him breathing. The man had a troublesome chest, she thought. Would Shauna catch more colds here? Would the poor child suffer that dreadful croup again?

The bride swallowed painfully against a rising sob. Eugene ... That had been a hurried marriage, too. With Cathy in her belly, Bridie had stood before a priest and had taken vows in the presence of two witnesses. Her first husband had been graceful when it had come to the signing over of all his unborn children to the Church of Rome. Eugene's voice popped into her mind. 'Does it matter, really?' he had asked. 'As long as they're strong and healthy, our babies can find their own way to God.'

'*Beati omnes qui timen ...*'

'Forgive me,' Bridie mouthed to God and to her dead husband. 'I need to get away. He will hit our children. Eugene, your family hates my Church.'

The priest saw the bride's lips moving. So she knew how to pray? Did she know how to get money out of an old fool? Ah surely not. Dad's will was made ...

Liam Bell had cold eyes, Bridie decided. That was the difference. His brother had the same colouring, the same build, yet these two were north and south poles apart.

At last, she was forced to look upon her bridegroom. He was slight, with thinning hair and a frayed edge to his collar. When all responses had been made, a ring was produced. The priest leaned forward. 'You must take off your other ring first,' he whispered, the quiet words seasoned with mockery.

Bridie glanced into the cleric's unfeeling eyes, then down at her hand. Eugene's ring still circled her finger. It had been there for over seven years. Well, she'd removed it when her hands had swollen towards the end of her second pregnancy, but apart from that ... She spoke silently to the man she had loved for eight years, the man whose memory remained sacred. 'It's for the girls,' she told him. 'It's for Cathy and Shauna, not for me.'

'You can't wear two,' warned Father Liam Bell.

She lowered her eyes once more, took off Eugene's wedding band and placed it on the ring finger of her right hand. Did nuns wear their bride of Christ rings on their right hands? she wondered. Or was it married women from other countries who—? Something made her look up sharply. The priest had folded his arms. Disapproval crackled in the starch of his alb, in the set of his chin. Clearly, he was not amused by the fact that the bold Irish upstart seemed unwilling to cast aside this one small symbol of an earlier union. Bridie's face was heating up again.

Sam Bell placed the badge of ownership on his new wife's hand, then they both knelt at the altar rail while Father Liam prayed over them. He prayed endlessly, first in Latin, then in English. Bridie's knees were aching; wasn't this meant to be a low-key wedding because of the time of year? It should be over by now, surely? After being tossed about on the wayward Irish Sea for half the day, Bridie was miserable, cold and weary. Shauna was adding her own touch to the proceedings by singing 'When Irish Eyes Are Smiling', and a few giggles had begun to spread like influenza throughout the sparsely occupied pews.

The priest paused. 'Would you take that child outside, please?' he asked eventually.

No movement followed this request.

Bridie raised her eyes, saw that the priest in charge of this unhappy service had fixed his nasty eyes on someone on her left. That someone was his brother, the man who was caring for her children. There was hatred and ... something else in Liam's expression. Was it jealousy? Was the expression sprinkled with a pinch of reluctant admiration? Whatever, it almost exploded in the air like lightning, yet Anthony plainly intended to remain exactly where he was.

The hand of God's intermediary raised itself. '*Dominus vobiscum,*' he said softly.

'*Et cum spiritu tuo,*' responded the solitary altar boy.

With painful slowness, the priest removed his stole, kissed the embroidered cross and folded the length of silk. Without stopping to dismiss the churchgoers, he left the altar and strode away into the sacristy.

Sam Bell touched the shoulder of his young bride. 'We have to go and sign now ... er ... Bridie.'

Meek as a lamb, she followed where her husband led. Two other people joined them. One was the best man; the other was a large, round-faced female with a big nose and a terrible hat.

'Where's your Liam gone?' asked the bulky woman.

'God knows,' answered Sam. 'You know what he's like, Diddy. Always on the move, that one.'

Bridie, who preferred not to dwell too closely on her

husband's face, spoke to the female witness. 'I'm Bridie O'Bri – I mean Bell, of course.'

'Elizabeth Costigan. Big Diddy, they call me. It was our Charlie who christened me—'

'I've met him,' said Bridie, anxious to make an ally in this strange city. 'In the shop.'

Diddy beamed. 'They say he's an idiot, but we know better – don't we, Billy?'

Billy nodded his agreement.

'If we were all as thick as our Charlie, we'd be experts. Anyway, Diddy was what he called me, and Diddy's been me handle ever since. Hasn't it, Billy?'

Billy nodded again.

Sam rattled the coins in his pocket. 'We should be signing the certificate. If our Liam's gone on one of his rambles, what shall we do?'

'We'll do just fine, so we will,' boomed a new voice. A short, almost spherical figure thrust itself into the room. 'Michael Brennan,' he announced.

Bridie found herself smiling properly for the first time in ages. Father Michael Brennan was as Irish as she was. His clerical collar hung loose like a fairground hoop circling a prize, and he was not much taller than Bridie. 'Good evening, Father,' she said. He had a speck of gravy on his chin, as if he had risen in haste from his supper. Quick, dark-blue eyes twinkled above fat, red cheeks, and he was struggling to fasten the belt around his protruding middle.

'Hello, Father Brennan,' said Big Diddy Costigan. 'Where's Father Liam dashed off to? Is he in a sulk because Anthony didn't take the baby outside?'

Father Brennan shrugged. 'He'll be rushing about trying to get back to Blackburn,' he said.

'Away from his brother, more like,' Big Diddy stage-whispered in Bridie's ear. 'Wants his own way. Always did. Holy Orders didn't improve him and—'

'Elizabeth?' Father Brennan beamed upon one of the more troublesome among his parishioners. 'Charitable thoughts, my dear. Remember to have charitable thoughts.'

Diddy winked at her old friend and adversary. 'My charity goes where it's needed, Father.'

The priest laughed. 'And sure we've heard about that, too. You and Billy will be in hot water if you don't watch out.' He opened the registration book, got Sam and Bridie to sign, helped Billy Costigan to clean a blot of ink from the table. 'Well, that's you all done and dusted,' announced Father Brennan. 'You can away now to all the shenanigans.'

Mr and Mrs Costigan pushed the bride and groom towards the door. 'Go on, then,' she urged. 'Down the aisle and off to our house. We've a fiddler booked and some ale to shift.'

On her way out of the church, Bridie Bell saw little, because her eyes became wet when she heard Shauna's reed-like voice delivering 'Danny Boy' to the amused gathering. Mammy used to sing that. Mammy, whose hair had been prematurely grey, whose hands had reddened from scrubbing, had hung on to her sweet, girlish singing voice—

'Mrs Bell? Mrs Bell?'

Bridie stopped, stared blankly at yet another new face. 'Yes?'

The man smiled, pushed something into her hand. 'Your wedding ring,' he said apologetically. 'It fell off.'

She nodded and took the band of gold from him. All in all, this marriage was off to a bad start.

*

The do had been arranged by no less a person than Big Diddy Costigan herself. In the very room where Sam Bell had been tortured into readiness for the service, table and dresser were swathed in white sheeting and spread with food, plates, assorted cutlery and a dozen pint glasses on loan from the Holy House.

'Our Maureen and our Monica's got this lot ready,' beamed Big Diddy. 'And there's a barrel in the back kitchen – neighbours chipped in for that.'

Our Maureen stood talking to Monica. Bridie recognized the latter as Nicky, the one who had helped earlier, and she sent a quick, grateful smile to the girl. But our Maureen was a different kettle of fish altogether. Never in her life had Bridie come across a person of such startling beauty. Ravenblack hair was folded in deep waves around a perfect, heart-shaped face. A creamy complexion did more than justice to eyes that sparkled like twin sapphires. Dark eyebrows, unnecessarily long, thick lashes and a pretty mouth completed the breathtaking picture. Maureen posed and pouted, was clearly aware of her appearance.

Big Diddy nudged the bride. 'We don't know where she came from, our Maureen. She's only thirteen, but she's like a film-star.' She removed her hatpin, threw the unbecoming headgear under the dresser-cum-sideboard. 'That hat needs a decent burial,' she remarked. 'I've had it fifteen years.'

'Hello, Maureen,' said Bridie. 'Good to see you again, Monica.' She pitied Maureen's plain sister. Although she was clearly the older of the two, she looked so vulnerable with her pale-grey eyes, nondescript hair and wide-spaced teeth.

Nicky straightened her shoulders. 'There's only me ma calls me Monica. I usually get called Nicky. Graham'll be coming, I think. We've been walking out, me and him. I'm fifteen now, see. So I can walk out.' She glanced sideways at Maureen, jerked a thumb in her direction. 'Our Maureen gets plagued with being nice-looking. But she's only thirteen. Anyway, she's saving herself for the stage, aren't you? She's Fairy Mary's star turn.' The 'Fairy Mary' came out as 'Furry Mury'.

Before Bridie could elicit an explanation, she was whisked away by the hostess. 'This is me husband,' pronounced the large lady. 'You can meet him proper now, not like in church. Best man in more ways than one, my Billy.'

Billy stuck out his chest, grinned broadly, then crushed Bridie's fingers between hard, calloused hands. 'Welcome to Scottie,' he boomed. 'We've not much to offer, but you just enjoy yourself.' He released the bride's aching digits and swept his arm across the room. 'Sit down and grab something before our Charlie comes home. He eats like a carthorse, you know.'

Bridie placed herself in a corner next to the fire and studied the ongoings. Charlie gangled in, mumbled a word or two into Sam Bell's ear, handed over a bunch of keys. The pawnbroker nodded before digging out a few coins as wages. Bridie took the opportunity to study her husband while he was unaware of her scrutiny. The groom was a man of moderate size, about five feet and six inches in height, with fading hair that threatened to become a monk's tonsure within the foreseeable future. Despite his slender frame, he owned a little paunch, an area of slackness that protruded slightly now that his waistcoat was unbuttoned.

She shifted her attention to Anthony Bell. He had entered by a rear door, was still in the company of Bridie's daughters. Shauna was laughing. 'Pigeons, Mammy,' she shouted. 'In the yard.'

Cathy came to stand by her mother. 'Anthony showed

us the birds. They're in cages, but they fly miles and run races and always come home.' The child was smiling, but Bridie could see that the tears were just a fraction of an inch away. Cathy would take a bit of time to settle, that was certain.

Bridie's eyes felt as if they were filled with grit. More than anything, she wanted to sleep. Food did not interest her at all, yet she wished not to offend her hosts, so she toyed with what Big Diddy had told her was a wet nelly, discovered the ample plateful to be a delicious concoction of cake and treacle.

More people arrived. There was Tildy whom Bridie had already seen near the landing stage, then the boy called Cozzer, some of his friends, a drunken fiddler in a battered hat. Fortunately, the inept violinist broke a string and was forced to stop torturing the battle-scarred instrument. Father Brennan, his collar straightened, joined the throng for a nip of Irish and a couple of salmon-paste sandwiches. Bridie's eyes would not stay open . . .

Someone was tapping on her shoulder. 'Bridie?' the voice said.

She opened her eyes. 'Sorry,' she mumbled. 'I must have fallen asleep for a moment or two.'

'An hour, you mean.'

Bridie heard a smile in the words. 'I am so sorry,' she repeated lamely.

Anthony Bell lowered himself into a squatting position. 'I took the little girls to my father's house. They settled down quite quickly. Tildy stayed with them. I think she crowbarred herself into bed with your little one.' This lovely young woman was easy to talk to. Would Dad appreciate her, look after her? His heart skipped a beat. She was beyond lovely; she was beautiful.

Bridie gazed round the room. 'Where's everyone else?'

Anthony shrugged. 'In the Holy House, I expect. That's

41

the pub next to the church. Big Diddy has gone off to round them all up.' He could have kicked his dad. Bridie and the children had travelled all this way, yet the groom was off in the company of others. Her eyes were so blue, so wide . . .

'My father?' She hadn't had sight or sound of Thomas Murphy since the wedding.

'At the stables,' he told her. 'In Newsham Street, opposite St Aloysius's school. I think he has some animals there.' He swallowed, turned his head. Did she know that her father had a lady friend on Scotland Road, that he had been sleeping with Dolly Hanson for many years? The owner of Hanson's news, sweets and tobacco was head over heels in love with Thomas Murphy. Rumour had it that she confessed her sin every time Murphy returned to Ireland, only to reoffend the minute the man set foot on English soil.

Bridie pulled herself upright, wondered fleetingly where her bridegroom had gone. 'Tell me about the Costigans,' she begged when her head cleared. Big Diddy could well turn out to be a friend in this strange new city. And, in spite of her weariness, Bridie had been touched by the warmth of the Costigan household.

'Do you have a week?' Anthony stood up and placed himself in front of the fire. He could scarcely bear to look at her. Sam Bell was such a cold fish. And that, thought Anthony, was a suitable metaphor to apply to a man who sat for hours dangling a line into rivers and streams.

'They seem to be good people,' said Bridie expectantly.

Anthony nodded. 'The Costigan story goes on and on, something new every day – usually a drama or a crisis. Diddy is really Elizabeth. Billy's a docker. They've five children. Charlie's the oldest – he's seventeen–'

'God bless him, poor soul.'

He looked at her now. 'Don't pity him. His body is

42

twisted and his speech is slow, but the brain's a good one. Then there's Monica. I think she'll be fifteen. She's often called Mouth Organ, but she answers to Nicky and she's a good girl—'

'Mouth organ?'

Anthony laughed. ''Ar Monica,' he said. 'Diddy gave all her daughters a name beginning with M – there's Monica, Maureen and Mathilda-Anne. Maureen's the only one who hung on to her name. She's the beauty. Tildy's ten and Jimmy – Cozzer – is nine. I could go on for ever about the Costigans, but you must be very tired after your journey.'

'A good family,' said Bridie. 'They treated me so well.' Anthony glanced over his shoulder at the mantel clock. He had to get away. He could not imagine this poor girl being happy in the company of a dried-up pawnbroker. She wanted fields, hills, freedom. 'I must be going soon,' he said at last. 'I'm up with the lark in the morning.'

She rose to her feet, smoothed the crumpled jacket. 'Don't worry about me,' she told him. 'As long as my girls are safe, I'll just stay here till . . . your father comes back.' She waited for a reply, received none. 'Do you live over the shop on Scotland Road, too?' she asked.

He shook his head. 'No. I've a house here in Dryden Street.'

The clock grumbled, spat eleven times.

Was he married? she wondered. He had come alone to the church, had mentioned no wife. 'Do you work, Anthony?'

He nodded. 'I teach.'

'Ah.' Bridie paused in the hope of further explanation, was disappointed again. He seemed such a pleasant man, so much nicer than his brother. 'Well, you go off and get your beauty sleep, then.'

The door flew inward. 'It's like trying to scrape barnacles off the bottom of a boat,' Diddy Costigan announced by way of greeting. 'They're all round the stables looking at Sam's new horses. Every one of my lot except Tildy's sitting down in the gypsies' parlour drinking cocoa. As for Billy and Sam and your dad,' she waved a hand in Bridie's direction, 'the three of them's up to their eyes in hay and horse droppings.'

'I didn't know my father had an interest in horses,' replied Anthony. As far as he knew, Sam Bell's single and very passionless passion was for angling.

'Well, he has now,' snapped Diddy. 'A very big interest and it's all over his shoes. Fine bloody bridegroom he turned out to be. Sorry.' She took a deep breath, shook her head. 'It's not your fault, lad. Go home and have a rest. I'll see to Bridie.'

Anthony made his goodbyes and left the house.

'Right.' Big Diddy eased herself into a fireside chair. 'Sam said he'd come for you soon and walk you home. God, I can't wait to get these corsets off and have a good scratch. I hope you know what you're taking on, girl. Me shoes are killing me.' She kicked away the offending articles. 'Some start you've had, eh? Your ring falls off before you get out of church, then the bridegroom buggers off to see the gypsies. And I'm telling you now in case you haven't heard – his mother's a tartar.'

Bridie said nothing.

'Did he write to you? He said he would.'

'I had a letter, yes.'

Diddy's eyebrows shot skyward. 'One? One bloody letter? Was Theresa Bell mentioned?'

'No.'

'Or his sons?'

'No.'

Diddy frowned. 'Still, I suppose your dad put you in the picture. I mean, Sam's a lot older than you, and his mother's nearly as old as God.' For several seconds, she

44

stared hard at the visitor. 'You weren't told any of it, were you, love? You've married a man you don't even know.'

Bridie shook her head in dismay.

With the air of a conspirator, Big Diddy looked over her shoulder as if reassuring herself about the room's emptiness, then dropped her voice to a whisper. 'What the bloody hell were you thinking of, girl? I mean, Scottie Road's all right and I wouldn't let anybody say different, but you've left the countryside for this? For him?'

'Yes.'

'Whose idea?'

'My father's.' That was not the complete truth, Bridie told herself. Lately, she had wanted to put the sea between herself and him. The O'Briens, too, needed removing from the horizon of her life.

Diddy wriggled and plucked absently at her clothing in a vain effort to ease a particularly troublesome length of whalebone in the hated corset. 'You'll be just a skivvy for him and his mother.'

'That's all I was at home once our farm was re-tenanted. When we had to move out, we lived for a while with my father, so I did all the chores for him. Anyway, Da was worried about my dead husband's family. They're Church of Ireland and Da thought they might try to influence Cathy and Shauna.' She sighed deeply. 'I'd had enough of Da. He was desperate when I married Eugene and he never forgave me. So I had to get away.'

Diddy nodded but kept her counsel. She knew a thing or two about Thomas Murphy and a certain female shop-keeper not a stone's throw away. Dolly Hanson had been 'looking after' Bridie's father for donkey's years . . . 'You've gone from one slavery to another. You won't even have a field for your children to play in, Bridie. Young ones round here are wise before their time. It's a pity you came. It's a pity I didn't get the chance to warn you.'

Panic paid another brief visit to Bridie's chest, but she dismissed it. For better or worse, she was a wife once more. ''Tis done now,' she told her hostess. 'No use looking back and dwelling on what might have been. If my mother had lived, if Da had been a better man, if you had written to me . . . We can't live while we keep looking back all the time.'

Diddy dropped her head in tacit agreement, chewed on her thoughts for a few moments. 'Sam Bell's not a bad man,' she pronounced eventually. 'And he's not a good one, neither. Like the rest of us, he's got his faults.' Light was beginning to break in the rear of her mind. Horses. Some snippets of conversation were weaving themselves into the thin curtain that separates the conscious from the subconscious. 'The horses came about a month ago,' she volunteered thoughtfully.

Bridie half smiled. 'Ah, yes. They would be ferried across in good weather and on quieter tides. He takes great care of his beasts. Da's famous for his horses.'

'Some were sold on.' Diddy clasped her hands tightly in her lap, as if trying to restrain herself. Given a chance, she would have clobbered Sam Bell and Thomas Murphy there and then. 'Two were kept with the gypsies. There's a stallion and a mare. The gypsies have been walking them miles and paying rent for fields where they could run about a bit. They're frisky, like. Specially the grey stallion.'

'Racers,' said Bridie. She ignored a flutter of excitement in her breast. Were Quicksilver and Sorrel here? Would she see them again?

'What?'

'They'll be racehorses. Arab–Irish are the best.'

Diddy eased herself out of the chair. 'Would you like a drop of ale?'

'No, thank you.' Bridie had never tasted strong drink.

'Cup of tea, then?'

'It's late. I must go and see to my children.'

The older woman laughed. 'Our Tildy's the best baby-minder in Liverpool, queen.'

'All the same, I'd rather—'

'Come on then.' Big Diddy Costigan forced her size seven feet into the size six shoes picked up from St Aloysius's rummage sale. 'We'll walk round to the stables and get your so-called husband to take you home.'

Bridie hesitated, forced herself to remember the letter. Sam Bell had promised not to trouble her except where the shop was concerned. She didn't really want to think about bed, could not encompass the idea of close contact with a man she had only just met. And he was old, with a terrible cough and thinning hair and a very dirty kitchen table.

Of course, there would be the cleaning, shopping, cooking, washing and ironing; there would also be his mother to tend and the girls to mind. Those things were a woman's lot, part and parcel of the institution called marriage. Compared to all those chores, the part-time running of a shop promised to be easy. If only he would give her a room of her own. She clenched her fists into tight knots and prayed that he would not touch her.

Bridie sat slumped in the midst of disaster and wondered whether she would ever be sane again. The walk from Dryden Street to Newsham Street Stables and thence to Bell's Pledges had been interesting, to say the least. The actual stables had been closed for the night, so Bridie had been denied the chance to see the two horses. She and Diddy had spoken to the gypsy whose husband owned the business, had been told that Sam and his companions had left some time earlier.

Flashes of what Bridie had seen outside kept leaping

before her mind's eye like cinema film that jerked its way over sticky spools. She had brought her children into a place of perpetual motion and constant bustle, it seemed.

She leaned back, allowed her eyelids to droop. Noises from the road continued – people shouting, running, singing. It was plain that every shop in the neighbourhood intended to trade until midnight. Bridie was frightened, scared almost to death of the Scotland Road folk. They were loud and emotional, as if their feelings dwelt just a fraction of an inch below the skin's surface. How easily they laughed, argued, fought. How quick were their eyes and movements, how rushed was their speech.

On hearing that Sam Bell and Thomas Murphy had left the stables before the arrival of Bridie and Big Diddy, the latter had shooed home her own offspring before dragging Bridie from Newsham Street into the Holy House, then had forced the new immigrant to face the crammed bar with its thick blanket of tobacco smoke and its stench of stale beer.

Bridie closed her eyes and allowed herself a little smile. As long as she lived, she would never forget that moment. Diddy had strode into the hostelry, had pushed aside anything and anyone in her path. 'Billy Costigan?' she had roared. 'Sam Bell? If you're in there, get out here. That goes for Thomas Murphy, too.' For several seconds, silence had visited the bar.

Bridie's grin widened. Perhaps the tendency to express sentiments so vigorously might even be fun? Perhaps the people hereabouts were all like Diddy – strong, kind and given to bouts of laughter? Oh, she hoped with all her heart that she might feel for others what she felt for this first friend.

Well. She tapped the arm of the chair. Here sat Bridie Bell, recently O'Brien, née Murphy, in a room filled with the clutter of travel, in the house of a man whose property she had just become. The ring was in her pocket. She could not wear it, because it was too big by a mile. If he touched her, she would surely die. If he touched her, she would run away.

Big Diddy Costigan was doubtless a trustworthy soul, as she had produced a key to the back door of Bell's Pledges. 'I keep this in case of emergencies,' she had said. Had the good woman been unable to gain access to Bell's, Bridie would have been spending her wedding night elsewhere. Wedding night. She would find her way upstairs in a minute, would seek out her daughters and her own bedroom and ... and the old woman. How many rooms? One for Mrs Bell, one for the girls, one for ... Would she be forced to sleep in the same room, in the same bed as a man old enough to be her father?

A key turned. Bridie froze, her ears straining towards the shop.

'Come in, Tom.' The voice belonged to Sam Bell. 'Sit on this stool while I find you a drop of good Irish.' Although the Liverpool accent was present in his language, the man spoke clearly, was easy to understand.

Bottle and glasses clinked faintly.

'I hope you're satisfied.' These words came from Thomas Murphy. 'You drive a hard bargain, Sam Bell. After all, she's young and healthy, strong and able. She works hard and doesn't complain. You should be paying me, man–'

'You wanted her settled,' replied Bridie's husband. 'I mean, it's not my fault if her husband's family's Protestant. And she's not on her own, is she? There are two children who'll want feeding and clothing.'

'Cathy can help in the shop. She's a bright enough girl, though she needs a firm hand.'

Bridie's heart beat feverishly. A firm hand? If anyone lifted as much as a finger, she would surely leave this place and take the children far away.

'I was all right,' said Sam. 'I'd no intention of getting married again. In fact, nothing was further from my mind. I'm set in my ways, you know, getting a bit long in the tooth for fresh starts.'

'Too late,' chortled the Irishman. 'The bargain's made and the wedding's over. You've two fine horses out of it, haven't you? Silver will fetch a pretty penny once he's broken properly. And the mare's as solid as a rock.'

Another drink was poured. Bridie leaned forward in her chair. Da had paid this pawnbroker to marry her. Her flesh crawled as if she had suddenly become infested by some particularly virulent parasite. Surely to God a father didn't go about trying to get rid of his only child?

'John Baker knows all there is to know about horse-flesh,' grumbled Sam Bell. 'He's not interested in either of the animals, says there's no call for them at the moment.'

'What?' roared Thomas Murphy. 'Of course he's interested. He's just acting the part in the hope of a better bargain. I'm telling you, man, Silver will be a good runner. It's all in the breeding. And, if you manage to race him without gelding, you'll have a pension from the stud fees.'

'I'm not so sure of that.'

The two men continued to talk. Bridie, shocked to the core, realized that her father had sunk to depths even lower than she had ever imagined. She had been sold. No, that was not the case, she told herself. In fact, if she had been sold, then she might have had some idea of her own value. Da hadn't even managed to give her away; he had paid someone to relieve him of his burden.

With her eyes adjusting to the dimness, she managed to make out the shape of a sofa. The reason behind Da's moment of hesitation in the church was now as clear as day. He had parted with two valuable horses, had been reluctant to give away so much. She was worthless in the eyes of her own father, simply because she brought no money in. Horses were, of course, a great deal more important than blood relatives.

Quietly, she rose and tiptoed across the room. A small case hung open. Little Tildy-Anne Costigan had probably raided this piece of luggage to find the girls' nightwear. Bridie lifted boxes and packages, placed them quietly on the floor. The wedding night problem was solved. She would sleep here on the sofa with her coat acting as a blanket. Tears threatened, but she blinked them back. Da could continue his journey towards hell, but she intended to make the best of an appalling situation.

Sleep did not come easily. When she finally dozed off, she was back in Ballinasloe. The old castle oversaw the ongoings, kept its many eyes on river, market and church. Cattle straggled along lazily, birds sang, Mrs O'Hara stood outside the forge while her husband laboured and sweated over horses' shoes. Brendan Gallagher rested against a wall, a glass of dark stout in his hand.

Mammy came along the street, her black skirt sweeping the dust, the snow-white apron starched and ironed, a shawl about her shoulders. She waved at Bridie before disappearing into the churchyard. Even in the dream, Bridie remembered that her mother was dead. But look, Eugene was coming along on that terrible, bone-shaking bicycle. His blond hair was sticking out in all directions, and his face was pink after toiling in the fields. Eugene had come back to her!

Bridie ran to him, touched his shoulder, breathed in the scents of the earth that always seemed to cling to his clothing. They would be married tomorrow.

Eugene kissed her, lifted her off her feet and onto the handlebars, took her along the bumpy street and struggled to keep the balance for both of them. She was so happy. She could hear him laughing, could feel the wind in her face.

She woke, looked around her. Sweet Jesus, what was she doing here? What would Eugene have said about this terrible business? No, no, she wouldn't cry. From the next room, the room that was a shop, Thomas Murphy's voice continued to drone. Wondering what Eugene might have thought and said was a waste of time. Had he lived, she would never have come here.

Sam Bell lit the gas, allowed the flame to glow for a few seconds before turning it down. Bridie was asleep on the sofa, had been here all the time, then. Had she heard? Did she know that her father had persuaded, cajoled and bribed in order to get someone to take her off his hands?

Big Diddy Costigan breathed down Sam's neck. 'You shouldn't have gone off like that after the wedding,' she whispered. 'And I've worked out what you and Thomas Murphy have been up to. Why, Sam? What possessed you?'

The pawnbroker lifted his shoulders a fraction. 'He wanted rid of her, I suppose. If anything had ever happened to him, her in-laws might have taken charge.'

'He didn't plan this out of love, you know.'

Sam nodded.

'You shouldn't have done it. It's bloody evil. I mean, look at her. That girl could have got herself a younger man—'

'He wanted her away from Ireland.'

Big Diddy dragged the shopkeeper out of the living room and into the small, lean-to scullery. 'He wanted?' she hissed through clenched teeth. 'What the hell does it matter? It's her life, not his. She must have been desperate to get away – desperate enough to fasten herself to some-body she'd never even clapped eyes on. Well,' she spat, 'I hope you get what you deserve, Sam Bell. I hope your horses never break into so much as a bloody trot.'

He pulled away from her. Diddy was not the sort of woman he wanted to cross. She was universally loved and respected. 'I'll look after her,' he muttered lamely.

'See that you do. Because you'll have me and Billy to answer to if any harm comes to her or the children. Your card's marked. We'll be watching you.' Her hand raised itself and the index finger jabbed in his direction. 'That dad of hers is a rotten bugger. He's been warming Dolly Hanson's bed for years – even before his wife died, I'm sure. This poor girl's not got a father – he's more of an excuse. So you make her a good husband or I'll break your puny little neck. And that, Sam, is a promise.' She flung open the door and marched out.

Sam returned to the kitchen-cum-living room. For several minutes, he lingered in his chair next to the range, watched the pretty young woman sleeping. This was his wife. He thought about Maria, who had given him twin boys before slipping away quietly with pneumonia brought on by the exhausting confinement. He thought about Muth, who had stepped in immediately to raise the motherless Liam and Anthony.

Sam Bell fixed his eyes on the dampened fire, wondered what the hell he was going to do with a child bride, two female youngsters and a couple of mad, scarcely broken racehorses. He shouldn't have listened to Thomas Murphy. The idea of taking on a resident nurse for Muth was sound enough, but marriage was a frightening step. As for horses – well – they had a leg at each corner. Four-legged furniture was something he understood, but valuable animals were not his forte.

Bridie shivered, muttered something in her sleep. A tear

made its way down her cheek. He hoped she wasn't going to be a moaner. She had been advertised by her father as biddable, strong and good-natured. The concept of a colleen wailing all over the house was not a happy one.

Silently, he crossed the room and turned off the gaslight. Bed was the best place for a man as exhausted and confused as he was. He checked that all was well in the shop, made sure that every bolt was fixed. Muth would be asleep by now. A young woman from Wilbraham Street had been instructed to feed and settle the old lady.

Bridie opened her eyes and listened while the man climbed his stairs. She had felt his scrutiny. A proper wife would have followed him to the upper storey, would have been glad to spend the night next to her husband. But Bridie was not a proper wife. Two horses had entered the bargaining arena. Mr Bell had required a great deal of persuasion, because he hadn't really wanted to remarry.

She struggled to her feet, dragged the coat about chilled shoulders. Tomorrow, her new life must begin. But for the rest of this night, she must remain in limbo.

Three

Cathy woke, discovered an elbow in her face. Where was she? Ah yes, they had come on a boat to Liverpool, everyone except Granda had felt sick, then Mammy had been married last night. The man Mammy had married was very, very old, because a lot of his hair had gone. It was all very frightening. It would have been so much nicer if they could have stayed at home. Cathy missed her own bed, her dog, her chicken and all the horses. Even living with Granda would have been better than Liverpool, though she had little love for her mother's father. But she must try to be a big girl, because Mammy had all to do for Shauna, who was not thriving.

Although a pall of darkness hung in the air, Cathy sensed that this was morning. She kicked out at the other person, who was extremely knobbly and sharp. 'Take your arm away, please,' she implored.

Tildy rolled to one side, hit the floor with a none too quiet bump. 'Jesus,' she muttered angrily. 'You're worse than our Nicky, you are. No need to throw me across the bloody room. After I looked after you, too.'

Cathy sat up. 'What are you doing here? And you shouldn't be blaspheming. You shouldn't say Jesus except when you're praying, and you should bow your head when you say it.'

'I'll say what I bloody want,' replied Tildy smartly. 'You've hurt me.'

'Is this your bed?'

'No, it's yours. But even if it is your bed, you shouldn't be kicking me out of it. I stayed with you, didn't I? Mr Anthony Bell told me to look after you and your sister – remember?'

Cathy remembered some of it. Mammy had gone to sleep in a corner. The pigeons had been asleep, too. There had been loads of food called spiceballs and ribs, and she had eaten two slices of something described as bunloaf. A man called Anthony had carried Cathy through the streets. 'Did you carry my sister Shauna here?' she asked.

'Yes. I got in bed with her at first, but she's a wriggler. So I climbed in with you.' She shivered. There had been a fire in the corner of the bedroom, but that had gone out hours earlier. 'Let's get dressed,' she suggested. 'And I'll show you round Mr Bell's shop. Our Charlie works here, you know. He's me brother and he's a clever lad. He looks a bit funny, but he's all right. Then our Nicky – that's Monica – runs a stall on Paddy's Market. She sells the stuff what gets left over downstairs – stuff what's not worth much. Me and our Cozzer help out after school, like, if she's busy.'

Cathy struggled into her clothes. She had often heard people saying that Galway was on the chilly side of Ireland, but this place was surely the coldest in the world. 'I don't like Liverpool,' she grumbled.

'That's all right,' answered Tildy. 'Liverpool might not like you. Me mam's always saying that. They say funny things, don't they?'

On that score, Cathy was forced to agree. She nodded swiftly, then rubbed her numbed fingers together.

They crept out onto the dark landing. Tildy, who seemed accustomed to the place, took a box of matches from a small table and lit a gas lamp. 'There's the new electric downstairs,' she informed her companion. Tildy pointed out the doors on the opposite wall. 'Old Mrs Bell's in there,' she whispered. 'You have to go through her room for a bath. There's a real bath with taps. I stop with old Mrs Bell sometimes when Mr Bell goes off fishing.' She sniffed. 'Me mam says fishermen are the most boring people in the whole world. He is a bit boring.'

Cathy, who was trying hard not to be even more scared, spoke up. 'Your mammy says a lot of things.'

'Well, she's always right. Me dad says she's always right.'

'My mammy's clever too.'

'Good,' beamed Tildy. 'They'll be fit for one another, then.' She pointed out Mr Bell's room, which was next to his mother's, then gave her attention to another pair of doors alongside the room in which Shauna still slept. 'Used to be two houses. That's why there's a lot of rooms. Me mam says Mr Bell's minted. Anyway, that's a storeroom and that's another storeroom.'

'What's minted?' asked Cathy.

'Got a lot of money. No rent book. He bought this place outright. He's got millions of stuff, millions and millions. There's these bedrooms packed to the ceiling, things in the roof,' she pointed to a trapdoor above her head, 'a storeroom in the back yard, one next to the kitchen and another under the stairs. Some people pawn things, and some people sell them to Mr Bell.'

'What's pawn?'

Tildy sighed in the face of such stupidity. 'On a Monday when there's no money, you take stuff to the pawnshop – clothes and boots and wedding rings. Then, on a Friday when you get paid, you redeem the things. Don't ask me what redeem is – it's a word for getting your clothes back.'

Cathy pondered for a moment. This girl was very, very

quick-mouthed. It might be best not to mention that the nuns at home talked about redeeming souls by the grace of the Holy Ghost. It was all very bewildering, but she did not wish to appear stupid, so she bit back a comment about the pledging of an individual's inner spirit.

They creaked their way downstairs and into the shop. Tildy had been right – the shop did have electric light. Cathy wondered briefly about this miracle, spent a few seconds clicking the power on and off. Then, finding herself in an Aladdin's cave, she followed Tildy round Sam Bell's kingdom. There were bicycles and bicycle lamps that worked when the pedals turned. There was a wigwam, a box of lead soldiers, a set of drums and a box of football rattles.

'This is the music department,' Tildy pointed to a dusty corner. 'That's a cornet, trumpet, mandolin, guitar, zither.' She stabbed a bitten, black-rimmed fingernail at the exhibits. 'He'd have pianos, only they won't come through the door. He had bagpipes once and our Cozzer borrowed them. Sounded like a load of cats getting tortured.'

Cathy wandered about looking at rugs, tin baths, bed-steads, chamber pots, butter dishes, hair clippers, gramo-phones, stock pots and fish kettles. At the front of the shop there was a huge window filled with all kinds of booty from sewing machines to cricket bats.

Tildy joined Cathy at the window. 'That's Scotland Road out there.' There was a kind of pride in her tone. 'The other window on the side looks out at Penrhyn Street. He keeps smaller things on show there, and new buckets and all that. The stuff with tickets stuck on,' she swept a hand around the shelf-filled walls, 'they're all pledges and they're kept away from the rest. Nobody can buy them while there's a ticket stuck on. But when your ticket runs out, he can sell your pledge.'

Cathy nodded thoughtfully. 'If you have no money when the Friday comes.'

Tildy grinned. At last, her attempt to educate Cathy seemed to be paying off. 'The dockers'll be walking past in a minute. They work on the ships, loading and unloading. Me dad's a docker. It's Friday, so this shop'll be busy tonight when people start picking their pledges up. They'll want their best suits and shoes for mass on Sunday. Mr Mellor's teeth'll be under the counter somewhere. He only has teeth at weekends.'

Cathy's stomach rolled cavernously as she thought about the poor, toothless Mr Mellor. 'I'm starving,' she decided. 'The boat made me feel so sick, I thought I'd never be hungry again. But I am.' As if underlining her words, Cathy's stomach rolled again magnificently.

Tildy knew all about hunger, though she had seldom appreciated it first hand. 'Come round to ours,' she said. 'Me mam'll have the porridge ready.'

The younger girl hesitated. 'What about Mammy? She won't know where I've gone.'

'Don't be worrying. Your mam'll still be in bed.'

'Where? There was no bed for her in our room.' At Granda's, Mammy had shared a room with her daughters.

'With Mr Bell, of course. Married people stay in the same room. Did you not know that?'

Cathy shrugged, blushed, hated her own ignorance. 'I know, I know. I'd just forgotten, that's all.'

'Never mind.' Tildy was the eternal optimist. 'You'll get used to it, girl. Come on, let's go for some breakfast.'

Bridie was beside herself. During the night, she had made her way upstairs, had managed to get about by lighting her path with a candle. The girls and Tildy Costigan had been fast asleep, so she had returned to the comfortless sofa to rest her travel-wearied bones. And now, at seven o'clock in the morning, one of her daughters seemed to have disappeared into thin air.

Shauna moaned in her mother's arms. 'Want Cathy. Where she gone?'

Bridie tutted, threw open a door, peered into a room filled with bulky shapes. The next bedroom was the same – piled high with junk, no sign of occupation. 'Are you hiding in there?' she asked fruitlessly. Then, in a room opposite the one assigned to Cathy and Shauna, Bridie finally found humanity of a kind. 'Who's there?' croaked a rusty voice.

Bridie hesitated, placed Shauna on her feet and advanced, the candle held before her like a very frail defence. 'I'm Bridie,' she said. 'And Cathy's gone missing, so I'm—'

'Hold the light up. Let's have a look at you.' The tone was imperious, and the accent announced a person whose origins were not hereabouts. 'So you're the new wife. Hmmph. Not much flesh on you. Will you be able to lift me? I need turning a few times so I won't have bedsores. It gets uncomfortable being stuck in bed all the while.'

Bridie couldn't have cared less about anything – including this rude old woman's various disorders. 'Look, can we talk about that later? My daughter is missing.' She pondered for a second. 'And there's another one gone, too, one called Tildy.'

Theresa Bell sucked briefly on her few remaining teeth. 'Go to Dryden Street after,' she advised. 'That's where they'll be, in Elizabeth Costigan's house. But first, I'll have my cup of tea, two sugars and no milk.'

Bridie stood her ground. 'I must find Cathy first,' she insisted.

'Then wake Sam,' snapped the old woman. 'He's always

got my breakfast up to now, so once more won't hurt.' She sniffed. 'He's not a lot of use to me, but he makes a good brew.'

Bridie turned, dragged her younger child back to the landing. There was only one door left. She knew he was behind it, because she had peeped in there a few hours ago when looking for the girls' room. 'Wait here for Mammy,' she told Shauna. After taking a deep breath, she approached the door.

He was awake and seated on the edge of his double bed. The remaining hair stuck out round his head like a slipped halo. 'Morning,' he mumbled. 'Have you seen to Muth?' He sneezed, coughed, fumbled with a hand-kerchief.

'Who? Oh, yes – I mean no. I've seen her, but I've done nothing for her because I'm worried about Cathy.'

Sam, too, was worried about Cathy. Last night, Thomas Murphy had painted a graphic picture of the older girl's carryings-on at the landing stage. Sam avoided trouble whenever possible. The feud between his sons was yet to be settled, but Sam had placed himself alongside the righteous. Oh yes, he had invested his faith in Liam, an ordained priest. Anthony would mellow in time, he felt sure. But Sam didn't fancy another cartload of mischief from his bride's offspring. 'What's Cathy done?' he asked.

'She's disappeared.'

He yawned. 'She'll be getting her breakfast round at the Costigan house. Tildy's probably with her, so she'll come to no harm, you can be sure of that.'

Bridie swallowed. No harm? At just gone seven in the morning, Scotland Road was lively. The drumming of feet along the pavement was almost continuous, might have belonged to a battalion of shabbily drilled soldiers. 'This is a busy place for a country child,' she said. 'I'll have to find her.'

He shrugged. 'Children don't disappear round here. They go off for hours, but they come back. I hope Cathy's not trying to be difficult. Running this place is hard enough without—'

'I shall look after my girls, Mr Bell, just as I always have.'

He dropped his head pensively. 'You'll have to call me Sam. And you can sleep in here from now on.'

Bridie's flesh crawled.

'There's no fire in here,' he added. 'The only rooms with chimneys are Muth's and your daughters'.' He stared at her sleepily. 'I'm a reasonable man, Bridie. You help me and I'll help you. That sounds fair, doesn't it? At least the nights should be warmer if we share a bed. It is a very cold winter.' He perked up slightly. 'Still, once the weather warms up and you've got used to the shop, I'll be able to go fishing.'

Unable to lay her tongue across a suitable response, Bridie dashed from the room and picked up her younger child. 'Come on,' she managed eventually. 'We'll go and find your sister.'

She ran along the pavement, the blanket-wrapped Shauna clutched to her chest. Men bearing small tin lunchboxes and billycans pounded towards her, and she almost collided with a woman who carried a huge pannier of fruit. Shops were already opening, their doors hanging inwards, customers popping in for the day's allocation of tobacco, milk and bread. Prams filled with washing rolled along like a wagon train, while early tramcars filled with human cargo clattered past on iron rails. For Bridie, this place was the ultimate nightmare.

At the corner of Dryden Street, she paused for breath. He wanted her to share a bed with him. He wanted his rights as a husband. Hadn't he said in the letter that he would not trouble her? Oh, she would think later, after

Cathy was safely home. She marched up the street, nodded at people who seemed vaguely familiar. If she didn't sleep with him, he might have the marriage annulled. And would that be an altogether bad thing? she wondered.

All the houses looked the same, and she couldn't remember which one she had visited the night before. She knocked on a door from behind which the sounds of human occupation could be heard. Annulment would mean returning to Da. Da would gloat endlessly about such failure.

The door opened. 'What do you want?' The speaker was pale and thin. An even paler baby mewled in the woman's arms.

'I'm looking for the Costigans,' said Bridie.

'Four houses up.' The door slammed.

Bridie covered the rest of the distance in a few strides.

'Come in,' smiled Big Diddy. She led Bridie through the small parlour and into the kitchen. Billy and Charlie were at the table finishing their breakfasts. Maureen preened at the mirror while Nicky struggled into a coat. 'It's cold round at Paddy's,' she told Bridie by way of explanation. 'Is he up?'

Bridie's eyes were fixed on Cathy. 'Why did you go without telling me? Don't you understand that we're in a strange place and that I would be worrying?'

Cathy ladled golden syrup onto her porridge. She was seated near the fire, was using the box-shaped wire fire-guard as a table. 'Sorry, missus,' said Tildy. She was at the other side of the range. 'It was my fault.'

'Is he?' repeated Nicky.

'I beg your pardon. Were you talking to me?' asked Bridie.

'Oh, never mind.' Nicky flounced out of the room.

Diddy descended on Bridie and prised Shauna out of her grasp. 'Sit down,' she begged. 'Have a cup of tea and a bite to eat.' She gave the three-year-old a shive of bread and jam. Shauna sat on the floor and watched Tildy shovelling porridge.

Bridie dropped into a chair. 'I won't have her running wild,' she told her hostess. 'At home, she never strayed far, and we knew everybody. Here, it's different. Cathy will have to learn to take care in these parts.'

Big Diddy nodded sagely. 'She'll learn all right. I've told you, they grow up quick round here.' When the tea was poured, Diddy kissed her departing husband, then dragged Maureen away from the mirror. 'If you carry on like this, you'll need laughing gas while we peel you off that bloody dresser. And the job'll be gone. Remember, no cheek and no batting the eyelashes. You're there to serve Dolly Hanson's customers, not to make eyes at anything in trousers.'

Charlie wiped his mouth on a corner of the tablecloth, belched and stood up.

'That's right, love,' said his mother. 'You go and help Mr Bell.'

Charlie shuffled out, almost colliding with the door while grinning at Bridie.

'He likes you,' announced Diddy. 'He's special, our Charlie. There's a lot more to him than what you see. Deep, he is.' She pushed a pint pot of tea at her guest, then ladled out enough porridge to feed a small nation. 'Put yourself outside of that,' she ordered. 'It'll line your ribs right through Christmas.'

Bridie tasted the porridge, found it delicious and said so. 'Do all your children work?' she asked between mouthfuls.

Diddy parted the digits of her right hand, counted off with the left index finger. 'Charlie's me eldest – he's seventeen and he works nearly full time for Sam. Our Monica

64

– she's very hard-working. Only fifteen, but she runs a stall on Paddy's, sells things from junkshops including Bell's.'

Bridie waited, watched the large woman's frown.

'I worry about our Maureen. Thirteen going on thirty, she is. This is her last year at school. She does a couple of hours in a morning for Dolly Hanson, then a couple more hours after school. She's getting dancing lessons at Mary Turner's.'

'Fairy Mary's?' asked Bridie.

Diddy nodded. 'You're catching on, girl.' She sat down opposite Bridie. 'There's always a crowd of lads chasing our Maureen, like flies round a jam pot.' She shook her head. 'There'll be trouble with her sooner or later.'

'Try not to worry.'

Big Diddy smiled at her newfound friend. 'Funny. I'm talking to you like I've always known you. Must be your face. It's very open.' She took a slurp of tea. 'Tildy-Anne's ten. She's another hard worker.' Diddy beamed at her daughter. 'Reminds me of meself at her age. Then Jimmy's the youngest. He's nine and everybody knows him as Cozzer. A good lad. But he's always losing his boots. Takes them off down the landing stage, pretends to be poorer than he really is. Says people feel sorry for him and give him work. He's a bloody character.'

Bridie admitted defeat and laid down her spoon. 'It's wonderful stuff, Diddy, but my stomach's full.' She eyed Tildy and Cathy. 'Wouldn't you like to take another look at Mr Costigan's pigeons?'

Big Diddy pointed to a carton on the dresser. 'You can feed them for me.' She waited until the girls had gone out with Shauna hot on their heels. 'He's a lovely feller, my Billy, but the pigeons get me down. Still, men have to have an interest, like. If they've got interests, they don't get into mischief down the pub.'

Bridie took a sip of tea strong enough to take the breath away. 'Sam's interest is fishing, I'm told.'

Diddy stirred a fourth spoonful of sugar into her own measure of the bitter brew. 'He just sits there,' she said. 'With a long pole and a hook and a little bucket full of maggots. Breeds the buggers in his meatsafe, so watch your food, 'cos they have been known to travel.' She blew into the blue-and-white striped mug. 'I don't know what he gets out of it, Bridie. Reels them in, measures them, chucks them back most of the time.'

'You don't like him,' said Bridie.

'I never said that.'

'No.'

'He's not a man you love or hate. He's just there.'

'Like maggots are just there?'

Big Diddy shrugged. 'Not as bad as maggots, not as good as angels. He's there like a lamp-post is there. Has his uses, but you don't really look at him.'

Bridie nodded thoughtfully. 'His mother?'

Diddy almost choked on her tea. 'Now, that one's a bloody star turn, all right. Went to bed during the General Strike, hasn't hardly moved since.' She giggled, sounded girlish. 'Well, let's put that another way. Theresa Bell thinks we think she's failing. But she's up and down them stairs like sh— ... like sugar off a shiny shovel when she feels like it. I mean, she's stood at that bedroom window for hours watching the world go by. It's as if ... oh, I don't know what I mean.'

'Try to know,' urged Bridie. 'I need to understand the household.'

Diddy pulled a cigarette stub from behind an ear, lit the blackened end, inhaled deeply. 'It's all about Liam and Anthony, I think. See, old Theresa loves the bones of Anthony, only Anthony doesn't visit no more unless his dad's out. In fact, it was a bloody miracle that he turned up at your wedding. Still, he was minding your girls, I suppose. He loves children.'

Bridie pondered. 'And Liam hates Anthony—'

'And Sam thinks the sun shines out of Liam's back passage. Now, if you're talking about not liking, well, I'll tell you now I can't stand sight or sound of Father High-and-Mighty Liam Bell. Old Theresa feels the same. So she's been sulking for about three and a half years.'

'Sam loves his mother.'

Diddy ground out the spent cigarette in her porridge bowl. 'Sam's a funny bugger. He doesn't have any strong feelings, never loses his rag, doesn't often smile, doesn't panic. When Maria died – she was his first wife – he never so much as flickered, or so I've been told. Theresa brought the twins up, 'cos they were only babies when their mam passed on, like.' She dropped her head for a moment. 'I remember my mam laying Maria out, poor soul. All skin and bone, my mam said.' Diddy raised her chin. 'But the root of all the trouble in that house is Liam, I'm sure. Anthony's dead straight, wouldn't harm nobody.'

'A teacher?'

Diddy's head bobbed up and down. 'They all love him, even the nuns. He takes the top junior class at Aloysius's.'

'And he isn't married?'

The older woman's face clouded over. 'Bridie, that lad's had one hell of a life. Valerie, her name was. Lived with her mam and dad in Virgil Street – nice family – and she got engaged to Anthony. It was about five years ago. She ... died, like.'

Bridie placed her mug on the oilcloth that served as weekday table cover. 'How?'

Diddy lifted a shoulder. 'She was found strangled down Sylvester Street at the back of the school. They hanged a man for it.' She stood up, stared into the near distance. 'From Bootle, he was. Right to the end, he said he never did it. But . . .' Her eyes adjusted themselves and she smiled at the visitor. 'I suppose they all say that, don't they?'

'I wouldn't know.'

Diddy picked up the dishes and began to stack them. 'Valerie's mother says to this day they hanged the wrong man.'

'Oh?' Bridie didn't know what to say in the face of such tragedy.

'She'd been interfered with. She was in a mess, or so we were told. The man they hanged was found fast asleep and drunk as a lord in a school doorway round the back. He'd been celebrating 'cos he'd got a job in one of the bonded warehouses, and he'd no memory of where he'd been. People who'd seen him earlier on spoke up for him, but there were a couple of hours missing. Bridie, he had a wife and two little boys. Gentle as a lamb, according to his neighbours. He wasn't a drinker. The whole of Bootle told the police he wasn't a drinker. Made no difference.' She sighed deeply. 'He was in the wrong place at the wrong time, so they made him pay for it.'

Bridie suppressed a shudder. Oh, what was she doing here? At home, her children had been able to run and play without fear. As far as she knew, no-one in Ballinasloe had been murdered or hanged . . . 'So Anthony's all alone now.'

'He is. Don't talk about this to Sam, not yet. Get yourself settled in first. He won't be drawn, anyway. He's a quiet sort, not much to say for himself. But he's no time for their Anthony. In fact, like I said before, we were all gobsmacked when Anthony turned up at the wedding. That must be the first time they've all been together in the one place since . . . I don't know when.'

Bridie thanked Diddy, collected her daughters and said

goodbye. On her way to the shop, she noticed ice on the ground, had to place her feet carefully. In less than a month, it would be Christmas. What sort of a festive season would Cathy and Shauna have? Would that awful priest arrive? Would his kinder brother be all alone in Dryden Street? She shook her head in reply to her own unspoken question. Big Diddy Costigan would allow no-one to be isolated at Christmas.

Sam looked up when she entered the shop. 'You found her, then?'

Bridie offered no answer, as Cathy's presence precluded the silly enquiry.

'Take her to school,' advised Sam. 'Nine o'clock, St Aloysius Gonzaga. It's behind the church.'

Charlie grinned. 'School,' he managed. 'It's a nice school. You'll like it, Cathy.' The words sounded as if they were battling their way through a barrier.

Bridie picked her way past mangles and prams, took her children into the kitchen. With the gas turned up high, it was not a bad room, she pondered. It certainly didn't seem as terrible as she had thought just before the wedding. The sofa on which she had tried to sleep was matched by three armchairs. There was a dresser, a long and very messy table with six dining chairs and, in the alcoves that flanked the range, glass doors allowed some very decent pieces of dusty china to be seen. Everything was covered in bits of dirt and rubbish, but she would sort it out in time.

She placed Shauna in a chair. 'Cathy, we must get you ready for school.'

Cathy stood with her back to the fire. 'I don't want to go. I'm not going. You can't make me go.'

Bridie considered these statements. 'First of all, we must all do things we don't want to do. Secondly, you are going.

69

Thirdly, you are definitely going and yes, I can make you go. I'm older than you, bigger and stronger. If necessary, I shall carry you in like a big baby.'

Cathy started to snivel.

Shauna decided to come out in sympathy.

'Want Bob,' sobbed the older child.

'Want Bob,' cried the younger echo.

'Who's Bob?' Sam surveyed the scene from the doorway.

'He's my dog,' screamed Cathy. 'I don't like you and I don't like your dirty house and I want my dog.'

Bridie turned to apologize, saw that Sam was nodding his head. 'I'll get you a dog,' he said.

'Do you think that's altogether a good idea?' Bridie asked. 'Giving in to her like that?'

Sam wanted a quiet life. The shop was trouble enough without a pair of screaming infants in the living quarters. 'I was going to get a guard dog anyway,' he told Bridie.

Cathy cheered up immediately. 'Can he sleep inside?' she asked.

Bridie drew the line. 'If you must have an animal, he can live in a kennel.' She turned to the man who was supposed to be her husband. 'Get a grown dog,' she advised. 'One that's good with children.'

He inclined his head, then returned to the shop.

'Cathy, you are not going to have your own way all the time. Where are you going?'

Cathy stopped at the bottom of the stairs. 'To find a clean dress for school.' She smiled sweetly at her mother before dashing off upstairs.

Bridie sat at the table and shook her head. She was not taken in by Cathy's sudden change of heart. That girl was going to be a handful – of that, at least, Bridie felt certain.

*

By the time Cathy and Bridie arrived at the school, daylight was finally managing to filter through cloud and smoke. A cold drizzle clung to everything, soaked through clothing within moments. Even the rain was different, Bridie thought. It felt gritty and sticky, as if it had fought its way down through layers of grime and grease. She glanced towards the docks, remembered that her father would be sailing back to Ireland on this very day. Where was he? she wondered briefly. Where had he slept last night?

The school was an imposing sight, bigger by far than the tiny village school back home. St Aloysius Gonzaga Infant, Junior and Senior School was a Victorian building with two floors, tall windows and four gables on the front. There was a railing-edged playground, a large double-doored entrance and a view of the arch-windowed rear of St Aloysius Gonzaga's church.

'It's big,' remarked Cathy, her tone dwarfed by the awesome sight and by the sounds of children at play.

'You'll be all right.' The confidence in Bridie's tone belied her own misgivings. At twenty-seven years of age, she was terrified by the idea of going inside. She must go in, but she could come out. Poor Cathy had to stay here for years ... 'You're my big, brave girl,' she told her daughter. 'There's nothing you can't do, for you have a fine brain.'

Cathy swallowed a lump of terror. She was Mammy's big, brave girl, and she must continue stalwart because Mammy had all to do for Shauna, who was not thriving. Shauna was having a great time with Charlie, the strange-looking but kind son of Mr and Mrs Costigan. Shauna was sucking on a barley sugar stick and playing house with some grand, real pots and pans in a corner of a very interesting shop. 'Mammy?' breathed Cathy.

'What?'

'There are so many children, hundreds and hundreds.'

'You'll be marvellous.' Bridie squatted down and straightened her daughter's collar. 'Seven sevens?' she asked.

'Forty-nine.'

'Subtract twelve?'

'Thirty-seven.'

Bridie smiled. 'Can you read?'

'Yes.'

'And what did Daddy always say about school and learning?'

The little girl swallowed again, this time tasting the grief that had arrived with the passing of her father. She took a deep breath. 'Daddy said to plough the field one furrow at a time. He said the job looked big, but to just get on and do a little bit, then a little bit more.' She paused. 'He taught me to read.'

Bridie nodded. 'He taught me, too, Cathy. And he showed me how to keep the account books and how to write without blots. We won't forget him. We haven't come here to forget about Daddy.'

'Then why?' asked Cathy. 'Why are we here?'

Bridie bit back the tears. 'We must make the best we can of a world without Daddy in it.' They were here because Thomas Murphy had bribed a widower to take them on. 'We'll be fed and clothed and comfortable.' They were here because Thomas Murphy was a bigot who could see only one route to God. 'You must call Mr Bell Uncle Sam. He will care for us.' They were here to escape from Da and from the O'Briens whose antipathy to papism had made them turn their backs on their son. 'Be good,' advised Bridie.

'I don't want to go in, Mammy, I—'

'Come on.' Bridie rose to her feet and marched Cathy across the playground and into the school. An inner door bore the message, PHILIP MAHONEY, head teacher. Bridie paused, drew breath, knocked.

'Come,' bade a voice from within.

They entered. 'Oh,' said Bridie. 'You're not Mr Mahoney.'

The man behind the desk put his head on one side, rose to his feet and stood before a small fireplace in which coals glowed and flickered. He looked in the mirror above the mantel. 'You're right,' he pronounced after a few seconds, 'I'm not Mr Mahoney.' He looked at Cathy. There was a humorous twinkle in his eye, and a corner of his mouth twitched in response to threatening laughter. 'I am definitely not Mr Mahoney. This is a different face altogether.' He looked over his shoulder as if expecting to discover an eavesdropper. 'I am so much better looking than Mr Mahoney,' he added.

Cathy giggled. 'Did you not know who you were when you got up this morning?' she asked.

The teacher scratched his head. 'I thought I did,' he answered slowly. 'It seems I was wrong.'

'Yes, you were.' Cathy was delighted with the performance.

'You must say "sir",' chided her mother.

'Sir,' echoed Cathy.

Anthony Bell turned his attention to Bridie. 'In school, I'll have to be a sir, I suppose.' He left a space for an answer, got none. 'Are you settled?'

'Not yet,' answered Bridie. 'We're barely unpacked.'

Anthony glanced at the clock. 'I'll have to go in a minute to take morning prayers. The real headmaster is in hospital, I'm afraid, so I'll have to do for now.'

He would do very nicely, thought Bridie as she made her way out of the school. On the other side of the railings, she stood with a group of mothers, some laden with shopping baskets, some with prams containing babies, others with prams housing the seemingly ubiquitous packages of dirty washing.

'You're new,' announced the nearest.

'Yes,' agreed Bridie, who felt new and old at the same time.

'Just over from Ireland?' asked the thin, weary-looking woman.

'That's right.'

'Ah well, you'll get used to it. We all do, I suppose.' She walked away with the shabby pram whose occupant's thin cries sounded too frail for survival.

Anthony Bell blew a whistle and all the children froze. A second blast sent them scurrying into lines, then a short, fat nun appeared in the doorway to shepherd in her charges. She had a round face whose sunny expression was at odds with such vile weather.

Satisfied that her older child was in good hands, Bridie turned towards Scotland Road, stopping in her tracks when she heard the unmistakable neighing of a horse. For a split second, she was back on the farm. Eugene was ploughing while she sat on the gate and watched the proud carthorses plodding along, tails twitching, large heads bobbing like sages who laboured over books and maps. Horses are wise animals, she thought.

When the moment of reverie had passed, Bridie followed her instinct across the street. Opposite the school stood a cobbled yard surrounded by stables. Above a pair of battered gates hung the legend MCKINNELL STABLES. A gaudy caravan was parked in the centre of the yard, while the door of a shabby dwelling hung inward. Dark-haired children ran in and out of house and caravan, while a woman screamed at the top of her voice, 'Get gone into that school. You're late.'

Half a dozen youngsters sped past Bridie, across the street and through the school gates.

The gypsy woman stood on the cobbles shaking a fist. 'Get right inside the classrooms. I've told yous before, if yous come out early, your dad'll rattle the bones of your heads.' She pursed her lips and blew out a puff of exasperation before giving her attention to Bridie. 'Did you want something, missus? Oh – you were here last night, weren't you?'

'Yes.' Bridie hesitated for a split second. Yes, of course she knew why she was here. 'Have you a grey stallion and a chestnut mare?'

'Thomas Murphy's horses?' asked the woman.

'Sam Bell's now, I believe.'

The gypsy woman nodded vigorously. 'Aye, they'll be his now, all right. Did you ever hear the likes? He knows nothing about horses, Sam Bell. We're trying to sell them.'

'Could I see them?' asked Bridie.

'Help yourself,' advised the gypsy woman. She waved a dark brown hand towards a pair of stables at the furthest point from the house. 'If you need me, I'll be inside having my breakfast.' She shook her already tousled head. 'Getting that lot to school is worse than threading a pony through the eye of a needle.'

While the woman strode off, Bridie almost managed a smile. Shouldn't the odd quotation involve a camel rather than a horse? The smell of equine life filled her nostrils, made her feel at home again. She had been bareback riding since she could walk, had been born with a love for horses. With the wind in her hair and a mane in her grip, she had coaxed many an animal halfway across County Galway.

She entered the first stall. 'Sorrel,' she whispered. 'Hello, my girl.'

Sorrel, whose name had been born because of her light colour, almost grinned at the well-remembered friend. She nuzzled Bridie as if begging to be taken out for a run.

'There's nowhere for you,' said Bridie. 'But I swear there will be.' She sniffed, wondered what had driven her to make such a rash promise. 'I'll do my best to get you out of here. And the gypsies exercise you, don't they?'

Sorrel nodded friskily.

'All right,' said Bridie. 'You win.'

She dragged a mounting block into the stable and jumped onto Sorrel's back. As soon as she gripped the animal's mane, she was elsewhere. Round and round the caravan she rode, eyes closed, cold drizzle wetting her face. No-one would take Sorrel away from her. There must be a way, there had to be a way. If she could only keep this mare, a degree of joy and freedom would always be available.

With Sorrel returned to her rightful place, Bridie entered Silver's stall. Quicksilver was a different kettle altogether. With his flaring nostrils and huge eyes, he displayed the intelligence and quickness so typical of Arab stock. Although he knew Bridie, he still reacted to human-kind in the age-old way, ears pricked, eyes rolling slightly as he prepared for flight.

Bridie leaned on the half-door and spoke to him. 'Silver, Silver, Silver,' she intoned.

He steadied, but continued to eye her warily.

'Grand fellow,' she told him. Apart from her children, horses were her greatest passion. Reading had opened up so much for her. She had learned about the physical construction of the horse, his needs, his weaknesses, his abilities, his pride.

'You've ploughed for us and died in battle with us,' she told him. 'You've jousted and hunted and pulled our heaviest loads. I saw in a book that the word chivalry comes from your kind. Chivalry means honour, and you are the most honourable of beasts.'

Silver quietened, listened to her. 'Did you know about Wellington's horse? Copenhagen was his name. Did you hear about him ever? He was buried with full military honours, so he was. Did you know there are paintings and statues of horses? You are so beautiful, so good...' She reached out and touched the quivering neck. 'Just to please us, you all work so hard. Will you hold me, Silver? Will you do that?'

He showed her his teeth, as if trying to answer her.

'Good boy. I see the baby teeth are gone. Is this you ready to begin racing? Would you run like the wind for a cup and a ribbon? Would you?'

The horse whinnied.

Bridie approached him, made sure that he could see her properly. She had no wish to take punishment from such powerful rear limbs. She placed her face next to his, could feel his breath on her neck. 'I shall own you,' she informed him. 'I don't know how – perhaps I must steal to make sure. But you and Sorrel will be my horses.'

He clipped the floor with a hoof.

Slowly, carefully, she opened the door and drew him outside. As he came alongside a fixed mounting block, she began to hum and stroke his side. For a split second, the horse tensed, then he relaxed as Bridie broke into song. The singing had no verbal pattern or rhyme, but the rhythm was steady. 'I shall climb on your back and ride you,' she sang.

When the ground was almost seventeen hands below her, Bridie gripped Silver's mane and waited to be thrown forward. For Bridie, riding was first, not second nature. It was a simple business involving a good seat, a sense of balance and firm use of hands and legs. 'Walk now,' she sang.

He walked.

77

The gypsy woman appeared in the doorway, her mouth hanging open. 'Mother of Jesus,' she breathed to herself. 'That one's lively.'

Bridie grinned. 'He's nearly broken,' she informed the spectator. 'He only needs to relearn his manners.'

Silver circled the caravan like a docile nag.

When the horse was safely back in his stable, Bridie approached the woman. 'Is your husband in?'

'No. He's out on business. Can I help you?' Admiration for the fearless rider showed in her tone. If this lady could manage the grey stallion, she should be fit enough for the devil himself on judgement day.

Bridie dug the 'new' wedding ring out of her pocket, then hesitated for just a second before pulling Eugene's ring from her right hand. Eugene would have approved, she told herself firmly. 'I've my mother's gold locket as well,' she said. 'I'll bring it tomorrow. There's not enough for the two horses, but the value should feed them for a while. All you have to do is tell me when someone tries to buy the mare and the stallion. Come to Bell's. Speak only to me about this.'

The gypsy picked at her teeth with a shaved match. 'You his new wife?'

'I am. Please say nothing to him or to anyone else.'

The woman nodded, slipped the rings into a pocket and looked over Bridie's shoulder. 'Hello, Mr Murphy. Did you come to see the horses one last time?'

Bridie swung round. 'Da,' she muttered.

'What are you doing here?' he asked.

'Introducing myself.' Bridie straightened her spine. 'I've just put Cathy into the school.'

Thomas Murphy grunted. 'I'm away now,' he told his daughter.

She made no reply.

'I'll see you when I bring over more stock.'

Bridie inclined her head, then turned her back on her father. 'I am very pleased to make your acquaintance,' she told the woman in the doorway.

Rosa McKinnell, whose instinct for horses and folk was strong, removed the match from between a gap in her upper incisors. There was no love lost between these two people, she realized instantly. And were she to take sides, she would definitely come down on the side of the new Mrs Bell.

Bridie walked out of the yard and towards Scotland Road. Silver. Had it not seemed like an insult to the animal, she might have considered renaming him.

She entered the shop, saw Shauna playing with a box of toy bricks. Yes. Thirty Pieces of Silver would have been a suitable tide. But she loved the horse too much to burden him. Now, all she had to do was find some money. To buy the two horses, she would need more than thirty pieces. A great deal more.

Four

By Christmas Eve, Bridie had quietly organized her new household. Curtains were clean, starched and pressed; furniture had been polished to within a hair's breadth of its veneer and all the cupboards were in good order. She had stocked up the meatsafe and food cupboards, had bought and wrapped gifts, had made a Christmas pudding and two dozen fancy cakes.

Her biggest worry was Cathy. Although the child had settled at school, she was beginning to run amok with Jimmy 'Cozzer' Costigan and his sister, Tildy-Anne. There was a wildness in Cathy, a freedom of spirit that had arrived with years of living on the edge of a quiet Galway town. And now, that selfsame foolhardiness was playing out its little dramas among trams, motor vans and the frenzied bustle that seemed to typify Scotland Road in Liverpool.

Three spattered miscreants stood unabashed in a row near Sam Bell's spanking clean kitchen dresser. Jimmy Costigan's socks lay in corrugated waves atop filthy boots, while his sister's hair was sticking out around her head like the bristling quills of a disturbed porcupine.

'Well?' asked Bridie.

Tildy scratched her tatty head. 'We was doing nothing wrong.'

'Were doing nothing wrong,' corrected Bridie.

'That's what I said. We never done nothing.' Tildy

beamed optimistically at Cathy's mum. She was a bit on the posh side, was the new Mrs Bell, always Brasso-ing and Zebo-ing and tidying up. But in spite of being as fidgety as Diddy Costigan, Bridie Bell was a good, decent sort of person who would never hit a child. Tildy thought up another case for the defence. 'Everybody does it,' she added, as if placing the final cherry on a well-decorated Christmas cake.

'I see.' Bridie nodded thoughtfully. 'So this nothing you haven't done is not being done by everybody else as well. That makes grand sense, Tildy.' She turned her attention towards her own daughter. 'I will not have you risking life and limb for a handful of molasses.' Bridie awarded Cozzer a withering look. 'And, as for involving my daughter in that disgraceful toss-gambling school – you should be ashamed, Jimmy.'

Cozzer hung his head for a split second, then bounced back, just as he always did. 'We were only dowsying,' he explained. 'We never joined in or nothing like that.'

Bridie nodded. Even after such a brief period of residence, she had learned snippets of the language. 'I don't care what you call it, Jimmy Costigan. Dowsying or dozying – it's all the same to me. You were keeping watch while men played illegal gambling games. Is that the truth, Tildy?'

Tildy nodded her reluctant assent.

'And I suppose you stayed there until all the fighting and arresting was over?'

Tildy shook her head. 'No. We ran off. We seen the bobbies coming and we legged it out of there.'

Bridie raised her eyes to heaven as if seeking guidance. 'You'll all end up in Rose Hill with a million questions to answer. Is that what you want, Caitlin O'Brien? Would you like to spend a night in the station bridewell alongside the snoring drunks and the howling thieves?'

'No, Mammy.' Cathy's voice was tailored to suit the situation.

'You don't fool me, any of you,' declared Bridie. 'It's no use saying sorry if you don't mean it.'

Cathy crossed her fingers behind her back and prayed that Mammy wouldn't find out about anything else.

'Then, of course, there was that desperate business with the rags.'

Cathy's fingers uncrossed themselves while her heart sank.

'Under a month we are in England, and you are well on your way to real trouble,' said Bridie.

'Everybody does it,' repeated Tildy. 'They're just old clothes what didn't get sold. Nobody wants them. Somebody comes the next day and takes them away and—'

'And weighs them in.' Bridie's voice remained even and soft. 'The poor man has an arrangement with the stall-keepers. He shifts the rubbish and he keeps the few pennies for his pains. But you went and took the things. You decided to weigh them in and you carried them to . . . to where, Tildy?'

'William Moult Street,' replied Tildy.

'And from the rag yard in William Moult Street, you took the wages of a man with a family to keep.' She shook her head in exasperation. 'Cathy – upstairs. You two get back to your mother. Tell her I'll be round later to discuss the matter.'

Tildy and Cozzer got out while the going was good. There were a few more things on the list, so they ran hell for leather towards home, each hoping that nothing else would come up on the prosecution agenda of the case.

Cathy stood at the bottom of the stairs. 'I want to explain,' she said.

Bridie saw herself as a reasonable woman. 'I'm waiting,' she said.

Cathy inhaled deeply. 'It's all for the Nolans,' she told her mother in hushed tones. 'There's Johnny, Denis, Martha, Alice, Pauline, Sidney, Bernadette, Eileen, Luke, Brenda, Stuart and Matt. Oh, and the mammy and daddy, too. The daddy drinks all the money, so the Costigans . . . help.'

'By stealing?' So that was why the parish priest had chided the Costigans about their charity work.

Cathy shrugged. 'Sometimes. And sometimes by up-ending.'

Bridie sank into a chair. 'Up-ending?' she asked resignedly.

Cathy was proud of her much improved knowledge. 'Mr Costigan and some other men up-end Mr Nolan to shake the money out of his pockets before he drinks it all. Then they give that money to Mrs Nolan for the rent and food.' She paused, thought about it. 'Mind, I suppose he must have spent some of it already, because he has to be drunk to be up-ended.'

Bridie shook her head. 'Upstairs with you, Caitlin.'

'Please, Mammy—'

'Upstairs. I don't know what I'm going to do with you. There's no excuse for stealing.' But as she listened to her daughter's hesitant ascent of the stairway, Bridie had to agree, albeit inwardly, that thievery was sometimes forgivable, even essential.

She kept an eye on Shauna, who was having her afternoon nap on the sofa. There was a dual morality among the Scotland Road people. Catholic to the last, they were fervent Christians who would hand their last penny into the ever gaping maw of the church. Yet they had to eat.

Bridie stirred the fire gently so as not to disturb the child. Almost every day, produce was stolen by young ones. They took from shops, market stalls, pavement vendors. She had been told that one boy, towards the end of the previous summer, had almost drowned in a container of rotten fruit behind a market, had been swallowed up by a mouldering sea of discarded plums and cherries. To eat, they risked their very lives. To eat, they stole. After which sin they would attend confession, only to reoffend on their way home from church.

Bridie smiled ruefully. The poor box would be rich in years to come, because the priest, before giving absolution, would be forced to ask his penitent about repayment. As the ability to make restitution would be non-existent, the parishioner would be ordered to put the value of each stolen article into the poor box at the earliest opportunity. The poor box remained empty. Should any of today's miscreants ever make his fortune, the poverty would be wiped out of the Scotland Road area in one fell swoop.

Cathy would probably turn out rampageous, then. The child had an excellent brain and a strong sense of fair play. God would scarcely figure in Cathy's calculations when it came to the bare necessities of life. If Caitlin O'Brien saw hunger, she would feed it. 'She's like me exactly,' Bridie whispered to the flames. 'And she's very like my mammy, too.'

Shauna opened her eyes. 'Cathy naughty again?' she asked.

Bridie looked at her baby. For one who was not thriving, she seemed very alert. 'Go back to sleep.' Would Shauna be like Cathy? Would Shauna risk her health to ride on the back of a cart for a bit of raw sugar? The mother nodded to herself. To appease her own hunger, Shauna might take a chance. But would she do that for a family of twelve whose father was a drunk? In spite of her show of defiance, there remained in Cathy a degree of selflessness that was not yet apparent in Shauna's make-up.

Sam put his head round the door. 'Five minutes then, Bridie?'

She nodded, watched him disappear. This time, he would not be going fishing. Sam would fare very well today, because it was Christmas Eve. He would take all the unredeemed pledges into the pubs and round the markets, would sell many pieces to those who had forgotten to buy gifts. Worse than that, he would probably accept down payments and charge a high rate of interest to those who might well continue to owe for presents by the middle of next June.

Bridie stared into the fire. It wasn't a bad life, she supposed. Apart from worrying about Cathy, she had few troubles. At first, she had been afraid of sharing a bed with Sam, but even that no longer frightened her. On Saturday nights, he went for a couple of beers, came upstairs and fumbled about apologetically for a few minutes. By keeping her mind on other things, Bridie managed to survive the man's clumsy attempts at love-making. He spent his spare hours fishing, always came back with a terrible cough, would not consider seeing the doctor. According to Diddy Costigan, Sam Bell had not visited a doctor in twenty-odd years.

She stabbed at the coals, stirred them to life with the brass-headed poker. Eugene. She missed him as much as ever. This would be her first Christmas without him. At the age of twenty-seven, she had been relegated to the ranks of middle-age, was fastened to a man whose life was more than half over. Eugene had been a thoughtful man who had loved her, body and her soul. Now, there was no love at all. Sam drank a little, breathed over her for a few moments, then rolled away and slept till morning. Bridie endured his behaviour just as she coped with housework, shopkeeping and caring for his mother . . .

She glanced up at the ceiling, wondered what old Theresa would do next. Well, it was time to enter the fray again. She crept from the room and made her way upstairs. Before going into the shop, she must check Sam's mother. There had been tantrums, arguments and tears, but Bridie was doing her best to stick to her guns and change Theresa's way of life.

Bridie opened Theresa's door. 'Nice to see you out of bed, Muth.'

The old lady turned rather rapidly for one in a supposed state of senile decay. 'Don't you "Muth" me, Bridie Bell. I'm no mother to you.'

The younger woman nodded and smiled. She had taken to leaving Theresa Bell's food on a tray by the door. Nothing had been said on the subject, but the food was disappearing each time. So, for a bed-ridden invalid, this old girl had a markedly good appetite and the ability to walk, pick up a tray and carry it to her bed. 'Will we get you dressed and bring you down?' asked Bridie.

'What the hell for?' Theresa sank onto the bed, this dramatic movement accompanied by a heavy sigh.

'For a change.'

Theresa fixed her beady eyes on Bridie's face. In spite of better judgement, she found herself liking Sam's new wife. She was clean, easy on the eye and a damned good cook into the bargain. Also, she had brought children into the house, had brought movement back to this place of decay. 'When I want to come down, I'll come. I don't need you carrying me round like a sack of spuds.' As ever, she spoke in flat Lancashire tones.

Bridie agreed. 'Sam wants you up and about again,' she said. In truth, Sam, still looking for the easy life, preferred to listen to his wife in this instance. 'Bridie says you need to move about,' he had begun to tell his mother. 'It'll do you good.'

'You'll bloody kill me between you,' the old lady screamed energetically.

But Bridie was not fooled, not worried. Theresa was eating well, was embroidering pretty squares of cloth, was arguing, had fire in her eyes. She approached the bed. 'If you can manage, I want you downstairs. You can sit with Shauna while I help in the shop. Sam's out, so Charlie's on his own. This is a very busy time, as you are well aware. Now, shall I dress you?'

'Bugger off.'

Smiling to herself, Bridie took this advice and carried the tray back to the kitchen.

'Mammy?'

Bridie lifted her head and looked at Cathy. The child must have followed her down the stairs. Cathy seemed so pathetic and downtrodden with her shoulders stooped and her hands hanging limply by her sides. 'I thought you were supposed to stay upstairs for a while?'

'Please, Mammy. It's Christmas. Let me go just outside on the pavement. I'll be good, I promise.'

Cathy had been deprived of so much. The child had been dragged from her home, had been insulted repeatedly by her grandfather, had lost her daddy, her farm, her animals. 'All right. Just for a little while, now.'

When Cathy had left, Bridie gave Shauna some toys, then went through to the shop, saw Sam making his way outside with a couple of cases. She greeted Charlie Costigan, flicked a feather duster over some books, straightened a row of ornaments. She actually liked the shop, had taken to spending the odd happy hour talking to Charlie and to customers. Charlie, once she had got to know him, was an angel. He had gentle, knowing eyes, a deep, booming laugh and a good rapport with customers. Bridie spoke to him. 'Go and get yourself a bite to eat, Charlie. We'll be open well past midnight, I shouldn't wonder.'

He loped out in the direction of home. There would be scouse in a pan, bread in the cupboard. Charlie and his siblings were among the luckier inhabitants of Scotland Road.

Bridie placed herself in the centre of the shop. There were four counters set in a square with two flaps for access. Below the counters, deep shelves held pledges, as did the floor-to-ceiling storage areas on the two window-less walls. The Penrhyn Street window displayed some new stock – buckets, mops, pans, brushes. During recent years, Sam Bell had expanded into chandlery. The Scotland Road display was made up of items judged to be antique – old mirrors, statues, brass and steel fire-irons, tea sets. These articles were usually sold to 'foreigners', people from Waterloo, Crosby and Seaforth Sands.

The bell clanged. Diddy Costigan ambled in. 'I've put your goose in the bakehouse,' she announced. 'And I've made you a couple of bunloaves.' She grinned at Bridie. 'I know the kids have been carrying on, love. Can we talk about it when the festivities are over? We can't cope with cooking and toss schools as well, you know. So shall I brew up?'

Bridie nodded. A cup of tea would be most welcome, but first, she wanted to talk to Diddy about something momentous, something other than Cathy's behaviour. She inhaled deeply. 'Diddy?'

The large woman paused on her way to the living quarters. 'That's me.'

'I . . . er . . .'

'Spit it out, girl. It's Christmas tomorrow, in case you haven't noticed. There's no time for messing about. That bloody bakehouse is packed, you know.'

Bridie tried to organize the words. 'I need some money,' was the best she could manage.

Diddy laughed. 'You need money? Try telling that to

Cissie Nolan. She's fourteen mouths to feed and her feller's drunk all his Christmas bonus before my Billy could get to him.' She nodded vigorously. 'Arthur Nolan's in the bloody bridewell again sleeping it off. Christmas? It doesn't mean a thing to them poor Nolan kiddies and their mam.'

Bridie felt ashamed. 'It doesn't matter,' she said. 'I don't mean the Nolans don't matter, it's just that—'

'What do you want it for?'

The younger woman swallowed. 'Horses,' she whispered.

Diddy crossed the shop floor with an agility that was remarkable in view of her bulk. She clasped Bridie's hands. 'The horses your dad gave to Sam?'

Bridie nodded.

'Worth a lot, are they?'

'Yes. Well, they could be.'

Diddy cursed under her breath. She cursed Sam, Thomas Murphy and the family of Bridie's dead husband. 'Bastards, the lot of them,' she murmured.

'Does everybody round here know?' asked Bridie.

'Know what?'

'That my father had to pay to get rid of me and the girls.'

Diddy hesitated for a split second before wading in. 'Rubbish,' she spat. 'That's not true. If you'd stopped at home, some bright feller would have picked you up.' She gazed at Bridie Bell. 'You're the best-looking woman in the whole of Liverpool,' she advised her companion. 'Anyway, I've told nobody about the horses. What do you want them for?'

Bridie thought for a few moments. 'To know what I'm worth,' she said slowly. 'To get them trained as runners so that I can show my father his error of judgement. He may be clever with animals, Diddy, but he knows not one thing about me. I'm easily as good as he is with horses, I must say that.'

The shop door opened, so Diddy went off to make tea while Bridie served. Diddy spoke to Shauna, gave the child a bit of chocolate. Sam Bell and Thomas Murphy wanted whipping, she thought as she waited for the kettle to boil. Poor Bridie had been treated like a piece of property – no – worse than that, she pondered. The young woman was not even merchandise in the eyes of her father and her husband. Bridie and her children were nuisances, irritations, things to be passed on as quickly as possible.

'Diddy?'

The visitor turned, looked at Mrs Bell the younger. 'What?'

'I don't know why exactly these horses are important. They just are.'

Diddy warmed the pot.

'They were in the wrong, my father and Sam. My father was more wrong than Sam, of course.'

'I know they were wrong, love.'

'The horses are my chance of becoming . . . oh, I don't know.'

'A human being?'

Bridie smiled. She had known all along that Diddy would understand. 'But they're worth a lot more than I've got to spare.'

When the tea was poured, Bridie picked up her cup and stood with one foot in the shop and the other in the kitchen. Diddy, silent for once, stirred in several measures of sugar to help her think. 'Take something from the stores and flog it in town.' She waved a teaspoon at one of Sam Bell's many hiding places – a walk-in cupboard which ran the length of the kitchen. 'I know it's locked, but my Billy could open it.'

'No.'

'You what?'

It was difficult to explain, but Bridie could not bear the thought of hurting Sam. He had done her no harm, had taken in her children, had sheltered and fed three strangers. He was wont to disappear from time to time with fishing rods and net, but that was no crime. 'Not that, Diddy. Not from Sam. I know he bargained with Da, but my father's a powerful man when it comes to persuasion. No, no, I'm not going to turn against Sam.' She left unspoken the certainty that Sam would never turn against her and the girls. She was developing a respect for her husband, a tolerance that bordered on concern.

'What else, then? There's stuff parked all over this house that's worth a fortune. It'll all go to that bloody Liam once Sam pops his clogs. Sam doesn't know what he's got, can't remember half of it. He'd not miss some bits of silver and jewellery.'

'I can't.'

Diddy drained her mug. 'Where else will you get the money?'

'I don't know. I've handed over my mother's locket and both my wedding rings so that Rosa McKinnell won't sell Sorrel and Silver without telling me first. But the value of my bits and pieces won't feed the animals through the winter.'

Diddy's mouth dropped. 'Does he know about the ring?'

'He thinks I lost it with it being so big.'

'Bloody miser,' said Diddy. She took a long, hard look at Sam Bell's bride. 'You getting on all right with him?'

'Yes.'

Diddy considered the problem. The horses must have been worth a few bob. Sam Bell didn't know a horse from an aspidistra. If someone could convince Sam that the beasts were worthless . . . Even so, Bridie would need a fair sum. 'Have you no money at all?' she asked.

'None,' replied Bridie.

'Housekeeping?'

'I just ask when I need it. But he gives me only a few shillings at a time.'

'Let me think on it,' said Diddy. 'It'll have to wait till after Christmas now.' She struggled to her feet. 'Billy'll fetch your goose round from the bakehouse when it's done. There was a bit of a queue this time. Must be a good sign if a few of us can afford proper meat too big for our own ovens.' She frowned. 'If you've any bits of food left over tomorrow, bring it round to our house for the Nolans, will you?' Diddy bustled off to carry on her Christmas preparations.

Bridie made a mental note to make sure that some 'leavings' found their way into the Nolans' house. Cissie Nolan was that poor, thin woman who had opened her door to Bridie when Cathy had gone missing on their first morning in Scotland Road. Twelve children. Bridie shook her head and wondered how anyone could possibly manage more than two. She glanced at the clock. Cathy was out again, of course, had probably forgotten her promise to be good. She was no doubt trailing all over Paddy's Market with Cozzer and Tildy-Anne.

'Bridget?'

The young woman froze, then turned slowly. Theresa Bell was fully dressed and standing on the stairs. 'Muth,' began Bridie lamely, 'so glad you've managed to get down the—'

'No time for all that,' snapped Theresa. 'You and I need a bit of a talk together. I've got ears, you know. There might be a lot wrong with me, but I'm not deaf, not yet.' She frowned deeply, making the channels of age more pronounced than ever in the withered face. 'It's time you and me got a few things straightened out, girl.'

Bridie saw Charlie entering the shop, fished around in

her brain for some excuse. She didn't want to talk to Theresa Bell. How long had Sam's mother been eavesdropping? Had she heard the conversation between Bridie and Diddy? Meekly, she made her way back into the kitchen.

Theresa Bell limped in, shooed Shauna into the shop. 'Right, lady,' she said to her daughter-in-law. 'I declare this meeting open. Just let me say my piece . . .'

Cathy O'Brien was in her element. Mammy was busy with the shop, with Uncle Sam's mother and with Shauna. There were no fields to run in, no horses to play with, but Scotland Road was like a large extension to Bell's Pledges – full of noises, sights, interesting things and people. In spite of Bridie's several warnings, Cathy had taken charge of herself, had grabbed a degree of liberty.

Since her father's death, Cathy had never imagined herself to be a part of anything. Her mother loved her and was good to her, her clothes were decent and she had a little sister who wasn't always a desperate pain, but she had been lonely inside since Eugene O'Brien's terrible accident. Now, Cozzer and Tildy were beginning to fill a corner of the void in Cathy's young heart.

It was Christmas Eve, so excitement hung in the air even here, where many people were too poor for lavish celebrations. The shops were busy, their windows decorated with dabs of cotton wool and twists of crêpe paper. People stopped for what they called a gab or a jangle, then rushed off to prepare whatever was within their means. The lamplighter handed out toffees, and a silly man in a Father Christmas suit sang songs and, when he thought no-one was looking, swigged whisky furtively from a bottle.

Cozzer had earned a few pence for carrying oilcloth, and these wages had been squandered in Scouse Alley, a café near the market. Tildy, Cathy and Cozzer had dined oh a feast of scouse and red cabbage followed by several helpings of syrup cakes. Cathy felt as if her stomach would burst at any moment, yet the memory of those syrup-soaked pancakes was precious. 'That was the best thing I ever ate,' she told her companions. 'Where do we go now?' Mammy wouldn't be looking for her yet, surely?

Cozzer shook his head. They had scoured the pavements outside the Derby, the Gaiety and the Gem cinemas, had found no dropped pennies. Fishing down the grids had yielded a shirt button and a single miserable halfpenny, and it was too early for drunks. Cozzer was clever with drunks. He would engage them in conversation, help them across the street, then pick their pockets before wishing them well. Of course, pocket-pickings were for the Nolans. Catholics did not steal, not for themselves, at least, not unless they were starving to death. 'We could have another wander round Paddy's,' he suggested.

They strolled down Scotland Road, their way lighted by gaslights that flickered unconvincingly, their breath hanging in chill air like miniature clouds. Vans carrying paupers' parcels coughed their way up and down the road. On a whim, Jimmy 'Cozzer' Costigan stepped out and halted one of these vehicles. 'Stop!' he yelled, a hand raised against the looming van.

A woman alighted. 'Boy, you will be killed,' she announced.

Cozzer eyed the charitable person. 'Have you done the Nolans?' he asked. 'Dryden Street, twelve children.'

She nodded. 'We left the food with Mrs Costigan.'

'Just as well,' commented Cozzer. 'Else Mr Nolan would have sold it for beer.' He stepped aside and allowed the Goodfellows to continue their gargantuan task of feeding the destitute.

'We'd best go home,' said Tildy. She jerked a thumb at

Cathy. 'Her ma'll be wondering where she is again. And we might have to go down Limekiln to the bakery.'

Cozzer shook his head. 'Me dad's picking our bird up. Let's go to Paddy's.'

'Why is it called Paddy's?' asked Cathy. 'Mammy says it's St Martin's Market.'

As they ambled along, Tildy instructed Cathy on the origins of Paddy's, told her about destitute Irish immigrants who had clothed themselves with stuff bought second-hand at the market. 'Everybody knows about it,' pronounced Tildy airily. She prided herself on her standard of education, most of which had been gained by listening to her mother. 'On ships, they call the main gangway Scotland Road. Even on the big liners what go all round the world. If you're lost, a sailor tells you to go up Scotland Road, then bear port or starboard. That means left or right.'

Paddy's was crowded. People milled about, some with purchases in mind, others just passing time and waiting for that magic moment when the Scotland Road butchers and fruiterers would be panicked into auctioning off their stock. Many a Christmas roast would be acquired at the last minute by folk whose purses were slim to the point of emaciation.

Cathy lingered near Nicky Costigan's stall. Nicky was trying to do business with a man who looked very strange. He was wrapped in several layers of clothing, and was wearing no less than six hats. Cathy understood the need for all the jackets and woollens, but was defeated by the sight of six precariously balanced bowlers above a brown, sea-weathered face and huge black eyes.

'What Johnny pay?' asked Nicky.

Cozzer grabbed Cathy's arm. 'Come on,' he urged. 'They're only Johnny Laskies.' He pointed to a long row of dark-skinned men, one of whom was struggling to carry what looked like a whole fireplace. 'Them in the middle of the line has the money,' he informed Cathy. 'So's they never get robbed. They're no use to us, not for the Nolans.'

But Cathy was riveted to the exotic sight.

'His Master's Voice,' the seaman told Nicky.

Nicky walked to the front of her stall, winked at her siblings and pointed to a gramophone. 'His Master's Voice,' she said. 'Two shillings, Johnny.'

Johnny shook his head, miraculously failing to dislodge the heap of hats. 'Libby's Milk,' he replied.

'This not Libby's Milk, Johnny,' said Nicky slowly. 'This from Bell's shop. Mr Bell not stick Libby mark on gramophone.'

Cathy's jaw hung open. How on earth could this man fail to distinguish a tin of milk from a gramophone?

Tildy nudged her female companion. 'Shut your mouth, you look soft,' she advised before offering an explanation for this strange scenario. 'Some stallholders have found labels on milk tins that look a bit like His Master's Voice. They cut them out and stick them on gramophones. Johnny's just being careful. Aren't you, Johnny?' she asked the Indian sailor.

Twin rows of perfect teeth smiled down on Tildy and Cathy. 'Johnny careful,' he agreed.

Cathy was finally dragged away by Cozzer and Tildy. 'Six hats,' she muttered. 'And gramophones and bicycles and somebody's fireplace.'

Tildy nodded sagely. 'All bought for tuppence and sold for a fortune when they get home. Like me mam says, that ship'll be low in the water tonight.'

They wandered on, listened to a band playing carols on foo-foos, strange little wind instruments out of which the locals produced improbably beautiful music. Cozzer took a comb and paper and joined in, made a fair stab at it.

'He's getting a foo-foo for Christmas,' said Tildy. 'Then he can join a proper band.'

A fight broke out in front of an improvised coconut shy whose owner had used weighted coconuts. Police arrived, missiles flew, and strong language filled the freezing air. Cozzer dragged his female charges out of Paddy's and through the narrow jiggers towards home. Then a thought struck him. 'I'm going to get them a bird,' he announced.

Cathy, who was still reeling from the adventure on Paddy's, leaned against somebody's back gate. The jiggers were awful places, narrow alleys running between back-to-back houses. The tiny yards were so close that children could climb on the walls and leap across from gate to gate. The rubbish-filled middens stank, even in cold weather, and the droppings of dogs were not easy to avoid in the darkness.

'I'm going for a bird for the Nolans,' repeated Cozzer.

'Where from?' asked Tildy scathingly. 'Top of the Liver building?'

'Shut up, you,' ordered Cozzer.

'I'm older than you.'

'And I'm a lad,' snapped Cozzer.

Cathy said nothing. It was hard to judge the time, but it felt late. Mammy would be angry, she felt sure. And this was Christmas Eve. Tomorrow, her dog would come. Uncle Sam had promised a dog for Christmas. 'I'd better go home,' she said.

'Scared?' asked Cozzer.

'No.' Cathy turned up the collar of her coat.

'She is,' announced Tildy.

'I'm not.'

'Prove it,' challenged Cozzer.

Cathy was becoming very uncomfortable. She knew about the Costigans trying to help the Nolans, had heard all about their dad's efforts to take money from Mr Nolan before he could drink it. Mr and Mrs Costigan turned a blind eye when things appeared magically, things that the Nolans could use. 'How do I prove it?' she asked.

Cozzer thought for a moment. 'You can get Mr Marks out of his shop for me.'

Cathy squirmed.

'How does she do that?' Tildy wanted to know.

'I'm thinking.'

The two girls waited while Cozzer thought. Tildy, who was used to being in trouble, didn't mind for herself. No matter what happened, no matter what she and Cozzer did for the Nolans, Mam and Dad would forgive them. But on Cathy's behalf, Tildy was concerned. 'Mrs Bell won't like it,' she whispered to her brother.

'She won't know,' he answered.

'She will,' insisted Tildy. 'She's one of them people that know things just by looking at you.'

'Don't talk so soft,' he advised.

Cathy moved from foot to foot, wished the cold would go away, wished the smells would go away, wished Cozzer would go away and stop involving her in all his naughty activities—

'I've got it,' he declared triumphantly.

'God help us.' Tildy sounded just like her mother.

'Tildy can have an accident,' proclaimed Cozzer.

'Thanks,' said the proposed victim.

'Just pretend,' he said. 'Lie on the floor outside the shop, then Cathy can go in for help and I'll run through, grab a chicken or something and leg off home.'

'Jesus,' exclaimed Tildy. She dug her elbow into Cathy's side. 'Don't start on about blaspheming,' she reminded her friend. 'That was praying. If we're going on one of our Jimmy's adventures, we'll need the Father, the Son, the Holy Ghost and every saint that ever drew breath.'

Cathy, too cold to mind about blasphemy, kept her counsel.

'Come on, then,' said Cozzer. 'And you can stop calling me Jimmy,' he advised his sister. 'Else I'll call you Tildy-Anne.'

Cathy followed the two miscreants through the alley-ways until they reached Great Homer Street. This was awful. She had to go into a shop and tell lies so that Cozzer could enter the same shop with a view to stealing. And it was Christmas. Surely sins committed at Christmas were worse than any other sins committed at any other time? It was Jesus's birthday. 'It's Jesus's birthday tomorrow,' she muttered.

Cozzer, whose hearing was acute, pushed Cathy against a shop window. 'Jesus turned water into wine.'

Cathy sniffed. 'What's that got to do with anything?'

'And he pinched five loaves and two fishes to feed the poor.'

'He did not steal,' insisted Cathy.

Cozzer was adamant. 'It says nothing in the Bible about Jesus paying for that bread and them fish. He just grabbed the stuff for the poor. And that's what we're doing.'

Defeated by Cozzer's undoubtedly flawed logic, Cathy followed the Costigans into their life of crime.

Bridie opened the shop door, looked left into Penrhyn Street, right into Scotland Road, saw no sign of her older daughter. This was getting well beyond a joke. Her husband was out selling gifts while his mother sat in the kitchen waiting for a private word. Bridie turned, closed the door, glanced at Charlie. He was making out a ticket for a customer who was pledging blankets for the where-withal to buy a Christmas dinner. This woman's family would eat, then freeze to death, thought Bridie.

Charlie laboured on, a corner of his tongue peeping from the twisted mouth. While he wrote with one pen, two others followed suit, the trio being joined by a length of wood. This time-saving invention allowed for the simultaneous production of three copies – one for the customer, one for the records and a third to be stuck to the pawned item. 'Can you manage?' Bridie asked.

Charlie stopped writing, nodded at his boss's new wife.

Bridie Bell dragged herself back to the kitchen. Shauna was leaning against Sam's mother's chair. 'Sing it again,' begged the child.

Theresa Bell delivered a reedy rendition of 'Sing a Song of Sixpence' for the umpteenth time, then sent Shauna to help Charlie. 'Well,' she said to Bridie, 'have you run out of excuses yet? This meeting's been adjourned five times.'

Bridie sank onto the sofa. 'Sorry,' she muttered.

Old Theresa sucked her top teeth. 'Horses,' she said eventually. 'All I know about horses is they fetch milk and coal and trouble.' She sniffed meaningfully. 'There's more bookies' runners round here than fleas. What do you want with horses?'

Bridie didn't know what to say, so she said nothing.

'Can you ride?'

'Yes.'

'Right. Tell me all about horses, then.'

The younger woman opened her mouth, but nothing came out. She felt like a child on her first day at school, all awkward limbs and no brain power. This old dear would probably tell her son all she had heard while skulking on the stairs. And Cathy was still missing, too—

'Cat got your tongue?'

They had no cat, though a dog had been promised to keep Cathy quiet. 'The horses are at McKinnell's stables,' she managed at last. 'A mare and a young stallion. He could be used for stud, because he's got good papers.

They've Arab blood, so they'll make fine runners with the right training.'

Theresa leaned forward. 'And who's going to teach them? Were you planning on exercising them, up and down the bloody tram tracks?'

Deflated, Bridie snapped her mouth closed.

'Good job you know me, then, isn't it?' Without pausing for an answer, she continued, 'Our Edith,' she said carefully, as if addressing an infant, 'me sister's girl – Sam's cousin. She might be some use after all. Great big lanky thing with ideas above her station. Married a doctor, she did. Got a lot of land over towards Bolton. She'll know somebody who knows somebody. I think they own some stables, if my memory serves me right.'

Completely at a loss, Bridie let the old woman drone on.

'I'm a Boltonian meself,' announced Theresa Bell proudly. 'I found a good man, a Liverpool man, but he died young like all good folk seem to do. It was Cedric – my husband – who moved us here. A sea captain, he was, very handsome.' The old face seemed to cloud over. 'He drowned. Sam was only a lad at the time, and my sister – Edith's mam – invited us to go and live with her. Oh aye, I'm not from round here, you know.'

Bridie had noticed the difference. Theresa's speech was broad and flat, easier to understand than the Liverpool accent. Until today, Mrs Bell Senior hadn't had much to say for herself, but now the words flowed like a burst dam.

'I'm a Lancashire lass,' grinned Theresa. 'But when Cedric died, I stayed round here, took his bit of money and opened the shop. It was only a little place then, just enough to keep me and Sam. Course, our Sam had ideas. Bought two houses and knocked them together.' She stretched the thin neck and nodded just once. 'This is my business,' she said softly. 'Not his. I started it. I worked in it year in and year out. I brought the two kiddies up when their mam died, God rest her.'

Bridie waited while the old lady collected her thoughts.

'She'll be coming New Year's Day.'

'I beg your pardon?' Bridie wondered how Sam's dead wife would manage to visit in a week's time.

'Not Maria. Our Edith. I've just told you, haven't I? I had a sister. She's dead now. And me sister had a daughter called Edith and they always come at New Year, Edith and Richard. Nice enough man, usually has his head in the clouds or in a book. Happen they can look after the horses. Oh, there's some money under a loose floorboard next to my bed. Take it and welcome.'

Bridie held her breath. Why was Mrs Bell helping her?

'He's boring,' pronounced Theresa.

'I beg your pardon?'

'Sam. Your husband. He's boring.' With this damning pronouncement made, Theresa closed her eyes and leaned back in the chair.

He was boring, thought Bridie. Every night, he sat in the same place and went through the same ritual. Ten small pieces of paper were always laid out on a wooden tray in front of him. Into these ten papers Sam Bell measured crumbs of tobacco which he flaked between his palms. When the cigarettes were rolled, he smoked one, then put the other nine in a tobacco tin for the following day.

On Mondays, Sam cut his toenails before going up for a bath. He was proud of his plumbed-in bath. It was in a small cubicle off his mother's bedroom. On Tuesdays, he had his hair cut at Razor Sharpe's. Eddie 'Razor' Sharpe trimmed a microscopic amount from the fading tonsure's edge and gave Sam a proper open-blade shave and a hot towelling.

On Wednesdays Sam Bell did his accounts, then on Thursdays he deposited his takings in the bank at the corner of Dryden Street. He went to confession every Friday night, to the pub on Saturdays, to mass and benediction every Sunday.

'Does he still do his toenails in here?' asked Theresa.

Bridie jumped involuntarily. Did this old lady read minds? 'Yes,' she answered.

'Always got on my nerves, did that.'

Bridie stared at her mother-in-law. The eyes remained closed, but the features were very much alive. 'Why are you offering to help me?' she asked.

'I don't know. Must be summat to do with being in me dotage.' She opened one eye. 'I'd nothing to get up for,' she said. 'After the General Strike, I couldn't think of one single reason for falling out of bed. I was no use, you see. When I'd finished rearing Anthony, there was nothing more to be done.'

A few beats of time passed before Bridie plucked up enough courage to ask, 'Didn't you look after Liam as well?' Surely the twins had been raised together?

The other eye opened. 'I told you before, I raised both, though I'm taking no credit for the way Liam turned out.' The word 'credit' was spat, as if it meant blame.

'He's a priest,' murmured Bridie.

'I know that.'

Bridie cleared her throat. 'Aren't you proud?' Catholic families back home were delighted when a child opted for the holy life. 'I've a cousin a nun, and her mother was thrilled fit to burst about it,' she added lamely.

Theresa made a guttural sound deep in her throat, as if trying to shift a terrible taste. 'There's good folk and bad folk, good priests and bad priests. I'd rather not talk about him if you don't mind. He got what he wanted, the bugger.

He's taken Anthony away from me. As for our Sam, he never did see sense. A dog collar's a wonderful thing according to your husband.'

Bridie leaned forward, decided to opt for a change of subject. 'Muth, I don't want to deprive you of your little bit of money. It doesn't seem fair.'

'There's nowt fair in this life, Bridie.' She shifted in the chair, flinched when her knee clicked. 'The horses mean something to you, love. I heard. I was listening on the stairs and, like I said afore, there's not much wrong with my hearing. Let's get your bloody horses back.' She sniffed, took a handkerchief from her sleeve. 'You fettle for me and I'll fettle for you.'

'Fettle?'

The old woman's face stretched itself into a wide grin. 'Help. Do for. Look after. You've got me out of bed. Your girls have given me something to laugh at.' She noticed Bridie's worried expression. 'Has she gone off again?'

'She has indeed.'

Theresa nodded. 'She's a rum one, is your Cathy. But then you've got to remember all she's lost.'

'Shauna's lost everything, too.'

The small head snapped upward on its shrivelled stem. 'That little one of yours is a tough nut, Bridie. She might be thin, but her head's screwed on the right road. Anyway, she was young enough to get over her dad's death. Cathy's on the sensitive side. She wants love. She wants attention and things to take her mind off this big move you've made. That's why she's running about with Diddy Costigan's tribe – there's always a bit of adventure.'

Bridie didn't like the idea of her daughter getting mixed up in Jimmy and Tildy Costigan's style of adventure. 'They steal.'

Theresa Bell chuckled. 'Eeh, you want to talk to Elizabeth about that. According to her, it's not stealing, it's redistribution of resources. She reads, you know. Yes, she's an angry woman, is Diddy Costigan.'

Bridie was about to ask a few questions, but a commotion in the shop made her rise to her feet and rush out of the room.

Charlie stood behind the counter, his face apparently frozen by the sight before his eyes. A policeman hung on to Jimmy Costigan, who, in turn, hung on to a very large and very dead turkey. 'It's for the poor,' the lad yelled.

The policeman turned on his heel in response to Tildy. Tildy, who was tough for her age, was beating her fists against the constable's back. 'Leave our Cozzer alone,' she screamed.

Behind Tildy, a tall, dark-skinned man lingered. Behind him, several more Lascar seamen were trying to crowd into Bell's. Six or seven bowler hats were deposited on the counter. A fire-surround blocked the doorway, and a small congregation of passers-by was assembling on the pavement outside.

After a few seconds, Bridie realized that one of the Indians was carrying Cathy. 'Johnny bring baby home,' the man said, bowing courteously. 'His Master's Voice,' he added, nodding towards a gramophone. 'From Bell's – not Libby's Milk.'

Bridie knew she was going insane. A very strange-looking man dressed in far too many clothes was cradling Cathy in his arms, talking about tinned milk and pointing out a gramophone on the floor.

Cathy looked at her mother and burst into tears. 'I did it wrong,' she wailed. 'I said Tildy had been knocked over, then I went to sleep.'

'She fainted,' said the policeman. 'And while the butcher tried to revive her, this young man stole a turkey.'

'For the poor,' insisted Cozzer.

One of the seamen dragged Tildy away from the constable, got kicked for his pains.

Bridie pushed her way through the throng and took her daughter. She passed the policeman and spoke to Cozzer. 'You will give that bird back now, Jimmy Costigan. Tildy – behave yourself.' She carried Cathy to the kitchen and placed her on the sofa. 'Don't move,' she muttered. 'Stay here with Muth.'

Back in the shop, she separated Cozzer from his ill-gotten gains, then advised the policeman to take the Costigan children back home. When only the Lascars remained, Bridie thanked them, then watched in amazement as they struggled their way out of the shop with hats, gramophone, fire-surround, pots, pans and bundles of clothes.

'Nice men,' offered Charlie.

Bridie sank onto a stool. This was a crazy place. Nobody made sense and her daughter was turning out badly. She looked at Charlie, comforted herself with the thought that this poor boy was a small piece of normality in a very confused world. 'Charlie,' she said. 'This is an end of it. I can take no more. We are going back to Ireland.'

Five

Sam Bell sat in his usual place next to the fire. On the table, slices of roast goose and beef were spread on platters covered in muslin, and the room sparkled with polish. In little more than a month, Bridie had changed the place into a real home. She was a worker, all right. She got on with her chores, helped in the shop, dealt very well with Muth and, best of all, she wasn't a moaner. But, worst of all, she was intending to return to Ireland in order to protect Cathy from the Costigans' bad ways. Sam was not a happy man. In spite of his firm resolution, he had developed a soft spot for his young Irish bride.

He lit the first of today's cigarette allowance, drew the smoke deep into his lungs, then coughed explosively. Christmas Day. Couldn't he allow himself the odd extra ciggy on this festive occasion? No. Moderation in all things had been Sam's creed so far, and he was getting too old to alter the ways of a lifetime. He took a deep, shuddering breath, then carried on smoking. He would miss her. She was lovely to look at, pleasant to the customers and, most of all, she was good to her husband.

In a few minutes, he would take a walk to the Holy House. Every man in the Scotland Road area strolled along to a pub on Christmas morning for a pint and a gab with his mates. The excuse given for this ritual was that males were keeping out of the line of fire and 'from under the wife's feet'. Many sought to anaesthetize themselves beyond the knowledge that their seasonal fare would be egg and chips, while others drank out of habit, just as they did every other day of the year.

Anthony would be here soon. He was probably out in the streets at this very minute, would be watching for Sam's exit from the house. Today, Anthony would visit Muth. Muth loved Anthony and Anthony loved Muth. The father of the Bell twins shook his head slowly. If only Anthony would make an effort. Liam was a bit on the sharp side, a sober-sided sort of chap, but he was a chosen man. Anthony had little or no patience with Liam, and Sam stood by his ordained son. A priest in the family was a status symbol, something to brag about. Sometimes, though, Sam missed Anthony. Sometimes, he wondered whether he had backed the wrong horse. No. Liam was a good man and Anthony should mend his ways and treat his twin with the respect a priest commanded.

The pawnbroker tapped away some ash and loose tobacco, tried to remember how life had been before Bridie. This was stupid, he told himself. He'd been a widower for years, yet he had grown accustomed so quickly to the comforts of this second marriage. As, indeed, had Muth. Until Bridie had arrived, Muth had stayed upstairs sulking all the time. As soon as Bridie returned to Ireland, Muth would, no doubt, go back to her life of self-imposed solitude, misery and constant whinge-ing. Living alone down here with his imprisoned mother upstairs held little appeal. The thought of this household struggling to survive without Bridie was not attractive. Sam had even cut down on his fishing expeditions in order to make a go of this new liaison. Up to now, the world had offered few diversions attractive enough to separate Sam from his hobby.

He took another drag of hand-rolled tobacco, looked at

the tree Bridie had decorated so prettily. There were bits of tinsel, some baubles, strands of cotton wool snow, and a pretty crêpe-clad fairy with a silver star-topped wand and feathery wings, teetering uncertainly on the topmost branch. A proper Christmas at last. And she intended to go hell for leather back to Ireland after Christmas just because young Cathy had got herself involved on the fringe of a couple of very lightweight skirmishes.

Bridie entered from the scullery with two pans of peeled veg. She stirred the fire in preparation for her cooking, opened the door of the range oven, assessed the time her potatoes would need to roast.

He cleared his throat. 'Where are the girls?'

'Upstairs,' she replied, 'playing in their room with their Christmas toys. The fire's lit, so they'll be warm enough.'

Sam threw his fag end into the grate. 'You're sure I shouldn't go and get that dog? After all, I did make a promise. She'll be expecting a dog, you know.'

'There'll be no need,' she said. 'We have a dog at my father's house. I don't want to be taking another across on the boat. The girls and the bags will be more than enough for me to manage without running after a dog.' She hated the idea of returning to Da. But what was the alternative?

Sam Bell broke every rule in his book by lighting a second cigarette while the first was still curling its way towards death in the coals. He didn't want to beg and plead, refused to demean himself by crawling to this woman or to any person of either sex, for that matter. Yet he needed her to stay. 'We're married,' he said. 'We should abide by our marriage vows.'

'I know that. I also know that my daughter is misbehaving. She's not used to being locked up inside. In Galway, children can have all the freedom they need without stealing and fainting all over the place while people thieve poultry.'

'She won't do it again,' said Sam. 'I'm sure she'll settle down in time. Just give it a chance.'

Bridie turned and faced him fully. 'I can't take that risk, Sam.'

He nodded pensively for a moment. 'And you hate living round here, don't you?'

Her answer astounded both of them. 'No, I don't think so. The place isn't great, what with all those terrible courts and people living so crowded and so poor.' She lowered herself into a dining chair. 'But it's . . . it's lively. You know, there's always somebody to talk to. It's never boring.' Well, it was often rather boring in here with Sam, but boring was preferable to Da's ranting. If only Cathy would behave.

She folded her arms as if trying to hold on to her resolution. 'I can't have them wild, Sam. It's not even the fault of Jimmy and Tildy-Anne. They do what they do because it's necessary while the Nolans starve. But Cathy's not used to this sort of life and I want her to be honest. We never had a lot of money to spare at home, but we wanted for nothing. In Galway, she would not be tempted into all this stealing and making up of tales. You see, if my daughter turns out wrong, then I will be to blame for it.'

Sam had never been one for the women, yet he recognized that Bridie was one in a million. He'd listened to all the dirty talk over the years, had heard tales delivered by seamen who pretended to have a girl in every port. But Sam Bell was not a lecher by nature. However, this one was a catch. Many men in the neighbourhood were jealous of a man with such a pretty bride. She was lovely to look at, she had a stable temperament, good housekeeping skills and, above all, she was marvellous with customers. 'Don't go,' he managed.

Surprised beyond measure, Bridie stared steadily at the man she had married. There was no harm in him. He had never hurt her or the girls, had always handed over adequate household funds, was even-tempered and ... and, yes, infuriatingly predictable and set in his ways. She felt a measure of pity for him, yet she could make no promises.

'Please,' he said eventually, 'give it a bit longer.' What would people say if she went off after such a short time? Would they mock him, accuse him of being too old and worn out for a woman of Bridie's tender years?

She looked down at her folded arms. 'Marriage is binding, I know that. But I've a duty to my daughters as well as to my husband.'

'Hang on for another week, then,' he said. 'Just till New Year. I'll talk to Diddy and Billy, see what we can sort out.' And he intended to acquire that dog, too. He needed an arsenal with which to defend himself.

'All right,' said Bridie. 'I'll wait a few more days, then.' She picked up a fork, polished it on her apron.

Sam stood up, threw away his second cigarette and made for the door. Had he been less sure of himself, he might have fancied that he felt love for this young woman. But no. Sam Bell had his head screwed on too tightly for that. Far too tightly ...

Anthony Bell waited until his father had disappeared into the pub. He blew warmth into his hands, then bent to pick up his parcels. She would like the pearls. He had spent more money on that single gift than all the others put together. He walked, paused, thought about what he was doing, why he was doing it. Perhaps he should swap the labels about and give the pearls to Grandmuth.

He greeted some familiar faces, made his way to Bell's and knocked. This was ridiculous. How would Bridie explain away the pearls? Dad knew his stuff, could recognize good jewellery at twenty paces. And was this pity that Anthony felt for Bridie? Was he just feeling sorry for a poor woman who had been dragged from her home and deposited here?

When Bridie opened the shop door, he noticed the bloom in her cheeks, colour borrowed from the kitchen where she would no doubt be preparing the festive meal. He shuffled inside, deposited his packages on the counter. 'Cold,' he muttered. 'If my hands weren't fastened on at the wrists, they'd snap off.'

'The kitchen's hot,' she told him. 'Come away in till I make you a nice cup of tea.'

Instead of following her immediately, Anthony transposed two labels and ignored the regret in his breast. Grandmuth was going to be happy about the necklace. But Grandmuth's skin was too old and slack for the wearing of these, the least forgiving of gems. Pearls wanted satin skin and bright eyes. They needed a bare young throat rather than a winter cardigan to show them off. Bridie had perfect skin, lovely hair, beautiful clear eyes. The visitor bit his lip. He was balancing on the brink of a precipice, yet he could not save himself. Was love at first sight real? Was it? Scotland Road on a cold November night, two children clinging to their mammy, a cold-hearted priest in a chilly church ... He must stop this, he really must.

Bridie basted her potatoes, took a tray of soda bread from the top shelf of the fireside oven. 'Did you have your breakfast?' she asked. 'I've butter and jam and this new batch just made. It'll be great when it cools off a bit.'

'Er ... yes, I have eaten. Thank you.' Anthony felt like a fourteen-year-old boy who lusted after the girl next door. No, no, it was worse than that. It was horrible. His father had taken a bride and he, Anthony Patrick Bell, wanted her. He had wanted her ever since that moment when he had met her out in the street just before the wedding. He had dreamed of her, had thought about her when he should have been doing his job. He had lingered at a window and watched her taming a wild horse with her gentleness and her quiet, unobtrusive confidence.

'Do you take sugar?'

His cheeks burned. He knew his catechism, knew, understood and obeyed the rules of the church. Consanguinity, affinity and spiritual relationship – those were the qualities that precluded liaisons between the sexes. Even if Dad died, Anthony could never live with the woman of his dreams. He pulled himself together. 'Just a drop of milk, thank you.' She had eyes he wanted to drown in. She had a waist he might have spanned with his fingers. She had ... she had a cup of tea in her hand and he must take it, now.

Bridie put her head on one side. 'Are you coming down with something?'

He was lovesick. He was a lovelorn loon and no, he didn't want Dad to die, even if his death would release this lovely woman. 'I'm fine,' he replied. 'It's the change in temperature, I suppose. Icy outside, very warm in here.'

'Oh, keep still a moment,' she ordered. She stood behind him and peeled off his heavy overcoat. 'There,' she said. 'Now, you'll feel the benefit when you go out.'

Anthony had not intended to go to his father's wedding. He and Sam had found little common ground in recent years. But Anthony had met Thomas Murphy on the road, and the man had assumed, naturally, that Sam Bell's son would be attending the service. Then, Anthony had seen her.

'Did you not hear me?'

Startled, he shook some tea into his saucer. 'Sorry,' he

113

muttered. Her father was a rat, he mused. Thomas Murphy had been carrying on with Dolly Hanson for ever and a day—

'It'll be a chill,' she repeated. Was he deaf? She placed a hand on his forehead, found his skin hot. 'Let's hope it's not the influenza. You should perhaps stay here with me and your father till I see how you are.' The devilment had gone out of his eyes. She had noticed that little bit of naughtiness, the tell-tale glistening of the irises in a poker-straight face. This was a joker, not a man of misery. 'Wait for your da,' she said again.

He swallowed. 'My father and I don't get on.'

'And I don't get on with people not getting on,' she said, her tone firm. 'Mind, I might not be staying anyway, so you'll be able to carry on with your little quarrels, won't you? Yes, when you're left to yourselves, Muth can stay upstairs and you, your father and your brother can fight like infant boys all the way to kingdom come. I hope St Peter will be pleased to see you.' She bustled off to find a clean saucer.

Little quarrels? He shivered, took a sip of tea, refused to think about his brother and his stupid, blinkered father. Suddenly, the words she had spoken registered. She was going. He took the clean saucer from her, found difficulty in meeting her eyes. 'Where are you going?'

'To the scullery for—'

'No. You said something about leaving.'

'Ah.' Bridie sat down. 'It's Cathy,' she told him. 'She's away all the while in the company of Jimmy and Tildy-Anne. The last scrape they got into spread as far as the police and a lot of Indians with fireplaces and hats and gramophones.'

'Lascars,' he said, fighting a weary smile. 'Yes, I heard about that.' He fingered the cup, forced himself to look at her. There was a pinch of white powder on her nose –

flour, probably. It was a short nose, but not snub. He wanted to wipe the blemish from a face he found perfect. 'She's a brilliant student,' he remarked. 'She'll do well here. The time for young women to succeed has finally arrived. Our teachers at St Aloysius's are thrilled to have her at the school. She is so well-read, so capable. The fact is that she will make more of herself here than she would in Ireland.' He felt so awkward, heard his own stilted words, might have been a lecturer delivering a sermon or something very dull, like inorganic chemistry.

Bridie processed the information. 'Ireland is not as backward as you seem to think,' she informed him. 'We do have schools and universities, you know. It's not all potato fields, cattle and poteen brewing in the stables.'

Anthony's cheeks were burning again. 'But there's more scope here.'

She nodded pensively. 'Aye, and there's more people, too. All crammed up together with no air to breathe, all pushed into a crowded classroom and sharing one arithmetic book between two. Did you see those courts? Have you looked at the living conditions in this area? Animals have better shelter.'

'Of course I've seen the poverty,' he answered. 'Many of my pupils come from very poor homes.'

Bridie shook her head. 'It's terrible,' she said. 'And I know why Diddy's children break the law and the commandments. I understand. But it's all a matter of what a person wants from life.'

He swallowed drily, took a gulp of tea to oil his throat. 'Cathy must be given the opportunity to find out what she wants, Bridie. Let her study here and—'

'It's their mother who keeps them safe,' she declared, absolute certainty in her words. 'While they're little, parents decide. Perhaps in ten years Cathy may come back. For now, I'm in charge of my children.'

He remained where he was after she returned to the scullery. Bridie wasn't a bit like Val. Val had been dark-haired and tall, almost willowy. She, too, had been a teacher after training at some dreadful convent in Southampton. When he closed his eyes, he could see and hear her still. 'We couldn't talk after nine o'clock, we had to wear a uniform and all our letters were censored.' Val had taken a strong dislike to all things Catholic after her two years of prison with the nuns. 'Ladies from hell', she had called them.

'Are you all right in there?' shouted Bridie.

'Yes.' So Val had decided to teach at a non-denominational school in Liverpool. That had caused a few ructions among the die-hard Catholics.

'I've a little gift for you.'

Anthony took the proffered package, opened it and found a diary, some pencils and a drawing. 'Shauna did the picture and Cathy bought the pencils,' she said. 'The diary is from me and Sam. It has a real leather cover.'

'Thank you.' He gave her the scarf. Grandmuth would love the pearls, he told himself again.

Bridie draped his gift round her throat. 'Just the thing,' she told him. 'It goes with my eyes.'

It did. Val's eyes had been brown. Anthony had identified the body, because her parents had been too distraught. On this Christmas day, he would go and eat with the family of his dead fiancée. The courts had charged the wrong man, had found the wrong man guilty, had hanged him.

Bridie laid some cutlery on the table. This poor young man was very sad, she thought. He was perspiring and he looked quite ill. There had been no jokes, no laughter. Beneath the tanned skin there lurked a pallor, though twin spots of feverish colour brightened his cheeks.

Anthony picked up the rest of the parcels and announced his intention to visit his grandmother and Bridie's daughters. He climbed the stairs, tapped at Grandmuth's door.

'Come in,' she ordered.

For a split second, he hesitated. Christmases came and went, and he still remained at loggerheads with his twin and his father. Years ended and began, yet nothing changed. Whatever happened, they had still hanged the wrong man. And Anthony Bell was condemned to live with that knowledge embedded into his mind. Determinedly, he blotted out a mental picture of Val, only to have it replaced by the image of a small blonde woman with flour on her nose.

He ground his teeth for a second or two. Love at first sight? He had loved Val at first sight, after knocking apples from her shopping basket at the fruit market. They had bent to retrieve the Cox Orange Pippins, had both seen stars when their skulls had met. Val. No, no, this was Christmas Day. He must not dwell on the past, must forbid himself to remember the sight of Val's broken body.

'What are you doing standing there like a bloody statue?'

He blinked, saw that his grandmother had opened her door.

'I've been waiting,' she snapped.

'Sorry.' He followed her into the room, sat next to her on the bed. 'I got you pearls,' he said.

'Hmmph.' Theresa Bell folded her arms. 'What's up with you? You look as if you've lost half a crown and found a bent tanner.' She loved this grandson. Even though weeks went by between meetings, she knew him like the back of her own hand.

'Here.' He handed her the gift.

Theresa opened it, grinned broadly, then sat still while Anthony fastened the necklace for her. 'They're lovely,' she told him.

He unwrapped an anthology of poetry, thanked his grandmother, asked how she was.

'Yon bloody Bridie's got me moving,' she said. 'Kept leaving me plate just inside the door, made me get out of bed to get the food.' She sniffed. 'I like her. I like her kiddies, too. They make a bit of noise, but the house is back to life.' Anthony might have had children if Val had lived. Theresa could have been a great-grandmother several times over. The idea of a non-Catholic wedding hadn't worried Theresa. And then . . . and then the lass had gone and got herself murdered.

'You know she's thinking of going back to Ireland?' asked Anthony. 'Bridie, I mean.'

Theresa scowled. 'Aye. I hope she stays here, though.' She watched him from the corner of her eye, saw how strained he looked. 'Is that job getting you down, lad?'

'No.'

'What is it, then?'

He shrugged. Grandmuth was a caution. She had the Scotland Road knack of hitting the nail on the head, and the inland Lancashire tendency to run at a small tack with a lump hammer. Diplomacy had never been Theresa Bell's catchword. She spoke the truth and shamed the devil, expected everyone else to be as blunt as she was. 'I'm all right,' he said.

'And I'm a monkey's grandma,' she replied smartly. 'Is it Val?' Anthony's girl had died in December, so Christmas had not been a favourite time of his for some years.

'It might be that,' he said pensively. 'I'm due at their house for my dinner.'

Theresa inclined her head. If she lived to be a hundred and five, she would never forget that dreadful day. 'It should be getting easier now, lad. You should be looking for somebody else. No use carrying a torch for a girl who can't see it, eh?' She tapped his knee with a bony hand. 'Find a nice lass and settle down, Anthony. I shall get no great-grandchildren from the queer feller, you know.'

Anthony sighed, made no reply.

'Go on, then,' she ordered. 'If you've brought presents for the little ones, you'll find them playing in their room.' She watched the slope of his shoulders as he left, noticed how heavy his footfalls seemed. If only he would shape up and pull his life back together. Val wouldn't have wanted this for him.

Theresa stared through her window and back down the years. Bonny lads, they had been. Even at the start, when they had been weeks old, Liam had commanded the attention. He had cried all night and all day, had fed voraciously, had seemed to dominate the situation right from the beginning.

The old woman fingered her new pearls. By the time the twins had started to walk, Liam's assumed supremacy had become evident. Anthony had been clouted, knocked down, bitten and bruised. Anthony's toys were always broken or spoilt or lost. Liam had stolen from the shop, from his grandmother's purse, from Anthony's little box of pennies.

Theresa had learned to hope that Liam would improve in time. But he was still an arrogant and unpleasant man. 'Damn you, priest,' she snarled under her breath. 'One day, Father Bell. One day, some bugger'll come along and mess up your playpen. And I can't wait for it to happen.'

Cathy loved Anthony. She admired him, enjoyed his company, respected him. 'Thank you,' she said. He had brought her a huge box of paints and a story book. For

Shauna, he had chosen a doll and a collection of nursery rhymes with colourful pictures. Anthony talked to Cathy and Shauna as if they were adults. He didn't tailor his language to suit the young; he used proper words at normal speed.

Anthony squatted down and helped the younger girl to build a tower of bricks.

'Sir?'

He looked across at Cathy and smiled. 'Anthony when we're not at school,' he reminded her.

'I might forget,' Cathy said. 'I might call you Anthony at school.' She perched on the edge of her bed. 'That's if we stay in Liverpool.'

He rose and warmed his hands at a small fire that danced in the iron grate in a corner of the bedroom. Perhaps Bridie was right, when she said he was coming down with a chill, because he felt cold, then hot. 'Do you want to go back to Ireland?' he asked.

Cathy thought about the question for a few seconds. She hugged the memory of Ballinasloe, often had dreams that she was running with Bob through fields and streams. But now, she had so many friends. At any time of day, she could go round to the Costigan house and chat with those who happened to be at home. There were always plenty of children outside, and they were all good fun. She enjoyed the company of Tildy, had even taken a liking to the school. 'I don't know. We'll just have to do what Mammy decides.'

He nodded.

'It's my fault,' she said sadly. 'Because of helping Tildy and Cozzer to get stuff for the Nolans. Cozzer says Jesus is on their side, you see. Jesus knows the Nolans are hungry, so it's not a sin to take things as long as they're for the poor. But in confession, Father Brennan gave me three Our Fathers and three Hail Marys and said I haven't to steal any more. I told Father Brennan about Jesus taking the loaves and fishes and never paying for them, but Father Brennan said that was different. He was laughing, too. I didn't know priests could laugh during confession. He called me a caution. Anyway, I put some money in the St Vincent de Paul box.'

Anthony patted the bemused child on the head, then made his way downstairs. Even at Christmas, the sharp-edged sword of poverty cut into people, made them bleed over the double standards that plagued the Catholic community hereabouts.

Grandmuth had got herself down to the kitchen. She was tucking into a plate of soda bread and strawberry jam. 'Manna straight from heaven,' she mumbled through a mouthful. 'This girl can cook, all right.'

Anthony smiled at Theresa. 'Who helped you downstairs?'

Bridie's head put in a brief appearance from the scullery. 'She helps herself, Anthony. I've been bullying her and building her up, you see. She complains about me all the time, says I'm a cruel and thoughtless woman.'

'That's why you've to stay,' croaked the old woman. 'You have to look after me.'

Anthony gazed round the room he knew so well, the place where he had been reared by the frail-looking lady who was currently demolishing a sizeable late breakfast. There was the dresser drawer against which he had been thrown by Liam. On that occasion, a doctor had been brought in to staunch the flow of blood. Anthony recalled how matted his hair had been once the blood had dried. To the right of the dresser stood a locked door behind which Sam Bell stored some of his too-good-to-sell treasures. Anthony had been trapped in there many times, had listened helplessly while Dad and Grandmuth had searched for keys hidden by Liam. To this day, Anthony remained uneasy in confined spaces, especially during darkness.

'You don't look well to me,' announced Theresa.

Dad had always saved things, had never managed to save Anthony from the flailing fists and boots of his twin. Dad hung on to pots and ornaments against the day when they would 'come back into fashion', was a wizard at assessing the potential value of inanimate objects. But Dad had never seemed to notice that Liam was odd and extremely dangerous in temper.

'Cat got your tongue?' asked Grandmuth.

'Sorry, I was thinking.'

She placed the plate on a side table. 'He's not here any more, love. He can't cut your head open or take an axe to your toys.'

Anthony shivered.

'Holy Orders was the only place for him to run,' said Theresa. 'He's not fit for the ordinary life, so he goes about telling everybody else how to live now.' She sniffed. 'As if he knows owt. Nasty bugger.'

The door to the shop opened and Sam stepped into the scene. For a split second, he stopped mid-stride, as if uncertain about his next move. 'Hello, Muth,' he finally managed. He had thought that Anthony would be well on his way by this time.

Anthony rose to his feet.

'Stop where you are,' commanded Theresa. 'Don't be dashing off just when you're getting warm. I've told you, you don't look well.'

Sam pulled on a piece of rope and dragged a large dog into the arena. 'For Cathy,' he told his mother.

Bridie entered from the scullery, blew a strand of hair off her face and fixed her gaze on Sam. He shouldn't have done it. He shouldn't have brought an animal home while she was still making up her mind about the future. She noticed that the two men seemed awkward, reminded herself that her husband and his son were not on proper speaking terms. But for the most part, her attention remained glued to the ugliest piece of canine creation that she had ever seen.

Sam puffed and panted, then fastened the hound to the handle of the storeroom door. 'Well, what could I do?' he asked helplessly. 'The man brought the dog to the pub. I couldn't ask him to take it away again. Nobody else wanted it, and I can't say I blame them. It takes some dragging along, the stubborn brute.'

The dog sat down and cast a lugubrious eye around the room.

'In all my days, I have never seen anything as miserable-looking as yon dog,' declared Theresa.

Bridie leaned on the door jamb. This unfortunate creature resembled an impossible cross between a tram and a long-haired carpet that needed hanging outside for a good beating. 'What breed is it?' she asked, her words emerging strangled.

'I don't know,' replied Sam. It was a huge dog, not much smaller than a Shetland pony. It had one brown eye, one dark-blue, and long ears that flopped all over a permanently puzzled expression. 'Nobody wants it,' he repeated.

Bridie pushed another lock of hair from her damp forehead. 'I'm not surprised. That will eat Cathy,' she pronounced. 'And it'll swallow Shauna whole for its pudding.' She approached the beast and offered the back of her hand.

Sensing a friend in this cruel vale of tears, the dog licked Bridie's hand and woofed a polite greeting.

'I'll be off,' said Anthony. 'I'm expected elsewhere.' He kissed his grandmother, nodded at Bridie, then left the room.

Theresa Bell stared at the animal. She knew what Sam was up to. He had brought the dog so that Cathy would make a scene about going back to Ireland. He was doing his best to get Bridie to stay, and he didn't care what means he used. 'Take it back, Sam,' Theresa said quietly. 'It's not fair. And you know what I mean, son.'

He coughed. 'The man's gone home now. He lives over the bridge – miles away. And it's freezing out there.'

'If Cathy sees that dog, there'll be no shifting her,' said Theresa. 'Don't you think it's time Bridie started making her own mind up, Sam? It's like the bloody horses all over again.'

Sam shifted awkwardly, curled a hand and coughed self-consciously behind it.

'It's all right,' continued his mother. 'She knows. Bridie knows you and Thomas Murphy have a habit of dragging dumb animals into things when you want your own way.' She eyed her daughter-in-law. 'And if she does decide to stop on in Liverpool, you can give her them papers, Sam.'

'Papers?'

Theresa sighed heavily. 'Horse papers. You can let Bridie have them two horses. I've not lived this long without knowing you. Oh yes, I know how to deal with me own son. So pin your ears back. You'd best give her the animals, or you'll have me to deal with on top of everything else.' She glared at the 'everything else' until it squirmed inside its matted brown coat. 'Your cousin Edith'll take the horses. She can get them stabled and all that.'

Sam looked at Bridie. So she knew all about it, then. 'It was your dad's idea, not mine. I ... er ... I'm glad you're here. You've made a difference to me and to Muth.' He paused for a second. 'The horses are yours whether you go back to Ireland or stay here.' He untied the dog's makeshift lead. 'And I'll get rid of this as soon as possible.'

He was a decent man, thought Bridie. He was not much

to look at, he was predictable to a point that made her want to scream sometimes, but he had a bit of conscience. If he had a bit of conscience, why wasn't he more friendly towards Anthony? Anthony was a lovely chap. Well, he was usually pleasant, though he had seemed a bit down in the mouth today.

Sam approached his wife, rope in one hand, a small box in the other. 'I got you a new one,' he said.

'I beg your pardon?'

'It's a wedding ring. Brand new this time.'

She couldn't leave him. Apart from the fact that marriage was for ever, he was trying so hard to please her. But what should she do about Cathy? Perhaps the child needed a lead so that she might be tied up like this stupid great dog.

The wedding band was beautiful. 'Twenty-two carat,' Sam said proudly.

Bridie swallowed a pain in her throat. This man was not a husband to her. The marriage had been consummated, just about, but Sam was ... perhaps he was the father she had never had. There wasn't much warmth in Sam Bell, but she forgave him for that because he had been a widower for almost thirty years. Yet Sam's presence in the house gave her a secure feeling, an idea that he would not allow her or the girls to come to any harm. She didn't know what to say to him, could find no words.

'And the horses are yours, too,' he told her.

Bridie lifted her head, looked at Sam, then at Theresa. She had some value after all. The man was standing here, was telling her that he needed her, that she was not a bitter pill sweetened by the promise of riches from racecourses and stud farms. She, Bridie Bell, was worth keeping. 'Thank you so much, Sam,' she managed. 'You have done your best to welcome strangers into your home. Please remember how grateful I am.'

Clearly embarrassed, the pink-faced man glanced down at the dog. 'What shall I do with this?' he asked.

Bridie squatted down and allowed herself to be almost drowned by an over-enthusiastic canine tongue. 'We'll call him Noel,' she said, 'because it's Christmas.' She rose, gave Sam the ring and allowed him to place it on her hand. Just as Diddy had said, this was not a bad man, not a particularly good one. 'The first sign of sun and you bathe this creature, Sam,' she said with mock-severity. 'And make sure he stays from under my feet.'

'Mine, too,' announced Theresa.

The dog glanced from one to the other, his ragged tail waving to demonstrate a glimmer of hope. They had food. He could smell it, could almost taste it on his lolling tongue. If he bided his time and made no sudden moves, his belly might be filled.

The feasting was over. Sam unbuttoned his belt and leaned back in his chair. It had been a grand day. Roast goose with good gravy, then Christmas pud and brandy sauce. Bridie was a pearl. He looked across at Muth. 'New necklace?' he asked.

Theresa fixed him with her small, bright eyes. 'Anthony got them for me. Remember him? He's the lad who was here just on dinner-time. I believe he's a teacher by trade. Think hard, now, it'll all come back to you. Lived here at one time, he did.' She sat up and leaned forward. 'He's a good lad, our Anthony, well thought of round these parts.'

Sam sighed and closed his eyes. The worst thing about Muth was the fact that she just couldn't leave well alone. He supposed they were like that, the Bolton folk. Muth's niece was the same, always speaking up for herself and laying down the law.

'It's not right that you don't talk to your own boy.'

He opened his eyes. 'He went too far last time,' he said softly. 'He should never have thrashed Liam. Yes, he went too far, Muth.'

'Did he?' Theresa shook a finger at her only son. 'He were grieving. He were upset on account of Val.'

Muth was upset too, now. He could tell she was worked up, because her 'wases and weres' got mixed up whenever she became excited. 'Leave it alone, Muth.'

Theresa struggled to her feet. 'Goodwill to all men? What sort of a Christmas is it when you can't be civil to a blood relative? You weren't here when they were little. You were always mithering over the shop and running about buying stuff. You never saw what I saw, Sam. Liam would have killed our Anthony if I hadn't rattled his bloody ear for him. He's bad through and through, and you're as blind as a bat.'

Sam remained in his chair, refused to rise to the bait in any way. Anthony had always been Muth's favourite. Liam was a wonderful man. He had gone away to a seminary and had kept up with the best of them. Few people realized how clever priests had to be, all that Latin and liturgy and moral law. There had been a scrap or two between the twins when they were very young, but nothing out of the ordinary. Then Anthony had started a terrible fight and he would not make his apologies to Liam.

Theresa Bell loomed over her son. 'You saw nowt, our Sam. He were allers good when you came home, that sly Liam. Oh aye, butter wouldn't melt, eh? He were a strong little beggar, forever shoving our Anthony in cupboards and pretending it were all a game. And you pretended too. Because you could never face what he was, and you can't face what he is to this day. Leopards does not change their spots, just mark my words.'

Sam pulled the tobacco tin from his pocket, took out

the last cigarette. 'Go to bed, Muth,' he advised calmly. 'You're getting worn out.'

The old woman stepped back a fraction. 'Have I not spent long enough in bed? I stopped up there all them years because there were nowt down here for me, nowt at all. I missed our Anthony. I still miss him. And yes, I will be going up in a minute, because that swine'll be paying his after Christmas tea visit, won't he? Oh aye, he'll be stopping the night with Father Brennan so he can come round here and plague the daylights out of me. Well, just keep him away from my room, that's all.'

Sam watched his mother making her slow way out of the kitchen. Bridie was upstairs putting the girls to bed. She was a grand woman, a good wife. A lovely dinner and a lovely tea – what more could a man ask? He tossed the end of his cigarette into the grate and answered his own question. A man wanted peace when his belly was full. As for Anthony – well – that one would have to apologize to Liam before he would be welcomed properly again.

The scullery door flew open and brought a draught with it. 'Sam,' puffed Diddy Costigan, 'it's Anthony. He called in to wish us all the best, then he had a turn at our house and we took him home and put him to bed. He's burning up.'

Sam sat up straight. 'Get the doctor.'

'We have,' answered Diddy. 'He said it's his bronchials.'

Bridie entered from the stairway. 'What's happening?'

Diddy told the tale again, then stood and watched while Bridie pulled on her coat.

'Where are you going?' asked Sam.

Bridie stopped in her tracks and looked at her husband. She had no idea what the quarrels were about, but she knew at this moment that she could spare no patience for the family feud. 'I'm off to look after your son,' she told him. 'I'll leave you to do the same for my daughters.'

It was a terrible night. The wind howled in the chimneys, rattled guttering, shunted slates along ill-formed rooftops. Flurries of snow twisted and turned, swirled like miniature tornados and prevented anyone from seeing houses across the way.

'God's in a temper,' declared Diddy. 'My ma always said that when the weather was bad. May the good Lord rest her.'

Bridie heaped more coal into the parlour grate. Billy had brought down Anthony's bed and set it up in one of the alcoves that flanked the fireplace. The sick young man slept on a mound of pillows, since the doctor had advised his neighbours to keep him as upright as possible. His breathing was audible, as if it rasped and tore at his lungs in order to find its way out.

Diddy sat by the bed with her knitting. Three doors away, members of her family were enjoying the final hours of Christmas, but Diddy was staying where she was needed. 'He doesn't deserve none of this,' she declared as she stabbed away at a half-formed cardigan in bottle green. 'It's always the good what suffer. Have you noticed that, Bridie?'

'Yes.' Mammy had suffered, had shrivelled away slowly and painfully. Now, this kind-hearted man who worked hard at educating the poor was desperately ill, too ill to be moved to the fever hospital. Sam hadn't even bothered to turn up at Anthony's bedside. 'What is going on with the Bell family?' asked Bridie. 'Why won't Sam call round to see his son?'

Diddy picked up a dropped stitch and tossed her

needlework aside. 'None of us knows the whole truth. The twins never got on as babies, everybody knew that. Liam used to batter Anthony and break all his toys. He didn't like Anthony having anything. I've heard tell that Liam bought Anthony's friends by giving them toffee and fruit, stole the money to get the stuff. Devious little swine, he was. And I don't think he's much different now.'

Bridie perched on the edge of a fireside chair. 'It's more than that, Diddy. It's bigger and more recent, but not yesterday or even a year ago.'

The older woman gazed at her friend. She had a full set of marbles, this Bridie Bell. She could sense the atmosphere in the Bell household, had worked out that something major must have happened. 'All I know is there was a big bust-up after Val died. It was probably something Liam said – I bet he was glad poor Anthony had lost his girl, because she was a lapsed Catholic, you see. But I've not many details for you, Bridie. The only folk with the truth about what was said are Liam and this one here.' She waved a hand at the bed. 'For the first time in twenty-odd years, Anthony turned on Liam and gave him a pasting the likes of which you only see at a bare-knuckle fight behind the market.'

Bridie stared at Anthony's ashen face. 'Was Liam ordained when this happened?'

Diddy nodded vigorously. 'Oh yes, he was fully-fledged, all right. Didn't have his own parish – still doesn't – but he was attached to St Aloysius's while he learned the ropes. It was after confession one night. At a guess, I'd say Father Brennan went looking for Liam and found him in the porch with Anthony standing over him. Our Charlie saw some of it. He was the last but one in the confessional box. When he came out to say his penance, Anthony went in. So there was only the twins and our Charlie in church at the time.'

Bridie stood up and poked the fire to life. 'Isn't it unusual to have a man confess to his own brother?'

Diddy fixed her eyes on the flames and sighed. 'I don't think he went in there for a blessing, Bridie.'

'Neither do I.'

Diddy frowned. 'Our Charlie's slow on his feet – you know what he's like. He was just outside the church when they rolled out in a ball, both kicking and screaming. Then Anthony picked his brother up and knocked seven shades of everything out of him. Charlie couldn't do nothing, so he came home as quick as he could and told his dad. And when my Billy got there, everybody had gone. I heard they were in the presbytery, but I'm not certain. Since then, there's been no love lost.'

'It's a terrible situation,' remarked Bridie. 'Sam should be here with his sick son.'

'He's all for Liam.'

'I know.'

'And Theresa Bell's all for Anthony. That's why she sulked for so long.'

'I know that, too.' Bridie crossed the room and stood over the man who was her stepson. He was in a deep sleep, the sort of sleep that sometimes precedes the end of life itself. She picked up a flannel and wiped his face. 'Sweet Jesus,' she begged, 'don't take him, not at this age.'

Diddy joined Bridie. 'Look, I've some balsam at home. There's an old girl down Hornby Street who makes it from an Irish recipe. You just stick it in hot water and let the fumes rise till it breaks up the phlegm.' She sniffed. 'Strips the bloody paint off your walls at the same time, like. Still, if it does him no good, it'll do him no harm.'

While Diddy went to do battle with the weather, Bridie settled herself next to the bed and held Anthony's limp fingers. He was so still. The only movements came from his upper body, which seemed to shake and shiver with each and every breath. She prayed, put all her energy into the effort. He had to live. He was young and strong and clever and good ... dear God, don't let him die, she prayed inwardly.

Eugene had lived for a day after the accident. She had sat like this right up against the bed with his hand in hers. There had been no marks on her husband's face. His legs had taken the worst of it. Had he lived, he would not have worked again, might never have walked unaided.

A tear slid down her face, was followed by another and another until her whole body was racked with sobs. She hadn't been able to cry. The children had needed her, the farm had needed her. Even now, she remembered standing in the churchyard dry-eyed and numb. Da hadn't attended the funeral. Da didn't allow himself to set foot inside any place of worship that wasn't Catholic.

And here lay a sad young man with no family around him. This wasn't right, wasn't human. She wept until she was exhausted. There was something about Anthony that reminded her of Eugene. She tried hard to work out what it was, because her first husband had been fair-haired and solid, not dark and tall like this man. Drier sobs were still coming from her throat while she attempted to find some similarity between Anthony and Eugene. As far as she could ascertain, their masculinity was the only common ground. There was the humour, she told herself. Like Eugene, Anthony had a sense of the ridiculous and didn't mind making a fool of himself.

Where was Diddy? she asked herself. She mopped the clammy brow again, straightened the bed covers, smoothed black hair away from his forehead. It was probably the mouth, she decided. Yes, Eugene's mouth had been like this one ... or was it the chin?

'Bridie?'

132

She jumped involuntarily. His dark eyes were fixed on her. 'Yes, it's Bridie,' she said eventually.

'A drink.'

Bridie placed an arm round his neck and supported him, guided him to the cup in her right hand.

After one sip, he was defeated. 'Thanks,' he managed.

Diddy bumbled in, brought cold air with her. 'It's always in the last place you look, isn't it?' She waved the bottle of balsam.

Bridie bit back a clever retort about things obviously being in the last place where a person looked, then helped Diddy to set up her cauldron and make the brew. After a few minutes, the air was thick with the smells of tar and eucalyptus. 'He woke while you were gone, Diddy.'

Big Diddy Costigan grinned. 'That's a good sign. The stink of this bloody lot should shift him one way or another.' She walked to the bed. 'See? He's breathing easier. You've been crying, Bridie. No need for that. This lad has a few more miles in him yet.' She patted the quilt. 'That's right, Anthony. We'll get you better. Just breathe easy, slow and easy.'

Bridie, too, breathed more freely as the night wore on. While Diddy snoozed in an armchair, the younger woman remained alert to the sick man's every intake of air. With luck and good medicine, he might just come out of this without getting pneumonia.

Towards morning, he woke again. Bridie was sitting next to him. Her hand rested on his and she was staring straight into his eyes. 'Thank you,' he said.

She smiled at him. 'Will you make it after all, Anthony?'

He nodded. While she was in the world, he would surely remain alive. As she bustled about pouring tea and medicine, he kept his eye on her. She was his father's wife. She was his father's wife and Anthony loved her.

Six

The first day in the fourth decade was crisp and bright. Children played out of doors, whipping new tops into dizzying whirls of colour, testing out footballs and skipping ropes, skidding along in carts consisting of orange boxes and old pram wheels.

Cathy lingered outside Bell's and thought about being good. She had been good for a whole week and, up to now, she had permission to keep Noel. But Noel would go back where he came from if Cathy broke any of the rules. She hadn't been near Cozzer and Tildy for days, was avoiding involvement in any scheme to improve the Nolans' quality of existence.

The dog squatted next to his new mistress, thought about scratching his ear, froze with a hind leg in mid-air. He had to be alert. Itching was a cross to be endured so that he could keep his mind on looking after Cathy. She had tied a red satin bow to his collar, and he had spent several hours trying to be rid of the indignity, but this was not the time to indulge in personal grooming. So the dog simply cocked one of his floppy ears and awaited instructions.

Cathy sighed heavily, wondered what to do. She missed Tildy and Cozzer. Mammy had gone along to Dryden Street with soup for Mr Bell, who was Anthony out of school, and with some more soup for the Nolans. Mammy was acting tight-lipped with Uncle Sam, something to do with Uncle Sam not visiting Anthony while he was ill.

The little girl made up her mind at last. She would walk along to Dryden Street and visit Anthony. With any luck, she might just avoid Mammy and bump into the Costigans. 'Come along, Noel,' she ordered.

Noel was a grand dog and he knew it. Life had been hard thus far, but he had come through with flying colours, one of which was currently fastened to the length of leather round his neck. The collar itself had taken some getting used to, but he owned a tolerant nature and a degree of self-control. Ignoring three cats and a yappy mongrel, Noel raised his tattered tail and walked proudly with his owner. He needed no lead, because he was so grateful to have shelter and good, solid food that he practised obedience and was almost perfect.

Cathy knocked on Mr Bell's door, was ushered inside by her mother. 'Can Noel come in?'

Bridie frowned. This dog of indeterminate origin was the size of a sofa. Unfortunately, she had taken a liking to the thing. It knew how to get round people, how to look sad, happy, mischievous and angelic. It was probably something to do with the eyes being two different colours. The dog's expression depended on the onlooker's point of view. 'He'll have to behave himself.'

Noel stalked in and parked himself on Anthony's feet.

Anthony stared down at the strange-looking creature, wondered whether it might have been a rag rug in an earlier life.

'He's a very good dog,' said Cathy cheerfully. 'He's not chewed anything since Christmas.'

Bridie suppressed a giggle. 'He picked on one of Sam's new slippers, I'm afraid, worried it to death in the back yard.'

'What breed is it?' asked Anthony.

'One of its own,' replied Bridie. 'God broke the mould when He saw the state of this article. There's mountain dog in him – St Bernard or some such kind, but Noel's a bit of a mixture and he eats constantly. Everyone keeps asking what breed he is. Anyway, he doesn't bite, and that's what counts.'

The dog lay flat, squashing most of the feeling out of Anthony's toes.

Bridie set a tray, placed a bowl of steaming soup next to a spoon and a chunk of bread. She moved the dog by simply giving it a long, hard look, then passed the tray to Anthony. 'There you are, some nice Irish broth.' He looked so much better. That foul-smelling brew of Diddy's had helped to do the trick, it seemed. 'Now, no going outside,' she ordered. 'Billy will be in later, and Diddy's making a pie for your tea.' She pulled at the dog's collar. 'Away now, Noel. You're only getting in the way.'

'Leave him,' begged Anthony. 'Let him and Cathy keep me company for a while.'

Bridie left them to it and walked home. She had delivered a pan of broth to Cissie Nolan, who now trusted Bridie sufficiently to allow her into the house. Bridie had discussed with Diddy the idea of getting the Nolans some furniture from the shop, but Diddy had squashed the idea. Anything that wasn't nailed to the floor in the Nolan household was sold and swilled down Mr Nolan's throat. Had there been a market for children, he would probably have let all his offspring go to the highest bidders.

Scotland Road looked better today. With frost and a sprinkling of snow, and without the dust that accompanies toil and transport, the area was more attractive. Bridie bustled on towards Bell's Pledges, her mind fixed on sandwiches, scones and cakes. Today, there would be three visitors. Liam, who had remained absent over

136

Christmas, was to grace the family home with his presence. He would be accompanied by Sam's cousin and her husband.

Bridie refused to be nervous in the face of this imminent happening. Her hands were trembling because of the bitter cold, she told herself. And the headache was just tiredness, wasn't it? Of course it was. She wasn't dreading seeing those awfully cold eyes again. No, not at all. She was just a little run down, no more than that.

Anthony's house was very interesting. There wasn't a lot of furniture – just a pair of armchairs in the tiny parlour, a table and chairs in the kitchen, a couple of rugs. But there were hundreds of books. Some were on real shelves and in bookcases, others were housed in orange boxes stood on end to look like cupboards, and many were stacked on window-ledges, mantelshelves and against walls. Cathy dashed about picking and choosing, finally setting on an *Atlas of European Countries*.

They pored over a map of Ireland. 'There it is,' said Cathy triumphantly. 'Ballinasloe. It's really spelt B-E-A-L, A-T-H-A, N-A, S-L-U-A-I-G-H-E. With lines over some of the letters. That's proper Irish. There's a castle to guard the river Suck and a big quarry nearby where they get the Galway stone. Great big men work there. They have to be strong to break the stuff. Sometimes, there's an explosion and your feet tremble. I used to pretend I lived near one of those mountains—'

'Volcanoes?'

'Yes. They spit fire and rocks.'

She was bright to the point of effervescence. Intelligence shone in her eyes, and she had humour, too. Cathy was like her mother, he decided. Although he had never known Eugene, he guessed that this little one would turn out to be very like Bridie. Bridie. He mustn't think about the fall of her hair and the arch of her brows. No, he should concentrate on what he did best, should stick to educating children.

He listened while Cathy prattled on about the forge and the church, while she passed on her mother's opinions about various neighbours. 'My daddy ran the farm, then he was killed in the machinery. Mammy took over, but the landlord wanted a man to have the place. Mammy told him she could read and count and do as well as anybody, but we were still moved. We lived with Granda. He's got angry eyes and bushy hair, but he plasters that down with stuff in a bottle. Granda has horses and cows and pigs. I had my own chicken and a dog, but now I've got Noel. Granda used to slap me. I think that's why Mammy said she'd come over and marry Mr Bell. We call him Uncle Sam. Mammy never smacks us and she doesn't like anyone else slapping us. Anyway, Uncle Sam's nice because he never shouts and he got Noel for me.'

They both gazed at the animal in question. 'He's a size,' said Anthony.

'I have to be good to keep him. Mammy says we're both on trial. But really, I'm the one who has to behave.'

He tried not to laugh. 'That shouldn't be too difficult. When Tildy and Jimmy want to go . . . want to find stuff for the Nolans, just walk away.' The child would never walk away from anything. She was an explorer, one of life's navigators.

Cathy studied this teacher and friend for a moment. 'Can I do that? Won't they laugh and call me a baby if I just go off and don't help to feed the poor?'

Anthony took the child's hand. 'Does it matter if they do?'

It did matter. What people thought was important. She was Mammy's big girl in the house, but when she went outside, she became a little girl who had to remember her mother's orders and stick to them at all costs. Following Mammy's orders meant she couldn't spend time with the Costigans, couldn't choose or decide anything for herself. Cathy told Anthony about this. 'I'm to be big and helpful at home, but not in the street.' She withdrew her fingers from his grip and folded her arms. 'It's like being two different girls altogether, one big and one small. I have to remember which one I'm being, and that's not easy.'

He understood her. 'Childhood is confusing,' he informed her. 'And parents don't always make the best sense. But your mother has your welfare at heart, Cathy. She wants you safe and sensible. Tildy and Jimmy have had a different life. Anyway, don't you want to go back to Ireland? Isn't that what you'd like to do?'

She really didn't know, and she told Anthony all about it. 'I like school. I like the shop, and Uncle Sam gives me pennies. Tildy is my friend, even though she's older and in a different form at school.' She pondered for a second or two. 'But I miss Bob and Chucky and the fields. I don't miss Granda, because I don't like him. Nobody likes him. If we do go back, it won't be to Galway, Mammy said. So . . .' She chewed her lip. 'So I'd rather stay here than have to go and live somewhere new all over again. It would be Ireland, but it would still be strange.'

The front door opened and Maureen Costigan stepped inside after a cursory little click of fingernails against the wood. She stopped in her tracks when she saw Cathy, then slinked her way into the room and stood in front of the fire. 'I just came to see how you are,' she informed the sick man. She smiled to show off her dimples, then fluttered the long, soot-and-petroleum-jelly-coated eyelashes.

Anthony breathed deeply. How much longer would this go on? Maureen was in her last year at school, for which he thanked God, but she was pursuing him relentlessly at every opportunity. During playtimes, she came down from the senior department and 'helped' him. 'Helping' was sashaying about with inkwells and gazing into his eyes across piles of books. 'I'm going to have a rest now,' he told the two girls.

Maureen pounced on the tray, carried it out to the scullery and clattered the pots.

Cathy placed a proprietorial hand on Noel's head and led him to the door. Sometimes, she didn't quite manage to like Maureen Costigan. At first, she hadn't liked Nicky-really-Monica, but Nicky was all right. Nicky had a boyfriend called Graham Pile. Graham Pile had a lazy eye that stuck in the corner next to his nose, but he was kind. When he got his hands on stale or spoiled stock at the bakery where he worked, he always wrapped it up and brought it to the Nolans. But Maureen was selfish and proud.

The little girl said goodbye and went out into Dryden Street. Maureen wasn't nice. She was usually chasing boys. Tildy was always telling stories about Maureen kissing people in the dark in jiggers and in shop doorways. As far as Cathy understood, kissing should be reserved for members of a family. For a brief moment, she imagined herself embracing one of the boys from school. When her stomach settled, she walked along to a group of children that contained Cozzer and Tildy. Within seconds, she had forgotten all about Anthony and Maureen.

The black-clad man alighted from a vehicle and stood at the bottom of Dryden Street. Anthony was ill, or so he had been told by Aunt Edith. He must go and visit his brother. After all, wasn't the tending of the sick a part of his ministry? And he rather liked the concept of praying over his prostrate twin. Was he still afraid of Anthony? Liam asked himself as he made his way towards the house. No. All that nonsense should be dead and buried by now. This was 1931, the first of January, the beginning of a new decade. Wasn't it time to forgive and forget? His mouth curled into a travesty of a smile.

The older O'Brien girl was here with some of those dreadful Costigans. He stopped for a few seconds and watched the group playing an unseasonal game of cricket. It was clear that the Costigan boy had been given a bat for Christmas, as he was dictating and changing the rules to the advantage of his own side. Gas lamps acted as wickets, and a monster of a dog kept running off with the ball. The O'Brien girl spotted Liam, ran towards him. 'You should be inside,' she cried. 'Mammy says you've to stay warm.' The child shunted to a halt. 'Sorry, Father. I thought you were . . .' Her words tailed away as she spoke.

Liam ignored the girl, straightened his shoulders and tapped at Anthony's door. Whatever happened in the next few minutes, he would emerge victorious. If Anthony accepted the attempt at reconciliation, Liam would get the glory. If Anthony would not negotiate, then the priest would still be wearing the halo.

He entered the house. Maureen Costigan was sitting opposite Anthony with a cup and saucer. The host, too, was sipping tea. Liam paused, took in the situation. This strumpet was dressed to the nines and her face was painted. It was plain that she adored the sick man. 'Anthony,' he said with a nod, 'I thought it was about time I paid you a visit.'

Anthony maintained the grip on his cup, but only just. Had Maureen not been here – and he fervently wished her in darkest Africa at that moment – he would have said a few short, sharp words. As things were, he could only sit and hope, however stupidly, that he was experiencing yet another nightmare from which he would wake in a moment or two. Of late, Liam Bell and Maureen Costigan had figured in the less pleasant of Anthony's dreams.

Maureen rose carefully and placed her crockery on the mantelpiece. 'Father,' she said, 'I've been looking after Mr Bell.' She smiled fondly at the recovering invalid. 'He's getting better now.' She tightened the scarf at her throat and awarded both men a smile that was supposed to be seductive. 'Ta-ra, Father,' she trilled. Then she turned to Anthony. 'I'll see you later,' she said, her tone suddenly husky.

When the young madam had left, Liam placed himself in the chair she had vacated. Like many priests, he treated the houses of others as if they were an extension of the church and presbytery. Even here, where his welcome was not assured, he made himself at home.

'What do you want, Liam?'

Anthony did not look ill at all. And he had been entertaining that cheap-looking girl, too. 'I heard you had been sick, so I came to see how you are,' said the priest.

When his teacup and saucer had been placed on the rug, Anthony rose to his feet. 'I don't recall asking for Extreme Unction – when I do need a priest, I'll send for a real one. And I don't remember inviting you in.' His voice was quiet.

'Do I need an invitation?'

'Don't hold your breath,' was the quick reply, 'because you'll never receive one.'

Liam remained very still. It didn't matter. This man could say and do nothing that would have the slightest chance of damaging an ordained priest. 'That business is long past and best forgotten,' he said. For much of the time, Liam really did forget the past. Occasionally, he even managed to believe that nothing had happened, that it had all been a strange story that he had read somewhere.

Anthony nodded. 'It's long past, I agree. And Val's long dead.' He concentrated on his breathing, prayed that he might stay free from one of his coughing bouts. 'It must be twenty years since you threw me in the river.' His tone was normal, conversational. 'I think we were eight when you broke my arm, a little bit younger when you knocked out two of my teeth.' The clock marked beats of time for a few seconds. 'And you killed Val five years ago.'

'Rubbish,' snarled the hallowed visitor.

Anthony nodded pensively. 'The police said the same thing. They thought I was in shock. But even if I was in shock, I knew you. I knew you then and I know you now.'

Liam stared straight ahead, seemed to look through his brother. 'I am only glad that my father and grandmother didn't get to hear about that foul accusation.'

Anthony laughed, though the hollow sound contained no joy. 'If my allegation had been empty, you would have run to Dad and told him. You would have been delighted to inform the family about how wrong and how cruel I was, how I had tried to blacken your name with the police. But you kept quiet.'

'I was a priest,' snarled Liam.

'And a murderer. Now, because of your sins, you are condemned to eternal damnation – isn't that the case? If you go to confession without telling all, if you partake of Holy Communion while in a state of mortal sin – isn't that a sacrilege?'

Liam continued to stare, but his eyelids blinked slowly. Anthony was saying all these things, but Liam could scarcely bring to mind the sequence of events that had led to the quarrel.

'You are so sick,' whispered Anthony. 'So sick and so evil. You forget, don't you? If the past is unsavoury, you just file it away in a drawer marked miscellaneous. You genuinely manage to wipe out all the things you don't need to remember. But I remember, brother. Oh yes, I can't erase any of it.'

Liam licked his upper lip. He was the priest; he was in charge. The things Anthony spoke of were part of another time, a different life. 'Anything I have done wrong has been confessed and forgiven,' he said clearly.

'Get out,' snapped Anthony. He leaned over the chair in which his brother sat. 'Even the pope himself could not absolve a murderer – not without the intervention of state authorities. To be absolved, you would need to confess to the church and to the police. Out, now. Or I'll find the strength to kick you the length of this street.'

Liam jumped up, staggered back, then threw himself out of the house.

Anthony, his breathing suddenly laboured, sank to the rug and gasped for oxygen. How could the man just walk in here like that? After a minute or so, his heart slowed and his head stopped spinning. As slowly as an old man, he placed his weary bones in the chair. He was cold, chilled to the marrow in spite of a healthy coal fire in the grate.

Icy sweat poured down his face, stung his eyes. Dear God, would he never be free of Liam? He remembered. Oh yes, he remembered, felt the pain in his head, in his arm, felt the water closing over his face. 'You'll die,' Liam had spat before throwing his twin into the Mersey. Anthony had been no swimmer, but a docker had rescued him. 'An accident,' Sam Bell had declared while visiting Anthony in hospital.

Girls. The girls had always found Anthony attractive. One by one, Liam had picked them off, had bought them little gifts, had bribed them so that they would change allegiance.

Anthony shifted his head and looked at a pale photograph of the mother he had never known. 'He came close to rape many times before actually committing it, I'm sure,' he told the faded picture. Of course, the assaulted girls had not lived in this parish – they had been culled from streets nearer to the city itself.

Liam had needed to be angry. In his calmer phases, he had not been particularly interested in females. Anger gave him false power, aroused him to a semblance of manhood. 'I should have spoken up then,' he whispered. 'Fourteen or more years ago when I heard about girls hysterical and with torn clothes.' He swallowed painfully. 'But I didn't. I was young and ashamed of him. And the Parliament Street girls never spoke up, either.' He nodded, swallowed a sob. 'He probably disguised himself, anyway. So clever, our Liam. And it's too late now.'

He closed his eyes and leaned back. Liam had become a priest for several reasons, none of them sound. Firstly, the priesthood would gain for him the acclamation he required – no – demanded. Secondly, he knew that Anthony would never match this wonderful achievement. Thirdly, Liam was incapable of leading a life that involved wife and children. Fourthly, the cloth would give him power and a degree of immunity. Father Liam Bell was now a worthy cleric. He toiled ceaselessly for the poor of Blackburn, was a guiding light in his parish, was intelligent enough to rise through the ranks – parish priest, Monsignor, bishop.

Anthony's eyes flew open. God forbid that the creature should ever become a cardinal. Liam had built a fortress around himself. The materials he had used were holy, impenetrable. If Anthony wanted to make a fool of himself by telling the church hierarchy that his brother was a pervert, Liam would ride any such storm without effort.

He stood up, poured medicine into a spoon, gulped down the foul-tasting concoction. It was his inability to warn the world that made him sad and fearful. Liam had taken away everything Anthony had enjoyed or valued, from toys to intended bride. The savage creature had probably placed everything in the one category. The killing of Val would have been no more significant than the loosening of a bicycle wheel. Absently, Anthony rubbed his arm. The upper bone had suffered a green-stick fracture when the bicycle had fallen apart beneath him on Great Homer Street.

Back in his chair, he coughed until his body was weak. He was weak, all right. There must have been something he could have done to impede Liam's destructive journey through life. He inhaled until the convulsive movements of his chest abated. 'I could have killed him, I suppose,' he said aloud. 'I could have descended to his level. By ridding society of him, I might have saved a lot of grief.'

But although he sat and pondered for hours, he knew he was covering familiar ground and that there was no solution. The fact remained that Anthony Bell was not a killer. The man with whom he had shared a womb was the murderer, but who would believe a tale as tall as that? The answer, as ever, was no-one.

Bridie's table glowed with pride and silver. She had spent the whole of New Year's Eve cooking, had risen today at five o'clock in order to set out the feast. According to Diddy Costigan, Richard and Edith Spencer were 'classy'. 'She grew into her face,' Diddy had proclaimed. 'She wasn't nice-looking as a young woman, but she's handsome in her middle years.' Bridie rubbed an imagined spot from a knife, folded muslin cloths around sandwiches to prevent staleness.

Sam came in and surveyed the scene. 'Our Edith will think she's got off at the wrong tram stop,' he said.

Bridie paused, cake-slice held aloft. 'Are they coming on a tram, then?'

He shook his head, even managed a faint smile. Bridie was getting to him. In spite of himself, Sam Bell was becoming rather fond of his wife. Had he loved before? he wondered. Had he loved poor Maria? 'By tram?' he asked, squashing a laugh. 'Oh no. They travel by car. Richard's a doctor, so he has to have his own transport. And Edith does a lot of charity work, takes sick children to Blackpool and helps out at the hospitals.'

'Are they rich?' asked Bridie.

Sam considered the question. 'Well, it depends what you mean by rich. They've land. Richard's dad was a gentleman farmer, and Richard kept the farm on, but it's run by tenants. They've livestock and big gardens. They've a sizeable house and no children. Yes, I suppose they're better off than most.'

Bridie glanced down at her wedding suit. It had come up fairly well after a spongeing, but it wasn't the height of fashion. She felt a bit shabby, a bit of a country bumpkin. Like many of those who had toiled under landlords, she had an overdeveloped respect for anyone who owned acreage. 'Do I look all right?'

Sam stared at her. 'What?'

'Am I dressed well enough?'

He blinked rapidly. She was lovely, she looked radiant and very pretty. 'Er ... yes, you look fine to me.'

Bridie considered her husband's suit. She had cleaned that, too, but it had seen better days, as had the shoes. 'Sam, you got married in that, didn't you?'

He glanced down. 'Yes, I did.'

'It's very old,' she told him. 'And you need shirts, too. With the girls and your mother and the shop, I can't spend a lot of time turning collars.' She straightened her spine. 'To be truthful, we all need clothes, Sam.'

He considered the problem. If he gave her everything she wanted, she could spoil and become demanding, even selfish. No, no, she could never be like that. If he refused to listen, she might go back to Ireland. He could not imagine life without her. This was the first day in January, and she had arrived towards the end of November, but his life was so different now. He had not imagined that a second marriage could be so free of stress. There were no neighbours popping in to see to Muth and make a bit of dinner. Snacks of bread and dripping or charred toast were things of the past. He was well-fed, his house was clean, and his mother had found a new lease of life. 'Get what you want,' he told her. 'And for the children, too.'

'Where?' she asked.

'I'll open an account,' he promised rashly. 'At Blackler's or Bon Marché. Take your pick.' Deliberately, he sat on the misgivings born of his frugal nature.

Bridie was flabbergasted, but she kept quiet. Back home, she had made her own clothes. The suit she wore at present had been ordered by post through a catalogue. A chance to acquire shop-bought clothes on a regular basis was very attractive.

The shop bell rang and Sam went off to greet the visitors. Bridie fussed with her hair, glanced at the clock and worried about Cathy. Shauna was upstairs with Muth, who had refused to come down until the 'queer feller' had been and gone. Cathy was with Anthony. Well, she hoped Cathy was with Anthony. What if the child had gone rooting around the back of Paddy's Market again? What if she'd become involved in another of the Costigans' naughty schemes?

The door opened and a tall, thin woman stepped in. She wore a simple black coat over a simple black suit, and everything about her screamed of money. Her shoes were good but plain, and she carried a vast handbag and a pair of kid gloves. 'Bridget?' She did not attempt a smile.

Bridie thought about curtseying. Timidly, she held out her hand. 'Yes, I'm Bridie.'

Edith Spencer grasped the proffered hand and studied the young woman. 'Do you eat properly?' she asked. Without waiting for an answer, she swivelled and called to her husband, 'Richard? Do come in, we are making a draught.'

Sam and Richard entered the room. Like his wife, Dr Richard Spencer was dark, tall and slender. He wore rimless spectacles, a goatee beard and a solid gold albert across his waistcoat. He marched in, shook Bridie's hand and asked how she was.

'Fine, sir,' she managed.

'Richard,' he reminded her not unkindly. 'My wife is Sam's cousin. Sam's mother and Edith's mother were sisters.' He lost interest and stalked off to correct the clock on the mantelpiece. 'A whole minute slow,' he informed his hosts. 'A life can be saved in a minute.'

Edith removed her hat and coat, pushed the gloves into her handbag, then thrust the bundle at Sam. 'Get rid of these,' she said. 'And tell Aunt Theresa I'll be up in a few minutes.'

While Richard Spencer settled down with an old newspaper, the two women stood by the table. Bridie felt doubly awkward, because the guest was so sure, so confident. 'Will I make some tea for you now?'

'Not just yet, dear,' replied Edith. 'Liam will be along soon. We dropped him off lower down the road. He has gone to visit his brother.'

'Oh dear.' These words slipped from Bridie's lips before she could check them.

Edith allowed a dry laugh to escape from her throat.

'Never mind, Bridget. God alone knows what gets into those two boys, but it's no worry of yours.'

The tension drained from the younger woman's body. This lady seemed very nice, full of humour and kindness.

'You've children of your own, I believe. You have enough problems. Oh, by the way, do you prefer Bridie?'

'Er . . . yes, I do.'

'Good. Bridie it is, then. Richard?'

The seated man glared over the top of his newspaper. 'The world is in a terrible state,' he declared, waving the sheet as if trying to kill it.

Edith lowered an eyelid in a half-wink. 'Richard does not like newspapers,' she explained. 'They make him angry, but he will insist on buying them. He's a doctor, so he should know how to cure his own disease, but he won't listen.'

'One has to keep up,' said Richard.

Edith winked again at Bridie. Bridie, shocked to see a lady winking, dropped into a chair and waited for the pantomime to continue.

'A British physicist is splitting atoms,' said the doctor. 'Do you know what that means, Edith?'

Edith didn't know, and she admitted her ignorance readily.

Dr Spencer glared at the daily paper, seemed to blame the inanimate object for all the woes of mankind. 'Energy,' he roared. 'Instant, cheap energy. No good will come of this discovery, mark my words.'

'Oh, we shall mark your words, dear,' murmured his wife reassuringly. 'By the way, Bridget prefers Bridie. Isn't she a pretty thing? Would you say she's thin, though? Perhaps cod liver oil and malt, Richard?'

He looked at Bridie over the top of his spectacles. 'Nothing wrong with her,' declared the doctor. 'Good Irish air has been her mainstay. Small bones, Edith. She would not carry weight, so she is better to remain on the slender side.'

Bridie bit her lip. She had been nervous to the point of terror, but now, while the two visitors discussed her physical construction, she wanted to giggle. It was a mixture of relief and hysteria, she told herself as the laughter escaped in spite of her best efforts. She leaned against the table and buried her face in her hands until she cried with the pain of mirth.

'Look!' said Edith. 'You've upset this poor child, Richard.' This statement sent Bridie into further uncontrollable paroxysms, as the poor man had done nothing wrong at all.

The doctor jumped up and came to the table.

Bridie raised her tear-stained face. 'You make me sound ... sound like a cow at the ... oh, saints preserve me ... at the fair. No, no,' she shrieked. 'More like a horse. A horse that's ... seen better days and won't ... oh dear ... won't carry weight. Am I ready to be melted for glue?'

Richard Spencer threw back his head and roared with laughter that seemed too big for his body. Edith joined Bridie at the table and chuckled loudly. 'Sense of humour, Bridie,' she declared, delight in her words, 'that will see you through many a crisis.'

A crisis chose this instant in time to announce itself through the scullery door. A very dirty Cathy was dragged in by the tight-faced Liam Bell, who, in turn, was pursued by Noel. The dog growled, because a stranger was manhandling Cathy.

Immediately, Bridie was sober, though the echo of unseemly merriment seemed to reverberate round the kitchen for several further seconds. 'Cathy,' she said finally, her tone carrying more sadness than anger, 'whatever have you been up to this time?'

Liam glared at his father's wife. He had heard the

conviviality, and was not pleased to discover that Bridie was enjoying life. She was just another jumped-up madam, a creature with her eye on the main chance. Well, he would speak to Dad later, would make sure that Sam realized that this colleen and her brats deserved nothing out of Bell's Pledges. Dad's money should go to the Church where it rightfully belonged. 'This child was with the Costigans,' he said tightly. 'I saw her and brought her home.' He curled his lip at Bridie. 'She should not be allowed to associate with those dishonest people.'

A coldness entered Bridie's breast at that moment, as if her inner core tried to reflect the ice in Liam's face. 'Children play,' she informed him. 'When a child is clean all the while, a mother worries. Little ones learn through play. We can't expect Cathy to be clean when the streets are dirty and wet.'

'What they learn depends on their choice of companions,' spat the cleric.

Bridie decided to ignore him, though she did wonder whether that might be a sin. After all, a priest represented the Holy Father in Rome who, in his turn, embodied the one true Catholic and Apostolic faith. But this Liam had a cruel set to his jaw and a face like a month of wet Sundays. She grabbed the child and pulled her towards the dresser. 'What were you doing?'

'Playing cherry-wobs.'

'She was on a bicycle,' interspersed Liam.

'Cherry-wobs?'

Cathy nodded. 'You flick fruit stones up a drainpipe and when they fall out into the gulley, they hit some other stones and then you win all of them.' She put a hand in her pocket and pulled out some disgusting cherry innards that looked as old as time itself. 'They've been vinegared and dried to make them last.'

152

'With no saddle,' said Liam.

Bridie tutted. 'You're filthy, child.'

'And no brakes. Her shoes will be ruined.'

Cathy sighed resignedly. 'I got on the bike after I'd won the cherry-wobs,' she said. She tried to look at the priest, could not quite manage to meet his eyes. He had very nasty eyes. 'And I can ride standing up on a horse or a bicycle,' she declared, mostly for his benefit.

Edith stepped to the fore. 'You'll come clean,' she advised Cathy gravely. 'But riding on a bicycle with no brakes can be dangerous. Shall we go upstairs to Aunt Theresa's bathroom and get you clean? Then you can tell me about your adventures.' She smiled at Bridie, nodded towards her nephew and removed the offending child from the scene.

'You should keep a closer watch on her,' said Liam.

Sam bustled in from the shop. 'Sorry,' he said. 'I heard someone knocking on my way downstairs. It was Mrs Charnley wanting her blankets, so I had to open up for her. Of course, she decided she needed a long chat.' He looked from Liam to Bridie to Richard. 'Where's Edith?'

'Cleaning the child,' snapped Liam. 'Catherine wants watching. I found her doing about fifty miles an hour on an old boneshaker of a bike. She shouldn't be out when you have visitors. That girl needs to be taught some manners. Her mother should be keeping a closer watch on Catherine's behaviour. The girl ought to have some discipline.'

Sam dropped his chin, thought for a moment. This was one of the many times when Liam was not quite likeable. 'The little girl's name is Caitlin, not Catherine,' he said finally. 'My wife knows exactly how to deal with the girls.' Then he raised his head and looked Liam full in the face. Bridie must stay. He wasn't going to stand still and allow

Liam to strengthen the case for returning to Ireland. 'Things are well in hand here, Liam. So you need not concern yourself.'

Bridie was dumbfounded for the second time this day. Here was Sam sticking up for her after he'd promised shop-bought clothes for herself and the girls. She knew what he was up to but, all the same, he wasn't a man who parted easily with money. He must value her, or he would not have volunteered to open a clothing account. Also, he was holding his own with Liam, who was usually discussed with reverence and in hushed tones.

Liam Bell's heart seemed to stand still for a second or two. Something told him not to inform Dad of the visit to Anthony's house. He had intended to take his father aside at some point, had meant to describe Anthony's attitude. But this was not the time, Liam advised himself. Not that he had anything to hide or regret. Oh no, he had atoned in full for any little sins he might have committed. Liam's work was the work of God, so righteousness was on Liam's side. Nevertheless, he would keep certain things to himself for now.

Noel crept past the dresser and tried to hide himself behind Bridie's skirt. Because of his size, he failed miserably, so he curled into a tight ball. The atmosphere did not suit him. Cathy had left the room, and he felt the tension.

'What is that?' snarled Liam.

Sam sat down in his usual chair. 'It's a dog.'

Liam shook his head. 'All the starving people in the world, and you decide to feed an animal.'

Bridie felt herself heating up. The ice melted beneath the ferocity of her anger, yet she remained outwardly composed. 'There are things of value in the shop, Father Bell,' she said. 'Noel is a guard dog. He earns his dinners.'

'I know there are items of value here,' said the priest meaningfully.

Richard Spencer broke the ensuing silence by clapping Liam on the back. 'Happy New Year,' he said jovially. 'Let's help Bridget – I mean Bridie – by making the tea, shall we? After all, we can't have the ladies thinking we are completely useless, can we?'

Sam and Richard shuffled about with kettle, teapot and caddy, but Liam Bell remained where he was. He stared hard at Bridie, was momentarily nonplussed when she did not lower her eyes. This one thought she was brave, then. She had travelled all the way from Ireland to get her hands on dad's money.

Without moving her eyes, Bridie dug in the table drawer. She held Liam's stare when she spoke. 'Sam?'

'What?' He turned from the fireplace.

'Here you are,' said his wife. 'A little gift to mark the new year.' She placed a packet of Players Weights on the table. 'That will save you rolling your own tonight, Sam.'

Edith Spencer sat with Aunt Theresa while Cathy splashed about in the little bathroom. Aunt Theresa looked ages younger than she had last year. 'Bridie's done a lot for you.'

Theresa grinned gummily. 'She has that. Forced me to crawl on me hands and knees to get me dinner. Always left it near the door, she did. Tricked me into getting out of bed.'

Edith kept quiet. Like everyone else, she knew that Theresa Bell's supposed inability to move about had been born of grief and obstinacy. Theresa had worshipped Anthony. After Liam's ordination, something major had happened between the two boys. Although no-one knew the precise details of the argument, Edith was not surprised by the rift. Liam had given Aunt Theresa one hell of a life, had made his twin's days miserable, too.

'Did you bring the queer feller with you?'

Edith nodded. 'We dropped him off along the road. He went to visit someone.'

'That'd be Father Brennan,' said the old woman. 'There's not many houses round here where that bugger could expect the welcome mat. As for red carpets – he'll see none of them.'

Edith thought about mentioning Liam's intention to call on his brother, but decided against it. Talking about the past was fine, but there was no point in causing the old woman to worry about any further arguments between her grandsons.

Edith Spencer's biggest regret in life was that she had never borne a child. Cousin Sam's wife had given birth to twin boys, then poor Maria had died within weeks. Edith had offered to rear the twins, but Aunt Theresa had kept them. And the boys hated one another. It was such a pity. Where there should have been joy, there had been years of agony. 'Liam was never easy to manage,' she said now.

Theresa let forth a hollow chuckle. 'I never had a minute's peace. Even before they were weaned, that one wanted more milk, more rocking, more attention.' Her face softened. 'Anthony used to just stop where I put him. Eeh, that lad's a good one.'

Edith fiddled with the cameo at her throat. 'Sam's hard to understand. He telephoned Richard and told him about Anthony's illness, yet he won't visit him. Whatever happens, Sam seems to stand by Liam.'

Theresa sighed. 'That's a Catholic education for you. They have it drummed in that they've got to have respect for priests, as if priests are perfect.' She paused for a moment. 'But deep down, our Sam knows. He won't face things, our Sam. Always takes the easiest road, never wants trouble. So he's sided with what looks like good. But he's not as daft as he makes out.'

Sam was not daft at all, thought Edith. He had built up a thriving business in an area of poverty, had taken on a capable young wife who would tend him in his dotage after caring for his mother. 'So you won't come down for something to eat, Aunt Theresa?'

'When he's gone. I've no intention of breaking bread with him. Whatever happened all them years ago, it must have been serious. Our Anthony's never borne a grudge for this length of time before. No, I'll come downstairs when Liam's gone.'

'When he goes, we go with him, I'm afraid.'

'Then I'll have my tea up here and I'll see you next time.' Theresa pursed her lips for a moment. 'Edith?'

'Yes?'

'We were good mates as well as sisters, me and your mam.'

'I know that.'

'I could ask her anything and she'd not let me down.'

Edith kept quiet, sensed that something of moment was about to be disclosed.

'There's these two horses,' said Theresa at last. 'A brown one and a white one.'

Edith maintained her silence.

'I want you to take them home with you.'

The visitor nodded slowly. 'Shall I put them in the front seat of the car or in the back? Or would they be better strapped to the roof?'

Theresa grinned. 'Don't start, Edith. I'm not messing now. See, our Sam got paid for taking Bridie on. Her dad's a miserable old bugger, wanted her out of Ireland and away from her dead husband's lot – they're not Catholics. So he gave our Sam these bloody racehorses. From what

157

I've heard, they've been leading the gypsies a merry dance. Any road, to cut a long story down to size, our Sam's given Bridie these horses.'

Edith was surprised. She did not think of Sam as a generous type. In fact, the spread downstairs was quite exceptional. In the past, when Edith and Richard had visited at New Year or while on business in Rodney Street, they had been lucky to get a cup of tea and a fish-paste sandwich. 'Why?' she asked simply.

The older woman shrugged. 'Well, for one, Bridie found out about the little arrangement, so happen our Sam's ashamed. And for two, Bridie's thinking of beggaring off back to Ireland.'

'Really?'

'Aye.' Theresa leaned forward and dropped her voice to an even quieter whisper. Cathy was singing in the bath, but children had good hearing. 'That one in there's running a bit wild.'

'Cathy?'

'She's a bright girl, a bit high-strung, but clever. Bridie doesn't want the child's cleverness to be turned to bad ways. A lot of criminals are clever, you know. If some of them in prisons had got a bit of a chance, they'd have used their brains well. Bridie's scared of staying here, so the horses are Sam's idea of getting Bridie to stay. She's horse mad. So's Cathy. She likes animals, that little girl. Have you seen yon dog?'

Edith nodded.

'If she loves that thing, Cathy must have a good heart. Anyway, we want these here horses stabled and trained.'

'I'll do all I can, of course.'

Theresa patted her niece's hand. 'I knew you would, love. Aye, there's a lot of our Ida in you.'

Edith went to get Cathy from the bathroom. For a few moments, she stood in the doorway and watched the child splashing and laughing, then she lifted her out and enveloped her in a towel. In that moment, while she dried Cathy's hair, Edith realized how much she would have loved a daughter. Especially one like Cathy.

Seven

Diddy Costigan picked her way through a few bags of clothing and several small pools of water. It was washing day in the Costigan household. Like many with large families, Diddy carried the bigger weekly items to the wash-house in Burroughs Gardens. This was the place to be on a Monday morning – not only to achieve clean clothing, sheets and towels, but also in order to collect the juiciest gossip or to keep up with neighbourhood events. Professional washerwomen used the facilities almost every day, but housewives dragged their dirty linen and the world's problems into this public place just once or twice each week.

The big woman opened her laundry sacks and made sure the colours went in one pile, the whites in another. She glanced around at a few familiar faces, wondered why everybody was so quiet. Armed with a bar of green soap and a scrubbing brush, she began her attack on the first of Billy's collars. Her movements slowed as light began to dawn in her brain. The wash-house had gone quiet because Diddy, or someone belonging to her, was the subject of today's discussion. She was the talk of the wash-house. How many times had she heard that said about some other woman? How many times had she uttered those words herself? In Scotland Road, you had to be in real trouble to become the talk of the wash-house.

She threw down soap and brush, raised her head, caught everyone in the act of swivelling to avoid her scrutiny. With her arms akimbo, Diddy addressed the assembly. 'Right,' she began, 'what have I done, when did I do it, where did it happen and who's going to clean it up?'

Every last woman in the room was suddenly engrossed in stain removal. The sound of bristle against fabric was all that broke the heavy silence.

Diddy bridled, breathed deeply, folded ham-like arms across her ample chest. 'Minnie Houghton,' she screamed, 'have you gone deaf all of a sudden?'

Minnie dropped her washboard. It hit the stone floor with a clatter that resonated for a second or two. 'Me?' Black eyebrows met in a frown of mock-horror.

'Yes, you.'

'I've done nothing,' said the woman in question, her eyes darting from side to side in search of support from other occupants of the vast room.

Diddy stepped into the aisle. 'No, it's me what's done it, isn't it? Will you tell me the details then I can run to confession and have my soul bleached while the whites soak? Because I'll get to the bottom of this, girls.'

Minnie squirmed. 'I don't know what you're talking about.'

Diddy's eyes scanned all the familiar faces. 'Elsie?'

The Elsie in question flew outside muttering something about forgotten starch.

Diddy began a slow march round the room. The slap of her shoes against the flags was loud, as if every thud accused a member of the Monday club. Whatever this was, it was big. If Jimmy had been up to his tricks getting food for the Nolans, all here present would have congratulated Diddy on her son's inventiveness. After all, survival was important, and anyone who helped the truly destitute became the hero of the hour. 'There'll be nothing done here till I get some sense,' shouted Diddy. 'Even if we're all here till Easter Sunday falls on the Tuesday before Christmas.'

Minnie Houghton lit a rolly, spat out some loose tobacco.

A woman with a crying baby opened her blouse and fed him. A few more lifted their heads and looked at one another.

Minnie coughed, took another drag on the thin cigarette. 'It's your Maureen,' she ventured. 'She's carrying on. Well, that's what we've heard, anyway.'

Diddy nodded. Their Maureen had been carrying on since learning to walk without falling over. Their Maureen had been born with the ability to obtain almost anything she wanted from men. As a beautiful baby, she had smiled for sweets. As an infant, she had danced and sung her way up and down Scotland Road for more sweets. These days, she won every amateur talent show for miles around. So what was new? What was different? 'Go on, then,' she ordered.

'She's set her sights,' announced Minnie, her wavering tone betraying a level of nervousness.

'Has she?' asked Diddy sarcastically.

'She has.' Minnie inhaled another dose of courage, coughed again.

'What are you smoking?' asked Diddy. 'Old rope? Will Dolly Hanson not let you have some baccy on the slate, Minnie?'

The spokeswoman caught her breath. 'Your Maureen's after Mr Bell,' she announced. 'According to what's been said, like.'

Diddy howled with laughter. 'What? That miserable old bugger? Him with the new wife, him with the . . . ?' Her voice died. 'You mean Anthony?'

Minnie nodded mutely.

'I'll kill her,' declared Diddy.

The atmosphere relaxed immediately. Women left their washing to care for itself while they gathered in a solid knot of support round their old friend. 'We were frightened of telling you,' said Minnie Houghton. 'With him being so much older than her. I mean, she hangs about with a few of the lads, like, but this one's a schoolmaster, isn't he? Oh, I hope there's nothing in it.'

Diddy's eyebrows raised themselves. Anthony Bell was a teacher, all right, but she reckoned their Maureen could fill in a few gaps in his education when it came to the sins of the flesh, especially those parts of the flesh that should remain hidden. 'I've tried to keep her busy,' she informed the multitude. 'Only you can't be on top of them all the time, can you? I mean, she does three or four hours a day at Dolly Hanson's, then there's school. But I can't follow her around when I've four others. Jesus, what next? Thank God Anthony Bell's got more sense than most. He's one of the few what doesn't keep his brains in his trousers.'

Sheila Turner decided to throw her hat into the ring. 'I know Maureen's a worry, queen,' she said. 'Same with my Dorothy. Up the spout at sixteen and no sign of a wedding ring. You don't know where to put your face. Shamed to death, I was. It never happened in our day.'

Those whose marriages had been hasty made no reply, but women who had been virgin brides or simply lucky nodded and made sympathetic noises.

Diddy leaned against a sink big enough to bathe a whole family. 'Right. Who's seen her and what's going on? Let's get at a few facts before I brain her.'

The fractured tale was put together until Diddy had a fair idea of the completed jigsaw. 'So she's going in there when she's supposed to be out with her friends? When she says she's visiting, he's the one she's calling on?'

A chorus of yeses formed the reply.

'He's too nice,' pronounced Diddy. 'He'd never say boo to a goose, and that's the truth. Only he'd be better locking his door. I mean, she's not a bad girl, our Maureen, but with her looks she's older than her years. I'll have a word. Thanks, girls. But next time, come out with it. I can't be the talk of the bagwash. I'd be grey before my time.'

They went about their business, steeping, scrubbing, bleaching, rinsing. While washing hung in the heated drying frames, they appointed guards, did their shopping in turn. Diddy Costigan folded her sheets, passed the time of day with her comrades. Then she went home to 'kill' their Maureen.

Michael Brennan had been a parish priest for almost twenty years, the last five of which he had served at the church of St Aloysius Gonzaga. During his ministry, he had come across all kinds of people, but he had never encountered anyone quite like the young Father Liam Bell. He could not fathom the man at all, could not place a finger on what it was that singled out this person. There seemed to be no humour in him, no ability to laugh at or with others. Liam took life far too seriously altogether, would certainly not laugh at himself, would never allow others to find him amusing.

Liam was perched on the edge of a brown leather sofa, his hands clasped as if in prayer. 'Have you made up your mind, Father Brennan?'

The older man took a sip of tea, then turned his chair so that he could study the man who wanted to attach himself on a semi-permanent basis to the parish. This priest had been here before, had brought trouble with him. 'What did the bishop have to say on the subject?' he asked.

'He says I know the area well, which is true, as I was born on Scotland Road. But the final decision is yours. I can assure you that I work hard and take my calling seriously.'

Father Brennan stood up and walked to the window. This was a busy parish, packed to bursting with large families whose problems were manifold. Poverty lurked on every corner, particularly in the courts where people endured conditions that were almost beyond belief. It was 1931, yet folk hereabouts shared space with all kinds of vermin, sometimes without the facilities to keep their own bodies properly clean and safe from infection.

Father Brennan was tired. For six months, he had been alone. He said at least two masses a day, heard confessions, took communion to the sick, held confirmation classes, visited the school twice a week, baptized the newborn, performed benediction services, comforted the dying. Help was needed. No man could keep up the pace, not on his own. And yet . . . He turned and looked at Liam. 'Did you make peace with your brother?'

'I tried.'

Michael Brennan remembered the fight. Liam had been newly ordained, had been travelling round Liverpool to gain experience of parish work. Just a few weeks into his own ministry at St Aloysius's church, Father Brennan had found the quarrelling twins, had separated them. He had not expected Liam to return here, was slightly bewildered by the bishop's suggestion. Yet he did not want to spoil a new priest's career by advising the diocese of a family dispute that had taken place years earlier. 'You should raise your hand to no man, Liam.'

'It was self-defence.'

Michael Brennan nodded. 'Anthony works in our school. How would it be if I sent you in to take a class?'

'Civilized enough, I should think,' Liam replied smartly.

'We are both professional men. There will be no further trouble.'

The parish priest wished with all his heart that the bishop had made a clean-cut decision. 'Liam, I can't say I don't need your help, because that would be a lie. These are troubled times. Since the police strike, when our parishioners were accused of looting, rumour has it that the Home Office has spoken about clearing Scotland Road. The houses are foul and the police have to walk about in threes. I believe we shall witness the break up of the Scotland Road community.'

Liam nodded just once. 'When the Liverpool police came out on strike, the people round here took advantage. They signed their own death warrant in 1919.'

Michael Brennan took a deep breath. Judgemental – that was the word for Liam Bell. 'Liam, if you had a wife and children and they were starving, what would you do?'

'I would not steal.'

'Then what would you do?'

The younger man shrugged. 'I'd get work.'

'And if there was no work?'

'I would pray.'

Father Brennan sat down again. 'Prayers are all very well, but a baby screaming with hunger can drive a man to despair. Families must eat, Liam. I don't condone thievery, but humankind can be pushed to extraordinary lengths by poverty. The parishioners here require some compassion, some hope. I can't condemn them to hell for feeding their offspring and keeping themselves warm, clothed and sheltered. We must not set ourselves on pedestals. We, too, are human.'

'The commandments are the commandments,' said Liam.

'Love thy neighbour as thyself,' replied Father Brennan. 'That instruction implies forgiveness and tolerance. Jesus said, "And the greatest of these is charity." To work here, you will need to relax your attitude. There are crimes far worse than stealing to sustain life. We are not talking about murder here.'

'I understand.'

Michael Brennan noticed a slight tic at the corner of the visitor's mouth. He did not like Liam Bell. Because he did not like him, he knew that he must give him a chance. After all, wasn't that what he had just been preaching? 'I shall speak to the bishop,' he said. 'I think a temporary stay here might help you. After all, when you get your own parish, you may find yourself in a situation not dissimilar to this one. However, if there is any problem between you and Anthony, I shall ask for you to be moved.'

Liam inclined his head. 'Very well, Father Brennan.'

When Liam Bell had left, Michael opened a bottle of whisky and poured himself a hefty measure. A strange sensation paid a brief visit to his spine, a chill that sent a message the length of his body and into his brain. There was something very wrong with Liam. He was too correct, too rigid, too decided.

The fire flickered and spat while the cleric gazed into its flames. He emptied the glass, poured in another drop. Sam Bell's son had come through the seminary with flying colours. He had gained distinctions in all subjects and at all levels, would soon be on his way to his own living and his own congregation. Too perfect, thought Michael Brennan. Too perfect, too sure and too ... cold to be a priest. But it took all sorts to make a world. He finished his drink and went up for a siesta. There were plenty of people on the sick list, so he grabbed his rest while he could.

*

Big Diddy Costigan needed no visa to enter a house in the Scotland Road area. She had laid out the dead, had nursed the sick, had even delivered twins during an interval at the Rotunda Theatre. To lock a door against Diddy would have been like struggling to hold back the tides or the sunset. The woman was a valuable ally and a fearsome foe, so she went freely in and out of homes, shops, churches and places of entertainment.

Without much more than a tap of the knuckles, Diddy entered Anthony Bell's house. She found him seated by the fire with a pile of books and with Maureen gazing at him from the opposite armchair. 'Out, lady,' commanded the matron. 'Get yourself home and I'll talk to you later.'

Maureen's jaw dropped. 'You what, Mam?'

'I said out. And don't come back in here, neither.'

Maureen stood up and smoothed her skirt. 'I'm only looking after him.'

'There's nothing wrong with him now,' said Diddy. 'In fact, if we were all as healthy as him, we'd be in the pink.' She stood her ground while Maureen left in a temper and surrounded by a pungent cloud of Evening in Paris.

Anthony grinned ruefully. 'I was wondering when you would notice,' he said. 'But she was safer with me than on the streets. At least we knew where she was.'

Diddy folded her arms. 'You knew, but I didn't. I'll have you know I've been the talk of the bagwash,' she told him. 'The air was thick with it when I got there. They'll need no starch in their collars today – the bloody shirts'll stand up by themselves. What's been going on?'

'Nothing. Maureen just keeps coming in and ... talking to me. She's older than her years. She just wants a bit of attention, that's all. But I knew you'd be worried about her spending so much time with a crusty old bachelor. At the same time, I didn't want to be carrying tales to you and Billy.'

He was a handsome man. Diddy tried to work out how completely identical twins could possibly be so different from each other. Liam and Anthony had dark brown hair that just missed being jet black, brown eyes, straight noses and square chins. They had both grown to approximately six feet in height, were well-made without being weighty, and they even shared some mannerisms, like the way they walked and held their heads.

'Diddy,' he said. 'I—'

'Hush, I'm thinking. Has she said anything to you? Our Maureen, I mean. Because I'm telling you now, she's got big plans and you're on the agenda at the moment.'

Anthony sighed. Maureen was only thirteen, so her mother had every right to know about her behaviour. Yet his instinct told him not to betray the young girl. Maureen had tried to hold his hand, had said how much she liked his eyes, had gone on about what a good teacher he was. 'She just kept making gallons of tea,' he replied. 'I'm thinking of changing my name to Horniman, because I'm swimming in the stuff.'

Diddy tapped the floor with the toe of a shoe. 'She's told Minnie Houghton's girl that you're going to marry her when she's sixteen. Marry our Maureen, that is, not Josie Houghton.' Diddy sniffed. 'I doubt anybody'll marry Josie, spiteful little cow. Anyway, you and our Maureen are having four bridesmaids, a papal blessing and a do afterwards at Fairy Mary's. All the dancing class will be there and she wants a three-tier cake.' Diddy's mouth twitched. 'They'd better hurry up and build us a cathedral, because St Aloysius's won't be good enough for you and our Maureen, will it?'

Anthony, too, was fighting his laughter.

'I don't know what to do with her,' complained Diddy, her tone suddenly serious. 'She's getting out of hand.'

'Exactly what Bridie says about Cathy.'

Diddy nodded her agreement. 'Yes, but Cathy can't get herself in the family way yet, can she? Our Maureen'll have me in my grave, I'm telling you.'

Anthony wondered what to say. He had no feelings for Maureen – no feelings for anyone except ... No, he was not in love with his father's wife. It was probably lust and a yen for the unobtainable. 'Take it slowly, Diddy,' he said. 'Don't go jumping down her throat and turning her away from you. She's neither child nor woman. It's a very difficult age.'

'Difficult? Difficult? She's always been the same, Anthony. I'll swear she had an eye for the men when she was still in the pram. What if she gets herself in trouble? She'll be no good as a singer and dancer with an eight-month belly on her.'

He understood only too well. Girls left school, married young in order to break free from their crowded homes, then went on to create a crowd of their own. It was a self-perpetuating problem, a downward spiral into which young people continued to jump before they were ready. 'Make sure she carries on attending the dance school,' he advised. 'At least you'll know where she is two evenings a week. And she is talented, you know.'

Diddy lowered her bulk into the chair Maureen had vacated. 'Sometimes, I wonder if I'm doing it all wrong.' It was funny, she thought, how she could open her heart to this man. He was educated – a teacher – and he had no experience of rearing a family of his own, yet he had no side to him. Going to college hadn't spoiled Anthony Bell. Perhaps losing Valerie had aged him, had made him more accessible than most.

'In what way?' he asked.

The visitor leaned back and rested her head. Washing for seven people took its toll sometimes. 'Well, the way I let them ... find stuff for the Nolans. And our Jimmy running barefoot round the docks begging for work, and our Nicky selling stuff on Paddy's for Bell's and other junk shops. They're old, Anthony. They're only young, but they're old.'

He understood completely. 'Diddy, you're the best mother you can be in the circumstances.'

She looked at him, her eyes bright and wet. 'When they put our Charlie in my arms down at the lying-in hospital...' She swallowed, inhaled deeply. This topic was not raised very often, because it upset Diddy so badly. 'He was a difficult birth, didn't want to put in an appearance at all. They took me from our front room to the hospital on the coal wagon, you know. I was as black as a pot when I got there. When they told me he was different, I broke my heart. And it's never mended, Anthony. I suppose I'll never get over it.'

Anthony knew. Charlie had been damaged at birth, had been dragged out by panicking doctors. He was stiff down one side, slow in his speech, hard to understand. He would have gone far had he not lacked oxygen during Diddy's first labour. 'He's a good boy, Diddy,' said Anthony.

'I know. What happens to him after me and Billy are dead? I don't want him to be on his own, but I don't like the idea of Maureen or Monica or Tildy-Anne being stuck with him.'

Anthony bit back a question about Jimmy. It was always assumed that the Cinderellas in a family had to be female. 'Charlie could manage by himself,' he told her. 'He's got more sense than most, and I think you know that.'

Diddy shrugged, the movement almost listless. 'Well, I suppose I won't be around to worry about that when it does happen. But our Charlie was only the start. I've four more. Are they growing up right, Anthony? You see, we've always helped people, me and Billy. And the children have just joined in. But Bridie set me thinking when she said about Cathy not being allowed to run about with them while they're looking for bits and pieces for the Nolans.' She paused, pondered for a moment. 'There's more to life than Scotland Road, isn't there?'

'Of course,' he answered softly.

'They might move away from here, my kids. They might go somewhere with gardens and velvet curtains. Or they might not be able to better themselves because of how I've brought them up. Then it would all be my fault.'

'No,' he said firmly. Anthony lived in hope. Although the cycle continued to renew itself through early marriage and large families, he knew that some of the older pupils at school had set their sights further afield. They wanted professions, indoor plumbing, fewer children and a full larder.

Yet he sympathized with this woman's dilemma. She had been born into poverty, had brought children into poverty. Diddy and Billy worked hard, kept their brood fed and clothed. But Diddy was beginning to look to the future, and she wanted better things for the next generation. 'They will educate themselves out of the trap,' he told her. 'Your children will move on, Diddy. They'll have opportunities that weren't available to you. And they'll be good people.'

'Promise?'

As far as he could remember, he had never heard Diddy sounding so uncertain. Maureen had frightened her. Diddy had realized today that life wasn't standing still, that her fledgelings were growing and preparing to leave the nest. She was hoping and praying that they would not allow themselves to repeat the age-old pattern of marriage, parenthood and the pain that came with deprivation. 'I'm sure they'll turn out fine, Diddy,' he said. 'All of them will turn out fine.'

Bridie was surprised to find Edith Spencer at the back door. 'I'm just ironing our Cathy's clothes,' she told Edith. 'They go back to school in a couple of days.' What was this woman doing here again? She'd visited at New Year and, as far as Bridie understood, the Spencers were not regular callers in Scotland Road.

Edith stepped through the scullery and into the kitchen. 'Where are the children?' she asked.

'Cathy's round visiting the Costigans and Shauna's in the shop playing. Charlie's very good with her.'

Edith looked round. Everything was as neat as a new pin, just as it had been when Aunt Theresa had been in charge of the household. 'I've come to sort out the horses,' said Edith. 'They will be moved tomorrow.'

'Thank you.' Bridie's heart raced. If only she could go to the Spencers' farm. If only she could climb into a horsebox and hide throughout the journey, then canter across meadows on Sorrel's back. 'Sam is making a gift of them to me.'

'And to your daughters,' said Edith. 'He stressed that.'

Bridie set the kettle to boil, carried a batch of scones to the table. 'He's good to us,' she remarked while splitting and buttering. And he was good. Sam was undemonstrative, predictable, quiet and hard-working. But he tried to be fair.

'Yes, he seems to care about you and the girls,' replied Edith thoughtfully. Sam was a Scrooge. If a fool and his money were soon parted, then Sam Bell was a genius. Yet for the first time, Sam seemed to be mellowing slightly. Perhaps he loved this woman, then. Perhaps his chainmail had been penetrated at last, because he'd shown little affection for his first wife, had parted with few gifts in poor Maria's direction.

'Will you take a scone, Edith?'

Edith nodded absently. 'This idea of yours about returning to Ireland – what's happening?'

Bridie shook her head. 'I really don't have the answer to that. It's strange, you know, because I like Scotland Road. I'm still shaken by the noise of it, but I've an affection for the people. And it's nice to have the picture houses and the theatre so close. We went to the pantomime at the Rotunda. It's a beautiful place. They get variety shows there, too. Then there's the markets and the street entertainers – never a dull moment.'

'But?'

'But Cathy's a very bright child. If she sees Jimmy and Tildy running riot, she'll end up not following them, but leading them into mischief.'

Edith Spencer swallowed her pride and a bite of featherlight scone. 'Would you stay with Sam if Cathy could be settled?'

'Yes, I think we would stay.'

The unexpected guest drained her cup. 'Then I'll have her.'

Bridie dropped the butter knife. She tried to absorb Edith's words, allowed them to dance about the surface of her brain for a second or two before taking them in. 'Split up my family?' she managed at last. 'I can't allow that, Edith.'

The older woman placed her cup in the exact centre of its saucer. 'Bridie, I live only forty-odd miles from here. Public transport means that we are almost neighbours. You see, Richard and I can afford to send Caitlin to a private and very exclusive school where her abilities will be directed positively. We own a great deal of land where she can use up her energies without getting into trouble. I am offering your daughter a future.'

Bridie bit her lip. 'She'll settle down here.' There was doubt in the words.

'And if she doesn't? What will you do when she gets into the next scrape? Will you threaten to return to Ireland again? Because those threats unsettle children. It would be better to go and be done with it rather than to keep mentioning it. You're going, then you're staying – how secure do your children feel in the face of such indecision?'

Bridie dropped into a chair. There had been so many changes in the girls' lives – and in her own. Happiness was something all three of them remembered. Happiness was Eugene coming up the lane for his supper, hay in his hair, cow droppings on his boots, the sun in his eyes. Happiness was warm soda bread eaten with butter next to the fire on a winter's evening, cups of tea consumed over books and columns of figures. He had wanted his own place, had started to save a little bit towards the dream of independence.

'Bridie?' Edith Spencer's dark eyebrows were arched by concern.

Heartbreak was a farm labourer running along that same lane with tears coursing down his face. It was a hospital bed that contained a man too small to be Eugene, then a wooden box, also too small for the man she had loved. Misery was Thomas Murphy screaming and ranting because his granddaughters had Protestant blood in their veins. Misery was knowing that she, Bridie O'Brien, must save her children from the wrath of a tyrant who had driven her mother into the afterlife. 'Let me think about it,' she whispered. And it hadn't turned out too badly, had it? They were secure here, warm, fed, well dressed. Leaving Galway and doing her father's bidding had not been such a bad thing after all. If only Cathy would behave. 'It's not a thing I can decide about quickly. And I have to talk to Sam before I do anything.'

Edith understood. How could a mother part with a child? And why should Bridie hand over her daughter to a woman she scarcely knew? 'Why don't you visit, stay with us for a few days? You can bring the girls – we'll use the car.' She cast an eye over the ragged animal who had stretched himself out in front of the grate. 'Noel will be welcome, too.'

Bridie looked at the dog. He was a fine animal in spite of his appearance. 'He'll mess up your car.'

'That's no matter.'

The hostess poured tea, sat with her guest and thought about Edith's suggestion. A bit of fresh air would do them all good, and she would be able to see how Silver and Sorrel would be stabled. 'What about Sam?' she asked. 'He won't leave the shop, and I'll not come without talking to him first.'

'Shall I ask him?'

Bridie shook her head. 'No, thank you.' It was her own responsibility, Bridie decided. She should talk to her husband about this. He would agree, no doubt, because he wanted her to remain in England. All the same, he deserved some respect, and she would seek his opinion before making any decisions.

Maureen Costigan flounced out of the house and ran down the jigger. Mam was being a real pest. Dad wasn't helping, either. He was just sitting there nodding, agreeing with everything his wife said. They didn't understand, didn't even try.

She stopped a few houses down from her own and opened the back gate. Maureen was in love. This love had lasted throughout the previous school term, right from the beginning of September when she had first looked closely at Mr Bell. He taught the juniors, but she made sure she saw him at least twice every weekday. There was a lot to do in a junior class. There was ink to mix, paper to cut, the blackboard to clean. Maureen did all those things while Mr Bell marked his books.

Anthony. It was a lovely name for a lovely man. He was going to be her man, because she had made up her mind. Maureen knew that she was beautiful, was sure that she could have any boy she wanted. But she didn't want a mere boy. The one she had fixed firmly in her sights was a man, a real grown man. However, she failed to understand how or why the present set of circumstances had arisen. Why wouldn't he notice her? Why was she getting nowhere with him? All her life, she had achieved her own way where males were concerned. There should have been no problem. She wanted him, therefore she should have him.

She pressed her ear against the scullery door. He was inside, was no more than a few feet and inches away, was probably reading or getting lessons ready for next week. When the door suddenly swung inward, she gasped and stepped back. 'You frightened me,' she told him.

Anthony buttoned up his jacket and tightened the scarf around his neck. For the first time since his battle with bronchitis, he was on his way to the Throstle's Nest for a pint. And here she was again, for the third time today. 'Maureen, I'm all right now. I've no temperature, no wheeze and no cough. So I can go and play in the Throstle's Nest.'

Maureen bit her lip. She wanted to touch him and kiss him and tell him about this pain that was love. He would be able to kiss properly, not like the sloppy lads at school. They would be happy together. She could move in here with him and still be right on top of her own family. Singing and dancing didn't matter any more. Nothing mattered except being wherever Anthony Bell went. 'I'll walk with you,' she offered hopefully. 'The fresh air will do me good, too.'

'No, Maureen.'

Tears sprang to her eyes. 'I'm going that way,' she said. 'I'm visiting Bernadette McManus in Kew Street. So I'll be passing the Throstle's Nest anyway.'

He sighed, pushed his hands deep into his pockets. She had to be told. From somewhere, he had to drum up courage and the words to match. Instead, he found himself giving a history lesson about the Throstle's Nest having been situated originally in the churchyard. 'It had a big tree outside, and it was hung with cages that held pairs of singing throstles. That's how it got its name.'

She tried to keep up in more ways than one, because he had long legs and was very clever. 'What's a throstle?' she asked.

'A song thrush.'

They walked past Bell's Pledges and to the corner where the Throstle's Nest stood. He glanced at her, saw gaslit tears on her cheeks and led her up the side of the pub and into Chapel Gardens. 'It has to stop, Maureen,' he said. 'You must go back to your friends, to people of your own age.'

Maureen pressed the heel of a hand against her nose. If it started to drip and run, she would surely die of shame. 'I love you,' she mumbled.

'No, you don't.'

'I do.'

He stepped away from her, took a handkerchief from his pocket. 'Dry your eyes,' he told her. 'Then off you go to visit Bernadette.' Teachers were in a vulnerable position, he supposed. He had heard about crushes, about young girls hanging round the houses of schoolmasters and following their heroes everywhere. It was a forbidden love, his mind's voice said. But it was no more forbidden than ... No, the foolishness about Bridie was over, wasn't it?

Maureen blew her nose.

He was so sorry for her. She was obsessed, no more than that. Young people often fell head over heels for a mature person, only to discover that the idol in question had feet of clay or bad breath or some other unforgivable failing. He reached out and touched her arm. 'Go on, Maureen. I'll talk to you at school.'

She nodded dolefully, then fled the way she had come, past Bell's Pledges and into Wilbraham Street, where she lingered for a moment to dry her face. Bernadette Mc-Manus could wait. Bernadette McManus had been a mere ploy.

Maureen did not notice a shadowy figure at the end of the street, as she was too busy preparing herself for home. Already in trouble with her parents for tormenting Mr Bell, Maureen didn't want to go into the house all shame-faced and tear-stained.

Liam smoothed his hair and stepped back into Scotland Road. He was on his way to catch the last train, had been privileged to watch that trite scene between Anthony and this Costigan girl. He had heard none of the conversation, but he had watched the little tears and the sharing of a handkerchief. Costigans. He sniffed, turned up the collar of his overcoat. Anthony had such poor taste in women.

As he made his way to the city centre, he thought about his twin's last dalliance, the one that had ended ... when? Ah yes, about five years ago. Valerie had been a strumpet. She had denounced the faith openly after leaving training college, had opted to teach in some saintless school away from her roots. Twice he had followed her – once to her place of work, next to ... no, he could not quite recall the second time. Had it been dark? Dark and cold like tonight? Had he pursued her into a dark place? Well, whatever, she had been found dead and the incident had been reported in all the national newspapers. A Catholic funeral, too, he mused, his teeth clenched against a chill wind.

It was cold. His breath hung in the air, and the soles of his shoes found poor purchase on the slick of ice that covered the paving stones. Surely that Costigan girl was still a child? Yet she had the body of a woman and a face that matched those found on hoardings outside picture houses. So, Anthony was looking for another soulmate, was he?

Liam's lip curled. For as long as he could remember, it had been 'Anthony did this' and 'Anthony said that'. Grandmuth had loved Anthony, yet she had not loved his twin brother. Liam had been forced to fight for attention, had urged himself to attain a status far higher than Anthony's. But even now, Anthony got all the praise, all the fuss from Grandmuth about being a handsome fellow and a marvellous teacher.

He turned into Lime Street, bought a paper, leaned against a lighted window and read the news. The words danced before his eyes, would not enter his mind. All he could see was that pretty, dark-haired girl having a lover's quarrel with Anthony. Anthony would marry, would have children. Dad might be won over when another generation of Bells put in an appearance. And if Dad got won over, Liam would be truly alone.

He sat on the train and looked at his reflection in the darkened glass. The vehicle lumbered over rails, chattered across points, struggled to achieve its regular rhythm. His eyes closed and he leaned back. As he slipped towards sleep, he heard the regular accent of iron on iron. 'Anthony Bell, going to hell, Anthony Bell,' chanted a voice in his head. His eyes flew open. Did he have to wait until the end of life before getting his due? Would things even out only then, when he entered Paradise and Anthony sank into Hades? No, no, he didn't want his twin to go to hell. He must save Anthony again, must make sure that Anthony made no mistakes. He had saved him before ... but the details were still vague.

Liam wiped an unseasonal sweat from his face and loosened his coat. Confusion ruled his brain, made his thoughts jump all over the place. Anthony. He loved him, hated him. He could not just sit back and let Anthony carry on sinning. Something would have to be done, something big. It would happen in a dark place and ... Yes, he would know what to do, he would remember. The answer would come before death, he would make sure of that.

Anthony drained the glass and asked for a second pint. He saw Billy Costigan lumbering towards him, hoped that the big man was not too upset. But he should have known that there would be no ill-feeling on Billy's part. Billy clapped Anthony on the back, asked the barman for a set of arrows and went off to wage war at the dartboard.

Someone touched Anthony's arm. 'Is this you drinking straight out of your sickbed?'

Anthony smiled down on Michael Brennan. The priest's head reached Anthony's shoulder, just about, though his girth filled enough space for two. 'Whisky, Father Brennan?'

'Oh, very well. Here's yourself leading me into the ways of sin. Mind, I have to tell you – I'm very easily led astray.'

They drank, found a corner and leaned against the wall. 'Crowded,' remarked Michael Brennan. 'Are they putting on turns tonight?'

Anthony shook his head. The pubs hereabouts were still famed for 'free and easy' evenings, nights when landlords did battle for business by bringing in a comedian, a singer or an illusionist. 'No, we've no entertainment tonight,' he told the priest. 'It's the football teams debating strategy. There'll be a ding-dong in Lock Fields next Sunday. They're competing for free beer. And the rest have come in to watch the fun and to thaw out.'

The cleric finished his drink and looked hard at Anthony. This was one of the best teachers he had ever encountered. The children respected him, felt no fear of him, trusted him. This was hardly the right place, but Michael Brennan had to come out with it, had to get it off his chest. 'Anthony, Liam is to be attached to our church for a while.' Well, at least he had said it. He had been wondering since early evening how he would break the news. But the scotch had loosened his tongue. 'Just for a few months,' he added.

Anthony dropped his chin and thought for a moment or two. This short, friendly priest was Anthony's confessor. Anthony had never mentioned Val in confession, had never unburdened himself. Could he do it now? Could he do it ever without sounding like a total idiot? 'Father, I'm ninety per cent certain that my brother raped and murdered my fiancée, though I'm sure he half believes he didn't. Or perhaps he thinks what he did was not a sin. Yes, he is a priest and yes, he will be coming back to our church simply to make my life a perfect misery.' Oh, that would sound great, wouldn't it?

'Anthony?'

The younger man fixed his attention on the man who was, he supposed, his boss. Without the support of a parish priest, no teacher could reign long in a Catholic school. 'Michael,' he said, 'you asked me ages ago to call you by your Christian name, and this seems a good occasion on which I might start.' He inhaled deeply, coughed out some second-hand tobacco smoke. 'I am asking you to release me from my contract.'

'What? What are you talking about, man?'

'The need to go, the need to get away from him.'

'Away from Liam? But why? I know he's not the kindest of men, and I remember the spat you had when I was new to the parish. But I put that down to you being upset. Didn't your fiancée get buried a month or so before I took up my post?'

Anthony nodded.

'Liam said he tried to make peace with you just recently.' The priest left space for a reply, got none. 'Is that the case?'

It was hopeless, thought Anthony. What was he supposed to say? 'I think he's sick,' he managed eventually. 'Sick in his head. Sometimes, I really believe he has no memory of the unsavoury things he has done.' He tapped his empty glass with his fingernails. 'If I were to tell you what I know, and what I think I know, you wouldn't accept it.'

'Try me.'

Anthony lowered his head. 'If you did give me credit, the Church in Liverpool could be lifted right off its foundations. Even then, Liam would win through. Winning through is what life is all about as far as my brother is concerned.'

A new shiver travelled the length of Father Brennan's short spine. Anthony Bell was a completely trustworthy man. Like everyone else, he was a sinner who attended confession, but there were very few stains on the soul of this teacher. 'Is he dangerous?' he asked quietly.

'Yes.'

'And you'll say no more?' Antagonism between siblings was not uncommon, but the Bell twins were surely taking their rivalry a bit too far? 'Will you wait till I replace you?'

'Of course. There are plenty who will be glad of the chance.'

'And where will you go?'

Anthony thought for a few seconds. 'Not too far away from Grandmuth, I suppose. Inland. Yes, I'll go a bit deeper into Lancashire.'

Father Brennan touched his friend's arm, then went forth to visit those among his flock who needed their priest. He stood for a while and watched a tram pulling up, listened to the Mary Ellens as they serenaded all the other passengers. A few of these alighted, fruit baskets empty after a day's toil at the Pier Head and on the ferries that cut across the Mersey several times each day.

Ragged urchins dashed about trying to rid themselves of their remaining newspapers. The smells of cabbage, pig's cheek and spiceballs lingered in chill air as people walked homeward with carry-out suppers. Michael Brennan loved this place, knew that his friend Anthony Bell loved it, too. Why was this happening?

He crossed the road and made for Tenterden Street where a mother was nursing three cases of measles. One of the children was extremely ill and might be in need of the fever hospital. On a corner, he paused for a while and watched an entertainer juggling with plates. Why did Anthony have to leave? Perhaps the bishop's opinion should be sought, but ... but what could a man say to a bishop about family feuds? Also, it would be wrong to blacken Liam's name, and yet ... And yet Michael Brennan trusted Anthony completely. He stared at the juggler and felt empathy with the man. A priest's job was not unlike juggling, trying to keep all the plates in the air, hoping they would not collide or crack.

As he walked towards the sickbeds of children, the parish priest of St Aloysius Gonzaga made his reluctant decision. He must let Anthony go, and he must keep an eye on Father Liam Bell. Like the juggler, the parish priest had to keep the show on the road.

Eight

Monica Costigan, usually known as Nicky, walked with the love of her young life along Dryden Street to the door of her home. Graham Pile, a boy with a good heart and an unfortunate appearance, carried a basket of stale bread from the bakery. At seventeen going on eighteen, he was almost ready to complete his apprenticeship, so he and Nicky would be married as soon as she had reached the age of sixteen.

'Mam'll miss Mrs Bell,' said Nicky. 'They're going to Bolton for Easter, Mrs Bell and her little girls. That Auntie Edith invited them just after Christmas, but Mrs Bell's only just made her mind up. I like Mrs Bell. We'll all miss them.'

'It's only for a fortnight,' Graham replied. 'And it's not as if they're going to Africa. Bolton's not that far away.'

Nicky stopped in her tracks and grabbed his arm. 'Right. Have you ever been to Bolton?'

'No,' he admitted.

'Where is it?' she asked.

'Over there.' He waved a hand in a direction he judged to be north-easterly.

Nicky clicked her tongue and carried on walking while Graham brought up the rear. Had Monica Costigan been able to see herself and Graham at that moment, she might have recognized a facsimile of her own parents. Diddy led and Billy followed, though he had been known to put down one of his very large feet whenever the various breeds of bee in his wife's bonnet buzzed too loudly.

Diddy was in full flood when Nicky and Graham entered the house. She shook a newspaper as if she wanted to throttle it. 'Not fit for human habitation?' she yelled. 'Have they only just bloody noticed? Why can't they make our places decent instead of threatening to pull them down?'

Billy, who was struggling with a tough piece of stewing beef, closed his eyes and allowed the storm to develop. Opinions about living conditions in Scotland Road had been the subject of editorials since the previous century. Nothing would get done, yet Diddy continued to panic every time she read one of these articles.

'Well, I'm not budging,' she declared.

Billy swallowed the offending forkful. 'They're not knocking us down yet, love,' he said mildly.

Diddy breathed in and prepared to deliver another piece of oratory. 'You'll be sitting there, Billy Costigan, when the big hammer takes the walls down. I mean, if we all just sat there chewing, who knows where we'd end up?'

'Sitting down,' came the response from Billy. 'If we all sat down, we'd end up sitting down, not squeezing the life out of the *Liverpool Echo*. Don't get yourself worked up.'

Diddy marched to the dresser, pulled out a large brown envelope, then scattered its contents onto the table. 'Just you look at them, Billy Costigan. Look. How long has my family lived here in this house? Since before the bloody turn. And I've kept all my mam's rent books and all ours.'

Billy sighed. It was lecture time. Diddy would be riding round the kitchen on a very high horse until she got saddle sore, fell off, or got pushed off. 'Don't start, girl,' he begged. 'I've had a hard day.'

Diddy pushed out her enormous chest and folded her arms beneath it. 'There's more bloody rules on them rent books than what they've got written down at the Old Bailey.' She picked up a few of the tattered articles. 'See, three bob a week in nineteen-o-eight. "The tenancy shall be subject to the rules ... the tenement is not to be used as a shop." They stopped my mam selling pie and peas through that very window you're staring at,' she accused.

Billy lit a cigarette. If she hadn't burnt herself out by the time he reached the end of his smoke, he'd be off out.

'Mam–'

'And,' Diddy glared at Nicky and Graham, 'look here, Monica – you, too, Graham – you might learn something. See that word? And there and there again. It says arrears, arrears, arrears.' She stabbed at the page with a podgy finger. 'It's all smudged because my mam cried over not being able to pay. Tears rhymes with arrears, doesn't it?'

Graham looked at Nicky, then placed his offering on the table. 'Bread for the Nolans, Mrs Costigan,' he said quietly.

'Thanks,' snapped Diddy. 'If the rotten government did its duty instead of sitting on its arse, there'd be no need for stale loaves. Course, they're like that bloody Marie Anton-etty, aren't they? No bread, let the buggers live on cake.'

Dock work was difficult, thought Billy, though a wife with a mission was worse. He cared. He cared just as much as she did. But his hand was sore in spite of leather glove and docker's hook. His shoulders ached from heaving bags of molasses and coffee beans, and all he wanted was a little snore behind the *Echo* and a bit of tranquillity in his own house. Which dwelling belonged, for the moment, to Diddy's mother. It would be at least ten minutes before Diddy reached the change of tenancy.

'Poverty?' she roared. 'We don't know the half of it. I've seen my dad go out to work with an empty belly and not a penny in his pocket. I've seen people dying in doorways, kids screaming with pain and nothing to pay the doctor with, and—'

'We've all seen it, love,' Billy managed to squeeze in.

'I know,' she yelled. 'I know, but we're all sitting here picking our teeth.'

'You're not,' he said placidly. 'You're disturbing the peace.'

Diddy pounced on the current rent card. 'Look at this one, then. Thirteen and six a week and what do we get for it? Where do they spend all our thirteen and sixes? Because they've not thrown any money back at Scottie Road, have they? There's buckets in bedrooms catching rain. There's people sleeping downstairs because the upstairs floors have gone. Thirteen and six.' She waved an arm at the door. 'Billy, "She's Out" nearly had that door down till you got work and paid the three quid we owed in back rent.'

Billy sighed, nodded. Matt Roberts, rent collector, was commonly known as 'She's Out', because that was the response he usually got when he knocked at a door. 'He was only doing his job, Diddy.'

'And you weren't doing yours, because you had no rotten job. There's thousands out there with no work.' She sat down, thought about what would happen here again if Billy became ill or stopped getting picked for work. It was literally hand to mouth round these parts. The Costigans were lucky, because Charlie earned a crust, Maureen got a few bob from Dolly Hanson and Monica ran a little stall at the market. Even young Jimmy fetched a copper or two home. But Billy was the mainstay. If Billy became idle again, if he lost favour on the docks, the arrears column would fill up to the point of eviction. 'They should do something for us,' she told her small audience. 'They should get our houses right and stop talking about pulling them all down.'

Graham backed towards the door. His girlfriend's mother in full sail was not a pretty sight. 'My tea'll be ready,' he mumbled timidly. Nicky followed him. 'Back in a minute, Mam,' she called over her shoulder.

Diddy was reading aloud again. '"The tenant is to pay for all broken windows, make good any damage and pay the total rent due before notice will be accepted." You can't even swap houses without filling in three forms.' She threw the piece of cardboard down and stared ahead as if trying to burn a hole right through the air and into the future. 'They'll tear the lot down, Billy. They don't care about us.'

Billy closed his eyes. The Scotland Road folk lived day-to-day. They didn't go looking for trouble in the *Echo*, didn't start ranting and raving when some journalist wrote about conditions. Of course, they weren't married to Diddy, were they? 'Pipe down, love. You'll have the neighbours in. The police'll be sending a posse round if you don't stop shouting.'

Diddy stopped shouting. She sat for a while and wondered what she'd been shouting about. The courts round here were a bloody disgrace. There were families living in houses with no windows at all at the back, with no slopstone, no indoor water, lavatory sheds shared between dozens of people. Perhaps they should pull the lot down, then. Perhaps Scotland Road ought to be flattened and abandoned. 'No,' she said aloud, 'it's the heart.'

'Eh?' Billy stared at her. 'Whose heart?'

She tutted impatiently. 'Yours, mine, Dryden Street's, Scottic's. It's not about houses, Billy. It's about us and the Nolans and the Bells and all the rest of them. It's like . . .' She searched for words. 'Like we're all a part of one another. Not blood, not related. It's soul, that's what it is. This place has a soul. And they'll kill it off. They'll split us up and shove us all over the place.'

'How've you worked that out?' he asked. 'They might move some of us out, then bring us back when the houses are rebuilt.'

Diddy shook her head. 'There's more to it than that. They want the community destroyed. I suppose if you look at it from their point of view, it makes sense. How many times has a lad run through this kitchen with a bobby behind him?'

Billy shrugged. 'How many feathers on a pigeon?'

'Exactly. And what do we do? Before we'll let one of our own kind down, we say, "Who? No, there's been no lad in here, Mr Policeman." By that time, the boy's three streets away tucking into his dinner, and the stuff he's pinched is hidden or eaten. So they're going to split us up. Divide and rule, it's called. But we all know it wasn't just us what done the loot. There were others at it, too, during the police strike. We're the ones who'll suffer, though. We're the ones who get the blame for everything.'

Billy sighed and thought about a nice, frothy pint. If Diddy would just shut up and get on with her chores, he would be able to nip out for a quick drink.

'Go on, then,' she said. 'Get down the Holy House and drown your sorrows. Dryden Street might still be here at closing time.'

Billy kissed his wife, dragged on a jacket and marched quick-smart out of the house. Sometimes, women were best left to stew on a low light until they calmed down.

Bridie folded the last of the clothes and packed them in the cases. Sam was watching her. He sat on the edge of the bed with one of his silly little hand-rolled cigarettes smouldering in his fingers. He watched her quite often, when he thought she wouldn't notice. But she did notice, and his vigilance had ceased to make her uncomfortable.

Sam loved her – in his own way. The word 'love' was, perhaps, too strong to describe Sam's feelings for anyone, she told herself by way of correction. He liked her, approved of her and needed her. 'That's all done now,' she told him. 'And thank you for so many new clothes.' Bridie and the girls were the proud owners of several shop-bought outfits. The man had not turned a single one of the sparse hairs on his head when paying the not inconsiderable bills for these luxuries.

Shauna came in, a teddy bear trailing alongside her. 'His ear came off,' she wailed.

Bridie studied her younger daughter for a moment or two. Shauna was becoming a bit of a madam. Fortunately, she was too young to play outside, so the trouble she caused remained indoors. 'I'll sew it on later,' Bridie said.

'Now.' A small slipper was stamped against the carpet.

'No,' said Bridie, 'later.'

Cathy entered the room. She was wearing a brand new nightdress and a dressing gown in a warm shade of pink. She smiled at Uncle Sam. 'I like my things,' she told him. 'Especially the blue dress. Thank you for my blue dress and the lovely shoes.' Blushing, she ran to him and threw her arms round his neck. He wasn't Daddy, but he was terribly kind to give so many presents to someone who was a desperate nuisance. 'I'll try to be good,' she whispered in his ear. 'I promise I will.'

Sam didn't know what to do with the child. He placed the cigarette in a saucer and stroked the little girl's hair. It was blonde, but darker than Bridie's, almost brown in parts. She was pretty. Both girls were pretty, though Shauna looked weedy next to the better upholstered Cathy. 'There, there, it's only a few bits and pieces,' he mumbled. 'You have to have clothes, Cathy.'

Bridie laughed. 'How does it feel being with young ones all over again?' she asked.

'Better than last time,' he admitted. He remembered the twins. Anthony had been placid enough, but Liam, because of his superior brain, had acted up. 'Liam was hard work. But the hard work paid off.'

'Did it?' asked Bridie.

'He's a priest.'

Bridie lowered her head. 'Anthony's a good sort. When he was ill, I noticed how gentle and kind he was. All the children loved him, Sam. They were heartbroken when he left the school and went off to work elsewhere.'

Sam lifted Cathy up and sat her next to him. He wished his boys would sort out their differences. Anthony had often complained about his twin's behaviour, but the real trouble had started after the death of that girl. That girl had not been suitable as a potential member of the Bell family, because she had left the Church. Following the murder, Anthony had turned completely against Liam. 'Talk to Anthony,' Sam told his wife. 'He's living in a cottage near Edith's house. Try to get him to see sense, will you?'

Bridie thought about that. If she had to go near either of those twins, she would definitely choose the school-teacher. She didn't like Liam at all, still felt chilled when she thought about him. He had been dreadful to her during confession, had preached a real sermon and given her miles of penance. When she had emerged from the box, people had stared at her because she had taken so long to get her sins off her chest. Since that one disastrous time, she had always confessed to Father Brennan. 'Come on,' she told the girls. 'Let's have you two in bed.'

She took them across the landing to their own room, covered them, prayed with them, renewed her promise to sew on Teddy's ear before leaving for Bolton, then returned to her husband. 'What do I say to him?'

'Who?'

'To Anthony.'

Sam looked at his watch. 'I'll have to go down in a minute. Charlie will be wanting to get home.'

Bridie sat in a cane chair. 'Sam, what do I say? And why should I be the one to say it? Liam is so ... unapproachable. I can understand Anthony's reluctance, because Liam seems to think he's better than everybody. How can I tell Anthony what to do? He won't listen to me. Anyway, I wasn't here when all the trouble happened.'

He pushed the watch into his waistcoat. 'Because you weren't here, you might be the best one to speak up.'

Bridie nodded. 'All right.' Sam looked after the girls, so she must do what she could for him. But she knew full well – as did every other parishioner – that Anthony had left Scotland Road because of his brother's return to the area. She didn't think much of Liam, yet she must do her best for Sam. 'I've sorted out the rota for Muth,' she told him, anxious to change the subject. 'There are two women to do the cooking and cleaning, then Diddy will make sure Muth gets out of her room each day.'

Sam rose and walked to the door. 'Bridie?'

'Yes?'

He tried to clear the embarrassment from his throat. 'Er ... I do appreciate everything you've done since you came.'

'I know that, Sam.' And she did know it. He never said much, but she often caught a hint of gratitude in his expression. 'Sam, will you get along to the doctor and have that cough seen to? There's a limit to what shop-bought pills and potions can do. You've been coughing such a lot lately.'

He nodded at her, gave her a hesitant smile. Sam had no intention of visiting a doctor. He'd seen too many people walking into a surgery in reasonable condition only to finish up within weeks in a hearse. Smokers coughed.

He could carry on coughing quite happily without the help of any medical man.

When he had left the bedroom, she tidied up, laid out her clothes for the next morning, went to close the curtains.

Outside, the road heaved with life. Bridie stood for at least five minutes watching the world into which she had been dragged just months ago. The weather was fair, so young men lingered on corners, their antics tailored to attract the attention of passing females. These girls pretended not to notice the carryings-on, but they laughed and joked as soon as they had passed the boys.

People sauntered by carrying basins into which pig's cheek and cabbage or meatballs would soon be placed. Policemen ambled along in twos and threes, while older men strode into the many public houses. Bridie had tried to count the hostelries in the area, had given up. There were pubs on the main road, and many more in side streets.

She drew the curtains, turned back the quilt on the bed. Tomorrow, she would see her horses. While she looked forward to that, she knew that she would miss the Scottie Roaders. Da had done Bridie a favour by bringing her here, and she thanked God for her good fortune.

Father Liam Bell turned slightly so that his right ear was almost up against the grille. The Costigan girl was on the other side of a very thin partition. He could smell the cheap, cloying scent she was wearing, could hear the sadness in her tone as she requested the blessing. 'Tell me your sins, child,' he whispered.

'Father Brennan?' she asked.

'He's out. I'm here in his place.'

She swayed from side to side in an effort to achieve

some comfort, because the plank of wood on which she knelt to repent was very hard. The priest at the other side was not Father Bell, she told herself. There had been quite a number of different confessors here lately, because the parish priests had been busy with a lot of sick people. Maureen assumed that Father Bell, too, would be out on his ministry, because this voice was nothing like his. Father Bell's voice was loud and strident, not gentle and kind.

'Are you ready to confess now?' he mumbled.

Maureen counted off her sins, told about pinching a few sweets from Dolly's shop, about arguing with her mother.

Liam waited until he heard her say, 'For these and all my other sins, I am very sorry.' He absolved her, listened to the formal act of contrition. When she stopped praying, he whispered again. 'There is something troubling you. Not a sin, perhaps, but a matter that preys on your mind.'

Maureen hoped the splinters hadn't made too big a hole in her stockings. This quiet priest sounded concerned about her. Should she tell him about her troubles? Mam had often said that the confessional was not just for sins, that it was there so that people could tell God, through a mediator, exactly what was bothering them. 'It's nothing,' she said. 'Well, it's not important.' It was important. She had just lied in confession, and that was a huge sin. 'No, it is important,' she admitted.

Liam leaned on his hand. He would get to the bottom of that little scene he had witnessed outside the Throstle's Nest. 'Go on,' he urged softly. 'I won't be shocked.'

So she told him. She told him that she loved an older man and that her parents were not pleased.

'His name?' asked the priest.

Maureen pondered. 'No, my mam says I've to tell my own troubles and nobody else's when I'm in confession.

But he lived round here, the man I've just told you about. He's gone now. He's gone away.' She cleared her throat and prayed that the tears would not flow.

Father Bell's fingers closed tightly around his crucifix. 'He loves you?' he asked.

Maureen, who had been loved by all and sundry since birth, could not imagine how any man could fail to become enamoured of her. 'I think so,' she answered. 'But I'm too young ... I think he went away because I'm too young and because of...' Oh dear, she had stepped into muddy waters without thinking. 'Somebody he didn't like came to live round here. But when I'm old enough, he'll come back for me, I know he will. I'm lonely now, though. I used to go to dancing class, but I can't be bothered any more.'

Liam took a chance. 'The person he does not like is Father Bell. Am I right?'

This was confession. This was the place for truth. 'I think so.' She felt a stab of fear. This man would know Father Bell, surely? And he would tell Father Bell what she had said ... No. The relief that flooded into her was almost painful. Father Bell would not be told, because priests had to keep the secrets of the confessional. Anyway, nobody in the parish of St Aloysius Gonzaga liked their new priest, because he was all doom, gloom and black looks. Perhaps the other priests didn't like him either.

'Say one Our Father and five Hail Marys,' he told her, his tone still soft. 'And I shall pray for you.'

Maureen Costigan blessed herself before going into the body of the church where others waited for a hearing or made their way through the apportioned penance. She said her prayers inwardly, then asked the Immaculate Conception to intercede on her behalf. After all, Mary was a woman, so she should know all about Maureen's sufferings.

In his secret cubby-hole, Father Liam Bell made the right noises while penitents told their sins. He suddenly felt rather ill and light-headed, attributed these symptoms to a rise in body temperature. The weather had been unpredictable, so perhaps he was coming down with a chill.

But he had no time to be ill, no time to take to his bed. On this occasion, brother Anthony had been clever, far too clever for his own spiritual good. He had left the area in order to shield the loose child who had pledged undying love.

'*Te absolvo...*' he murmured automatically to some invisible man. He must save Anthony from himself, must prevent his brother from making a terrible mistake. A Bell to marry a Costigan? No, that would never do. Maureen was cheap, common, a little street urchin with a pretty face. A very pretty face...

The confessional door opened, closed, opened again. Another man offloaded his list of wrongdoings, laid bare his weaknesses. Anthony was a damned fool—

'Father?'

'Yes?'

'Will you absolve my sins, please?'

Liam apologized, explained that he did not feel well.

'I'll pray for you,' said the invisible sinner.

'You do that,' replied Liam. And he meant it.

It was almost time to go. At any minute, Edith Spencer's car would appear outside Bell's Pledges, then Bridie, Cathy, Shauna and Noel would be off on holiday.

Bridie sat upstairs with Theresa Bell. 'You will get up and go downstairs every day?'

Theresa shrugged. 'I suppose so. But it won't be the

same, not without you and the girls.' She loved Bridie's daughters, spent hours knitting and sewing for them. They and their mother had become the centre of her universe, her reason for struggling her way out of bed each day. 'Don't forget to talk to our Anthony,' she said. 'And get down to Bolton Market, you'll like it. And have a look round the shops. One of these days, I'll get back home for a visit. But for now, I'm depending on you to tell me all about Bolton.'

'I'll telephone Sam,' suggested Bridie.

Theresa grinned broadly. 'What? And you're the one who won't even answer the damn thing when it rings in the shop. All right, get yourself gone and I'll see you in two weeks. Tell Anthony I'm thinking about him.'

Bridie bent down and kissed the top of Muth's head. This old woman was special and precious. She was also easier to understand than some of the born and bred Liverpudlians. So perhaps Bridie would manage Bolton very well if they all spoke in this accent.

'Look after yourself,' called Theresa as her daughter-in-law left the bedroom. She leaned back on her mound of pillows. Things had bucked up no end, but she was becoming very tired. The Grim Reaper hovered, especially at night when she was alone. How much longer did she have before the spectre called Death led her onward? A month, a year, a day? Still, she had enjoyed the last few months.

'Grandmuth,' sang a young voice from the road outside.

She left the bed and walked across the room stiffly. Cathy was below in all her new clothes. Theresa waved, then sat down by the window. They would be back in a matter of days, she told herself. Her bones creaked with arthritis these days and, sometimes, a pain visited her chest. She hoped with all her frail heart that Bridie would see Anthony and cheer him up. He liked Bridie. Well, everybody liked Bridie – except Liam, of course. Liam loved God and himself, not necessarily in that order.

Theresa watched the scenes on the road below, waved again at Sam's stepdaughters. She didn't like brooding about Liam, wished that she could wipe him out of her mind altogether. He wasn't akin to other people, had never been like other children. A broody, silent boy, he had stuck to his books whenever taunting his twin had become too boring.

How was poor Anthony getting on? she wondered. Did he like the school in Bolton, was he eating properly, was his house warm and dry? Such a good baby, he had been ... Her head nodded as she dozed and dreamed of days when she had been mother and grandmother to Anthony. But when Liam entered the pictures in her mind, the sleeping woman moaned. Because there was something not quite right about Liam Bell.

Big Diddy Costigan bustled along Scotland Road with a wicker basket held in front of her. A Mary Ellen across the way hailed her. 'Diddy? Are you setting up in competition?' The lady pointed to her own large pannier which was balanced perfectly on her head.

Diddy laughed. 'Yes, I am, so you'd best watch out. You all right, girl?'

The girl in question was well over sixty. Her skin had weathered to the point where it looked as if a tanning factory might have played a part in achieving such texture and colour. 'Second trip,' she yelled. 'Sold the first load by half past eight this morning. Your lot all right, are they?'

Diddy replied in the affirmative, then carried on to Bell's. She had to get Muth out of bed, then make sure that Amy McMahon turned up to do the cooking. She swept into the shop like a ship in full sail. 'Sam?' She beamed at him. He was in her good books at last, because he was looking after Bridie and the children, and because he had given Bridie the horses. So he couldn't have been such a bad old bugger after all.

Sam looked up from his ledger. 'Morning, Diddy. Your Charlie's in the back drinking a cup of tea. The girls have followed him in there. They've been in and out looking for Edith's car and sending me and all the customers dizzy. Oh, and Bridie's upstairs putting her hat on.'

Diddy absorbed this information. 'Yes,' she remarked finally. 'I think I'd put a hat on if I was going out with your Edith.'

A corner of Sam's mouth twitched. Edith probably did look rather forbidding until you got to know her. 'She's not that bad,' he advised the visitor.

'Neither are you,' retorted Diddy before marching through to the living quarters. The little girls looked a treat decked out in all their new finery. 'I've brought you some pasties and pop,' she told them. 'In case you get hungry on the way.' She beamed at her older son. He was the best lad in the world, their Charlie. He'd had a rough trip as a child, what with all the other lads calling him names and imitating his strange way of walking. Diddy had banged a few heads together in her time. 'Hello, Charlie.'

The ungainly youth smiled at his mam. He was so happy now. The shop had livened up no end since Bridie, Cathy and Shauna had arrived. Many a time, he was left in charge of the youngsters, and he enjoyed their company and their laughter, because they seemed to treat him as if he were like everyone else.

Diddy smiled to herself. Many of those who had taunted their Charlie were out of work, but the one they had called 'Cripple' was in almost full-time gainful employment. She turned round as Bridie entered the room. 'Bloody hell,' she said. 'Who got you ready, queen?'

Bridie felt like a queen, too. She wore a tight-waisted suit of light navy with emerald green accessories. Her hat, the outfit's crowning glory, was green with a petersham ribbon in navy round its brim.

'Nobody got Mammy ready. Mammy dresses herself,' said Shauna. 'After she dresses me. Cathy dresses herself, too.'

'What a clever family,' exclaimed Diddy in mock-surprise. 'Who dresses Uncle Sam?'

'He does it himself,' laughed Cathy.

Diddy shook her head. 'Well, he needs lessons, then. He looks like a bag of rags some days, even days when he gets married.' She passed the basket to Bridie.

'We'll be there in an hour or so,' said Bridie. 'We won't need anything to eat, surely?'

'Then have them for your dinner when you get there,' advised the guest. 'Or give the food to Anthony. And tell him we all miss him, especially the kiddies at school.'

Edith Spencer breezed in, greeted everyone and examined the dog, which looked far too big for the car. The girls should have worn old clothes, she thought, because the animal would probably be all over them, shedding and dribbling and indulging in all kinds of canine behaviours. 'Are we ready?' she asked.

The children screamed their 'yeses' and dashed out of the room. Charlie struggled to his feet. 'Mrs Bell,' he mumbled, 'I hope you have a good time.'

Bridie remembered what Anthony had told her that first day. She had learned for herself that Charlie Costigan had brains to spare. It occurred to Bridie in that moment that she actually loved the Costigan family. Jimmy and Tildy-Anne were cautions, of course, but they were fine children in spite of being a bit wayward. Diddy and Billy were grand – not just the salt, but the whole seasoning of God's earth. Nicky was plain, honest and very attached to the homely Graham Pile, and Maureen was ... Maureen was a lost child who hid behind great beauty.

'Changed your mind?' asked Diddy.

Bridie threw her arms as far as they would reach around the large woman. 'You're like my own,' she said. 'All of you, all the Costigans.'

Diddy pushed her friend away and swiped at a disobedient tear that tried to travel down a rounded Costigan cheek. 'Get gone,' she muttered. 'And hurry up back.'

'We will.'

Outside, a small crowd had gathered round Edith Spencer's car. Holidays were a rarity, so everyone was pleased to know that some among them were going away for a while. Eddie 'Razor' Sharpe waved his neck clippers. 'Shall I give that dog a bit of a shave?' he asked.

The dance teacher, commonly known as Fairy Mary, twittered about waving her hands and skipping like a five-year-old. Gob Stopper, really Peter Cavanagh, stepped out of his shop with somebody's dentures in his grip. 'Smile,' he told the false teeth. He clicked the dentures, pretended to be a ventriloquist. It was this sort of thing that kept them all going, thought Bridie. Their humour was their salvation.

Bridie got into the front passenger seat, laughed at the farewell gathering. Occasionally, at night, she missed Galway. But she could not have come to a better place. She spotted Sam in the doorway of his shop. He wasn't smiling. 'Back soon,' she mouthed through the windscreen. The car lurched forward, Noel barked, and they were on their way.

Maureen broke into a run. She had been visiting a friend down Limekiln Lane, was making her way homeward in the dark. A man had started following her when she had passed the end of a narrow street that ran between the lane and Scotland Road. She hadn't stopped to look at him, especially while the light was so poor, but she knew that he was tall and broad. Inwardly, she cursed herself. She should have cut through to the main road earlier on, because Limekiln Lane was quiet tonight.

The heel of her shoe gave way and threw her off-balance. He was getting nearer. She opened her mouth to scream, felt a hand on her face, struggled to breathe. He heaved her backwards, dragged her down the side of St Martin's church and into the recreation ground. This wasn't happening, couldn't be happening. In a minute, she would wake. Tildy would be rolling off the bed and Nicky would have pinched all the blankets again. From behind a curtain that divided the bedroom, she would hear Charlie's snores.

The man threw her face downward in the grass, placed something like a narrow scarf around her neck and pulled tightly until breathing became almost impossible. She felt the pressure on her throat, saw red and green lights dancing behind closed eyelids. Was he going to kill her? Why was he hurting her like this? Everyone loved her; everyone was always kind to her.

With a desperate surge of energy, she bent a knee and kicked upwards and backwards, made contact with a leg, felt him flinch. Mam would be waiting for her. Maureen was late, had been told to get home by nine o'clock. She flailed and kicked again, but her foot found nothing but air this time. He had moved, was tightening the scarf again.

A tremendous agony visited her spine. He was kneeling on her body while he strangled her. Then he knelt astride her, put his face near her ear. She could hear his breath, was suddenly aware of a smell, a familiar scent that she could not place. As she sank into unconsciousness, Maureen Costigan's last thought involved her mother. Mam would be mad about this. Mam would certainly kill the man who was killing Maureen.

Flash Flanagan carried all his worldly goods in an unwieldy barrow fashioned from a crate and the wheels of some long deceased pram. This creaking container held his one-man band, some tattered clothes, his wooden puppets and a bottle or two of beer. He usually slept where he landed, often finishing up in somebody's coal shed or doorway, but he had been promised a berth tonight by a widow in Blenheim Street. In exchange for the privilege of sleeping indoors on a horsehair sofa, he would be expected to do odd jobs – a bit of painting, sanding down, some scrubbing, perhaps.

This free soul, whose life was dedicated more or less to drink and to the entertainment of children, ambled his way up from the dock road, a tambourine clattering in the cart, one foot rather damp where cardboard in his boot had failed to keep out the rain. He paused, opened the beer and took a swig, looked round for a place where he might relieve himself. Several gentlemen of the road had been arrested of late for indecent exposure, so he took himself well off the beaten track. Even in the gloom, some folk round here could see for miles, it seemed.

He stumbled across grass and narrowed his eyes to look for a discreet spot before parking his cart. A man had to be careful these days, because things got stolen even from a poor itinerant. As he fumbled with buttons, he heard the first groan. Flash was a gentleman, so he forgot his own needs and followed the sounds. 'Hello?' he called softly from time to time.

A bundle of rags lay on the ground. He bent, touched

what felt like wool, allowed his hand to travel until it found flesh. With shaking fingers, he struck a match and caught a brief glimpse of the body before a skittish breeze extinguished the flame. It was a girl. He was in the middle of a field in the dark with a dead girl. No, she wasn't dead, because she was still moaning.

He left his cart and ran out of the recreation ground. From a torn pocket of his army greatcoat, he took a whistle and blew until he felt his lungs would burst. Doors opened and a couple of people stepped out into Sylvester Street. 'Get the police,' shouted Flash. 'Somebody's been hurt.'

He turned round and went back to the playing field. She was very still now, but he knelt and heard her rasping inhalations. As quickly as he could manage, Flash removed his dilapidated coat and covered the girl. She had been beaten, he thought. Someone had tried to murder this poor young girl. His hand made contact with something soft and silky, so he struck a match and examined the find. It was a priest's stole. A cross was appliqued to the centre of the vestmental piece. Someone must have pinched this from a church. Either that or the attack had been committed by a . . . no.

Flash straightened, pondered for a moment. Although not a regular attender of mass, Flash had been reared Catholic. The Church must be protected. From layman to cardinal, all the Church's members must strive not to hurt the faith. For a split second he paused, then rammed the stole down the neck of his jersey. A girl lay half-strangled, and the weapon was holy. Still, the less he told the police, the better. If they got their teeth into him, they might keep him for days answering their questions.

A policeman arrived and dragged Flash away. 'What happened?'

Flash held onto his dignity. 'I found her,' he said. 'I

don't know what happened.' The police were not Flash's favourite set of people. They were always moving him on, always going on about where he had been when things had gone missing. 'I only found her,' he repeated.

A crowd gathered, then ambulance men fought their way through with a stretcher. Flash stood and watched helplessly while torches pierced the dark to reveal the true horror of what he had found. The girl had been hit about the face. A dark weal across her throat confirmed that some crazed person had tried to strangle her. 'It wasn't me,' he kept saying. She had been garotted by a priest's stole. 'I found her.'

A young policeman came to Flash's side. 'Don't worry, Flash,' he said. 'Nobody will suspect you. You did all you could.'

Flash swallowed. 'Is she dead?'

'Not far off,' was the bald reply.

The old tramp was taken to the station and given hot, sweet tea and some biscuits. He drank the former, gagged at the thought of food. 'Who would do something like that?' he asked the sergeant.

'A sick man,' answered the seasoned lawman. 'Sick or evil – take your pick.'

Flash Flanagan looked at his belongings which had been parked opposite the desk sergeant's counter. He didn't fancy the idea of going out again, was afraid that his legs might not be up to it. 'Got a spare cell?' he asked. 'Because I don't feel like walking.'

The policeman lifted the flap and came to stand by Flash. The poor old lad was probably in shock, because colleagues had described the condition of the victim. 'Come on, then,' he said. 'It's not the Ritz, but we'll do our best.'

'Thanks,' said the tramp. For the first time in his life, he would welcome the sight of a cell. As for the widow who expected him, she would have to wait until tomorrow.

Diddy Costigan flew along the corridor. In spite of her bulk, she was well in front of Billy. Someone had hurt Maureen. Like a tigress, Diddy was ready to take out the eyes of the creature who had injured one of her young.

A woman in a dark-blue dress pursued the couple. 'Where are you going?' she asked.

Billy stopped. 'We're looking for our daughter. One of the police recognized her. Maureen. Maureen Costigan.'

The ward sister fixed an eye on Diddy's back. 'She can't run about like that, you know. This is a hospital. There are a great many sick people here.'

Billy, whose knees were shaking, stared hard at the nurse. 'Don't you dare tackle her.' He waved a hand at his wife, who was just about to disappear round a corner. 'Or she'll flatten you. Right? Now, tell me where Maureen Costigan is before I lose my temper.' He was too traumatized for tantrums, but he wasn't going to admit that, not to somebody with a face like a smacked bum and what looked like a half-eaten wedding cake perched on her head.

The woman indicated the direction in which Diddy had launched herself. Billy cursed his disobedient legs and staggered after his wife. He found her in an open doorway with two policemen who were trying to hold her back. He watched while she rained blows on the nearest man, decided that he did not have the energy to go to the aid of Diddy's innocent victims. For a larger than average male, Billy was certainly a weakling at the moment. The law had arrived at the Holy House half an hour ago, had advised him that Maureen had taken a battering.

Diddy clouted a constable. 'She's my daughter—'

'The doctor's with her,' said the second policeman. 'Trying to save her life.'

Diddy began a verbal attack, her voice loud enough to wake the dead. 'If my little girl's dying, I have to be with her.' The tears flowed, but she continued furiously. 'You've no right to keep me away from our Maureen.'

Billy sank into a hard wooden chair. 'Did,' he shouted, 'stop it.'

She looked at him. He was grey about the mouth, and a film of sweat covered his face. 'Billy, I want to see her.'

The relieved officers stepped back and closed the door before resuming their positions of guardianship.

'They're sorting her out,' Billy Costigan told his wife. 'They can't have folk interfering while they're trying to mend her.'

'We're not folk, Billy,' she cried. 'We're her mam and dad, we're her next of kin.'

A young nurse hove into view. She carried a tray. 'I've brought you all a cup of tea,' she said. 'Please don't upset yourselves. We're doing all we can.' She set the tray down on another chair, then squatted down beside the weeping woman. 'Try to drink some tea. I've put sugar in.'

Diddy knew full well that she would be sick if she drank anything. The seriousness of the situation was beginning to filter through at last. This wasn't a case of a lost tooth or a broken limb after a fall. Most of her children had damaged themselves at various stages of their lives. But the police were here. Doctors toiled at the other side of a door where Maureen was lying between life and death. 'I'll be quiet,' she told the nurse.

Billy accepted a cup, lost most of the contents because he was shaking like a leaf. He dabbed at his jacket with a handkerchief, kept an eye on his wife. It wasn't like Diddy to give in and sit quietly.

'She's so pretty,' announced Diddy suddenly. 'I don't

know where she came from, because she's nothing like the rest of us.'

'Keep praying,' said Billy. 'That's all we can do now.'

Diddy dragged a rosary from her pocket, tried to say the words in her head. But all she could hear was Billy screaming at her as he came up the street. She had been standing at the door waiting for Maureen to come home. Maureen had not come home, but Billy had run up from the pub, grabbed his wife and told her about Flash Flanagan finding Maureen on St Martin's recreation ground. Anthony Bell's Valerie had been found near a church, she remembered. Yes. St Sylvester's.

The door opened and both Costigans rose to their feet. A doctor smiled kindly at them. 'I think she'll make it,' he told them.

Diddy charged at the startled man and hugged him almost to a pulp. 'Thank you,' she wept. 'Oh, thank you.'

With the help of the policemen, the doctor was released from Diddy's powerful hold. 'We're not out of the woods yet,' he said, recovering spectacles and dignity. 'She will need a lot of care and nursing.'

Billy mopped his face with the tea-stained handkerchief. 'What happened to her?' he asked.

'She was attacked and beaten, probably without much warning,' the medic replied.

Diddy lifted her head and looked at the nearest officer. 'Get him,' she said. 'Because if you don't, I'll find him and kill him myself.'

The doctor bowed his head. This was not the time to tell this mother that her daughter had been half-strangled, that the poor girl had been raped, too, probably while she was unconscious. The truth would have to come out, but not now, not yet. 'You will be able to see her for a few minutes later on. Meanwhile, try not to worry.'

When the doctor left to tend his other patients, Diddy

kept watch over the police who, in turn, were keeping watch over Maureen. In spite of all advice, she worried about her little girl and prayed constantly.

'It'll be all right,' said Billy in an effort to comfort his wife.

'Will it?' she asked. 'Will our Maureen ever be all right again?'

To this question, Billy found no answer.

Nine

Bridie walked out of the house and fixed her eyes on the landscape. She hadn't expected anything quite like this. Bolton lay below her, a sepia-stained place with dozens of factory chimneys that belched steam and smoke into the sky. But here, on the outskirts, moors rolled away like a carpet of many greens, square-patterned by boundary walls and hedges. It was lush, beautiful, teeming with fertility. She remembered the area around Liverpool as flat and uniform, but Bolton's setting undulated gently towards the horizon. 'It's lovely,' she told Edith. 'So very pretty. Like a green counterpane trying to settle on a bumpy bed. It's not fierce, you know, like mountains. This is friendly and peaceful.'

Edith nodded. 'We're used to it, I suppose. Mind, I wasn't always used to this. My mother and Sam's mother grew up together and worked together there.' She indicated the hollow in which the city-sized town sat. 'Aunt Theresa was a doffer and my mother was a weaver. They were born in a tiny house just off Deane Road and in the middle of all the mills. Aunt Theresa married a sea captain and went off to Liverpool. My mother and father remained in the Deane Road area. Theresa and Ida – my mother – had just one child each. So there's Sam and there's me.'

Bridie looked over her shoulder and cast an eye over Edith's magnificent house. It was like the mansions that belonged to landowners at home, broad and tall, with many windows.

'I married well,' said Edith.

Bridie nodded. 'Richard is a nice man.'

'And wealthy, I suppose. Money isn't everything, but it helps.' Edith watched the children playing with Noel. 'Those two are your riches,' she informed her guest.

Bridie felt Edith's sadness. This woman would have loved children, would probably have made a good mother, too. And a house of this size cried out for a family to enliven it.

'I lost three,' said Edith softly. 'Two girls and one boy.'

'I'm sorry to hear that.'

'Yes, it is a pity.' The older woman's gaze was fixed on Cathy. Yesterday, when the guests had arrived, Edith had spent some time with Cathy. The child was alert, eager for knowledge. She needed an education, a proper chance in life.

Bridie scolded her untidy daughters and took them into the house which was called Cherry Hinton. They lingered for a while in a wide hall with a fireplace, a sofa, some Queen Anne chairs and a huge, circular table covered in items of black Wedgwood. A cabinet next to the fire boasted Waterford and Stuart crystal. In this entrance room, a family of five or six might have lived without being cramped.

They ascended a curving stairway, their progress muffled by dense carpet in a dark maroon colour. Noel followed them, overtook them, lay in waiting on the wide landing. According to Edith Spencer, Noel was a mess, but he was one of the family. Even the dog was subdued and well-behaved, as if recognizing and respecting such opulence. Large, gilt-framed paintings lined the wall to their right, while on the left, the hall remained visible through intricate banisters of carved and varnished wood.

Bridie and her daughters had been allocated two rooms with an interconnecting bathroom between. She told the girls to wash, then went to sit in her own temporary home, a green-and-cream palace with carpet, wall tapestries and the most comfortable bed in the world. It was odd, but she felt settled here. Richard and Edith were very normal in their ways, were not the sort of stuck-up people one expected to find amid luxury such as this.

In the bathroom, Cathy washed her little sister's face. The towels were beautiful, far too pretty to dirty, so she made sure that Shauna's face was sparkling before allowing the child to dry herself. This room was gorgeous. The taps were made like fishes and the soap bowls were all shaped into shells. Next to the bath lay a rug with a leaping porpoise woven into it. A collection of shells and pebbles was spread across the window-sill, and some of the tiles were decorated with sea horses. Cathy loved it.

Shauna dabbed at her face with a thick, soft towel. Once dry, she looked for something to add to her collection, picked up two of the shells. While Cathy was engrossed in sea horses, Shauna ran into their pink-and-gold room and placed the bounty in her little case. She would take them home and show them to Charlie. In less than a day, she had acquired two tiny matchcases in silver, a small book with gold on the edge of its pages and a pot with roses on the lid.

'Put those things back.'

Shauna jumped, turned and looked at her big sister. 'No,' she replied. 'I want them.'

Cathy stood her ground. If she told Mammy about Shauna's stealing, Mammy might decide to go back to Uncle Sam's right away. Also, Mammy might blame her older daughter for the younger's delinquency. After all, hadn't Cathy been involved in schemes set up by Cozzer and Tildy to provide for the vast Nolan family? She wrenched the case from Shauna's hand.

Shauna screamed. In Cathy's opinion, Shauna's screams might have put to shame the sirens of large ships on the Mersey.

Bridie rushed in. 'Whatever is it?' she asked.

Cathy sighed, gave the case to Mammy. 'Aunt Edith's things,' she said, 'Shauna has been taking them, and they were for herself, too, not for people who need them.'

Bridie relieved Cathy of the stolen goods. 'Shauna, these things are not ours. You must put them back where you found them.'

Shauna looked from Mammy to Cathy, then turned again to her mother. 'I want them,' she said clearly.

'Why?' asked Bridie.

'To show to Charlie. Charlie shows me things in the shop.'

Bridie sank onto Cathy's bed. Two of them. She had two of them growing up with no morals at all. Where had she gone wrong? She had tried to teach them the early sections of their catechism, had explained about commandments and sins. Of course, Cathy had picked up her waywardness from the Costigans. In a sense, Bridie had come to understand the Costigans' dual standards. But now, Shauna was becoming a thief, too.

'Don't read too much into it,' said a voice from the doorway.

Bridie jumped to her feet. 'I'm sorry, Edith. Shauna's only a baby. She doesn't know the difference between right and wrong, not yet.'

Edith eyed Shauna. The child knew, all right. She had been mollycoddled, overindulged because of her slightness of frame and her unwillingness to eat a full meal. Shauna O'Brien might well grow up believing that the world existed just for her amusement. 'She will return those things. Won't you, Shauna?'

Shauna looked at the unsmiling lady. Something in Aunt Edith's expression made Shauna realize that no foolishness would be tolerated. She took the case from Mammy and went to put back the treasures.

'I'm sorry,' said Bridie.

'It's no matter,' said Edith, her tone reassuring. 'Most children do that sort of thing. We must remember that Shauna is not turned four yet.' All the same, Edith Spencer could not quite manage to like Shauna. Which was ridiculous, she tried to tell herself firmly. Children of Shauna's age were not fully formed, were still growing and learning. She smiled at Cathy. Cathy had stolen in order to help her friends who, in their turn, were keeping alive a family of twelve. Instinctively, Edith knew that Cathy would never steal on her own behalf.

Cathy broke the tension. 'Aren't we going to see our horses today?' she asked.

'Indeed we are,' replied Edith. 'It'll mean boots, because there may be mud. Boots are kept in the rear porch.'

Cathy ran down to invade Mrs Cornwell's kitchen. The cook grinned, sighed, thought wistfully of her mistress's sad lack of children.

Bridie took Edith's hand. 'Thank you for stabling the animals,' she said. 'And for understanding about Shauna. She misses her daddy. They both miss him.'

'And you?'

Bridie knew that she would miss Eugene for the rest of her life. But she was married to this lady's cousin. 'I'm over it,' she lied.

Edith heard the lie and said nothing.

*

Anthony Bell was living in a cottage on Far Moss Lane. From his upstairs front window, he could see Cherry Hinton if he stood on tiptoe on a chair. Which, he told himself, was an extremely silly position for a man who was headmaster of the local school. Also, he would never see Bridie from here, not without some very strong binoculars.

He stepped down from his perch and sat on the bed. Had fate dictated that Bridie should be sent here? Anthony had left Liverpool for two reasons. Firstly, he needed to keep a great many miles between himself and Liam. Secondly, the feelings Anthony had for his father's wife were not appropriate. He remembered the touch of her hand when she had nursed him, the sound of her voice, the kindness that seemed to radiate from her.

He was content in his work, happy with the cottage. Built of stone, it stood alone on the lane. Opposite the house was one of the farms owned by Richard Spencer. The Spencers had been gentleman farmers in these parts for several generations, but Richard had broken the mould by becoming a doctor. Now, the crops and animals were tended by tenant farmers, though Richard maintained his deeply ingrained love of the land. Whenever he had time to spare, Richard Spencer could be seen striding about in long boots and old trousers. He birthed calves, ploughed fields and looked after all who worked for him.

Anthony loved the tranquillity here, though he missed many of Scotland Road's colourful characters. This district was quiet and sparsely populated, a far cry from the hum and bustle of Anthony's birthplace. At the bottom of the lane, in a slight pleat between two moors, rested the village of Astleigh Fold. It boasted a public house, a post office, a few dozen houses and the school where Anthony worked. Children from other villages travelled to Astleigh

Fold Junior Mixed and Infants, but the numbers were still low enough for the classes to be of a decent and manageable size.

So he should be happy. He stared at the brass bedstead as if his distorted reflection in one of its decorative orbs could give him some answers. But there were no answers. He had loved Val, had lost her. He had fallen almost in love again, this time with a woman who was totally out of reach.

His hands curled into tight balls. He knew. He carried the knowledge in his head, and it was heavy, far too weighty for any one man to support. Sometimes, he thought he would go insane, because his nerves had been worn to transparency by the near certainty that Father Liam Bell had murdered Valerie. There was no proof, nothing tangible that could link the then newly ordained priest with that heinous crime. How on earth could Anthony have stuck to his guns? Apart from one small outburst in the police station, he had nursed the feelings close to himself, because no-one would ever believe him. A priest? A Catholic priest committing rape and murder? The desk sergeant and his officers had declared Anthony to be out of control due to shock. And the scratches on Liam's face had been made by an illmannered dog belonging to a parishioner . . .

No! Anthony leapt up and smashed his fist against the nearest wall. The pain seemed to cleanse him, because he was calm in an instant. Was he like Liam, then? Was his temper just a fraction below the surface, was he capable of damaging others while in a rage?

He forced himself to sit down again. Red-hot needles of agony shot through the digits of his right hand. Mercifully, the school was closed for Easter, so he would not need to write for a couple of weeks.

Liam. Liam had bribed away most of Anthony's girlfriends. The twins had been young then – fourteen or fifteen. But about a year later, just before entering the seminary, Liam had begun to conduct his own social life well away from Scotland Road. Once he had managed the spoiling of Anthony's friendships, Liam had hunted elsewhere, in the seedier areas of the city centre. Girls had been beaten; some had been scarred for life. The man who had assaulted them had worn a balaclava helmet and an eye mask. Both Anthony and Liam had been bigger as youths than most grown men.

So, ladies of the night who had plied their trade on Lime Street had taken to walking in pairs and threes. When Liam had gone into the seminary, no further attacks had occurred. Of course, none of those anonymous women had been murdered, because Liam had saved his worst behaviour for Val. He had punished the prostitutes, had killed the one woman who had been close to his twin brother. Had he prayed over the corpse? Anthony wondered.

The street girls of Liverpool had enjoyed some peace once Liam had left the city. Coincidence? wondered Anthony. No, oh no. The bruises and the scratches had been visible on his brother's hands. With a blinding conviction, Anthony had perceived that Liam Bell's sexuality was empowered only by fury. He was a woman-hater, a man who needed to wreak his sadistic and sick revenge on females. Yet it was more than that, more than simple misogyny. Liam despised people and believed that he had been put on earth to punish and cleanse them. Almost every one of the prostitutes had reported that their attacker had mumbled over them, as if he had been praying. He punished, then he prayed. The women of the streets were lucky, as they had been allowed to live. Unlike poor Valerie whose life had been terminated by a very sick man . . .

Anthony shifted in the chair. Liam was guilty, but Liam was ill. Anthony hung on to that idea for a few seconds, ordered himself to feel pity instead of rage. And he did feel pity. Not for Liam, but for the victims. 'Sweet Jesus, help me,' he prayed aloud. But would Jesus help him? After all, Anthony had deliberately taken a post in a non-denominational school. He smiled to himself, realized that he was probably as brainwashed as most Catholics. Jesus was there for everybody, not just for the followers of Rome.

Anthony had no quarrel with the Church, hadn't stopped going to mass. But he was confused. How could the one true faith harbour in its fold a monster who maimed and killed people? Liam should be in an asylum. If he were locked away, the world would breathe more easily.

He leaned back, closed his eyes and tried to ignore the throbbing hand. Grandmuth had told him all about the birth. Maria Bell, the mother of the twins, had suffered an appallingly long and painful labour. Anthony had been born first, a healthy and robust child. Liam, smaller and weaker, had arrived some fifteen minutes later. Was it possible for a person to remember, however subconsciously, that a sibling had commanded the best nourishment in the womb? Had Liam wanted to take revenge because he had been squashed for months behind the stronger baby?

Anthony shook his head. 'Jesus,' he mumbled, 'I'm serious. Put a stop to him, please.' Liam had killed Val because Val had been important to Anthony. Must Anthony remain celibate for the rest of his life so that the population could be safe?

He went downstairs and set the kettle to boil, wincing when his fingers ached again as he turned the tap. While not exactly primitive, the cottage offered just the rudiments necessary to sustain human habitation. It had a cold tap in the kitchen, a grate with an oven attached, and a hob that lowered over the fire for cooking. The kitchen housed a table, two chairs and a dresser with blue-and-white plates, cups and saucers spread along its shelves. In the living room, the furniture consisted of a sofa, some bookshelves and an overstuffed armchair. The lighting was provided by oil lamps, and the bath hung on a nail just outside the kitchen door. A cast-iron grate and a Victorian whatnot completed the living room.

Richard had offered to get the place decorated, but Anthony, unsure of how long he would remain in Astleigh Fold, had refused any help. He liked things the way they were, anyway. And he had his luxuries. The shelves were crammed with books, and a wireless stood on a small table beneath the front room window. He had to get the accumulators charged at the post office each week, but that was a small price to pay for concerts, plays and up-to-the-minute news broadcasts.

He warmed the pot, spooned in some tea, made the brew. This afternoon, he intended to walk the short distance to Cherry Hinton. He was going to see Cathy, he told himself.

When someone knocked at the front door, he put down the teapot and hesitated before walking from the kitchen, through the living room and into the small vestibule. Few people called at the lone cottage.

He opened the door and tried hard not to show his pleasure. She was wearing blue, and the colour did justice to those magnificent eyes. 'Bridie,' he managed, 'come in. I'm just making some tea.'

She entered and placed a basket on the sofa. 'Pasties from Diddy,' she explained. 'You'd have thought we were going on safari to Africa, the amount of food and lemonade she packed for us. We saved them for you. Mrs

Cornwell kept them cool overnight. They have a refrigerator, you know, at Edith's house. Did you hurt yourself?' She noticed that he was nursing the right hand by cradling it with the left.

'It's nothing,' he answered. 'Where are the girls?'

'With Edith.' She sat down next to the basket. 'She wants to keep Cathy. She wants to send her to a good school with a uniform and strict nuns.'

He nodded. 'That'll be Sacred Heart. It's near Richard's practice in Bolton.'

He was a teacher, so she might as well ask him. 'What would you do? Is it a good school?' The man had warm brown eyes with laughter lines already taking up residence along the temples. His brother had lines, too, but Liam's were around his mouth and just above the nose, nasty furrows caused by frowning and scowling all the time.

Anthony placed himself in the armchair. 'They've been getting girls into Oxford and Cambridge. They have high standards, they expect perfect behaviour and the fees are colossal. As for what I'd do – well – I've never had a child, so I can only hypothesize.' He paused, pondered. 'Cathy is unusually clever. She is already receiving a good education, but the chance to go to Sacred Heart can't be dismissed lightly.' Why did he always lecture her? Why couldn't he sit here like a normal human being having a normal conversation with another normal human being?'

'What'll I do, Anthony?'

He loved the way she spoke, the softness of her voice, the way she caressed the consonants lightly, as if words glided like molten silver . . . He was becoming poetic, albeit inwardly. She had wonderful ankles, too. He cleared his throat. 'I can't make the decision for you. But let me think about it for a while. It is important that you see the school and meet the nuns first. After that, you would need to know what was on offer, wouldn't you? Informed decision's essential.'

She smiled at him. 'Would you go with me?'

'Of course.'

'And, if I do decide to allow Cathy to live with Edith, would you keep an eye on her? It's not that I don't trust Richard and Edith to look after my child, but you have taught Cathy and you've seen her happy in school. So you would know what to look for.'

He gave his promise. 'Will you have that cup of tea?'

'No, thank you. I'm off to see the horses again – this time by myself. We took the girls over this morning, but I'd like to look at the horses alone. You know, I remember both of them being born, the filly and the colt. Silver looked like a huge spider – all legs, he was. Sorrel's a gentle soul. I think I might let her brood, for she'd make a wonderful mother.' She stood up. 'In fact, if I'm any judge of horses, we could earn enough from those two to pay our own school fees.'

Anthony followed her to the door. 'I watched you riding,' he said when she was outside on the short path. 'At the stables. No saddle, no bridle.' He laughed. 'Judging from what I saw then, you'd do well in a circus.'

She felt the heat in her cheeks. 'If I'd known about the audience, I would have lost my seat.'

'Would you?'

She paused for a moment, slightly bemused by the expression on his face and the tone of his voice. 'Probably,' she replied, 'though I've been riding since I could walk, and there wasn't always a saddle to suit me.'

He looked her full in the face, tried to memorize the shape of her features, the eye colour, the skin tones.

'Are you all right?' she asked. 'Will I bandage that hand?'

'I'm fine.'

She backed away, waved, swung into the lane and walked off.

He stood at the door until she had disappeared round a bend in the track. She had read him, he felt sure. She had seen him for what he was, a total idiot who was finding his own way to hell. The Bells, he mused, were all in a bloody mess. Dad was as cold as ice, Grandmuth was failing, Liam was ... Liam.

The tea was stewed past drinking. He started again, filled the kettle, stoked the fire, spooned out tea. His hand didn't hurt much any more. But he was still in pain, because he was a fool. Heartache was an acquaintance with whom he had been on nodding terms for many years. So Anthony did what he always did at times like these. He picked up a book and buried himself in someone else's turmoil.

Bridie idled her way back to the stables. She needed some time to herself, because the last few days had been so exciting, buying clothes, packing, travelling. The air was good here in spite of those factories down below, and she was enjoying the greenness of everything. Why had he looked at her like that? Was he asking some sort of a question without words?

A man entered the lane and lifted his cap to her. She watched him leading the cows home to their shippon. Bridie had always liked cows. They appeared stupid, with their soft eyes and docile expressions, but they were far from that. The Friesians apportioned her a few cursory glances, then carried on with their journey, tails swishing, udders swollen with milk.

Why had he looked at her like that? Buttercups danced in the ditch and a few pink-tipped daisies struggled to survive among denser weed. Eugene had looked at her like that. A pair of thrushes walked along in front of her. Strange how some birds hopped and some walked. Thrushes were watchers. Many times at home she had got close to one of these feathered eejits. They were too inquisitive for their own good. He had been trying to tell her something with his eyes.

It was a good school. But Cathy might feel rejected if Bridie let her leave the family home. He had dark-brown eyes. They were not gentle like a cow's eyes, but they were not harsh like Liam's. And it seemed the most desperate cheek to allow Edith to pay for Cathy's education. Mind, if the horses came good, things might be different after a while.

Bridie stopped and sat on a tree stump. Her mind was all over the place. She looked at a cabbage white that fluttered among the long grasses, felt a degree of empathy with the creature. Like her, the butterfly settled on nothing. He just blundered along softly, stopping for a split second then wandering off again. Like her, he was bewildered. The man whose house she had just visited seemed confused, too. She was his father's wife. Bridie shook herself and stood up.

No, she had to be wrong, surely? Anthony could not possibly feel anything for her. If he did – and he didn't – that would be totally against nature. She was supposed to be his stepmother, for goodness sake. A handsome man like that one did not need to make eyes at the person who had just married his father.

Yet her heart was beating a little faster and, somewhere inside, she was smiling. Was it possible to smile inside and not outside? 'Pull yourself together, woman,' she muttered. 'You've horses to visit.' In spite of this reprimand, Bridie walked the rest of the way with excitement staining her cheeks. Unfortunately, she was the sudden victim of emotions over which she found no control.

Edith Spencer was ensconced in her small library with Bridie Bell's daughters. The younger one, armed with wax crayons, was inflicting grievous bodily harm on a sheet of writing paper. Cathy had her eyes glued to a prospectus. 'Is there any fun at all at Sacred Heart?' she asked. It looked such a grim building. There was a photo of some girls standing in a row of dark-grey misery. The uniform was so desperate that anyone at all would be unhappy in it, stupid skirt with box pleats, stupid hat with a horrible brim.

Edith had to think about that. 'There's organized fun,' she replied. 'Tennis, netball, gymnastics and rounders. Sometimes, the nuns hire a charabanc and take the girls for day trips to Chester or York.'

Cathy studied the face of the headmistress. The headmistress had a page all to herself. She was so ugly. 'Do they all look like her?' The nuns at home in Galway and at the school in Scotland Road had been ordinary, sometimes pretty, often young. The headmistress of Sacred Heart had a big nose, wire-rimmed glasses and a wart on her chin. The wart had three hairs sticking out of it. 'I don't like her at all. Tildy's mother would say this face is like the back end of a tram.'

Edith didn't laugh. It was true that Mother Ignatius had an appearance fit to stop clocks. 'She's a very nice lady, Cathy. You may go and meet her if you wish.'

Cathy sat bolt upright. The thought of coming into contact with such an eyesore held little appeal. Of course, Mammy was always saying that beauty was skin deep and that many ugly people had hearts of gold, but the little girl could not quite manage to believe that anyone with such steely eyes might have an ounce of kindness hidden beneath the wimple. 'I don't want to meet her, thank you,' said Cathy. 'And why should I meet her?'

Edith took a deep breath. 'Because Uncle Richard and I want to send you to that school. Of course, you would have to pass an entrance examination and you would need to live in or around Bolton.'

Cathy blinked. 'Are we coming to live here, then?'

'No. Not all of you. And you need not stay with us and go to Sacred Heart if you don't want to. It's just that you are such a clever girl. There are excellent teachers at Sacred Heart. They take very few pupils under the age of eleven, but their kindergarten would give you the best possible start in life. You would be glad in the end, Cathy. You could even go on to university.'

The child closed her book to shut out the offending photograph. She could not imagine attending any school whose boss looked like the back of a tram. 'I want to stay with Mammy,' she said.

Edith decided not to go into the business of cajoling and persuading. She could have told the child about all the freedom she would enjoy on the farms, could have reminded her of the animals that were housed on Spencer land. Instead, she simply turned to Shauna and looked at the drawings.

Cathy didn't know what else to say, didn't know what to think. She liked Aunt Edith and Uncle Richard, but she was happy enough in her latest resting place. Until May of last year, she had lived with Mammy and Daddy and Shauna on a farm. Then Daddy had died, and she had lived with Mammy and Shauna on the same farm. The move to Granda's had not been a happy one, and the relocation to Liverpool had brought its problems. The idea of further upheaval was not attractive. Did Mammy not want her any more? Were the Costigans fed up with her, too? 'What does Mammy want me to do?' she asked finally.

Edith turned away from the prattling Shauna. 'Your mother wants the best for you, of course.'

Cathy had worked out that what grown-ups thought best for a child was not always what the child would have chosen. Castor oil or California Syrup of Figs were often listed and administered as the best thing. Going to mass on Holy Days of Obligation was another best thing, even when the weather was cold and the bed was warm. 'The best is not always the best,' she said, almost to herself.

Edith smiled and kept her counsel. The remark made by Cathy proved a point, the very point on which Edith Spencer was pinning her hopes. Cathy was perceptive. Sooner or later, she would require the kind of education that was offered only by schools like Sacred Heart. And Edith would still be here when Cathy needed her.

The Spencer Stables were situated on Spencer land, though Robert Cross Esquire was very much in charge of all equine and human life on the acreage he ran for Richard Spencer. The house in which he lived was a total shambles. A die-hard bachelor by nature, Bob Cross put horses first every time. The stables and yards were spotless, but finding a chair on which to sit in his kitchen was almost impossible.

He allowed Bridie to enter his domain, sweeping a pile of clothing from a battered but once ornate monks' bench beneath the window to provide her with a seat. 'Got you a saddle here,' he said. 'Best leather, straight out of Walker's Tannery not long back. It's a good one.'

Bridie examined the specimen, thought it was brand new. 'Did Richard buy this for me?'

'Nay,' said Bob. 'I've had it cleaned up. See, there's hardly any wear to the seat, and we've shined all the brass. It'll adjust all right to suit you.'

Bridie examined it closely, ran a hand over pommel and cantle, checked stirrups and cinch. 'It's in very good condition,' she told him. 'Actually, I often ride bareback.'

He nodded, stuck a match between his teeth and chewed for a moment. 'Them's damn good horses you've got there, Mrs Bell. They want training. There's many a mile in that there stallion. Rum bugger, mind. Not beyond kicking somebody into the middle of next Tuesday, yon feller.'

Bridie grinned. Bob Cross's accent was very like Muth's. Edith had honed her vowels to match her status, but her aunt, Theresa, remained very much a Lancastrian, as did this chap. 'He needs to get used to a saddle, then.'

'Oh aye,' replied Bob. 'He's not keen on tack, your Silver. Won't take no bridling, no halter, not yet. Only there's not many races run bareback, tha knows. Stable lad's had a go with Silver, got a lead rein on him after about half an hour of murder, but the horse didn't take to him. Lad's leg's nearly all reet now.'

It didn't seem quite proper to smile when some poor boy's leg had felt the business end of Silver's not inconsiderable strength, so Bridie made her expression sober. 'I'd like to ride Sorrel today. She has a pleasant nature, as I'm sure you will have noticed. Silver responds to singing, by the way.'

The man stared at her and ran a hand through hair grizzled enough to resemble a horse's short-cut mane. 'I'm no good at singing,' he said seriously. 'Not since me voice broke. But I can get a lend of one of them wind-up gramophone things. Does he like Richard Tauber? Or will he need one of them Eye-talian singers with moustaches and big bellies?'

He was laughing at her. She could see from the twinkle in his eyes that he was unsure about this tiny Irish filly's ability to handle highly-strung stock. 'I saw him born,' she informed him. 'I was there when he took his first steps. He had legs right up to the barn ceiling then.' She lifted her head, 'I do know quite a lot about horses, Mr Cross.'

'Aye, and so do I. That stallion'd kill you soon as look at you. Shows the whites of his eyes a lot. But there again, yon's the spirit as wins races. Shall I walk you down?'

'If you wish.' Bridie knew better than to wander about on Bob Cross's sacred soil without his company. He adored horses, tolerated people. She kept up with him, just about, because his stride was long. As they turned into the stable yard, she came upon a sight that almost took her breath away. Her opinion of Bob Cross changed in an instant. He did love people after all. 'How long have you been doing this?'

He scraped a dirty hand across his ill-shaven chin. 'A while,' he answered.

Little ponies trotted meekly round the yard, each one accompanied by an adult. On these mounts sat children, some of them so disabled that they required holding in position by their guides. A blind boy grinned widely, his sightless eyes rolling at the sky. A tiny girl with callipers lay belly down across a blanket, her hands stroking her pony's flank. 'It's a good man you are, Bob Cross,' said Bridie quietly. 'Though I'll tell no-one your secret.'

He cleared his throat. 'Childer has what you might call an affinity with animals,' he said gravely. 'And these particular kiddies need to touch things, to learn, like. Ten minutes twice a week does them the world of good.' He nodded at a lady who supported a thin, wasted infant. 'Ponies is from the pits,' he added. 'Used to toil, they are. Getting them used to light were another matter, I can tell thee. Near blind, they were. Good as gold, and all, never a minute's trouble out of any of them.'

Bridie bit down on her lower lip. She would cry in a minute, she really would. That a bachelor should understand so well the needs of these special children . . .

'Animals and childer is same thing,' he said, as if reading her mind. 'All they need is good grub, a warm bed and a kind word. So they belong together.'

'That's the truth,' she told him. 'And God bless you for what you do here.' She was learning all the time, she reminded herself. She was staying in a grand house whose owners refused to be grand. She had met a bachelor with a love for animals and for children.

He looked her up and down. 'How much longer have I to stand here holding this saddle of yourn?' he asked. 'I've better things to do with my time. Just get yourself off to number four – Sorrel's in there. And I'll talk to you again about jockeys and suchlike. We shall make a bob or two out of your Irish–Arabs.' He dumped Bridie's saddle on the floor and went to help with the ponies.

Bridie walked to stable four and smiled to herself. Today, she had met a rather remarkable man. Down the road a little way, there was another remarkable man in a stone cottage with a pocket handkerchief of a garden at the front. He had looked at her as if she had been the only woman in the world.

In the stable, Bridie greeted her friend. There was no time to think about Anthony Bell's eyes. She had better get on with the business in hand. After all, she had responsibilities here. And Sorrel was so pleased to see her.

Bob Cross lit a Craven A and leaned against the stile. 'I watched her mounting,' he told his companion. 'And she has a goodly shape to her, right proportions for a jockey. Still, she's not a bloke, so she can't enter races, more's the pity.'

Anthony stood next to the stable-keeper. What Anthony knew about horses could have been written on the back of a twopenny stamp with plenty of room to spare. He'd come across a few beasts in the McKinnells' stables on Newsham Street – had even been on sugar lump terms with the coalman's nag, but leaner and glossier creatures with good breeding and mile-long pedigrees were hardly his forte. 'Is she safe perched up there?' he asked. She was so far from the ground. What if she fell off? What if she fell off and rolled under those thundering hooves?

'Her's a natural,' pronounced Bob, admiration in his tone. 'If she'd been born on a desert island with no horses within a thousand miles, she'd still have ridden straight off as soon as she'd got back to civilization and clapped eyes on a horse. She'd not have needed no help from humankind to teach her horsemanship. See, with her, it's hard to tell where the animal finishes and she starts. If I were one of them with a fanciful turn, I'd say I were watching a piece of poetry in motion. She's a gradely rider, is yon Mrs Bell.'

Anthony could see where she ended and where the horse began. She was so tiny, so compact. The beast beneath her was huge, with rippling muscles and limbs that stretched on forever. Yet he could see a little of what Bob meant, because Bridie was plainly unaware of anything beyond herself, her mount and the direction in which both were cantering. 'She's very good at it,' he admitted.

'Good?' Bob puffed on his cigarette. 'See how she changes her seat when she wants a different pace?'

'No,' confessed Anthony. 'But I can tell that she knows what she's about.'

Bob Cross watched woman and horse greedily, almost like a cat lapping up cream. She was certain of her balance, was plainly commanding each slight change of gait. She was relaxed, completely at home. Sorrel, too, was happy, because she obviously felt no tension, no pressure at all. 'Her hands are working perfect,' the sage announced. 'There'll be no bit-bruising in that filly's mouth. That's a magic touch, tha knows. Eeh, I wish she were a man.'

Anthony was very glad about Bridie being female, though he made no comment. After a few more minutes, he began to understand more fully the comments made by Bob Cross. Bridie's spine was as straight as a die, and she seemed not to bounce around even when dictating a change of gait and speed. It was clear that she noticed little beyond the direction in which she travelled. Her riding was natural, instinctive. When Sorrel galloped, her rider flattened herself in order to make a streamlined shape which cut through the air easily. 'Now, she's one with the horse,' said Anthony.

'A shorter stirrup and she'd be halfway to Manchester.' Bob Cross had come across many riders in his time, a few of whom had achieved a level of competence sufficient to keep themselves in the saddle for a decent length of time. Clients had entered little shows, had taken the odd rosette. Bob Cross had been content with that, as his mission in life had been to introduce people to horses and vice versa with a view to enjoyment for all concerned.

This, however, was another matter altogether. Was he qualified to deal with animals of such value? He had not felt as excited as this for many a year. The chestnut mare looked every inch a winner. And Quicksilver, that devil without disguise, was probably the fastest thing on four legs – with the possible exception of a cheetah. A combi-nation of fear and elation touched Bob's spine. He was sixty-five, had been mulling over Dr Spencer's offer of a little cottage over towards Doffcocker, had been looking forward to a few years of relative idleness before shuffling off skyward. Not now, though.

Anthony suddenly felt like an intruder. It was as if he stood about idly watching someone doing something very personal, undressing for a bath, perhaps. Bridie was more than human at this moment. She was travelling not just round a field, but also into a dimension understood by very few people. Like Mozart and Constable, Bridie was exploring a God-sent gift. Anthony said goodbye to Bob, then wandered off towards his lonely home.

Mother Ignatius, undisputed monarch of all she surveyed, was a grim-faced Irishwoman of about four feet and nine inches in height. She had a figure as puny as a sapling and, for a woman of sixty, she moved remarkably quickly, allowing for no dawdling and few human errors on the part of other, less fortunate beings. She believed in God, the value of discipline and the fundamental unwhole-someness of most young people.

Cathy moved from foot to foot, tried to take her eyes off a hideous painting of Jesus on the Cross with blood all over His face and a hole in His side and—

'Caitlin?'

Cathy blinked. The nun was staring at her over the tops of a pair of glasses which looked as if they had been cut in half, because they had bottoms and no upper halves. 'Yes, Mother Ignatius?' In a minute, she would get out of here. She would run like the wind all the way down Blackthorne Road and she would never, ever return. In the flesh, that three-haired mole was worse than ever.

'Nine nines?'

'Eighty-one.'

'Do you know your catechism?'

Cathy nodded.

'Did the cat eat your tongue?'

'I have no cat, Mother. Just a dog called Noel. Uncle Richard says Noel has all the charm of an exploded straw pallet.'

The nun's mouth twitched almost imperceptibly. Sometimes, too rarely, she came across a child who did not fear her. The Bolton children had all heard of Sacred Heart Grammar School for Girls, had lived since infant school under a cloud whose constituents were an improbable combination of hope and terror. They wanted to get into the school, yet they dreaded the day, because Mother Ignatius's reputation was widespread. But Caitlin O'Brien had heard none of the stories.

Cathy noticed the twitch. 'He eats slippers,' she continued. 'But never in pairs. Mammy says the most annoying thing is losing half of a pair. Like gloves. Mammy says it would be better to lose the two, because you'd know somebody had the use of them.'

Mother nodded. 'There's some sense in that.' There was sense in the teller as well as in the tale. 'What do you want to be, Caitlin?'

'I'm not sure yet, Mother. I suppose I'd have to be older to know that.'

'Yes.' At least this one hadn't come out with a lot of old rope about wanting to be a nun or a missionary in darkest Africa. 'Have you a wish to come here, child?'

Cathy hesitated. It would be very difficult to tell lies while in the presence of Jesus Christ, who was bleeding heavily all over the wall behind the headmistress's head. 'No,' she said, 'I don't want to come here.'

Mother Ignatius was unused to such veracity. She wriggled in the high chair, set the small of her back in a more comfortable position. Comfort was not easy to achieve when one's feet dangled inches from the parquet. 'Why not, Caitlin?'

'Well.' Cathy searched for words, pretended to cough in order to create a bit of thinking time. 'I was happy in Ballinasloe, then Daddy died and the landlord threw us off the farm and we lived with Granda.' She paused, inhaled. 'Granda is not a nice man. He hit me sometimes. No-one likes him, even Mammy, and she's his little girl. So we came to Liverpool and I got in trouble falling asleep in the street while Cozzer – that's Jimmy – stole the turkey for the Nolans. The policeman said I hadn't gone to sleep, really. He said I'd fainted, but it was very like going to sleep. There are twelve Nolans and the daddy drinks.'

The mother of the convent was fascinated. This Caitlin child had few inhibitions and much to say for herself. Also, she was Irish. It was nice to hear a young Irish voice again. Some of the immigrant parents retained their accents, but the school was populated by Boltonians. 'Go on,' she urged.

'Well, Mammy went mad, Mother.'

'Did she?'

Cathy nodded gravely. 'She said I was going to turn out wild.'

'And will you?'

Cathy shook her head. 'I don't know. I'm not old enough to know what I'll be. But the Nolans are starving. Anyway, I don't play with Tildy and Cozzer any more when they're looking for things for the Nolans. So I don't need to be sent away from Scotland Road, do I?'

Mother Ignatius, head of the convent and Superior to all her sisters in Christ, wanted this girl. Caitlin O'Brien, given the right grounding, might become almost wholesome. She had a positive attitude to life, no fear of speaking up, and the qualities that constituted a good teacher or a writer or a member of some decent profession requiring brains. 'Will you not think about coming to Sacred Heart?'

Cathy thought about thinking about it. It did no harm to think, she supposed. 'I will think, Mother.'

Edith Spencer wanted the girl, too. Edith Spencer had been lavishing praise via the telephone for several days. 'Would you go outside now, Caitlin?' asked the nun. 'And ask Mrs Spencer and your mother to step in.'

Out in the corridor, Cathy sat on a polished bench that looked very like a church pew. Yards away, two nuns in sacking aprons scrubbed the marble floor. The pictures along this wide passageway were a lot more cheerful than the one in the headmistress's office. Our Lady was the favourite on one side. She was the Immaculate Conception standing on a cloud, then *Mater Perpetui Succurus* with the Baby Jesus. Further down, she was in black and white with *Respice Stellam Voca Maria*. St Bernard's name was written underneath, so he must have said those Latin words.

Behind Cathy, St Theresa of Lisieux kept company with St Francis of Assisi, who had no shoes on in spite of the fact that he had once been a wealthy man. Everybody loved him, especially nuns and priests, because he had stopped being rich and had given away his shoes on purpose.

Cathy wriggled and fidgeted. Why were they here? Mr Bell had been expected to come with them, but he had a bandage on his right hand, something to do with a quarrel with a wall and the wall coming best out of it. They were strange creatures, grown-ups. Always talking in riddles, seldom making sense. Whoever heard of a wall winning a fight?

Mammy was a long time in there. Cathy rose and

walked casually to the headmistress's door with a view to eavesdropping, but she quickly rid her soul of that intended sin when one of the scrubbing nuns clanged the handle of her bucket by way of warning. The little girl wandered off, poked her head into a library, then a class-room with V1 B over it. 'That's the lower sixth,' whispered a tiny voice.

Cathy swung round and faced one of the scrubbing nuns. 'Oh,' she said, wondering what was expected of her. She added, 'Sister,' to punctuate the pause.

'Will you be starting here soon?' asked the nun.

'No.'

'Ah well, God go with you.' The woman picked up her skirt and walked up a flight of stairs with brass edges. When she reached the summit, she knelt and began to clean the brass.

Cathy returned to her seat. There was something going on behind that door, and it was all connected with her. No-one seemed to care about what she wanted or where she preferred to live. Aunt Edith and Mammy had been weeks in there. Was Cathy going to be thrown aside into this place? Would Mammy allow a dwarf nun with an ugly face to take away her daughter?

She counted the stars round Our Lady's head, counted the number of tiles that made up one of the mosaics on the floor. There were four pieces of red glass, eighteen white, four yellow and four green in the window at the end of the corridor. The Sacred Heart on a plinth held out His hands, and a night light in a red glass container flickered below his bleeding feet. The whole place stank of disinfectant and wax polish.

The door opened and Mother Ignatius stepped into the corridor. Mammy and Aunt Edith were behind her. They shook the tiny woman's hand, then led Cathy out through a door marked STAFF ONLY.

Cathy had nothing to say, so she honoured the promise she had made to herself by running helter-skelter down Blackthorne Road until she reached a tram stop. Had a tram arrived with THE NORTH POLE announced as its next port of call, Cathy would have jumped aboard gladly.

Ten

Billy Costigan stood outside the hospital's main door and cried like a baby. He was glad that Diddy wasn't with him. If Diddy had been here, the whole hospital would have been blasted to kingdom come by her pain and temper. Fortunately, Billy had been alone when the doctor had finally told the full and very grim tale. Rape. The sound of that word even tasted bad. How could a sound have a taste? he asked himself. Maureen, poor little Maureen.

A hand gripped his arm, and Billy flinched. 'How is she?' asked a familiar voice.

Billy gazed through saline into the frigid eyes of Father Liam Bell. Diddy detested the arrogant young priest. If he were to be thoroughly honest with himself, Billy might have admitted his own strong dislike for this new addition to the parish. 'Hurt,' he replied eventually.

'Did she say anything?'

'What?' Billy shook himself inwardly, as if trying to waken his brain after a too long sleep. He could scarcely remember sleep. Nights had been spent comforting Diddy; days continued the same – lift the sacks, move the crates, knock off at dinner-time for a pie and a pint or to eat the carry-outs prepared by wives.

'Maureen,' said the priest, an edge to his determinedly patient tone, 'has she said anything about what happened?'

Maureen hadn't said anything about anything since being brought into hospital. The doctor blamed shock for her inability or unwillingness to communicate. 'No,' replied Billy, 'she's still too weak to talk.'

Father Bell tightened his hold on Billy's arm. 'Do they have any idea of who did it?'

Billy shook his head, wiped the moisture from his cheeks with the cuff of a sleeve. 'No, they've mentioned nothing. But I can tell you this much, Father Bell. The man who did this to our Maureen isn't right, he's not normal. He should be hanged, because he's killed her childhood. She's like . . .' He couldn't carry on, didn't want to tell this miserable-faced cleric that Maureen was looking so old for her years.

Maureen Costigan had never been a child, Liam told himself silently. She had flaunted herself for as long as he could remember, gallivanting up and down Scotland Road in her dancing frocks, singing for anyone who would throw her a penny. Lately, he had heard talk of her kissing boys in the jiggers, too.

'If I catch him, I'll strangle him,' continued Billy.

Liam inclined his head. 'Perhaps I'll visit her.'

Billy considered this for a fraction of a second. 'No,' he said firmly. 'Father Brennan's been going in and trying to talk her round.' Father Brennan was a damned sight more cheerful than this holy Joe. 'She needs the rest.'

Liam's stole was missing. He had a replacement, of course. He was grateful that the vestment had been a green one, because he had several in the more commonly used green. Had it been purple, he would have been in a spot of trouble, because he owned just one stole in that shade, and its absence would have been noticed, especially during Lent. 'The newspaper said someone tried to strangle Maureen.'

Billy nodded miserably. 'And more,' he mumbled.

'I beg your pardon?'

Billy decided that he could no more talk to this bloke about rape than fly to the moon on a yardbrush. 'I'd better get home. Diddy'll be expecting me.'

'Did they find a weapon?' asked Father Bell.

'Eh?'

'A weapon.' The priest spoke slowly, as if he were addressing a very young child. 'Did they find the ... the rope?'

'What rope?' Billy's eyes ached. The tears had stopped, but he was tired enough to fall asleep crying on a clothes line. Why was this man talking about ropes and washing lines?

'The rope she was strangled with.'

'Oh.' The older man scratched his head. 'My brain's not straight, Father.' He sighed. 'I don't know nothing about what they found and didn't find. They've searched that field a few times, though. Nothing's been said, not to me, anyway.' He walked off and left Liam Bell standing in the company of several unanswered questions.

The priest walked round a corner and stood in the shadow of the hospital. He had been so careful. He had been so careful that a piece of vital evidence was missing, was possibly in the hands of the police. What a damned fool he was! 'It wasn't you,' said a small inner voice, but Liam ignored it. The last time this sort of thing had happened was so long ago. He could not quite remember certain events, but he recalled this episode well enough. He had been doing his duty, no more and no less, he told himself. People had to learn and learning was a painful process.

He walked again, stopped, walked a little further. Should he go in? Perhaps if he went into the hospital, he might find out a few things. And that girl could recognize him, identify him ... No, she had seen nothing.

The trouble was, he could not remember everything. Like Billy Costigan, he seemed to be suffering from a degree of absent-mindedness. It was so difficult now that Anthony had left the area. Liam needed Anthony as a focus, as if Anthony provided the lenses for his eyes, the reason for his continuing existence. But Anthony had moved across the county. Of course, Liam had almost saved his twin from yet another mistake. Almost. The girl was alive. Shocked into silence, but still alive.

He sat on a form and stared at some miserable daffodils as they nodded their way towards death. She was potentially dangerous. Alive, she might even pose a threat. But he could not walk into the hospital and finish what he had started. And if he fled the area, the finger of suspicion would certainly point in his direction. The stole. Where was it? Why hadn't it been found? Or had it been found, and was he being watched right now, in the dusk? And was that where he had lost it? Had these past few days been a nightmare? Or had he really put a stop to Maureen's whoring? Yes, he had. Yes, he was the one who could be called guilty by those who misunderstood his vocation in life.

Made furtive by his fear, he glanced around, saw no-one lurking or staring at him. But the police were clever. He must remain on his guard and stay away from the hospital. Maureen Costigan's memory might return, might not return. 'She won't know you,' he whispered. 'She never saw your face.' But if he hung around here looking guilty, he could very well give himself away.

He forced himself to recall what he could. It had happened in the field – yes, he had dragged her there. She had struggled, had kicked him on the shin. Not a word had been spoken. Or had it? Oh, he wished his powers of recollection would buck up. The full punishment. That was right – he had disciplined her thoroughly, had attempted to make her sorry for all those sins of the flesh. Had she died, she might have repented during those final moments, could have entered purgatory rather than hell. He had hurt her. Retribution for sins of the flesh had to be extremely agonizing.

His mind wandered again to other women whose lives had been altered by him. They had been allowed to live, of course, because those street girls had not been connected to the Bell family, had posed no threat. But the other one ... the last one ... yes, she had died.

A man had hanged for that. But he had deserved to hang, because he had been found drunk. So Liam had taught the world two lessons. Two birds with one stone? Drunkenness and sacrilege had been justly condemned on that occasion. The woman had left the Church. Anthony could not be allowed to marry a non-believer. In fact, a lapsed Catholic was worse than a Protestant. Some of the latter were simply ignorant, uninformed. But the one called Valerie had thrown away the only true faith. He had promised himself that he would not think about Valerie any more. God had directed him, had spoken to him, had guided his hand. He needed no priest to ask on his behalf for God's mercy, because the disposal of Valerie had been a part of God's plan.

Maureen Costigan was not a suitable candidate for the Bell family. She had not seen his face, he told himself firmly for the umpteenth time. As far as he could recall, he had not seen hers, either, not on that occasion. He had worked from behind. He had been careful, had made sure that he had been almost invisible. For much of the time, she had been barely conscious, so what could she say? Nothing. No, no, she would never accuse him. But all the same, he worried about that stole.

*

Billy stumbled through the doorway of Bell's Pledges. Charlie, who was in charge for the moment, saw the pain in his father's features. It was etched deeply, as if ingrained by a chisel into stone. 'Dad?'

'Where's Sam?' asked Billy.

'Kitchen.'

Billy crossed the shop, passed the bottom of the stairs and entered Sam Bell's kitchen. Old Theresa Bell was huddled over the fire, while Sam sat at the table writing in a ledger. 'Billy? Are you all right?' asked the pawnbroker.

Billy dropped into the chair opposite Sam's. 'I can't tell Diddy,' he said. 'I can't, Sam.'

Sam laid down his pen. 'Tell her what?'

Billy flicked a meaningful glance in Theresa's direction.

'It won't go no further than these walls,' promised the old lady. 'If I hear owt, I'll say nowt,' she added with her usual Lancashire bluntness. It was a tragedy. That young girl hurt for no reason. 'I've prayed for her,' she told Billy.

The large man swallowed. 'Sam, she'd been interfered with.'

It was difficult to know how to reply to this statement. 'I'm sorry. Is that what you can't tell Diddy?'

Billy nodded.

'Wants bloody castrating,' spat Theresa. 'Men like that should be sent somewhere for a seeing to.' She rose stiffly, walked to the table and placed a claw-like hand on Billy Costigan's shoulder. 'Lad, I'll pray for you and yours again tonight.' She left the room and made her slow and painful way upstairs.

Sam rose and reached for a bottle, took two glasses from a cabinet next to the range. He poured a moderate amount of whisky for himself, a double for Billy. 'Here, drink that.'

Billy swallowed the lot, allowed Sam to provide a refill,

emptied the glass again. 'Don't give me any more, Sam,' he said. 'I need my thinking brain tonight, and it's been on strike all week. I can't tell her. I'll have to let our Maureen do it when she's ready. The policeman and the doctor promised to say nothing to Diddy. It's already made her ill. She's not sleeping, not eating, not looking after herself. Her nerves are shot to bits.'

Sam nodded. The Scotland Road folk often told him their troubles, because they knew he could keep a secret. 'Bridie would help her if she was here.'

Billy agreed. 'Don't bring her home, Sam. Let her have a bit of a holiday with her horses. Rosa McKinnell was saying last week how good Bridie is with horses.'

The shopkeeper sat and stared at Billy Costigan. He had known Billy from birth, had watched him grow up, marry, become a father five times. He was changing. Since marrying Bridie, Sam Bell had developed one or two chinks in his armour. Bridie had made the house into a home, had got Muth out of bed, had contributed to the running of the shop. And he missed her. 'She's a good soul, is Bridie,' he told Billy. 'If she knew about this, she'd be back to help, I know she would.'

'There is no help, lad.'

'Never say that,' urged Sam.

'I don't know what to say, don't know what to think,' answered Billy.

'Be positive. Try to be hopeful.'

Billy's hands were clasped so tightly that the whiteness of his knuckles showed through work-stained skin. 'I'll kill him, Sam.'

Sam nodded.

'I'll geld him, then I'll cut his throat. If I can bloody well find the swine. Police are getting nowhere with it. They've spent days with a fine-tooth comb searching the playing field. And he's still out there walking about a free man, whoever he is. That bastard's laughing up his sleeve at us. Who'll be next, eh?'

Sam could provide no reply.

'They say Maureen can come out of hospital in a couple of days. She wasn't as badly hurt as they thought, thank God. The bit of her throat that got damaged is all right now. Course, they had to stitch her face and one of her legs. She's got bruises all over her body and a big purple mark on her neck. And she won't talk. But they'll not keep her much longer.' The massive hands lifted themselves then crashed loudly onto the table. 'I'm so damned useless,' Billy cried.

'Stop it,' pleaded Sam. 'You've got to be strong for the rest of your family.'

The docker's head moved slowly from side to side. 'I know I'm built like a brick lavvy shed, but Diddy's been the strength in our house. I just earn the money when I can, only it's her what does all the working out and paying bills and tending the kids. Her strength's on the inside. Mine's just in my body. But if Diddy found out that our Maureen's been raped, she'd crack. She's not far off breaking up as it is. Without Diddy in one piece, our family would fall apart, Sam.'

Sam thought about this for a moment or two. 'They both need a rest,' he said finally. 'I'll send Diddy and Maureen to our Edith's. Maureen shouldn't be round here. A change of scenery would do her and Diddy a world of good.' He pondered again for several moments. 'They were supposed to go just for the fortnight, but they can stop on a bit longer, Bridie and the girls. Another week or two off school won't do Cathy any harm.'

Billy blinked several times, looked for all the world like a man waking from a long sleep. 'Hasn't Mrs Spencer got enough on her plate?' he asked. 'She's already got Bridie and the girls, then your Anthony's there, too—'

'Anthony's in a cottage,' interrupted Sam. 'And Edith's got a heart of gold and enough bedrooms for a battalion. Leave it to me, Billy. Go home and get your head down.'

Billy Costigan rose from his seat and stared for a while at the pawnbroker who employed two of his children. Nicky, who ran the stall, worked for other dealers, too, but Sam was the mainstay. Then Charlie was nearing full time here, and the lad enjoyed his work. Billy reckoned he had known Sam Bell for most of his life. Yet he hadn't known him.

'Go home now,' said Sam.

The pawnbroker had pretended to listen in the past, had nodded and grunted. But now, he was listening, answering, thinking about solutions. 'Thanks, Sam,' he said. Then Billy Costigan went home to nurse his wife and his terrible secret.

Maureen lay flat, hands on top of the white coverlet, her hair spread out against a pillowcase of cheap, coarse cotton. She had been here for a long time. Sometimes, it felt as if she had been here for ever. But she hadn't. She lived in Dryden Street with Mam, Dad, Charlie, Nicky, Tildy-Anne and Jimmy. They had scouse twice a week, tripe and onions on Thursdays, boiled eggs and toast on a Saturday morning and, like most other families on Scotland Road, they had salt fish cooked by Dad every Sunday morning.

Maureen didn't like salt fish. It was grey and sad-looking, sludgy and full of bones. There was a pigeon on the window-sill. She turned her head and looked at it, wondered if it might be one of Dad's come to visit her. The pigeons were kept in the back yard next to the scullery. Dad was very gentle with his feathered pets, very tender with his children, too. He was a great big man, well over six feet in height, but he had a delicate touch.

Mam. Mam kept crying. When she visited the hospital, she was always talking about needing the toilet or going to see the doctor. Really, she was going outside to cry in the corridor. It wasn't like Mam to cry so much. Mam was crying because of what had happened, because of ... No, no, Maureen told herself. Don't try to remember, don't think about it. You never saw his face. They keep on asking you the same questions, but you didn't get a look at him. He came from behind ...

There was a big mark on the ceiling of this hospital room, as if something or other had spilled and filtered through from upstairs. She was in a small ward of her own. People came in with food and drink and medicines, but she was alone most of the time.

Fairy Mary had visited her star pupil. She had gone on and on about Maureen getting better and being picked up by a talent scout. 'We'll see you on the professional stage yet,' Mary Turner had chirruped. 'This won't make any difference, so don't worry, because the scars will go.' Maureen could not quite manage to worry about the scars.

The man had not just strangled her and left her for dead – he had also left his marks. There were the blemishes on the surface of her body, and there were those inside. Apart from being hit and strangled, she hadn't been aware of or conscious during anything else. But she was sure that he had done the really bad thing, the thing she and the rest of the girls had been warned about. 'No man will want you for a wife unless you keep yourself to yourself,' Sister Agnes had said. Maureen had had no choice.

The door swung inward and Father Brennan rolled in. He was a fat man with a jolly face, yet she didn't want to look at him. He said some Latin and held out the host, but Maureen tightened her lips. She didn't want Holy Communion. She just needed to be left alone. 'Open your mouth, child,' said Michael Brennan. On no less than three occasions, Maureen had refused.

'Maureen?'

She looked straight at him, kept her mouth firmly closed.

'Why, Maureen?'

She didn't know.

Father Brennan sighed. 'Child, let me help you. I'll do anything, anything at all if you will only let me. Can't you talk to me? Can't you allow me to comfort you?'

Maureen simply stared at him until he went away.

The day wore on. She slept occasionally, was glad when she woke, glad when the dreams stopped. Her throat remained sore, but she was able to swallow soup and rice pudding. She had heard them discussing her voice box, had listened while they had gathered to wonder aloud about damage to vocal chords. So, once safely isolated again, she had tested her power of speech, had found it to be rusty, but competent.

The lights went on outside in the corridor. She had nothing to say, and that was why she remained silent. After a while, they might get fed up and go away with their questions. Why should she talk about it? Why should she let herself be forced into encouraging the recurring nightmares?

A nurse came in. The nurses always wore bright smiles and over-white aprons that hurt the eyes and crackled with starch. The woman switched on the light and gave her patient a cup of cocoa. Once propped up on pillows, Maureen sipped at the drink and avoided eye contact with her minder. They were all waiting and watching. If she uttered one single syllable, the police would swarm like flies in summer all round her bed.

'Would you like a biscuit?'

Maureen made no reply, did not nod or shake her head. Let them all think she was struck dumb, then she might get some peace.

'A hot water bottle? Shall I fill your decanter for you?'

The patient closed her eyes.

'Your mam been in yet?'

They were so annoying, so persistent. Never an hour went by without them trying to trick her into some kind of response. But she was going home soon. Mam had told her that she could come home and rest in the kitchen on Grandma's old sofa. Maureen remembered Grandma, just about. After her death, Mam had taken over the rent book. Mam had lived in Dryden Street for ever.

When the nurse had left, Maureen closed her eyes and let out a sigh of relief. Another day accomplished without being forced to talk. Talking would have been useless, because she had nothing to say. Where was she? Ah yes, she had been thinking about home and how Mam had always lived there. It was a drab house. No matter what colour the walls got painted, they inevitably attained a brownish tinge after a while. Dad was always on the roof sticking felt over leaks. The tap in the back kitchen was stiff, sometimes needed a quick belt with the hammer.

Maureen Costigan had envisaged something better for herself. The London stage, perhaps, or the wireless. She had a nice singing voice. Well, she used to have a good voice. Until ... Who was he? she wondered. And where was he?

All her life, Maureen had been proud of her looks and her abilities as an entertainer. But it was as if her attacker had removed all ambition and all interest in herself. She didn't want to live round here any more, only she no longer thought about moving towards something. Maureen felt more like running away, just running and running until she got as far as possible from ... from him.

A tear made its slow way down her cheek. At just under fourteen years of age, Maureen was certain that her life was over.

Michael Brennan smothered his chips in vinegar. He was partial to a nice bit of cod with chips and sloppy peas. Across the table sat the bane of his life, one Liam Bell. Liam was staring at him, was tacitly condemning the older man's greed. On Liam's plate, there lingered a sliver of steamed yellow fish, two boiled potatoes and a sprig of cauliflower. 'You don't like your food much, do you, Liam?'

Liam prodded the fish with his fork. 'I don't believe in overindulging,' he replied pointedly.

The parish priest lay down his cutlery. 'Liam, do you have to be so hard on everyone – yourself included? It's like living with a saint. Saints are all very well in their place, but I imagine that many of them would be slightly less than interesting company. Can't you let the halo slip just a little?'

Liam chewed on a bit of cauliflower, took a sip of water. 'It's just how I'm made,' he muttered. 'I'm sorry if I cause offence.'

'Well.' Michael pushed away his plate. He would warm the food later, though it would not taste the same, he thought sadly. His housekeeper was a good cook who enjoyed the pleasure her employer got from the meals she made. Liam Bell had upset her, too. 'You know, I'm packed to bursting at confession. I don't know what sort of penances you've been giving, but it's my door they're all coming to.' It seemed that no-one liked the young priest. 'Even your father comes to me.'

'So he should,' said Liam quickly. 'I told him to go to you.'

Father Brennan sighed. This man was so correct, so completely sure of himself. 'Have you no faults, Liam?'

'Of course I have.'

'And to whom do you confess your sins?'

'I go into the city, just as you do. After all, we can't be living in one another's pockets, can we?'

Michael Brennan fought a familiar shiver that made its way like a cold finger all the way along his spine. Occasionally, in a certain light, he caught an expression in Father Bell's features, a look that seemed akin to madness. It was rather like being in the company of a reptile, some kind of large snake with staring eyes and no ability to blink. He gazed at his assistant, watched the man eating slowly, carefully, as if he counted the numbers of chews before allowing food to enter the sanctum of his stomach. For more than a minute, Michael kept watch. His companion blinked just twice in that time.

'Are you going to leave that?' asked Liam.

Father Brennan picked up his knife and fork, attacked the tepid meal. In all his days as a priest, he had never encountered another ordained man as soulless as this one. Liam Bell was strange, even weird.

'Did you see Maureen Costigan?' asked Liam, his tone rather lighter than normal.

'I did.' The coldness had returned to Michael's spine.

'How is she?'

'Silent.'

Liam cut a small potato into four pieces. 'Did she have Holy Communion?'

'No.' It was like watching a surgeon at work, thought the parish priest.

'I wonder why.'

Father Michael Brennan dropped his fork. It crashed against his plate and bounced to the floor. He noticed that his companion did not react to the sound, that he simply carried on eating. Liam Bell was in some world of his own, was living in a place where few things touched or worried him. Michael picked up a dessert fork and used it to finish his meal.

'Do you know why she refuses Holy Communion?' asked Liam.

'No.' The older man's appetite suddenly deserted him. 'I've no idea at all,' he said. 'Have you?'

Liam ran his eyes over the face of his senior. 'Of course not,' he replied. 'How should I know what goes on in her head?'

'Exactly,' said Michael Brennan, rising to his feet. 'If you will excuse me, Father Bell, I feel the need to pray.'

Diddy Costigan put the last few items into a suitcase loaned by Sam Bell. Edith Spencer would be here shortly. In other circumstances, Diddy might have felt rather uncomfortable at the thought of travelling in the company of Edith, but such minor concerns had been relegated to a rear compartment of her mind. Her sole aim now was to do anything she could for Maureen.

Nicky passed a blouse to her mother. 'Don't worry. I'll look after the others. It'll do you good to get away.'

Diddy paused. Maureen had never been anywhere. None of the Costigan children had travelled further than New Brighton on the ferry for a day trip. 'Monica, you're a good girl.'

Nicky was thinking about their Maureen and she felt a bit guilty. She'd never had much time for their Maureen, because their Maureen had spent years floating about in a cloud of self-admiration. But now, Maureen had given up. She'd given up talking, singing, dancing, hoping and looking in mirrors.

'Don't forget to make your dad's carry-outs.'

'I won't.'

'And stay in when it starts getting dark. Or make sure Graham's with you.' Scotland Road had always been such a safe place. The Scotties looked after their own, loved their neighbours in the truest sense. There were some on-going differences, of course, but people round here would back a hated neighbour if that neighbour had any trouble from 'outside'. And it had come to this. Gone were the days when a daughter could nip out late on a Friday night for ribs and cabbage. 'God, this is terrible.' Diddy sank into a chair. 'We'll all be looking over our shoulders.'

Nicky squatted down next to Mam. 'It was a one-off. It was a stranger, Mam. I bet he's moved on now.'

'How do we know that?' asked Diddy helplessly.

'Because it's never happened before.'

Diddy patted the hand of this sensible girl. It had happened before. Val had died, though. And a man had hanged for the murder. She shivered. 'What's the world coming to, girl?'

'I don't know, Mam.' That was the truth. Nicky and her siblings had invariably felt protected from all harm since infancy. There was a permanence about Scotland Road, a feeling that the place would be here for ever. People pulled together and helped each other out, minded children for sick mothers, made sure a poor family had a bite to eat. One bad person had shaken everyone's faith in an area where most folk were decent.

'Poor Maureen,' moaned Diddy for the hundredth time.

'You can't put it right, Mam,' said Nicky gently. 'You can't stop it happening, because it's already happened.'

Nicky was wise. Diddy touched her daughter's cheek.

She was plain, yet still beautiful. 'You're a good girl,' she said again.

The uncomely young woman bared her teeth in as near a grin as she could manage. 'I've got a good mam, that's why.'

Diddy drew her daughter close and let the tears flow anew. She didn't want to be weeping when she arrived at the hospital to pick up their Maureen. She didn't want to be crying in Edith Spencer's posh car. Nicky had been Diddy's backbone during the past few days. 'I'm sorry,' she blubbered. 'You're too young for all this, Monica.'

'No I'm not,' replied Nicky truthfully. After what had happened to her sister, Monica felt as old as the blue-misted hills of Wales.

Maureen Costigan got out of the hard bed and put on the clothes Mam had brought in yesterday. She wasn't going home. She was going to some sort of a farm outside Bolton to stay with Mam, Mr Bell's cousin and cousin-in-law, Bridie Bell and the two little girls. Anthony Bell was there, too, living in a cottage.

Mam had chattered away about Bolton, had used the special voice that emerged only when she was upset and pretending to be all right.

Maureen stepped into her shoes. It was funny, but she wasn't looking forward to seeing Anthony Bell. She didn't seem to have feelings any more, didn't want to laugh or even cry properly, couldn't be bothered with any of it.

At the small mirror, she combed the black hair, saw how bruised her face was, caught sight of a small scar, didn't bother to study herself closely. Soon, she would be able to talk – if she wanted to. At least she would be away from the Rose Hill mob, the policemen who had gone on and on about how much they wanted to catch the man, about how Maureen was the only one who could help. 'What if he does it to somebody else?' they had asked repeatedly. Maureen couldn't manage to care, not yet.

She sat on the one chair and waited for Mam and Mrs Spencer. It occurred to her that this room had been home since the attack. She had been secure here, had been able to lie still and allow life to continue without her help or hindrance. Now, she must go out and join the race again. A small finger of fear touched her heart, the first emotion to visit her spiritless core. But it was a mere shadow, and it passed in an instant.

Limekiln Lane. The recreation ground. A hand across her mouth. Dragged down. Something round her neck. Narrower than a scarf. Wider than rope.

Her heart maintained its steady rhythm. She would allow in no panic.

It was over, it had happened, nothing to do now. His full weight on her back, a big man kneeling astride, pulling hard, no breath.

She studied her fingernails. Her hands were pale.

A smell, just a smell, thick and sweet, where? No talking yet. A smell, forgotten, hidden away in her head.

The door opened. 'Hello, love.'

It was Mam. Mam was big and strong and she had always been there. But even Mam had cried, so Mam had no answers, either. Because there were no answers. It was no use.

Maureen stood up while Mam gathered up a spare nightie, a hairbrush, a comb. They walked out of the sanctuary and into the body of the hospital. People moved about the corridor and made noise. Maureen Costigan carried on putting one foot in front of the other, because there was no choice. Time and tide waited for no man.

That had been one of Grandma's sayings. The future was there, so she simply walked towards it while her heart continued its perfect and undisturbed beating.

Diddy Costigan was seeing the world for the first time, would now be able to tell her friends at the bagwash that she had been to Lowton, Leigh, Atherton and Bolton. Bolton was grander than she had expected. Everyone thought of the mill towns as shabby, dirty and dull, but this, the largest town in England, seemed to be thriving in spite of recession.

She took in the civic buildings which formed a perfect, crescent-shaped backdrop for the Town Hall and its magnificent clock, decided that there must be money in cotton if these structures had risen out of spinning the stuff. Maureen wasn't taking in much. 'Look,' said Diddy, 'a Bolton tram. I wonder where it's going. Have you seen all the chimneys? Thousands of them. This is where they make the quilts we have on our beds.'

Maureen stared through the window. She had never ridden in a car before. They had driven through some towns, past fields, over and under bridges. Mam and Edith had tried to keep up some sort of conversation, but Maureen hadn't spoken yet. So she would speak now and get it over and done with. 'I don't want any questions,' she said.

Diddy, who was sharing the rear seat with her daughter, simply sat and allowed her mouth to hang open.

'What did you say?' asked the driver.

'No questions,' repeated Maureen in answer to what was obviously a question. 'About what happened to me, I mean.'

Edith understood. This poor young thing was plainly in shock, could take months to get back to somewhere approaching normal. 'There'll be no inquisitions from me or from Richard,' she promised.

Maureen turned to her mother. 'Sorry, Mam,' she said softly.

'What for?' Diddy asked eventually.

'For getting into trouble. For not talking in the hospital. Only I didn't know what to tell them. If I'd opened my mouth, they would have gone on about how tall was he, how strong, was I sure I hadn't caught a glimpse.' She swallowed painfully. 'It would've been like going through it all over again, Mam. And I don't want to. Don't let them make me.'

'I won't. I'll keep you safe, love.'

Maureen closed her eyes and leaned back. Coming away was probably the right thing, because nothing would be expected of her. Perhaps she might even start to feel better or worse or different. Feeling anything at all might be a step in the right direction. If she could just care about how she looked, what she did, where she went. Was worrying about not caring a feeling, she wondered? And was she really worrying, or was she merely thinking?

She remembered being a tree in a show about ten years earlier. As a new pupil of the dancing school, Maureen had simply stood in her tap shoes and tree costume, her arms outstretched, fingers dropping paper leaves onto the stage. She was a tree again. If the wind blew, she might bend, but exterior forces would have to be in charge. Edith Spencer was wind and weather at the moment. Edith Spencer was dictating pace and direction. Like a three-year-old sapling, Maureen must stand still and let things happen.

'You all right, queen?' asked Diddy.

'Yes,' replied Maureen. She wasn't, but she didn't want to go into any details.

*

Anthony Bell stopped outside the village post office. He had acquired a rather ramshackle bike, and he leaned this untidy object against the wall of the shop. There wasn't much doing today. An improbably blue sky was dotted with cotton wool clouds kept mobile by an intermittent breeze. A dog barked, the till drawer inside the shop clattered into the closed position, Bridie Bell emerged with her shopping basket.

She stopped in her tracks. Anthony could tell by her demeanour that she had been rendered uncomfortable by his unexpected presence. 'Good morning,' he achieved after a small and rather unwieldy silence, 'how's Cathy?'

'Both the girls are fine, thank you.'

He thrust his hands into his pockets. 'Damn,' he muttered, 'I've forgotten my money. I'll walk back with you.'

Bridie fiddled in her purse. 'I can lend you two shillings,' she offered.

'Forgotten the list as well.' He indicated the basket attached to the bike's handlebars. 'Shopping on wheels from now on.' She wasn't looking at him, not fully. She knew. Women were like that, he supposed. They were capable of receiving messages loudly and clearly when not a single word had been uttered. Perhaps they had hidden antennae or a sixth sense.

Bridie tried to smile, but the effort gave birth to no more than a nervous flicker. 'Diddy's coming today,' she said. 'We found out just last night that Maureen was attacked. So she's coming with Diddy to stay at Cherry Hinton.'

Anthony froze. 'Attacked?' The pitch of his voice had risen. 'When? Where?'

Bridie sighed. 'We don't know the full tale yet, but the poor girl was in hospital for days. Some man came up behind her and tried to strangle her. She was found by a tramp – you know the fellow – he pushes an old cart round, has a one-man band and a puppet show.'

Flash Flanagan, thought Anthony. Flash had been entertaining the children of Scotland Road for about half a century. 'Does Maureen know who did this to her?'

'No.'

Anthony swallowed his instinctive terror. No, no, it could not possibly be Liam, not this time. Maureen was only a child. Light dawned slowly at the front of his mind. Maureen. Maureen Costigan had been making eyes at Anthony. Liam allowed no-one to do that. But Anthony had left the area, was well out of Maureen's reach. Had Liam felt that his twin had moved away to wait for Maureen to come of age? Was it that blind fury again, the special rage that had driven Liam for years to break bones, to throw his brother in the river, to … to kill Val? 'Jesus,' he whispered.

'Anthony?'

His legs refused to move. The upper part of his body was trying to push the bike, yet his feet remained planted firmly on paving stones.

'Anthony?' she repeated.

'I … er … I'll be all right in a minute.' He sat down on the ground after deciding that sitting would be better than falling. The bike went with him, of course, and he lay that on the flags. Bridie threw aside her basket and crouched next to him. 'Are you ill?' It was important that he should not be ill again. Bronchitis could be the very devil to shift, could lead to a permanent weakness in the chest, even to bouts of pneumonia. The idea of him being ill again panicked her beyond reason. 'Shall I get help?' she asked.

'No. There is no help.'

Fear stabbed into her heart. Did he have some degenerative illness that took away the power of movement from time to time? Was he going to lose the ability to walk? 'Tell me what's wrong,' she pleaded.

'I can't.'

'Why not?'

He shook his head. 'Go away from me, Bridie. People who associate with me always meet trouble. Val died, you know. Now, poor Maureen Costigan, who had a little schoolgirl passion for me, has been half-murdered too.'

'Nonsense.'

'You must listen to me,' he persisted. 'You know I'm fond of you, too fond, perhaps.' He cursed himself inwardly. Those words should never have been spoken. If such a declaration were to meet the light of day, it should be made in better circumstances. Better circumstances meant not sitting in the street like a fool and not being the son of the loved one's husband. 'He'll find out, Bridie. He always does. He'll know how I feel about you.'

She rose and stared down at him. This was Samuel Bell's son, and she loved being near him, hated being near him, felt warm, excited, terrified, sick. 'Sam would not hurt you or me,' she said, mistaking his meaning, 'and we can't be carrying on fond of each other anyway.'

He lifted his head so quickly that a red-hot crick of pain shot up his neck. She cared. Anthony could see it in her expression, could read it in her eyes. 'I am not talking about my father finding out,' he said quietly. 'My brother is the dangerous one. Liam is the murderer.'

'What?' Bridie backed away and leaned against the post office wall. 'What did you say?'

'You heard me. I don't need to repeat it. He killed Val and he tried to kill Maureen. No-one would ever believe that, not without proof. You must say nothing. I don't need proof. Yes, he is a priest and yes, I may sound crazy, but he and I are identical twins. I've known him for almost

262

thirty years. We were born at the same time and we grew up together. The fact that I survived to adulthood is nothing short of miraculous. Liam is ill. The illness makes him evil.'

Bridie could not lay her tongue across one sensible word. Yet she knew that she believed what this man said. He was kind, clever and good. He was also humorous, but no sign of fun appeared in his face today. The level-headed Anthony Bell was not the sort to make unfounded allegations.

'I'm sorry, Bridie.'

'Pardon?'

'Sorry. If I've frightened you.'

'I'm tougher than I look.' She wanted to question him, to try to reassure him, but they were in a public place. Anyway, she needed time to absorb the concept of an ordained killer.

He struggled to his feet. She reached out to help him, withdrew her hands as soon as he was upright. 'Did I burn your fingers?' he asked.

Bridie hid her face by turning to retrieve her shopping. This was terrible. The shock in her fingers seemed to have transmitted itself to him. He had felt her pleasure.

'Bridie?'

She swung to face him. 'Come on, let's get you home,' she said in the no-nonsense voice that was usually reserved for Cathy and Shauna. 'We can't have you falling down all over the place, can we? Wheel the bicycle – it will support you.' Liam was an unpleasant fellow. Was it possible that a man of God could be a cold-blooded murderer? And what about confession? Priests went to confession just like everybody else. Was Liam receiving absolution while nursing a mortal sin? Because absolution would surely be refused in the case of a murderer. And if he did not confess the crime, Liam would be damned for ever more. All these thoughts spun around in her head while she waited for Anthony to right his bicycle.

They walked in silence up the paved street and along the dirt track that led to Anthony's cottage. At the gate, they stopped and looked at each other. 'Are you going to be all right?' she asked. Could he hear her heart pounding?

'Yes, thank you.'

She placed the basket on the garden wall. 'Will I come in and make you a cup of tea?'

He smiled sadly. 'That could be extremely dangerous, you know.'

Bridie did know.

He left his bike outside the door and went into the cottage. He would not look back. What had happened to Val and Maureen must never happen to Bridie.

In the kitchen, Anthony pulled a shopping list from one pocket and a ten shilling note from the other. He had forgotten nothing on his recent shopping expedition. With the possible exception of his principles. He should not have told her about Liam. He should not have dragged Bridie into such murky waters.

It was the shock, he supposed. Bridie must say nothing to Maureen or to Diddy. But she wouldn't. He had known Bridie for just a few months, yet he realized that she would never hurt anyone, not intentionally.

Which was more than could be said for Father Liam Bell.

Eleven

Anthony Bell jumped off the tram before it had stopped moving. He leapt onto the pavement and immediately looked around for Flash Flanagan. Flash Flanagan was one of those people who were always there. Like birth, death and dirty washing, Flash was one of life's undeniable inevitabilities. But the old man, his puppets and his tambourine were neither visible nor audible today.

Anthony glanced across the shop fronts, took in the Maypole Dairy, Razor Sharpe's barber shop, the premises that housed a mender of false teeth who was known as Gob Stopper. He walked along, peered into Daly's tobacconist's, Dolly Hanson's, the pork butcher's. There was no sign of Flash, his cart or his gaudy marionettes.

Alice Makin, a mountainous woman who worked on Paddy's Market, was being 'escorted' from the Throstle's Nest by two unfortunate policemen. She had one in a stranglehold under a massive arm, while the second was enduring heavy blows delivered by the man-sized boots she wore.

'Mr Bell?'

Anthony swivelled, saw Nicky Costigan. 'Monica. How are you?'

'It's Nicky, sir.'

'Sorry. Tell me, Nicky, have you seen anything of Flash Flanagan?'

'I haven't,' she replied. 'Not for a week or two. You live near the Spencers now, don't you? So have you seen Mam and our Maureen?'

'Not yet,' he said. 'I'll visit them tomorrow, perhaps. I'm only here for the day.'

'Look out,' warned Nicky, her tone heightened by a mixture of amusement and anxiety, 'here comes trouble – watch you don't get knocked over.'

Alice Makin had taken both policemen into firm custody, was holding one under each arm. 'Mind yer backs,' she screamed as she approached Nicky and Anthony. Her face was scarlet and running with sweat as she fought to hang on to the struggling prey.

Anthony and Nicky stepped back. 'Alice?' called Anthony.

'What? Can't you see I'm busy?' A half-strangled policeman peered at Anthony. 'Get some help,' he managed. He had lost his helmet. There would be trouble at Rose Hill Police Station when the sergeant found out about that. The missing headgear would be adorning some chimney pot by this evening, another trophy acquired by the youth of Scotland Road.

'Have you caught sight of Flash lately?' Anthony asked the woman. He knew better than to tangle with Alice. As well as running her stall on the market, Alice Makin had a long-established moneylending business. Which must have been doing well, thought Anthony, as Alice was usually arrested on Saturday nights only. Now, she seemed to have the cash to be drunk and disorderly on a weekday lunch-time.

'He's been moved on by these buggers.' She nodded at her hostages. 'Other side of Liverpool by now, poor lad. Course, with him finding your Maureen,' she gave Nicky a smile that was meant to be sympathetic, 'they questioned him for bloody days before kicking him off the

266

patch. He's a nuisance, see. Like me, old Flash is nothing but a pest. The police don't want him frightening everybody with the tale of how he found your sister.' She nodded at Nicky. 'All the best, queen. Tell Maureen we're all thinking about her.'

Alice continued onward to deliver her prizes to Rose Hill, after which mission she would be charged and allowed to dry out in the bridewell. She knew the form well enough. Rose Hill had been her resting place on Saturday nights for as long as she could remember.

Nicky touched Anthony's arm. 'When you see our Maureen, give her my love.' She blushed, because she and Maureen had never been close enough to talk about loving one another. 'She is my sister, so I do worry about her. And I wish they'd find who did it. Everybody's walking about in twos and threes just in case he tries it again. We're not used to it, Mr Bell. We've always been safe round here.'

Anthony sighed, wished he could give Nicky some reassurance. He would not attempt to search the whole city for Flash – Flash probably knew little, anyway. The tramp had discovered Maureen, but he had obviously been interviewed by the police. So roaming the streets of Liverpool on the off-chance that Flash might divulge something new could be a waste of time.

Anthony had nowhere to stay, because his house in Dryden Street had new tenants. His father would not be overjoyed to see him, so he had no intention of going to the shop. If Dad found out about Anthony's true reason for visiting Liverpool, there would be trouble.

He made his farewell to Nicky, then turned and strode towards the church of St Aloysius Gonzaga. With only a few hours to spare before catching his train, Anthony would have to do what he could within that time. Gone was the slight doubt that had held him back in the past.

Gone was the fear of being considered foolish. He had to talk, had to speak up. Nevertheless, he experienced a degree of nervousness as he approached the priests' house.

Father Brennan opened the presbytery door. His housekeeper had just left to go shopping, and Father Bell was out visiting parishioners. 'Come in, Anthony. It's good to see you. Are you thinking of rejoining the fold here at St Aloysius? Because we'd be very glad to have you back with us.'

'No, Father Brennan.'

'Michael. Call me Michael.'

They walked into the living room and placed themselves in chairs at the dining table. 'Will you have a cup of tea?' asked the priest.

Anthony declined the offer. 'Where's my brother?'

'Out on parish work. Did you want to see him?'

'I never want to see him again, so it's as well he's not here. You are the one I need to talk to.'

Michael Brennan sat and waited. He could see the tension in this young man's expression, had learned long ago to simply sit and wait when a parishioner wanted to get a load off his chest. Anthony Bell would speak when he was good and ready, not before.

'Do you remember separating me and Liam when we were caught fighting outside the church?'

The priest nodded. 'Yes, I was new to the parish. It was quite a shock to find you and your brother brawling like that. That was the last thing I might have expected.'

'I should have killed him then. I'm sure if I had killed him, God would have absolved me. Because Liam's death would have meant the safety of others.' Where should he begin? At the beginning, in the middle, or with Maureen's unfortunate experience?

Michael shifted uncomfortably.

'I don't know what you can do, what anybody can do. I suppose I'm just asking you to watch him.' Anthony kept his voice low. There was no point in getting worked up, because he wanted this man to believe him. 'What you think of me isn't important. If you judge me to be hysterical, then I shall have to accept that. But I am sure that Liam killed my fiancée. I am also certain that he was the one who attacked Maureen Costigan.'

Michael Brennan swallowed audibly. His flesh crawled slightly and he tugged at the dog collar. He knew full well that there was something unusual about Liam. He was also aware that the twins had been at loggerheads since learning to walk and talk. Their father and Diddy Costigan had told him about the boys' mutual dislike. 'Anthony, this is a very serious allegation. Shouldn't you talk to the police instead of discussing the matter with me?'

'I did tell the police,' replied Anthony. 'Over five years ago. And they sent me away with a flea in my ear. Liam was aware that I had spoken to the police. He is so cocksure of his own superiority that he feels the law will never touch him. Liam is above and beyond the law.'

'Not God's law.'

Anthony folded his arms. 'Liam is God's law. Liam is on a special mission. He is here to punish all who indulge in sins of the flesh. He started his campaign in the city centre a very long time ago.'

It was difficult to talk to a priest about sex, but it had to be done. 'To be intimate with a girl, Liam needed to be angry. Some of those prostitutes remembered their attacker praying over them afterwards. Of course, no-one was particularly interested in what had happened to mere street women.' He paused, drew breath. 'To be blunt, my brother is crackers. Until some doctor discovers that fact, we're all helpless and useless.'

Michael cleared his throat. 'Did Maureen Costigan mention prayers?'

'I haven't seen her yet,' said Anthony. 'Apparently, she is unwilling to talk at the moment.'

'And she's refusing Holy Communion,' remarked Michael. 'But Anthony, surely your brother could not do anything so brutal. He would have to be evil ... or very, very sick.'

'Exactly.' Anthony suddenly felt more than tired. 'He's dangerous, Michael. He's just ... dangerous.' What more could he say?

The priest rose and began to pace about. 'But if he has committed a murder, how does he manage to continue as a priest? The commandments are clear enough – so is the church's attitude towards those who kill. Liam is always going on about the commandments – I have found him rather rigid, in fact. After murder, he would not receive absolution, Anthony–'

'He doesn't tell the sin, Father Brennan.'

The older man stopped in his tracks. 'Sacrilege? He carries out his ministry while he himself is past redemption?'

Anthony closed his eyes and took a deep breath. 'He's different. His own rules apply, don't you see? No matter what he reads or understands, Liam is in contact with something he imagines to be God. My brother is the most unusual person I have ever met. He has his own set of rules. I think he sees himself as a second Moses, a bringer of more rules.'

Michael Brennan excused himself and left the room quickly. In the kitchen, he turned on the tap and dabbed cold water on his brow. He had a great deal of respect for Anthony Bell. Anthony was sensible and decent, was certainly not given to bouts of mindless hysteria. But ... but Liam was a priest.

Outside, a thin drizzle had started to fall. He stared into it, tried to imagine how on earth he was going to handle this problem. Liam Bell's confessor would be pledged to silence, as were all those who heard the sins of others in the privacy of the sacrament. If Liam had confessed to murder, he would not have been absolved until or unless he had informed the guardians of justice. It was probably right to assume that Liam had not confessed the supposed crime. Therefore, by withholding a mortal sin in confession, Liam was damned. In this parish, a pastor with sacrilege on his soul was blessing and distributing Holy Communion, was saying mass, advising sinners, preaching ...

On the other hand, Anthony could be mistaken. Michael Brennan was sure that Anthony would not lie deliberately, but perhaps the whole business had been blown out of proportion. In which case, why did he, parish priest of St Aloysius Gonzaga, feel so uncomfortable in the presence of his assistant?

He walked back into the living room. 'Without concrete evidence, Anthony, I can do nothing. I am as helpless as the police were when you reported your suspicions.'

Anthony understood completely. 'You can know, Michael,' he said, deliberately using the priest's Christian name. 'Even if you find difficulty in believing me, you can bear in mind what I have said.' He reached out a hand and picked up an old Bible from a side table. 'With this in my hand, I tell you that I am almost one hundred per cent sure that my brother is a very ill man who has injured several people and killed at least once.'

Michael swallowed. 'What would you have done had Liam been here?'

'I would have asked to see you in private. Or I would have returned later.'

The priest took the Bible from his visitor. 'I'll keep my

eyes open,' he promised. 'And I'll pray.' He stood at the door and watched Anthony walking away. The young man's shoulders were stooped as if he carried a great weight on his back. Of course, he did bear a heavy burden.

Michael closed the door and leaned against it. Sometimes, prayer was not enough.

Maureen Costigan gazed through the drawing room window. Outside, a sweep of lawn met the semicircular gravel driveway, and a fountain played in the centre of the grass. She found the water comforting, liked to see it pouring from the urn that sat on the shoulder of a stone cherub. Beyond the lawn there was a shrubbery and a small orchard. Soon, when she had stopped being so tired, she would go out for a walk in the grounds.

Diddy was sewing. As Edith and Richard Spencer had refused money for keeping herself and Maureen, Diddy had appointed herself chief seamstress of the establishment. The cook-housekeeper, one Milly Cornwell, was glad of Diddy's help. 'Me eyes is not what they was,' she had told the visitor.

'They talk funny, don't they?' mused Diddy. 'They talk so different from us, but we're all living in the same part of the world.'

'They're nice,' replied Maureen.

'Oh, they're nice. I'm not saying they're not decent. It's just how they talk.'

Maureen knew what Mam meant. The people hereabouts had very mobile faces. Their mouths stretched and pouted when they spoke, something to do with trying to be heard above the clatter of machinery, according to Edith Spencer. She was nice, too. She had given Maureen and Mam a lovely room with yellow bedspreads and pretty wallpaper with flowers on. 'I like it here,' Maureen said. 'You don't have to think when you're here. It's like being asleep even though you're awake.'

Diddy snapped a thread between her teeth. 'It's called relaxation, love. Nearest I get to that at home is a good chinwag round the bagwash. I hope they're managing all right. There's not many can fold a double sheet as straight as me.'

Maureen looked at her mother. Elizabeth Costigan had been a good mam, continued good. She did everything she could for her family, kept them warm and fed, kept them safe ... 'If I'd come home early that night like you told me,' she began, 'then it might never have happened.'

Diddy was instantly alert, though she continued sewing, tried not to look startled. Maureen still hadn't said much.

'He was very big,' the girl continued. 'Tall. I ran, but he caught me and dragged me to the field. He leaned very hard on me, on my back, then knelt down with one knee at each side of me. It was like a scarf, the thing he used, but it wasn't a scarf. And it wasn't screwed up or wrinkled – it was flat and it felt shiny.' And the smell. She could not quite define that sickly aroma that had risen from him.

Diddy pricked her thumb, held the pad of it against her cardigan so that she would not bleed on Edith's linen. And she didn't want Maureen seeing blood, not now, not when she'd just begun to allow her mind to open up. No questions, Diddy told herself firmly.

'I couldn't breathe. He breathed very loud. Then I just blacked out. Another man came. He was nearly crying. Afterwards, the police told me it was Flash Flanagan who found me. I remember Flash. He used to do puppet shows for us. I used to sing with him when I was little, for pennies.' She paused for a moment and inhaled deeply.

'My face was sore.' It was not easy, but she would say it here and now, while the garden fountain poured and the world was quiet. 'And inside me, I was sore.'

Diddy dropped the needle, saw blood appearing on Edith Spencer's linen. It was only a pillowcase.

'He did the bad thing, Mam. I never felt it, but when I woke up, I knew it had happened.'

Tears rolled down Diddy's face. She sat perfectly still in a beautiful room while birds twittered and fussed outside, while her daughter framed words that were terrifying.

'I listened to the doctor telling Dad about it. They thought I wouldn't hear them in the corridor, but I got out of bed and put my ear against the door. I wasn't talking, but I noticed most things that went on while I was in the hospital. Dad was crying. He said you hadn't to be told.'

Diddy prayed for strength, held on to her sobs, kept them caged inside her chest.

'Funny, I forgot most of it just before we came here. I even forgot about what the doctor had told Dad. I was me, but I wasn't me. Like a dream. Sitting here like this, I've let it all come back. Nobody will marry me now. The nuns said no man wants a girl who's done the bad thing.'

Diddy jumped up. 'This is different, Maureen. You haven't done anything wrong, girl. It was the man who did wrong, not you.'

Maureen nodded slowly. 'It doesn't make any difference,' she said flatly. 'It's been done. The girls at school used to talk about who'd been broken in and who hadn't. I've been broken in.' Maureen had enjoyed something of a reputation at school, but she had always known when to make the boys stop. She needn't have bothered, she supposed now, because her virginity had been ripped from her anyway.

Diddy tossed aside her mending, jumped up and

hugged her daughter tightly. 'You'll be all right, love,' she kept saying. Was she comforting Maureen or herself? After a minute or so, she released Maureen and began to pace up and down the room. Why hadn't Billy told her the full story? Then she remembered how she had been, crying over the dinner, her tears watering down the corned beef hash or the pea and ham soup. Billy had been trying to protect his wife for as long as possible. 'I bet your dad left you to tell me when you were ready. And you have done. Christ, I'll kill that bloody man, whoever he is.'

'I don't want anybody to know about the bad thing, Mam,' said Maureen. 'Our Nicky – there's no need for her to find out. The neighbours and all that lot – keep it from them.'

Diddy nodded just once. 'We will, I promise. There's only me, you, your dad and the doctor who know all about what happened.'

'And the police,' said Maureen softly. 'And the man who did it. The trouble is, if he gets another girl, people will say we should have spoke up.'

'They can say what they like, queen. Whatever you decide, we'll all stick by you.'

Maureen continued to look out at the beauty of Cherry Hinton's gardens. She wouldn't mind staying here for ever. It was so peaceful after Scotland Road, so beautiful and quiet. 'Mam?'

'That's me.'

'I'm not going back to school. I should be leaving in July, anyway. I don't care what anybody says, I'm not going. I'd only get asked questions. They'd all be pointing at me and whispering about me. It'd be terrible.'

'All right, love.'

Maureen inhaled deeply. 'It's the same with church. I mean, I suppose I'll go to mass and confession and all that in time, but I don't feel like it yet.'

'You just please yourself,' answered Diddy.

That was enough for now, Maureen decided. She wouldn't tell Mam yet about the other plan, the one Edith Spencer had cooked up. If Maureen wanted to, and if her parents would allow it, she could remain at Cherry Hinton as a helper for Mrs Cornwell. Mrs Cornwell had arthritis in her hands and bunions on her feet. The bits in between were all right, the cook was always saying, but, in the woman's own words, her 'extreme bits was playing up something monumental.'

In a day or two, Maureen would ask Mam if she could stay in Astleigh Fold. Whoever he was, he would not come here. Would he?

It was a very silly way to carry on. In Bridie's opinion, a horsewoman as experienced as she was should not be falling out of the saddle and landing on her head. The riding hat had rolled away, was sitting upside down in a small indentation between field and ditch. Sorrel wandered about chewing grass while Bridie nursed her sore head. She would get up in a minute. It was the shock, she supposed, because this had been the first fall in years – in fact, she had been younger than Cathy the last time she'd taken a tumble as nasty as this one.

Bob would be as annoyed as his surname, she told herself. Cross by name and furious by nature, no doubt. The guardian of the Spencer Stables was not watching, and Bridie was grateful for that. Sorrel had to be looked after. Bob Cross would be more concerned about the mount, because he didn't want Sorrel to think she could toss away her burden whenever the fancy took her. Bob Cross had planned a big future for Bridie's horses.

On New Year's Day in 1932, both Sorrel and Quicksilver would have their legal third birthday. So, in just over twelve months, one or both of them could be entered for the Derby if they showed good form in the meantime. Before the Derby, the horses would be tried at York and Chester. Bob Cross had been in touch with Dad, had acquired documentation that traced the animals' ancestry all the way back to a long ago Arab–Irish mating. And she, Bridget Bell, had just come off the more peaceable of the pair. She rubbed her head. God help anyone who tangled with Silver, because that feisty beast would throw St Francis Assisi himself out of the saddle if given a mere fraction of an opportunity.

'Hello?'

She sat up, turned, saw Anthony leaning over a stile. 'Oh. Hello,' she replied.

'Are you hurt?'

'No. I fell on my head, so I didn't feel a thing.' Her heart was all over the place again. She wanted him to climb over the fence and come to her, wanted him to go away – preferably to China – wanted him to touch her, talk to her . . .

He came into the field and helped her to sit up properly. 'You have a bump on your forehead the size of Everest,' he told her.

'No sense, no feeling,' she said flippantly. 'Is the horse all right?'

'You're as bad as Bob Cross,' he said. 'Horses first, people second. She looks fine.' He dropped down beside her. 'It's a long way to fall, Bridie.'

She was in trouble; she was in love. Was it love? she asked herself. Or was this plain and simple lust? Whatever, it was a condition from which she had never suffered before. 'I'm tough,' she said. 'The main thing is to keep the horse safe.' She fixed her gaze on the placid young mare. Sorrel was not in the least way concerned about any of it. 'Sorrel and Quicksilver are expected to have a big future.

That's what Bob Cross thinks, anyway. There's a jockey coming tomorrow to try the pair out. If he's any sense at all, he'll stick to this one. I only hope he sticks to her better than I did.' She waved a hand towards the pale chestnut. 'She has an even temper. The other fellow can act up like the very devil, you know, when the mood takes him.'

'Yes, Bob Cross did mention it in the pub the other night. Apparently, your Silver has a tendency to kick out. The stable boy had a limp for three days, I understand.'

'Silver's highly strung,' she said defensively. 'It's in his breeding. Lord knows it's sensible to fear humans. Sometimes, when horses show you the whites of their eyes, you know they're thinking of fight or flight. That's when I picture them roaming the plains away from humankind. We exploit them.'

'Yet you'll enter Sorrel for the races?'

'Yes. She's already in captivity, and she's happy enough, so she might as well earn some money. And she's a stayer as well as a sprinter. She has the breathing capacity to go the full distance. The Derby's a race for horses like Sorrel and Silver.' If she could carry on talking about horses, things would turn out fine. If she didn't look at him and—

'I went to Liverpool yesterday. I told Father Brennan about Liam.'

'Ah.' She got up and retrieved her hat. 'Have you tried confiding in Sam about Liam? You should tell your father,' she insisted.

Anthony laughed mirthlessly. 'He would have me committed to an asylum.'

'I still think you should talk to Sam. He's not as stubborn as you make out.'

He stood up and brushed a few pieces of grass from his trousers. If he looked downwards, he would not have to watch her. His eyes were hungry for the sight of Bridie in that quaint divided skirt she always wore when in the saddle. Her hair had tumbled about her face in ringlets made bright by the spring sunshine. He would not look at her again; he would walk away and climb over the stile and—

'Anthony?'

He looked. She was unbearably lovely. 'Yes?'

'Try not to brood.'

He dropped his gaze again. 'I shall do my best. Anyway, I had better be on my way,' he said. But his feet seemed to have taken root again. 'Bridie, I—'

'Come along, Sorrel.' She took the rein and led the horse back towards the stables. He was staring at her. She could feel the heat of his eyes boring into her spine. 'God help me,' she muttered. Prayer was the thing, she reminded herself. Anthony was one of the temptations in her path. She must take a circuitous route, must steer herself away from him. Soon, she would return to Liverpool. Things would be easier then.

'Bridie?'

She froze. 'Go away,' she begged.

He walked around her, placed his hands on her shoulders. 'You know how I feel, don't you? Stand still, for goodness sake.'

'Why?' She looked straight at him. 'I can't stand still, Anthony. I have two daughters to rear and a household to run. I have a good husband. The girls and I want for nothing.'

'What about love?' he asked.

She bowed her head for a moment, then lifted her chin in defiance. 'I am married to your father,' she whispered, 'and I respect him, Anthony. Respect endures, but love can pass away very easily. I will not hurt him. He is so good to me and Cathy and Shauna—'

'Gratitude,' he said.

'What's wrong with that?'

He touched her hand, flinched when she drew away from him. 'Do you want to spend the rest of your life being grateful?'

Bridie's grip on the rein tightened. 'That's no matter,' she told him gravely. 'But I don't want to be worrying about adultery, either, for the next twenty years.' Courage, courage, she told herself. 'You are my stepson. And that's an end of it.' She marched away with the horse.

Anthony hated himself. He had got her involved by relating his innermost secret, by inviting her to worry about Liam and his crimes. Also, he had allowed his love for her to show. 'You're a fool,' he told himself aloud. 'And a fool gets what he deserves from life, no more and no less.' With a heavy heart, he trudged back to his little house.

Bridie stumbled onward, her vision impeded by unexpected tears. Noel ran towards her with Cathy. 'I'm all right,' Bridie told her daughter. 'Just a little fall.'

Cathy took her mother's hand and led her back to the stables. She was Mammy's big girl, and Mammy had been crying.

Michael Brennan was becoming increasingly sure of one fact. He was not designed to be a policeman or a detective. His spherical shape was aerodynamically unsuited to quick movement, while everyone in the Scotland Road area recognized him as soon as they clapped eyes on him.

He sidestepped two boys in mangled steeries – carts made from old boxes, pram wheels and rope – then became involved with a crowd of children who had appointed themselves as entertainers for tram travellers. When the tracks had been cleared of singing, dancing and leapfrogging infants, Father Brennan wagged a finger at the young daredevils, then set off for Rose Hill Police Station. Surely he could ask questions without giving away all his reasons? After all, Maureen Costigan was a member of his congregation.

He entered the station, tried to keep clear of a pair of marauding drunkards. 'Father!' screamed the nearest of the two. 'He's pinched me last drop.' Anxious to get rid of the inebriated men, Michael helped a constable to direct them towards the cells.

'Starting already,' complained the desk sergeant. 'And it's only half past seven. What can we do for you, Father Brennan?'

Michael looked around. Apart from an officer who was distributing police clothing to some ragged children, the area was reasonably clear. 'I've seen you busier,' said the priest.

'So have I.' The sergeant took a noisy sip from a mug of tea. 'You should have been here when we had the loot, Father, during and after the police strike – a bit before your time. There was more stolen stuff going through here in 1919 than I've seen in all my other years put together.' He glanced round the room. 'By those standards, I suppose we're quiet. Just shows – police should never go on strike. Without us and your lot, this place'd go straight to the dogs.'

Michael leaned against the counter. 'Maureen Costigan,' he said. 'The whole parish has been concerned and praying for her recovery. Was Flash Flanagan the first to find her and what have you discovered about the person who injured her?'

The policeman, who was too near retirement to care much for protocol, gave his answer immediately. 'Flash Flanagan found her and no, we haven't got any idea who committed the crime,' he replied. 'We gave Flash his marching orders while things settle down a bit. He would have frightened everybody to death with his tales if we hadn't shifted him.' He swung round. 'I've eyes in the back of my head, Bobby Flynn,' he told a lad who was creeping through to the cells. 'Get back here and find some trousers. The arse is out of the ones you're wearing.'

'I want to see me dad,' moaned the boy. 'It's a matter of life and death.'

'We know all about that,' said the sergeant. 'Your mother'll batter him to death if she doesn't get his wages. Well, he's been drunk since dinner-time and I've locked him up for his own good. Go home and tell her I found three bob and a couple of coppers on him. If she'll come round, she can sign for it.'

The lad ran out bearing the good news and a pair of brown corduroy trousers.

'He'll not wear them,' said the policeman sadly. 'They don't like wearing the police clothes. They stink when they're wet, them trousers. Still, we can do our best and no more.'

'I'm worried about this attack,' Michael continued. 'I've heard that Maureen was almost strangled.'

'Yes, but we found no evidence apart from the state she was in.'

Father Brennan picked up his biretta.

'Hang on,' said the sergeant. He leaned forward. 'We think it was more like a scarf,' he said softly. 'Rope leaves a definite mark, different from the bruise on that poor girl's throat. But that's all we know. Oh, and we've took a bit of a collection for her. She can get herself a new frock or something when she feels better.'

'Was she raped?' Michael Brennan spoke in a whisper.

His companion nodded just once. 'I know that'll go no further,' he said.

Michael Brennan stepped outside, watched the toffee ponies clopping their way home after delivering sweets to all the little shops in the area. These favourites of the local children were small piebalds with round bellies and well-polished tack. He waved at the driver, crossed the road, made his way through a maze of streets.

From a cellar, an excited voice called, 'House!' Michael grinned to himself. There was not much work about, and many young men spent their time organizing football teams. These were financed by illegal gambling but, like the police, the Church turned a blind eye. They were better off playing lotto than stealing and getting into fights. At least the football matches helped to burn off some of their surplus energy. With the takings from the bingo, they would buy boots, socks and a proper inflatable football.

A couple of Mary Ellens approached him, their baskets empty after a long day's toil. They swayed when they walked, as if still balancing the panniers of fruit on their heads. Each wore a long black skirt with loose pleats, and a dark shawl around her shoulders. 'Hello, Father,' they chorused. 'How's business?'

'Fair to middling,' he replied, as always. 'How's yours?'

'Picking up,' laughed the nearest. 'Picking up all we've dropped before the kids pinch it.' They sallied onward, their pace unhurried, boots slapping the pavement rhythmically.

He crossed Scotland Road, saw a fight going on outside the Prince of Wales, stood with his arms folded until the warriors separated, shame on their faces because their priest had seen them brawling.

In the Throstle's Nest, he ordered a pint of ale and sat on a stool. Where was the man? And for how much longer could he, Father Michael Brennan, PP, follow his second in command around the streets? There were other matters waiting for attention, like sick people to visit and sermons to write.

Molly Barnes plonked herself next to him. Molly was a lovable woman of easy virtue whose looks had faded. So she was off the streets now and running a home for girls who worked the city centre and the dock road. 'I've come to thank you,' she said, her face broadened by a smile. 'For lending us your Father Bell.'

Michael took another sip of beer. Molly was not the best company to keep, because she paid little attention to personal hygiene. Her idea of social acceptability was to spray herself liberally with cheap perfume. This did not disguise the scent of unwashed flesh; it merely added to the unsavoury bouquet of aromas that battled with each other for dominance as they rose from her clothing. She had mentioned Liam. He would take his time, get what information he could from this lady. 'I beg your pardon?'

Molly downed her gin and stared into the empty glass. 'Father Bell. He's working at the Welcome Home.' She was very proud of her establishment. It provided a safe haven for those who wanted a rest from the weariness that accompanied prostitution. The little nest had been lent to her by a charitable organization. 'The committee's very pleased with me,' she boasted. 'I've got two married off and four who've gone back to their mothers.'

Michael placed his glass on the counter, tried to appear nonchalant. 'How long has Father Bell been involved?' he asked. 'I seem to have forgotten.'

'Oh, just a couple of weeks. He prays with us after tea when he can, when he's got time, like.'

He prays, thought Michael. Afterwards, he prays over them. The priest suppressed a shudder. 'Does he help in any other way?'

Molly pouted while she thought. Powder had caked and settled into the network of fine lines around her eyes and mouth. The lips were brightly painted, looked as if they had been in contact with the blood of some recently killed animal. 'Well, he talks to the girls, advises them on how to try and get a proper job. Sometimes, he brings bits of fruit and cake. I mean, he's a sobersides, but he does his best.'

Michael bought another gin for Molly, finished his pint, then left the pub. Liam Bell was working with prostitutes. He heard Anthony's voice, went through all that Father Bell's twin had said. According to Anthony, Liam had associated with street women before, though he had hardly helped them. Dear God, what could a very ordinary Irish priest do about this mess? Should he go to the bishop? What could he tell the primate of Liverpool? That there was a possibility that Liam Bell had the makings of a mass murderer? Anthony could have been wrong, for goodness sake.

He went back to the presbytery and sat in the living room until the daylight faded completely. Tonight, he did not want to see Liam. He climbed the stairs, undressed, donned his pyjamas and lay on the bed. The more he pondered, the further from an answer he seemed to travel. He would sleep on it. He would sleep on it for the third night in a row.

Soon, Maureen and Diddy would return. If ... if Liam had attacked Maureen, would the child recognize him? And would Liam finish the job in case she did remember him? Or had Liam been innocent in the first place?

He heard sounds from downstairs, knew that his right-hand man had returned from his evening of charitable work among the women in the Welcome Home. With a heavy heart, Michael got up, collected his rosary from a side table and knelt at his small prie-dieu. He looked up at the Virgin Mary, asked her to intercede on his behalf. 'This is too much for me,' he told her. 'Please stop him – if it is him. And if it isn't him – stop whoever it really is.' He said a decade for Maureen, another for Liam, then one for himself.

The stairs creaked. Father Brennan was not a fanciful man, but it occurred to him that he might be sharing a house with an ogre. He swallowed his own fear, said his last Glory Be, then climbed into bed. At times like this, it was better not to think.

Through the wall that divided the two front bedrooms, he could hear the young priest moving about. Tomorrow, he would ask about the Welcome Home business, would try to discover Liam's motives. Fat chance of that, he pondered as he drifted towards sleep. An innocent man would not react to questioning. And a guilty man would not react, either.

Twelve

It was another way of life, Bridie thought as she took a sip
of water from a crystal glass. Dinner was served in the
evening at Cherry Hinton. The midday meal was called
lunch, then afternoon tea consisted of thin sandwiches,
small cakes and tea from a china pot. Mrs Cornwell did
the cooking, while a woman from the village cleaned the
house. Occasionally, the woman's daughter helped with
housework, too, but Edith Spencer preferred to preside
and serve at her own table.

Edith was a wise woman. Although she was proud of
home and husband, she had chosen not to forget her
beginnings. She appreciated her staff, but she liked to feel
that she was running the household. After the main meal,
dishes were usually left for the cleaning staff to clear away
and wash, though the mistress of Cherry Hinton sometimes helped and hindered her employees in the kitchen.

The tattered dog known as Noel was allowed to wander
the house as freely as he wished. With Edith and Richard,
there were few rules, so every guest felt important and
welcome – even Cathy's disgraceful mongrel was treated
with respect. This was a valuable house and a happy home.
The Spencers had found that elusive happy medium between house-pride and sociability.

Cathy and Shauna's meal had been served earlier, and
the two little girls were in bed. Around the oval table in

the dining room sat Diddy, Maureen, Edith, Richard, Bridie and Anthony. After soup, there was roast lamb with home-grown baby potatoes, fresh peas and carrots. On the sideboard lingered Milly Cornwell's speciality – a huge apple and cinnamon tart with a jug of custard sauce.

Bridie, who had been placed opposite Anthony, kept her eyes on her plate. Being in the same village was hard enough; eating a meal with him was torture. Even with her eyelids lowered, she could see him, as if the image had imprinted itself permanently on her brain. Another reason for not looking at him was the devilment in his eyes – he was quite capable of making Bridie giggle at the most unfortunate times.

'Bridie?'

She forced herself to answer him. 'Yes?'

'More potatoes?' he asked.

She shook her head. He had made the word 'potatoes' sound like forbidden fruit in some biblical garden where snakes played in the trees. People would begin to notice, she thought. Her cheeks were warm and she was having difficulty swallowing food. Any minute, he would crack a joke about people who couldn't stay on a horse.

'Your bump's gone down nicely,' he told her.

Ah yes, here came the teasing. She attempted no reply.

'That was quite a tumble,' he continued.

Bridie raised her head and looked straight at him. 'Did you ever notice that it's always the people who can't do something who criticize others for doing that same thing and making a small mistake?'

He placed his knife and fork on the plate. 'Somewhere in what you say there must be logic,' he mused.

Bridie held his gaze levelly for a second, then carried on eating. He was a child, she told herself. All men were children, especially those who made eyes at women across tables.

Diddy broke the spell. 'That's the best bit of meat I've tasted in ages,' she told the hostess. Diddy loved being here. If Maureen could just be all right, this would turn into a holiday to remember. Her heart missed a beat, because Maureen might be staying on at Cherry Hinton. Still, this was a decent place, wasn't it? The Spencers were rich, but they had few airs and graces. If you used the wrong knife, nobody was bothered. 'Maureen's enjoying it – aren't you, love?' At least the girl was eating now.

Maureen smiled at Richard. He had been wonderful with her. He had sat with her for hours explaining why she felt sad, what she could do to make herself better, how she should take a bit of exercise every day. He had asked no questions, yet he seemed to have cleared her mind. She had started going for walks, and the scar on her face had begun to fade. Dr Spencer was a good man.

Diddy burped politely behind a snow-white napkin, made herself sit still while Edith collected plates and put them on the sideboard. Diddy had been allowed to sew, but was forbidden to do any other chores. She was growing fond of Edith Spencer, had ceased to feel awkward in her company. Edith was just an ordinary woman who had married well and enjoyed sharing her good fortune. 'I'll get used to this, you know,' Diddy chided playfully. 'When I get back, my Billy'll have to wait on me hand and foot. And Sam'll have to do the same for Bridie. Won't he? Bridie? Have you dropped off to sleep in the middle of your dinner?'

Bridie jumped. 'Were you talking to me?'

'I was,' said Diddy. 'You've a head full of straw these days. It's all horses, isn't it?' She caught Anthony staring at Bridie. Oh, surely not? Diddy sat back thoughtfully. She recalled how Bridie had cared for Anthony during his illness, remembered the expression in the young man's eyes when he had looked up at his nurse. Could these two be falling in love?

Maureen was quite comfortable in Anthony's company. The schoolgirl crush had died, had been throttled to death by a cruel stranger. Anthony was nice to her, and that was an end to it. He didn't interrogate, didn't try to baby her. Anthony was just another decent man like Richard Spencer.

Diddy broke into her portion of tart. That wasn't the heat of a summer evening staining Bridie Bell's cheeks, as spring was still in the air. No, it was something else altogether. She hoped it hadn't happened, hoped it would never happen. Life in the Bell household was complicated already. Yet Diddy's heart, already made heavy by her daughter's tragedy, was saddened again, because Anthony and Bridie seemed so right for each other. Had the circumstances been different, they might have made an ideal couple.

Richard spoke to Diddy. 'Well, we're all friends here, so I'll just get it said. We have already mentioned to Diddy that Edith and I would like Maureen to stay on for a while. The country air is doing her good, and we should perhaps consider Maureen's inner well-being. She is safe here.'

Diddy suffocated the pain she felt whenever she considered losing one of her children into that gaping maw called life. She glanced at her daughter. 'What do you think, love?'

Maureen lifted her head. 'I want to stay.'

The big woman sighed. It had to start some time, she supposed. Charlie would always be at home, bless him, but the others would start leaving one by one. Monica was courting Graham Pile, now Maureen was thinking of staying on here. Still, Jimmy and Tildy-Anne could be in Dryden Street for a few years yet. 'All right, Maureen.' She turned her attention to Richard Spencer, apportioned him a watery smile. 'Give her something to do, though.' Maureen had been destined for the stage. Diddy remembered pawning many house-hold items repeatedly just to keep up the dancing lessons. Now, all that seemed to have come to nothing.

Dr Spencer nodded reassuringly at Diddy. 'Maureen is going to help Mrs Cornwell. Mrs Openshaw from the village is getting old, so your daughter can step into her shoes – once Maureen feels a little better, that is.'

'I am better,' declared Maureen. She tossed the black curls. 'He's not going to win,' she went on, her voice lower. 'What he did to me was awful, but I can't let it finish my life.'

Bridie watched Anthony's facial muscles tightening. She hated his pain, almost wished that he would simply carry on with his teasing and joking.

'The dancing lessons can be resumed eventually,' said Edith. She reached along the table and patted Diddy's hand. 'She will gain strength, my dear. There's the physical pain and the mental anguish. The attacker took control of Maureen's life, deprived her of her own decision making ability for a while. Richard has explained all this to Maureen. That's what takes time to heal, you see. Physical hurt is easier to mend.'

Maureen felt the blood rising to her face. 'I just want to thank everybody for being so good to me,' she mumbled. 'I don't know what I would have done without all of you. Even the little girls helped by being there and chattering like they do.'

Bridie smiled encouragingly. Maureen was a different person. She remembered the Maureen she had met after the wedding, that shallow and beautiful girl who had seen the world as her own personal playground. This had been a terrible way to grow up, though. She noted that Anthony was still looking grim, because he was certain that his brother had been the cause of Maureen's misery.

When the pudding dishes were empty and after everyone had groaned at the thought of cheese, coffee was served in the drawing room by Mrs Cornwell. She bumbled about on sore feet, smiled benignly upon 'her' family. She had taken to Maureen, was glad that the young woman might be moving in. Cherry Hinton was a happy house. The Spencers were good employers, careful to ensure the welfare of their staff, and Maureen deserved a bit of luck.

The weather looked fair, so Richard suggested a walk to help digest the feast. Everyone followed him through French windows and into the rear garden. Spring bulbs were past their best, but there was a promise of summer in the fine evening.

They walked to the front of the house and across the lawn, then Maureen sat with her mother on a bench facing the fountain. Noel pranced about for a while before settling at Maureen's feet. He had appointed himself guardian to this quiet girl. Also, the dog seemed to have acquired a modicum of decorum during recent days. Perhaps he recognized that he was leading the good life at last.

Maureen fixed her gaze on the flowing water, found it soothing. Richard and Edith lingered among rose beds while Bridie carried on towards the little orchard. The apple trees were burgeoning, blossom swelling the buds and threatening to erupt at any moment. Cherry trees, too, were ready to bloom, as were the plums and pears.

'We're alone,' said Anthony. 'Look at the cherry trees – hundreds of them. I suppose they gave the house its name.'

She jumped. 'You shouldn't creep up behind me like that.' She looked over his shoulder, noticed that the rest of the party had failed to follow her. 'I'd better get back,' she said. 'In case the girls wake.'

'Mrs Cornwell will watch and listen,' he told her.

Bridie sighed. He was still in a state. A frown had crept across his forehead, seemed to be trying to knit its way into both eyebrows. 'There's nothing you can do,' she said softly. 'Stop worrying about what can't be changed.'

'You read minds, too?'

'No. But I understand what's bothering you.'

He plucked at an overhanging branch, rained a few leaves onto the ground.

Bridie turned and began to walk back towards the house. She had to get away from him, had to keep her distance. As she moved, she began to realize that she was trying to escape not just from him, but also from herself. If they could only stay apart, things might settle down. Separately, she and Anthony would carry on as normal. He would teach, she would rear the children and run his father's house. But together, they might destroy everything. It was as if some chemical reaction took place whenever they met. Sometimes, substances that were benign on their own became explosive when mixed. Where had she read that? In one of Sam's many second-hand books?

'Bridie?'

Something akin to temper rose in her throat, and she turned on him. 'We are not children.' But there was no chance of remaining angry, not with him. He was so sad, so frightened. She wanted to smooth his brow and tell him that everything would turn out fine. But he was not her child. 'I'm sorry,' she said. 'I'm tired.'

'Tired enough to fall off a horse?'

'Yes, I suppose so.' She did not trust her eyes, her ears, herself. Diddy was near. She would turn and run to Diddy and Edith. Women were the strong ones in situations such as these. Women were the strong ones, anyway, because they had to be. Men followed their instincts, lost reason where love was concerned. They didn't have to bear the grief or the babies.

'I won't hurt you,' he said.

'I know that.'

'How?'

She knew because she loved him. 'I just do.'

He lowered his chin and thought for a moment. 'Be safe,' he said. 'Watch for him, stay away from him.'

Bridie made no reply. Her throat was dry, probably because of the nervousness he engendered. She wished with all her being that she could offer him some comfort, but any gesture of sympathy could be misconstrued. She feared touching him.

'Bridie?'

'Yes?'

'I am deadly serious. Keep away from him.' Liam didn't need evidence to attain his proof. One careless word, and he might home in on Bridie. 'And don't talk to my father about the rift. If you speak up for me, and if Dad then speaks to Liam, my dear brother will assume that you are on my side. With him, being on my side is as good as being at my side. Do you understand?'

She nodded.

'He knows things. He's uncanny, almost weird. It's as if he has a sixth sense, but no common sense and no decency.'

Bridie heard his misery, wished for a miracle. 'You must not concern yourself about me. I'm a grown woman.'

'And he's a big, strong man.'

'How could you possibly be twins? Apart from colouring and build, you are like chalk and cheese.'

He tried to smile. 'I am the chalk, I suppose, because I

use enough of it in my job. Somehow, I don't see my brother as half a pound of Cheddar.'

They walked back together, each painfully aware of the other's proximity. Bridie saw Maureen sitting peaceably with Diddy, hailed Richard and Edith as they plotted over which roses to prune before summer began.

Anthony Bell said his goodbyes and went home. He lit the lamps, turned on his wireless and opened a bottle of beer. The news would be on the Home Service soon, and Bridie loved him. Because of that love, he must stay away from her. But he found no solace in his radio, was aware only of that special loneliness which comes to those forced to live without company. 'If he touches her, I'll kill him,' he informed the fireplace.

Outside, birds practised evensong, and a skittish breeze ruffled leaves. While Anthony ached for Bridie, the world simply carried on turning.

A tall, dark man strolled through the village of Astleigh Fold. He wore a charcoal suit, white shirt, black tie and black shoes. He was on his way to visit his second cousin, Edith Spencer, but first, he intended to call in on his brother.

Liam stopped for a while and studied the village stocks, crude boards with holes positioned to trap the hands of miscreants while the rest of the village hurled abuse and rotted vegetable matter. The stocks had been a good idea, he thought. Anthony should go into the stocks, for the simple reason that Anthony was trying to betray his brother.

The collar and tie felt strange, because he had grown so used to the life and garb of a priest. But there was nothing in the rules that forbade a day off, so he was having a change. People stared less at a man in everyday clothes.

He walked on towards the cottage where his brother stayed. Anthony had been to visit Father Brennan, it seemed. Liam was annoyed. It was plain that his twin had said something to Michael Brennan, because the latter had begun to act quite oddly. He was questioning Liam at every opportunity, had taken him to task about helping in the Welcome Home, was always probing for information about Liam's movements. Once, Liam had caught sight of his parish priest lurking in a doorway. Fortunately, Brennan was a very visible man, so Liam was now on his guard. What had Anthony said? Wasn't all that business over with?

One thing was certain, thought Liam. The weapon used on Maureen Costigan had not been found. God had protected His true servant by making sure that the stole would never be discovered. Had anything turned up, the police would have spoken by now. So. There was no further need for concern in that direction. This near knowledge had provided Liam with a degree of confidence, enough to allow him to sally forth and see his brother.

He arrived in the lane, stopped at the garden gate, looked through the window and saw Anthony sitting reading a newspaper. Liam stood still for a few seconds. As ever, he felt a degree of confusion when he looked at Anthony. Liam loved his brother and hated him. Sometimes, the strong feelings bubbled over and pushed Liam to act on his brother's behalf. But he protected Anthony, made sure that Anthony's path was swept free of sin and temptation.

He steadied himself on the gatepost, blinked, tried to remember. There was the first girl, then a hanging. Then a second girl had come along . . . ah, yes. Today, he would see Maureen Costigan. She did not know him, would never recognize him. A man who did God's bidding was safe from creatures like Maureen Costigan. With his shoulders squared against the vagaries of life, Liam Bell walked up the path and knocked.

The door opened. 'Bugger off,' said Anthony.

Liam pushed his way in. 'You invaded my territory,' he snapped. 'This is the return visit.' He walked into the living room. 'Cosy,' he remarked, a sneer on his lips.

Anthony crushed the newspaper and gripped it hard as if holding on to his temper, then he cast it to the floor. 'I don't want you here,' he said slowly and clearly. 'So get out.'

Liam sat down. 'I think you should see a doctor.' His tone was mild. 'There's something wrong with your brain. What have you been saying to my parish priest?'

Anthony opened his mouth to speak, closed it quickly. He must tread carefully, must avoid giving Liam a reason to turn on poor Michael Brennan. 'You should never have gone back to Scotland Road,' he said. 'You ought to have taken a post elsewhere.'

'Why?'

'You know why, Liam.'

The priest folded his arms. 'Tell me, Anthony.'

Anthony leaned against the doorpost, was glad of its solid support. 'Because of Valerie,' he said softly. 'And because of Maureen.'

'Who?'

'Maureen Costigan. The girl you molested.'

Liam's lip curled. 'Rubbish,' he spat. 'There is nothing to connect me with the attack on Maureen Costigan. As for the woman you intended to marry – the murderer was hanged.'

It was no use. Anthony stood in the doorway and realized anew that he was in the company of a very ill man. Liam was probably aware of most things he had done, yet a part of his mind rejected his misdeeds. Liam was the one who needed a doctor – and a padded cell, no doubt. 'Don't you remember killing Valerie? What about the girls in Lime Street and Bold Street – those who were merely mauled about?'

Liam shuddered, tried to hide the involuntary action. He was not here for an inquisition; he was here to do the asking. 'Have you spoken to Father Brennan about these insane theories?'

'No.' Sometimes, a lie was the lesser sin.

'Are you sure?'.

'I'm sure.'

Liam leaned back. Perhaps he was mistaken, then. Anthony invariably told the truth. 'He is acting strangely,' he said.

'He's keeping strange company.'

The priest let out an exaggerated sigh of impatience. 'Anthony, I am an ordained man.'

'Some of the Borgias were men of the cloth,' replied Anthony.

Liam nodded. 'Why do you hate me?'

'Oh, come on, for goodness sake. Why did you try to drown me? Why did you break my arm and knock out a few of my teeth?'

The man in the chair glowered. 'Children do those things.' A picture came into his mind. Anthony was falling, falling very slowly into the Mersey. Grey waters parted to receive his flailing body. As he relived the half-forgotten moment, panic entered Liam's throat, caused him to gasp. Anthony had to live. Anthony must not drown. Who had pushed Anthony into this murky river?

'Not your most pleasant memory?' asked Anthony.

A man jumped in, his body displacing dark, scum-crested ripples. Another man threw a lifebelt. The dripping body of Anthony Bell was lifted out. Men worked on the child, pumped the filthy water out of him. He was alive. 'I was so glad you didn't drown,' Liam said now.

Anthony bent down and picked up his wrecked newspaper. He didn't know what to do or say. It was as if Liam had a split personality, two sides that seldom came together, an almost distinct pair of individuals, each of whom carried no crosses for the other. Liam's dominant self was cold, unfeeling – rather like Dad's. But beneath the calm exterior dwelt a fiend over which there could never be control. Where had such a creature been born? 'Liam, you really don't know what you're doing when you hurt people. Am I right?'

The frigid eyes fixed themselves on the man in the doorway. 'No, you are not right,' he replied.

'But you have raped women. You have killed. I know.' He hammered his ribs with a closed fist. 'For God's sake, don't you need to get all that off your chest? Don't you want to confess and be done with it?'

Liam's eyes seemed to cloud over, so he blinked to clear his vision. He had done nothing wrong. He had simply tidied his brother's way through life. He and Anthony were joined, bound together for the rest of their days. 'I pray for guidance every day,' he said. 'And God is with me in all I do.'

Anthony stepped into the room. 'Do you hear the voice of God?'

'Sometimes.'

'Are you sure it's His voice, Liam? Remember the story of Jesus's temptation – Satan had the temerity to try to fool the Son of God. After having a go at Jesus, the devil might find you to be very easy meat.'

'No.' Anthony was doing his best to play tricks. 'I am a priest,' said Liam quietly. 'Because that is my calling. As a priest, I do God's bidding and no-one else's.'

'And do you also obey your parish priest?'

Liam laughed mirthlessly. 'The man's a fool. A good enough fool, I daresay, but not equipped for the post he holds. I expect he will be put out to pasture soon. Of course, I may well be offered his position, because I know the area so well.'

'Including the various church playgrounds and sports fields.'

Liam inhaled deeply and leaned back in the chair. 'Anthony, you are mistaken about me. If you need proof, I am going now to visit Edith. Maureen Costigan is there, I believe?'

'Yes, she is.'

'And she will not recognize me.'

Anthony leaned over his brother's chair. 'No, she won't,' he said. 'Because you attacked her from behind.'

Liam kept his hands firmly in his lap. He would not strike his twin. The room spun slightly, as if the earth had suddenly quickened on its axis. But Liam intended to remain calm. There was no point in hitting out at Anthony, not now. Anthony was the loser, because he was a mere teacher. Whereas Liam, the superior twin, had graduated with honours from the toughest seminary in England. 'I shall go now,' he said. 'To visit Edith.'

Anthony stood aside and allowed his brother to pass. The front door slammed shut and Anthony breathed a sigh of relief. But Bridie was up there. Bridie was at Cherry Hinton with her little girls. No, he told himself firmly. Liam would not do any harm in daylight. But Liam disliked Bridie already. She should be warned, must be forced to listen.

He sank into a chair and steered his breathing towards an even pattern. If he went to the main house, there might be trouble. So he sat and waited, hoping with all his heart that the woman he loved would be safe. Again, that familiar sense of uselessness invaded him, making him weak and suddenly weary. The unfortunate truth was that Liam would remain free as a bird until someone else died or got hurt. Even then, Liam might not be caught.

Anthony closed his eyes and prayed for Bridie, Maureen and Bridie's little girls. He prayed also for Liam, remembered the story of Jesus on the cross. The Saviour had looked at His tormentors, had forgiven them. 'They know not what they do,' the Lord had said. Like Liam, they had not been in control.

Silver was in a mood. He showed Bob Cross the whites of his eyes, nodded angrily, snorted, tried to free himself from bridle and rein. He kept Bridie well in view, because he remembered and tolerated her, just about, but he raised a hoof each time Bob Cross came within striking distance.

Bridie observed. Quicksilver seemed to have forgotten many of his manners. The horse was, without doubt, one of the most beautiful sights she had ever beheld. He was perfectly proportioned, with a large, well-covered ribcage, rippling shoulders and hard, muscular thighs. This fellow was built for running and staying the course. But he had a wickedness in him, and this was the quality she admired above all others. Silver's naughtiness was born of intelligence. He had the sense not to trust on sight, but now, he needed to accept a human friend. Once courted, the horse would be a gallant and loyal steed.

Bob Cross, stablemaster and would-be monarch of the stallion he surveyed, grunted and gave up. He dragged the rein to Bridie and placed it in her hands. 'He'll do better for you,' he said grudgingly. 'I hear from our new headmaster that you can charm this blinking horse. So get charming.'

Bridie did not move. She didn't want to get too close,

because she would soon return to Liverpool. Silver needed to ally himself to someone else, and she hoped that the 'someone else' would be arriving at any moment. 'No,' she told Bob. 'I want him to forget me. This fellow will take only one master, and it's best if he gets used to ... what was his name?'

'Robin Smythe. Well, Harrington-Smythe, really.'

'My goodness, what a mouthful.' She turned her head and saw the 'mouthful' walking towards her, riding boots polished, crop slapping his shin. He wasn't even a mouthful, she thought. He looked like a child who had aged prematurely.

Robin Smythe held out his hand. 'Robin will do,' he said, performing a comical little bow. 'Mrs Bell?'

'That's me.' She shook his tiny hand. 'And Bridie will be quite all right, thank you.' He had kind eyes and his face looked weathered, as if he spent a lot of time outdoors.

Bob Cross came over. 'This one's a bugger,' he said, pointing out the wayward stallion.

'And that bugger's a winner if ever I saw one,' replied Robin. He threw down the crop and sidled over to the horse. 'No nonsense now,' the tiny man told Silver. 'You and I will be friends if I have to kill you. Understood?'

Silver tossed his mane and tried to run away, but Robin grabbed the rein from Bridie and swung himself onto the horse's back. Silver took exception and began to buck and rear like a newly caught wild yearling. But Robin held on.

'He's good,' remarked Bridie. So far, she was impressed by what she had seen of Robin Smythe.

Bob nodded. 'He's heartbroken. We're lucky to get him to visit. He's between horses, and he makes the same mistake as you and me, love. He gets fond of these wearisome beggars. He loved his last one, loved it too much for his own good.'

'And was his last horse difficult?'

Bob jerked his head and guffawed. 'Difficult? He was a raving bloody lunatic till Robin bested him. There's no beast in existence that doesn't fall under Robin's spell.'

Robin Smythe lay flat across the withers and along Silver's neck. Like a streamlined bird, man and horse cut through the air as if welded together. Bridie held her breath and prayed that the jockey would remain on board. Silver had a strong desire to be the boss, but he would surely respond once he respected his rider.

'That's the York races won,' laughed Bob. 'Let's watch the Derby.'

The horse streaked past with Robin hanging on like grim death. 'I want Robin to ride for us,' said Bridie excitedly. 'He'll manage Silver. Try to persuade him, Bob.'

Robin and Silver ground to an unbecoming halt. The jockey jumped down as easily as stepping off the last rung of a ladder. Silver cocked his head and looked at the small person who had just driven him to run at least a quarter of a mile. He thrashed the earth with a hoof, then bent to sniff the grass.

Robin Smythe left the horse chewing and blowing. 'I'll take him,' he said. 'But I'd like to try the other one, too.' He grinned at Bridie. 'I lost my favourite a few weeks ago. They've nothing else I want to ride, which is why I'm looking round. This one is interesting.' He turned back and placed a hand on Silver's neck. 'See? He never flinched. He knows who's in charge.'

Bridie spoke to Bob. 'I can't pay for all this. Edith's already feeding and stabling the pair.'

The old man smiled. 'She'll get her money back, don't worry.'

Bridie wished she could be sure. The horses looked good and ran well, but there could be many a slip between now and next year's races, many a strained muscle. 'Then who pays Robin?'

The miniature man joined them. 'That's not for you to worry about,' he said.

Bob Cross laughed out loud. 'Robin could buy and sell the Spencers without touching his bank account. He's a very rich man.'

The jockey pretended to punch Bob Cross. 'Shut up, man,' he said. 'Or you'll have all the ladies after my money.' He led the horse in the direction of the stable yard.

'Keep your fingers crossed,' said Bob. 'He's the best.'

Bridie nodded to herself. If Robin was the best, then he deserved the best. From the way Bob had been talking, Bridie had gathered that Quicksilver and Sorrel were among the finest two-year-olds in the North of England. 'I must get back,' she said. 'Diddy will probably have had enough of Cathy and Shauna.'

Bob clapped a hand to his mouth. 'I forgot to tell you,' he cried. 'That nun's at the house.'

'Nun?'

'Sacred Heart,' said Bob. 'Maureen asked me to tell you. There's some sort of exam going on, like an entrance test. Are you sending Cathy to Sacred Heart, then?'

Bridie pondered for a moment. 'Well, let's see does she have the brains for it,' she said finally. Sacred Heart was another kind of race altogether, she reminded herself. But there again, Cathy was a fine runner and a stayer. The trouble was, Cathy might just shy away from the starting pistol. 'See you later,' she told her companion. Then she walked back to the lane and towards the big house.

Liam Bell made his way in the direction of Cherry Hinton. This was one of the days when he didn't feel very well. Lately, he'd had to concentrate really hard, had been forced to keep a tight rein on himself because his mind was playing up. Things he knew by heart were eluding him – names, addresses, bits of the Holy Mass. If he didn't pull round, he would be drying up in the pulpit, and that would never do.

It was tiredness, he supposed. The workload was heavy, especially since he had taken on the Welcome Home. He was finally in control, he kept telling himself. He could work with the wayward without being tempted to punish. It was strange, but he got a great deal of pleasure out of helping that handful of whores. The work made him feel good, especially when one of the girls decided to turn straight.

He glanced to his left and saw a tiny man leading a horse out of the field. A jockey, he thought. Then a woman leapt over the gate, her ankles just showing beneath grey culottes. It was Bridie. It was the Irish widow who had married his father.

Bridie dusted herself down, saw a man approaching. Her heart skipped a beat, then she realized that this was not Anthony. Breathing was suddenly difficult. Liam was here and he had probably visited his twin brother. A picture of a battered and bruised Anthony touched her consciousness for a split second. The need to run to the cottage was acute, yet she knew that she must stand firm. She could soothe the priest. She could pander to his ego in the cause of peace. She could lie.

He stopped, looked her up and down.

'Father Liam,' Bridie managed, 'how well you look. And it's lovely to see you again. Did you visit Anthony?'

'Yes,' he growled. She had the temerity to stare straight into his eyes. She was so sure of herself.

'Are you going to the big house?' she asked.

'I thought I might call in, yes,' he replied.

'Then walk with me.' Her insides were churning, but she kept the smile on her face. 'Keep safe,' Anthony had ordered. 'Stay away from him.' Well, she couldn't, but she might as well have a stab at diverting the priest. She swallowed, inhaled deeply. 'It's so strange,' she managed, 'you and Anthony are unalike. There's the physical resemblance, of course, but you're so much more sensible.' She put a hand to her mouth. 'Oh, I am sorry, Father. I should not criticize your twin, should I? Still, I'm sure you will keep my opinions to yourself.'

'Of course.'

Bridie sighed dramatically. 'My quarrels and differences with Anthony are my concern, not yours. But thank you for listening.' With a tremendous effort, she reached out and touched his sleeve. 'Pray for me, Father Liam. I do so hate family quarrels. But Anthony is so ... so inclined to interfere with my rearing of the girls. Of course, he does it out of kindness, I'm sure, but these teachers are fond of lecturing, don't you find?'

He did find, and he nodded his agreement.

They walked together towards Cherry Hinton, Bridie gabbling nervously about flowers and birds, then she excused herself and ran in to change. She felt sick, yet she continued up the stairs. Her hand was dirty, because it had touched his arm. She scrubbed herself for five whole minutes before sitting down to think. Liam was not the only item on her mind. Cathy was sitting an exam. Bridie had been soothed by the suggestion that Cathy might come to Sacred Heart not immediately, but in four years. The monster was in the house where her daughter's future was being decided.

Liam dallied in the garden for a while. The Irishwoman and Anthony were at loggerheads, it seemed. The idea pleased him. Anthony deserved few friends, because he had rejected his own twin, had accused him of all kinds of crimes.

Satisfied that his brother's life was no bed of roses, Liam stepped into Cherry Hinton with a new spring in his step.

Cathy scribbled the last answer and placed her pencil on Aunt Edith's desk. It was three-fifteen and she was supposed to linger here for another quarter of an hour. Sister Ignatius was rattling her rosary and staring at Cathy over the tops of those silly half-spectacles. Outside, blackbirds sang and the sun shone while Cathy basked beneath the eagle scrutiny of an extremely ugly nun with a three-haired wart. Noel skulked under the library table and Cathy didn't blame him. Sister Ignatius was enough to strike fear in the heart of any dog, even one as brave and uncomely as Cathy's mongrel.

'Would you like to check your answers?' asked Sister Ignatius.

'No, thank you.' The test had been fairly easy. For the first few minutes, Cathy had been tempted to put down all the wrong answers, but she did not wish to appear stupid in front of this tiny, hard-faced woman. Anyway, Mammy had promised that Cathy didn't have to think about going to Sacred Heart until she was eleven. Four years was a tremendous length of time. Anything could happen before Cathy reached the grand age of eleven.

'Then you may go.'

Cathy leapt up and made for the door with Noel hard on her heels.

'Have you nothing to say to me child? Normally, these examinations are held at the school. Because of my friendship with your aunt, I took the unprecedented step of interrupting the Easter holidays to bring the mountain to Mohammed.'

Cathy had seen no mountains, and Sister Ignatius had travelled in Aunt Edith's car, so the little girl failed to see what all the fuss was about. 'Thank you for coming, Mother,' she said. 'Come on, Noel.' The dog shot like greased lightning across the room.

'Very well. You may go.' Sister Ignatius waited until child and dog had left, then she fetched the test paper from the bureau. She scanned the first couple of pages, assessed the score. As expected, the child had achieved satisfactory marks in a test that was usually aimed at girls of ten or eleven years.

Edith appeared in the doorway. 'How did it go, Sister?'

'Caitlin O'Brien's intelligence quotient is high. I shall work it out later, but she has an adult reading age and her comprehension is excellent. We shall probably offer her a place. If she cannot take it up now for the kindergarten, we shall see her again at a later date. But she has passed the entrance hurdle.'

Edith smiled. Cathy was a clever girl. Now, all Edith had to do was court her away from Scotland Road. Sacred Heart was one of the best schools in the country. It could hold up its head with the finest of them, and Edith wanted to be around when girls from so-called working class families started to attend universities. With any luck, there would be more scholarships soon and further help from national and local governments. 'We need female doctors, lawyers and the like from all walks,' Edith told her friend. 'Not just from the ranks of the rich.'

Sister Ignatius agreed wholeheartedly. 'You find brains and stupidity in every class,' she remarked. 'And a school such as ours should cast its net wide to find the pick. That girl is a case in point. She needs us, Edith.'

'I know.'

The door opened and Liam Bell entered the room. He came to a dead stop when he saw the visitor, ran his eyes over the uncomely guest. 'Ah. Good afternoon, Aunt Edith. Sister?'

'Ignatius,' replied the seated woman.

'Liam Bell. Father Liam Bell.'

Mother Ignatius stared at the collar and tie, waited for further information, received none.

'It's a long time since you were here, Liam.' Edith was anxious to fill the awkward pause. 'And I see you're in civilian clothes.'

Liam made a quick response. 'Ah well, no-one takes notice of a man in a suit. The dog collar does tend to give away a priest's position. I've been working on the dock road, trying to get some of the women off the streets.'

Mother Ignatius nodded just once, the small movement emerging stiffly. This man had not been scouring the streets of Liverpool for fallen women. His mode of dress was wrong for such a role and anyway, he must have been travelling for much of the day. When had he found time to walk the dock road? And weren't the street women called ladies of the night? Surely they would have spent the mornings asleep?

Liam approached the chair in which the headmistress sat. 'Parish duties have kept me away from my aunt and uncle,' he said. 'So I decided on a whim to visit today.'

Priests were not allowed whims, had no time for such luxuries. Mother Ignatius smiled faintly, picked up Cathy's paper and walked to the door. 'I must take this chance to have a walk in your lovely gardens,' she said. 'I shall see you later, Edith. You too, Father Bell.' She laid great emphasis on the 'Father'. 'I shall find Cathy's mother and talk to her about the child's promising result.' She left the room, closing the door quietly.

'What was all that about?' asked Liam.

'Oh.' Edith closed the lid of her writing desk. 'We're thinking of securing a place for Cathy at Sacred Heart.'

'Really?'

Edith noticed the curl of his upper lip, heard the sneer in his tone. 'She is an exceptional child.'

'Is she?'

'Yes, indeed,' replied Edith.

Liam kept his mouth closed. He and his twin would probably figure in the last will and testament of Edith Spencer and her husband. So he needed to take care and put a rein on his tongue. 'It's very generous of you to help,' he said. 'I hope the child and Bridie are grateful.'

Cathy was far from grateful, and Edith was well aware of that fact. The child was enjoying her stay in the country, though the idea of living here did not appeal, not yet. In time, Cathy would come to realize that everyone was acting in her best interests. 'I'm sure they are grateful, Liam.' She kept the edge in her voice, allowed him to hear her displeasure.

He cleared his throat. 'So my father's wife is enjoying her stay?'

'Yes.' Edith had never found conversation with Liam easy. 'I think so.'

'And ... er ... Anthony?'

'He is settled.'

'In a non-Catholic school.' This was not a question.

'Anthony is a Christian,' replied Edith. 'Wherever he teaches, he will instruct the children to love and respect God.'

Liam coughed again. 'Do he and Bridie get on all right?'

Edith shrugged. 'I suppose they do, yes. They seem polite to each other, at least.'

He decided to hold his tongue. If the Irishwoman had quarrelled with Anthony, Aunt Edith might well be unaware of any such argument.

Edith muttered something about tea before leaving the room. Liam, momentarily alone, sat at the table and looked through the window. His heart did not flicker as he saw Maureen Costigan walking towards the house. She was from another time and another place, and she had merited her punishment. Now, she was here in Astleigh Fold, was living within a stone's throw of Anthony. In fact, the way things had turned out was probably to her advantage.

When the door opened, he did not turn.

Maureen came in and replaced a book she had borrowed.

'Good afternoon,' said Liam.

'Hello, Father Bell.'

He glanced at her. She was a decorative girl, rather striking with that dark hair and clear eyes. But she was not right for Anthony. 'How are you?' he asked.

Maureen put her head on one side. 'I'm all right.' He was horrible. He didn't care how she was, wasn't concerned at all. There was no expression in his tone, nothing on his face. He might have been asking about the weather.

'And the man who attacked you? Do you remember him?'

There was just a smell. She had seen no part of him, not even a foot or a hand. 'No,' she replied. The smell still eluded her. It was a familiar odour, yet her mind seemed to have blanked it out.

'That's a pity.'

Maureen dropped her chin and stared at her shoes. A finger of ice crept partway up her body, though the day was warm and sunny.

'Have you seen my brother?'

She shrugged. 'He came for his dinner once. And I think I saw him walking down the lane the other day. But I've been busy looking after Shauna and Cathy. Mrs Bell's been at the stables a lot.'

He breathed more easily after that. Maureen Costigan had lost interest in Anthony, it seemed.

'When are you coming back?' he asked.

'I'm not.' She straightened and looked at him. 'Mam says I can stay here for a while.'

'Ah.' So she was being careful. She was deliberately pretending not to care about Anthony. He would have to keep a watch on this situation, though supervising the young madam was going to be difficult. How on earth could he be in two places at once?

Maureen shifted from foot to foot. This was not the sort of man to be alone with. He was a priest, but he was not good. In fact, there was something quite nasty about him, as if he were criticizing people all the time, as if he considered himself to be a cut above everybody else. 'I . . . I'll go and help in the kitchen,' she said.

Alone once more, Liam Bell sat down and stared into space. Maureen Costigan had emerged very well from her ordeal. She would be living in comparative splendour, would be close to the object of her desire. Liam's hands closed into tight fists. She should have died. He would think about this later, would try to come up with a plan. A marriage between a Bell and a street urchin must be avoided, no matter what the cost.

Thirteen

Anthony picked up a book, flicked through the pages, scanned pale and closely packed print. Somewhere inside a volume such as this, he might find a clue, perhaps a whole set of ideas that could account for his brother's madness. He sighed, took a mouthful of tea. There were probably no answers. At best, one of the tomes would contain reasons, diagnoses, explanations of syndromes, suggestions about treatments and medications. He was not about to discover a solution to the problem by reading, though literature was as good a place as any to start, he supposed. The main question was how to get his twin brother removed from society. 'How?' he asked himself quietly. 'Who the hell will listen to me?'

The chapter on psychopathic disorder fell open, as if previous borrowers of this library copy had perused that particular part more frequently than the sections covering more mundane matters like anxiety and insomnia. His eye flew across the lines, searching greedily for a prompt.

The word 'psychopath' covered a multitude of sins and omissions, it seemed. The term referred to all kinds of sufferers, including those who failed just minimally to integrate with society. 'Eccentric?' mused Anthony. 'No, this is more than mere eccentricity.' He read on, discovered a few alarming paragraphs whose subject was nearer to home. Sweat beaded his forehead, dripped into his eyelashes. Liam was here, was written down and accounted for.

He raised his head. A strange feeling of comfort began to mingle with the fear in his chest. Someone knew. Whoever had written this book had seen the signs, had made notes about people like Liam. Father Liam Bell was odd but clever. Although the author of the borrowed book tended to concentrate on patients of low intellect, he had outlined a case concerning a mentally sick doctor who had damaged many in his care. Anthony quoted, 'Some disordered personalities function quite well within the confines of respectable professions. Many manage not to offend for long periods. However, colleagues may notice a certain oddness, an occasional tendency to offer inappropriate replies to questions. Sufferers occasionally fail to hear instructions or forget what they should be doing at a certain time. Nonetheless, the gifted psychopath can conceal his problem for much of the time.'

Anthony leaned back and remembered. How careful the young Liam had been when in the presence of adults. 'Me?' Liam would ask, the dark eyebrows arched in convincing dismay. 'It wasn't me. I'd never do a thing like that.' The embryonic monster had developed into a teenage terrorist whose targets had been chosen with meticulous precision. Liam had sharpened his illness to perfection while tormenting girls from areas other than Scotland Road, had graduated into manhood by 'punishing' prostitutes. Anthony swallowed. By the time Val had come along, Liam had been honed and ready for murder.

Maureen. Would Liam try again? Would he attack Bridie, too? After all, Bridie had married Dad, and Liam had expected to fare rather well after the demise of Sam Bell. 'God, will You please tell me what to do?' groaned Anthony. 'No-one will listen. Everybody thinks he was a young tearaway who straightened himself out and became a priest. Come on,' he pleaded. 'Omnipotence. Do something with Your omnipotence, Lord.'

The handbook for psychiatric staff rambled on about behaviour and emotional reactions. Reactions. Liam seldom reacted unless angered. Anthony could not recall a solitary positive response. Had Liam ever loved at all? No. Liam cared for no-one, pitied no-one. A few sentences leapt from the page. 'The patient presents himself as hard and uncaring. He suffers no guilt, pity or remorse. Concerned only with himself, he sometimes experiences, very briefly, a slight amount of pleasure or satisfaction when interfering successfully with another person's life.

'On the other hand, he may occasionally overreact as a result of some imagined slight, or he may enthuse disproportionately over a trivial matter.'

There followed a case history of a woman who had set out to destroy the lives of her relatives. She had haunted a sister's husband for weeks on end in order to 'prove' his infidelity, had divided the family into factions by means of malicious gossip, had sent 'anonymous' letters to her many victims. This unhappy female, having found herself to be unloved and unlovable, had assumed a power that might have compensated for her terrible loneliness had her plan worked. Having endured years of ill-treatment and bullying, the unfortunate husband of the sick woman had been admitted to a mental hospital. After questioning this man, doctors had realized that the wrong patient had been locked away.

A movement in the garden caught Anthony's eye. He stared through the glass, tried to smile as his heart sank. Maureen was here. Surely all that silly business was not about to start all over again? He would have to get rid of her. Liam had been on the loose in the neighbourhood. He might be planning to follow the girl, might be plotting another attack. Anthony dived through the house, threw

315

wide the door and stepped outside. Except for Maureen, the lane was deserted.

'I came,' she said proudly. 'All on my own.' Today, she had taken the giant step of venturing out unaccompanied. It had something to do with Father Bell, she suspected, because the desire to get away from him had been so strong. Still, whatever the reason, she was now able to walk about without an escort.

'I beg your pardon?'

Maureen sniffed and dashed a suspicion of moisture from her cheek. 'I'm going for Mrs Cornwell's messages in the village,' she told him. 'For meat and stuff, like. And I thought I'd call round here and say sorry. For . . . for what happened.' He was a decent bloke, she told herself. Just an ordinary, good-looking man who worked in a school and made people happy. It was a pity about his brother, though. Father Bell was a dull, nasty bugger.

Anthony scratched his head.

'When you were ill and I kept on visiting you.'

'Oh. That's all right.'

She stepped back. 'Are you looking for somebody?'

'No.'

Maureen felt the man's nervousness. She knew all about fear, could sense it here and now.

'Have you seen Liam?' he asked, his tone measured.

'Yes.'

Anthony cleared his throat. 'Where is he?'

'Talking to some nun in Mrs Spencer's garden. The nun came about Cathy going to her school.'

He studied the unwanted visitor closely. She did not flinch when speaking of Liam. 'Are you feeling better?'

She blinked slowly, looked as if she might be emerging from a reverie. 'He was tall.'

Anthony folded his arms and leaned against the jamb. 'Who was tall?'

'The man. The one who hurt me.'

Anthony shuddered.

'I could tell he was tall. He had long arms. I've not told anybody about his long arms. He was as big as you.'

Here came the truth, then. Well, as much of the truth as Maureen was capable of recalling. Anthony's fingers bit into his upper arm as he fought the rising panic. He could say nothing, could do nothing. But at least she was talking. 'Anything else?' he asked.

'Can't remember.' On the fringes of her memory sat another factor. It might have been a smell. She was almost sure that it was a smell or a taste. 'It was dark,' she added lamely. 'I couldn't see nothing. And I went and passed out 'cos he strangled me.'

'Maureen.' He stepped nearer to her. 'You're a survivor. You come from a family of survivors. Please look forward, not backwards.'

Maureen attempted a smile, though the result was unsure and watery. 'I can talk to you,' she told him. 'We all can, all the Scottie Road kids. And I will look forward, 'cos I've a lot to look forward to. Mrs Spencer's sending me to a dancing school in Manchester. She's nice. So is the doctor. He said the same as you. I'm young and I'll get better. Anyway, thanks for everything, Mr Bell.'

If only she knew how little he was doing, how limited he was. But if one syllable of Anthony's suspicions about his twin reached Diddy's ears, she would send her Billy out to deal with Liam. No matter what ideas he came up with, Anthony was powerless to act.

'I don't think he should have been a priest.'

Anthony inclined his head. Poor Maureen's thoughts were all over the place. Perhaps an almost inaccessible part of her mind had connected with Liam—

'Nobody likes him,' she added.

'I know.'

She sniffed. 'I don't think Father Brennan likes him, even. Nobody goes to confession when Father Bell's on. I'm sorry, 'cos I know he's your brother, but—'

'It's quite all right, Maureen. We can't choose our families, can we? Fortunately, we do get to choose our friends.'

She put her head on one side. 'Mr Bell's all for him, isn't he?'

'I suppose so.'

'And you belted Father Bell a long time ago.'

'Five years ago, yes.'

'Why?' She blushed. 'Sorry, I shouldn't have asked. It's your own business, not mine.'

He reached out and touched her shoulder. 'Go and do your shopping, Maureen. Don't worry about me and mine, just concentrate on yourself.' He stood and watched as she walked towards Astleigh Fold. Was it his imagination, or were those black curls of hair stiller than they used to be, less bouncy and free? Suddenly, Anthony realized that he was watching a woman, not a girl. Maureen Costigan was almost fourteen, and she was almost old.

Bridie rapped on the door sharply. He had to answer, had to be in.

Anthony finally opened the door. 'Bridie?' Her face was flushed along the fine cheekbones. She was so small, so vulnerable. He wanted to gather her into his arms and into his home, wanted to look after her and keep her from all harm. And she was the last person he could ever expect to enter his life as lover and soulmate.

Displaying an unexpected level of physical strength, she thrust herself past him and into the house. Her breathing was shallow and rapid, as if she had run all the way from Cherry Hinton. 'He's gone,' she whispered. 'I wondered if he had hurt you. He was on the lane earlier and I spoke to him.' She caught her breath. 'Richard came home after surgery and took him to Trinity Street in the car. About ten minutes ago.'

'Thank God for that. Are you all right?'

Bridie nodded, struggled to control her rapid inhalations. She had to tell him that she believed him, had to make sure that Anthony was not alone. ' 'Twas he who did it, Anthony,' she managed at last. 'I tried so hard to hope that you were wrong. I tried.' Her voice faded to nothing.

He drew her across the room and placed her in a chair. 'Please calm yourself,' he advised quietly.

She gazed at him silently for a moment. 'He looks so like you, yet not at all like you.' She didn't know what she meant. 'I saw the devil in his face,' she muttered by way of explanation. 'Anthony, he did it. He did that to Maureen, and she doesn't even remember. Can we make her remember?'

'No, Bridie. She will take her own time. And I doubt he'll strike at Maureen again, because he knows I have his measure.'

'Dear God.' She took a handkerchief from her sleeve and patted the moisture from her face. 'I feel so hot,' she said. 'I'm all of a work, as Mrs Cornwell would say.'

Anthony sat himself in the opposite chair. 'What happened to make you so agitated?' he asked.

'Nothing. Nothing at all. And that's the eejit truth of it.' She was strangling the handkerchief now. 'Nothing I can put a finger on, at least.'

He nodded, waited.

'I just looked through the window and saw the both of them together. The way he looked at her. That's all it was. He said little, did less, just stood there. But his mouth went tight and a corner of his lip lifted a bit, like a sneer. And his eyes ... well ... I never before saw an expression

319

like his. Just a second, it lasted, but I finally understood you.'

Anthony leaned forward, arms bent, elbows resting on knees, his head in his hands. 'Thank you,' he whispered.

'For what?'

'For coming.' He sat up straight, pushed the shock of dark hair from his forehead. 'For believing me.'

Bridie stared into the near distance. 'Has it occurred to you ever that he can't help it?'

'Of course it has. A mad dog can't help biting, so we remove him from society. If Liam isn't managing to control his behaviour, then we must remove him.'

Bridie froze. 'You don't mean . . . kill him?'

'I mean we put him away where he can do no more harm. But will he get put away because you don't like the way he looked at Maureen? Or because I have this strange notion that he killed Val and attacked other women including poor little Maureen Costigan? Do you know what that was about? Have you any idea how he came to pick on Maureen?'

'No.'

He closed his eyes for a couple of seconds, saw Maureen's bright young face in his mind's eye. The Costigan girl was still beautiful, but she was so much quieter these days. 'Maureen imagined a fondness for me, kept coming round to my house and feeding me tea and toast. He must have noticed. No-one must ever come near me, you see. He's . . . obsessed with our "'twin-ness".'

'That's terrible. It's unbelievable.'

'I know. That's why I am grateful for your faith in me. And Bridie, I'm beginning to think there's more than one Liam.'

Bridie bit her lip. 'I have to talk to Sam, Anthony.'

Anthony sat bolt upright. 'And Dad will run straight to

Liam with the tale. Do you want to die?' His tone was low, almost inaudible.

'No, I do not.'

'You want your children safe?'

A thrill of ice-cold fear made its slow way up Bridie's arms.

'He is so treacherous,' said Anthony. 'And I won't allow you to put yourself in any danger.' He jumped up and paced about. 'You must stay away from me and from him. Even though I love you...' His voice died for a few seconds. 'If he realized how fond I am of you—'

'This isn't the time for all that kind of talk,' she retorted almost snappily. 'In fact, there's never a right time for such foolishness. I have to talk to my husband, Anthony.'

'No. Don't you understand?' He crossed the room in two strides and stood over her. 'You must do and say nothing.'

But Bridie's mind was made up. Her marriage was not exactly the stuff dreams were made of, but she trusted the man who had taken her in. 'I shall talk to him,' she insisted. 'I have a lot of faith in your father. He is very good to me and my girls.'

'Dad won't listen.'

'Oh, he will.' She nodded thoughtfully. 'He will listen to me, Anthony. It's time he understood the quarrel between you and your brother. If you won't tell him, then some-body should. And I am probably the best somebody for the job.'

Made powerless by the forcefulness of her tone, Anthony returned to his chair. 'What a bloody mess,' he remarked.

'Yes, it is so,' she said to herself. 'It won't be easy. I don't expect it to be easy. But all the same, it has to be tackled.'

'It will hurt my father,' he told her.

'I know that. But Val, Maureen and yourself have been hurt. Unfortunately, more pain must be caused before the problem can be wiped out.'

'I'll miss you,' he whispered.

She knew what he meant. 'I'll need to be going,' she answered.

He saw tears in her eyes. 'Telling Dad what we know about Liam will damage him,' he said.

She walked to the door. 'I have weighed it all in my mind, Anthony,' she announced clearly. 'And I shall be talking to Sam.' Her heart lurched as the words were spoken, because she might well be putting herself, Cathy and Shauna at risk. Even Sam could become a target for his own son's vileness. But Bridie's sense of right and wrong dictated that the problem must be addressed. 'Goodbye,' she said softly. 'Be safe.'

'But will you be safe?'

She dropped her chin and stared at the ground. 'I have never been safe. Neither have you. Yet we have survived till now, so we'll probably be all right.'

He went inside, stood at the window and watched as she walked towards Cherry Hinton. The pit of his stomach ached with emptiness, though Anthony's real hunger was not for food.

Flash Flanagan ambled along behind the cart that contained all his worldly goods plus a few items whose origins he had conveniently forgotten. A gentle soul who would never willingly hurt another, he was not averse to picking up 'lost' articles, some of which had not been thoroughly misplaced when Flash had 'found' them. But his mind dwelt on just one small parcel – a paper bag with a length of green silk folded into it.

He stopped at the Pier Head, watched a train puffing its cityward way along the dockers' umbrella. The overhead railway sheltered many people from rain, and Flash used its protection regularly as one of his stopping-off points. He picked up a penny, two cigarette cards and a half-eaten apple.

'Flash?'

It was the law. 'This is my penny – I dropped it.' The defensiveness left his tone as he continued, 'I'm not moving on. There's no life at the other side of Liverpool. I'm doing no harm here, anyway.'

'You're a vagrant,' replied the constable.

'I'm as English as you are,' said Flash, deliberately choosing to misinterpret the policeman's words.

'Go to the Sally Army,' suggested the officer.

'I don't want saving.' Flash's feathers were ruffled. 'And I got fleas last time.'

'Fleas? You breed your own, Flash.' The younger man shrugged his shoulders. 'Just keep moving, then. Don't be loitering with intent.'

Flash glared belligerently at the policeman, did not blink until the man turned and walked away. A bloody nuisance, they were. Thought they owned the place just because they wore a daft hat and boots big enough to use as tugs. He did not trust the keepers of the peace. Had he enjoyed any faith in the law, Flash would have handed over that murder weapon. The girl had survived, but the stole had been used with a view to ending her life.

He turned towards the river and stared blankly at the horizon. The green stole had been stretched to a point where the stitching had failed. The green stole had probably been stretched across Maureen Costigan's throat. Flash remembered Maureen well, as she had often joined him in his efforts to entertain the people of Scotland Road. The girl had shared in his takings, had performed many a song and dance while Flash had rattled his marionettes or his tambourine.

A priest? Gulls whirled over his head, their plaintive cries echoing along the waterfront. Or had someone stolen the stole? He allowed himself a wry grin when the play on words hit his consciousness. Who stole the stole?

A seagull perched itself on the handrail that edged the Pier Head. It kept one eye on the river and the other on Flash's recently acquired half-apple. 'Loitering with intent,' Flash advised the bird. 'Keep moving, or soft lad'll be back with his truncheon.'

The gull sped away over the water.

'Whoever did it, it'll be my fault,' Flash told himself aloud. 'Every time anything goes missing, it's always down to me. Anybody would think I was a robber. They'll say I pinched it. But I never hurt little Maureen, did I?'

A woman stopped. 'Did you say something?'

'Not to you, no.'

She walked on and wondered whether the tramp's brain was drink-addled.

Flash collected thoughts and cart, then continued his noisy journey. The cart's wheels squealed like injured cats, and various substances clattered together inside the cart's body. Several people recognized Flash and greeted him, asked him where he had been recently.

On a whim, he turned right and made for Scotland Road. He didn't feel up to much, wasn't in the mood for puppets and music. But on Scotland Road there lived a man who was a good listener. Flash would go to Sam Bell and see if he could squeeze an opinion out of the pawnbroker. Sam was a quiet man, but he owned a degree of common sense. Perhaps Sam could work out what should be done about the stole.

When he reached Scottie, Flash stood for a few seconds and drank in the sights and sounds that he loved so much. The barber leaned against his door jamb, a white apron covering him from head to foot. A butcher chased a dog out of his shop, while trams and horses rattled along the road. 'This is my bloody home,' Flash told himself. 'I'm not getting hunted out of here again.' He straightened his travelweary spine. 'Just let them try,' he muttered.

This was no time for talking to walls and seagulls, he told himself firmly. Although the vestment in his cart weighed very little, it was the biggest burden he had ever carried. In his possession, Flash had the evidence that might send a man to the gallows. Although the day was warm, the tramp pulled up the collar of his coat before crossing over to Bell's.

Charlie grinned broadly, allowing Flash Flanagan the sight of perfectly even teeth. 'I'm in charge,' he boasted. 'Mr Bell's been fishing three times this week.'

Flash processed the poorly pronounced statement. 'Is he fishing now?'

Charlie shook his over-large head. 'Down Paddy's with a load of stuff for Nicky's stall.'

The visitor leaned against the counter. 'How's Maureen?'

Charlie's smile vanished. 'With Mam on a farm. Getting better. Mam's coming home. Maureen's stopping at the farm.'

While Charlie made out a ticket for a customer, Flash had a root round the shop. He turned the mechanism of an oil-starved wooden mangle, fiddled with a chloride house-lighting battery and a James Autocycle that had seen better days, then sat on a cane chair to wait for Sam's return. Poor little Maureen.

Flash closed his eyes and saw her dancing outside the

Rotunda, shining curls bouncing, cheeks dimpling in the three-year-old face. Even the hardest of hearts had melted when confronted by such a beautiful and talented child. She would run along the theatre queue and beg for money, would always bring it back to share with Flash. 'I looked after her,' the tramp said to no-one in particular.

'Mam likes you.'

Flash opened his eyes. The Costigans were a good lot, decent and caring. 'I like your mam, too, Charlie.' They had trusted him to look after little Maureen, had left her in his care for many an hour. 'Safe as houses with Flash,' Diddy had always said.

Charlie counted takings, made laborious notes in a ledger.

'I'm tired,' said Flash. It suddenly occurred to him that he was about seventy-five. Without the benefit of complete family or birth details, Flash had been forced to guess at his age. 'I might even be eighty,' he added. 'Or bloody ninety.'

Theresa Bell poked her face into the shop. 'Hundred, more like,' she pronounced cheerfully. 'If only the good die young, you and me must be as old as Father Time.'

Flash closed his surprised mouth. 'Who got you up?' he asked.

'Meself.'

'Enough to give me a heart attack. Must be years since you set foot in the shop, Mrs Bell.'

Theresa sniffed. 'Get in here,' she told him. 'And I'll find you a bite to eat.'

Flash asked Charlie to keep an eye on his cart, which was parked outside the window. He walked into the kitchen and sat opposite Theresa at the table.

'Well?' she said.

'Well what?'

'What have you found? What are you selling? More to

the point, where is it, do they know they've lost it, how much would you be asking for it if it was yours and do you take sugar?'

'Two sugars,' he answered. She looked marvellous, as if she had found a new lease of life. 'I just want to talk to your Sam, that's all.' He grabbed a scone and bit into it. 'She's done a lot of good round here, that new daughter-in-law of yours.'

'What about?'

'Well, it's clean and cheerful and—' He spluttered on a mouthful of scone.

'What do you want our Sam for?'

'Private.'

'Oh, I see. Man talk, is it?'

'I suppose so.'

Theresa sipped at her tea and waited for more information.

Flash wriggled beneath her scrutiny and under the weight of his own unsavoury thoughts. 'How's Father Liam?' he asked eventually.

Old shoulders lifted themselves. 'How the hell should I know?'

No, the tramp told himself. It couldn't have been a priest. Even one as nasty as Liam Bell. Some bad piece of work had pinched the stole from the vestry ... Funny thing to pinch, though. 'He was a tearaway at one time, your Liam.'

Theresa Bell sniffed meaningfully. 'Aye, he was. Near put me in my grave, he did. Near put our Anthony next to me and all. Why are we talking about him?'

It was Flash's turn to shrug. 'I don't know.'

'Oh, don't come that with me, Flash Flanagan.' Flash was not a particularly talkative man. The only time he spoke up was when defending himself in front of that universal enemy that called itself a police force.

'I want to talk to Sam,' he insisted.

'Please yourself.' Theresa scraped back her chair, nodded curtly, then took herself off upstairs.

The visitor leaned back and gazed round the room. The fireside cupboards were stuffed with valuable ornaments, but Flash made no move in their direction. He was a man of principle, a man who would never steal from a friend. In fact, he seldom took anything unless his chances of getting caught were negligible.

The back door opened. 'Flash?' Sam was surprised to see the guest. 'What are you doing here?'

The tramp rose from his chair, his movement stirring dust in clothing that was rather less than clean. He walked to the stairs, made sure that Theresa had not lingered.

'What's happened?' asked Sam.

'I don't know. But I never done it.' Flash returned to his seat.

'Then why are you here?' Sam's much admired steadiness of temper had diminished of late. He missed Bridie. What would she have said had she seen Flash Flanagan sitting at her table in all his muck and glory? 'Come on, I haven't got all day.'

Flash dropped his chin and thought for a second or two before dragging a package from his pocket. He set it on the table and pulled back his fingers quickly, as if the small parcel had been on fire. 'I found that,' he whispered. 'As God is my judge, I never done nothing. Except for finding that.'

'What is it?'

'It's not a matter of what, Sam. It's a matter of where.'

'Eh?' Sam scratched his head.

'Where I found it.'

The pawnbroker leaned against the dresser. 'I've a shop to run. There's no time for guessing games. Just spit it out and then I can get on with business.'

Flash inhaled deeply. 'It belongs to a priest,' he said.

'Then take it to the presbytery. Father Brennan'll sort it out. I don't sell that kind of stuff.' Flash often called in with something he had acquired on his travels. 'And I certainly don't want holy bits and pieces that have been found before they went missing. There'll be a sin attached to whatever that is.'

'Oh, there's a sin to it, all right,' Flash replied quietly. 'Just about the biggest sin going.'

A feeling of unease visited Sam's stomach. He had known Flash for years. Flash was not one for getting himself worked up over nothing. 'You're making a big mystery out of this,' he said. 'Open the bloody thing.'

'I'd rather you did. I've been carrying it round for ages, ever since I found it. Course, they asked questions down the police station, but I kept a lid on this. I mean, it's not normal, is it? You can't walk into the copshop and show them something like this. Where would it all have ended?'

Sam strode to the table and ripped open the paper bag. A length of green silk tumbled out. 'Where?' he asked, the word emerging strangled from his parched throat. He coughed. 'You'd better tell me all about this, Flash. Where did you get it?'

'I picked it up next to little Maureen Costigan. It's been stretched to buggery, Sam. I reckon it was used by who-ever attacked her. That man tried to kill Maureen with a priest's stole.'

In that moment, Sam's world stopped moving. He heard the ticking of a clock, the rattle of a tram, some hissing from the fire when pockets of air freed themselves from within the coals. But all these sounds seemed to be coming from a different place, from another dimension.

'Sam?'

No, no. None of it was true. Anthony had exaggerated all his life, had blamed Liam for the least thing. And for the bigger things, too. Sam had stood by a hospital bed and watched the almost drowned Anthony coming back to life. He had consulted dentists about Anthony's broken teeth, had visited doctors while limbs had been set. Anthony had been a clumsy child. Anthony had always blamed Liam.

'Sam?'

The shopkeeper swivelled and looked at the storeroom. Liam had sworn repeatedly that his twin brother had locked himself in there before pushing the key under the door. Broken toys, broken friendships, Anthony silent and unsmiling, Liam grinning covertly in a corner. 'He's a priest,' said Sam now.

'What?' Flash was beginning to worry. Sam Bell looked ill and pale.

The stole was Liam's. It came from a full set of vestments that had been stitched by some retired Augustinian sisters in the city convent. The crosses on the garments were ornate and unusual, had been crafted lovingly in celebration of the new priest's ordination.

'I'll leave it with you,' mumbled Flash. He rose to leave.

'Hang on,' said Sam. 'Say nothing. I want you to swear that no matter what happens, you'll tell nobody about this stole.'

Flash looked hurt. 'You know me better than that,' he said. 'I'll say nothing to nobody.'

'Swear,' insisted Sam.

'I swear, all right? I swear on my own life that I'll never breathe a word.'

'Thanks.' Sam Bell lowered himself into a dining chair. He listened while Charlie Costigan and Flash Flanagan passed the time of day, waited until he was truly alone. Then he reached and picked up the stole. It was creased and squashed where a pair of strong hands had held it firmly, was stretched to bursting point along its narrowest part. Stitching had broken so that the cream-coloured lining had parted company with the layer of emerald green silk. This was a murder weapon.

He closed his eyes in an effort to shut out the sights of normal life. There had been trouble. Always, always, there had been trouble. From the periphery of memory, sounds and pictures crept into his head, so that the inside of his eyelids formed a screen against which the past played itself. Things he had half-seen and half-heard, comments Muth had made, angry words scalding the air between Liam and Anthony – all these filled his brain until he thought he might just explode. The angry words had usually come from young Anthony, as Liam seldom got riled.

After several moments of stillness, Sam opened his eyes, picked up the stole and stared at it. He folded the silk, took a key from his pocket, then locked the offending item in a part of the storeroom known only to himself. No-one in the world knew about this secret hiding place. He had to think, had to collect more information. With a heavy tread, he walked to the bottom of the stairs and picked up the phone. Moments passed while he waited for the connection to be made. 'Edith?' he said at last. 'Send someone down for Anthony, please. I'll call back in half an hour.'

Thirty minutes was a dreadfully long time. Sam checked on Charlie, left him in charge. He brewed tea, threw it away, smoked three cigarettes. There was something wrong with the clock, he felt sure. It ticked very slowly, seemed sluggish and in need of winding. But the six-day mechanism had been tightened only yesterday. The fire flickered. Bridie had made the room so nice, so cheerful. Bridie had married a man whose son was a . . .

A priest. 'I'm blind,' he announced to the mirror. 'I've always been bloody blind.' He had blinkered himself deliberately, he decided. 'Such a good little lad, Liam seemed. It was as if Anthony wanted to get his brother into trouble all the time. Why didn't I see? I should have listened to Muth.'

At last, the half-hour was over. Sam threw a fraction of cigarette into the fire and returned to the phone. For the first time in ages, he was going to give his full attention to Anthony.

Father Liam Bell let himself into the presbytery. A creature of habit, he followed the same routine as ever by removing his shoes and easing his feet into sensible brown slippers. He hung up his cloak, stood the biretta on a hall table, tapped the nearby barometer. Father Brennan was hearing confessions tonight. As few of the congregation wanted to open their hearts to the younger priest, Liam had been given the night off.

The barometer promised rain. Liam walked into the kitchen and took a covered plate from the top shelf of the meatsafe. Michael Brennan's dinner sat on a pan of water on a gas ring waiting to be reheated. Father Brennan loved his stomach, but Liam stuck to salads, vegetables and a small amount of meat or fish. The sins of the flesh should not be committed, especially in a presbytery. He carried his meal through to the dining room, whispered his grace, began to eat slowly and without pleasure.

Maureen Costigan had landed on her feet, it seemed. There had been gossip about her staying on with Aunt Edith and Uncle Richard. She would be near Anthony, of course. Perhaps Liam should abandon his twin to whatever fate lay in store for him. Perhaps marriage to the little madam was what Anthony deserved. Yes, that situation was best left alone for now. Let Anthony find his own way into the bottomless abyss.

Liam chewed on a piece of ham, tasted nothing. The Welcome Home project was doing him a lot of good. Even the bishop had remarked upon how well the young priest was doing. Yes, Liam had proved something. He could save souls. He was capable of sitting down amongst the lowest of street women and persuading them to mend their ways. That was preferable to the other kind of penance, he supposed. Punishing people by demonstrating physically the error of their ways had been an untidy business.

The door opened. Feeling a slight draught, Liam turned. His father was entering the room. 'I wasn't expecting you,' Liam said, voice and face expressionless.

Sam steadied himself against the sideboard. This was his son. Even now, Sam tried to turn from the inevitable. Surely not? Surely Liam was not a killer? 'You forgot to lock the door,' was the best he could manage. As if seeing Liam for the first time, Sam studied his son's face. There was no warmth, no humanity in the features. Liam was a good-looking man with a bad-looking soul. He had empty eyes and an unyielding jaw.

'Are you ill?' asked Liam.

Numbed almost to the bone after the lengthy telephone conversation with Anthony, Sam simply stared at the other twin. Gooseflesh rose on his arms and a cold sweat bathed his brow. God, why hadn't he noticed before? Why hadn't he cared enough to notice? Bridie, he told himself inwardly. Since her arrival in his life, Sam had become more perceptive.

'Dad?'

'I've come . . .' Sam's voice failed him, so he cleared his throat. 'I've come to confess,' he managed finally.

Liam dropped his napkin onto the table. 'Father Brennan's in church. He's hearing confessions.'

'I know that.'

'Then why are you here?'

Sam advanced and stood next to the table. 'I've a very big sin to tell,' he said. 'And I have to tell it to you, because you will understand it. Well, you might understand it.' Split personality, Anthony had said. Sam wondered who Liam was at this moment. Was he the Liam who could absorb information, or was he the one who killed? The unspoken question answered itself. The other Liam, the murderer, was the unseen man, the one who crept up from behind and . . .

'Ah.' The younger man pushed himself away from the table. 'Just wait until I get my stole,' he said.

Sam sighed. 'The green one? Will you use the green one? I remember the sisters making those vestments for you, Liam. The needlework was beautiful. I was so proud of you. So proud and so damnably stupid.'

Time ticked away a few seconds, then the mantel clock chimed the hour.

'Remember the green one, Liam?' repeated Sam.

The priest made no reply, but a small warning arrived, a soft voice telling him to beware.

'Where is it?' Sam asked.

Liam shrugged. 'Well, I've several green ones, of course—'

'Cream lining. The crosses outlined in real gold thread. Gold and green fringe on the ends.'

'I've mislaid it, unfortunately.' The hairs on Liam's neck stood on end as he walked into the hallway. He opened his case, took out a stole, kissed the central cross and placed it around his neck. Something momentous was about to happen.

Sam was waiting for his son. 'Bless me, Father,' he began.

Liam raised his hand and formed the sign of the cross.

'The biggest sin, the worst sin,' said Sam. 'That's what

I've come to talk about. You see, I had no time for my children. If I had made time, I would have noticed what was going on.'

The priest mumbled a blessing.

'Anthony was always in trouble,' continued Sam. 'Broken toys, bruises all over him, missing teeth. I took the easiest way by listening to you and not to him. My mother tried to tell me what a bad lot you were, but you were so quiet and angelic in the house. You didn't interfere with business, you see. Your brother's complaining kept me from my shop, so I lost patience with him, then ignored him. I had a living to make.' He paused, took a deep breath. 'It is three weeks since my last confession, Father,' continued the penitent. 'My biggest sin is that I bred a monster. You are my fault, Liam. I take full responsibility for what you are.'

Liam dropped into the chair he had recently vacated. 'What on earth are you talking about?'

Sam stared into those familiar dark eyes, noticed that his son scarcely flinched. 'Valerie. Little Maureen Costigan. Those street girls in Liverpool. I'm talking about rape, murder and attempted murder.'

'Nonsense,' snapped Liam. 'You've been in touch with Anthony, I take it?'

Sam nodded.

'He's hated me right from the start. How do you think I felt when he threw himself into the river and blamed me for the incident? He used to go into the cupboard and push the key under the door. He broke his arm and said I'd done it. Everything that goes wrong for him is my fault, or so he insists.'

Sam clucked his tongue. 'You'll fool me no longer,' he muttered. 'I've seen the light.'

'What light?'

'The stole.'

335

Liam picked up his cutlery and laid it neatly on the plate. 'I told you earlier – the stole went missing from the vestry. Anyone could have taken it. Perhaps one of the altar boys, or–'

'No.'

'Dad, I am a priest. Being a priest is difficult enough without all this. I have done nothing wrong. Anything I do is for the good of the Church and her members.'

Sam walked across the room and stared through the window. He looked at the school where Anthony had taught until recently, where young Cathy had enjoyed herself since arriving in Liverpool. St Aloysius's was a marvellous school with an excellent reputation. 'Anthony's a good teacher,' he said, almost inaudibly.

Liam heard the words. 'That has never been in doubt.'

'Then why did he leave?'

'I don't know.'

Sam swung round and faced his son. 'Because of you. He left because he can't stand to be near you. He's been reading some medical books, stuff about mental cases, says you're ill. Are you ill?'

'No.'

The pawnbroker inclined his head in thought. 'Then why do you hurt people? What the hell gives you the right to go round raping women and murdering them?' He held up a hand. 'No, don't deny it. Anthony put me straight this afternoon. There's no way he could have made all that up. Too many coincidences, you see. I should have known without needing to be told. Perhaps I did know, only I didn't want to face what you are. Because I'm a failure as a father, Anthony has been forced to carry the weight of your sins without my help. It's been a heavy burden for the lad.'

Liam glanced at the clock. Depending on the number of customers, Father Brennan might be back within half an hour. 'You should sleep on this.' There was a steely edge to the words. 'After all, you can't go running around with accusations of this nature, can you? I think you should—'

'Don't think for me,' snapped Sam. 'Don't treat me like a child whose fingers have been in the collection plate. I'm sick of your patronizing attitude. You killed Anthony's girl. You tried to squeeze the life out of Diddy's daughter. When Billy hears about that, you'd better be in a different country or a different bloody galaxy.'

Liam's eyes were fixed on his father's face. Never before had he seen Sam Bell in a temper. Sam had been a placid man, one who usually followed the easiest course through life. It was the Irish bitch who had changed him, of course.

'Why, Liam?'

'I beg your pardon?'

'Why did you kill?'

Liam's face was devoid of expression. 'I followed orders,' he answered at last.

'From God?'

The young cleric nodded.

'Voices?' Anthony had mentioned voices, had told Sam that many diseased minds played tricks.

'Sometimes.'

'Then you are ill,' Sam said. 'You need help. And those around you need to be kept safe.'

Liam did not understand any of this. Other saints had followed orders straight from God. St Joan had persisted until the flames had swallowed her. St Stephen had been stoned to death. Many apostles had been martyred because they had obeyed the voice of the departed Jesus. 'I do what has to be done,' he announced clearly. 'The punishment must fit the crime.'

Sam nodded rhythmically for a few moments, as if deliberating over his son's words. 'Then you must hang.

If the punishment is to fit, you must feel that noose tightening around your throat. That's what Maureen felt. The only difference was that her noose was holy and made of silk.'

Liam's head shook in disbelief. 'Maureen was throwing herself at Anthony and—'

'And that's no business of yours.'

Liam jumped to his feet. 'It is, it is!' His tone rose in pitch until it resembled the wailings of a spoilt child. 'Anthony is the other half of me. I have to save him.'

Sam Bell feared for his own sanity. He was watching his son dissolving before his very eyes, as if the man's face were melting into an unrecognizable shape. The eyes were burning like coals, and his mouth kept twisting as if something nasty rested on the taste buds. 'You're crackers,' breathed Sam. 'You are one hundred per cent off your bloody head, Liam.'

Liam checked himself, literally pulling himself together until he felt taller and stronger. 'Yes, it is your fault,' he breathed. 'If you had taken better care of my mother, she would have been there to care for me. Instead of a mother, I had that old dragon. She always despised me, always loved Anthony. My mother died because of your neglect.'

Sam staggered back as if he had just been hit. Liam had struck a nerve. Poor Maria. He closed his eyes and saw her, a little waif of a thing with a belly swollen in pregnancy. Maria had had no family to take care of her. Sam, busy making ends meet, had found little time for his exhausted wife. Muth had tried her best, of course, but Maria had still slipped away quietly. Maria had done everything quietly, and Sam had not appreciated her. 'I wish I'd done more,' he admitted. 'I wish I'd got to know your mam better.'

'Then that's the sin you should be confessing,' snarled the priest.

The older man's eyes flew open. 'Whatever I've done or failed to do, my behaviour was nothing compared to yours. I suppose you'll kill me now. But before you do, remember this. Others know about you.' He nodded jerkily. 'There is no way of silencing all who know the truth, Liam.'

'Who? Who are they?' Panic trimmed the words, causing Liam's voice to rise yet again. 'Who?' he screamed.

'Apart from your brother, who has always known your guilt, the rest are not family members.' There was only Flash, Sam told himself. No, no. There was Richard. Anthony had spoken to him, and the good doctor had agreed. According to Richard Spencer, Liam Bell was probably a lunatic. Had Anthony told Bridie? God, were they all in danger?

Sam swallowed the rising panic. 'Anthony has left the decision-making to me. He tried five years ago to have you arrested for killing Valerie. Now, he feels that no-one will ever believe him. But there's proof at last, Liam. There's the stole. Once that's given to the police, they'll start listening to your brother.'

'Where is it?' The priest spoke through gritted teeth. He had to find that wretched stole.

'In a safe place,' replied Sam. It was locked in a box behind a loose brick in the storeroom, hidden while Sam decided what to do next.

'Anthony? Is he going to have me arrested?'

Sam shook his head wearily. 'Anthony, strangely enough, is on your side. He's been thinking about ... doctors. You should go into hospital for treatment.'

'Never!' roared Liam. 'There's nothing wrong with me. Look at my exam results; look at all I've achieved. No mentally sick person could do what I've done.'

Sam dropped his head. 'Your cleverness is part of your illness,' he said sadly. 'And that's the unfortunate thing.

You were born with a magnificent brain and you have used your natural superiority to do damage. I'm sorry, son. I'm so sorry for you.'

Liam leapt across the room. Soon, he would work out what must be done. As God's chosen messenger, he must carry on with his work. 'Will you hang me?' he asked. 'Or will you have your own son locked away for life with insane people? Where is the stole?'

Sam saw the devil in his son's eyes and backed away.

'Where is it?'

'No.' Sam pulled at his collar, which was suddenly tight. He had to get out, had to get away from the madman. The world had fallen apart since Flash Flanagan's visit. Until a couple of hours ago, Sam had been the father of a priest. Now, he was the father of a maniac.

'Tell me!' commanded Liam.

A red-hot pain shot through Sam's chest. It travelled swiftly down his arms and into his wrists. There was no air in the room. Knowing that he was dying, he thought briefly about his pretty young wife, his poor old mother and the son who had gone to work in Bolton, the son he had neglected.

Liam stood by helplessly while his father dropped like a stone. He bent down and shook Sam's arm, recognized immediately that the man was dead. Like an animal, the priest lifted his head and roared at the ceiling. His father was gone. More importantly, the stole had been found and he, Father Liam Bell, was in danger.

Fourteen

The pavements were packed with people, yet a strange quiet overhung much of Scotland Road. Old enemies rubbed shoulders, all differences forgotten in the wake of recent events. United by tragedy, friend and foe stood together to mourn the passing of a man whose shop, like all the others, was closed for the first time in years.

Outside Dolly Hanson's, a *Daily Herald* poster had been knocked to the ground, 'PRIEST STILL MISSING' screamed the headline. Sam Bell had died of a heart attack in the presbytery of St Aloysius Gonzaga, and his son had disappeared without trace on the same evening.

'I suppose he might be upset, like. In shock or sent crazy with grief,' said Alice Makin, doubtfully. Alice, money-lender and seller of second-hand clothes, had woken this morning in her own bed rather than in the bridewell. Out of respect for the deceased, she had stuck to brown ale for several days. She had also taken the unprecedented step of leaving her market stall unopened. The gigantic woman, surrounded by other 'Paddy's' traders, waited with everyone else for Sam's coffin to be borne out of Bell's Pledges. 'For all we know, Father Bell couldn't take no more, so he ran off when his dad dropped dead.'

The pot stall woman grunted. 'He never cared about nobody, that Father Bell. He once gave me a dozen decades for swearing. Twelve bloody decades. My old man got no tea that night because I kept forgetting how many times I'd been round the beads. Horrible, that priest was. I can't see him dashing off just because his old feller keeled over. More to it than that, Alice.'

Alice Makin sighed. 'I've met nobody what liked Father Liam, the po-faced bugger. But Sam Bell thought the world of him, loved his bones. Never had no time for their Anthony. Sam was the only one what loved Liam. So now, Liam hasn't got a friend on this earth. I wonder where he's buggered off to?'

'He doesn't want friends,' snapped the pot-seller. 'He likes people not liking him. Cut above us all, that one. No, he's not gone off grieving, Alice.'

The trams had stopped running, were spilling their human cargo onto the road. Drivers got down and removed their hats. A postman lingered with his sack, waited with everyone else for Sam Bell to make his final journey to church.

At the back of the crowd, a thin blue line was forming.

'Police,' breathed Alice.

'Never mind – you're sober,' replied Alice's colleague.

'I bet they're looking for him,' decided Alice Makin.

'For Father Bell?'

'Yes. Told you, Polly. There's more going on than what meets the eye. I've got a funny feeling about this lot,' she whispered. 'I keep hoping he's just run away because he's sad, but my flesh carries on crawling. There's something wrong.'

But the woman who was usually called Potty Polly wasn't convinced that the boys in blue were looking for Father Bell. The police were here because the Protestants were here. She cast an eye over familiar faces, noticed Jews among Christians, Methodists in line with Catholics, nuns side by side with uniformed members of the Sally Army. 'He never had a lot to say for himself, Sam Bell,' she decided aloud. 'But he was fair. Did you ever see the likes of this, Alice? There's that kosher butcher, the one what always pays to have his fire lit by a Christian lad on Saturdays. And look – that lot over there marches with the Orange every year. They've all come out for Sam Bell. If I hadn't seen this with my own eyes, I'd never have believed it, not in a month of Easter Sundays.'

Alice nodded and folded ham-like arms across her ample chest. 'There'll be no fighting,' she advised her companion. 'Not at a funeral. Police aren't here because of the crowd. No, there's got to be something else.'

Potty Polly smiled sadly. It was nice to see everybody together like this. For years, there had been trouble on 'walking days', when Catholics paraded through the streets with brass bands playing behind statues carried by strong men. On walking days, the Protestants had to keep their distance from Scotland Road.

The little old woman who had sold pots on Paddy's Market for almost half a century thought about the Orange marches, too, when Catholic children threw fruit and abuse in the direction of King Billy's horse as it ambled through the streets with a child on its back. The poor lad who pretended to be Billy inevitably ended up spattered and filthy. Yet today, because a quiet and rather cool-mannered pawnbroker had died, the people stood united in an almost silent wall of tribute. 'He was respected,' said Polly.

'He was honest to a fault,' agreed Alice. 'But I still wonder why the Rose Hill mob have turned up. And there's coppers from other stations, too. They'll be up to no good, as usual.' Alice's antipathy towards the guardians of the peace was a legend in her own lifetime. 'They say Anthony made peace with Sam just before he died.'

'Who says?'

Alice shrugged her huge shoulders. 'People.'

'Diddy Costigan?' asked Polly. Alice and Diddy were good mates. Diddy was always a reliable source of information. 'Was it Diddy that told you?'

'Yes. But that was all she said. There was a lot she didn't say.'

Polly scratched her nose. 'How do you know there was a lot she didn't say if she didn't say it?'

'I just do. Shut up, Polly. Here comes poor Sam, God bless him.'

Complete silence visited the road while Sam was brought out of his shop. Six bearers carried him, with Billy Costigan and Anthony Bell at the front. The other four were dockers who had forgone a morning's pay to help Billy with his tragic burden.

Alice Makin sniffed and wiped her face on a corner of her grey shawl. She fixed her eyes on Bridie Bell, a small figure in black. The young woman's face was hidden by a veil. 'She'll have her work cut out,' breathed Alice. 'No bigger than a child and with a business to run.' She could not imagine Bridie emptying a house or giving a hand with a chest of drawers. 'Good God,' Alice exclaimed, 'it's old Theresa.'

Bridie steeled herself at the sight of so many people. She clung to her mother-in-law's arm, wondered who was supporting whom. Theresa had not cried, had shed no tears for her departed son. The old lady had simply sat for several days with cups of tea and a grim expression. 'Liam did it,' she had said from time to time. 'Liam killed our Sam.'

When the dreadful news had reached Cherry Hinton, Bridie had decided to leave her daughters at the farm. It was no use dragging two little girls through a procession and a Requiem Mass. Strangely, Bridie had grieved for the man she had married. She had not known him long, but he had done his best for her and the children. Kindness always made Bridie cry. Mammy had been kind. Until Sam, Mammy had been the only kindness Bridie had known at close quarters.

Of course, Da had turned up. There was a saying about bad pennies, and Thomas Murphy was a full half-crown's worth. Since his arrival from Ireland, he had worn a smug grin, had stalked about looking like the cat who had eaten the cream. Was he expecting his daughter to return defeated to live with him?

She shuddered. Da was a bad man. Bridie chased a thought from her mind, forced herself to stop wishing that the coffin contained Thomas Murphy instead of Sam Bell. Fourth commandment, she told herself sternly. Honour thy father and thy mother, even if thy father is the wicked creature who drove thy lovely mother to an early grave.

'You all right, love?' whispered Theresa.

'Yes. And you?'

'I'll be lighter when yon so-called priest is locked up or hanged.'

Muth knew nothing, yet she knew everything. It was probably something to do with being very old, Bridie decided. The police were here, were standing shoulder to shoulder behind the crowds. There would be no trouble, Sam's widow thought. People were here just to say good-bye to Sam.

The cortège turned left and entered the small forecourt of St Aloysius Gonzaga. A glass-sided hearse waited to carry Sam's body to the cemetery. In front of this vehicle, two black horses stood still, jet plumes on their heads disturbed only by the breeze.

Michael Brennan led the way. Sickened by what had happened recently, he felt as if he were in some kind of dream. But no, this was real. He had blessed Sam's cooling body with holy oils, had sent the bad news to the next of kin. And Father Bell had disappeared from the face of the earth.

The priest turned and looked at the packed church. He raised his right hand. *'In nomine Patris, et filii, et Spiritus Sancti,'* he began. *'Introibo ad altare Dei . . .'*

Diddy Costigan knelt and prayed. Her heart pounded. Sam Bell had dropped dead in the priests' house. According to what the police had gathered, Sam and Liam had been alone. Father Brennan had returned from hearing confessions to find a body on the floor and no sign of Liam.

Liam had not killed Sam. But had Sam died because of Liam? she wondered. Had guilt about something or other driven the young priest away? With a great effort, Diddy forced herself back into the present. This was going to be a long mass complete with the *Dies irae* and all the other lengthy prayers that accompanied a proper requiem. She must concentrate. But her eyes slid towards her Billy and she continued to wonder why Liam Bell had run away so suddenly.

The piles of sandwiches had diminished to a few crusts and crumbs. Diddy continued to run about with a teapot, while Nicky Costigan doled out dishes of trifle. Bridie sat by the fire, her bones chilled in spite of the flames. Anthony was avoiding her. She was glad about that, grateful for his thoughtfulness. He had cried in church. There was a certain strength about a man who cried in public, she thought. His father was dead, so he grieved. She thanked God that the rift had been healed, felt heartily sorry for Anthony and Sam. Their peace had been achieved via Sam's broken heart, and that injured organ had stopped as a result of shock.

'Cup of tea, queen?'

Bridie shook her head. Would Diddy remain friendly once the whole truth was aired? Would she be offering cups of tea when she discovered that a Bell had tried to murder Maureen?

'You've had nothing,' accused Diddy.

'I'm not hungry.'

'Just a drink, then.'

'Later,' promised Bridie.

Michael Brennan made his way across the kitchen, a glass of stout in his hand. He was seriously worried. Anthony had alerted him weeks ago about Liam's state of mind, but the young priest had been visible then. Now, suddenly, Liam Bell had disappeared into the sunset and Anthony was almost beside himself. 'He'll not be found,' Anthony had said earlier. 'He's clever and cunning and he'll hide till the fuss dies down. Then he'll be back for me, for Bridie and for anyone else he decides to hate.'

Bridie awarded the parish priest a smile. 'Thank you for the service, Father. And for your kind words about Sam.'

'He put bread on many a table, Bridie. He seemed cold – distant, you know – but he wasn't.'

She nodded.

'There'll be the will to read, I suppose.'

'Yes.'

The short man dragged a dining chair across the rug and sat next to the young widow. 'What'll you do?'

Bridie blinked. 'About what, Father Brennan?'

Michael took a sip of beer. ' 'Twas well known that Sam intended to leave his worldly goods to Liam and the Church. I imagine Sam will have made arrangements for his mother, but what about you and the girls?'

Bridie could find no answer. She glanced across at Edith and Richard. 'Maureen's minding the children over at

Cherry Hinton today,' she said. 'And perhaps that's how it's going to be for a while – one day at a time.'

'Of course, if Liam cannot be found—'

'Surely he'll go to prison eventually?' Bridie shook her head. 'I can't believe that he will remain free, Father. Sam told Anthony that there was evidence of some kind. But he didn't live long enough to explain properly.'

Michael Brennan nodded. 'The police have been told very little. They know about his rages – they took some convincing, of course, but they listened to me. And Anthony told them of his suspicions about Valerie and those other girls.' He glanced at Diddy's back. 'We decided to say nothing about Maureen. It seemed ... wrong to bring that up just now. But I think Anthony and I managed to convince the police that Liam's a potential danger. That should be enough.' He shook his head. 'What'll you do, Bridie? Will you go to Edith and Richard? Or will you return to Galway?'

'I shall stay where I am for now, Father Brennan.'

Thomas Murphy blundered across the room. He had obviously poured several measures of whisky down his gullet. 'Well, is this you on your way back home?' he asked his daughter. 'Because if you do come back, things will be the same as they were. You'll not let the O'Briens get their Protestant hands on my grandchildren, not while I live and breathe.'

The parish priest of St Aloysius Gonzaga held his tongue. While people like Thomas Murphy lived, the ecumenical movement would make no progress. Poor Sam Bell had done more in death than this fellow would ever achieve while still breathing. Methodists and Catholics had watched with Church of England nuns when Sam had been borne through the streets. Thomas Murphy carried the bigotry that had waged wars for too long in the name of Jesus Christ. This was a wicked man, an unfeeling man.

Bridie looked at her father, stared him full in the face. She was no longer afraid of the bully. 'Our coming home would not suit you, Da,' she said sweetly. 'After all, you may come to Liverpool more often if your grandchildren are here.'

She paused, turned her head and nodded towards Dolly Hanson. Dolly was resplendent in a dark-grey coat with a dead fox wrapped across its shoulders. According to local gossip, Thomas Murphy and Dolly had been lovers for a great many years. 'You'll see your ladylove regularly if we stay here, Da. After all, your journeys with horses don't happen too often these days, do they? You seem to have parted with the best of your stock. Grand horses, Silver and Sorrel. Still, you will come to visit Cathy and Shauna, won't you? And I believe you've kept company with Mrs Hanson for some time.'

Thomas Murphy glanced at the priest, reddened, staggered back a pace. 'That is none of your business,' he snapped.

Bridie inclined her head thoughtfully. 'It was none of Mammy's either, I suppose. Yes, I've been told. You were keeping company on this side of the Irish Sea long before Mammy's death.'

Murphy steadied himself and stood tall. 'I want those horses back,' he said.

'Horses?' Bridie's eyebrows rose. 'And which horses would they be, now?'

'You know what I mean,' said the large Irishman. 'You mentioned them seconds ago.'

The young widow pretended to search her memory. 'Ah, yes. The horses you gave to Sam.'

'They're the ones.' Thomas Murphy had heard the

rumours. Although the Spencer Stables were trying to keep a low profile, there was a buzz going round some racing circles. Quicksilver and Sorrel were champions in the making, it seemed.

'You bribed Sam to marry me by giving him those horses.'

The room was suddenly quiet. Diddy placed the teapot on its stand, Billy coughed into the silence, Dolly Hanson picked at her fox fur as if searching for fleas.

'They're mine,' spat Thomas Murphy.

'Really?' Bridie rose to her feet. 'We just buried a man twice your size, Da. Oh, he wasn't very tall, but at least he was a man. He gave me the horses, Father, dear. He gave me the papers, too. Any income from race or stud goes to me, Cathy and Shauna. Any foal of Sorrel's is ours. Any stud fee from Quicksilver goes to me and mine. The horses are ours to sell or to keep.' She nodded slowly. 'Sam looked after us, you see. He was a proper husband. He was the best guardian my daughters could have hoped for. So take your . . .' She looked at Dolly Hanson. 'Take your friend and go, because you are no comfort to me or to any here present. Except for Mrs Hanson, of course.'

Michael Brennan stood beside Bridie and placed a hand on her arm. 'Go easy, now, Bridie,' he whispered.

Thomas Murphy shook with rage. He balled a fist and waved it under his daughter's nose. 'Flesh and blood is all I am,' he roared. 'Your mother was sick and I met Dolly—'

'You met her before your wife was sick.' Diddy Costigan squeezed her substantial frame into the space between father and daughter. 'You met Dolly years ago, just after her husband died at sea.' She nodded at the embarrassed woman. 'It's all right, Doll. You were in pain yourself. And by the time you knew he was married, you'd fallen for him.' She sniffed. 'Mind, you should get your eyes tested, like.'

Murphy let forth a roar that sounded like the bellowing of a bull. As he raised his fist, a hand clamped itself onto his collar and dragged him backwards. 'Don't touch her,' said Anthony Bell.

Richard Spencer was not far behind his second cousin by marriage. 'Don't touch anybody,' he said, the cultured tones making the order more firm.

Thomas Murphy measured Anthony with his eyes, decided that youth would win through if a fight started. 'If I were younger, I'd lay you out,' he shouted.

Neighbours parted to make a path through the room. Anthony pushed Bridie's father out of the living room and into the shop. 'Don't come back,' he said to the man's neck. 'If you know what's good for you, stay away.'

Released at last, Murphy shrugged himself back into his jacket. 'Dolly?' he roared.

The short, plump woman entered the shop.

'We're away,' he snapped.

Anthony waited until the two had left, then he shot home the bolt on the shop door. He leaned his forehead against cool glass, wished with all his energy that his mind would still itself. Had he said enough to the police, had he said too much? Where was Liam, would he come back for Bridie, for Maureen, for his twin brother? Were any of them safe?

'Come away inside, Anthony,' said Bridie.

He swung round and stared at her. 'What are we going to do?' he asked.

'We'll be fine,' she said with a confidence she did not feel.

'Will we?'

Bridie nodded. 'He's miles away.'

'How do you know?'

'I just do.' She knew no such thing, but she sought to comfort the man. 'Stop worrying. Your grief is heavy

351

enough, Anthony. It's no use concentrating on something you cannot control.'

'I suppose you're right. The police haven't found him. They want to question him about Dad's death, so they've been looking. There's no more to be done.'

'Do you think we should have said about Maureen? About what we believe Liam to have done?' she asked in a whisper.

'No.' He paced about, almost falling over a brass coal scuttle. 'Maureen needs a rest. They would have questioned her again. Aunt Edith and Uncle Richard will keep their eyes open. Maureen will be safe.' He smiled sadly at Bridie, then crossed the shop and closed the door to the living quarters. 'He changed his will. Dad, I mean. After talking to me, he went to see his lawyer.'

'The day he died?'

He nodded. 'He was going to see the solicitor before facing Liam. Everything comes to you. Liam will be livid if and when he finds out.'

Bridie sat down on a frayed piano stool. She fingered a brass Buddha and some old belt buckles. 'I'll miss him. It's almost as if he knew he was going to die. He changed his will and then ... Oh, Anthony, I don't deserve it.'

'Why not?'

'Because ... I didn't love him. Not like I loved Eugene, not like I love ... like I should have loved him.'

The dead man's son pondered for a moment. 'Amazing how a phone call can change your life. We talked for about forty minutes. A lot of catching up to do, I suppose. And we told each other everything. We crammed a lifetime into that conversation. He said I must look after you if and when anything happened to him. Perhaps he thought Liam might kill him.'

Bridie lifted her face and looked at him. 'Everything? You told him ... ?'

'I told him that I love you, yes. And he smiled. I could hear the smile in his voice.'

Bridie's tears spilled again. She wept silently, simply allowing the water to flow down her face and onto her blouse. 'He seemed so distant, your da,' she said softly. 'With his little tins of money and tobacco and receipts. But,' she brushed a hand across her tear-bathed cheek, 'I'd catch him looking at me – you know? Just looking. Or at the girls. He'd be satisfied inside as if he'd found some sort of answer to a question he'd never asked aloud.'

She took a deep breath. 'Your dad annoyed me with his little habits. Cutting his toenails and rolling those thin cigarettes of his night after night. But he got me a new ring.' She held up her hand. 'And it wasn't just the money he spent, Anthony. This wedding ring was him saying, "It's a new start, Bridie."' She allowed herself a faint smile. 'And when he brought home that dog, well, I could have crowned him with my rolling pin. That dog was his army. That dog was bought to keep me here.'

Anthony thought about offering comfort, but he held back. She had to cry, had to grieve.

'He would have given me anything. Even on the very day he died, he gave me . . .' The words faded. Sam hadn't given Anthony to her, because she could never have Anthony, not as a husband. 'Knowing Sam has been a humbling experience. It's all about books and covers and not judging folk by what you first see.'

'Dad loved you,' said Anthony. 'He told me that day. Said you were the best woman in the world.'

'I'm not.'

'He thought so. I think so.'

She fixed her eyes on him, looked at him through a cloud of tears. 'Not now, Anthony.' Not ever, she told herself again. 'I miss him.'

'I know that, Bridie.'

'He was a comfort. He was solid, always there, always the same. He was our safety.'

'Will you stay here?'

She nodded. 'Oh yes. Someone must care for Muth and look after the shop. Sam would want me to do that. And Charlie will help. All the Costigans will help.' She paused. 'Until the truth comes out. Until they know that your brother tried to kill Maureen.'

Anthony swallowed. 'There's something else, Bridie. A piece of evidence, Dad said. He wouldn't give me any details, said he'd hidden whatever it was. But somewhere, there's proof that Liam was Maureen's attacker.'

A policeman knocked at the door. Anthony drew back the bolt and allowed the officer into the shop.

'Nothing,' said the constable. 'He's not round here, Mr Bell. And I have to say it wouldn't be easy trying to pin something on him that happened years ago. A man hanged for it, too.'

Anthony shook his head. 'He has disappeared because my father told him a few home truths at last. My brother's a dangerous man.'

The policeman sighed. 'He's gone off to grieve somewhere on his own and—'

'No.' Bridie stepped forward. 'Father Bell killed my husband. He took no weapon to him, but he caused that heart attack. I know you don't believe us.' She wanted to tell him about Maureen, longed to spit out the vile truth, but she couldn't manage it, couldn't bear the thought of Maureen being dragged out of her hiding place and into the glare of publicity.

'Mrs Bell.' A heavy layer of patience was applied to the name. 'You are upset. Everybody's upset. We can't carry on looking for a grown man who's decided to move on. If he'd turned up at his dad's funeral, we would have questioned him. But our orders are to let this lie unless there's any new evidence. There is no actual evidence.' These last five words were spoken slowly, the syllables separated so that they would be understood perfectly.

Bridie fixed her eyes on Anthony. There was evidence. Somewhere nearby, Sam had hidden an item of proof. Or if poor Maureen could just remember something, anything . . .

'I'll be off, Mrs Bell,' said the policeman. 'We're very sorry about your husband.'

Bridie and Anthony watched helplessly while the constable walked up Scotland Road. 'He's a priest, you see,' said Anthony sadly. 'Priests don't commit crimes.'

'Then why were the police out in force this morning?' asked Bridie.

Anthony raised his shoulders. 'Protestants and Catholics together always attract the law. And, of course, Father Brennan expressed his worries about Liam. So they had to show their faces.' He bolted the door. 'It'll all die down now,' he said. 'Until next time.'

Across the road, Flash Flanagan pushed his cart towards the city. His weathered brow was further creased by worry as he shuffled along in a pair of 'new' boots that were on the small side. The stole was no longer in his keeping, but Flash could not manage to feel relief. Sam was dead. Liam Bell might know something about the attack on Maureen Costigan. Should Flash go to Rose Hill and bare his soul?

He glanced up in the direction of the police station, paused on the corner for a few moments. 'All right, Sam,' he said under his breath, 'a promise is a promise. I told you I'd keep my mouth shut, lad.' Flash Flanagan carried on until he reached the next pub, then he parked his cart and went inside to drown his sorrowful secret.

*

Cathy looked from Uncle Richard to Aunt Edith. 'But I don't want to stay away from Mammy,' she said. 'My friends are all there, too. It's not fair. Shauna's going back, so why must I stay?'

Richard squatted on his haunches and touched the little girl's hair. 'Noel will be here,' he told her.

Cathy eyed the dog. Noel had been washed. There had been terrible scenes in the garden, because Noel hadn't liked coming clean. His fur was soft and silky, and he had tried to remedy this sad state of affairs by rolling in soil. 'He looked better before,' said Cathy.

Noel stuck out his tongue and panted.

'He doesn't suit being clean,' added Cathy.

Edith was forced to agree. 'Yes,' she said. 'Noel is a professional mongrel. No matter what we do, he'll always be a mess. But we like him that way, Cathy. We like you too. We want you to stay here in the fresh air until you get better.'

Richard dragged himself up into a standing position. Little Cathy O'Brien had anaemia. The fainting spell outside a butcher's shop at Christmas had been an isolated incident, but she had complained recently of feeling tired and, as she had put it, 'as if I just turned round and round very fast.' Fortunately, Richard had taken a look at her, had found her blood to be low in iron.

'It's nice here,' the child continued. 'But it's nice at home, too. And Mammy needs me.'

The doctor shook his head and smiled at her. Despite her condition, she continued to be talkative. He was relieved beyond measure, because he had suspected for years that Sam Bell had needed a doctor. Sam's cough had been typical of TB, yet the stubborn man had refused to seek treatment, had feared being isolated from his home and his business. At least Cathy's illness was eminently curable.

Cathy stared hard at the man she called Uncle Richard. 'I hate liver,' she advised him. 'And spinach, too.'

'You have your iron medicine,' he said.

She grimaced. Iron medicine was the worst thing she had tasted in seven whole years. It was black and nasty, and the taste lingered for hours. 'I'm not ill,' insisted Cathy. 'I'm never ill. Shauna's the one who needs all doing for her.'

Edith sighed. The frail-looking Shauna was as healthy as a newly minted sixpence. But Cathy, who appeared robust, had succumbed to anaemia. Edith was certain about one thing. This child should not return to Liverpool until her health improved.

'I'm not going to that school,' said Cathy angrily. She chided herself for being rude, but she felt desperate. She didn't want to disappear forever into the clutches of a black-clad dwarf with a hairy wart on its chin. 'I want to go home. Uncle Sam's dead and Mammy's on her own. She'll want me for messages and watching Shauna.'

Cathy hadn't expected to be so sad about Uncle Sam. After all, she had known him for such a short time, and he hadn't been like Daddy. But she missed him. She missed him in a part of her being that had no words, because she was unable to explain to herself why she was so sad. He had been good to her, she supposed. When she thought of him, she felt hungry, but not in her stomach. It was all terrible and Mammy was going to need her big girl.

Dr Richard Spencer looked at his watch. He pushed it back into his waistcoat and told himself to hurry up. A young woman on Noble Street was nine months pregnant with her thirteenth child. If he didn't shape up, there could be a dozen orphans by tonight – a baker's dozen if the new baby survived. 'Cathy,' he said. 'You either stay here or you go into hospital for injections and a great deal of spinach. Liver, too,' he added gravely.

'But I'm not ill,' Cathy repeated.

'Not yet,' replied the good doctor.

'Then wait till I am!' Cathy balled her fists and shouted, 'I'm going back to Mammy.'

Maureen entered the room with Cathy's little sister. She picked up Shauna and sat her on a sofa. 'Don't shout,' Maureen advised Cathy.

'They're trying to make me stay.'

'For your own good,' said Maureen.

Cathy knew that for-your-own-good things were grown-ups' ideas. If something was for her own good, it would be boring, painful or both. 'They'll send me to that warty nun.'

Richard shook his head. 'There'll be no school, Cathy.'

Cathy considered this. 'No school?'

Richard shook his head. 'Most children would be delighted by the promise of a few weeks' or months' holiday.'

'But I like school. I like St Aloysius Gonzaga's, anyway. Our school's fun. We have nice nuns with no warts.'

'You can't live on Scottie for a while,' said Maureen. 'Too many germs.'

Edith studied the young woman who had been a child until a few weeks ago. Maureen was beautiful again, but she was mature, far older than her years. What a pity that she had been forced so cruelly into what was called common sense. 'Maureen's right,' Edith told Cathy. 'You need the moors. You need the wind and the sun.'

Cathy needed her mother. At the risk of being judged a baby, she allowed her tears to flow. She babbled on about falling behind in her school work, about Mammy being lonely, about being needed in the shop.

Edith pulled the child into her arms. 'We shall look after you,' she said, wiping up tears with a spotless handkerchief. 'Uncle Richard and I will teach you. You'll be able to run about with Noel and your horses. Mr Smythe will be practising for the races, so he'll need plenty of stable staff. Cathy, it won't be for ever. Just now, you're weak – you'd catch everybody's colds and coughs.'

The sobs abated. 'I'll stay if Noel can sleep in my room. And I'll need books like at school.'

Richard pretended to glare. 'Bargaining already?'

Edith smiled at him. 'We'll get her well,' she told her husband.

He gazed at his wife with the child in her arms. In a few moments, he would be setting out to visit a woman with too many children. If only one of Edith's babies had survived . . . Richard gathered up his bag and went out to do his job in an unfair world.

As he motored down the moor and towards Bolton, Richard considered all that Anthony had told him a week ago. Anthony believed that Liam was unstable. The young priest's disappearance seemed to verify that. Richard had known for a long time that all was not well with Anthony's twin, though he had never considered a definite diagnosis. 'Didn't think of looking for anything like that,' he muttered aloud. 'Paranoid schizophrenia? Sounds as if he's well on his way to being dangerous, then.'

He drove down Tonge Moor Road and round Turner Brew. Anthony was sure that Liam had attacked women in Liverpool, had been responsible for the death of Valerie Walsh. What about Maureen? the doctor wondered. Had she been another of Liam's victims? Anthony had mentioned nothing about the young girl, but it was something to think about, wasn't it? Nothing could be done, of course, while Liam was missing. Richard carried on to Noble Street and the job on hand. He had no time for hypothesis, not while a patient waited.

*

Bridie Bell sank in an exhausted heap. The armchair was comfortable, and she leaned her head back, closed her eyes and allowed her thoughts to take their own course.

Well, whatever that piece of evidence might be, it was not downstairs. The idea of fighting her way through storage areas on the upper floor did not appeal, yet she could not rid herself of the notion that Sam was trying to guide her. 'Sam?' she asked the empty room. 'Where is it? What is it?'

The only answer came from the mantel clock.

Cathy was ill with anaemia. 'Eminently curable,' Richard Spencer had stressed. Bridie hung on to that, clutched at it fiercely. There was no need to worry about Cathy, because Cathy was in good hands. All the same, she prayed frequently, used her mother's beads to count the decades.

The house attached to Bell's Pledges, where five people had lived, was currently occupied by just two. Shauna would return tomorrow, but Cathy would not. Sam would not return at all. For now, only Bridie and Sam's mother were residing here.

Bridie's mother had been of the opinion that God never sent anyone a burden too heavy to carry. 'With every responsibility, God sends strength,' Mammy had been wont to say. Bridie's energy was sapped. Losing Sam had been dreadful. She had just begun to understand him, had been learning to take care of him and his home. Yes, he had been predictable, but predictability brought safety. They had been secure here.

Her eyelids raised themselves. Would any one of them feel safe ever again? No-one knew where Liam was; no-one knew how or where to begin searching for him. He might be outside now, could have climbed over the back gate and into the yard. This was nonsense, she told herself firmly. He was unlikely to show his face for some considerable time . . . Except . . . oh God, if Sam had told Liam about the hidden evidence, then perhaps the priest might try to break in to find it.

She felt the hairs on her neck rising. There was no man in the house. Anthony had returned to Astleigh Fold, thank goodness, and Charlie had gone home an hour ago. The shop was closed. 'You must not turn to Anthony,' she told herself aloud. 'He is not for you, can never be for you.'

Something moved in the yard. She wished with all her heart that Noel could be here. The dog was daft, but he always growled and barked when disturbed after dark. What must she do? Muth was in bed, was too old to be of help, too old to share Bridie's fears. Was it the wind? Was there a cat outside?

'Keep calm,' she whispered. 'It'll be nothing, nothing at all.'

Outside in the yard, Liam Bell squatted next to the coal shed. There was no moon. He moved forward on tiptoe, peeped through a small gap in the curtains. She was there. She was inside his house, sitting on his chair, sitting on his inheritance. A pretty woman, he supposed. But he wasn't fooled by her, not for a moment.

For several days, Liam's place of abode had been a derelict warehouse on the dock road. Like a common tramp, he had rummaged in bins for food, had been forced to comb the streets during hours of darkness. He was cold, hungry and weary. He had returned to Scotland Road in order to acquire the means with which to travel towards a different and easier life. The Irishwoman was comfortable in his father's house. Liam was shivering in the back yard, and he was furious.

He kept his eye against the window, studied Bridie as closely as he could. The stole was in that house. A million and one things were in there, too, bits and pieces collected over the years by Bell's Pledges. Really, the place would need ransacking.

Someone walked down the jigger. Liam stiffened, listened while a girl giggled. 'Stop it,' she shouted. 'Just you wait till I tell Mam, Graham Pile.'

It was Monica Costigan.

'I've done nothing wrong, Nicky,' replied the boy.

'No, but you will if you get the chance. I've told you, I'm risking nothing before I get a wedding ring.'

A few more giggles reached Liam's ears. He crept towards the gate and listened closely. 'It's funny without Mr Bell,' said Nicky eventually.

'Are you still selling for Bell's?' asked the boy.

'Oh yes. Mrs Bell's in charge now. That Liam got his eye wiped, didn't he? Not a mention of him in the will, Mam said. It's all gone to Mrs Bell and the little girls. Except for books and a few hundred pounds. That's what he left Anthony. And he left some pots for us – nice cups and that with roses on.'

'I wonder where Father Bell is?' mused Graham.

'Who cares?' asked Nicky. 'Not me, not any of us. He was a right bloody misery-guts. Even Father Brennan's glad to see the back of him.' She paused for a second or two. 'Graham?'

'What?'

'My mam thinks Father Bell's really bad. Not just miserable – evil, like.'

'Does she?'

'She says he ruined Anthony's life when they were kids. But she reckons there's more to it. She thinks he might have made his dad have that heart attack.'

'Well, Father Bell's gone,' said Graham. 'And good riddance to him. Come on, your mam'll have the supper on.'

Liam stood by the gate until the footsteps faded away. So Dad had found time to change his will. Stunned to the point of numbness, he leaned against the gate for several minutes. He had nothing, nothing at all.

When a modicum of composure had returned, he swivelled silently on rubber soles, stared at the building he had expected to inherit. He could have gone a long way in the Church, could have made a massive donation to the diocese. And now, he was being denied his rights by that female intruder who sat in Dad's chair pretending to be sad.

Heads were going to roll, he told himself. But not yet. He had been foolish to come here, but life had been far from comfortable during recent days. The first thing he needed was money. He must get into the house and find cash or small items that would be easy to sell. Living rough in a draughty warehouse had not been easy. Tonight, he would take what he could and get away.

He squatted in a dark corner and waited for her to go to bed. There was a place he had heard of, a monastery in Lancashire where refuge was granted to travellers. From what he had read, Liam knew that some down-and-outs stayed long-term and helped out with menial tasks. He swallowed a stab of pain. A monastery? He was almost a parish priest, not a mendicant. Care would be needed, he reminded himself. No sign of his superior education must show. Like the rest, he would have to act the part of a vagrant.

She was riddling ashes. Liam rose and watched her. She looked every inch the grieving widow, all tangled hair and slow movements. She picked up Dad's tobacco tin and opened it, pulled out his cigarette papers and a bit of loose tobacco. With what almost amounted to reverence, she replaced the tin on the mantelpiece. This was the usurper. Liam needed plenty of time to think. He would go as soon as possible to Lancashire, would hide himself among the brothers.

Bridie would keep for a while. For the moment, Liam's prime duty was to survive.

Bridie heard him and did nothing. With her heart pounding, she sat on the edge of the bed she had shared with Sam and waited for Sam's son to go away. There was a telephone at the foot of the stairs, but the staircase ran down the centre of the house, its small, ground floor lobby forming a natural division between shop and domestic premises. To summon help, she would have needed to put herself in danger.

He was quiet, but not quiet enough. Bridie's ears tuned in to the opening and closing of drawers, the lightweight complaint of a key in a lock. The safe was empty. Since Sam's death, small items of value had been stored in the vault of a bank.

Liam would be stealing a few bits and pieces, was possibly searching for a certain piece of evidence at the same time. Sam had believed Anthony at last. Bridie pictured that final scene between Sam and Liam, imagined what had been said. Sam had accused; Liam had denied. The heat created by these opposing poles had caused Sam's heart attack. He must have died a broken man.

Would Liam come upstairs? Would he search the storerooms on the top floor, would he try the roof space? If he came upstairs, she would surely die of fright. No, no, her heart was stronger than poor Sam's. She had two children to live for, two little girls whose father and stepfather had died recently. Bridie had no intention of being scared to death.

What about Muth? Muth had a knack of appearing to be deaf when it suited her. All too often, Muth heard things that even the sharpest of young ears might miss. If Muth went downstairs ... Keep still, Bridie told herself severely. Just wait. If you can find some patience, Liam will clear off eventually. The locks would have to be changed. She thanked God that Cathy and Shauna were away. Had the girls been here, she might have been panicked into doing something crazy.

A stair creaked. With her heart clamouring like a bass drum, Bridie slid between the sheets. Her teeth chattered. Slowly, she reached for the pewter candlestick on a bedside table. Hugging this chilly item, she lay on her side and tried to breathe evenly. Her pores were open and she shook like a leaf in the wind. He was across the landing, was opening the door of one of the storerooms. The door remained open. Had he shut that door, Bridie might have been tempted to come out of her bedroom, but she remained where she was for fear of being seen on the landing.

Surely he didn't expect to get away unnoticed? He was audible; she imagined she could hear him breathing. What was he looking for? Maureen had been strangled. Had Sam come by the rope? If so, how had Sam been so certain that this particular length of rope had been used by Liam?

Thoughts darted about like moths looking for light, each idea fluttering away in the wake of another concept. If only Sam were here. If Sam were here, Liam would not be here. Liam would have been out doing his good deeds or murdering someone. He was becoming careless. If Muth heard him . . .

He was on the landing again. One door closed, then another opened. He was still in the storerooms. Again, Bridie heard the movements quite clearly, could visualize Liam's actions. She had worked hard in those two rooms, had been in the middle of sorting out all kinds of tangles.

Suddenly, her eyes opened wide. What if he found the evidence? He would be able to return to Scotland Road with an excuse about having been driven away by grief. With the tangible proof removed, he would be able to continue his reign of holy terror.

But what if he didn't find it? Would he return again and again to search? Oh, she didn't know what to hope for. And she missed Sam, missed the father figure he had become. If only Sam could come back, she would never again complain about toenail clippings on the rug. Sam could not come home. She bit back sobs of grief and panic, forced herself to lie still.

The door handle squeaked. Sam had talked about oiling it, had never got round to the task. Liam Bell, priest, rapist and killer, was padding his way towards the bed. He was not wearing shoes, she thought irrelevantly. And if he killed her, Cathy and Shauna would be orphans. Edith had affection for Cathy, but she seemed not to have the same feelings for Shauna.

The quality of blackness in front of Bridie's closed eyelids intensified. He was looming over her. She must remain completely still, must breathe slowly and evenly. Did he have a knife? Had he picked up the poker or a hammer or a second-hand cricket bat? Would it hurt, would it be quick? Were Sam and Eugene waiting to greet her on the other side of some frail curtain?

She opened her mouth and let out a sigh that was supposed to convince him. He was completely immobile. This could not continue for much longer, because she would be unable to bear it. Was that a hand on the quilt? Was he touching her? Would he attack, rape and kill her?

Bridie's right hand was wrapped so tightly round the candlestick that it felt stiff, almost spastic. No feeling remained in the fingers. Surely he would leave now? He could not spend the rest of the night standing next to her bed.

With painful slowness, she allowed her eyelids to lift

just a fraction. She had seen Cathy and Shauna sleeping with their eyes not quite closed. A shadow moved across the room, pulled at a drawer. She could hear him fingering the contents, rifling through clothing. He closed the drawer, opened another. When he had finished the search, he crept out of the room and closed the door.

A scream stuck in her throat like unchewed food. Bridie forced her face into the pillow and forbade herself to make a sound. There was the old lady to think of. If he killed once, he would kill again. Muth must not be disturbed, because her very life depended on total silence.

He went downstairs. Bridie waited, her ears attuned to every slight sound, but she heard nothing. For the remainder of the night, she lay as stiff as a board, not daring to move until the light came. If he left, she did not hear him. If he continued to scour the place, she was not aware.

But when morning finally came, Bridie went slowly down the stairs and found a house that showed not the slightest sign of having been entered. There were things missing from the drawers and from the storeroom, and five pounds had been taken from the caddy where coal, milk and insurance monies were kept. Apart from that, Sam's house and shop were exactly as she had left them the night before.

Nevertheless, the locksmith was summoned. By teatime, Bell's Pledges would be a fortress.

Fifteen

Les Frères de la Croix de Saint Pierre had settled before the Great War in a black-and-white Tudor-style mansion in the middle of nowhere. With their cows, pigs, chickens and acres of vegetables, the brothers maintained themselves as far as possible, though expeditions to Blackburn and Bolton, their nearest towns, were undertaken on a fortnightly basis.

The Brothers of St Peter's Cross asked few questions. Their original purpose had been to offer shelter to newly released French criminals in a refuge near the Pyrenees, and they had spread their wings throughout Europe in the hope of rescuing and reforming those who offended Christ. They believed in hard work and the inherent goodness of mankind. The long-dead founder of the order had enjoyed a great fondness for St Peter, who, ordained by Christ Himself, had gone on to deny Jesus three times. Peter had cried for days when the Lord's prophecy had been fulfilled. It was Peter's humanity that had made him culpable and forgivable.

Inside the open porch, a sculpture of Peter stood on a marble pillar, his face scored deeply in accordance with descriptions from the gospels. According to the New Testament, Peter's face had been marked by channels born of prolonged weeping. Across the porch, on another plinth, stood an image of the all-forgiving Christ, the right hand raised in an eternal blessing.

Liam Bell placed his worldly goods on the flagged floor. He had brought with him some cheap clothing and boots, a couple of pounds and a much thumbed missal. Before him, a huge black door was studded with ancient bolts and long hinges. Above this portal, the motto of the order was painted in gold. *TOUJOURS AVEC TOI, MON ENFANT*, declared the flowery script. Liam sat on a bench and pondered.

He had read about the monks, was fairly sure that they would not search him or ask for a potted history, but he wanted his account of himself to be convincing. As long as he lived a good, clean life, the brothers should allow him to stay. Because of a stringent regime, the house was not a popular place, so there should be room for one more sinner. Only the truly down-and-out or the genuinely convinced Christian could survive in this place. Liam intended to endure at all costs.

He pulled at the collar of his jacket, hoped it looked old enough and poor enough. His new name was Martin Waring. Smith, Jones and Brown had been rejected as too obvious, so Liam had opted for a more convincing persona. In a moment, he would ring the bell. A large iron pull hung down just behind Jesus. At the other side of the door lay months – perhaps years – of punishing toil. But he had no fear of hard work. In fact, he was rather looking forward to the change and to the discipline. Father Michael Brennan had been far too easy-going for Liam's taste. Discipline and order were essential within the calling of a priest. Each priest was a missionary, whether he toiled in Africa with the heathen or on Scotland Road with the thief.

Of course, Liam was no longer a priest. In fact, he had decided that Martin Waring had discovered the one true faith while reading his way through a prison sentence. Here, he would be baptized and confirmed anew. God had sent him to this monastery. It was all a part of the Divine plan for Liam. The projected stay with the brothers was a mere stepping stone along the path to greatness.

He tugged at the bell-pull, waited for admittance. The door was drawn inward and a small, round face peered up into the tall man's eyes. 'Do you seek refuge?'

'I do.'

Liam was guided into a cold hallway. This flagged area was being scrubbed by two brothers. They wore blue-grey habits and sacking aprons. Buckets clanged against stone, while stiff bristles scratched the flags.

The small man stopped and beckoned. 'Follow me, friend.' He led the way into a tiny room that contained a table and two chairs. 'Sit, please.' He indicated the less ornate of the two seats.

Liam sat, placed his belongings on the table.

'I'm Brother Timothy.' Tiny blue eyes shone like twin jewels in the weathered face. 'Do you wish to give a name?'

'Martin Waring.'

Brother Timothy grinned broadly, causing his plump cheeks to swallow the bright eyes for a split second. 'Brother Nicholas will be here shortly.' He disappeared through an inner door.

Liam waited. He had the uncanny feeling that he was being watched, so he remained still and calm. Thick stone walls seemed unlikely places for peepholes, yet he felt as if a million eyes were on him.

The inner door creaked open and Brother Nicholas came in. He was a large man, well-muscled and with dark skin. 'Please remain seated,' he said before placing himself in the tall-backed chair. A beam of light crept through the high window and sat on the monk's deliberately bald pate.

'Are you the abbot?' asked Liam.

'No. We have no titles here, as we are all brothers in the true sense. But I am the senior, because I have been here for many years. We try to be democratic, though we do have a committee. Its members are drawn from the order and from the lay residents.' He folded his hands inside the wide sleeves of his habit. 'Are you a sinner?'

'Yes.'

'Have you paid for your crime?'

'Yes.'

'So what do you seek? Some of our gentlemen require a bed and food for a few days. Others stay indefinitely.'

'I wish to stay, Brother.'

The monk nodded thoughtfully. 'We have little to offer beyond hard work, sustenance and shelter. Feel free to leave whenever you wish.'

'Thank you.' Liam fished some notes from his pocket. 'This is all the money I have.'

'Then keep it,' advised Brother Nicholas. 'In a few days or weeks, you may decide to move on.'

Liam hesitated. He must appear 'normal', must act like a man released from jail. 'I have been reading about you,' he said carefully. 'We were given leaflets about the brothers. I also read about the Catholic church while I was away. That is why I am here.'

'A convert in the making?' Brother Nicholas beamed over his spectacles. Like Timothy, he had a happy face, though this was an altogether more personable man. His eyes were quick and clever, and he seemed to be trying to sum up his latest refugee. 'We do have several brothers here who joined the order after prison. It takes many years to become a Catholic, Martin.'

'I am prepared to wait and work.'

'And to learn?'

The ordained priest nodded. 'I learn quickly,' he said.

'Then you must have been a successful criminal,' replied the monk. 'Even so, you were caught. Being caught is the best thing, you know. Many offenders take the opportunity to study themselves during confinement. Is that a missal?' He pointed to the book on the table.

'Yes, Brother.'

'You know the order of the mass?'

Liam smiled inwardly. How many masses had he said in his time? 'Yes, I think I do.'

'Good. Come to chapel whenever you wish. Except during hours of work, that is. We keep animals and grow much of our own food.' He paused. 'What was your job?'

The new recruit remembered his script. 'I was a clerk in a shipping office.'

Brother Nicholas rose. 'St Peter was crucified,' he said, 'but his biggest cross was not the one on which he died. St Peter's sin was heavier than any gallows, Martin. He denied Our Blessed Lord. God loves sinners. The first pope was a sinner. Here, you will find peace and forgiveness.'

Nicholas left, then Timothy bumbled his way through the inner door. 'Come. Let's get you settled, Martin.'

In the hallway, the scrubbing was finished. The monks were dusting rows of holy pictures that lined the walls. 'All right?' asked the nearest.

Liam froze. The accent was definitely Scouse. 'Very well, thanks,' he managed finally. 'Are you from Liverpool?'

'Yes.' The man crossed the floor. 'Are you?'

'No.' Liam cleared his throat. 'Any more here from your neck of the woods?'

'Not as far as I know,' replied the monk. 'They're mostly from this side of Lancashire. I served my time all over the place – a lot of us did.'

Liam studied the man's clothes. 'Are you a member of the order now?'

'Yes.' The monk sounded pleased with himself. 'Been here fifteen years next October.' Liam heaved a sigh of relief. This Liverpudlian probably knew nothing at all about the Bell family. Even so, the utmost care must be taken. Although the brothers' heads were shaven, one or two had beards. He would grow a beard.

Brother Timothy led the way down a corridor and into a very small room. There was a bed, a table, a chair and a little chest of drawers. 'This is yours,' said the brother. 'There are overalls in there.' He pointed to the drawers. 'Today, you must have some rest. Tomorrow, you will be assigned work. When the bell sounds, I shall collect you and take you to the refectory.' He made a little bow and left the room.

Father Liam Bell put away his few possessions, then lay on his bed. There was a tiny window, but it was high on the wall, too far up to afford a view. It was like a prison cell, except that the walls were painted cream and there were faded flowers printed on the bedspread. He had found somewhere safe. With his head propped by an extremely hard pillow, Liam Bell said goodbye to himself and welcomed Martin Waring into this new world.

'He was here?' Anthony stared at her in disbelief.

Bridie nodded. 'He was poking about all over the place, probably looking for whatever Sam hid – money or jewellery.' She paused. 'Or evidence. I just waited until he went away.'

Anthony took a deep breath to steady himself. Because of his father's death, he had been given five extra days' compassionate leave, so he had taken the chance to visit Bridie again. She should not be alone, should not be expected to face such dangers. 'You should have telephoned. You should have sent for me. Good God, he could be miles away by now.' Worse than that, he could be here . . .

Bridie felt light-headed, as if she were really elsewhere. A great wedge of guilt had positioned itself somewhere between her heart and her throat. Had she looked after Sam well enough? Had she looked after Cathy well enough?

Anthony pushed a strand of hair from his forehead. 'He might have killed you.'

'What?' Cathy had anaemia. Sam had died and left everything to his wife of just a few months. She didn't deserve it. She had not been a good wife, was not a good mother.

'Did you hear me?' asked Anthony. It was plain that she had not slept for some time. Dark shadows sat beneath her lovely eyes, making her older and sadder.

She pulled herself into the present day. 'He might have, but he didn't. Please, please, don't talk about it.' She lowered herself into a chair. 'I got the locks changed . . . Billy sent a man from the docks. He looks after warehouse security.' She was bone-weary, exhausted by several wakeful nights. So many emotions had clamoured inside her head and heart these past few days. 'I feel like a wet rag,' she said. 'My poor, poor Cathy. I never noticed. I never noticed that Sam was ill, either.'

'Dad's death was an accident waiting to happen,' said Anthony. 'He must have had a weak heart, Bridie. I feel so sorry for him, sorry for myself, too, because we were going to be closer. But I'm sorriest for you, Bridie. Two husbands dead in such a short time.'

Bridie said nothing, though her brain would not be still. Somewhere in England, a man who had killed and raped was on the loose. Even now, after poor Sam's death, the police were scarcely interested. Someone had hanged for

Valerie's murder, so the law was satisfied. Bridie suspected that the guardians of civil order might be embarrassed if and when the truth came to light, because the hanging of the wrong man would be viewed as quite a substantial accident. She had not reported her burglar, had been too tired and too busy to pester a police force whose disinterest was so apparent.

'Bridie?'

'I'm all right,' she said almost snappily. The Costigans would arrive shortly. A summit conference was to be held in Bridie's kitchen. The subject of discussion was to be the shop's future. Bridie was going to need help, and the Costigans were happy to offer their services. How would that family feel once the truth came out about Maureen's attacker?

Anthony sat down and watched the woman he forbade himself to love. Dad had changed his will. On the very last day of his life, Sam Bell had decreed that the shop and all its contents were for Bridie. Dad had loved this girl. He had been a passionless man, but the young Irishwoman had made his last few months almost happy. 'My father cared for you. Everyone said how much happier he was after your arrival.'

Bridie lifted her head. 'Charlie told me that Flash Flanagan visited Sam on the day he died. Muth said the same. If you recall, it was Flash who found Maureen. Perhaps he found more. And Sam told you that there was concrete evidence.'

Anthony considered the statement. 'Evidence? But Flash was questioned repeatedly. He complained all over the place for days about harassment. Surely he would have told the police?'

Bridie sighed. 'According to Muth, Flash has no time for the law. He's been locked up as a vagrant so many times that he just keeps out of the way as often as possible.' She hesitated. 'Also, the nature of what he found might have surprised him.'

The clock chimed. Anthony stared into thin air. 'Something of Liam's?'

She nodded. 'And Sam went round to see Liam—'

'Not right away. He called in to see his solicitor first.' The light dawned so suddenly and so intensely that it seemed to hurt Anthony's eyes. 'He changed his will there and then, Bridie. He must have described to Liam whatever had been found. Then he confronted Liam and ... and the stress of that killed him.'

Bridie's handkerchief was a knotted wreck. 'There's proof in this house, Anthony. I am so sure of that. Liam knows it's here, he must, and—'

The door burst inward. Diddy, panting as if she had just run a marathon, leaned against the jamb. 'Donald Bentham's office got wrecked a few days ago,' she said breathlessly. 'I've just heard. All ripped to shreds, it was.' She shook her head sadly. 'I mean, I can understand folk stealing to eat, but ...' She shrugged as if giving up on an insane world.

Bridie and Anthony exchanged glances. Donald was Sam's solicitor. Liam must have hunted there, too, for evidence.

'There's nothing been took,' continued Diddy. 'Donald and his mates and the coppers have been playing jigsaws all week – putting stuff back together. There was money in a tin – tea and milk money – it wasn't touched. But the bloody office was wall-to-wall torn paper. What the hell's the world coming to? There's wills and deeds and all kinds damaged. Nobody round here would do that. There's no sense in it, nothing worth pinching.'

To cover her confusion and distress, Bridie got up and bustled about with kettle and teapot.

'The locksmith's round at Donald Bentham's,' continued Diddy. 'Same fellow who changed your locks. Have you been burgled?' she asked.

'No,' replied Bridie rather quickly. 'But with Sam gone, I need to feel safe at night. There are a few valuable pieces here.'

Diddy agreed. 'Better safe than sorry,' she said.

Muth came in. 'Them bloody stairs is getting steeper,' she complained. Her expression changed when she saw Anthony. 'Eeh, lad, it's time you came home.' A tear made its way down a wrinkled cheek. 'He did for my Sam, you know. Frightened him to death, he did, and that's why he's done a bunk.'

Anthony said nothing. He led his grandmother to a chair, wiped her face with his handkerchief. 'Don't worry,' he said. 'I'll visit you as often as possible.' Should he give in his notice and return? He glanced at Bridie, wondered what she would want. Given the circumstances, she might feel safer with him here. There again, she might feel safer if he stayed away. What a mess.

Bridie scalded the teapot and heard the words. He was intending to visit on a regular basis. Strangely, she felt little reaction. She was probably too tired to feel anything at all.

Anthony walked into the shop, stood behind the counter in the very spot where Sam had reigned for years. What would happen when everyone's grief had run its course? he asked himself. Could he keep his distance from Bridie for ever?

'Why did he bugger off like that, Anthony?'

He jumped, turned and looked at Diddy, saw a picture of Maureen's face in his mind. 'I don't know,' he said.

'Something must have happened,' said Diddy.

'Yes,' he replied. 'But only two people know exactly what. And one of them is dead.'

Diddy stood and watched while the young man

377

returned to the kitchen. She understood that Anthony and Sam had reached some kind of truce, and she was glad about that. The window blinds were closed, making Bell's Pledges dark and lifeless. Diddy shook her head and looked up to heaven. 'It's all right, Sam,' she told him. 'We'll be open in the morning. Business has to go on, old lad. Hasn't it?'

The meeting had been declared open. Charlie was in charge at the start, because his experience of Sam Bell's methods was the longest. 'I can manage,' he said. 'Selling and doing tickets and finding pledges. But I can't clear houses and all that. Mr Bell used to get help with the big stuff. I'm no use at lifting.' At the end of this unusually long speech, Charlie sat down.

Bridie smiled encouragingly at Charlie, her mainstay in the business, then she addressed his father. 'Billy, would you give up the docks? We'll be needing a fine, strong fellow like yourself. What do you think?' she asked.

The large man pushed a hand against his breast. 'Me? I've been a docker all my life. It's the only job I've ever done. I've never thought of any other kind of work. I've always worked the docks.'

'She knows that,' said Diddy tartly. 'You've told her about three hundred times.' Billy was famous for his dockside stories.

Nicky cleared her throat. 'What about the stall? Mr Bell and a few others paid for the patch, so are we keeping it on? Only we've regulars, see. The Johnny Laskies always come to me, because they know they'll get good stuff. Will I be carrying on working on Paddy's?' She loved the market, could not imagine life without it. She got her dinner every day in Scouse Alley, bacon ribs with as much cabbage as she wanted, then a wet nellie dripping with warm syrup. 'Can I keep it open?' she begged. Bell's was Nicky's biggest supplier. Other businesses sold stuff through Nicky, but she could not imagine surviving without Bell's.

Bridie nodded and smiled at the homely young woman. Nicky lived and breathed Paddy's Market. Her ambitions in life were to rent a few more yards of selling space and to marry Graham Pile. Graham, once out of his apprenticeship, would perhaps make cakes to sell from another stall. 'Oh yes. That will continue just as before.' Bridie gave her attention to Diddy. 'It might be an idea for you and Nicky to run the stall between you. I've always thought it was a bit much for a young girl. Anyway, your children are grown, so a little job would be just the thing.' She returned her scrutiny to Billy. 'I'd like you and Charlie to run the shop. Proper wages, of course. Billy, you would be in charge of moving large furniture and clearing houses. The McKinnells will continue to hire out the cart and horse, I'm sure.'

Billy studied his calloused hands. The biggest section of hard skin sat across the palm of his right hand, a diagonal line at the base of his thumb. This had been produced by a docker's hook, a murderous piece of curved metal attached to a piece of wood. 'Shifted some stuff,' he mumbled. 'All weathers, too.' He lifted his head. 'I always get picked, you know. Sometimes, I look at them who never get much work, and I could kill the bloody bosses.' He sighed, swallowed. 'Right, queen. I'll work for you. Same difference, I suppose. I'll still be heaving stuff between hither, thither and Tuesday dinner.'

Bridie closed her eyes and tried not to worry about Cathy. For twenty-four hours a day, she was thinking or dreaming about her older daughter. A mother should be with her daughter—

'Where's Shauna?' asked Muth. Muth was huddled over

a newspaper next to the fire. She was going through the deaths column in search of redundant household goods. This had been Sam's job. After a death announcement, he would present a card to the family in case they wanted to sell any of the deceased's belongings. It was a morbid task. 'Where's Shauna?' she repeated.

'Edith took her out,' replied Bridie. Edith and Anthony had brought Shauna home this morning. Cathy had stayed with Mrs Cornwell and Maureen at Cherry Hinton. Bridie hoped with all her fast diminishing energy that Shauna would be good while out with Edith. Edith didn't care for Bridie's younger daughter. Shauna had a habit of acquiring things, anything and everything that took her fancy. Shauna had been the weakling, yet Cathy was the one with the blood disorder—

'Bridie?'

'Sorry,' she replied. 'I was elsewhere.'

Billy smiled sadly. 'We've all been in the wars lately, haven't we? Never mind, God's good.'

'So you'll come into the business, then?' Bridie asked the Costigans. 'I'd feel happier if you would, because I trust you, all of you.'

Nicky sniffed meaningfully. 'If you trust our Jimmy, you want your head testing. Mind, he'll settle down, I suppose.'

Muth poked her head out of the newspaper. 'I want you all to keep your eyes open. That bugger's out there somewhere. He knows he killed his dad. I don't know owt about what went on in that presbytery, but that so-called priest finished Sam off. That's why he's disappeared, bloody rotten coward, he is. Fancy leaving Sam like that. He might have been saved if the doctor had come.'

Anthony glanced at Bridie. The strain was showing on her face. He jumped to his feet and made for the door. 'I've got to go out,' he told the small gathering. 'A little bit of business to attend to.'

Bridie closed her eyes again and leaned back in the chair. Muth didn't know the half of it. And now, Anthony had probably gone to search for Flash Flanagan.

'It'll be all right, queen,' said Billy Costigan. 'We'll not let you down.'

Bridie buried her face in her hands and wept. She cried for the dead man who had cared for her, for Maureen's damaged life, for Cathy, for Eugene. Most of all, she grieved for the poor man who had just left the house, because he had shared a womb and a home with Liam.

Diddy patted Bridie's shoulder. 'You thought a lot of him, girl.' There was surprise in her tone.

Bridie looked up. 'You said he wasn't good and he wasn't bad. You said he was just there, like a lamp-post is there. You said he was something we all just took for granted. Well, he isn't there. Not any longer. The lamp-posts are all right, still standing. But Sam fell down, Diddy. I wish I'd done more . . .' Her voice cracked.

Diddy bit her lip. 'You did a lot for Sam, girl,' she finally managed. 'He was happy – wasn't he, Mrs Bell?'

Theresa Bell stared into the fire. 'Happier than I'd ever seen him,' she declared. 'Don't cry, Bridie. We've to carry on, you see. That's what it's all about, carrying on.'

Bridie heard the words and knew the sentiment behind them to be valid. But she still cried.

Anthony walked down Dryden Street, looked along Great Homer, strode the length of Rachel Street and headed back to Scotland Road again. How many times in his life had he seen Flash Flanagan squatting on some street corner with his puppets and his banjo? Of course, the man was nowhere to be seen today.

He continued his circular journey, hands thrust deep into pockets, eyes scouring the road. A tram rattled past in the direction of the city, then another clanged its heavy way towards the Rotunda. Where the hell had Flash disappeared to? Was it possible that Liam had...? Oh no, please, no. The fact that Flash had found Maureen after the attack was well known. Had Liam put two and two together? Had he killed the tramp?

'Hello, Anthony.'

The young man swung round. 'Father Brennan. Michael.' He grabbed the priest's arm. 'Have you seen Flash today?'

'Have I seen him?' Michael Brennan's eyebrows shot skyward. 'Oh, I've seen the miserable wretch, indeed I have. He made a big show of sweeping up the church paths for me. Broke the broom – probably through leaning on it – then demanded his money. Yes, I've seen the old reprobate. And I'll tell you this – he'll say nothing about Maureen's attacker. I've questioned him several times, so if you're thinking what I think you're thinking, forget it. He's sealed up his mouth with cement.'

'I'll get it out of him,' swore Anthony. 'If he knows anything, I'll make him talk.' He let out a sigh of relief. 'Thank God the old dog's alive, at least.'

The two men lingered outside Razor Sharpe's barber shop. 'I don't know what to worry about first,' said Anthony. 'There's my brother on the loose with heaven knows how many names on his list. With so many in danger, I can't work out where to start.'

'Mine's probably one of those names,' said the priest. 'He'd no time for me, considered me to be a greedy pig because I enjoy my food. Sins of the flesh. He always had a lot to say about the sins of the flesh.' He glanced down at his protruding belly.

'Where did he go?' asked Anthony.

'Liam?'

'No, Flash.'

382

Michael removed the biretta and scratched his head. 'There's no answer to that, because Mr Flanagan moves in mysterious ways. There are some people who feed him, of course. He has a sort of timetable, tries not to hit the same target two days in a row. But there are several soft-hearted ladies who dish up a plate of scouse for Flash. He'll turn up. Doesn't a bad penny always make the rounds? Wait till the pubs open.'

Anthony leaned against Razor's painted window. A crudely printed message above his head read, 'It'll be all right when it's washed.' Children who returned home fretful after being shorn by Razor's enthusiastic scissors were always persuaded by mothers that they might look human again after a quick scrub and a dousing. Razor, whose sense of humour was legendary, had incorporated the advice into his advertising.

'Michael, my brother's out there and he's dangerous.'

The priest knew exactly what his companion meant. 'Proof, Anthony,' he said quietly. 'Theory is all very well, but the police want a little more than that. And they think Liam's gone absent because he saw his father's death.'

'He caused it,' replied Anthony.

Michael Brennan shook his head before replacing his biretta. 'You know that. I know it and God Himself definitely knows the whole truth of the matter. But the police force needs something a little more tangible than ours and the Almighty's certainties.'

'Do you think Liam will have heard about Dad's new will?'

'I doubt it. He'll be too concerned with other matters. Staying free is probably his main goal for now.'

Anthony turned this way and that, saw no sign of Flash. 'If and when he does hear about the will, he might well go for Bridie.'

'Do you think so?'

'Yes.' Anthony's heart raced. His father was only just buried. Anthony did not love Bridie, would not love her. 'She thinks he was in the house the other night. And he tore Dad's solicitor's office apart, too. Looking for something, obviously. We – Bridie and I – think Dad told Liam about some evidence. He was searching for whatever that is. Flash knows exactly what Liam was looking for. That's why Flash must be found.'

The priest turned round and stared in the direction of his church 'There's another way of looking at this,' he said, almost to himself. 'If we can't find one thing, we can surely look for all the others.'

Anthony repeated this sentence in his head, failed to solve the riddle. 'I beg your pardon?'

'You are absolutely sure that Liam attacked Maureen, aren't you? And, to be perfectly honest – like every priest should be – I tend to agree with you. The man's weird.'

Anthony nodded mutely.

'Now, the item – if there is an item – that was discovered at the scene must be easily identifiable.'

'But–'

'Hear me out.' Michael removed his hat again, as if the action would allow his brain to breathe more freely. 'Sam saw Flash. Flash gave something to Sam. Sam changed his will, then came to the presbytery–'

'Without the evidence?' asked Anthony.

'Probably.' The cleric thought for a few seconds. 'If Liam had retrieved the very thing that might damn him, he would have stayed here. Unless, of course, he thought your father had spoken to other people. But Liam has been searching, hasn't he? A few nights ago, he was still looking for this article.'

'He's been scouring the area, certainly.'

'Then we look at what is left,' said Michael Brennan. 'He ran, you know. He must have left as soon as Sam fell down. His cupboards are still full. There was no sign of packing. So, let's look at what we have in order to find out what we haven't.'

Anthony followed the parish priest towards St Aloysius's. On the way, several people spoke to Father Brennan, while not a few stopped Anthony to offer their condolences.

'Your father was a well-liked man,' said Michael while hanging up their coats in the porch. 'Come in while I make a pot of tea.'

They drank tea, ate a couple of biscuits, talked about the future of Bell's Pledges. 'You've a fondness for her,' said Michael after hearing Bridie's plans for the business.

Anthony, startled almost out of his skin, simply nodded.

'For your stepmother.'

'She was not my stepmother for very long,' replied Anthony warily. 'And I never lived in that household, so she was no mother substitute for me. Anyway, she's younger than I am.'

Father Brennan dipped a Marie biscuit into his second cup of tea. 'Did Sam know how you felt about his wife?'

Anthony nodded again. He didn't know what to say or where to look.

'Did Sam mind?'

'No. He sounded pleased. Almost as if he knew that death was near. As if he wanted someone to look after her.'

The priest collected cups and saucers, made a pile of them, clattered teaspoons onto a tray. 'There's affinity, Anthony.'

'I know.'

'As things stand, you can never be married to her.'

'I know, I know!'

Michael Brennan rose from his seat and walked across to the fireplace. He leaned an elbow on the mantelpiece and stared at himself in the mirror. Reflected in the glass was a painting of Jesus and Joseph at a carpenter's bench. Next to that was a reversed view of St Peter's in Rome. Rome would not allow this young man to express love for a woman who had been married to his father. 'What is sin?' he asked of himself. A fat old man stared back at him, the same question on his lips.

Anthony remained seated. 'Sin is hurting others,' he replied.

'Or hurting God Himself.'

'God is in us, or so we're told,' replied Anthony. 'He is concerned that we respect one another's needs.'

The cleric turned round. 'Yes,' he said eventually. 'It's a wonder that you weren't ordained instead of himself.' He walked back to the table and sat opposite his guest. 'I've been in love, you know,' he said. 'Three or four times. Priests wear no body armour against the onslaughts of nature. Of course, I never did anything about it.'

Anthony stared at the round-faced man, waited with bated breath for the story to continue.

'Loved a girl back home first of all. I was about sixteen, all spots and enthusiasm. Her family came over to England and I never saw her again, never heard from her.' His eyes clouded over and he rubbed them with the heels of his hands. 'Margaret, she was called. Hair like buttercups and a voice as sweet as heaven itself.' He pulled himself together. 'During my ministry, I've become over-fond of a couple of other ladies.'

'Here?' managed Anthony.

The priest smiled. 'Here and there – 'tis no matter. So I know how difficult this is for you. Forbidden love.' He retreated into his thoughts for a few moments. 'There are bigger sins, Anthony.'

'Yes, I'm sure there are. Michael,' said Anthony slowly,

'even the state itself would be unlikely to encourage a union between a man and his stepmother.'

'Does Bridie care for you?'

Anthony raised his shoulders. 'I think she does. Of course, she's grieving for Dad, because she did become fond of him. And Cathy's had to stay behind in Astleigh Fold. Then all this with Liam is terrifying. You know, she will need somebody once she settles back into life.'

'Then why should that not be you?'

Stunned, the younger man stared hard at the priest who had been his confessor for years. The Catholic faith was extremely rigid with regard to matrimony, adultery and fornication. 'But the Church,' he began. 'The Church would—'

'Sometimes, we need to look past the Church and into the face of God Himself. But first, we must look into your brother's belongings.'

Bridie placed a bunch of large white daisies on her husband's grave. Across the sea, in Ireland, there was another grave. Eugene's grave. She shivered and pulled her coat tightly across her chest. Slow, sad people moved about the cemetery with flowers and containers of water. Surely she was safe here in broad daylight? 'Liam's gone,' she whispered under her breath. 'He isn't here any more. I'd know if he was still around here.' Sam was a mere six feet below this piece of ground. 'You were a fine man,' she told the earth. 'And I wish you were here now to meet Anthony and to know him.'

Anthony. She really should not think about him. It was not right for a new widow to want to run her fingers through thick, dark hair. She needed comfort, needed someone to care for her. The people she was allowed to love – Shauna, Cathy and Muth – were her dependants. If only she could turn to that strong man. Anthony would look after her if she gave him the chance. She was cold and lonely and terribly afraid.

She walked across a narrow path of gravel and perched on a bench, her eyes still fixed to the fresh mound of earth that covered Sam. A cross of flowers wilted among smaller wreaths and bouquets. Like the poor man they covered, the flowers were fading away to nothing. He would have a stone. She would make sure that Sam and his first wife would be remembered, that their names would be carved in fine Italian marble for all to see.

Leaning further back, she closed her eyes and thought about Sam. How scared she had been when Da had first brought her to Liverpool. How terrifying those trams had been, how loud this new world had seemed. But Sam had been good to her. Sam had provided for her and the girls, had removed them all from Thomas Murphy's field of vision. Da. He was staying at Dolly Hanson's, Bridie supposed. Poor Dolly had fallen in love with Da long before Mammy's death. 'He'll be hanging around to see what I do with the horses,' Bridie told Sam now. 'But he'll not get his hands on them, so don't you be worrying.'

She had come here to be alone with Sam. The funeral had been busy, hectic and noisy. Bridie felt as if she had not been allowed to say goodbye. She had been elsewhere when the heart attack had happened. Only Liam knew how Sam had died. 'If I'd been there, would I have saved you?'

Edith was back at the house with Shauna. Sticky-Fingers was Great Aunt Edith's name for Bridie's younger child. Everything had been returned, but Edith had been tight-lipped on her return to Scotland Road. Shauna had done the rounds in Woolworths, had acquired several penny whistles and some brightly coloured rubber balls. There was something wrong with the child. She needed, so she took. Shauna's physical requirements were well catered for, so from which part of the child's being did her need arise? Was she starved of affection? Did she miss her daddy?

Sam would have put everything into perspective. He would have lectured Shauna for a minute or so, would have explained that stealing was wrong. Now, there was no-one to share in the guilt, the powerlessness. What was she going to do without him? He had been a father to her, a better parent than Thomas Murphy could ever have been. And she was selfish, because she was worrying about her own future when she should have been grieving for the departed.

'Mrs Bell?'

A hand touched Bridie's shoulder. She turned. 'Ah. Mrs Hanson.'

The chubby little shopkeeper walked round the bench and laid a small bundle of freesia on the grave before placing herself next to the widow. 'What must you think of me?' she asked Bridie.

Bridie made no reply.

'I didn't know,' muttered Dolly Hanson. 'In the beginning, I didn't know.'

'What?' Bridie resented the intrusion. She had come here to say goodbye and to work her way through her own thoughts and memories. At home, behind the shop, Edith and Muth were chattering and reminiscing while Shauna played. Diddy and Billy were in and out all the time with soup and cakes, and Charlie was stumbling about in the shop tidying up and doing paperwork. 'I came here to be alone,' said Bridie. 'To think. I don't mean to be rude, but it's been difficult to find a chance to think these past few days.'

Dolly nodded. 'I'll not stop.'

Bridie smiled apologetically. 'Look, I don't blame you.

Mammy was ill for a long time, and I suppose he needed someone.'

'He won't marry me.' Dolly regretted the words immediately. She should not have aired her troubles in the company of this poor young woman.

'You're lucky,' replied Bridie. 'He married Mammy, and she never thrived. My father is one of the cruellest people I've ever known. If he did marry you, there would be a reason. If and when he does ask you, think about the shop. It would be his if you died.'

Dolly nodded. 'My first husband was a bugger. I seem to go for the wrong sort.' She thought about her son, an engineer with a merchant fleet. The shop was for him, she supposed. Sailors had hard lives and often needed to retire early. 'He'll need the business,' she said aloud. 'Our Stephen. My husband died at sea before Stephen was born. The shop's for him, for my lad.'

Bridie smiled again. 'Get rid of Da. Tell him to get back to Galway and rot.' She straightened her shoulders and stood up. 'I've changed my mind, Mrs Hanson. I'll walk back with you and tell you all about your lucky escape.'

Bridie took one final look at Sam's resting place. He had done a lot for her in such a very short space of time. Sam had given Bridie some confidence, some security. She didn't need to think any more. 'Thanks, Sam,' she said. 'I'll never forget you.'

Sixteen

Anthony sat back on his heels. His knees ached after taking his full weight for ten minutes or so. He had emptied the wardrobe and was picking out the last of Liam's belongings. 'That's all the shoes and boots accounted for,' he said. He grabbed a penny from the floor of the old wardrobe, handed it to the priest. 'Here. Put that in the collection plate.' He got up and walked to the bed. 'So – are all his things here?'

'As far as I remember. We brought a couple of albs over from the vestry – they were miles too long for me, and they would never have covered my dignity.' He patted his substantial paunch. 'As far as I can tell, he took little or nothing with him when he left here.'

The younger man gazed round the room that had contained his brother. Mushroom-coloured walls were adorned with holy pictures of St Anthony of Padua, St Aloysius Gonzaga, John the Baptist and several prints of Our Lady. A statue of the Immaculate Conception sat on a chest of drawers, an extinct candle in a blue glass container at the figure's feet. In front of the chest, a prie-dieu with a leather kneeler bore marks left by a series of praying priests. 'I'll look in the drawers,' he said.

Underneath socks and underwear, Anthony discovered a faded photograph of his mother. He turned this over, found pencilled words on the reverse side. WHY DID YOU

LEAVE ME? was printed in a childish scrawl. 'See?' He handed the picture to his companion. 'Always, he resented being motherless. He blamed her, my father, me and anyone else who dared to enter his field of vision. To this day, he's punishing mankind. Well, womankind, mostly.'

Michael looked at the photograph. 'A bitter child who grew to be a bitter man.'

'A sick man.' Anthony lifted out a wooden box. He pushed at the lid, but it refused to budge. 'Locked,' he said. 'Do you have a screwdriver?'

Michael Brennan smiled grimly. 'Not about my person, no. It may seem strange to you, but I've never found the need for one. Are you going to break that box open?'

Anthony shook the container. It was about the same size as a canteen for cutlery, but its contents did not rattle. 'Papers, I'd say.' He glanced at the priest. 'If I'm committing a crime or a sin of some sort, go out while I do it.'

Michael Brennan allowed his frustration to show. 'Look at us,' he said angrily, 'we've jobs to get on with, and here we are doing detective work. How do I make the police listen? I keep telling them we've a man missing and that he's a hazard. Twice, I've done that. How many more times must I do it before they take notice?'

'What was their response?'

'The police say he's a grown man who can come and go just as he pleases. They're neither worried nor interested. They seem to think we're making up half of it – though Dr Spencer's had a go at them, told them that Liam's not right in the head.' He glanced at the box in Anthony's hands. 'You're Liam's next of kin, so do what you like with the box.'

'Right, I shall. We must investigate for ourselves. This box may contain an answer.'

Michael pondered for a second or two before leaving the room in search of a screwdriver.

Anthony sat on the bed. Next to him were draped items of Liam's vestmentry, greens and purples and golds laid out on top of the counterpane. The bed was mercilessly hard. It must have been like sleeping between the tram tracks on Scotland Road, Anthony mused. But that was typical of Liam. The sins of the flesh were to be eradicated. Warmth and comfort were probably iniquitous indulgences. Liam had a fondness for big words. Iniquitous was one of Liam's words. He would never use a monosyllable when a longer word could be found.

Anthony placed the box on the floor and picked up a black stock. It hung limply from its dog collar, the four ties drooping from its sides. Liam had owned several of these false fronts. 'Where are you?' he asked the garment. 'Where the hell have you gone?' The clothing gave no answers. Everything was clean and folded. Not one stain lingered on Liam's garments. He wasn't real, wasn't human, wasn't reachable in any sense.

The absent priest's cope hung on a brass peg attached to the door. This plain black cloak with its hook and chain fastening was draped over a wooden hanger, the folds neat and precise. Everything else, with the exception of several albs, lay on Liam's bed. Maniples, chasubles and stoles made a rainbow of colour on the plain coverlet. Each piece looked new, almost unused. Liam, even during infancy, had never come home from school dirty. When his hands had been slightly soiled, he had scrubbed and scrubbed until his skin had turned almost red-raw.

Anthony got up and picked Liam's albs from the bottom drawer. He unfolded the white, long-sleeved shifts, looked for clues, found nothing but tissue paper placed carefully so as to avoid creasing. Outward perfection had hidden so much. Never a hair out of place, never a mark on a shoe, never a straight thought in Liam Bell's mind. Oh God, where was he?

'Screwdriver.'

Anthony jumped, placed a hand at his throat.

'You're nervous,' said Michael Brennan. 'Would a drop of scotch steady you?'

'No. Thank you. Liam's a burden, but he hasn't driven me to drink just yet.'

The priest produced some paper. 'I hope you're ready for this, Anthony. It's a letter from Liam to me. It must have been delivered since we came in. He says he has been called to Africa. Well, I heard nothing about that. Neither did the bishop, I'm sure.'

Anthony took a deep breath. 'Why didn't I speak up earlier, Michael? Why didn't I scream and yell until somebody noticed? I'd a brother hearing voices while I did nothing at all. Why didn't I make someone understand?'

Michael touched Anthony's shoulder. 'Because you would have finished up screaming in a padded cell. You were never a hundred per cent sure, were you? In your heart, you felt sure that Liam had done harm, but there was always a shred of doubt in your mind.'

'A shred of hope,' said Anthony. He unfolded the single sheet of paper and read aloud. '"I have booked a ticket to Southampton and will be leaving soon for Africa."' Anthony shook his head. 'Why Southampton? He could have sailed from Liverpool.' He continued to read aloud. '"The light dawned suddenly at the very moment when my father's soul departed. God reached out to me in my grief and told me what to do. Please make my apologies to the diocese and to my family. I shall pray for the repose of my father's soul. Father Liam Bell".'

'A load of nonsense, of course,' said Michael. 'He's no more in Southampton than I am. Here – open that box. My curiosity is getting the better of me.'

Anthony removed the screws and unhinged the lid. The interior was lined with green felt. He pulled out some envelopes and a writing pad, threw them onto the chest of drawers. At the bottom of the container lay a few frail cuttings from newspapers. There was the announcement of Val's death, a piece about the murder and an account of the trial. This last article bore the headline, 'GUILTY'. 'An innocent man,' said Anthony. His voice emerged thick and his hands shook. 'Here's one of the best arguments yet against capital punishment.' He waved the yellowing newsprint. 'And there's still not a scrap of proof in here, nothing we can show to the law. After all, Liam was merely collecting the sad tale of how his poor twin's fiancée was murdered. So clever. So very astute. How can a deranged man be so brilliant?'

'Well now,' replied Michael Brennan, 'isn't that the question and the answer all in the one sentence? There's but a fine line between brilliance and lunacy. Your brother crossed back and forth so quickly and so often that we never noticed.'

'I noticed,' said Anthony. 'And I waited for others to notice, too. But no-one ever did.'

'I did. I thought he was a queer fellow altogether, but he functioned adequately. Don't blame yourself. With the grace of God, Liam is gone for good.'

Anthony shook his head wearily. 'He'll be back. You mark my words – we have not seen the last of him.'

Mother Ignatius occupied a small section of a leather armchair in Dr Richard Spencer's study. The chair was so big that the tiny woman seemed in danger of being swallowed up by the vast expanse of dark-brown hide. However, any lack of stature was compensated for by the expression on her face. Had Diddy Costigan been present, the little woman's visage might well have been described as 'fit to scrape your bloody boots on.'

Mother fixed a gimlet eye on Cathy O'Brien and fought a sigh. The girl was difficult. She might, with good nursing and God's help, recover from the blood problem, but the stubborn streak was probably here for life. 'Have you nothing to say to me, child?'

Cathy hated being called 'child'. Granda used to scream 'child' when he wanted something doing for him. She tapped the toe of a shoe against the rug. Mother Wart-Face was here without Aunt Edith. Aunt Edith had gone out to register the horses for racing or some such thing. And the warty nun had arrived uninvited.

'Speak up,' said the nun.

Cathy had nothing to say, because life had become the most desperate mess. Uncle Sam was dead. He'd been a bit on the quiet side, but he had been terribly kind. Uncle Sam had got Noel for Cathy. She glanced round the room, noticed that the dog had curled itself into a corner beneath a shelf of medicine books. The medicine books had rude pictures in them. Cathy blushed, because it didn't seem right for Hairy-Warty-Face to be in the same room as a girl who had looked at rude pictures.

'Cathy?'

Naked men and women. 'Mother?'

The tiny nun edged forward in her chair so that her feet might dangle a little nearer to the floor. 'I've brought you some books.'

'Thank you, Mother.' The books would not have medicine type pictures in them.

'You'll be studying at home.'

Cathy looked the headmistress straight in the eye, which was an easy thing to do, as both sets of eyes were on the one level. 'My home is in Scotland Road with Mammy and Shauna.' It was happening again. Shauna was getting all the love while Cathy got all the work. Only this time, the work had arrived disguised as a dwarf in black with a pile of dusty-looking books. Cathy was partial to reading, but she resented this unbidden intrusion. 'I'm ill,' she informed the nun.

'Your blood is tired, that's all,' replied Mother Ignatius rather smartly. 'With good food and fresh air, you'll be ready to return to school before you know it.'

Cathy refused to cry for Uncle Sam and for her own misery. She would cry later, on her own. Life was so terrible that she was even forced to plan her crying times. Perhaps she should make a timetable with Crying Time written just below Bedtime. 'My own school will send some books,' she said.

'You are advanced for your age. You are ready to work alongside ten- and eleven-year-olds.'

Cathy didn't want to be different. She wanted to run about Paddy's Market with Cozzer and Tildy, wanted to play rounders with lamp-posts as bases. She wanted to sneak down to the city when Mammy was busy. Liverpool was so exciting. Sefton Park was the largest in the world and it had a great huge palm house. Cozzer had been thrown out for messing about with a strange-looking spider on a big plant and—

'What do you want to be when you grow up?' asked Mother Ignatius.

Cathy's sole ambition was to be a person who could make up her own mind about her own life without nuns and people telling her what to do. She wanted to work at Blackler's with all those other happy-looking girls. The shop had canopies that went right round a corner and it sold everything. Blackler's went on trips in the summer, closed its doors so that employees could run races and eat picnics on beaches and in parks.

'This is dumb insolence,' remarked Mother Ignatius.

'I'm thinking,' said Cathy sulkily. 'Uncle Sam is dead and I want to be with Mammy.' She could cheer Mammy up by taking her to the Edinburgh café and Woolworths. They could walk down Lord Street and look at all the street traders standing with their backs to the traffic and with trays hung round their necks. They sold funny little wind-up toys and matches and tea towels that were no good. Uncle Sam said the cloth was rubbish. But he would never say that again. He'd never let Cathy hold his baccy tin while he made his rollies. And he'd no longer be sitting staring at Mammy with that special little smile on his lips. And she would not cry till bedtime. Tonight, she would cry for Daddy, too.

'You can't go back to Liverpool,' said the nun, the crisp edge honed carefully from her voice. 'You need the air and the fields. Your mother will visit you.'

'I don't want to be somebody she visits. I should live with her all the time like Shauna does. Why do I have to stay when I don't want to? I'm the big girl, Mother. Mammy has all to do for Shauna, because Shauna is not thriving.'

Shauna was thriving, thought the head of Sacred Heart Grammar School for Girls. Shauna had led Edith a merry dance after the death of her stepfather. In Bridie's absence, Shauna had sulked and screamed and indulged in magnificent tantrums all over the house. The child had a marked talent for theft, though she was a bit young to be damned just yet. All the same, it was plain for everyone to see that the younger O'Brien girl had been overindulged by her protective mother. 'Shauna is doing very well,' added Mother Ignatius. 'She's stronger than she looks.'

Cathy gazed sadly at the ugly, shrivelled-up person who sat before her. 'Mother, I know my mammy is missing Uncle Sam. She didn't know him for a great while, but she was happy. So was I. He didn't shout like Granda. He didn't frighten me like Granda. I am frightened of being

398

frightened again.' Why had she said that? What on earth had prompted her to confide in the enemy?

The nun bowed her head. 'The fear of fear is as bad as fear itself,' she said quietly. The head raised itself. 'Put your trust in God, in Edith and Richard. And in me. I can do so much for you. Please allow me to help you, Cathy.'

Cathy took the bull by the horns. 'I'm frightened of you,' she said bluntly. 'I'm scared of your school. It's all uniforms and lisle stockings and silly hats.'

The nun's mouth twitched, but she kept her composure. 'Go on. I'm listening.'

'Well, I'm not sure I want a lot doing for me. I like being at St Aloysius's school. We have a good time. There are nuns, but we don't have a uniform. And all my friends are there. There's Cozzer and Tildy-Anne, then Mavis Burns who sits next to me – she has crossed eyes when she takes her glasses off.' Mavis always removed her eye furniture during religious lessons so that everyone would cheer up a bit, but Cathy couldn't tell that to a holy woman. A lot of people had been chastised for explosive laughter during religious lessons. Nobody would ever laugh in front of this sister or mother or whatever she called herself. 'And we've steam lorries and trams and a man with a barrel organ.'

Mother Ignatius nodded, waited.

Cathy began to listen to herself. A very short time ago, she had been terrified of trams and steam lorries. 'Sometimes,' she began thoughtfully, 'things that frighten me start to be interesting.' She and Cozzer and Tildy-Anne had been thrown out of the Fruit Exchange and the Cotton Exchange on several occasions. After the first few times, the fear and the excitement had evaporated. 'And sometimes, things that used to frighten me stop being interesting.'

'That's the way of it,' pronounced the nun.

'Is it?'

'I'm afraid so.'

Cathy eyed her adversary. 'What is it that you want to do for me?' It was no use being afraid, Cathy decided. A lot of bad things had happened, including Uncle Sam's death, so fear of this forbidding-looking person was a waste of time. Those who had looked after Cathy were fast disappearing, and she had better speak up for herself, stop acting like a scared rabbit.

'I want to educate you.'

'At that school?'

The nun smiled, causing her wart to wobble. The three stiff hairs separated and quivered with the unexpected movement. Cathy thought the hairs might fall out with the sudden shock of being fastened to a smile, but they didn't. 'Not yet,' answered Mother. 'For a while, you will have to stay away from other children in case you catch a cold. Anaemia makes colds worse, so you have to stay safe.'

'I feel lonely,' admitted Cathy.

'I know.'

'And there's no fun at your school. I suppose you want me to go there when I'm better, but there's no fun.'

Mother Ignatius sighed deeply and glanced at the clock. Young people seemed to set so much store by what they called fun. Fun often involved destructive or stupid acts like swinging from lamp standards and throwing balls near windows. 'Achievement is the greatest reward,' she said finally. 'And we have netball, tennis and gymnastics. There is always something to do.'

Cathy picked up the nearest book. It was a French dictionary. 'French?' she asked. She was still having trouble with the various kinds of English she had encountered. There was the language spoken in Liverpool, then the totally different tongue used in Lancashire and by

Uncle Sam's mother. On top of all which, Cathy had to contend with the King's English as spoken by Richard and Edith Spencer. 'I don't think I'll be very good at French.'

Mother Ignatius smiled again. The wart moved. 'French is easy. If you're very lucky, you get to learn Greek in the sixth form.'

After staring at a few very odd words, Cathy replaced the book on the pile and decided to hang for a sheep. 'Why are you a nun?' she asked.

'I was called.'

'Called?'

'By God. He wanted me to devote my life to Him. And teaching was what I did best, so I combined the two and here I am, headmistress of Sacred Heart.'

'I'd never be a nun,' said Cathy. 'The clothes are horrible and you don't have children.'

Mother Ignatius wagged a bony finger at this bold child. 'Caitlin, I have six hundred daughters and thousands more who have gone out into the world. So I answered the call of God and I still have my children.'

Cathy brought to mind a conversation she had overheard between Uncle Richard and Anthony, who had been Mr Bell at school. 'Father Liam hears voices,' she announced. 'He thinks they're from God, but Anthony says they're from a sick part of his mind. Uncle Richard says Father Liam's got . . . skip-so something.'

Mother Ignatius pricked up her ears. Schizophrenia? She recalled the young priest, the coldness of his eyes, the confidence in his stance. 'Is he the one who went missing?'

Cathy nodded vigorously. 'Africa or somewhere. I heard Aunt Edith telling Uncle Richard that Father Brennan had been sent a letter from Father Liam. But Uncle Richard says he doesn't think Africa is the truth.'

'Really?'

'Priests don't tell lies, do they?'

'Not as a rule.'

Cathy thought about that. 'Do they sometimes?'

'We all sin, Caitlin.'

'Do you, Mother?'

'Yes. It's a part of being human.'

Cathy put her head on one side and scoured the nun's features. She had bright blue eyes that were fading towards the edges, as if someone had painted a white-ish line around the irises. The nose was small, not pointed, and the rest of the face was ordinary except for the wart and a lot of lines. The woman was human, then. 'They think Father Liam has some kind of illness in his head, Mother. But he's clever all the same. Uncle Richard says he's gone to ground for the time being.'

So the priest was in hiding. 'He didn't go to the funeral?'

'No. He ran off. I think he was with Uncle Sam when . . .' The tears threatened. She closed her eyes tightly and thought about timetables. 'Uncle Sam was nice.'

Mother Ignatius saw and heard the little girl's pain. She edged her way towards terra firma and stood on the rug. 'Just look after yourself, Caitlin O'Brien,' she said. 'Because some of us have great plans for you.'

Cathy waited until the headmistress had left, then she claimed the leather chair. It was still warm from the nun's body. Cathy hugged herself and let the tears come. Sometimes, timetables didn't quite work.

It was something Bridie could not quite put her finger on, an elusive quality that defied description. But she could hardly bear to be in a room with Anthony Bell, yet she wanted him to stay. The feelings of guilt that had been stirred up by her husband's death seemed to be at war with other emotions, and Anthony was part and parcel of this terrible, silent conflict.

'Bridie,' he began. 'Michael – Father Brennan – and I have been to the police again. Richard Spencer has written to the Chief Constable. Richard is fairly sure that Liam is schizophrenic. The force is keeping an eye open for Liam. Try not to be afraid, but, at the same time, keep watch.'

Bridie sat down in Sam's chair. She could smell him, could almost taste the tobacco he had used to make his cigarettes. 'I miss your father,' she said softly. 'More than I expected to. Anyway, put your mind at ease, because no-one will get in here again. The locksmith did a very good job. We've more keys than doors. Stop worrying. Your worrying will only make me worry, too.'

'I'm sorry,' he replied. 'I just wanted to make sure of your safety before I go back to Astleigh Fold.' He could not stay here, not yet. Astleigh Fold was a safe distance away, yet near enough for regular visits.

Bridie's internal war broke out again. Her heart leapt about and the palms of her hands were suddenly clammy and cold. He must go. He must get as far as possible away from Scotland Road, from her, from ... from the love she had for him. Love? How could she think of love when Sam had only just died? Anthony must go now. No, no, she would be truly soothed only if he were here with her.

'Bridie?'

He had lost his father. She reminded herself yet again of this man's grief. In the space of a single day, Anthony had rediscovered Sam, only to be deprived of him almost immediately. 'I'll be fine, so I will,' she told him. 'You just get along to your work and leave us to sort out this end of things.'

'My brother won't come back, not for a while. He may have more than one personality, but he will always guard himself, no matter who or how he happens to be at the time. I've known him for long enough to realize that he'll remain hidden. And Richard has almost convinced the police that Liam could be dangerous.'

Bridie swallowed. 'What about the Costigans? Do they know that Liam is being looked for in connection with Maureen?'

Anthony cleared his throat and his mind. Bridie looked so beautiful today. Her hair was all over the place, had broken free from its anchorage to settle in frail wisps around her face. Better not to look. He stared at the fireplace. 'No,' he said. 'Richard advised them that Maureen is too injured for any further probings. There is no point stirring up the neighbourhood without proof. If the people round here had a hint of Liam's suspected involvement, all hell would break loose. But once Liam reappears, he will be detained for questioning.'

Bridie didn't know how she was going to be able to look Diddy in the face. She needed Diddy, needed the strength of that big-hearted lady. For Bridie, Diddy was Scotland Road. She embodied the strength of it, the colour and the sheer, dogged determination of an area that refused to be pushed under.

'I love you, Bridie,' Anthony said. There was no taking back the words, no erasing the sentiment behind them.

'I know that,' she replied. 'And it's as well that you're going away again.'

'Michael Brennan says there are bigger sins.'

She searched his face as if trying to make a picture of it, something to which she might refer during his absence. 'You told him, then.'

'He didn't need telling.'

'It must be very obvious if he can see it.'

Anthony took a step towards her, thought better of the move and fixed his eyes on a point above her head. 'Michael's a romantic soul,' he said. 'Had he not been a priest, he would have enjoyed an interesting love-life.'

Bridie giggled, then wondered immediately how on earth she was able to be here laughing when her husband was dead and her little girl was ill and in a different place. 'Bigger sins,' she repeated.

'He would want me to take care of you.'

'You mean Sam, of course.'

'Yes.'

She pushed a thread of hair from her face. 'Your dad changed my life altogether and for ever. Until the day I die, I shall be grateful to him. Things started off so badly, what with the horses and my father being involved.' She shook her head slowly. 'Everything Da touches is soiled, including poor Dolly Hanson. In her eyes I see an expression that was often in my mammy's eyes, too. Confusion and self-distrust. But in spite of my father, Sam and I came through. We would have been fine, you know.'

Although he kept his eyes on the window-sill behind Bridie's head, Anthony could still see her. He ached to comfort her, longed to draw his own solace from touching her, holding her and saying those silly things which can only be spoken in whispers. With the length of a hearth-rug between them, he could not open up his heart. 'Come here,' he said.

Bridie paused, placed her hands on the arms of her chair, raised herself slowly into a standing position. 'No good will come of this,' she murmured as he stepped towards her. She was dreaming, was drugged. Like a piece of base metal, she was drawn to him, because he was her own particular magnet. Shauna was asleep upstairs. Muth, too, had gone up early. Would either of them come down and witness Bridie's terrible sin?

'I need you,' he told her. 'Wherever he is, Dad knows that. And I think you need me.'

No words would come from Bridie's lips. She tried to speak, even framed a syllable with her lips, but her senses were filled by his nearness and by the fear that always accompanied his presence in her life. If he touched her, she would die. If he didn't touch her, she would die. It was all the same, all the one thing. Need and dismay made an uncomfortable cocktail, caused her heart to beat erratically. She stood at the edge of the rug and at the rim of hell, yet paradise was so very close.

Anthony buried his face in her hair and let his grief go. He cried soundlessly for the father he had scarcely known, wept because the woman he held so closely was precious, special and forbidden. Michael Brennan had talked about bigger sins. The biggest sin of all had run away, was in hiding. 'Can God make mistakes?' he whispered at last.

'I don't think so,' she replied with difficulty. 'If He could make mistakes, then He wouldn't be God.' Breathing was difficult. She needed him to hold her for ever. She needed more than holding, and the desire made her cheeks hot.

'Then did He make Liam deliberately?'

Bridie kicked her brain into gear. 'We made him, Anthony,' she told him. 'The world makes mistakes. Liam is an example of what we all might become.' She breathed in and out slowly, tried to take charge of her own mechanism. Even talking about Anthony's twin did not take the edge from her terrible longing. 'There's a bit of the Lucifer in all of us,' she murmured. 'But there's too much of the devil in your brother.'

Anthony kissed her forehead and her cheeks. 'Not here,' he said, pulling away from her. They could not become lovers on a hearthrug while a child and a grandmother slept above their heads.

She wiped his face with her handkerchief, shivered, was cold without his closeness. 'Dear God, this is wicked,' she managed. 'Sam's hardly buried, and I lost another good man last year, yet here we are—'

'Being human, Bridie. And we're hurting no-one.'

'Isn't this our bit of Lucifer, Anthony?' She might never have met him. Had she not come to England, this encounter would never have taken place. How strange fate was. Thomas Murphy had brought love into Bridie's life. He had intended to send his daughter into misery, had wanted to punish her for marrying a Protestant, yet the same man, her da, had been instrumental in bringing true love into Bridie's life. 'How many never meet the other one?' she asked.

He understood immediately. 'Someone worked out that there are about six people for each of us. The chances of walking into a certain room on a certain day are very remote. So we usually settle for the seventh or the seventieth. Yet one of those six could be living right next door or across the street—'

'Or he could be your husband's son.'

'Or your father's widow.'

She took his hand and held it tightly. 'Whether this is right or wrong, it's here,' she whispered. 'What would God have us do?'

Anthony smiled ruefully. 'If God's a Catholic, He'd be a bit put out. But if He's an ordinary all-round sort of chap with a sense of humour, He'd not damn us.'

Bridie found herself smiling again. 'I never had such feelings for anyone before,' she confessed. 'I loved Eugene, but that was quieter altogether. And Sam – well – I came to appreciate him. As I said before, we would have been fine, your dad and me. But this is ... like an illness that won't go away.'

He stepped back and sat down in an armchair. 'The first time I saw you, on the day you arrived, I felt uncomfortable. I couldn't understand why you were marrying a man so much older than yourself. You know, I think I was jealous of poor old Dad.'

'Bigger sins,' she muttered.

'That's right, Bridie. There are bigger sins than the one we are about to commit.'

The routine was rigorous and boring, yet the sameness of each day was exactly what Martin Waring wanted.

He rose at six in the morning, as did all lay members of the community. The *frères* themselves were up at five o'clock praying, lighting fires, making porridge and baking bread, tending the cows, pigs and hens. Martin wanted to be up and about alongside the monks, but he had to keep his head down on the iron-hard pillow. In accordance with the sketchy history of Martin Waring, he was forced to act like a recently released thief. Of course, he had been driven by his parents' poverty into a life of crime. His parents had died, rather conveniently, during Martin's brief spell in jail, and Martin had seen the light.

The *frères* asked few questions. Often, the men who stayed with them reverted to type after leaving the house, but the brothers carried on regardlessly in pursuit of their founder's dream. In the copperplate and gilded rules of the order, it was written that the aim was to save just one soul. The parable of the shepherd leaving his flock to search for a single stray lamb was quoted as part of the order's holy constitution. Martin Waring, né Liam Bell, had done sufficient research to learn that the *frères* took each lay resident at face value. They had even been known to grant asylum to runaways, though every offender, Catholic or otherwise, was guided subtly towards that healing sacrament called confession. A resident suspected of major crime was always handed over to the police.

Frère Nicholas listened to the news on the radio each morning. If he recognized a suspected murderer or rapist within his community, he would send for the law. But the architects of major crimes rarely sought refuge within these thick stone walls. The brothers simply strove to guide their mistaken flock towards a healthier and crime-free way of life.

Martin lay on his bed and waited for the rising bell. There were just five laymen here. The other four were creatures of no importance, petty thieves whose inadequacies were immediately apparent. Martin's 'job', the area in which he was expected to specialize after his farm chores were completed, was to teach two of his fellow refugees to read.

He sniffed. He ought to have been serving mass, conducting benediction, administering the holy oils, handing out the body and blood of Jesus Christ. And he was teaching idiots a for apple and b for box. Nevertheless, he was smiling inwardly. Brother Martin. *Frère* Martin. He rather liked the sound of that, rather liked the idea of a fresh start. His beard was growing very nicely, though it was still at the prickly stage. *Frère* Nicholas, who was wary of beards, had asked Martin to give a reason for wishing to alter his appearance.

'I'll shave it off gladly if you wish, *Frère* Nicholas,' Martin had replied. 'But I am hiding from myself, you see. I look in the glass and see a thief. I am trying to become a new man, a different person altogether. My parents must have been so ashamed of me. Even through the worst years, they endured their poverty without turning to crime.'

Brother Nicholas had agreed to allow the beard. Martin Waring fitted the description of none of the major criminals who were currently being pursued by the authorities. It did not do to ask too many questions. Many of these sinners had been frightened off by too close scrutiny, and Brother Nicholas realized that his latest lodger was of a liturgical turn. Already, Martin could respond at mass, was begging for baptism and confirmation, seemed sad when the brothers took Communion while he remained in his pew. At the next council meeting, Brother Nicholas intended to raise the subject of Martin Waring's intention to become a Catholic.

The intended 'convert' took up his missal and allowed it to fall open. The displayed page announced the third Sunday after Easter, and the epistle seemed appropriate. He read aloud, '"*Carissimi: Obsecro vos tanquam advenas...*"' Martin smiled to himself as he translated, '"I call upon you to be like strangers and exiles, to resist those natural appetites which besiege the soul."' Hadn't he preached this all along? '"... let them see from your honourable behaviour what you are..."'

He laid the book down. God was speaking to him again, so he must listen. The passage to which God had directed him had decreed that Martin Waring must remain in exile and wait for a sign. The epistle had even referred to the punishment of criminals and the encouragement of decent men. God had sent him here. Soon, the voice would return, would guide him along the path towards... towards the chastisement of sinners.

He stared through his cell window and watched the dawn glimmering its slow way towards morning. Dad's widow was a sinner. She had come from Ireland to take Dad's affection from his one true son. Maureen... what was her name? Costigan. He should write that down in order to remind himself. She had been punished. Anthony. As always, he was vague about Anthony, but the light would guide Martin and Anthony along a righteous path.

A bell sounded. Martin fell to his knees and prayed for the soul of his departed father, for the salvation of Anthony Bell, for divine retribution against the Irish widow.

The door opened a crack. 'Martin? Ah, I am sorry. I did not wish to intrude while you were at prayer, but *Frère*

Nicholas asks if you will sing again at benediction this evening.'

Martin allowed Brother Timothy a tight smile. 'Of course, Brother. The plain chant is so easy to follow, and I'm sure I'll master the Latin pronunciation in time.'

The monk backed his way out of the cell. He stood in the corridor and gazed at a print of St Francis Xavier. But *Frère* Timothy did not see the saint. In his mind's eye, he held a picture of Martin Waring, so holy, so correct, so uncaring. There was something amiss with this soon-to-be-bearded lay member of the fraternity. But Nicholas, the senior monk, would hear nothing against his protégé. It was because of the man's beautiful tenor voice, thought Timothy. The choir had not been blessed with a decent soloist since the untimely death of *Frère* Anselm. Nicholas was, perhaps, blinded by Martin Waring's abilities.

Brother Timothy crossed himself and walked towards his breakfast. As an ordained monk, he should not entertain such un-Christian thoughts. And he hoped that his porridge would still be hot.

The room was starved of light because of high windows, but the gloom had been deepened considerably by the liberal application of paint in all shades of brown from sepia to chocolate. Below a dado rail, thick gloss in an unattractive mud colour adorned the walls, while the upper sections seemed to be advertising the exhalations of a thousand smokers. Bookshelves framed the doorway, and photographs of grim-faced policemen in domed hats hung from every spare inch of picture rail.

Inspector Chadwick, a Mancunian who had moved west against his better judgement and in spite of his wife's protestations, had wedged his corpulence behind a huge square desk with a virgin blotter set into its centre. A handlebar moustache of indeterminate colour was suspended beneath a shiny, pitted nose. Thick, wet lips peered out below the foliage, and several red chins hung over a too tight collar.

The inspector's fingertips completed an inverted V created by angled elbows. 'Well?' he asked. 'To what do I owe this pleasure?' The last word was spat as if it tasted bad.

Without waiting for a formal invitation, Father Michael Brennan took a seat at the other side of the desk. Manchester's loss was Liverpool's loss, too, he mused. 'I've Flash Flanagan outside in the corridor with Anthony Bell.'

Piggy eyes widened slightly. 'What the dickens are they doing here?' He needed Flash Flanagan like he needed a dose of smallpox. The tramp was a source of irritation for every policeman in the Rose Hill district. 'I've a station to run, you know. I can't be sitting here listening to the ravings of an alcoholic.'

Michael Brennan sighed, lowered his head and looked at the floor. Even the floor was brown. He wondered, not for the first time, why this singularly uncharitable person had opted for a career which brought him into contact with people. Inspector Chadwick hated Irish Catholics, Jews, people with dark skin, prostitutes, homosexuals and most women. He treated children like vermin and was impatient with those unfortunate men who served under him.

The priest lifted his chin and looked across the desk. Power. It was all about control, dominance, dominion. Most people who hated as strongly as this man were inadequates who tried to prove their worth by demonstrating the foibles of others. While concentrating on the failures of mankind, Chadwick attempted to justify his own existence and thus to boost his supposed worth in the eyes of others. Or so the inspector hoped. Really, his major achievement so far was the great job he had done of generating hatred for himself. No-one liked him. Rumour had it that his own wife had tried to remain in Manchester when Chadwick had moved to Liverpool. Michael understood the wretched woman only too well.

'I've no time for this.' The huge policeman made an elaborate fuss of matching his watch to the clock on the wall, winding, moving the half-hunter's fingers, running his beady eyes over an inscription on the gold case. 'There's a meeting in half an hour.'

The priest assumed that the Manchester force had been glad to pay that nine-carat gold price to be rid of the man. 'I'm visiting you for a reason,' he snapped. 'There seems to be proof that Father Liam Bell has committed an offence. Perhaps several offences.'

The lard on Chadwick's face quivered for a split second. He was used to papist criminals, but the idea of a crooked priest promised to be immensely amusing – the lads at the lodge would be in pleats of laughter once a Catholic clergyman sat in the bridewell. 'What did he do?' he asked, the tone of voice deliberately cool.

'The man's ill,' replied the cleric. 'We think he has some sort of mental disorder and—'

'Are you a doctor?' Bushy eyebrows leapt upward.

'No, but we have consulted a medical practitioner. I understand that Dr Spencer has communicated his concern to your chief constable.'

'I see.' Fingers as thick as pork sausages were spread wide on the blotter. 'And the offence?' he asked again.

'He has probably attacked some women – quite a number of women – over the years.'

Chadwick nodded sagely. 'The Costigan girl?'

'Possibly.' He would not commit himself, would not subject Maureen to a grilling until the time was right.

'And the proof?'

'Flash Flanagan had it.'

'Ah.' The monarch of Rose Hill and several other small stations leaned back in his chair. Flash Flanagan. The man was about as reliable as the English weather. 'The last time we had the pleasure of Mr Flanagan's company – about two months ago – he was wrestling with a snake in his cell. The snake was the rope that held up his trousers. On that occasion, his trousers fell down, because he was busy strangling the rope. He's a drinker. If he can't afford whisky or whatever, he mixes methylated spirit with wine. The man's totally useless.'

Father Brennan shook his head sadly. 'Even the worst of us is of some use, Inspector Chadwick. He found Maureen Costigan.'

'We know all about that. He was drunk and disorderly for days afterwards. In fact, we moved him on to prevent a riot. He was stirring up the populace into a state of terror.'

Michael Brennan sat quietly for a few seconds. 'There's a stole missing. Anthony and I went through Father Bell's vestments in the presbytery. We counted them twice. All the sets but one were complete. But there was just that single piece missing from the ordination vestments. Flash Flanagan found the stole next to Maureen Costigan.'

The policeman raised thick eyebrows once again. 'He said nothing when he was questioned.'

'The man's a Catholic. He was frightened by what he found.'

Frank Chadwick had little time for Romans. In fact, he had often mused about the word 'Catholic', had been known to hold forth about its similarity to 'alcoholic'. The two words shared several letters, and the inspector often joked about the fact. Also, the 'one true Apostolic Faith' begged to be altered to 'the one true Alcoholic Faith'.

They were all the same, these papists. Down on their knees in the gutter on a Saturday night, down on their knees in their church nine hours later, bowing and scraping to rows of statues. Their women wore green knickers when the Orange Lodge marched, lifted their skirts to show their colours to the enemy. They sinned, then confessed, then sinned all over again. Even this priest was not averse to swilling the odd pint in the company of parishioners. 'He was probably pickled at the time.'

Michael stared through the window at the sky. It hung low and grey like an ill-washed blanket, all patches and stains. 'Anthony Bell is convinced that his twin murdered Valerie Walsh about five years ago. At that time, he tried to tell the police of his suspicions, but they refused to listen.'

'A man hanged for that murder,' replied the inspector.

'Ah yes. But was he guilty?'

'Of course he was. Look, bring in Flash Flanagan's so-called evidence and I'll have it looked into.'

The priest inhaled deeply. 'He hasn't got it.'

'I thought you said—'

'He had it. I said he used to have it.' This was hopeless. 'Look, there's a man on the loose somewhere out there.' He waved a hand at the door. 'God alone knows what he'll do next.'

The inspector folded his arms and looked with mock pity at the ageing cleric. 'There are many men out there, Father. There's enough stuff stolen from the docks every year to feed a small battalion plus half of Liverpool. I know the criminals are there and so do you. Finding out who they are is another matter altogether.'

Father Brennan nodded. 'And as long as somebody has hanged for a crime, then that particular book is closed.'

The moustache twitched.

'Do you and the courts of justice never make a mistake, Inspector Chadwick? Are you different from the rest of us?'

The inspector offered no reply. He had a meeting in ten minutes, and he had no time to be sitting here philosophizing with a silly old man.

'When his fiancée was murdered five or so years ago, Anthony Bell came into the station and told your officers that he believed she was killed by his brother.'

'They were not my officers. I was in Manchester.'

'Whatever. No-one listened to him.'

The policeman shrugged. 'I've heard rumours, of course, about how those twins never got on. There can be great hatred among families, because people are forced to live together even if they can't stand the sight of each other and—'

'And most violent crime is perpetrated within a family situation,' said the priest. 'That is a well-known fact. Mr Bell is also sure that his brother committed rape and bodily harm in the city. Many women were beaten and worse, and several said that their attacker had prayed over them. Then, as suddenly as the trouble had started, it stopped. I think you'll find, if you care to check a few records, that Liam Bell was in the seminary during that lull. Valerie Walsh was murdered after Liam returned to the area. Valerie was engaged to Liam Bell's twin. The girls in Liverpool were probably mere experiments to prepare for the real thing. Valerie Walsh was the real thing, because she was about to marry Father Bell's brother.'

'And the rest of the victims were prostitutes?'

Michael Brennan hung on to his temper. 'All the victims were women. Whatever their sins, they had the right to live without persecution.'

Chadwick wasn't sure about that. Some people got what they deserved, but he kept his mouth shut. 'Wheel them in,' he said resignedly.

Flash Flanagan's odour preceded him. He came into the room reluctantly and with Anthony acting as pilot. Once inside, the tramp shook himself free of his companion's arm. 'I promised a dying man,' he protested. 'And these two tricked me, told me they knew about the stole.'

The inspector toyed with a pencil, drew a square on his pristine blotting pad. 'You were questioned, Flanagan.'

'That's right, I was. And I got two measly cups of tea. I was faint for lack of nourishment.'

'And you withheld evidence.'

'I'm a Catholic.'

The pencil clattered on the desk's surface. 'What's that got to do with anything?'

Flash shrugged, causing more malodorous dust to rise from his person. 'It was a priest's thing, something what they wear on the altar. I could have got struck dead if I'd snitched on a priest. So I kept the bloody thing.'

Inspector Chadwick exhaled loudly. 'Then give it to me.'

'He can't,' said Anthony.

The policeman ran his eyes over Anthony Bell. 'Why not?'

'I gave it to Sam, that's why,' shouted Flash.

'And my father died,' said Anthony. 'We've questioned his solicitor, because Dad changed his will about an hour before the heart attack. But the man knew only that Dad had altered his will.'

'So has the lawyer got the stole?' asked Chadwick.

'No,' replied Anthony.

The pencil was employed again, this time to tap the desk impatiently. The inspector addressed Anthony. 'So a drunken tramp found this stole thing next to Maureen Costigan.'

Anthony nodded.

'And he kept it until the day of your father's death?'

'Yes.'

'So where is it now?'

'We don't know,' the priest replied. 'Sam must have hidden it.'

Inspector Chadwick nodded, causing the number of chins to vary according to the position of his head. 'Have either of you seen this stole?' He looked from the priest to Anthony, then back again.

'No,' they answered simultaneously.

'Then those who saw the evidence are this fellow,' he waved the pencil at Flash, 'and a dead man. And there's not much to choose between them, because our gentleman of the road is usually the worse for drink.' He gazed at Anthony. 'To be honest with you – and I'm sorry for your loss – I would probably get more sense out of your father than out of Mr Flanagan.'

Anthony closed the gap between himself and the policeman in one long stride. He was angry, so furious that he deliberately held himself in check. Somewhere, a dangerous man was on the loose. Anthony no longer felt any affection for or kinship with his brother. All he cared about was the safety of others, especially Bridie and her girls. 'When the killing starts, I shall rub your fat face into every piece of horse muck on Scotland Road,' he said softly.

Michael touched his friend's arm. 'Anthony—'

'Guardian of the law?' Anthony went on. 'Guardian of yourself and your own comfort.' This obese and ugly man belonged to two lodges – one Masonic and the other of a colour that screamed its garish hatred of Catholicism at every opportunity. 'When the next woman is raped or killed, I shall come for you, Inspector Chadwick.'

The inspector bared his teeth. 'You want me to find a priest? You want me to hang out your dirty Irish linen for all the world to see?'

Anthony smiled grimly. 'My brother is sick,' he said. 'What's your excuse? Were you born insufferable, or has it taken practice?'

'Careful, now,' came the warning from behind the desk.

'Or what?' Anthony waited for a reply, received none. 'Get off your fat behind and find my brother. If you don't, I promise you that this day will be forever in your mind, a reminder of your own crass stupidity.'

Chadwick blinked two or three times. 'Where do you suggest I begin the search?' he asked.

Father Brennan placed Liam's letter on the blotter. 'He says he's gone to Africa. We think he's still in England. Find him.'

The inspector was genuinely perplexed. If the information was correct, then a nationwide search might be warranted. But without hard evidence, no extensive manhunt could begin. 'I'll do what I can,' he said reluctantly. 'Now, if you will excuse me, I have to be somewhere else in a few minutes.'

Flash strode out of the room as quickly as possible. When Anthony and the priest caught up with him, he turned on both of them. 'See?' he said. 'I told you. You'd get more sense out of the bloody Liver Birds.' He marched outside, collected his cart, then went off in search of liquid sustenance.

Anthony leaned on the wall. 'Liam's hiding,' he said with certainty. 'He'll come out when he's ready and not before.'

Priest and teacher walked together to the presbytery. Like Flash, they needed a drink.

Seventeen

Martin Waring sat on the edge of his comfortless mattress. Another day had passed, then another and another. He had been at the monastery for weeks. The house, called Tithebarn, was creaking its way towards midnight, floorboards groaning themselves into position, ancient windows cooling and settling their frames against age worn stone.

He had a candle. If he ever became a *frère* – and he would achieve that status, surely – he would be unable to burn a flame once he had undressed and prayed. But, as a lay member of the fraternity, he retained the privilege of light whenever he wanted it. Tonight, he needed the light.

Martin was strong now. He was bearded and brown, muscular and calm. The outside work was monotonous, yet he enjoyed the predictability, the security of knowing exactly what would happen each day. After breakfast, there was mass. After mass came work. He hoed, weeded, fertilized and pruned various fruit-bearing trees until lunchtime. Occasionally, he fed the pigs and hens, though he avoided that particular task whenever possible. He felt no affection for animals, no kinship with creatures from the lower orders.

Early afternoons were spent helping in the kitchen and collecting slops for the swine. He disliked pigs immensely, but the pigs were part of his penance, part of his preparation. When supper was over, he attended benediction and sang with the choir, often as soloist. Recreation was spent among books, games of chess, painting and even tapestry. He had discovered a flair for carving and was making chess figures for the brothers to sell.

The whole community was in bed by nine o'clock. Laymen could go out if they chose, but Martin did not need to wander away from Tithebarn. He was safe here. He could plan here. He could finally read the whole of the letter.

Several items of value were buried beyond the monastery's perimeter wall. Naturally, these objects had been his to take from the pawnshop, because Sam Bell had been Liam's father. When the time came, the new Martin Waring would be able to recover those assets and give them to the Catholic Church. Everything should have gone to the Church. Sam Bell had promised that he would leave the bulk to Liam and the Church. But now, there was this letter. The letter had been in Bridie Bell's sewing basket. Obviously, the widow had missed it. Obviously, God had been on the side of the just, because Liam had knocked over the basket, apparently by accident. Yes, this had been God's work again, Martin decided.

A few times, he had scanned the letter's contents, but the anger had overcome him and God had started to speak to him. Sometimes, Martin was not fit to listen to God, although he was becoming more robust. If God spoke tonight, His servant would hear Him and remain tranquil. He took a deep breath, reached for the letter. Addressed to Mrs Bridie Bell, it currently rested inside a missal.

Martin picked up the book and removed the loose pages. He continued to breathe deeply and slowly, ordered himself to remain composed. Control was essential. If he became angry, his thoughts could emerge muddled.

He spread out the two sheets and moved the candle-stick to a better position. This time, he intended to read the whole thing. Knowledge was power, he told himself. Knowledge and self-control would see him through.

'My dear Bridie,' the message began.

'I hope you will not have to read this, but I have a bad feeling. Something may happen to me today. If it does, you must take this letter to Rose Hill, because I think Liam might just turn on me. If I survive, I shall tear up this message and you may never know how much I have come to care for you. The spoken word has not come easily to me.'

Martin Waring wiped a solitary bead of sweat from his forehead.

'I have been a stupid man and very selfish. But before I tell you all about that, I want to thank you. Since you came from Ireland, I have been a different man. The difference might not show much, but I am so much happier than I have ever been. If Liam kills me today, please know that I shall die thinking about you.'

The man on the bed shook the page and flattened out the creases. Bridie Bell had done her job so well.

'I have talked to Anthony and am going now to see Bentham, my solicitor. Everything I have is yours. I leave you to decide what will go to Anthony, as I am in a hurry and I trust you to be fair with him. All I ask is that you look after Muth until she dies. The will has been changed half an hour ago, and all I need is my lawyer and a couple of witnesses.

'Until today, Liam was to inherit most of my estate for the church. I have been so unfair to my other son. But sometimes, I did wonder about Liam. I suppose I didn't want to know the truth. Anthony complained so much about his brother's behaviour that I lost patience with him, particularly when they both came to blows on the church doorstep. Now, I know the reason for Anthony's quarrel with Liam, and I realize that I have not been much of a father, because I buried myself in the shop and took no notice of anything.

'Bridie, Liam is a murderer. Those words were very hard to write. He killed Valerie Walsh, who was going to marry Anthony. He tried to kill Anthony when they were children, but that was different, or so Anthony says. Liam used to hurt Anthony so that he could save him, body and soul. Liam thinks he owns Anthony's body and soul, you see.'

Martin Waring's lip curled. What had this dead man known about Father Liam Bell, servant of God? Sam Bell had never heard the voice of the Almighty.

'Anthony thinks that Liam attacked Maureen. I can't imagine a priest committing rape, but Liam's ordination stole was picked up next to the injured girl. Flash Flanagan found the stole and panicked. You know what Flash is like – drunk half the time and playing with puppets when he's nearly sober. Anyway, I have the stole. It is stretched and torn.

'In the downstairs store behind the cabinet for old receipts there is a loose brick. No-one will ever look there, as the cabinet is difficult to move – I almost broke my back shifting it. The stole is in the wall. I put it inside an old cash tin – green metal with a handle on the lid. I've hidden it because I'm going to face Liam in a few minutes. If I took the stole with me, he would get it and burn it.

'I pray that you'll never read this letter. I hope I come home later and burn it before turning my son over to the police. If I don't make it, please look after yourself, Muth and the girls. Get someone to shift the cabinet, then take the stole to the police station straight away and show the desk sergeant this letter. Tell Muth and Anthony that I'm sorry. All those years I never listened, Bridie. My son was a priest, so I thought he was a good man. Anthony says Liam is sick. He hears voices. Try to get him locked away in an asylum. The doctors might help him.

'Thank you for everything,

Your husband,

Sam'

Martin read the postscript.

'PS My son Anthony loves you. Not as a son, but as a man. If anything happens to me, go to him. I've realized that God's blessing is not something we get just in church. Anthony has had a sad life. He tells me that he is very fond of you.

'If you break the law of the Church and the state, you will do it with my blessing.'

In spite of firm resolve, Martin found himself screwing up the pages. His hand had closed like a steel trap, and he had to concentrate on loosening the fingers. Carefully, he smoothed out Sam Bell's piece of writing, stood up, steadying himself by holding the table. He flattened the pages of small, neat handwriting, and lifted down a picture of the Sacred Heart. He removed the glass, then inserted Sam's letter into the frame before replacing the original icon. Knowledge was power, he told himself.

So. The stole was behind a loose brick. She would never find it. Even if the cabinet was moved, the Irish whore would fail to notice the missing mortar, because all the walls in the store cupboard were scarred. Dad had been such a fool. He must have used a lot of strength on the day of his death, must have strained his heart in order to protect his sweet colleen.

He should never have allowed himself to be talked into such a marriage. Anthony was very like Dad. Anthony's senses deserted him when he saw a pretty face and a neat figure.

He fell back onto the bed. Anthony loved her. Even

Dad had known that, and poor Dad had been the woman's husband. Martin Waring remembered a day when he had visited Cherry Hinton and Bridie had spoken of her dislike for Liam Bell's twin. She had been angry with Anthony, probably as a result of some lover's tiff. Worse than that, she had probably lied.

Balled fists beat against the mattress. Anthony was in clover now, because Dad had shuffled off the mortal coil. Anthony Bell was sleeping with his own stepmother. No, no, screamed an internal voice. Martin stilled himself. Control was the key. Perhaps, this time, Anthony would not be saved.

Martin Waring blew out the candle, tried to sleep, failed. The summer sun rose early, thrust its rays through the high window, rested on the Sacred Heart behind Whom the letter was hidden. 'I'll be strong,' he said aloud. 'It isn't time for Liam to go back yet. He can stay here until they've all forgotten.'

Somewhere inside Martin Waring, the recently buried Liam Bell wept. Liam's grave was shallow, but he remained where he had been put. For now, someone else was in charge.

Maureen rose early, made her bed and prepared to go downstairs. Her duties as housemaid were light, but she put in extra hours in an attempt to demonstrate her gratitude. But for the Spencers, she would have been living in Dryden Street and wondering when the next attack would happen.

She had managed to clear her mind at last, and the improvement in her outlook was due in no small part to her surroundings. Astleigh Fold nestled like a small child in the arms of its mother, a tiny village cradled by the moors. There were so many shades of green on the gentle slopes, too many to count. Maureen remembered Irish relatives who had mused at length about Eire's lush foliage, but surely nothing could be greener than this place? She was comfortable here, protected and content.

She stood at her window and watched the sun as it began to bathe the fields and woods. Beautiful. With the window thrown open, she thought she could smell the green, could almost taste the dew as it evaporated towards the sky. This was heaven. If only Mam and Dad could live here. A picture of Jimmy and Tildy-Anne haring about the lanes filled her mind. If they lived here, they would be stronger, healthier, browner.

The bedroom door opened. Maureen turned to see Cathy with a finger to her lips. 'Shush,' the child said. She was supposed to be in an airy attic with the windows permanently open. She was supposed to avoid close contact with the rest of the household in case she caught germs before her strength returned. 'I'm lonely,' she complained.

Maureen nodded. 'Sit on the bed for a minute,' she whispered. 'I've got to do my hair.'

Cathy sat. 'Are you still going to be a dancer?'

Maureen shrugged. 'Don't know. I'm not bothered.' Much to her surprise, Maureen had found within herself a liking for housework. Putting things in order, maintaining control over dust and dirt brought an unexpected degree of satisfaction and contentment. Everything that had mattered didn't seem to count any more. All Maureen wanted was peace and quiet, a job and to be safe. 'Dr Spencer says he'll take me to the classes, but I can't get myself interested.' It was like being asleep, she thought. She was in a wonderful dream, a lovely fairy tale that had followed swiftly on the heels of a nightmare.

Cathy studied Maureen. She had wonderful black hair, blemish-free porcelain skin and eyes like blue jewels.

'You're not proud any more,' the child announced. 'But you are very, very beautiful. That scar you had has gone now.' Maureen had blossomed. She was fuller in the chest and her face had filled out slightly. Maureen no longer bore the marks that come with city poverty. The pallor had gone from her cheeks, and her eyes shone with health.

Maureen put the last grip in her hair. 'I'll do, I suppose,' she said.

'Wish I looked like you. Wish I didn't have anaemia. It's all vitamins and stuff, stupid drinks and hundreds of oranges. And liver, Maureen. They make me eat liver and spinach and porridge that's all thin and sweet. They keep dragging my eyes wide open to see how pink my eyelids are on the inside. There's nothing wrong with me,' she insisted. 'It's desperate. I'm always being prodded and looked at.'

Maureen smiled. 'You'll be well soon, just see. And when you grow up, you'll be all blonde and gorgeous. Boys like blonde girls.'

Cathy sniffed. 'Who said anything about boys? I want to look nice for me, not for a great stupid lump of a lad with scabs on his knees.'

The older girl laughed out loud. She thought about her own childhood ... had she ever been a child? Since the day she had learned to walk, Maureen Costigan had been coped over and fussed over. Her remarkable beauty had made her noticeable, and she had been encouraged to dance prettily, to sing and recite and carry on like an oversized doll. She had used her assets to get money, had performed for queues at the Rotunda and the cinemas, had earned her keep since infancy. 'Like a little prostitute,' she said absently.

'What?'

'Nothing.' Maureen had used her physical self to good

advantage. Until that night when some vile piece of humanity had used her body for his own purposes.

'You all right, Maureen?'

Maureen nodded.

'You look sad.'

'I miss Mam and Dad.'

Cathy swallowed. She missed her mammy; she even missed Shauna sometimes, though Shauna was not the sister Cathy might have wished for had she been given a say in the matter. Shauna was a brat. Brat was a word Cathy had acquired from listening to Aunt Edith. Cathy was a great listener, had dedicated herself to the art of eavesdropping just to break the monotony of being anaemic. Being anaemic meant eating the right things, breathing deeply even when the weather was cold and staying away from germs for much of the time. She was good at creeping and excellent at secreting herself behind Cherry Hinton's many luxurious drapes. Her vocabulary was improving. Shauna was a brat because Aunt Edith said so, and Aunt Edith was a genius.

'Do you miss your mam?' asked Maureen.

Cathy nodded sadly. 'And Uncle Sam. He isn't even in Liverpool. I won't ever see him again. Of course, Shauna's on the pig's back again, getting all her own way while I'm not there.'

Maureen grinned. 'Don't grow up too quick, love,' she said. 'I've been grown up for years, and it's not a good idea.'

Cathy plucked at the front of her nightdress. 'I'd better go in case they blame you for breathing on me.'

'I'll stop breathing, then,' promised Maureen. She held her breath, then exploded into giggles.

The younger girl sighed dramatically. 'I'm fed up with the attic and the fresh air. If somebody rides up on a horse

428

and tells me to let down my hair, I won't be able to. Rapunzel's hair was dead long.'

Maureen laughed at the Scouse 'dead'.

'I'll be stuck up there forever with liver and porridge and Mother Ignatius. She has germs. Why can't I keep away from her germs? Are her germs holy?'

Maureen carried on laughing.

'Why did she have to choose me, Maureen? She keeps coming to teach me all about French and algebra. The algebra is really stupid, because it's all letters instead of numbers. Why did they bother inventing numbers when people like Mother Ignatius use letters for counting? Three times a week, she comes. She says my education's too important to be worrying about germs. Why can't she have anaemia instead of me?' Cathy folded her arms after the long soliloquy.

'Don't wish anybody ill, love. It's cruel.'

Cathy shrugged with pretended nonchalance. 'As long as I get rid of her and her silly books—'

The door opened. 'Come along, Cathy.' There was no anger in Richard Spencer's tone. 'Go and wait for your breakfast. I'll be up to see you later.' She was recovering at an acceptable pace but he wanted her to have a few more weeks' rest and exercise.

Cathy walked out grumbling about cold stethoscopes and short hair.

Richard walked across the rug and stood behind Maureen. 'Are you feeling well?' he asked.

'Yes, thank you.'

He sat on the bed. 'Don't let Cathy get too close. She's doing very well, but her blood's still carrying too little oxygen. We must try not to cough or sneeze near her.'

Maureen sat on the edge of her stool. In the dressing table mirror, she saw herself and Dr Spencer. He was about to say something. He was going to say something she didn't want to hear. 'I'd better get to the kitchen,' Maureen said.

'No. Stay where you are for now.'

Her eyes pleaded with his reflection. If he would only go away. If he would leave, everything would get back to normal.

'Maureen?'

She swallowed audibly.

'Maureen?'

'Yes?' It was going to start again. The lovely dream was about to be shattered, then the nightmare could continue.

'Do you know why I've come up to talk to you?'

Maureen nodded mutely.

'Have you been sick?'

'No, Dr Spencer.'

'But your clothes are getting smaller.'

Her clothes were exactly the same size as they had always been. He was telling her kindly that she was growing fat. Mam was fatter than she used to be. Perhaps obesity ran in the family, then.

'Maureen, you may be carrying a baby.'

She rocked to and fro, her head shaking slowly from side to side. The man had entered her body, had left himself inside her. It was dividing, growing, a living piece of evil that would tear its way into the world in ... in about five or six months. 'I don't want it,' she said, her voice rising in pitch and quickening towards hysteria. 'This isn't my fault. I didn't do anything, anything. I didn't, I didn't, but he did and now I have this thing...'

Richard stood up and placed his hands on the girl's quivering shoulders.

'Where is God?' she screamed. 'Where was God when this happened to me? If there's a God and all saints and stuff, why is there all this badness?'

He had often wondered about that. Many, many times, he had stood and watched a child edging its way towards death while the drunken sot who had fathered it thrived on beer and whisky. It wasn't fair. That was the one certainty, the one truth. The doctor watched his little housemaid disintegrating before his eyes. As a medic, he had to protect her and her unborn secret. As a man, he wished that he could tear the burden from her.

'I want me mam.'

'We'll get her,' he said. 'Edith will telephone Bridie. My dear, I am so sorry. I wish there was something I could do—'

'There is!' Maureen swung round and jumped to her feet. 'You can kill it.'

Richard felt her hands clawing at his jacket, heard the terror in her words. 'I'm sorry—'

'You can, you can. At school, we heard about it. Somebody's mother had it done. You can get rid of it. You have to get rid of it before I go mad.' She broke down and fell into his arms.

He held her closely and blinked away his own tears. Edith stood in the doorway. 'Send for Diddy,' he said.

Edith Spencer dried her face and went slowly down the stairs into her graceful hallway. Everything was so beautiful in this house, so lovely and empty and meaningless. If a child had scribbled on the wallpaper, if a child had ruined the carpets, then life could have been so much richer.

She picked up the telephone and barked the number. Upstairs, a cluster of cells was multiplying in a womb that didn't want it. In Edith's heart, there was a huge hollow place where the damped down pain of disappointment had been carefully tucked away.

With a heavy sigh, Edith gave the message to Charlie Costigan, then replaced the receiver. Instinct told her to run, to get out of the house, to visit the stables, perhaps. In the stable yard, Mr Cross would be celebrating with Robin Smythe. Quicksilver and Sorrel were serving their apprenticeships at local courses, were showing great promise.

But the lady of the house remained where she was, waited for Maureen and Richard to come downstairs. Maureen was pregnant, and there was reason to believe that Edith and Richard would be blood relatives of the unwanted child.

The grandfather clock struck the hour and Edith shivered. That poor girl was carrying the sin of a priest whose malevolence might possibly match the evil of the Borgias. This was no time to be visiting the stables. First, this household must deal with the iniquity of the human race.

Bridie considered Dolly Hanson to be a decent body. Although the keeper of Hanson's News, Sweets and Tobacco had been Thomas Murphy's lover for many years, she was not a bad woman. Bridie's father was the adulterer. He had neglected Mammy and had found for himself a comfortable nest where he could rest his bones while in England. Dolly did not visit the pawnshop very often. She had her own business to run, and she had been without help since the departure of Maureen. But one Thursday in July, Dolly Hanson closed her customers' door and crossed the road. She had to talk to Mrs Bell.

Charlie Costigan had gone home in a rush for his dinner, leaving Bridie to mind the pawnshop while Billy did the rounds and picked up furniture. Charlie had muttered something about a telephone message for Mam, so Bridie was temporarily in sole charge. She was picking up the business quickly, had become quite adept at handling the strangest pawned items. The Scotland Road folk pledged anything and everything from rugs and brasses to silver-plated crucifixes. As Bridie sorted through a pile of tickets, Dolly entered the shop. 'Hello there,' said Bridie, her tone conversational. 'Have you found another assistant, then?'

Dolly shook her head. She always felt uncomfortable in the presence of her lover's daughter.

'What can I do for you?'

Dolly swallowed. 'It's him,' she managed.

'Who?'

'Your father.'

'Ah. Himself, is it? He who must be served first at all times?' Bridie closed a ledger with a loud snap, noticed Dolly's startled jump when the noise occurred.

'The horses.' Dolly took a handkerchief from her pocket, mopped her head. It was a hot day. Schools were closed, and the road was packed with children. Perhaps the young ones were using up all the oxygen, Dolly mused.

'Which horses?' asked Bridie.

'The ones he ... the horses he brought over for—'

'To Sam? As a bribe so that he would marry me and remove me from the threat of what Da calls Protestantism and perdition?'

Dolly nodded quickly.

'They're mine now,' said Bridie softly. 'Sam gave them to me for myself and my girls.'

Dolly lifted her head. 'Doing well, so he's heard.'

'That's right.'

The visitor dabbed at her brow with the soggy rag that had begun life as a decent handkerchief. 'He came over yesterday. He wants his horses back.'

Bridie's spine stiffened. 'His horses?'

'That's what he said.'

Bridie glanced at one of the more reliable clocks. It belonged to a Mrs Hartley from Dryden Street and its

German mechanism was in reasonable condition. 'Where is he?'

Dolly shrugged. 'Wherever the horses are.' She stepped back, peered through the window at her shop. Except for funerals, Hanson's had never been closed in the middle of the afternoon. 'I've finished with him,' she muttered sadly. 'He promised for years that he'd marry me, but there was always some reason why he couldn't. He's run out of excuses, so I read out the marching orders.' She bit her lip for a second. 'I didn't know he was married, Bridie. And by the time I did find out, it was too late, because I loved him. Over twenty years I wasted on that man.'

Bridie wondered how on earth any sane person could manage to love the unlovable person who had fathered her, but she said nothing.

'Anyway, I've said what I came to say.'

Bridie smiled. 'It was never your fault,' she said. 'Don't worry about the past, and thank you for warning me.' Da would not get 'his' horses. Da would not get past Bob Cross, because Bob Cross minded his stables too well.

Dolly Hanson was swept aside by Diddy. Diddy and Billy were now full-time employees of Bell's, though Diddy still left the market or the shop every lunch-time to produce her family's dinner. 'What does Edith want?' she demanded of Bridie. 'Our Charlie says there's a message on that thing.' She waved a hand towards the phone. 'From Edith, he said.'

Had Bridie not known better, she would have found the sight before her truly terrifying. With her sleeves hauled up above reddened elbows and her feet planted well apart, Diddy Costigan seemed to fill the shop. Her huge bosom heaved with emotion and as a result of running in the heat, while a couple of steel curlers drooped from the front of a very holey hairnet. 'Well?' asked Diddy impatiently.

Bridie scratched her ear. 'I was upstairs with Muth till Charlie left,' she said. 'So he must have answered the telephone.'

Without waiting for an invitation, Diddy crossed the room and stood at the bottom of the stairs. The phone was on a small table in this no-man's land between shop and living quarters. The large woman rifled through Sam Bell's personal telephone book, found Edith's number, then barked it into the ear of some innocent operator.

Dolly touched Bridie's arm. 'All right, girl? If anything happens to your horses, you'll know who to blame.'

Bridie smiled absently. She waved at the departing Dolly, then tried not to eavesdrop while Diddy shouted all the way to Bolton. Diddy did not believe in the telephone. She used it infrequently and with great reluctance, and she always spoke very clearly and with actions so that the unseen conversationalist would be in no two minds about Diddy's intentions.

'You what?' Diddy threw up her free arm. 'She's what? Holy Mother of God.'

Bridie stopped smiling. The older woman was pressing her spine against the door jamb as if seeking support. 'She can't be. She's only a baby herself.' Diddy's voice reached its crescendo. 'I'm coming, I'm coming. Bridie'll come with me.' She turned and used her eyes to plead with her employer.

Bridie nodded her agreement.

'But she's only ever been with . . .' The large woman's voice cracked. Her little girl was pregnant. The unborn child was the son or daughter of a rapist. 'God, what shall we do?'

The new owner of Bell's Pledges staggered backwards and grasped the counter. Rays of the afternoon sun glared at her accusingly, making her close her eyes against the light. But her mind would not be stilled.

'Bridie?'

She opened her eyes, saw the confusion in Diddy's face. 'Oh, Diddy. She's pregnant, then?'

Elizabeth Costigan wept. A curler slid down her sweat-slicked face and clattered to the floor. 'Billy'll go mad,' she said. 'He's done the rounds, and he's on the stall with our Monica, happy as a pig in muck, in the middle of selling a canteen of cutlery when I left him.'

Bridie held her companion's hands. She could say nothing, must say nothing. Proof, proof – where was the damned proof? 'We'll go together,' she said. 'Nicky can move in here. She'll take good care of Muth and Shauna.'

Diddy mopped her face on her apron. 'I wanted so much for our Maureen. She's such a pretty girl. And talented, too. I thought she'd go a long way, but she won't now, Bridie. He stopped her. That rotten animal ruined my little girl's life.'

Bridie, who enjoyed a fondness for creatures, did not agree. Few animals would have sunk to Liam Bell's depths. He was not comparable to an animal, she told herself. Liam was the worst creature in the world, because he was humankind at its basest.

'I'll go and get some things together,' said Diddy. 'And I'll send our Monica round. Charlie'll see to the shop.'

Bridie sat and waited for Charlie to return. Shauna played with a basket of toys. The child who had been a weakling was thriving among dirt and poverty. Cathy, a robust and cheery soul, was away being cured of a debilitating disorder. Life was full of strangeness, Bridie thought. Poor young Maureen was carrying an unwanted baby, while Edith had spent years craving for a child. And so the world went round on its crazy axis.

Muth came in. In spite of the heat, she was wearing a thick shawl and winter boots. Muth was another mystery, because she was old, yet infantile again. Since the death of her son, Mrs Bell Senior had gone downhill fast. 'Have you seen me mam?' she asked now.

Bridie shuddered. Would Nicky Costigan manage an errant infant and an old lady whose mind wandered further from reality with every day?

'Where's me mam?'

'In heaven,' replied Bridie. This was getting worse. Even yesterday, the bewilderment had been less noticeable.

'But I've not had me tea.'

Bridie sighed. Perhaps a further burden would soon be delivered to Edith's door. Edith had already offered to care for her confused aunt. So a new baby and an old baby might reside at Cherry Hinton. The world was truly upside down. No, no, Bridie told her inner self. Old Theresa would not be going to Bolton. Sam would have insisted that his mother should stay here with Bridie. That had been his final request to his solicitor on the last day of his life.

'I'm hot,' declared Muth peevishly. 'I shouldn't have boots on in this weather. What were you thinking of?' she asked her daughter-in-law. 'Telling me to wear me boots in the middle of summer.'

Bridie reached out and put her arms round Theresa Bell. 'God bless you,' she said.

Muth tutted. 'Get this shop tidied up,' she snapped. 'And leave go of me. I'm too hot for all this carrying on.'

Bridie watched helplessly while Muth tottered into the living room. She had to go with Diddy to Bolton. She wanted to see Cathy, needed to reassure herself that the child was getting better. And Diddy was going to need support. It was no use – she could not expect young Nicky to cope with everything. Once Charlie returned, Bridie would go out and seek a neighbour's help. That was the beauty of Scotland Road, she reminded herself. On Scotland Road, no emergency was too big. When Jesus had said that the greatest virtue was charity, He must have imagined a place like this.

Maureen sat down at the edge of the small orchard. Little pears were forming above her head, their peculiar shape already apparent in this early stage of growth. She stared up at the tiny clusters, wondered how much bigger they would grow before the mellow season.

Inside her belly, another small thing was developing. For some time, Maureen had wondered about her body's altered mechanism, had pushed away the idea that she might be pregnant. But today, Dr Richard Spencer had made the situation real and undeniable. She was harbouring an embryo and she hated whomever this tiny person was going to become. Bitter resentment filled her mind and heart, coloured every moment of this day, haunted her thoughts and left her exhausted. It must die. She had to find a way of making it die. Surely God did not want this terrible thing to be born?

She lay back and placed her hands on her abdomen. It was scarcely rounded, yet Maureen was sure that she could feel something hard, like a fruit stone in the centre of her being. Every morning, she felt a bit sick, though she was managing, just about, not to vomit. The doctor had noticed her nausea, had diagnosed the unacceptable.

Leaves swayed above her head. She didn't know how to kill the unwanted presence. She didn't know where to look, how to find a person who would undertake the murder of this small but heavy being inside herself.

Dr Spencer could have done it. Well, he probably knew how, but he had not mentioned the possibility. Maureen had heard tales at school about gin and hot baths and knitting needles, but the specifics had never been made clear. Did the gin go in the bath or in the expectant mother's stomach? And what would she do with a knitting needle? Oh no, surely not?

The foliage rustled gently. Through green-framed gaps, she caught glimpses of a deep-blue sky. 'I could have been happy here,' she said aloud. 'Except for this.' She smashed a fist into her belly. 'I'll kill you myself,' she muttered. 'And if I ever see you ... if you ever come out of me...' The very thought made her heave. That vicious man had done this to her. Not content with ruining her dreams, he had also left his dirt inside her. His filth was spreading like a disease. The thing that grew would be ugly, deformed, evil. She was poisoned inside.

Hot tears ran down her temples and into her hair. She would get fat soon. The fat would be the outer sign of inner corruption. No amount of baths or washes could possibly eliminate the contamination. Like the whited sepulchre in the Bible, Maureen would be eternally putrid on the inside.

Through the earth beneath her, she felt the beat of a horse making steady progress towards the trees. Perhaps she would be crushed by pounding hooves. If that happened, the devil's child would die. But so would she. Death had become an option during the last few hours. She had thought about sitting with Cathy, poor little Cathy who had to stay upstairs most of the time with all the windows thrown wide open because she needed air. Maureen remembered Mr Bell, who had died recently. Mam had said for ages that Mr Sam Bell had TB, though no doctor had ever got close enough to put a name to that hacking cough. How could she manage to catch TB, and would it kill her before this thing got born?

The horse was nearer. It was not going at its fastest speed, but it was cantering. She would leave the decision to God. If God wanted to finish her, He could do it now.

Through a gap between two apple trees, a huge white horse appeared. It was Quicksilver. In spite of his reputation, Silver was a sensible animal. As he neared the branches under which Maureen rested, he seemed to grind to a jarring halt. The unseated rider shot over the stallion's head and fell with a loud crack. Silver snorted, eyed Maureen and the crumpled man, then bolted off in the direction of his stable.

Maureen held her breath, waited for the man to move. A thick, red substance poured from his head, and she noticed that a partly buried stone was acting as a pillow beneath the man's neck. But a stone did not provide the properties of a cushion, especially when contact between bone and masonry had been so sudden and so violent.

She recognized him, knew that he was out of context. This was not an Astleigh Fold person. He was ... he was big and rather old to be riding a mount as uncertain as Silver. Even Robin Smythe had trouble remaining seated on the grey. The only person who could handle the temperamental Irish–Arab was Bridie, and she had enjoyed a close relationship with the earth on several occasions.

Robert Cross appeared. He ran to Maureen, made sure that she was not hurt, then bent over the prostrate figure. 'Who is he?' Bob asked. 'Do you know him?'

Maureen nodded.

'Who?' asked Bob again.

The young woman rooted about in her memory. 'I think he's Bridie's dad.' The blood looked black against the grass. 'Yes, he's Bridie's dad.' She felt sick again. The man was dead, or nearly dead. If she could organize a similar fall for herself, then her troubles could well be over.

Bob sought a pulse, found a weak flutter in a wrist. 'He stole the horse,' he said. 'We'd saddled Silver for his

440

morning exercise, then this fellow came in and took him away.'

The jockey arrived, whip in hand, short legs encased in khaki jodhpurs. 'Is he dead?'

'Not far off,' answered Bob. 'Get down to the house for help. Did the horse come back?'

Robin nodded. 'He passed me in the meadow. At least we know he's a homing pigeon.' He set off in search of Richard.

Thomas Murphy groaned. 'My horses,' he muttered, though the words were drowned. He was dying. Dolly had told him to bugger off, so he had come here to claim his property. Strangely, he felt little pain. The life was ebbing out of him, leaving him cold, diminishing all his senses.

Maureen vomited quietly, wiped her mouth on a handkerchief. Bridie had lost her first husband and her second husband and she was now losing her father. All the people who hadn't needed to die were dying, while Maureen contained a life that nobody wanted. She should have been the one. Had the horse killed her, the problem would have been solved. 'Should have been me,' she said.

Bob was kneeling over Thomas Murphy, looked at Maureen. 'Rubbish,' he said, 'you've your whole life in front of you, love.'

Maureen wept softly. It was a life she didn't want.

Anthony led Bridie into his little sitting room. The funeral had been quiet, just himself, Bridie and the Spencers, because Diddy had remained at Cherry Hinton with her daughter. The possibility of returning Thomas Murphy's body to Ireland had been discussed, but Bridie had dismissed it after sparse consideration. Thomas Murphy was now interred in Tonge Cemetery in the Bury Road area of Bolton. He had been given all the trimmings including a full Requiem and a graveside service, though no-one had truly mourned the man's passing.

'Cup of tea?' asked Anthony.

'No.' She just wanted to sit and think. 'I've needed you,' she said, her voice devoid of emotion. The fact that she needed him was nothing to do with love. It was his strength, his down-to-earthness that she missed. She also missed his humour, though that had been dampened by recent events, she realized. The love was another matter altogether.

He pushed her into a chair and knelt at her feet. 'Cathy's getting better,' he told her. 'Richard says that she might be able to attend school fairly soon.'

'And Shauna's getting worse. She stole fruit the other day.'

'Don't worry,' he said. 'She'll grow out of it.'

'I hope so.' She could not manage to feel any grief for her father. She was sad, but only because her own life had changed so much in recent months. 'Signposts along the way,' she muttered absently.

'I beg your pardon?'

Bridie looked into the velvety brown eyes. 'Life's like a road,' she told him. 'With little pointers at the edge of it. You go to school, start working, follow the way as best you can. Then things happen. Somebody ... adds the punctuation. And you don't know when or where the next full stop will come, because the road winds about a lot. Suddenly, you're alone, because some of those signs have the word death printed on them.'

'I'm so sorry,' Anthony said. He was helpless and useless and head over heels in love.

'The worst of it is, Anthony, that sometimes we are pilots as well, with young ones clinging to our hands. So I'm not alone, not while Cathy and Shauna depend. I mean, isn't it hard enough finding your own way through the mess without having to guide others? I'm so very tired.'

He took her hands. 'He wasn't a good father. He never showed you the way, did he?'

Bridie shook her head. 'Mammy was the guide. Then Eugene, then Sam. Your daddy was not a young man, so he was almost like a father to me. The way he had of never worrying, of never showing or sharing any troubles he might have had. That was a steady man. And he's gone, and my Cathy is ill and Shauna's a terrible, selfish little madam.' She managed a tight smile. 'Do you know how dangerous we are together?'

He did. 'No,' he replied. 'I haven't thought about it.'

'You have. Oh yes, you have thought. You're my stepson.'

Anthony understood her only too well. He remembered his first sight of the new bride, realized that feelings as strong as his must have communicated themselves to her almost from the start. And whatever he had felt for her had been reciprocated and therefore magnified. 'What shall we do?' he asked.

'You sound like Cathy. You are another child, I suppose, the son of my dead husband. Such a cold man he seemed at first.'

'You warmed him.'

'Yes, I did. I respected your father.' She shifted her weight, leaned away from him, but made no effort to free her hands. 'We were fine together, Sam and I. But I was aware of you all the same.'

He squeezed her fingers. 'We're supposed to be looking for *A Christmas Carol*. Your daughter wants to read it again.'

Bridie closed her eyes and rested her head against the chair's back. 'Maureen is expecting your nephew or your niece,' she said wearily. 'And there's no way of telling what

443

Diddy will do if the truth ever comes out.' Her eyelids flew open. 'What if the child is like its father? What if poor Maureen gives birth to another Liam?'

This thought had crossed Anthony's mind more than once in recent days. 'We can do and say nothing without proof.'

'Even with proof, it would be a difficult task.' She was suddenly more than tired. Would Liam be back? Was Cathy going to make a full recovery, was Muth about to lose her mind completely, did Shauna steal for devilment, how was Maureen going to manage a baby when she was just a child herself?

He pulled her to her feet. 'Come on,' he whispered. 'You need a rest.' He led her up the steep staircase, noticed how tightly she gripped his hand.

Bridie lay on the bed of the man she loved, allowed him to cover her with the quilt. 'They'll wonder where we are.'

'Let them wonder,' he replied.

She folded the cover back and reached out for him. The lassitude she felt seemed to have dulled the sensible side of her mind. She wanted and needed him, and the love was now a part of the need. It was all the one thing, she told herself. Anthony was Anthony and Bridie was Bridie. And whatever existed between them was another of those signs on a road they were destined to share.

Anthony held her for a long time before kissing her. She was vulnerable and precious and he could not bear the thought of her regret. 'Are you sure?' he asked.

She stared hard into his face. 'Sure is something we can never be, Anthony Bell. But I love you and I need you and we have to start somewhere. And we know that Sam won't mind. Sam's blessing is good enough for me.'

Eighteen

Father Michael Brennan pursued the shambling figure of Flash Flanagan across Scotland Road, musing on the miracle of the tramp's survival. Flash looked neither right nor left, simply stepping into the road and waving grimy hands at anything that dared to come near him. When the offending article was a tram weighing several tons, Flash treated it with the same contempt he showed for horses, carts, motor vehicles and steam lorries. He was a true king of the road, allowing no respect for any obstacle in his path.

'Flash?' yelled the priest.

The old vagrant took no notice. He had a bellyful of scouse and red cabbage, and he was on his way to perform on the corner of Penrhyn Street. A passing Mary Ellen might throw him a penny or an apple, and the 'girls' returning from the bagwash were always ready to stop for a bit of a jangle about the price of fish.

He parked his cart, took out a pair of battered marionettes and started to pick at all the tangled strings.

'Are you deaf?' asked the priest.

Flash sniffed. 'That is not one of my afflictions, not yet,' he replied. 'Though a drop of whisky would help my cold.'

Michael took a shilling from his pocket. 'You are supposed to contribute to the support of your pastor,' he complained. 'But it seems to be working the other way, doesn't it?'

Flash shrugged, struggled with a knot. 'How do these things manage to get all tied up?' he moaned. He threw the puppets into the cart and fished around for the components of his one-man band.

'Flash, you know and I know that a piece of Father Bell's vestmentry is missing. His room, the church and the whole presbytery have been searched. We must find that stole,' said the priest.

Flash eyed his adversary. They'd had a few run-ins in the past, he and Father Brennan. The priest should have been more understanding. In Flash's opinion, they were two of a kind, since each of them depended on others for their subsistence. 'It's nothing to do with me,' he said. 'I gave it to Sam and I've not seen it since. And I promised Sam I'd say nothing. You wormed things out of me, Father Brennan.' He looked up at the sky. 'Did you hear that, Sam? I done me best.' He returned his attention to Father Brennan. 'A priest lost it in the first place, so a priest can bloody well find it.'

Michael squared up to the beggar. 'Listen, Flash. Sam must have said something about his intentions—'

'He said nothing,' yelled Flash.

Some children who had been dangling twine down a grid stopped and stared at the two men. Their 'angling' had yielded nothing, so they decided to watch the priest and the tramp for a while.

'Go away,' said Father Brennan.

'Bugger off,' yelled the tramp.

'He sweared,' said a little girl with a torn dress and hair like a bird's nest. During school holidays, the younger residents of Scotland Road got a bit untidy. 'He sweared and it's a sin.'

'Your dad's always bloody swearing,' said a boy in odd boots.

'He's not,' answered the girl-child angrily. 'He never

446

swears, my dad.' The urchins backed off, then began to creep closer again.

Michael gave his full attention to Flash. 'Look, poor Sam mentioned nothing about the stole to his lawyer,' he whispered. 'But surely, when you left the article with him he gave you some idea of what he intended to do with it?'

'No.' Flash clattered his cymbals to the ground. 'I'm dead serious now, Father. I don't know what he did with it. It'll be in the shop somewhere, or in the house. Can't his missus look for it? And why won't the police try to find it? I can answer that one – they don't believe any of it. They never believe me. They never believe nothing I say, contrary sods.'

Michael Brennan sighed. 'They don't believe me or Anthony Bell, either.'

Flash pulled a harmonica from his pocket and rubbed it along the sleeve of his filthy coat. 'You think Father Liam's a bad swine, don't you?' He spat on his finger, wiped some grime off the mouth organ. 'And you're not wrong. I've seen him.' He nodded quickly several times. 'The way he looked at women – well – the devil was in his eyes.'

The priest turned to the children and shooed them off once more. 'Flash, if you remember anything – anything at all – please come to me immediately.'

'I will. And good luck with it.' Flash played a few discordant notes. 'Where's he gone, anyway?'

'Father Bell?' Michael shrugged. 'He sent me a letter about Africa, but I don't think he's gone there. God alone knows where Liam is.'

Flash thought about that. 'I'll keep my eyes peeled and my ears pinned back. I can't say fairer than that, can I?'

Cathy disliked Mother Ignatius. Well, she worked hard to dislike the ugly little nun, but Cathy's determination was

447

matched by her visitor's persistence. 'And what did you think of Mr Scrooge?' asked Mother. 'What sort of a man was he?'

Cathy fixed her gaze on the wart. This was one of the wart's purpler days. She longed to get the tweezers from Aunt Edith's room. Those tweezers would have made short work of Mother Ignatius's three bristles. 'He was cruel,' the child replied absently. 'Then the ghosts made him sad, so he stopped being cruel. He liked his money too much.'

The headmistress picked up Cathy's homework. 'I notice from your essay that you felt sorry for Mr Scrooge.'

'Well,' sighed Cathy, 'he'd no sense. He could have bought coal for his bedroom, but he didn't. And if he'd been a bit nicer to everybody, he wouldn't have seen the ghosts.' She was getting rather bored with Scrooge. Half the stuff was hard to understand, and the rest was on the miserable side. And Maureen was going to have a baby and she wasn't even married.

'We'll make a scholar of you yet,' declared the visitor.

Noel lifted his head and eyed Mother Ignatius. Mother Ignatius remained unimpressed by him. He always stayed out of reach when the tiny woman came to see Cathy.

'You'll be able to come to school in a few weeks,' said Mother.

Cathy frowned. The school was probably packed with nuns as ugly and snappy as this one. Cathy had no intention of attending Sacred Heart Grammar School for Girls, but she said nothing. These days, she had to be good. Being good meant open windows and long walks with Uncle Richard and Noel. Being good meant eating everything on her plate and putting up with Mother Ignatius.

'It'll be university for you,' added the nun. 'You've a fine brain for a child your age.'

Being brainy was boring. Stupid would have been more fun, because stupid people read books with coloured pictures and words inside bubbles. 'Maureen's having a baby,' she said.

The nun pursed her lips.

Cathy had been through most of Uncle Richard's books. She was good at creeping, so she had taken to tiptoeing silently downstairs when everyone was asleep. By the meagre light of a couple of candles, she had found the interesting bits. There was a drawing of a see-through woman with a baby curled inside her. 'At Christmas, Maureen's baby will be born,' she informed her unwelcome guest.

The wart quivered as the nun's narrow lips tightened even further.

Cathy wondered how the baby was going to get out of the see-through woman and out of the very solid Maureen. The nun would have no answers. 'Diddy keeps crying because Maureen's having a baby,' she said. 'And Mammy spends most of her time with Maureen instead of sitting with me.'

Mother Ignatius's tongue clicked. 'Maureen needs a lot of support just now.'

'Why?'

'Because of her situation.'

'Is the baby her situation?' asked Cathy.

In the opinion of Mother Ignatius, clever children were a blessing and a sore trial. This desperate and wonderful girl was probing for information she was too young to digest. Also, a bride of Christ was not a suitable candidate for a conversation like this. 'Yes,' she snapped eventually. 'Now, about the mathematics—'

'There's no daddy.'

'That's right. The long multiplication is what we'll tackle next.' A not quite eight-year-old ready for long multiplication and division? This little madam was most promising.

'I've no daddy.'

'I know.'

'He died. Uncle Sam died, too.'

'We must pray for their souls,' said the nun.

'Maureen's daddy's not dead. He's called Billy and he has pigeons and he used to work on the docks, only he works for Mammy now. He's got really big hands. So will he be Maureen's baby's daddy?'

'Grandfather.'

Cathy was not satisfied. The unborn baby had to have a daddy. 'Is he dead?'

Mother Ignatius cleared her throat. 'I don't know, Caitlin.'

'Does Maureen know if he's dead? She must do, mustn't she? Is that why she's sad? Has he had an accident like my daddy? Or a heart attack like Uncle Sam?'

The headmistress glanced at the clock, sighed meaningfully and gathered up her books. 'I shall return when you are in the mood for work,' she said grimly. 'Do you realize how much trouble I am taking to give you an education?'

Cathy stared at the small person in front of her. In spite of her better judgement, Cathy had a grudging respect for the shrivelled-up woman. Mother Ignatius was really tiny. Even when standing, the woman was minute. In fact, she was probably taller sitting down—

'Caitlin?'

'Yes, Mother?'

The china-blue eyes were so innocent, thought Mother Ignatius. The child would, no doubt, melt the hardest of hearts with her prettiness. But Mother Ignatius had processed an army of pretty girls in her time. 'Some questions,' she said slowly, 'are best not asked. Maureen Costigan is in pain, but it's a very private pain.'

Cathy considered the statement. 'Uncle Richard can give her something to stop her hurting.'

'It is not that kind of pain, child.'

The light began to dawn. 'Is it feeling sick pain, like when your daddy has died?'

'Yes.'

'Oh.' The little girl chewed her lip. 'Mother?'

'Yes, child?'

'Is it all right not to feel sad when your grandfather dies? Nobody liked him. I don't think Mammy cried, even though he was her daddy. But I think we should be sad, really.'

'Grief is not necessary,' replied the nun. 'But prayer is. You must pray for his release from purgatory.'

'I think he's in hell,' remarked Cathy. 'It would be a waste of time to pray for someone in hell. So I'll tell God that the prayers are for Granda if he's in purgatory, or for Maureen if Granda's in hell.'

Mother Ignatius left the bedroom rather quickly. On the landing, she organized her books and her face, fought back the laughter that bubbled beneath her habit. Transferable prayer? Now, that was an idea to conjure with . . .

Diddy was beside herself. She wept into her teacup while Edith and Bridie wondered how to calm her. The UCP on Bradshawgate was hardly a good place to cry. Several customers looked at Diddy, then glanced away quickly, embarrassed by the public show of emotion.

'She's a strong girl,' said Edith.

Bridie nodded. 'Maureen'll come through this, Diddy. She has your backbone.'

451

Diddy sniffed loudly. 'Her backbone got broken by that filthy bloody man.'

Bridie lowered her eyes. How much longer would the charade continue? Yet she knew that she could say nothing, because any words she might frame would serve only to deepen her friend's distress.

'Her mind's going,' wailed the big woman. She blew her nose. 'Only fourteen and she's acting crackers.'

Edith patted Diddy's arm. The shopping expedition had been planned in order to take Diddy away from the house for a while. Maureen had been left with Anthony, who had promised to take her for a quiet walk. 'Look, you aren't alone. Richard and I will do all we can to help Maureen.'

Diddy took a slurp of tea. 'You've been so good to us,' she said. 'I'm grateful, you know. None of this is your fault, but here you are with our troubles in your house.' She let out a sigh that shuddered its way through grief. 'I think I'll take her home, Edith. She should be with her own people.'

Edith Spencer toyed with an egg custard. 'No-one knows Maureen here, Diddy. She can have her baby, then she can decide what to do about it. We can arrange an adoption. Richard will look after Maureen's health. There are your neighbours to consider. Can you imagine how it would be for your daughter? Everyone would be asking questions. Leave her here, please.'

Bridie agreed with Edith. 'Living with Edith and Richard is probably best.'

Diddy looked into Bridie's troubled eyes. 'I'm so tied up with our troubles that I've given you no thought. I should be working on the market with our Monica. You've enough problems, queen, what with Cathy being off-colour and poor old Mrs Bell losing her marbles. Then your dad went and died. Oh, I'm sorry.'

Bridie stared into her teacup. As well as all the afore-mentioned, she was having an affair with Anthony Bell. They had made love only once, but she had sinned. When she was with him, she was happy, undeservedly so. He had taught her about joy. She felt the heat in her face, hoped that the two women would not notice. No-one should enjoy physical pleasures as acutely as she did. The sins of the flesh were suddenly real.

'Bridie?'

'Oh.' She dropped her paper napkin and bent to retrieve it from the floor. 'Did you say something?' she asked Diddy.

'Are you ill? You've gone all flushed,' said the big woman.

'It's warm in here,' Bridie said. 'Shall we get some air?'

They strolled through Bolton, bought groceries, sweets for Cathy and a pair of shoes for Maureen. 'Her feet swell,' said Diddy. 'And she's months to go yet.'

Edith tried to hide her concern about Maureen, though she was reaching her wit's end. The girl was decidedly strange these days, was spending too much time alone in her room. Several times, Edith had found Maureen stretched out on the bed with her face turned to the wall. What did she think about as she lay so still and quiet? Edith had told no-one about the gin episode. Maureen had consumed half a bottle of the stuff, had been found almost comatose in one of the stables.

They climbed into Edith's car and began the journey home. Bridie felt her heart quicken as they neared Astleigh Fold. He would be waiting for her. She knew that Anthony would always be waiting for her. Sometimes, the guilt was almost overwhelming. Here she was, twice widowed, recently orphaned and with two children to rear, yet she was happy to the point of ecstasy every time she saw Anthony or heard his voice. When he touched her, she

453

was in heaven. It must not happen again, she said inwardly. This stolen happiness would have to be paid for, she told her inner self. It was wrong to be so joyful.

'Where was God when this happened?' asked Diddy of no-one in particular. 'How could he let a baby be made out of my girl's suffering?'

Bridie stared at the road ahead and Edith just carried on steering. Diddy had voiced a question to which there was no answer.

'She did nothing to deserve this,' continued the grieving mother.

Although they agreed wholeheartedly, Diddy's companions had no comment to make.

Martin Waring was taking daily instruction from *Frère* Nicholas. This was a difficult task, as Martin had to pretend to know very little about the Catholic faith. He was simply a newly released thief who had spent his time in jail among books. As the prison librarian, he had taken the opportunity to read about various Christian religions, and had emerged from incarceration with a burning desire to be received as a communicant within the Church of Rome.

Following his daily stint of gardening and kitchen work, Martin was closeted for three-quarters of an hour with the senior brother. Professing to find trouble in learning the basic catechism was not easy. After all, his alter ego had sailed through the seminary with flying colours and distinctions at all levels. But he persevered, frowned a lot and mispronounced a word here and there. Acting stupid required a degree of genius that tested even his indisputable breadth of skills.

He had been at the Tithebarn for three months when he made his first journey outside the property. With a healthy growth of beard, he was completely unrecogniz-able. In fact, he was often taken aback when he caught a glimpse of his own reflection. It was time to sally forth and find out what was happening to Liam Bell's twin brother. Anthony needed Liam, and Martin was the link between the two. He was beginning to enjoy his new life, took pleasure in his assumed identity. For the time being, Liam was dormant and Martin was in the lead.

The *Frères de la Croix de St Pierre* owned several acres of land. They were virtually self-sufficient, seldom needing to venture out to purchase the basic necessities. But in spite of their meticulous husbandry, some things could not be grown on the farm. As a lay brother, Martin was expected to do his share of shopping and, since he was not a monk, he was able to venture forth in ordinary working clothes. Today, he was going all the way to the market in Bolton to search for cheap bed linens. He had assured the fraternity that the prices in Bolton were lower than in Blackburn.

It was about noon when he reached Astleigh Fold. The sun blazed mercilessly in a cloudless sky, making Martin wish that he could rid himself of his facial hair. But the beard was Liam's curtain. Liam had been forced to hide for a while behind Martin in order to be safe.

He walked past Liam's brother's cottage, noted that the windows had been thrown open to allow in air that seemed too lazy to stir in any direction. In a field further up the lane, he saw Bridie Bell's horses grazing lazily, their tails swishing gently against the threat of flying insects.

Confident that no-one would recognize him, the lay brother folded his arms, placed them across the stile and leaned his weight forward. The rest was pleasurable. He had been working for up to ten hours a day for over two months, was tired as a result of all the physical labour. Yet the back-breaking toil was important, because it was helping to ease him into the character he was planning to become. Liam was no longer necessary except where Anthony was concerned, he told himself frequently. Liam had served his purpose for the present.

A car passed him. He turned confidently and marked its progress towards Cherry Hinton. It was Richard Spencer's car, though Edith was at the wheel. A blonde woman sat next to the driver. That was Bridie Bell. Martin had ordered Liam not to worry about Bridie. She was a person of no particular significance, even if she had deprived Liam of his birthright.

As the vehicle left the lane, Martin thought he saw Diddy Costigan sitting in the rear seat. What on earth were the Spencers thinking of? The Costigans were low-life; they had no place in the elegant setting provided by Cherry Hinton.

Martin's heartbeat remained steady. Nothing could anger him, because he was now a lay brother who would eventually become a *frère*. Liam's anger was buried well below the newly constructed surface. Liam's anger would be kept damped down for years, if necessary, until it was required again.

He walked slowly up the lane. Monks were perfect. Because they aimed for spiritual purity, they were separated from the common run of mankind. The monastic life was simple and severe, its austerity deliberately planned to lead its members towards oneness with God. The brothers were meant to help the fallen without becoming too closely involved in a criminal's future choices. If a sinner wanted to stay, he could, but there were no restrictions. Lay people came and went, just a handful remaining as permanent lay members or as ordained brothers. All were blessed and forgiven; few were rejected by the order. Martin would be ordained.

He climbed over a fence and made for the Spencers'

little orchard. When he stood at the edge behind a particularly gnarled pair of apple trees, he could observe the house without being seen. They were all on the veranda, a small, paved area outside the dining room. A dark-haired girl stared absently into the near distance. She was another Costigan, the one who had been dealt with by Liam. Maureen, her name was. The strumpet had once had designs on Anthony Bell. Where was he?

Anthony came out through the French window. At his side walked Bridie Bell, the Irish whore. Big Diddy Costigan bent over her daughter and offered her something on a plate. The girl refused the food, then Diddy sat down next to her.

Edith poured tea while Mrs Cornwell fussed about with saucers and sugar bowl. Anthony and Bridie were sitting together. Hadn't they quarrelled not long ago? Martin recalled a time when Liam had visited Astleigh Fold and the Irishwoman had spoken to him, had criticized Anthony. The supposed argument seemed to have died down, because they looked quite at home in their little cast-iron garden seats. They were in love, weren't they? Hadn't that all been written down in a letter behind the Sacred Heart in his cell? Sometimes, remembering Liam's details was difficult for Martin.

After half an hour or so, the party began to break up. Maureen Costigan went inside with her mother. Mrs Cornwell cleared the table while Edith had a shouted conversation with a child. The girl hung out of an upper window, her arms waving as she laughed and joked with her hostess. It was Caitlin, the older of the two O'Brien immigrants. The Irish visitors were certainly getting a taste of the good life, it seemed.

Bridie Bell began to walk towards the orchard, so Martin backed off. He crept through the plum trees and secreted himself behind some light-starved raspberry canes and the bole of an ageing pear tree. She stopped, seemed to be waiting. Martin thought he could hear her breathing.

Then she turned and threw herself at a man. The man was Anthony Bell. He picked her up and kissed her, swinging her round in a small clearing. Her hair cascaded from its pins and tumbled down her back like a waterfall, the silken waves pouring down until they reached her waist.

Martin Waring held his own breath. What he was witnessing owned a certain beauty, rather like a properly choreographed *pas de deux*. These two people were almost fused together, the dark head and the pale, the man and the woman. Limbs folded and melted in the leaf-mottled light until their bodies seemed inseparable.

He felt no anger. The control he had over Liam was total. When the lovers pulled away from the embrace, Martin realized that their relationship had advanced well beyond this single lingering kiss. These people knew one another in the biblical sense. He must keep the information to himself. Liam was going to find out eventually, of course, but Martin felt no need to wake the dormant ghost just yet.

They left the orchard, the woman turning towards the field where her horses grazed, the man striding off in the direction of his cottage. It was half past one.

When a few minutes had passed, the intruder stepped out from his hide, diving back quickly when he heard someone else approaching. He flattened himself against the ground, tried to breath quietly and evenly. Weeds and grasses swished as the person came near. A couple of dry twigs snapped, then all movement ceased. 'No!' cried a female voice. 'I won't have it, I won't.'

A heavier person arrived. Martin could hear the laboured breathing, had guessed the identity of the woman before she spoke.

458

'Go away, Mam,' yelled Maureen Costigan.

'You're making yourself ill,' wheezed the girl's mother.

Martin's fingers closed around some foliage. He listened intently while mother and daughter argued. The subject under discussion was the younger female's pregnancy. 'Look,' said Diddy, 'there's nothing we can do except wait. You can't get rid of a baby, Maureen. It would be murder.'

'I won't have it. I'll kill myself, I will, I'll—'

The sound of a none too gentle slap reached the eavesdropper's ears. So. The girl was going to have a child. Anthony's? he wondered. Or could it be Liam's? Hadn't Liam . . . ? No, priests didn't have babies.

The Costigans walked away, each sobbing and wailing and stumbling towards the house.

When all was quiet, the lay brother sat up and dusted his jacket. Moss and bits of dried grass clung to the fabric, and there were greenish stains on a lapel. He brushed and scraped, rubbed at the discoloration with a handkerchief. Anthony was with Bridie Bell. They were probably sleeping together, the stepmother and her stepson. And Maureen Costigan was trying to get rid of an unborn child. Liam would have to be told eventually, but it was best not to dwell on such matters just yet. Baptism, confirmation and ordination were more important than these stupid people.

Pleased with all he had gleaned, he walked out of the orchard and towards the lane. The newly acquired knowledge would be useful one day, he told himself. For Liam, it would be vital. With his pulse as steady as a rock, Martin Waring gathered his thoughts and checked the money in his small leather wallet. He was going to buy the unbleached cotton sheets that were a part of the brothers' constant penance. Liam's news would keep.

*

Bridie Bell and her stepson lay on the rug. They did not touch one another, yet their intimacy would have been apparent to any witness. There was a languor about them, a total at homeness that spoke volumes about the depth of their relationship. Within a very short space of time, each had found a soulmate.

'She'll kill herself,' said Bridie.

'No, I think she's too strong for that.' He stroked a blonde tress which had fallen across his chest.

'Maureen thinks she's carrying the child of a devil,' continued Bridie. She could tell this man anything and everything. He would never judge her as stupid or hysterical. 'While she cannot blame the poor little creature, she will never welcome a baby who was made by rape.'

'God help her if and when she finds out the identity of her attacker.' Anthony sighed heavily. 'What an unholy mess. You and I know his name, as does Father Brennan, as does Richard Spencer. We can prove nothing at all, so we keep quiet. The police are doing precious little to find him. They think we're all mad.' Occasionally, Anthony hung on to a thread of hope, an insane desire for Liam to be innocent. It was a hopeless hope, he told himself yet again. Liam was ill; Liam was dangerous.

Bridie closed her eyes and wished away a threatening headache. Sometimes, she felt Liam Bell's presence, had even looked over her shoulder a few times as if expecting to find those dark, expressionless eyes staring at her and right through her. 'Diddy's beside herself. She told me last night that she was praying for a miscarriage. She's been down to St Patrick's in Bolton to ask forgiveness because she's willing her own grandchild to die.

'Everything's such a mess,' she groaned. 'Maureen wants an abortion, but she can't have one.' She looked at him. 'I want you and I can't have you. It's all so wrong.'

'You and I are in the wrong, I suppose. I have to agree

with you on that score,' he admitted. 'But I won't let you go free, not ever. In fact, I'm thinking of having you fitted with a ball and chain.'

'But we're hurting no-one,' cried Bridie.

'Your daughters may be damaged by our love,' he whispered. 'Not yet, but eventually.'

It was different, Bridie told herself. Her sin was born of love, not hatred. Anthony's sin, too, had been committed for love. Yet he was right about Cathy and Shauna. 'How am I going to tell my daughters that their stepbrother is my lover?'

'That's a big question, and it's not our concern yet,' Anthony said. Their main aim must be to steer clear of Liam. 'You know, I can feel him today, as if he's just around the corner. Weren't you cold in the orchard before you went to see the horses?'

'No,' Bridie lied.

He had felt chilled. He had shivered as if he had just been pulled out of the Mersey's grey depths. 'We've both lost our fathers,' he said. 'And you've lost two husbands. There's enough grief hanging in the air without looking over our shoulders for Liam, yet we must. God, I wish somebody would find him.'

Bridie thought about that. 'He'll find you, Anthony. When he's ready, he'll . . .' She didn't want to think about it.

'And Maureen's carrying his child.' There was a hollow quality in Anthony's words. 'Have you looked at her face lately?'

Bridie nodded, then placed her head on his chest. She could hear his heart beating its steady rhythm against her cheek. 'Maureen's desperate,' she said. 'And old. Diddy's at her wit's end, trying to get some sense into the girl, but she's getting nowhere.'

'I could kill him,' declared Anthony. He looked up into

the clear blue eyes and smiled ruefully. Reaching for her face, he used his finger to trace its outline. She would be returning to Liverpool very soon, and he wanted to hold this moment until their next meeting. They had made love only once, because he could not allow her to carry any more guilt. Restraint was difficult, but he was managing, just about. 'I'll get a job in Liverpool,' he told her. 'Then we can live together. After all, I'm your stepson, so—'

'No.' Bridie shook her head until his face was hidden beneath her tumbled hair. 'You must not live with us. It would be far too stressful.' She inhaled deeply, pulled the long tresses away from his face. 'It would be better if you stayed here.'

She was right and he knew it. He imagined how confused the girls would become if they ever found him with their mother. He imagined the tongues wagging outside and inside the church of St Aloysius Gonzaga, the jibes Bridie would be forced to tolerate.

She sat up, began to pin her hair. 'Your grandmother is descending quickly towards senility, Anthony. I have to get back and care for her. Sam asked me to do that, and I do love the old girl. But . . .' Her voice trailed away.

'But what?'

She smiled at him, wished that she could iron the lines of worry from his forehead. 'Silver will win the Derby next year.' She spoke with great conviction. 'And I shall be a wealthy woman. Perhaps I'll buy a cottage in Astleigh Fold, a place for holidays and for . . . for us.' A pang of guilt cut into her chest again, but she breathed it away determinedly. He needed her and she needed him. Their union could never be blessed by the Church, but Sam was blessing it. 'When the girls are grown and gone, we shall be outrageous. We shall live in sin and get ourselves excommunicated. Have you ever wondered how it will feel to wear sackcloth and ashes?'

Anthony shook his head. 'The nearest I came to that was when I fell in our midden twenty years ago. But won't the idea of excommunication bother you?'

'No,' she replied with certainty, 'it will not.' She was Catholic to the core, yet she loved this man too much to worry about something as unimportant as her own salvation.

Diddy Costigan placed the last of Bridie's clothes in the suitcase. Diddy felt guilty about not going back to help Monica on the stall, but she could not leave Maureen, not yet. 'I'm sorry, queen,' she said for the umpteenth time.

'It's no matter,' answered Bridie. Diddy was worried to the point of distraction. Maureen was refusing food, was staying in bed, was weeping softly and silently into her pillow for hours on end. 'I understand why you must stay here. Nicky can take care of things – she's a capable girl. And Billy's there to help with any heavy work.'

Diddy sniffed away her sadness. 'To be honest, I don't know how Maureen'll get through this, Bridie. I mean, to have all that pain for a baby you don't want – it's bad enough when the baby's coming into a happy family. I've cursed Billy through every one of my labours.' She bit her lower lip. 'Our Maureen won't know who to scream at, will she?'

Bridie swallowed, turned away to hide her face. Liam's child. Well, it probably was Liam's. 'Stay in Astleigh Fold as long as you need to.' She picked up her hairbrush and threw it into the case. 'Keep in touch, though.'

'I will.'

A loud crash caused them both to stiffen. Diddy put a hand to her throat. 'What the bloody hell was that?'

Bridie was the first to recover. She crossed the room, threw open the door and ran onto the landing. Maureen Costigan lay in a crumpled heap at the bottom of the staircase. A small pool of blood had seeped from her head, was spreading its scarlet rivulets across the marble floor and into the fringe of a Persian rug. 'Jesus,' breathed Bridie, 'let her be alive.'

The front door opened and Richard Spencer stepped into the hall. He threw down his bag and rushed to the prone figure. 'Edith!' he yelled. 'Ambulance – quickly!'

Cathy, who had now recovered sufficiently to move out of her attic and into the land of bacteria, emerged from her airy bedroom and ran to her mother. 'Mammy? Did Maureen fall?'

No, no, replied Bridie silently. She has killed herself. Aloud, she told her daughter to return to the bedroom. No sooner had she rid herself of Cathy than Diddy was upon her. 'Stay where you are,' ordered the younger woman. 'Richard's with her.'

Diddy let forth a primeval howl and pushed Bridie aside as if flicking away an annoying fly. She tore down the stairs with Bridie at her heels. 'Maureen!' she screamed. 'Don't die, you mustn't die, girl. We'll get rid of it, we will, we will. We'll find somebody, won't we?' she asked Richard.

The doctor knelt beside Maureen and found a pulse. 'Edith is getting the ambulance,' he said. 'This poor girl's too badly hurt to go in the car.' He pulled back one of the unconscious Maureen's eyelids, watched the pupil as it shrank against light. She was not comatose, not yet. 'We must get her there as quickly as possible.'

Diddy frowned. 'Where? Where are you taking her?'

'Into hospital, of course.'

'I'm going with her,' pronounced Diddy. 'And I'm staying with her till she's right.'

Richard counted the beats of Maureen's heart, pushed the half-hunter back into his waistcoat pocket. 'We must not move her until we have a stretcher and some help.' He watched Diddy as she crawled on hands and knees around the motionless body of her daughter.

'Will the baby die now?' asked the large woman.

Richard glanced at Bridie. 'Embryos are tough,' he said.

Diddy lifted her head. 'If somebody doesn't do something, our Maureen's going to die. She might not die this time, but if she comes round still pregnant, she'll jump again and again until she manages to finish herself off. All she needs is to get rid of that rotten bugger's baby.'

Richard cleared his throat. He blinked away some moisture from his eyes, wished with all his heart that he could pick up this child, carry her to his office and perform a miracle. But miracles often went wrong. He had watched several patients die after the execution of a miracle in some seedy kitchen.

'The blood's stopped coming from her head,' ventured Bridie. 'Can't we pick her up and make her comfortable?'

Richard bent down again, made sure that the bleeding had not stopped due to heart failure. But Maureen was very much alive, though one of her legs seemed to be broken. 'Leave her where she is,' he advised again. 'We can do a lot more harm than good if we move her.'

Diddy struggled to her feet with Bridie's help. Her eyes seemed to burn as she spoke. 'Will she be all right, Bridie? Will she die today?'

Bridie dragged her friend to the stairs and forced her to sit on the second step. 'I don't know,' she replied truthfully. Why was all this happening? Was God reaching down to punish Bridie and Anthony because of their unholy alliance? Was He watching Bridie's new found ecstasy, was He annoyed because she was finding pleasure through the joining of her flesh to Anthony's? Surely not? God wasn't like a soldier in the front lines. God knew where to send His darts – He did not hit the wrong man or the wrong woman.

'What have we done to deserve this bloody lot?' asked Diddy.

Diddy had done nothing, thought Bridie. She had married, had raised her children, had borne the pain of watching her eldest son struggling against physical handicap. Diddy had worked like a dog, had remained cheerful and strong through adversity, had loved and fed and clothed her family. She was well-respected in the community where she continued to serve as unqualified midwife and nurse, where she laid out the dead and comforted the bereaved. Diddy had even taken up arms against local and national governments, because she believed that the Scotland Road people were going to be ousted, separated and sent to live miles away from their roots. She was a fighter on the verge of conceding defeat because her daughter was in tremendous mental and physical distress.

'Bridie?'

'Yes?'

'She moved her arm.'

'Good. Isn't that great? They'll be here for her in a minute.' Bridie watched Richard as he ran his hands over Maureen's limbs in search of fractures.

Edith came into the hall with a tray of tea. She heaped sugar into Diddy's cup, then forced it into her hands. 'Drink it,' she ordered. 'It will help you to help Maureen.'

Obediently, Diddy sipped at the hot fluid. Bridie shook her head against the offer of sustenance, then left the scene. Upstairs, she had a daughter of her own with tired blood and a terrible thirst for knowledge. She pushed open the door, found Cathy weeping on the edge of her bed. 'Come on, child,' she murmured. 'Maureen's going to hospital to be cared for. Everything will work out fine, you'll see.'

The child clutched at her mother. 'It's that baby,' she said. 'Maureen doesn't want it. Why does she have to have it, Mammy? Mother Ignatius won't talk to me about it. Maureen won't talk to me at all—'

'Maureen isn't talking to anyone, Cathy.' Bridie sat down next to her daughter.

'What happened to her?'

Bridie sighed and held onto the trembling girl. 'There are things you don't need to know about just yet,' she said. 'Grown-up things. I remember when I was about your age, I used to think what a wonderful time grown-ups had. They decided what to do and where to go, then they decided what I had to do. It seemed so unfair. When I grew up, I found out that things weren't quite so easy. You see, Cathy, being an adult is as difficult as being a child. In fact, we never really grow up fully, you know. We're never sure that we are doing the right thing.'

Cathy rubbed her face with the heel of her hand. 'What happened to Maureen, Mammy?'

It was no use. Bridie realized, not for the first time, that this almost eight-year-old was really going on forty. Life had been hard for Cathy. She had lost her daddy, had feared her granda, had lost a stepfather, had been weakened by anaemia. Richard had said that the disease was in a mild form, but this poor little girl was lonely and bored due to enforced rest. Cathy was a great collector of information. Like a sponge, she soaked up everything without discrimination. She had been discovered by Richard reading medical books in the middle of the night. She read geography and history books, was using the published word to fill the empty and schoolless days.

'Mammy?'

Bridie took a deep breath. 'Someone hurt her. The baby is part of the hurt. Babies are made by a man and a woman who love each other. The father of Maureen's baby did not love her.' Liam loved no-one, was incapable of love. 'And that is all you need to know, young madam.'

'Did Maureen jump, Mammy?'

Bridie nodded.

'Did she want to die?'

'I don't know.' That was the truth. Had the girl leapt from the landing to promote a miscarriage, or had she wanted to end her life? 'It's possible that even Maureen has no answer to that question, Cathy.'

The child hung on to her mother. 'I want to come home with you,' she said. 'To help with Grandmuth and to stop Shauna stealing. I know all about stealing, 'cos Tildy and Cozzer do it to feed the Nolans. Mammy?'

'Yes, Cathy?'

'Don't things get sad and desperate all at once?'

'They do,' agreed Bridie. 'But it's our duty to pray and to stay cheerful for the sake of others.' Inwardly, Bridie groaned. She sounded like one of the nuns giving the Monday morning homily to a group of children who couldn't have cared less. But Cathy cared. That was the difference between Cathy and Shauna. Although Shauna was younger, she displayed none of Cathy's traits. Even at three, this older girl had been sensitive. 'I took advantage of you,' confessed Bridie. 'When Shauna came along, you were given too much responsibility altogether.'

'I don't mind,' said the child.

'No, but I do,' answered the mother. In that instant, Bridie made a bold decision. Cathy would stay here with her dog. As soon as the illness cleared, Cathy would go to Scared Heart and get an education. She needed love, organization, a timetable. Scotland Road was a fine community, but Bridie wanted a better life for this special child. 'You're a good girl,' she said now.

Cathy dried her eyes. 'I do try,' she replied, the blue eyes rolling dramatically. 'But it's very boring except when I go for my long walks. Uncle Richard says I have to be a patient patient. Mother Ignatius is seeing to my education.'

'Don't you like her?'

Cathy shrugged. 'I hate the wart, but she's fine underneath. She's teaching me.' Then the little girl remembered about Maureen out in the hallway with her head bleeding. 'Please let Maureen be all right,' she said. 'We shouldn't be talking about our own selves,' she chided her mother gently. 'Not while Maureen's hurt.'

Bridie pulled the child close. 'Cathy, I love you so much,' she said.

They heard the ambulance arriving, continued to sit together until the vehicle pulled away. Shauna would be missing her mammy, Bridie mused, and Muth needed watching. But first, Bridie had to remain in Astleigh Fold until Maureen was better. Or worse. Scotland Road must wait a little longer for the pawnbroker's widow to return.

Nineteen

Bridie Bell watched Robin Smythe as he led Quicksilver through the bathing pool and into the refurbished paddock. Rippling muscle in the grey's flanks reflected rays of a morning sun, while the horse tossed his head as if responding to an ovation. Silver was growing used to applause. Irish colts had made their mark on English racecourses in the past, but not until 1907 had Orby placed the sign of the shamrock on the Epsom Derby. Greys were rare winners, too, so Silver, with his eyes flashing and his tail erect, seemed to realize how thoroughly remarkable he had become. It was 1932, and Quicksilver had more than quadrupled his own value by running like the wind with the purple-and-silver-silked Robin in the saddle.

The horse's triumph was now Bridie's. Silver had romped home in several races, had left a huge gap between himself and the field a couple of weeks earlier at the Epsom Derby. 'I'm rich,' Bridie mumbled to herself almost incredulously. 'And you,' she mouthed at the horse, 'are no shabby little grey.' Silver had been compared with Gustavus, a horse of the same colour who had secured first place in 1821, though Gustavus, short in leg and neck, had taken the racing community by storm after his unexpected win. But Silver was a champion right down to the bone. He acted like a superior being, seemed to have been born with a sense of his individuality. Silver was a natural monarch.

Bridie smiled at the jockey, glanced down at the little fob watch pinned to her blouse. Eight o'clock. In a few moments, she would return to Cherry Hinton for breakfast.

Robin brought the horse to his owner. 'There's a queue a mile long for this chap.' He stroked the stiff, silver-white mane. 'Though I think you should be less hasty, Mrs Bell. It's a bit early to let them settle to breed. You could make a fortune racing these two.'

She shook her head. A widow for almost a year, she had become an astute businesswoman, but she drew the line at running her horses into the ground. Sorrel, who had performed solidly and successfully in Lancashire and Yorkshire, would be matured for breeding. Silver was to be the backbone of the Cathshaw Stables. As a stud, he was worth his weight in platinum.

Robin leapt down from his high horse and became tiny again. He looked far too frail to be stablemaster, but few mounts had ever bettered him in the war of the wills between horse and jockey. He was ready to abandon the circuit, was preparing to invest time and money in Bridie's venture. Bob Cross, who had died a happy man at a Chester meeting, was to be replaced by this diminutive character. 'The house needs fumigating before I can move in,' he told his partner. 'There are newspapers there from 1885, and I'm sure Bob must have fed the mice. They're almost tame.'

Bridie laughed. Bob probably had looked after his vermin.

'And how's Cathy?' asked Robin.

Bridie chuckled again. 'Strangely enough, the young madam is happy, though she'll be the death of me, Edith and several of those poor nuns. And the trouble we had persuading her to go to Sacred Heart. She loves it, has the school near to riot, always questioning and disagreeing with everything. Richard says she's a genius, but I know better. She has the wisdom to become a very clever woman – manipulative and cute. But she's no Sophocles. Says she's going to be a doctor, may God help and preserve us all.'

Robin released the horse and watched as he ambled off in search of food. 'And Shauna?'

Bridie's face was instantly sober. Shauna was five, had started attending school and was a different kind of trial. She was determined to have her own way at all times and at all costs, was given to tantrums and displays of temper. She was currently in the care of Nicky Costigan and her mother, Diddy. 'She'll improve with keeping, I suppose,' replied Bridie. She prayed that Shauna wasn't causing too many problems on Scotland Road while in the care of good friends.

'You're hard on her,' commented the little man. He was now a close enough friend to make such remarks.

Bridie nodded thoughtfully. She had favoured Shauna, had always loved her too much. The child was spoilt and ill-mannered, was capable of a petulance that had never been a part of her older sister's make up. Bridie had named her stables Cathshaw, had altered a letter from Shauna's name, had put Cathy first. She must remember to keep on putting Cathy first, because poor Cathy had been forced to grow up so early. 'Shauna continues difficult,' she said eventually.

'She'll alter,' said Robin.

'She'd better,' answered Bridie. She made her goodbye and began the walk back to the house. Richard and Edith had sold Bridie their stable for a ridiculously low price, but those good people would be repaid. They had done so much since Sam's death, had cared for Cathy, had welcomed Bridie, Shauna, Diddy and her brood for holidays.

Bridie, Edith and Richard were due to visit Maureen this afternoon. Maureen was locked away again in a secure wing of the Good Shepherd Catholic Asylum just outside Manchester. Augustinian nuns and lay nurses were doing their utmost to help Maureen regain her equilibrium, though the results of their labours were not yet encouraging. During the past eighteen or more months, Maureen had shrivelled into herself, had spent a great deal of time in the asylum. The girl was terrified, had been traumatized to the point of breakdown by her unwanted pregnancy.

'Oh, Maureen,' muttered Bridie, 'come out of it, for goodness sake. Don't let him win.' She stopped in the orchard, listened to the crying and fussing of wood pigeons. Even now, Bridie could not think about that fateful day without feeling sick. In her mind, there was a picture of Maureen's blood pouring, spreading, soaking into the Oriental rugs and staining dark-red the cement between marble tiles. It had been a hard landing for the distraught girl. She had not regained consciousness after three days, had been confined to bed for weeks, had suffered a messy miscarriage while sitting with her leg in plaster. And in all that time, Maureen had uttered not one solitary syllable.

'Diddy, my friend,' breathed Bridie as she watched a blackbird carrying worms for its young, 'how you tried.' Month in and month out, Diddy had stayed near her daughter, returning to Liverpool only when her presence was absolutely essential. The Scotland Roaders, in spite of their own poverty, had dug deep to send fruit and little gifts for Maureen. Diddy had prayed, cajoled, shouted and pleaded, but Maureen had remained silent. The girl's quietness had been broken only by her screams. Bridie pictured Maureen sitting in her bedroom, rocking, wailing, howling.

'Maureen,' muttered Bridie now, 'you can do it. I know you can face it.' She prayed to Our Lady, to St Anthony of Padua, to St Jude, to Thomas who had doubted, to God Himself. An orchard was surely as near to God as anywhere, wasn't it? But would the heavenly host listen to a woman who was carrying on with the son of her dead husband? Their love had been consummated only twice, but it was still a sin. However, there were worse faults than hers and Anthony's. Father Michael Brennan was always saying that.

There was Liam. There was Liam who had put Maureen where she was, who had murdered his brother's fiancée, who had disappeared completely from the face of the earth. Even Africa had thrown up no sign of the man when Father Brennan had written to the various missions.

Cathy ran through the trees and hugged her mother. 'Isn't it great?' the child beamed. 'Everyone at school wants to be my friend because we won the Derby. I've even heard the nuns talking about it. They say, whenever they have visitors, "There's Caitlin O'Brien whose mother bred the Derby winner." Do they like their pool?'

'Yes, they seem to.' Bridie believed in the strengthening power of water where horses' legs were concerned. 'Sorrel would like to swim, I think, but we're digging no deeper, or we'll be coming up in Australia. Have you eaten?'

Cathy nodded. 'So has Noel, but it wasn't his dinner. He's in disgrace again for eating Uncle Richard's bacon. Aunt Edith has banished him to his kennel.'

Bridie grinned. Edith had a soft spot for the leggy mongrel, and had probably given him a huge bone to gnaw for the duration of his sentence. Noel had never stayed in his kennel for more than an hour, because Edith was soft-hearted and Noel could howl like a wolf. If only

Edith would try to like Shauna. There was something about Bridie's younger daughter that made Edith Spencer's hackles rise, though she fought to hide her distaste. 'Will you stay here while we go to see Maureen?'

Cathy's face was immediately sad. 'Bring her home, Mammy,' she pleaded.

Bridie placed a hand on Cathy's cheek. 'We can't, Cathy. She's not ready yet.'

'But it's been a long time. And there's no baby to worry about now.'

Bridie thought about the little soul whose life had ebbed out of its mother's broken form. Liam's child was long dead. Perhaps that was for the best, though it was a pity all the same, because the unborn baby had done no wrong at all. Even so, Bridie shivered when she imagined how a child of Liam's might have turned out. 'No, there's no baby,' she replied.

'But Maureen's still waiting for it,' said the little girl.

'How do you know that?'

Cathy blushed. Listening to adult conversation was one of her hobbies. 'Uncle Richard thinks so.'

It was difficult to tell. After months of silence, no-one really knew what Maureen was thinking. She had suffered little or no discernible brain damage, was able to read, sew, dress, eat, clean herself. Tests for deafness had been used, and the young woman was certainly alert to noise. Diddy had talked to her for endless hours, as had Bridie, Edith and Richard, but none of them was able to elicit any response. Over and over, each had told Maureen that the baby was no more, that she had only to ask for what she needed, that she could come home whenever she was ready.

'She doesn't want to come out of that place,' said Cathy.

Bridie, who considered her daughter to be too old in the head, ruffled the girl's blond curls. 'Cathy, we can't know what she wants until she speaks. And she'll speak when she feels the need.'

While her mother went inside to eat, Cathy paid Noel a visit. He was licking his lips over a huge bone. 'I have a plan,' said the child to the dog.

The dog listened, chewed things over, crunched his way through to the marrow.

'What do you think?' asked Cathy. 'Will I do it, Noel?'

The dog woofed and carried on crunching.

Although Maureen Costigan appeared to be in a state bordering catatonic trance, she was very much aware of her surroundings. When her environment became too much for her, she simply retreated, took herself back to another life, a different time inside her head. Sometimes, she was dancing and singing outside the Rotunda, her audience entranced as she postured and performed the actions to her little ditties. It was her grandmother who had taught her songs from the old country, pretty Irish airs whose rhythms were tapped out by the shoes of queuing theatre-goers and by the percussion section of Uncle Flash's one-man band.

Maureen had been in and out of the asylum for a long time, or so everyone kept telling her. There was Mam, who always brought pasties and soup, then Dad, who just sat and held Maureen's hand. Sister Paul Mary, whose long legs covered the whole ward in fifteen steps, was always telling Maureen to pull herself together. Sister Agnes, who needed nineteen or twenty strides to clear the room, was more understanding. She would sit by Maureen's bed and whisper to her, 'Maureen, I know you're hiding. It's safe now. You can come out. But you'll not come out till you're ready, will you?'

Sitting very still and saying nothing was the secret.

Little could happen to someone who made no mark. If she didn't move, she would not be noticed. If she wasn't noticed, then the bad thing would never happen again.

There was a tap in the washroom that dripped constantly. Others found it annoying, but Maureen liked the sound of water. It was clean, gentle, peaceful. The drip-drop often matched the beating of her inner mechanism. A man with spanners had tried to take away the irritation, but it always returned to keep Maureen company.

Some memories were unpleasant; some memories were beautiful. When the nastier times plagued her, Maureen would empty her mind and sit motionless in the green moquette chair next to her bed. Water plopping from the tap helped to clear her mind. Then the nicer pictures usually arrived, snatches of childhood, or an orchard, a proper fountain and green lawns. A child with hair like dark honey, a very leggy dog, roses on the teapot, a tall, thin lady and her tall, thin husband.

A man on a horse. Falling, falling, blood on a stone. Banister railings, a marble floor, colours in the carpets, falling, falling. Was it dead? Was it really dead? Her hands pressing into her belly, feeling and prodding, searching for that hard knot of evil. Keep still. The tap dripping, dropping, a moquette chair, green. Sister Agnes, nineteen or twenty strides, Sister Paul Mary, fifteen. If she stayed as still as possible, she would be all right.

Riding in the boot of a car was not as simple as Cathy had expected. Also, there was the problem of getting out unnoticed, which was going to be no mean feat. Banking on Richard's slight tendency towards absent-mindedness, she had placed herself between the petrol cans and spare wheel before attaching a string to the boot handle. With the aid of this, she held the door in a more or less closed position while being bumped and jostled all over the place. Had Uncle Richard checked his boot, she would have been discovered before leaving Cherry Hinton.

It was a long ride along the Manchester Road, and Cathy was becoming quite bruised by the lumps and holes in the road's surface. From time to time, she felt like jumping out when the car stopped, but she had come this far. If she gave up, all her agony would have been for nothing. So she gritted her teeth, hoped that she still had a full complement of incisors and molars, and prayed that she would arrive at the Good Shepherd with most bones intact.

At last, the car stopped and the three adults got out. She could hear their feet crunching on gravel as she extricated her numb hands from their string prison. Now, the real problems would start. She didn't know where she was or how to get home, and she had no idea of where to look for Maureen.

Fortunately, the weather was good, so those patients who were trustworthy and calm were taking tea on the lawn. Cathy saw her mother sitting at a table with Aunt Edith, Uncle Richard and a dark-haired girl wearing a plain blue dress and a grey cardigan. So far so good, thought Cathy, though she didn't know what to do next. She had planned – rather vaguely – to hang around after Mammy and the others had left. Once alone, she would have been able to scour the place and find Maureen. Getting home would have been another job, though her sketchy idea had been to alert a nun and ask for someone to telephone Cherry Hinton. But hiding until everyone had left was going to be the hard part.

She skirted the pathway, followed a line of privet hedge, finally arriving at a place that was almost opposite the table where her family sat. Uncle Richard was holding Maureen's hand while Aunt Edith spoke to the girl. The nuns had scraped back Maureen's hair and tied it with a ribbon. Maureen looked older than Mammy.

So. There were a couple of possibilities, Cathy supposed. She could stay here until the party had left, or she could show herself now and take the consequences. What would the nuns do if they found her later on? she wondered. In Cathy's experience, nuns always did the right thing. She remembered ruefully how she had fought against going to Sacred Heart, how scared she had been of the sisters. At the end of several family meetings, Cathy had been persuaded to try the school for a year. And she loved it, though the nuns were so terribly correct. If these nursing sisters found her before she found Maureen, she would be despatched with haste. It was perhaps better to stand up now and be counted.

Slowly, Cathy rose from her hide. The bushes had been cut quite low, and she was able to see over their tops, just about. Now Mammy was holding Maureen's hand and Uncle Richard was doing the talking. Poor Maureen simply stared ahead as if dreaming. Her eyes were dull, reminding Cathy of a house with no lights, a place where no-one lived. It was really sad. She would cry in a minute, she really would. Maureen used to be so pretty, so alive . . .

Cathy raised a hand above her head and waved. Nobody reacted, so she lifted up both arms. Everybody seemed to have gone blind, because not one of them took the slightest notice. A nun pouring tea just carried on pouring, while a second nun doled out little sandwiches and cakes. Cathy's stomach rumbled angrily. She was starving. If she didn't get something to eat soon, she would probably faint from lack of nourishment and catch anaemia all over again.

Then the unexpected happened. A sister in a sacking apron appeared at the door and waved to one of her colleagues. A whispered conversation took place, then

Aunt Edith and Uncle Richard were summoned to the house. Aunt Edith turned to Mammy. 'Cathy's gone missing,' she shouted. 'Mrs Cornwell's on the phone.' The whole party dived inside, leaving Maureen gazing into her teacup as if seeking to read her fortune in the leaves.

The missing Cathy squeezed through a gap and ran to the table. 'Maureen!' she shouted. 'It's me – it's Cathy.' A nun leapt across the lawn and collared the intruder. 'Whoever let you in, child?'

'Myself,' managed Cathy.

'Far too young,' tutted the good sister, tightening her grip on the back of Cathy's blouse.

The child coughed. 'I'm not too young,' she gasped. 'Ask Mother Ignatius. She thinks I'm old, so does Mammy. I'm old in the head and I go to the big school even though everybody else is eleven. This is a good blouse, Sister.'

The nun was in no mood for negotiation. Because most of the Good Shepherd's residents were mentally ill, children were strictly forbidden to visit. 'How did you arrive here?' she asked.

'I came in Dr Spencer's car,' came the swift response. 'And he paid for the blouse from Henry Barrie's. Henry Barrie's is on Churchgate. It's exclusive, Aunt Edith says. Exclusive means very expensive.'

The Augustinian nursing sister was not amused. 'I suppose Dr Spencer told you to remain in the car?'

'No,' replied Cathy truthfully. 'He didn't say anything to me.'

Dr Spencer was well-respected by the sisters. He had given a great deal of his time to the Good Shepherd, had become involved with the community when Maureen had first arrived here. Although he was not a psychiatrist, he was a well-educated man with a genuine interest in sick people. 'You'll have to go,' said the nun.

Cathy struggled, used her eyes to plead with Maureen.

But Maureen simply sat and displayed no reaction to the scene.

'Come along now,' said the sister. 'We'll go inside and—'

'Maureen!' screamed Cathy mightily. 'Help me!'

Everything froze. Visitors and patients at the various tables stopped eating and chatting. Every eye was fixed on the angry young girl in the nun's grip.

Cathy kicked out, made contact with layers of serge and cotton, missed the sister's legs by a mile. She was genuinely furious. She had come miles and miles in the smelly boot of a car, had missed death by inches each time the car had rattled over a bump, had held on grimly when the boot had tried to fly open. She was tired, hungry and generally fed up with people, especially with nuns. They had no imagination. She had heard Uncle Richard saying that they were good people, but that everything in their minds was as black and white as their habits. 'I am not a little girl,' she shouted. 'And my Uncle Richard will be very cross if you tear my blouse.'

The nun released her grip. Cathy, suddenly free but still pulling away, fell over. The sister picked her up. 'Don't move,' she advised.

Cathy nodded at the black-clad figure. 'I am going to be a doctor when I grow up,' she said, her tone as dignified and threatening as she could manage. It was hard to put weight behind words when her clothes were messy with petrol and grass stains. 'You will need people like me one day, Sister.'

The nun fought a ready answer, turned it into a cough.

Cathy waved a hand towards Maureen. 'She is my friend,' she announced. 'And I am here to visit her.' She sat down next to Maureen, grabbed a cake and took a bite.

Richard appeared in a doorway. He was closely attended by his wife and Bridie. 'Would you ever look at that?' asked the latter. 'She's there as large as life and twice as much trouble.'

Cathy swallowed the cake in two bites before leaning sideways towards her companion. 'Maureen?' she began. 'Nicky's getting married soon to Graham if they can save enough. He has the strangest eyes. And I'm going to be a doctor. Come on, we'll have a little walk.' She tugged at the older girl's hand.

Maureen stood up and went where she was led by the child with dark honey hair. They strolled towards Richard, Edith and Bridie. 'When are you coming home?' Cathy asked Maureen.

'Umm,' Maureen replied, her tone guttural. There was nothing in her eyes, yet she had made a sound, and she had fixed her black gaze on Cathy.

'Will you come for dinner, Maureen?' asked Cathy. 'You don't have to stay still all the time, you know. I used to lie very still in my bed so that the nightmares wouldn't find me. You haven't any baby left. It's gone. Even if you move and talk, it won't find you. I know all about it.' She smiled encouragingly.

Edith Spencer mopped her face. Cathy seemed to be opening a line of communication with Maureen, even though no words had come from the older girl.

Bridie held her breath and prayed.

'There's no baby, you know,' repeated Cathy. 'You're all right now.'

Maureen stopped, dropped her head and studied the floor. 'Catheee,' she said softly. Upstairs, Cathy had been. She had stayed in bed with all the windows open, had gone for long walks with ... with that man over there, the tall, thin man with the tall, thin wife. Nice people, the Spencers. He was a doctor and she did charity work.

Richard Spencer dabbed at his face with a large hand-kerchief. During the time since her suicide attempt,

Maureen had spent the occasional weekend at Cherry Hinton, but Bridie had removed Cathy each time before Maureen's arrival. Cathy had been judged too young to cope with the older girl's strangeness.

For how long had Diddy Costigan sat and talked to her daughter? Richard asked himself. How many times had the girl been assured that she was not carrying a child of rape? 'Out of the mouths of babes,' he muttered. 'If we'd brought Cathy along earlier . . .' But would Maureen have been ready to listen? Was this a coincidence? Perhaps the girl's mechanism had been due to click back into gear, perhaps she was always going to begin talking again on this particular day.

Maureen looked at Bridie, frowned as if forcing herself to focus. 'Cathy,' she said, her voice rusty and dry. 'Cathy.'

Richard spoke to Bridie. 'There you are. I told you that your daughter is exceptional.'

Bridie nodded quickly. 'You're a good girl,' she told her elder child. 'But how did you get here? Everyone's searching Astleigh Fold.'

Cathy recounted her adventure. Richard fixed his gaze on Maureen, saw that she was retreating again into that part of her brain that felt little pain and no pleasure. 'Maureen?' he said.

'Cathy,' replied the girl.

The doctor turned to his wife. 'We get her out of here immediately,' he said. 'Cathy is the key.'

Edith touched her husband's arm before returning to the telephone. She would tell all at Cherry Hinton that Cathy was safe. Then, she would have the great pleasure of phoning a certain shop on Scotland Road in Liverpool. At last, Diddy's daughter was on the mend.

*

'She's Out', really Matt Roberts, was a mild-mannered man with a squeaky bicycle and dark, slicked-back hair. As an agent for landlords, he collected rent on a weekly basis from households in the Scotland Road area. His apparent gentleness was misleading, as he was not averse to sending in bailiffs whenever debts got out of hand. He would, however, listen to a case and assess its merits. Often, it was his accurate judgement of character that kept a family sheltered when money was scarce.

Diddy opened the door. She had finished her stint on the market with Nicky and was preparing a pan of scouse. 'She's Out' raised his hat and showed off the oily hair. 'There's a deputation hanging about, Mrs C,' he told her. 'Looking at the state of the houses. A couple from welfare and one or two from the council.'

Diddy paid her rent and thanked him for the information. Her stew was thickening nicely now that the potatoes had fallen, so she pulled on her coat and sallied forth to view the party from the corporation. There were rumours about rehousing, and Diddy wanted to say her tenpenn'orth before anything happened.

She stood on the road that had been no more than a cart track along which travellers had journeyed to and from Scotland, wondered how it had looked a couple of hundred years ago. Of course, inns had opened, then the docks had bred doss-houses and eating places. And now, it was a world apart, an area where people stood together in the face of many adversities. 'They' were going to break it up. 'They' had marked the streets for demolition ten years ago, just after the police strike and the loot. The Catholics were blamed and the Catholics would be condemned without the benefit of a trial.

Diddy glanced round, watched the children at play. A gang of lads chased a 'football' of rolled up newspapers, while girls jumped about on a chalk-drawn hopscotch grid. There were jacks and bobbers on the go, cherry wobs being rattled down drainpipes, while a slightly richer child shared her spinning top with a crowd of admirers. Down a side-street, a glass-sided hearse and two plumed horses waited outside a house whose windows were draped in the traditional Irish white sheeting.

She spotted them straight away. There was a fat woman with a loud voice, a cheery soul called Betty Something-or-other. Craddock, Diddy thought. This was an unusual female, a member of the council who would call in to see a poor family, often staying on for hours to cook, clean and wash up all the pots. That one would be on the side of the righteous, thought Diddy. With Fat Betty stood some weary-looking men in shiny boots and dark suits. The enemy. These were the ones who would dot the is and cross the ts when condemning Scotland Road.

Feigning interest in Bell's side window, Diddy listened to the conversation. 'Many of them sleep in the streets during hot weather. Their homes are riddled with vermin,' declared one of the men.

Betty from the council chipped in, 'And where are you planning on putting them all, Mr Swarbeck? In a bloody field? Shall we pitch a few tents while we're here?'

Diddy grinned. She liked the cut of Fat Betty's gib.

Swarbeck tut-tutted impatiently. 'There's a fortune spent on disinfectation, Mrs Craddock. A house went up in flames not long ago because the father used a blowlamp to burn the bugs off his children's bed springs. And all those free dinners are costing quite a sum.'

'Oh well,' sighed Betty Craddock. 'Like that French-woman with the piled-up hair said just before they cut her head off, let 'em eat cake while there's no bread.' She turned her attention to another, shorter man. 'And don't you start, Ernie Boswell. Your mam lived round here most of her life, brought you and four others up in a court.

485

Remember? Queueing up every morning for your water? It never did you any harm.'

Swarbeck bridled, while the unfortunate and skeletally thin Ernie Boswell shrank further into his over-large collar. Diddy, her nose almost pressed against Bell's window, thought she could hear Swarbeck's bristly moustache stiffening even further before he spoke. 'Are you suggesting that we let these conditions continue, Mrs Craddock?'

'No, I'm not. But we must take measures to rehouse the residents in stages.'

'Where?' boomed Swarbeck.

'Pull a few down and shove a few up,' snapped the fat lady. 'Do it in phases.'

The third man chipped in. 'Scotland Road needs gutting,' he said. 'There's plenty of space further inland where we can give these people a better chance. If we pull down houses and build more on the same site, the filth will simply spread. Eventually, all this lot will have to come down. In fact, if we wait a year or so, much of the area will fall down without any help from us.'

Diddy moved her head and saw the other side of childhood. While the young ones played, their slightly older brothers struggled along with rolls of oilcloth and baskets of bread. Yet they were happy. The Scotland Road children accepted cheerfully their responsibility towards their families. And, like Ernie Boswell, many moved on and made good when their time came, mostly because they were not afraid of work. Scotland Road should die a natural death. In a couple of generations, the young would get up, get out and build their own new world in their own good time. There was no need to put the road down like a sick cat.

'That windmill's an eyesore,' grumbled a member of the deputation. 'Some child will get hurt up there soon.'

Diddy glanced in the direction of the mill, knew that

486

her own children had been up and down the building since learning to walk. From the top, there was a wonderful view right down to the river and all the way past the Rotunda Theatre towards Bootle. They couldn't shift everybody, surely? But in her bones, Diddy knew that it was only a matter of time before the bigwigs turned up with a yardbrush and a handful of meaningless promises. It would be Kirkby and Huyton, families split up, grandparents miles away, kids heartbroken.

She thought about the schools, those Victorian piles where several generations had learned to read, write and calculate. What would happen to them and to the churches? What about the businesses hereabouts? The time had come to speak up, she told herself. With a smile plastered across her face, she addressed Mrs Craddock. 'Nice to see you,' she said brightly. 'Last time you were here was during that scarlet fever, wasn't it? I remember you bringing fruit for the Nolans.'

Betty recognized Diddy. Mrs Costigan was an ally. She didn't want to see the area broken up, didn't trust her elected representatives to do the right thing. 'Hello, Mrs Costigan. Dryden Street, isn't it? Let me see – you've a Maureen, a Monica and a Mathilda – am I right?' Betty prided herself on her grass roots approach.

Diddy looked the men over. Her Billy would make ten times the three of them put together. 'That's right, Mrs Craddock,' she replied sweetly. 'I know you, Ernie Boswell,' she continued. 'You were in my class at school. Remember when your mam sent you down the ha'penny plunge to get clean?' She winked at him, then addressed his companions. 'His cozzy was an old wool jumper sewn up at the hem with two holes for his legs. He had very thin legs, did Ernie.' She sniffed, looked at Ernie's trousers. 'I reckon they're still on the puny side. Anyway, he jumped in the plunge and his cozzy got waterlogged. Came up as naked as a newborn, didn't you, lad?' She awarded the unhappy chap a hefty blow across his shoulders.

Betty Craddock took a sudden interest in a chest of drawers in Bell's window. Her broad back shook with suppressed glee, but she didn't like to be seen making fun of folk.

Diddy addressed the delegation. 'Going to pull us all down, are you? This is a thriving area, you know. There's none of us'll go quietly. Can you imagine taking thousands of us out of here all kicking and screaming?'

Swarbeck made much of checking his watch.

'Look,' said Diddy, 'over there – best piano shop in Liverpool, that is. Then there's Annie's Antiques – she gets people from all over the world buying her stuff. Same with Bell's.' She jerked a thumb towards the shop. 'We work for Bell's, me, my husband and two of my children. There's a big future on this road, because everybody knows where to come for a good deal. You'll take the belly out of Liverpool if you rip down Scotland Road.'

The men shifted from foot to foot.

Betty turned round, her features back in order. 'It would be better to make a positive plan to improve and revitalize,' she said.

Diddy nodded vigorously. 'You can start with the Comus Street courts,' she suggested. 'We'll take care of our own while you build some decent places. The families can spread round and double up, or they can go and stop with relatives for a while.'

Betty agreed up to a point. 'There's sense in that, Mrs Costigan, though we'd need a better plan for temporary rehousing. But I take your point.' She sniffed the air. 'Do you know, I can smell Thorn's Cocoa Rooms from here. That pudding they make with the sugar crust – I remember having two helpings with custard. Then there's Polly's in Currie Street–'

'Stuffed heart, ribs and cabbage,' said Diddy. 'Tuppence a bowl, all you can eat.'

'We are not here to discuss menus, Mrs Craddock,' snarled Swarbeck.

'What are you here for?' asked Diddy. 'For the good of your health?'

A muscle twitched in the man's cheek.

Diddy rattled on. 'What about the Gaiety and the Gem and the Adelphi? What'll happen to the picture houses if there's nobody here to buy tickets?'

Swarbeck sighed deeply. 'Mrs Costigan, the density of population in this area dictates that something must be done. The children are in danger. They are begging for food from the dockers, they hurt themselves leaping across from one entry wall to another, they get drowned in the canal.'

Diddy knew that he was speaking the truth. Jim Clarke, the strongest swimmer in the city, was always being sent for to drag children out of the water. Sometimes, Jim was too late. But however often the young were told, they still spent time leaping into the 'Scaldy', a stretch of waterway heated by the discharge of hot fluids from Tate's sugar refinery. 'They'd play wherever they lived,' she answered. 'Children are always doing daft things. My Jimmy could have an accident in an empty room – that's how lads are.'

'There are too many children here,' replied Swarbeck.

Diddy's eyebrows shot up. 'Oh well, that's because we're Catholics. All we do is booze and breed – didn't you know? Ernie'll tell you about that, because he's a Catholic.' She looked at Ernie and Ernie looked at the pavement.

Two boys shot round the corner on bicycles hired from the Penny Rip. For a penny an hour, they had the dubious privilege of travelling at great speed, usually without the benefit of brakes. Any child who insisted on luxuries like brakes was deemed to be yellow. One rider stopped his progress by colliding with Diddy, sending her reeling against the shop wall.

'Now, do you see what I mean?' asked Swarbeck, his eyes gleaming.

Diddy pulled herself together with the help of Betty Craddock. 'Listen, you,' she said to Swarbeck, 'come near my house and I'll bloody swing for you. Get the places cleaned up, but leave us where we are.'

Betty held on to Diddy's arm. 'Are you all right, girl?'

'Yes,' snapped Diddy. 'But I won't be if these buggers don't get back where they came from. Go on,' she yelled. 'Back to your big desks and your leather chairs.' She nodded at Betty Craddock. 'It's all down to you,' she told the woman. 'And there's only one of you.'

Betty smiled. 'Yes,' she agreed. 'But let's face it, I'm a bloody big one, aren't I?'

Diddy watched the group as they walked away. She tried to see Scotland Road through their eyes, tried to imagine what they would think of her piece of Liverpool. It was a bit smelly, she supposed. There were children cavorting about on tram tracks, children climbing lamp-posts and racing about all over the place.

She thought about Astleigh Fold, its quietness, its cleanliness. It was all right for a holiday, she thought, but she couldn't live there. She needed the trams and the bagwash and the Mary Ellens. She could not bear to consider the prospect of life without Paddy's Market and the street entertainers who crowded the area on Friday and Saturday nights. Even drunken brawls provided a degree of entertainment.

The door of Bell's flew open and Billy stepped onto the pavement.

'They're looking again,' she told him, her eyes still fixed on the departing committee. 'Bloody corporation, bloody welfare do-gooders.'

'Diddy,' he said.

Something in his voice made her swing round quickly to face him. 'Billy? What's happened?' She had seldom seen her Billy crying like this.

'It's Maureen,' he managed.

'What?' She clapped a hand on her chest. 'Billy? What's happened – tell me!'

'She spoke,' he muttered. 'Diddy, she spoke. Edith just told me on the phone. Our Maureen's coming out of it.'

Diddy gathered her thoughts quickly. Maureen had come partway out of her trance before, and Diddy had always hoped for a total recovery. 'Get our Monica off the market, Billy. I'll fetch somebody to look after Mrs Bell while Charlie and Monica run the shop. Jimmy and Tildy can stop at Bell's, too. We'll take little Shauna with us. Run down to Hanson's for her.' Dolly Hanson had been taking care of Shauna during Bridie's absence. It was strange, mused Diddy, how well Bridie got on with her dead da's bit of stuff.

Diddy's heart was all over the place. 'We're going to see our girl,' she told her husband repeatedly as if trying to make herself believe the good news.

Before leaving, Diddy went up to see Sam Bell's Muth. The old woman was standing in the middle of her bedroom, hands reaching out as if twisting and turning some invisible handle. 'What are you doing now?' asked Diddy. 'Florrie Moss is going to look after you for a couple of days while me and Billy go—'

'You'll have to speak up,' yelled Muth. 'I can't hear you over all these bloody machines.'

'What are you doing?' shouted Diddy.

'Piecing me ends,' replied Muth. 'Pass us that skip of tubes, will you?'

Diddy found herself wheeling an invisible container across the bedroom. 'Here you are, Muth.' God forbid that

491

Maureen would emerge from her silence like this, confused and agitated. 'Florrie'll do your dinner.'

The old woman's hands dropped to her side as she paid a brief visit to the present day. 'No dumplings,' she said. 'I can't be doing with Florrie Moss's dumplings. Like bloody lead weights, they are.'

'It's all right,' answered Diddy. 'I've a pan of scouse ready, so our Jimmy can fetch that round.' She watched for a while as the aged lady carried on doffing tubes and piecing cotton ends. 'God forbid,' Diddy pleaded as she descended the stairs. 'Please God, forbid.'

Brother Nicholas always felt uncomfortable in the presence of Martin Waring. This lay member of the community was knowledgeable – far too well-read for a man from a supposedly poor family, a man who had been driven by deprivation into a life of petty crime. Yet there was nothing on which Brother Nicholas could lay a finger. Waring was correct, hard-working and an eager student. 'It's as if you have always been a Catholic,' he said.

Martin sat bolt upright. He had not been a Catholic, had not even existed until recently. However, Martin had been on close terms with a baptized and confirmed member of the faith, but Liam had to stay out of things for now. Liam was not yet needed and Martin was forced to stand alone. 'I have not been a Catholic,' he replied. 'But I have read many books about my chosen religion.'

The senior brother wiped his brow. He had not felt so ill at ease for many years, not since a murder suspect had been arrested just outside the Tithebarn's walls. His flesh almost crept beneath the unflinching gaze of this tall, dark-eyed personage. Perhaps the beard had added to the sinister appearance. The man's hair was as black as jet, while the eyes seldom displayed emotion of any kind. 'So, you will receive your baptism tomorrow. Will you keep your Christian name?'

'Martin John,' came the swift reply. 'John for the apostle dearly loved by Jesus.'

'I see. A very good choice.' The monk shuffled some papers on his desk. 'Will any of your family attend the service?' He kept his tone light.

'No, Brother.'

'Oh. What a pity.'

'Those who are alive are antagonistic towards Catholicism,' said Martin. 'In fact, I happen to have relatives who are members of an Orange Lodge. They would not be thrilled at the idea of my conversion.'

'Quite.' Brother Nicholas glanced at the clock, tried to appear nonchalant. 'Where do you come from?'

'St Helens.'

The reply was rather glib, thought Brother Nicholas. 'I know St Helens,' he said. 'Which part?'

'Eccleston.' Martin's mind shifted into a higher gear. 'Latterly, that is. I lived with an aunt for a while.'

'Near to the park?'

'Quite close, yes.'

Eccleston was not the poorest area in St Helens. So Martin Waring's aunt must have been comfortably placed. 'You stayed with her after your release from prison?'

'Until I came here, yes. Her husband – my uncle – is a lodge member. I could not have remained in his house.'

Brother Nicholas played for a second or two with the idea of research. Perhaps he should look into the Warings of St Helens. But the aunt might have been from the mother's side, and names were always changed by marriage. He sighed. 'There's a task for you on Tuesday,' he said. 'I want you to accompany Brother Timothy to a school in Bolton. It's Sacred Heart. We have been invited to talk to the older girls about our work here. You have a way with words, so perhaps you might like to listen to Brother Timothy. He likes company.' He coughed. 'In this case, I think he will be grateful for company. The headmistress is a Mother Ignatius. She has a reputation as a tartar, but she is open to new approaches within the syllabus.'

Martin swallowed. The name Ignatius was touching a slightly sore spot in his mind. But he could not refuse. Although the term 'abbot' was not applied to Brother Nicholas, the man was the undisputed leader of the *frères.* 'Gladly,' Martin replied.

Brother Nicholas nodded curtly. 'You may return to your duties,' he said.

Martin escaped from the office and stood in the corridor. Liam knew Ignatius, he thought. But Ignatius did not know Martin, so everything would remain under control.

Mother Ignatius swept along the corridor like a very small black ship in full sail. Girls from the sixth form stood quietly by the walls. They were accompanied by three postulants and two novices whose education was being completed while they waited to be received into the sisterhood.

Cathy O'Brien, who had toothache and a passionate dislike for algebra, was seated outside Sister Josephine's office. Sister Josephine was a jill of all trades. She served as bursar, school secretary, meals supervisor, welfare officer and troubleshooter. Because of her total faith in iodine, Sister Josphine enjoyed a reputation for grievous bodily harm. Girls had been known to suffer in silence rather than take themselves off to Sister Josephine for first aid. Many opted to drop blood all over the homeward-bound tram rather than choosing to put themselves in the grip of Sister Josephine and her iodine. Toothache was all right, though. With toothache, you got a bit of cotton wool soaked in oil of cloves. As the good sister did not like to invade the mouths of pupils, girls were in trust to apply these dressings themselves.

Mother Ignatius ground to a halt. 'Why are you here, Caitlin?' she asked.

'Toothache, Mother.'

'Since when?'

Cathy raised her eyebrows and thought. 'Since lunchtime, Mother.'

'I see.' The nun rattled her rosary, put Cathy in mind of one of those ghosts in *A Christmas Carol*. Marley. Marley had rattled his chains. 'What are you missing?' asked Mother.

'Algebra,' whispered Cathy.

'I beg your pardon?'

'Algebra, Mother.'

'Ah.' Mother Ignatius put her head on one side. 'So. It's algebra that gives you trouble, is it not?' The algebra was probably the cause of the child's toothache.

'Yes.'

'Yes, what, Caitlin?'

'Yes, Mother.' The trouble with nuns was that they always demanded their full title. Sometimes, they could be quite pleasant and friendly, lulling their charges into a sense of security that was usually false. Because as soon as a girl slipped into normal speech, she was dragged over the coals because of a missed 'Mother' or a forgotten 'Sister'.

'Do you really have toothache?' asked the headmistress.

'Yes, Mother. It's a pre-molar coming through before the milk tooth has fallen out.'

Mother Ignatius squashed a smile. Young Caitlin had been at Richard Spencer's medical books again. 'You will ask Miss Cookson for extra algebra homework. It is important that you keep up.'

Cathy didn't care about keeping up, since most of the girls in her class were two years her senior. She could always repeat a year. Mammy was rich now, because she had bred the Derby winner and—

'Do not make the fatal error of becoming complacent,' said Mother Ignatius. 'It is so easy just to sit back and think that everything will come easily for the rest of your life. I have had clever little girls in my school before. They sometimes burn out as quickly as a firework. You must strive, extend yourself, reach for better and better results.'

Cathy swallowed a sigh. 'Yes, Mother.'

'And don't sit all hunchbacked. You'll end up with a curvature of the spine.'

Cathy had read about curvatures. According to Uncle Richard's bone book, a curvature was more likely to be something a person had from birth. But she closed her mouth, straightened her shoulders and decided to shut up. Often, silence was preferable, as few of the nuns admired a clever-clogs whose knowledge went beyond the school curriculum.

A sixth-former giggled and won one of Mother Ignatius's steely glares. The headmistress looked along the rows of star pupils, fifty young women who were hoping for university places or a chance to go to teacher-training colleges. 'The two gentlemen we expect will be coming from a monastery. Their order is called *Les Frères de la Croix de St Pierre*. Translate, please.' She prodded her nearest victim.

'The Brothers of St Peter's Cross, Mother.'

Mother Ignatius continued. 'They work to help all those who have sinned. We have all sinned, have we not?'

'Yes, Mother,' chorused the girls.

'But some sinners offend the state as well as God. Stand still, Gloria Baker. You will never be awarded a place at Oxford if you carry on fidgeting. Now, where was I? Ah yes. Men who leave prison are often sad souls. Their families may have moved on or rejected them. So they need a place where they can sort out their future plans. The brothers provide such a place. Work like theirs is admirable.'

'Yes, Mother.'

'You will listen carefully and you will ask intelligent questions when the lecture is over.'

'Yes, Mother.'

'Carry on into the hall. Sit still and wait. You may talk quietly amongst yourselves once you are seated.'

'Thank you, Mother.' The twin crocodiles set off at a sedate pace along the corridor.

Mother Ignatius returned her attention to Cathy. 'Do not avoid algebra,' she said gravely. 'Algebra is the basis of all logical thought.'

Although Cathy disagreed, she smiled brightly. 'Yes, Mother.'

'Mother Ignatius?'

The nun turned to find two men in blue-grey habits making their way towards her. 'Brother Timothy?' she asked.

'Indeed,' said the plumper and shorter man. 'This is Brother Martin, Mother. He is a lay member of our house.'

Martin nodded curtly. He had chosen to wear the uniform of a monk for two reasons. Firstly, he wanted to be anonymous because of Liam. Secondly, he was supporting a brother on a mission to spread the word.

Mother Ignatius swept an arm in the direction of the school hall. 'Our sixth formers are waiting for you,' she told the visitors.

Brother Timothy smiled at Cathy. 'Toothache?' he asked.

She nodded, kept a hand against her cheek.

'This little one would be too young for our lecture, I

suppose,' chuckled Brother Timothy. 'So Brother Martin and I must cope with your older girls.'

Mother Ignatius rattled her beads again. 'Caitlin O'Brien's mother owns the winner of this year's Derby,' she told the monks.

Martin blinked slowly. Liam knew Caitlin O'Brien. Those horses should have belonged to Liam's father. And this was the daughter of the Irish whore. She, her sister and her mother had deprived Liam Bell and the Catholic Church of their rightful inheritance.

'Shall we go?' asked Timothy.

Mother Ignatius remained at Cathy's side for several minutes after the men had disappeared. Sister Beatrice was in charge now, and she would be introducing the *frères* to their audience. The headmistress fixed her eyes on a large statue of the Sacred Heart. The nightlight was burning low in its red glass container. She would change it in a moment.

A door opened to reveal the large, cheery face of Sister Josephine. 'Ah, Caitlin,' beamed the happy woman, 'toothache, is it? Come away in now till I find my oil of cloves.'

The door closed.

Mother Ignatius was not a fanciful person. Although the day was warm she shivered in her summer-weight habit. A glance at the thermometer reassured the chilled lady that the temperature was in the mid-seventies, yet she remained cold. In her mind's eye, a pair of dark eyes glowed dully, almost malevolently, above a lush growth of beard.

Mother glanced towards the hall where her sixth formers were currently in the company of the one who owned those eyes. Silly, she told herself inwardly. She was far too busy to be standing here shivering in the heat.

She renewed the flame beneath the statue, then carried

on with her duties. Having accused many of her pupils of day-dreaming, she was not allowing herself to be guilty of the same misdemeanour. But the pores on her arms remained open for much of the afternoon.

Twenty

Monica-usually-Nicky Costigan looked almost beautiful in her borrowed frock. With excitement staining the pale cheeks, she lived up to her five feet and two inches by walking proudly on this, her last hundred yards as a single girl. The small wedding procession made its way up Scotland Road towards the church, while bystanders placed their shopping on the pavement, clapped, cheered and whistled at the bridal party.

Nicky, at eighteen, was about to embark upon a new life with Graham Pile, the love of her dreams. She progressed slowly towards the future, not because of reluctance, but so that all around would get the chance to ooh and aah over the wedding dress. Mam had drawn the line at allowing Mrs Bell to buy a new outfit for Nicky, but Mam hadn't been able to prevent Edith Spencer from sending over a borrowed one from Bolton. The last girl to wear this lovely piece of silk was now a person of substance who had married a foreman in a textile mill.

Alice Makin narrowed her eyes and took a furtive swig from a medicine bottle. The medicine was a passable breed of gin that had been decanted into a container bearing the legend All Fours Cough Cure. Beside Alice stood Molly Barnes, the retired prostitute whose life was now devoted to the running of the Welcome House. A few of Molly's girls lingered behind the two women. Molly turned to them. 'See?' she said. 'You can get yourselves a proper man and a proper church wedding if you change your ways.' She prodded a very tall girl. 'Lily – what have you come as?'

Lily shrugged. Knowing what to wear was one thing, but having nothing beyond working clothes was another problem altogether. She had rummaged through her sparse wardrobe, had come up with a pea-green blouse and a tight black skirt. Her make-up was toned down to include scarlet lips and a smaller than usual dab of rouge on each cheek. 'I've got nothing else,' she replied.

Molly decided that Lily might fit in very well with a travelling circus troupe, though she said no more. Encouragement was the thing. She had to be positive, had to boost the morale of her lodgers and find them proper jobs.

Alice Makin took another swig of disguised gin. 'It's Bells to the left and Bells to the right,' she grumbled. 'With a few Costigans in between.' Alice's business had suffered because of the Bells. Since Sam's death, Mrs Bridie Bell had set herself up as a moneylender. The difference between Bridie and Alice was a matter of interest. 'Ruined me, she has,' mumbled the huge woman.

Molly Barnes flicked an eye over her companion. 'If you don't stop this daytime drinking, you'll be waking up dead,' she commented, her tone not unkind. 'Mrs Bell doesn't go doubling their payments if they run short of cash,' continued Molly. 'And that's why they all borrow off her instead.'

'It's the interest what keeps me alive,' moaned Alice, her treble chin trembling with indignation. 'She can afford to lend cheap, 'cos her old man left her a bloody fortune and she makes a packet with her stud farm.'

'Shut up,' said Molly. 'If you've nothing nice to say, say nothing at all.'

Alice grunted, then swallowed more 'cough medicine'.

Her business had dwindled to a mere trickle. 'Bloody upstart,' she cursed quietly. Still, Bridie Bell would be getting her eye wiped any day now. Alice had whispered a few choice words into a few choice ears, because it wasn't right. Nobody else seemed to bother about Bridie and Anthony Bell, but Alice's long-ignored religious knowledge was being used at last. The bold Bell trollop and her stepson were going to be knocked off their high horses, even if those horses had been racing certainties.

Molly Barnes, a true romantic at heart, smiled tearfully as she watched the ongoings. Bridie Bell's two daughters were bridesmaids, as was Tildy-Anne Costigan, but there was no sign of Maureen. The girls looked lovely in their little blue dresses, though Tildy was making a pig's ear out of the proceedings by waving and yelling at everyone she recognized.

Billy Costigan walked tall, his elder daughter by his side. Diddy would be waiting in the church with Bridie, the whole of Dryden Street and Sam's mother. Sam's mother was slipping away into a world of her own, but she remained a caution. Maureen should have come, he told himself. She was doing all right, was working at the Sacred Heart school alongside young Cathy.

Nicky groaned. 'Slow down, Dad. Let them all see my frock.'

Billy obliged. 'Sorry, love,' he said. 'I must have quickened up without thinking.' He measured his pace to suit hers. Their Maureen would not go near a church. She hadn't been to mass since . . . for three years or more. As a patient at the Good Shepherd, she had screamed and created when the nuns had tried to get her into chapel. At Sacred Heart, the sisters knew about Maureen's strange aversion, so they never asked her to attend services. Maureen cleaned corridors, emptied bins, replenished ink and chalk supplies, polished furniture. She lived with

Cathy at Cherry Hinton, worked for Edith and Richard, seemed unable to wind down, was always, always on the go.

Nicky waved to her friends. 'Look, Dad, there's Sarah Millington. She's getting married next month.'

'Very nice, love,' replied Billy. Maureen hadn't even been invited to this wedding. She hadn't visited Scotland Road for over a year, seemed happy and fulfilled where she was. Happy? he asked himself inwardly. Would his little girl ever be happy again? But this was a joyful occasion, he reminded himself. Determinedly, he relegated Maureen to the back of his thoughts and led his older daughter up the aisle.

Michael Brennan took a bite of cake, then brushed the crumbs from his stock. The wedding had gone very well, and the reception was loud enough to wake the dead. A ceilidh band played Irish jigs while the populace whooped and clattered about all over Fairy Mary's dance floor. Mary Turner herself was well gone. She had consumed large amounts of alcohol and was giving lessons in Irish dancing, a feat made difficult by limbs which were suddenly disobedient.

'Look at her,' smiled Anthony Bell, 'she's enjoying herself.'

Fairy Mary was a dignified woman who usually stuck rigidly to tap, ballet and ballroom. However, the Irish blood in her veins was responding to the energetic music, so all thoughts of propriety had disappeared fast.

Michael Brennan cleared his throat. 'How's the job?' he asked his companion.

Anthony, depending on lip-reading, smiled. He was enjoying his work in Astleigh Fold. The only fly in the ointment was the fact that he and Bridie were not together permanently. He nodded towards the exit, opened the door and went out to the landing.

Michael joined his friend.

'What's the matter?' asked Anthony. The priest was redder than usual about the face, was twisting and turning the glass in his hand. 'Michael?'

The cleric shrugged, swallowed the last of his cake. 'There's been a slight problem,' he said. This was not the time, but when would he see Anthony again? 'People hereabouts know about you and Bridie. These things do have a habit of getting out.' He sighed heavily, his head shaking slowly from side to side. 'The diocese has been on to me.'

'Oh yes?' Anthony pushed back his shoulders, waited. Let them all think what they liked, but he and Bridie had made love only twice. Anthony had been celibate for almost three years, but that was his own business, his and Bridie's.

Michael shrugged, as if trying to make light of his difficulties. 'Bridie still comes to Communion,' he began.

'I know.'

'And ... well ... someone has spoken out of turn, Anthony. I was sent for. Two monsignors accused me of condoning adultery. They put forward the usual argument – a sinner must intend not to re-offend if he wants absolution.' He coughed, drank some whisky. 'My marching orders would be on the doormat within days, they said, if I didn't make a certain promise.'

'Did you make it?'

'No.' Michael Brennan placed the empty glass on a window-sill. 'If I had absolved a murderer, I would understand. You and Bridie were made for each other – anyone can see that. Folk around these parts know about your relationship. Some don't approve, some couldn't care less, others are happy for you. But one particular person has complained.' It was Alice Makin, he felt sure. Alice Makin had been making a lot of noise about Bridie's cheap money-lending. 'The result is that I am now...' He searched for words. 'I am now blackmailing the Church.'

Anthony gasped. 'How?'

The priest laughed mirthlessly. 'I told the posse all about Father Liam Bell, the missing stole and the probability that he has committed rape and murder.' He lifted his shoulders. 'Stalemate,' he said. 'You know, Anthony, I think I might go in for chess. Strategy is my middle name.'

The younger man ignored the banter and homed in on the main issue. 'So they are worried that you might spread the word about Liam. Will you?' Anthony knew the answer before it came.

Father Brennan sat on the top step and waited until Anthony was seated beside him. 'Too much suffering lies that way,' he said quietly. 'There's Maureen and her family to think about. But I put the clergy in a tight corner, I can tell you. Then, I started to wonder. About wheelings and dealings within the Church, about compromise, about people starving while Rome prospers. It's not the first time I've entertained these thoughts.'

Anthony nudged his friend. 'Will you give up the ministry?'

'Will I hell!' chuckled the priest. 'Why should I? I'm priest right through to the bone, and that's an end of it. There's corruption wherever you look, because where there's humanity there is sin. However, the whole thing took my breath away for a while.'

'I'm sure it must have.' Anthony would tell Bridie. Bridie could go elsewhere for confession. Although she had not committed adultery, had not been guilty of recent fornication, Bridie was in love in spite of Rome's rules on the subject of affinity. The poor girl would be continuing to confess sins of thought and word, because she expressed her love each day on the telephone and each week in writing.

Oh, well. St Aloysius Gonzaga was not the only Catholic church in the Scotland Road area. When she had done the rounds of the immediate vicinity, she could go further afield and confess her sins all over Liverpool. 'Cathy's becoming aware,' he said quietly, 'and we worry, Bridie and I, about the example we are setting.'

Michael rose, walked to a window and stared down at the road. A scuffle had broken out near the Throstle's Nest and the police were having difficulty in rounding up the participants. 'You could buy an annulment, I suppose. Film stars have done it. While the poor and the battered stay tethered, those with money can break free of previous marriages. All Bridie has to say is that her marriage to Sam was not consummated.'

Anthony joined his friend at the window. 'But it was consummated.'

The priest shoved his hands deep into the pockets of his dark jacket. 'Sam wouldn't mind,' he said.

'But it would be wrong,' cried Anthony. 'You know how Bridie is – she won't lie unless she has to.' He lowered his chin and his voice. 'Michael, are you condoning this sort of behaviour, this buying of annulments?'

'Yes,' replied the parish priest. 'My faith is firm, Anthony. It's old-fashioned and long-established, because it goes right back to Pope Peter, to Jesus and to the Almighty God who sent Jesus to us. We mess about with the faith. It's only natural, only human. I want to see you and Bridie married. The smaller sin. You must always remember to measure the odds.'

'So you mean—'

'I mean that the future is more important than today is and than yesterday was. The example you set for Cathy and Shauna will set them up for life.' He rattled some coins against a rosary, dug deep until he held the cross between hidden fingers. 'Anthony, I am in a position from which I might bargain. Bridie will be able to make a substantial donation toward diocesan improvement. And I can assure you that Sam will give his blessing the day you marry Bridie. Let me negotiate an annulment. Of course, there is a second and much more powerful argument, because the poor girl was coerced – even forced into her marriage with Sam.'

Anthony took a deep breath and pondered. Bridie was what Grandmuth called 'a bugger for stubbornness'. Would she barter her principles in order to achieve matrimony with him? Would she be prepared to lie? 'I'll need to talk to Bridie,' he told Michael. 'For a quiet woman, she can be as determined as a mule. But she may well agree if you take the tack about her being pressed by her father to marry mine. I do know this much, Michael. We would both be prepared to lose our Church in order to have each other. That would be later, of course, after the girls are grown and gone.'

'She loves you.'

'I know.'

'Depend on that,' said the priest. 'And the rest will simply follow.'

Diddy Costigan's hat was at a rakish angle, the veil dangling over one eye, a feather pointing due west towards the sea. 'Shauna! Get back here,' she roared.

Shauna O'Brien stuck out her tongue and ran off past Bell's shop. Her dress was ripped right across the empire-line seam, its blue folds tripping her as she made her escape. The upper bodice was smocked and elasticated, and it rode up towards her neck as she fled. Cathy was after her. She could hear Cathy screaming and shouting as she overtook Mrs Costigan.

'Shauna, you'll be flayed,' cried the older sister. 'Come back at once.'

Shauna wasn't going back. She was fed up with bridesmaidship, wanted to get out of the stupid long frock and into something a bit more easy. Also, she didn't like Nicky, Graham Pile, Mrs Costigan, Mr Costigan, Cathy, Mammy, or anyone else in the neighbourhood.

Cathy caught up with her sister, grabbed an arm and swung the angry child round. 'You shouldn't have done that, Shauna.'

'Well, it's true,' replied the younger O'Brien girl. 'She is ugly. Graham's ugly, too. And Big Diddy's ugly and—'

'You're the ugly one,' said Cathy mildly. 'Would you ever take a look at yourself?' She dragged Shauna to a shop window and forced her to view the reflected picture. 'There you are, so,' Cathy said, knowing that she sounded just like her mother. 'With your face all twisted in temper and the dress ripped to shreds. Your ugliness is inside, Shauna, and you'll have to work very hard to keep it hidden.' She shook the small body. 'Badness inside makes badness outside. You'll be a hideous bride, Shauna O'Brien, if anyone is silly enough to marry you.'

Shauna stuck out her tongue, yelped her dismay when her older sister smacked her face. 'You are not to hit me!' she howled.

Cathy was so annoyed that she could not contain herself. Nicky was not a pretty girl; Graham was hardly a handsome man. But madam here had behaved dreadfully, had lost her temper good and proper.

Diddy joined the two girls. A couple of detached hairpins had found purchase in the pale-mauve netting of her

508

brand new hat. 'Don't . . . don't smack her, love,' the big woman advised Cathy. 'She's only a little girl.'

Shauna didn't want Big Diddy Costigan sticking up for her. 'I'm not little,' she said. 'And I'm not fat, either. I'm just right.'

Cathy stamped her foot. 'Shut up, Shauna. You are just about the most horrible, desperate sister a girl could ever have. You steal, you cry and howl for your own way, you upset people on their very special day.' She turned to Diddy. 'Bend down, Mrs Costigan, till I straighten your hat.'

Diddy tore off the offending article. 'It was driving me soft, anyway,' she said. 'Feathers sticking in people's ear holes and me eyes going funny through the veil.'

Shauna stopped whimpering. 'Graham has got funny eyes,' she declared. 'I told the truth.'

'The truth doesn't always want telling,' replied Diddy sadly. 'Sometimes, we just keep quiet about how people look, because they already know how they look. You see, Shauna, you aren't perfect. Nobody's perfect.'

'I'm pretty,' mumbled Shauna.

'But Cathy's prettier,' said Diddy. 'Because she has a sweet face and she tries hard to be nice. You don't. No-one will like you, Shauna, if you carry on upsetting folk.' Diddy liked Shauna, though. She saw past the mischief, past the noise and into a sharp little soul that would settle down and turn out marvellous.

Bridie arrived on the scene. She glanced at the hatless and breathless Diddy, took in the sight of Cathy and Shauna. Cathy was well again, had recovered completely from the iron deficiency. And Shauna was developing into a strong, healthy child and a pain in the neck. Poor Cathy, who had been the big girl for so long, was trying to control the spoilt and spiteful infant who was currently preparing to run off again. 'Move at your peril,' said Bridie without raising her voice.

Shauna froze. Mammy went extra quiet when she was really cross. Diddy sniffed, took a handkerchief from her pocket and wiped her brow.

'What happened?' asked Bridie.

Cathy, arms akimbo, told the tale. 'Graham offered Shauna some cake, and Shauna refused. He asked her why she wasn't eating, and she started complaining about the dress.'

'It's a stupid dress,' remarked the younger girl to no-one in particular.

Cathy picked up her tale. 'She tore the front seam, then told Nicky she was ugly.' Cathy smiled at Diddy. 'And she's not ugly, because she looks great and everybody said so.'

Bridie shook her head slowly from side to side. 'Shauna, you will not be allowed to play for a week. You will bring home no friends, and you will sit in your room after your tea.'

Shauna shrugged. She never brought friends home anyway, and she had grown tired of playing in the shop with Charlie Costigan and his father. Charlie was boring. Everything was boring. Cathy had the best of it, because she lived out in the countryside with horses and very rich people. 'I don't care,' she said defiantly.

'You will,' said Bridie coldly. 'You will care, Shauna O'Brien.'

Shauna kicked the paving stones with the toe of a white shoe. 'I want to go and live with Cathy.'

'No, thank you,' replied Cathy. 'Anyway, Aunt Edith wouldn't have you. The way you carry on, no-one will want you, no-one at all.'

Shauna bit her lip. Nobody loved her. She was beautiful and nobody loved her. Except Anthony, but he liked everybody whether they were beautiful or not. 'I shall run away,' she declared.

Bridie inclined her head. 'Run if you like,' she said thoughtfully. 'But try to be nicer when you reach wherever. Otherwise, you'll be running for the rest of your life.' Bridie spoke to Diddy. 'Bring Muth home, will you?' she asked. 'She's in a corner with a plate of jelly. Then I'll sort her out once I've sorted out this cheeky madam.' With a plate of jelly, Muth could be described as armed and dangerous. Bridie dragged her younger daughter along the road towards a short prison sentence in her bedroom.

Cathy took Diddy's hand. 'Anthony says our Shauna'll improve with time.'

'Course she will,' came the cheerful answer. 'Let's face it, love, she couldn't get much worse. Could she?'

Martin Waring sat on a backless stone bench in the garden at the rear of Tithebarn. With deliberation, he kept his eyes on the book in his hands, refused to listen to Liam. Liam was becoming impatient. Liam was worried about something hidden in a storeroom at the back of a shop. Liam was a nuisance.

He gave up, closed the book, closed his eyes. The sun was warm on his face, though a tiny breeze provided a pleasant fan that ruffled his hair and his beard. 'Go away,' he said inwardly.

Battle commenced. 'You don't give a damn about me,' declared Liam. 'I am the one who hears the voice of God.'

'I hear Him, too,' replied Martin. 'And remember, it was I who held you back. It was I who taught you self-control.'

'You? I invented you,' roared Liam. 'And now, I'm the one in danger.'

Martin was not in danger. He was a baptized and confirmed Catholic who was studying to become a *frère*.

The interruptions from Liam Bell were slowing his progress. An annoying fact was that Liam could have helped with the scholarship, but the priest was too engrossed in his own business. Martin vowed that he would not listen to Liam.

'You'll fall if I fall,' said Liam. 'You can't survive without me.'

Martin was annoyed. He had gone out of his way several times for Liam, had made sure that Liam was up to date with developments in the Bell family. 'Go away,' said Martin wearily.

A shadow loomed. 'Brother Martin?'

He opened his eyes.

'Sorry to disturb you,' said Brother Nicholas. 'May I join you?'

'Of course.' Martin shuffled along the bench to make room.

'You seem preoccupied.'

'Studying,' explained Martin.

'Ah.' Nicholas lifted his head and looked at the beautiful day. He had watched Martin for several minutes, had noticed the lips moving, the facial expression changing as the man struggled to learn enough to become a full member of the brotherhood. 'I think we may have a job for you,' said Nicholas.

Martin gave his full attention to the senior brother.

'We are sending deputations to America and to London,' he said. 'With a view to establishing our order in the new world and in the capital.' This fellow still made Nicholas feel ... strange. It was difficult to know Martin Waring, because the man was too careful, far too perfect. He was almost artificial, Nicholas decided. Brother Martin, still a lay member of the fraternity, did his job well, never complained, was never late for mass or benediction. Yet he had made no friends, because he did not discuss himself, made no mention of his earlier life. It was as if Martin had materialized out of thin air, a new but adult creature who had knocked at the door and begged to be admitted. Who was he? 'Six will be going to America,' Nicholas added. 'Or, if you would prefer it, you may opt for the East End of London.'

Martin sat up and listened intently.

'We feel that you would be very useful,' continued Nicholas. 'You are obviously a clever man and I feel that you would find such missions stimulating. Of course, you would return here eventually. What do you think of the idea?'

Martin breathed slowly, in, out, in, out. Liam kept quiet. This was a decision that Martin should make alone, yet he was fully aware that Liam would speak up as soon as Brother Nicholas had left. If only he could leave Liam Bell behind for ever. If only he could step out into the world without carrying that other person. 'I'm honoured that you have asked me, *Frère* Nicholas.'

'You need not give your answer yet,' said Nicholas. 'Take a day or two to think it over. If you have any questions, please feel free to come to my office during evening recreation. Your ability to teach adults to read and calculate is of inestimable value in our field of work. Literacy breeds confidence among offenders. They are more likely to obtain proper employment once they can read and write. America needs us, Brother Martin, as does London.'

Martin watched Brother Nicholas as he walked away.

'Well?' asked Liam. 'What are you waiting for?'

Martin was waiting for a sign from God.

'I'd be safe over there,' said Liam. 'We would both be safe.'

America. America was a very sinful country. Chicago, prohibition, gang warfare, Mafia, speakeasies. The country had gone through some troubled times. 'We're needed,' insisted Liam.

Martin nodded. He was needed, and Liam would be quieter in America or in London. The concept of putting a few hundred or several thousand miles between Liam and his missing property was attractive.

'Are we going?' Liam's tone was excited.

'Yes,' said Martin. 'We're going.'

'Good. Because that's what God wants us to do.' Liam Bell, having said his piece, was quiet for the rest of the day.

Maureen was waiting for Cathy. Whenever Cathy went away without her, Maureen was quiet, almost sulky. But Richard and Edith had decided that visits to Scotland Road might upset the older girl, so Cathy had gone to Nicky's wedding in the company of Anthony.

Richard watched Maureen as she ran down the path to greet Cathy. He looked at his wife, shook his head sadly. 'Cathy won't be here for ever,' he said. 'And I worry in case Maureen's close attention might impede Cathy's development in some way. The poor child is shadowed constantly.'

Edith sighed, put down her book and removed the reading glasses she had been forced to wear of late. 'Mother Ignatius expressed the same concern,' she said. 'It's all very well Maureen having a job at the school, but it's as if she depends on Cathy for her sanity.'

Richard moved the curtain and studied the two girls. 'That's it exactly,' he declared. 'Nail on the head again, my dear. Without Cathy, Maureen is a lost soul. I wonder why.' Tears sprang to Edith's eyes. For a supposedly tough woman, she had certainly been emotional in recent years. It had not been easy for anyone, but Edith had taken to

514

heart the fact that Maureen's attempted suicide had happened in her house. She should have watched the girl more closely, should have been there to help and advise. 'It's Cathy's innocence, I think,' she said eventually. 'Her cleanliness is what attracts Maureen. Maureen cannot be a child ever again, but she stays as near as she can to what she remembers of childhood.'

Richard saw his wife's expression. 'There is nothing you could have done, Edith.'

'And there is much that my nephew should not have done,' she answered.

This was haunting Edith. As a doctor, Richard felt that he should know what to do, how to help and offer comfort. But Edith was too intelligent for platitudes. The police had found no trace of Liam. Richard had contacted the Liverpool force on several occasions, but there seemed to be no trail to follow. 'I wonder where he is,' he said now to himself.

'God knows,' replied Edith. 'Only God and the devil can be sure of Liam's whereabouts. Mere mortals have no chance of finding him. You know, he was strange as a child.'

'I remember.'

Edith closed her eyes. 'And now, of course, we have Anthony and Bridie to worry about. I spoke to Bridie on the telephone this afternoon. She has confined Shauna to her room for misbehaving. The child tried to spoil the wedding breakfast.'

'Up to her tricks again?' Richard smiled inwardly. Unlike his wife, he had a grudging respect for the difficult girl.

'Father Brennan has suggested that Bridie should apply for an annulment. Bridie refuses. She says she might consider the dissolution once Aunt Theresa has died. Theresa still has moments of clarity, it seems.'

'Will an annulment be granted?' asked Richard.

Edith nodded. 'She was forced into the marriage by her father. Also, Bridie is a rich widow. Most things are purchasable these days.'

The doctor touched his wife's arm. 'It's not like you to be so cynical, my dear.' After thirty years of marriage, he knew this good woman like the back of his own hand. She was generous to a fault, hard-working, cheerful in the face of all kinds of adversity. 'Sam wanted them to be together,' he said softly. 'Sam knew how young she was.'

'They should be married,' insisted Edith. 'It's so difficult, because I love both of them. But Cathy is . . .' Her voice tailed away as she looked through the window at Maureen and Cathy.

'Cathy is not ours,' Richard reminded her yet again.

Edith inclined her head. 'She is the nearest we have, just as she seems to be the nearest Maureen has. And I hate to think of Cathy growing up confused because of our nephew and her mother. Things should be tidier.'

Richard sat down. There were bigger issues to think about. 'There will be war,' he said after a silence. 'Before the end of the decade, Hitler will be growing far too big for his boots.'

Edith simply sighed. 'They know he's a rabble-rouser,' she replied. 'The German people are not stupid, Richard.'

A year earlier, Richard might have agreed with his wife. Even six months ago, the power of Hitler seemed to have waned with the loss of two million votes and thirty-four seats. Yet, in January of this year, an ageing President von Hindenburg had declared Hitler Chancellor of Germany. 'Senile decay,' muttered the doctor under his breath.

'Yet she remains physically healthy,' replied Edith, whose hearing was very sharp.

'I beg your pardon?'

'Aunt Theresa. She's sound in body, absent in mind.'

'I was referring to von Hindenburg.'

Edith sometimes wondered about her husband's fixation with German politics. He concerned himself with atom bombs, chemical weapons, the Reichstag, Italy. There was enough at home to worry about without taking Europe on board. She left the room and went to discuss supper with Mrs Cornwell.

Richard Spencer rubbed a hand across his aching brow. A hysterical and uneducated megalomaniac was about to stamp his mark on the world. The jumped-up little madman would goose-step his way across France, no doubt, would threaten Britain by shaking a small, leather-clad fist across the channel.

With the burning of the Reichstag, Germany had lost more than its architectural seat of government. Thousands had stood by helplessly to watch the funeral pyre of their democracy. Hitler had instigated a decree suspending all human rights in Germany. Freedom of speech and of the press was a thing of the past, while the German people were forbidden to assemble for any reason. Radio stations were now in the clutches of fascism, their programming organized by Dr Goebbels, an expert in propaganda.

'Where will it end?' sighed Richard. Jews were being cast out of their jobs, were forbidden to teach in schools and universities. Works by Jewish writers had been incinerated, while their businesses were being forced to close. Hitler aimed to create the perfect Aryan race. Dr Goebbels was encouraging the masses to rid themselves of the 'Jewish vampires'. Jews were migrating in their thousands all over Europe.

'It's the perfection that's terrifying,' Richard told himself. 'Because from perfection come the largest flaws.'

Cathy ran in, put her arms round Uncle Richard's waist.

He smiled at her, ran a hand through her hair.

'What are you thinking about?' she asked. He was always thinking, always reading or writing.

He was thinking about war. 'I was waiting for you,' he said. The lie was the smaller sin.

Twenty-one

She missed him most when the bombs fell, when she and every other living subject felt naked, unsure and childlike.

It was not too late to escape, Bridie kept telling herself. The war was some twenty months old. If the Luftwaffe's current performances continued, hostilities could go on indefinitely. Why would she not go? Why didn't she pack up, get Muth dressed and ready, take herself, Shauna and the old woman to Astleigh Fold, into relative peace and comfort?

'I just can't,' she said aloud. Many of those who had chosen evacuation had returned to take their chances alongside the rest of their families. Heroes populated every pub, every shop, every office. Men, women and children went out daily and nightly to dig, often with bare hands, in rubble that contained remnants of life and death. This was a brave city. Battered, bruised and bloody, Liverpool remained defiant.

Muth would not move, anyway. In her clearer moments, Theresa Bell stood at her window and cursed Hitler passionately; at other times, she screamed her ire at the Kaiser, the Boers and the warden who waved a stick at her whenever she showed a chink of light. 'Bastard,' she howled. 'It's my bloody house and my bloody shop if you must know.' Often, she called out for Sam and for her dead husband. With her mind and body withered, poor old Theresa was in no fit state to be shifted. She refused to sleep in a Morrison, refused to leave her bedroom except during the hours of daylight.

Bridie sipped at her tea, stared through candlelight into the cage where Shauna and Tildy slept. If Anthony could just be here. If only he were nearer, close enough to visit occasionally. But Anthony had a school to run. He and Edith were in charge of a hundred displaced children.

She stood up and carried the candle across the room until she reached the fireplace mirror. Sam's tobacco tin remained where it had always been, between the clock and a large brass candlestick. Sam had been a good father to Bridie, had managed, in just a few short months, to compensate for years spent in the dubious care of Thomas Murphy. Even in death, Da had been a bad influence, because Maureen Costigan's attempted suicide had been a copy of Thomas Murphy's accident. That last act of Da's summed up the whole of his life. He had taken from people, had seldom contributed to life. He had ridden into death on the back of a stolen horse that was destined to win a classic race.

Bridie placed the candle in Sam's candlestick, looked at her reflection. Candlelight was kind, she told herself. It ran a smoothing iron over thirty-eight years of life, rendered her young again. Anthony. Even unspoken, the name made her shiver with anticipation. With Eugene, there had been warmth and the joy that accompanies youth. Sam Bell had minded her, had altered his spartan lifestyle to encompass Bridie and her daughters. But Anthony . . . Anthony was different.

She shivered, felt chilled to the core because she could not have her man. The Church had removed the padlocks from its gates, had granted an annulment on the grounds of Bridie's original antipathy towards the marriage to Sam. But Muth remained alive. Already confused, Theresa might have been shocked to death by a union between her grandson and her daughter-in-law. It was another waiting game, Bridie mused. They waited for the war to end, waited for Muth to die. And since Bridie and Anthony loved Muth dearly, they wanted her to remain alive, happy and as healthy as might be possible for a woman of almost ninety.

Anthony was forty-odd miles away. In her mind's eye, she saw him standing beside their bed of sin in his little cottage. He was tanned, muscular and very, very beautiful. He was also outrageously funny, causing her to scream with laughter at the oddest moments. When he touched her, she came to life. Without him, she was nothing, nobody.

Bridie smiled sadly at herself and sat down in Sam's chair. Sam wanted her to be with Anthony. Sometimes, when Anthony spoke to her, she saw a little of Sam in his frown.

'Even if we marry, it will be a sin,' she whispered now. The pleasure they had taken from one another was too intense to be pure. Yet hadn't God created man? Hadn't He decreed that the race must continue through acts of love? What on earth was a woman to do when she found the perfect lover? She would not think of him. She would tear up the old sheets she had found, would create some makeshift dressings for the rescue parties. It was silly to sit here remembering the feel of his hands, the sound of his laughter, the scent of his body.

It began. Flinging aside her bandages, Bridie snuffed out the candle and stood still for a few moments. Anti-aircraft fire boomed its quickening temper into the skies. In a lull between explosions, Bridie heard the sickening drone that foretold the coming of Heinkels. The Germans had long ago demolished the fake Liverpool built on the Dee's banks. In early raids, the enemy had killed rabbits and birds, had unearthed coffins in a cemetery, had thrown their loads onto farmland and into rivers. But they were getting better at their job; they were preparing to destroy English cities. Liverpool, a thriving port, was a prime target.

'Jesus save us,' Bridie prayed. She lowered herself into the Morrison. 'It's all right,' she told Shauna.

Shauna sighed, fell asleep again. Tildy, whose ability to remain unconscious was legendary, snored, coughed, turned over.

The ground shook. Bridie pulled a rosary from her pocket and prayed that this prison of steel girders and mesh would save them. A Morrison was supposed to support, pending rescue, the weight of a whole house, though Bridie had her doubts. Yet the thought of being trapped with others in a large shelter was unbearable.

As the bombs hit their targets, she heard Anthony's voice again. 'Look, the Costigans will stay in Liverpool no matter what. Leave the place, please, please. Bring Grandmuth to Edith. Marry me, live in the cottage with me. We can get a bigger place, then Cathy will live with us, too. You cannot stay there—'

A tremendous explosion passed through Bell's Pledges and jarred the bodies of its occupants. 'Our Father, Who art in heaven...' Bridie's fingers clutched the beads tightly.

'Mammy?'

Even Tildy was wakeful. 'What the bloody hell was that?'

Had the occasion been different, Bridie might have remarked on Tildy's language. 'It was near,' was all she managed.

Shauna was sobbing.

'I want you to return to Astleigh Fold,' said Bridie. More bombs fell.

'No,' answered Shauna. 'I ran away last time and I'll run away again.'

Tildy sat up, banged her head on the cage. 'Bloody hell,' she repeated.

The smell of fire hung in the air despite tightly closed doors and blacked-out windows. Many of the people Bridie loved were out there at this moment in this mess. Diddy was with the WVS, Billy had become a fireman, Nicky's Graham and Charlie Costigan were wardens. Graham Pile had been declared unfit for active duty because of his eyes, and Charlie had never been built for war. Dolly Hanson ran her shop during daylight, manned a first aid post at night. Father Brennan, older and fatter, wandered the streets night after night, helping where he could, blessing when no more could be done.

'Nicky'll be in a shelter,' said Tildy. Like Bridie, she had been accounting for those close to her. Everyone was very proud of Nicky. She worked at Littlewood's, which had become a centre for the censoring of all parcels and written messages. Nicky had unearthed from within herself a tremendous talent for code-breaking. She opened the parcels and the letters, scrutinized everything that passed through her hands. 'I hope me mam's not hurt,' added Tildy.

Bridie held on to the weeping Shauna. The bombs were dropping fast, crashing into buildings and making the earth shiver. Then a new sound arrived, half-screech, half-drone, the unmistakeable death-throes of a doomed bomber.

'We've got one,' declared Tildy.

Where would it land? Bridie wondered.

Tildy listened hard. 'Fighters,' she said after a moment or two. 'There's Spitfires out there, Bridie.'

The bomber exploded, caused further detonations, then the raid ceased. Bridie and Tildy listened to the enemy's retreat, heard the ack-ack of British fighters bidding a less than fond goodbye to the intruders.

'It's getting worse,' grumbled Shauna petulantly.

Tildy prodded the girl with a none too gentle finger. 'Do as your mam says – get to Astleigh Fold.' Tildy had a fondness for Shauna, saw in the fourteen-year-old a replica of herself. People thought Shauna was naughty, but she wasn't particularly so. In Tildy's book, Shauna was merely clever and determined. She knew what she wanted and she went for it, allowing nothing to stand in her path. The girl's enormous love for her mother was what kept her here in this city of hell.

Bridie finished her decade, blessed herself and turned once more to her daughter. 'You are selfish, Shauna,' she accused. 'I love you. You are my daughter and I want you to survive.'

Shauna dried her tears and sniffed. Mammy was a nuisance. She didn't understand, didn't try to understand. Mammy would not die as long as Shauna was with her. If Shauna moved away, then the worst would happen. 'I'm not leaving you. I told Anthony I wouldn't leave you. At least he understands even if you don't.'

Bridie sighed resignedly, clambered out of the shelter and groped for matches. When the candle was lit, she set about making bandages. Going outside and getting in the way would not be a good idea. She could hear the running, could smell the burning, but she simply carried on with her task while the proper units cleared away the worst of the debris.

Tildy lay back and closed her eyes. Tomorrow was going to be a long day. As a librarian, she was helping to move valuable books and manuscripts into areas of the civic centre that had been deemed safer. Documents from London had arrived, were to be stored here as a protective measure. London was taking the worst hammering, but would pieces of English heritage have a chance of remaining intact up here?

There was no safety. Tomorrow – or was it today? – after her stint at the library, Tildy would take one of her twice-weekly turns on the telephones. The frailty of Liverpool's defences was only too clear to a woman who sat for two nights a week with a receiver clapped against one ear and a wad of cotton wool against the other. While bombs fell and buildings ignited, Tildy screamed, 'Speak up,' until the message became audible.

She courted sleep, could not relax. Mam and Dad were outside somewhere, as were Charlie and Nicky's Graham. As for Jimmy, he was crawling about on his belly in foreign soil and gore. 'Remember the turkey?' she asked suddenly.

Bridie stopped tearing. 'Oh, I do,' she replied.

'Shop filled with Johnny Laskies and hats and fireplaces.'

'And gramophones,' added Bridie.

'You thought Cathy was naughty, didn't you?'

'I did.' Bridie picked up a second sheet.

'She wasn't. Neither is Shauna.'

Bridie found no answer. At fourteen, Shauna O'Brien was a blonde version of Maureen Costigan. The exquisitely pretty girl had a following of young men, some of which number wrote as regularly as the war allowed. There were letters from all over the globe, plus a few from the middle of some God-forsaken stretch of mined ocean. A twenty-two-year-old Canadian sailor had pledged to marry Shauna when the war ended. Shauna approved of him because he had volunteered.

'I'm no worse than anybody else,' said Shauna now. She had a strange accent, half-Irish and half-Liverpool. 'I don't steal any more and I've ruined no weddings since Nicky's.'

Tildy grinned into the semi-darkness. Shauna spoke her mind and shamed the devil. Shauna had a special courage that few seemed to have noticed so far. She had survived several dunkings in the canal, had become an expert at petty theft, was the sort of friend who would do just about anything for a laugh and to protect those nearest to her. All Bridie could see was the bad side. 'She's as clever as Cathy,' remarked Tildy.

Bridie knew all about that. She also knew that Shauna was a pest. 'I spoiled you,' admitted Bridie. 'And here's you now, tough as old boots.'

They carried on making pointless conversation until the all-clear sounded. It was always like this. The worries and fears were not allowed to show in faces or voices, were kept banked down beneath platitudes, silly anecdotes and, sometimes, singing and dancing.

When the all-clear died away, Bridie ordered the two girls to stay where they were. She stepped out into chaos, heard the shouts, the pounding of feet, saw that the area was well lit by fire. A hand touched her shoulder. 'Bridie? Are the girls all right?'

'Diddy.' The older woman's face was black. 'What are you doing here?'

Diddy trembled, gripped her friend's hand. 'I'm the only one alive,' she managed. 'Twelve dead. Rest Centre. I was out at the back getting spuds. All me mates, Bridie. All me lovely mates, girls from the bagwash.'

'Are you hurt?'

Diddy shook her head. 'Only inside meself,' she replied. 'Only where it doesn't show.' She sneezed away some dust, ran her free hand across her forehead. 'They've bombed the ciggy factory. Flash Flanagan's down there seeing if he can save any.' She achieved a watery grin. 'He must be all of ninety-five, and he's digging for bloody victory.'

Whenever she heard Flash's name, Bridie thought

about Liam. Even now, after ten years, a part of herself continued to expect his return. 'For tobacco, you mean,' she said. 'Come away in till I make you some tea.'

Diddy shook her head. 'No, love. I'm going back. I just wanted to make sure you were all right. Our Charlie's in one piece – I've seen him. Nicky's shelter's still stood up. As for my Billy . . .' She gazed at all the flames. 'He's in the hands of God tonight.'

Brother Martin Waring had not been to America. After due consideration, he had opted to work in London. At first, Liam had wanted his own way, but Martin had stuck to his guns. America might have been complicated for a man without a birth certificate. Born in Ireland at the turn of the century, Martin had lost all his documentation. 'They'll never believe that,' Liam had sneered.

'Can you think of a better one?' Martin had asked.

In 1939, Brother Martin of the *Frères de la Croix de St Pierre* had returned to the North. Although the brothers' original mission remained the same, the order had involved itself in offering temporary shelter to those whose houses had been bombed during 1940 and 1941. Martin and his brothers toiled among the human debris of war, feeding and clothing the victims of air raids.

Brother Nicholas, not quite in his dotage, took it upon himself to ensure that the monks took a few days off from time to time. Many managed to visit family, while others, like Brother Martin, stayed at Tithebarn and took long walks in lieu of a proper holiday. When Brother Martin asked for leave, the senior *frère* was surprised. 'Where will you go?' he asked.

Martin's answer had been prepared by Liam. 'To Liverpool,' he said. 'I want to visit some people who used to know my father. As you know, I have no living relatives, but Mr Dorgan was very good to my parents when I was young.'

'Do you know where to find him?'

Martin shrugged. 'I'll take my chances, Brother Nicholas. The city has received some punishment, I hear.'

'Yes.' The man had never mentioned friends before. Could he really have friends? Within the order, Brother Martin treated everyone with the same cold indifference. He taught with reluctance, seemed content with his own company, had become an exceptional sculptor in wood, retained a magnificent singing voice. Occasionally, Martin made an effort to engage in conversation, but the results always seemed stilted, false. 'Be safe,' said Nicholas. 'And we shall expect you back some time during next week. Of course, you may have difficulty getting there and back. Transport is badly disrupted.'

'I'll get there,' declared Martin.

'You certainly will,' echoed Liam.

Maureen had discovered over recent years how much she loved the countryside. At the age of twenty-four, she remained a pretty woman, but a streak of silver running right through her hair made her older than her years. She spent most of her free time with Cathy, whom she loved dearly, yet she sometimes opted to walk alone for miles across the moors. While walking, she remembered. She remembered how she used to be, recalled dancing in the streets, singing with old Flash Flanagan, lessons with Fairy Mary, the joyous household in which she had spent her childhood. 'I will come home, Mam,' she often said aloud. 'When I'm ready, I'll come home.'

On this bright May morning, Maureen sat on a mounting block and watched the horses. Quicksilver, who was not as quick or as shiny as he used to be, had learned some decorum. With his head over the stable door, he lifted his lip and whinnied at Maureen. He liked her. She often walked about with a pocketful of carrots and crusts from brown bread.

Sorrel was next door to Silver. A gentle mare and mother to several exceptional foals, she made no noise. If Maureen had carrots, she would surely save one for Sorrel. Along the row, more horses looked out at their visitor. It was a happy stables. Robin Smythe kept everything up to scratch, was content in middle-age to produce winners instead of riding them.

Maureen jumped down and dug out the spoils. With everything divided more or less evenly, she fed the beasts, felt their warm breath on her hands, stroked their heads. Horses were lovely. They asked for little and gave their all in return. Occasionally, during sadder moments, Maureen found herself moved to tears by their undeniable beauty.

She wandered off across the fields, picked a few pink-tipped daisies, sat down on a stone and looked at the view. Sooner or later, she was going to make herself recover. Her life was not completely wasted, especially now, because there was much to do while city children needed shelter. But the direction of Maureen's existence had taken a turn some ten years earlier, and she needed to get back on track. The urge to sing and dance had dissipated. Although Richard and Edith Spencer had offered to have her trained, Maureen's wish to go into theatre had died. Would it have died anyway? Or was this the work of the man who had attacked her?

Maureen had killed a baby. For a long time, she had not been able to think straight. Months of her youth had been spent in hospitals, and she retained few clear memories of her time as a patient. But compared to the child she remembered, Maureen Costigan was quiet, withdrawn and joyless. 'I didn't know what I was doing,' she said softly. 'So it wasn't a sin.' Killing the baby had been the worst thing. In her dreams, she often saw a pale child with its arms outstretched towards her. 'I was ill,' she told herself yet again. 'It isn't a sin if you're ill.'

Church was another long-ago memory. Church was the last place she wanted to be, yet she failed to understand why. As a child, she had attended mass each Sunday, had observed the Days of Obligation, had confessed her sins fortnightly like all the other Catholic boys and girls. Then suddenly, everything had changed. He was responsible. That big, dark man had altered the course of Maureen's life. He should not be allowed such importance, she kept reminding herself. Things happened to people all the time, mostly because of other people, some of whom were bad. A wicked man had done a wicked thing, and Maureen continued to pay for it.

The sun kissed her face, encouraged her to lift her head, close her eyes and soak in the warmth. She felt safe here among wild flowers and rough grass. Where else had she managed to feel so secure? At Sacred Heart. Yes, that had been a peaceful experience. With Cathy's education now complete, both girls had left the school. After the war, Maureen would return to Scotland Road and Cathy would go to medical school.

The sound of distant voices reached her ears. Maureen opened her eyes and saw Anthony Bell with a crowd of children. Like the Pied Piper, he led pupils and evacuees across a moor, stopping now and then to point out something of interest. Cathy's mother and Mr Bell were lovers. With her second marriage annulled, Bridie Bell would become Mrs Bell all over again once the old Mrs Bell had died. And that, thought Maureen, was a mix-up. Still, most people had now accepted the fact that Bridie and Anthony were destined to be together. Mrs Spencer had been tight-lipped for a while, but even she recognized true love.

Sighing, Maureen lay down. True love. Had she ever felt that? No, no. As a girl, she had developed a passion for Mr Bell, but, since the attack, Maureen had kept herself to herself. A few youths from the farming community had shown interest, and she had not encouraged them. Now, all who could walk and see straight were away at war. And she didn't want to be married.

What was the alternative? she wondered. Would she go home and live with Mam and Dad until they died? Would she stay in Scotland Road and look after Charlie? Would she become an old maid, an object of pity and the subject of gossip at the bagwash? And did it matter?

Maureen had few talents. She was good at cleaning up after people, had once been a singer and dancer. Her sewing was adequate and her cooking was fair. What could she become? At present, there was enough to do, as the evacuated children required a lot of supervision. But after the war, what would happen? Dr Spencer was getting old, had stopped practising as a doctor. Because of the war, he helped out in emergencies, but he was an old man, was ready to retire completely. Mrs Spencer didn't really need Maureen. Where would she go?

'I've needed Cathy more than I've needed Mam,' she said quietly. Cathy, at eighteen, remained Maureen's closest friend. Soon, Cathy would go off to university. 'I've got to get home,' Maureen said. 'I can't stay here for ever.'

Dressed in ordinary clothes, Martin Waring edged his way along the lane. He had seen Liam's brother in the distance, had heard the sound of childish laughter drifting across the fields. Martin's head was sore. The headache was not full-blown, but it threatened to erupt at any moment. Something was happening to him. Liam was loud, was pushing himself forward so strongly that Martin imagined himself to be shrinking physically.

'It's my turn,' growled the inner voice.

'Not yet,' breathed Martin. Martin was capable of a degree of self-control. If Liam took over, anything might happen.

He sat on a tree stump by the wild hedgerow, closed his eyes against a brightening sun. Liam had brought him here. Liam had forced him to ask for leave, had directed him to this village.

'My turn,' repeated Anthony Bell's twin. 'This is my business.'

The headache broke loose, scattered shards of coloured light across the insides of Martin Waring's eyelids. Crushed by pain, he stretched himself out on the grass and waited for the inevitable. Lately, there had been several battles between Liam and Martin, but the monk had always managed to keep a rein on the priest.

Sleep arrived eventually. Liam roared his way into the dream. 'I've been patient,' he screamed. 'You've had your own way for far too long.'

Inside the nightmare, Martin Waring was powerless. He seemed to be tied down by ropes, strapped to some unyielding surface that made his back ache. Liam was returning. 'It had to happen!' shouted the priest. 'I am your creator and God is mine. It's time for me to pay back all who stole from me.'

As the sun made its journey towards the west, the sleeping man stirred. He raised a hand, fingered the lush beard that covered his lower jaw. A sparrow chirped, scuttered about in the hawthorns.

Liam sat up, took out a white handkerchief and wiped his face. At last, he was back. At last, his time had arrived.

Maureen lingered outside the church. It had been her idea to come here. Cathy, who was fully aware of her friend's antipathy towards places of worship, leaned against the stone wall of St Patrick's. To her left stood Trinity Street Bridge, an iron structure under which trains puffed their way into and out of Bolton's main station. On the right, people bustled up and down Great Moor Street, some with shopping baskets, others in uniform, many bearing a canvas or cardboard gasmask container. 'I looked it up,' Cathy informed her companion.

'Looked what up?' Maureen shook slightly, ordered herself to be still. There was something she had to remember; today, she would remember it.

'It's the feast of St Athanasius.'

'Who?'

'That's exactly what I thought,' answered Cathy. 'You choose to come back to church on Friday the second of May, so I wanted to know why you had picked today. You must be celebrating the feast of St Athanasius. He sounds Greek to me.'

'Yes.' Maureen lifted her scarf and tied it round her head. 'Shall we go in?'

Cathy nodded. 'It's up to you. If you decide to go home, I'll understand.'

'That's not home,' answered Maureen softly. 'I'm getting ready to go back to Liverpool. This is part of it.' She waved a hand towards the church. 'I only want to sit in. I can't go to Holy Communion because it's years since I confessed.'

Cathy was concerned. 'I think he was a bishop.'

'Athanasius?' Over the years, Maureen had become used to Cathy's mercurial mind.

'That's the one.' Cathy watched her friend covertly, saw the trembling. Maureen had worked at Sacred Heart for seven years. She had washed and dusted statues, had cleaned classrooms and corridors, had worked in virtual silence amongst the non-teaching sisters. But Maureen had avoided the chapel, had even refused to clean rooms and corridors in its vicinity.

'If I don't do it today, I never will.' Maureen swallowed, then took a deep breath. 'Come on,' she said. 'Let's say a prayer to that Greek bishop.'

'He might not be Greek.' Cathy kept her tone light. 'He could be Russian. Or Turkish.'

Maureen smiled weakly. 'Does it matter? He's dead and he's holy. That should be good enough for us.'

Liam had managed to get most of the straw out of his hair. A barn was not the best place to sleep, but it had been better than the open air, he supposed. No-one knew him. He had followed these two girls, had ridden in the same ramshackle bus from Astleigh Fold to Bolton, had stood outside a café to watch them lingering near the church.

The dark one was Maureen Costigan. She had been punished, seemed to have benefited from the lesson. The other girl was probably the Irish whore's older daughter. They had landed in clover, these wretched people. Seeing Maureen Costigan had prompted him to dwell on the stole. Was it a stole? Yes. It was in a secure box in the downstairs storeroom. The Irishwoman did not know about it. There was a letter behind a picture in his cell.

He entered the church, genuflected, knelt in the rear-most pew. Nine o'clock masses on weekdays were not well attended except on Holy Days of Obligation. Even so, St

Patrick's was almost half full, because shoppers often popped into a town centre church. The two girls were about three pews further in and on the opposite side of the aisle. Maureen Costigan was kneeling. The Irish one was seated, one of her hands resting on Maureen's shoulder. Liam bowed his head and prayed, wished that he could have a parish like this one. Martin would have to go. Liam would clear his name, would return triumphant, would find a church of his own.

Maureen blessed herself, sat down next to Cathy and waited for the service to begin. She watched the altar boys preparing for mass. 'It's incense,' she whispered to her companion.

'What?'

Maureen turned and looked Cathy full in the face. 'The reason why I've never been to church is incense. Sometimes, I could smell it at your school, especially near the chapel.'

'It is a bit sickly,' agreed Cathy.

Maureen bit her lip. 'Father Brennan probably had it on his clothes, too. I wouldn't take Holy Communion when I was in hospital the first time. The Good Shepherd was the same. Nuns kept on tormenting me about mass, but I couldn't go. It's the incense. It was on . . . on him.'

Cathy felt a tingle in her spine. 'The one who–?'

'Yes.'

A man in front turned and frowned at the girls. Talking in church was not encouraged.

Cathy ignored him. 'Do you know who it was?'

Maureen sighed. 'He was big. He was strong and he stank of incense. I think he was a priest.'

Cathy's hands curled into tight balls of tension. 'Father Bell?' she asked quietly.

Maureen nodded. 'Yes.' Her voice was strangely calm. 'I think it was Father Liam Bell.'

Twenty-two

Diddy Costigan stood in the centre of Bell's Pledges, her arms folded beneath a whalebone-supported bust of immense proportions. In the open doorway, several women were squashing their way into the shop. 'Bertha Thompson?' barked Diddy. 'What the bloody hell's up with you this time?'

Bertha, elegantly decked out in steel curlers, scarf, slippers and her husband's old grey mac, made her way towards Diddy. 'It's everywhere,' she said. 'Not just in Liverpool. There's food riots down in London.' She lifted a hand and pointed towards the road. 'There's talk of the army taking over.'

'What army?' asked Diddy. 'They're all fighting abroad in case you haven't noticed.'

Molly Barnes, ex-prostitute and ex-runner of the Welcome Home, stepped in with her contribution. 'Some say it's worse than what we've had,' she declared. The bombing of the Welcome Home had been taken as a personal insult. No-one had been hurt, but Molly had developed a degree of paranoia since losing her house. 'They say the whole country's like this, all burst water mains, hardly any gas, millions dead and thousands of houses flattened.'

Big Diddy nodded. 'What a shame,' she said. 'What a shame that you lot have nothing better to talk about.' Inside, Diddy felt a degree of empathy with Molly Barnes, because Hitler seemed to be on the same side as Liverpool corporation. If this caper carried on, there'd be very little left for the council to demolish.

Alice Makin thrust her large personage onto the scene. 'There's a rumour that Hitler's landed,' she said gloomily. 'Them with blond hair and blue eyes'll be kept alive for breeding purposes. The rest of us have got no chance.'

'Hitler? Here?' Molly Barnes' eyebrows shot towards the ceiling.

Diddy sniffed one of her more meaningful sniffs. 'He's here all right,' she said.

Silence fell.

'I've seen him,' Diddy continued. 'Sold him a full set of Crown Derby this morning. He was very pleased, even though one of the cups was cracked. He said danker-churn – I think that's thanks – then I said *heil* Hitler and gave him a cup of tea. He's gone down to Champion's for a bed. I told him it'd cost him sixpence, but he wasn't bothered.'

'I'm serious,' insisted Alice.

'So am I,' said Diddy, her tone grave. 'He came in at the landing stage this morning. The Mersey's full of submarines and there's a couple of thousand soldiers goose-stepping up the dock road as we speak. Flash Flanagan's entertaining them, then there's a welcome party with jelly and custard this afternoon.'

Alice Makin waved a fist at Diddy. 'Don't you start, girl. I've had enough of you and madam as it is. I ran a decent business till Fancy Knickers started lending money.'

Diddy drew herself up. 'If you mean Mrs Bell, the proprietress of this establishment, like, she is doing her ablutions.'

Alice frowned. 'Gone to church?'

'Ablutions, not absolution,' said Diddy with mock-patience. 'She's having a wash. All right?'

It wasn't all right. The people of Liverpool saw devastation wherever they looked. Understandably, they believed that every part of Britain was receiving the same savage treatment. 'What if he has landed?' asked a thin woman in a torn frock. 'What if it's over, Diddy?'

Diddy Costigan shook her head and tutted sorrowfully. 'Listen, girls, get down to the water and have a look at the Liver Birds. There was talk earlier on of an ugly little bugger with a moustache. He climbed the building and he's trying to strap an engine to one of our birds. Sounds like Hitler to me. Sounds like he's trying to get back to Germany.'

Alice Makin relaxed. 'Are we talking daft?' she asked of no-one in particular.

'Yes,' replied Diddy. 'And that's what that evil little sod wants. We've Haw-Haw on the wireless going on about riots on Scotland Road. He said we'd tied white flags to our chimneys. Do you know what the German pilots really saw on the chimneys?' The women shook their heads.

'Chambers. Guz-unders. Piss-pots, girls. Some soft sod decorated the empty houses with them. And that's what it's all about. There's no food riots, no martial law, no giving in and—'

'Mrs Costigan?' It was a young voice. The congregation parted to allow the boy in. He strode across the floor and handed the dreaded piece of paper to Diddy. 'Sorry, missus,' he said.

Diddy trembled. The telegram in her hand shook like a leaf in a gale. All around her, the women closed ranks and hemmed her in. They created this wall of support instinctively, as many had received visits from telegram boys in recent months.

Finally, she opened the envelope. 'Missing,' she breathed.

'Missing's not dead,' said Alice.

'I can read,' snapped Diddy. 'Now get out and do what you should be doing. Hitler can take a running jump.'

Alone, the large woman allowed a few tears to wash her face. Jimmy. A real tearaway of a lad, a typical Scottie Roader with his quick wit and quicker movements. No, they wouldn't get Jimmy. Jimmy was a fighter, a stayer, a good boy.

Bridie came in. 'What was the commotion?'

Diddy shrugged. 'Jimmy's missing. You've to go down William Moult and pick up some dressings. Deliver them to all the first aid posts. See if they've any spare gas masks – that soft lad of Mary Johnson's has dropped his in the canal.'

'I'm so sorry, Diddy.'

'He's not dead. He'll be looking for something to eat. He was never any good on an empty stomach.'

Bridie watched her friend drying away the tears. There was nothing she could say, nothing anyone could say these days. Children were dying in their beds; shelters, hospitals, churches and homes were being battered and burnt nightly. Each person hereabouts could quote names and addresses of many dead friends, acquaintances and relatives. Words were no use.

Bridie touched her companion's arm, then went out to do her own war work. The telegram made everything more meaningful, because the fight had to carry on for the sake of all those in the forces. Soldiers, sailors and airmen looked into the face of death every moment of every day. As she picked her way over rubble and across stretches of firehose, Bridie squared her shoulders. The Germans must not win.

She stopped and watched while the remains of a house were pulled down by firemen, saw children playing in debris, noticed women queuing for food. In spite of all the mess, Scotland Road continued alive and as well as could be expected.

Maureen sat as still as a stone on the train. Cathy, pink about the face after arguing, slumped next to her friend. 'You shouldn't be doing this,' she said hopelessly. It was too late now. They had stood for twenty minutes in Trinity Street Station beneath posters saying CARELESS TALK COSTS LIVES and IS YOUR JOURNEY REALLY NECESSARY?, but Maureen had refused to listen to Cathy's argument. 'Aunt Edith was screaming at me on the phone,' Cathy added. 'She said she was going to send Anthony after us.'

Maureen sighed. 'Get off at the next stop. I didn't ask you to come with me, Cathy.'

'But I couldn't let you take off on your own like that. The trains aren't running properly. You might have got lost.'

'I won't get lost.' Since smelling the incense, Maureen had been strangely content. It was easier now. She knew the identity of her attacker and she was about to see the police. 'He wants locking up,' she muttered.

Cathy leaned back and closed her eyes. 'How can they lock him up when he's been missing for ten years?' Maureen must be mistaken, she thought. Liam was a priest. But why had he run away so suddenly? Why did Mammy and Anthony talk about him in hushed tones? Cathy felt sure that her mother was afraid of Father Bell. Even so, how could an ordained man do such a thing to Maureen?

'He ran because of what he'd done,' replied Maureen. 'My dad'll kill him. That's if my mam leaves enough of him for my dad to kill.'

'If they find him.'

'They'll find him,' Maureen's tone was almost serene. She sat back and wished the train onward, willed it to keep going until it reached Manchester, prayed that a Liverpool connection would arrive. She had to get home, had to face the past, had to help her family to survive and find a future.

'My mother will not be pleased to see me,' said Cathy. 'She'll have plenty to say, I'm sure.'

'Then go back.'

'No.'

Maureen listened to the train as it clattered about on its tracks. It went slowly, as if expecting to be derailed by some previously unnoticed broken rail. 'I know what I'm going to do with my life,' she announced. 'I've made my mind up.'

'What?'

'I'll have to tell Mam and Dad first. But I decided this morning. You'll be the third to know.' She turned her head. 'You've been good to me, Cathy O'Brien. Sometimes, looking at you was what kept me sane. You see, I had to get away from home, but I needed to be safe. Really, I don't know how I would have managed without you.'

Cathy groaned inwardly, thought about her mother. It would be, 'Oh, now I've the two of you to worry over,' and 'Why did you not have the sense to stay with Edith and Richard?' Mammy was a quietish soul, but she was capable of being quite angry in the face of foolishness. 'You would have managed,' Cathy told Maureen. 'You would have found somebody to talk to.'

Maureen was not too sure about that. After her attempt at suicide, after the baby had died, Cathy had become her touchstone, her contact with reality. That baby had been Father Bell's. The dread of going near a church had been

541

born on a terrible night many years ago, when she had smelt incense on his clothing. 'All along, I knew some of the truth,' she said now. 'And I couldn't face it.'

Cathy wondered what would happen when Maureen's truth finally came out. She felt sure that her mother and Anthony were already suspicious of Liam. He was seldom discussed in Cathy's presence. Even Aunt Edith and Uncle Richard showed a marked unwillingness to talk about their ordained second cousin.

The Costigans were probably unaware of the identity of Maureen's attacker. Had Diddy known his name, she would have plastered it all over the county. What would happen when Maureen finally spoke up? Cathy shivered. It would be like trying to find a ghost, because no-one had heard from Father Bell in ten years or more.

'He's sick,' said Maureen.

'Father Liam?'

Maureen nodded. 'He must be sick to do what he did.'

Cathy squirmed. Being related to Liam, albeit by a marriage which had since been annulled, was not a comfortable state of affairs. And Mammy would marry Anthony after Grandmuth's death, so Mammy would continue to be a Bell. Cathy shuddered inwardly. 'Does that mean you forgive Father Liam? After what you went through?' Maureen's hospital years had been so thoroughly miserable.

'I don't know.' That was the truth. Maureen didn't know what to feel any more. The deep anger had dissipated along with the lingering smell of incense in St Patrick's church. There was a peace inside her, a contentment of spirit that she had not expected. 'It's really funny,' she said. 'Not funny to laugh at, but queer – you know? As if it all happened to somebody else. Or perhaps it happened to a different me. Yes, I think I've changed. But he has to be found, Cathy. He has to be stopped. If he did that to anybody else, I'd blame myself.'

'Yes, I understand that.'

They reached Manchester, only to discover that no trains were going on to Liverpool. The derailment of a goods wagon was to blame. Maureen and Cathy sat in the Ladies' Waiting Room. Cathy wondered why a request to save empty Brylcreem jars had been placed in an exclusively female area. It was probably because women were in charge of the war, she supposed. Women made bombs and bullets, drove tractors, built aeroplanes and tanks, saved Brylcreem jars.

It was noon. Cathy's stomach grumbled like a threatening storm. She read through a leaflet entitled YOUR HOME AS AN AIR-RAID SHELTER, glanced around at all the grim faces of those who hoped for trains. There was a silence in the room, a kind of quiet acceptance. Women had become professional waiters, Cathy mused. They waited for sons and husbands to come home, stood for hours in lines outside shops, waited for the sound of an all-clear. During war-time, a woman's whole life was a waiting room.

'Go back,' whispered Maureen. 'Your journey isn't really necessary.'

Cathy flicked through a thin copy of *War Illustrated*, scanned a guide for the woman at home and the man in the street.

'Go home,' repeated Maureen.

'I am going home. I've as much right as you to visit Scotland Road.'

'What if something happens?'

Cathy turned the page, found that she was being invited to give an extra penny a week to the Red Cross. Bile Beans were advertised to anyone who wanted radiant health and a good figure, then Rodine claimed to do away with rats and mice. 'Something happens every day. Look.' She showed her companion a picture in the magazine. WANTED, DEAD OR ALIVE was printed next to a cartoon of Hitler. 'Here's the one who started it. He probably blew up the railway track, which is why we're sitting at the station.'

A woman in the corner spoke up. 'We could be here all day,' she said gloomily. 'Come dark, we'll all have to go in a shelter.' She picked up her shopping basket. 'I'm off home,' she announced to no-one in particular.

Maureen touched Cathy's arm. 'We'll have to try for a lift.'

'No. Let's give it another hour or so.'

The older girl frowned. A sense of urgency was brewing beneath the calmness. After all these years, it seemed silly to be in a rush, but she simply had to get home. 'Let's go for a cup of tea,' she suggested.

As the two girls left the waiting room, a bearded man shrank back into the shadows. The station was crowded, buzzing with talk and movement. He watched while Maureen Costigan and the Irish whore's daughter entered the refreshment room. Soon, very soon, his time would come.

Liam Bell folded his arms and leaned back against the wall. He was in no hurry, no hurry at all.

Bridie was used to explosions. She sometimes wondered how she had managed to believe that Scotland Road was noisy. When newly arrived from Ireland, she had found the area almost unbearably busy with all its trams, cart-horses, lorries and people. But now, in May 1941, she was beginning to know about real noise.

This latest blast was awesome. There had been talk of a ship in dock carrying explosives and weapons. Rumour had become part and parcel of everyday life, with the result that many exaggerated statements about defences, fallen planes and bombs went unheeded. On this night, however, all who lived in Liverpool knew about the *Malakind.* She burst wide open, scattering huge sheets of metal across miles and lighting a very easy path for the Luftwaffe.

The attack from the air was prolonged and merciless. No sooner had the *Malakind* exploded than the bombers intensified their onslaught, wave after wave of them dropping incendiaries and bombs onto Liverpool, Bootle and Seaforth.

Tildy sat up, poked a finger into her ear, then stretched her arms. She peered at Bridie's face in the candlelight. 'What was that? It's nearly shaken me out of my cage.'

'A ship, I think. Probably the *Malakind* – I heard it had arms in its hold.'

Shauna clutched her mother's arm. 'Will they get us tonight, Mammy?'

Bridie dropped her chin and said nothing. Shauna should have been away from all this, should have stayed with her older sister in Astleigh Fold. It was probably quiet up there. Bridie had not spoken to Cathy or to Edith for a day or so, because the telephone had suddenly stopped working.

She felt a trembling in her bones as a bomb rattled window-panes, ordered herself not to chide Shauna about being here. If they died tonight, she did not want her last words to Shauna to be angry or critical. 'With God's help, we'll survive,' replied Bridie. She thought about Muth in her bedroom, nearer to the Lord, nearer to the Germans and to death. 'Lie down,' Bridie told the girls. 'The shelter will save us, please God.'

Anthony. While her young companions slept, Bridie allowed her tears to spill. If only he were here with his arms around her. She could almost sense the touch of his hands, was able to recall the scent of him. Fiercely, she clung to the shadow of the man she loved. He was safe, she told herself. Cathy was safe, too.

Shauna, whose sleep was never as deep as Tildy's, moaned. Bridie heard the crashing of glass, felt the ground quivering beneath the mattress. How did Germany manage to have so many planes? A loud cracking sound was followed by the noise of masonry tumbling nearby. It was so close, not much more than a hair's breadth away. The air in the room thickened as plaster parted company with the walls. Someone shouted, pounded on a nearby door, shouted again.

A thin scream pierced its way through all other sounds. 'This is ours,' mouthed Bridie silently. She stretched herself across the heads of Shauna and Tildy, prayed inwardly for salvation as the scream grew louder. Miraculously, the bomb landed behind the shop. The Morrison rattled as if preparing to break. Shauna screamed and pushed Bridie away, while Tildy stirred and muttered a few words about not being able to breathe.

After settling the girls once more, Bridie crawled out of the shelter. The raid had lasted for six hours or more, yet it showed no sign of abating. In spite of falling missiles, she managed to hear the warden. 'Anybody with a Morrison stay in the house,' he called.

She crept past the stairs and into the shop, peeled back the blackout to create a tiny gap. Hell was just outside her front door. Dolly Hanson's bed was hanging out of the upper storey, while the little sweetshop itself was untouched except for a total absence of glass. In the centre of the tramlines stood an angry little woman with an umbrella. As incendiaries landed all around her, she shook her brolly at the enemy. 'Bastards,' she screamed. 'Come down here and I'll wipe your bloody eyes for you.' Kicking and screaming, the old lady was dragged away by the warden.

Bridie bit her lip. There were fires everywhere. Each street that ran off Scotland Road seemed to be blazing. The German pilots, plainly delighted to have such well-lit objectives, carried on depositing their loads on Liverpool. 'Jesus, Mary and Joseph, help us,' prayed Bridie. She could see sticks of bombs sliding down on the city centre, could hear every crash. Liverpool was being put to death, and Bridie could do nothing.

She moved the blackout, picked up some tape and prepared to seal down the dark material. A movement caught her eye. There was someone out there, someone without a helmet. Her heart seemed ready to burst apart when she realized that the unprotected moving target was Anthony.

He crossed the road, hammered on the door and waited until she opened it. He had to see her, had to make sure that she was alive in the hell-pit. After a day spent travelling in wagons and carts, Anthony was ready to drop, but he forced himself to remain alert. Bridie must not be alarmed, so he would measure his words carefully.

She threw back the door, dragged him inside and held him close. 'Oh, Anthony,' she wept. 'Why are you here? It's dangerous. Knowing that you are safe in Astleigh Fold keeps me alive.'

He kissed her, wiped her tears away. 'Bridie, are you alone?' he asked.

She told him about Shauna and Tildy in the Morrison, advised him that Muth, awkward as ever, was up in her room. 'But why did you come to Liverpool?' she asked.

Cathy and Maureen were not at the shop, then. He could not tell Bridie that her elder daughter was roaming about somewhere between Manchester and Liverpool. 'I ... er ... I've mislaid a couple of children,' he told her.

547

'Evacuees. They ran off, and I expect they will be trying to return to their families.' He touched her face, stroked her hair. 'I must go,' he said. 'But I'll see you later.' He dashed out before she could reply.

Bridie paced about in the shop, thought about Shauna and Tildy, tried to organize her priorities. The girls needed her. But they were in a Morrison while Anthony was unprotected. What must she do? Back and forth she trod, hands twisting together, sweat making her hair damp. She struck a match, found a steel helmet behind the counter and opened the door. She would find him and make sure that he wore the helmet. With an old cardigan pulled about her shoulders, Bridie left the safety of her home. The girls would not look for her if and when they woke. She had left them many times to go up to Muth's room.

Keeping close to remaining walls, she walked in the direction of the city. Doors, huge shards of glass and piles of bricks impeded her progress, forcing her to walk out in the open. Above her head, the Heinkels continued to drone and spit out their lethal cargo.

When she reached Newsham Street, she saw that the stables were on fire. Horses screamed hysterically while firemen pulled them free of the building. The gypsies ran about with old prams and carts containing a few worldly goods. Further down, more firemen fought to quench long tongues of flames that licked a terrace of houses. Incendiaries continued to float down from the sky, while bombs fell all around the area. As Bridie stood and fought for oxygen in the hot, smoky air, a hand clapped itself on her shoulder. 'Go home,' said a man's voice.

She spun round, half expecting to find Anthony. But the man behind her had a beard and his eyes looked wild. It was the fire reflecting in the irises that made his face forbidding, she told herself. 'Who are you?' she asked.

He smiled, displaying teeth that were perfectly white

and even. Anthony's teeth were ... 'Liam?' she managed. 'Father Bell – is that you?'

The man inhaled deeply. 'The Irish whore,' he said. 'You know me. Oh yes, you know who I am.' He had arrived in Liverpool half an hour earlier, had made the journey in a van carrying medical supplies to the stricken city. She was shivering. He licked his lips, could almost taste her fear.

Bridie's body was suddenly devoid of muscle and bone. In order not to tumble over, she placed a quivering hand against the wall. The helmet intended for Anthony tumbled down and rolled away towards the gutter. 'Wha ... what do you ... want?' He had killed Valerie. He had raped Maureen, had almost killed her, too.

'From you?' He sneered, showed his teeth again. The light from fires flickered over him, making him look like the devil incarnate. 'Not much. Not yet. Adulteress,' he hissed. He remembered the two of them in an orchard, the man and the woman entwined in an unmistakeably intimate embrace.

Bridie swallowed painfully. The dry air had seared her chest, making breathing almost impossible. Anthony was here. Did this man know that his twin brother was in the district? 'My marriage was annulled,' she achieved finally.

'So, have you married my brother?' he asked.

'Not yet. Perhaps we shall marry when Muth dies.' Would this answer calm him? she wondered.

He laughed menacingly. 'The old hag isn't dead yet, then?'

Bridie inclined her head, said nothing.

'Get back to the shop,' he said. 'To the shop that should be mine. I'll find you when I'm ready. That is a promise, Mrs Bell. I always keep my promises.'

She looked round frantically, strained her eyes for a sight of Anthony. Liam would kill him if he found him. Or would he? Hadn't Liam always wanted Anthony alive and suffering? 'Anthony and I have not seen each other for a while,' she gabbled, anxious to say anything at all that might distract the monster. 'Perhaps he no longer wants to marry me.' The smaller sin, she told herself. A lie was sometimes vital. 'You can have anything, anything you want.' Her teeth were chattering violently. When she spoke, she bit her tongue. 'If you will go away and leave us alone.'

'Don't offer me bribes or compensation,' he snarled. 'I shall take what I want without permission from you.' He clapped a hand against his head. 'Shut up, Martin,' he said, his tone impatient.

Bridie looked around, saw no-one near enough to be the Martin to whom Liam was speaking.

'I'm not listening,' he said. 'This is my turn.'

Thinking that she must be insane, Bridie took a step away from him. Then she remembered. Liam was mad. Anthony had studied, had talked to Richard. Liam needed locking away. 'I'll ... I'd better get back,' she muttered lamely. Could she walk? Would her knees hold her?

Liam stared at her, remembered who she was and where he was. 'I shall deal with you later,' he said.

Bridie ran, was urged along by a warden. In her panic, she promised God that she would not make love to Anthony ever again, not until they could marry, at least. Inside the shop once more, she dived for the telephone, listened uselessly to the instrument's total silence. She was locked in a house with two girls and a very sick old woman. Outside, the Germans attacked from above, while an earthbound madman waited to pounce. She should have alerted the warden, should have asked for help. But everyone was busy saving lives and drowning the flames of war.

Anthony was somewhere along Scotland Road, was

searching for missing children. Why hadn't he come back to the shop? Bridie grabbed her mother's rosary and placed it round her neck. With trembling hands, she picked up a large kitchen knife and Sam's brass candlestick. The thought that Liam might kill Anthony crossed her mind, but she could do no more, could not go out again.

Immobilized by terror, Bridie sat in the Morrison with a candlestick at her side and a knife held so tightly that it felt welded to her right hand. She held on to her daughter, and Shauna flinched and complained because Bridie was hugging her too tightly. Tildy snored, the clock ticked into the few short silences between bombs. Surely morning could not be far away? Bridie prayed for Jimmy who was missing, for Anthony who was in special danger, for the survival of Liverpool, tried hard to quell the fear she felt on her own behalf.

The ground shook as another delivery was made from the skies. Bridie released her hold on Shauna and tugged so fiercely at the beads around her own throat that they snapped. This had been her mother's rosary and she would mend it when daylight came.

She did not sleep, but the nightmares visited her in spite of wakefulness. She could see the man. He was bearded, insane and totally evil. He had come back. He had come for her, for Muth and for Anthony. He had returned to wreak his revenge.

Billy Costigan dragged out the last of the horses. The terrified creature gradually calmed itself once the flames were at a safe distance. The man who led him was big, strong and trustworthy. 'You'll be all right, lad,' Billy kept repeating to the huge shire. He bent down and shifted a sheet of buckled metal with some rivets still in place.

These pieces of the *Malakind* were strewn far and wide, some on roofs of houses, others hanging from windows and impaled in doors. 'God help us,' Billy mumbled. 'And find our Jimmy for us, too.' Diddy could not stand much more punishment. She continued to grieve for Maureen, was now fretting about Jimmy.

The horse whinnied and allowed Billy to lead him into the school playground. A couple of classrooms had been flattened in earlier raids, but the front of the building remained intact. Inside the school, Father Brennan ministered to man and beast alike. Horses chewed happily on hay in a straw-carpeted corridor, while the gypsies settled themselves on chairs and old mattresses in the school hall.

'Is that everybody out, Billy?' asked the priest.

Billy nodded. 'Three dead further up. The ambulance took them away. Is the presbytery in one piece?'

'Yes. I think I've the luck of the devil.' Michael Brennan gave a shive of bread to a tousle-headed gypsy child. 'Have you seen Diddy at all?'

Billy lowered his head. 'They've taught her to drive,' he said.

'I beg your pardon?'

Billy grinned ruefully, raised his face. 'She's been promoted into the Queen's Messenger Convoy. It'll be more than the Germans now, Father. With my Diddy loose in a van, you'd better stock up on holy oil. There'll be broken bodies from here to Dingle. The only driving Diddy's good at is driving me mad.'

Michael Brennan crossed the room and placed a hand on the large man's shoulder. 'I've said a mass for Jimmy, son.'

Billy Costigan wiped his sooty face with a cuff, left a streak of relatively clean skin where the material made contact. 'I'll get back to the job,' he said. 'We lost a young fireman tonight, Father. Pray for him, too. He had the makings of a grand man. Flat feet and poor hearing kept him out of the army, but he died all the same. He was training as a law clerk with some firm in town. Where's the sense?'

Michael Brennan watched the volunteer fireman as he walked away with his shoulders bowed. Night after night, the hastily trained service fought to put out fires, to save lives and minimize damage to property. There were shipping clerks, dockers, lawyers and accountants who worked all day before taking their turn at the pumps and ladders. The local window cleaner, the barber and the baker, all too old for active service, had enlisted to do the same dangerous job. 'Let it end,' prayed the priest.

He checked on his lodgers, then returned to the presbytery for a quick cup of tea. Soon enough, he would be sent for. Soon enough, he would anoint the broken body of some recently departed man, woman or child. As he opened the door of his house, he saw a candle burning on the hall stand. 'Hello?' he called.

'Michael?' Anthony came out of the living room. 'Have you seen Cathy and Maureen?'

The priest grabbed the hand of his friend and shook it. 'No, I have not seen them. Aren't they in Astleigh Fold?'

'They were.' Anthony shook his head as if trying to clear it. He was almost too tired to think. 'Cathy telephoned from Bolton to say that she and Maureen were coming here today. Edith tried to contact Bridie and yourself, but—'

'The phone lines are down.'

'We realized that. So I was appointed to come. Edith is demented. She has several new evacuees to place, so she couldn't get away herself.' He stopped talking during a particularly loud explosion. 'I'm glad Aunt Edith didn't come into this horror. But where are the two girls?'

Michael Brennan had no idea. 'In a shelter somewhere,

553

I hope. So Bridie doesn't know that Cathy has left Edith's house?'

'Probably not. I called at the shop. The girls had not arrived there, and I wasn't going to alarm Bridie – she has enough on her plate. Diddy probably continues to think that Maureen's safe, too.'

The priest sat down and lit another candle. 'Jimmy's missing. Poor Diddy has had enough. I'm not sure that she can cope with much more.'

Anthony placed himself at the opposite side of the table. 'Michael, Maureen went to mass this morning.'

'But she hasn't been near a church in ages.'

'In ten years,' said Anthony. 'After mass was over, Cathy telephoned Edith and told her the tale. It seems that the smell of incense has become distasteful to Maureen.' He paused, took a deep breath. 'She is sure that her attacker was a priest. Somewhere deep in her brain, Maureen remembered the smell. Her decision to avoid attending church services was prompted by that half-hidden memory.'

'Does she realize exactly who it was?'

'Yes. Cathy told Edith that Maureen intended to travel to Liverpool and speak to the Rose Hill police. Cathy is with Maureen.'

Michael ran a hand over his head. 'Is Maureen distraught?'

'Quite the opposite, according to Cathy. But her pennies ran out before she could draw the full picture. We know that the pair of them headed this way. We must search for them. Bridie thinks I'm looking for escaped evacuees, by the way.'

They rose simultaneously. Michael Brennan walked towards the door, turned and looked at his friend. 'I'll see you later,' he said. He reached for the door handle just as the wall collapsed.

Anthony was thrown across the room. He landed against a bookcase, sent its contents flying, then instinctively used his hands to cover his head. Thick dust entered his nose and mouth, and he coughed convulsively against the threat of choking. Michael was buried. Anthony crawled across the floor, his hands clawing at debris, his eyes streaming against particles of dust beneath the lids.

'Anyone there?' It was Billy Costigan's voice. 'Father Brennan?'

Anthony opened his mouth, coughed again, could not speak.

Billy pushed his way into the room. When he had cleared away the bricks, he picked up the door and threw it aside.

'Didn't I say I've the luck of the devil? But don't stand on me, Billy.' Michael Brennan spat out some bits of rubble and tried to stand. 'The door saved me. I've cursed its heaviness so many times—' He spat again, coughed, tried to stand. 'And will you stop shining that lamp in my eyes? Anthony?' he shouted.

'I'm here.'

'Thank goodness for that.'

Billy helped the priest to his feet. 'Are you sure there's no bones broken?'

'I'm tough,' declared Michael. 'After working in these parts for so many years, I've got to be tough. Go and help Anthony.' He struggled to remain upright, sank down to the floor again and grazed himself on a pile of wreckage. His hands shook and he had no control over his lower limbs.

Billy cleared a space, righted the table and a couple of chairs, then dragged Anthony into a seat. Chaos continued to reign outside. There was no sign of a let-up in the onslaught. 'Where the bloody hell are they finding all the ammo?' asked Billy of no-one in particular. 'Because if we're getting this lot, I bet London's in a pickle.'

Michael Brennan had another go at righting himself, managed to reach a seat before collapsing again. He held on to the edges of the chair with his hands.

Billy stood his torch on the table's surface. When the three men looked around, not one of them could understand how two of them had survived. The wall that separated the living area from the hallway no longer existed. A support joist above the door hung drunkenly over collapsed brick and plaster. Pictures and statues were broken up and scattered all over the place with books and papers. Yet above the fireplace, a crucifix remained perfectly in place even though the contents of the mantelpiece were spread all over the floor.

'A miracle,' breathed Michael when he saw the cross. 'Though if God had intended a miracle, He might have saved my whisky. That was a Waterford decanter and a very fine Irish, too. Still.' He brushed at his sleeve and tried to smile. 'It's probably God's way of telling me that I drink too much.'

Anthony ordered himself to stop trembling. It wasn't just the shock that made him shake; he was also worried about what Billy's reaction might be when Maureen finally put in an appearance. Had Billy already seen Maureen or Cathy? Probably not. Surely he would have mentioned such a sighting?

'You chose a fine time to visit the old neighbourhood,' Billy said to Anthony.

'Yes.' The single syllable emerged rusty and dry.

Billy picked up his torch. 'You'd better get out of here,' he advised. 'Tomorrow, somebody will have a look to see if it's safe for you to use the other rooms, Father. For tonight, you'd better sleep with the gypsies or in a shelter.'

He turned to Anthony. 'Where will you go? Bridie's Morrison will be full, because our Tildy uses it, too.'

'I'll . . . I'll stay with Father Brennan,' replied Anthony. He still could not bring himself to tell Billy that Maureen was missing.

Billy guided them out through the rubbish that had recently been the hallway, pushed them in the direction of the school. 'Stay out of the presbytery,' he repeated before taking off in the direction of more fires.

Anthony and the priest stared into a crater that had once been Newsham Street. Father Brennan, who was used to nights like this, sniffed the air, detected no gas. 'What do we do now?' he asked his companion.

'We find Maureen and Cathy,' replied Anthony. He gazed round, listened to the falling missiles, saw flames everywhere. 'They've hammered the docks,' he said.

'It's needles and haystacks,' remarked Michael. 'The two girls could be anywhere. They could be right under our noses, or in the middle of Liverpool, or—'

'Dead,' said Anthony.

'Don't say that.' Michael Brennan loosened the dog collar and grabbed Anthony's arm. 'Come on,' he muttered. 'We'll find nothing while we stand here. And if the lunatics in the sky carry on like this, I'd prefer to be a moving target.'

'Father?'

Both men swung round. Beneath layers of grime, Cathy's face was troubled. 'We just got here,' she said. 'Maureen's in the school talking to the horses. She's become fond of horses.'

'Where have you been?' asked Anthony. His heart did a somersault. They were alive and well and he could have danced for joy had he not been exhausted. 'And why on earth did you come back here? Couldn't you have waited?'

Cathy pushed a lock of hair from her face. 'Maureen was the one who wouldn't wait. I don't blame her, either, because everything came back to her in a terrible rush at St Patrick's.' She fixed her gaze on Anthony. 'Was it your brother? Was it?'

'I think so.' Anthony forced himself to meet her eyes. 'We told the police years ago, Cathy. But he disappeared. Maureen didn't want to talk about things, and we had no tangible proof, so ... so that's why it has dragged on. Forcing Maureen to go over the event would have damaged her even further. I'm sorry.' He felt useless and stupid, tired beyond measure.

Michael intervened. 'You are not responsible in any way for your brother's sins,' he said. 'Cathy, you must not blame Anthony.'

'I don't,' she answered.

'And Liam...' began Anthony. 'He's sick. He's always been sick, I think.' He glanced upward, saw that the sky was still populated by planes. 'Inside,' he ordered. 'We'll get under the headmaster's table.' He led the way into St Aloysius Gonzaga.

Maureen was stroking the white-blazed nose of a chestnut carthorse. She was cleaner than Cathy, was certainly calmer. 'Father,' she said, 'how are you?'

Michael Brennan took the girl's hand. 'I'd be well enough if the fellows above would kindly stop trying to kill me. And yourself?'

'Better,' she replied. 'Better than I've been in years.'

'That's good news.' The priest shunted everyone into the headmaster's office. After checking the blackout, he lit an oil lantern and ordered everyone under the sturdy table.

'Three different trains, two lorries and a very long walk,' remarked Cathy. 'We got a cup of tea from a first aid post.

Some of the lines are up, so the trains can only go short distances.' She patted Maureen's hand. 'Maureen never flinched through all this.' Cathy waved a hand upward. 'I was scared to death. How long has it gone on?'

Anthony, whose watch had stopped, judged the time to be about three in the morning. According to Father Brennan, the raids had begun just after eight o'clock. 'Seven hours or so. Are you wearing a watch?' he asked the priest.

'No. But this has gone on all night. There were a couple of lulls lasting ten or fifteen minutes, but they seem to want to carry on for ever. There will be a lot of casualties, I fear.'

'Where's my mother?' asked Cathy.

'In a Morrison at the shop.' Father Brennan covered his ears, waited for another near-miss to happen. When the earth stopped shaking, he carried on with the conversation. 'Maureen's daddy is a fireman – he's somewhere fairly near – and Diddy's driving a lorry or a van. She's rescuing the newly bombed.' He decided to say nothing about Maureen's missing brother. 'Charlie's a warden, doing a grand job. Tildy-Anne will be with Bridie, and Nicky goes to a public shelter. Everyone is safe, please God.'

Maureen smiled. 'Have you heard from Father Liam at all?'

Anthony felt his pores opening.

'No,' replied Michael Brennan. 'Not for years.'

'He disappeared into thin air,' said Anthony. 'He was supposed to be going to Africa, but we're sure he didn't.'

More bombs fell. 'Will there be anyone alive tomorrow?' asked Cathy of no-one in particular.

'You'd be amazed,' answered the parish priest. 'They crawl out of the smallest and silliest places quite unhurt. There was one poor fellow slipped down inside the tippler lavatory. He was stuck there all night until a warden found him. I'm told he complained more about the smell than the bombs.'

After an awkward silence, Maureen spoke again. 'I have come here to report everything that happened. I must talk to the police. You see, I'm afraid that he might do something to someone else. I couldn't bear to think of another girl going through such a terrible time.' She looked at Anthony. 'I'm sorry,' she murmured. 'Sorry for you.'

Anthony could manage no reply.

Cathy reached across and squeezed the hand of the man who was loved by Bridie. When Grandmuth died, Anthony would cease to be a stepbrother and would become a stepfather to her and Shauna. 'Anthony, it's all right. We all know how he used to hurt you. Like you said, he's sick in his head and can't help himself.'

Anthony bit his lip. 'Give us a few minutes, girls,' he managed eventually. 'Then we'll go to Bridie and get a bite to eat. The police will be up to their eyes in trouble tonight, so you'd better leave seeing them until daylight. Just let this raid die off a bit.' He thought about Diddy and Billy, wondered how they would react, what they would say when they found out that Anthony, Bridie and Father Brennan had suspected Liam for so many years.

They stayed under the table for a long time, each with his or her own thoughts, every one clinging to the nearest person while bombs crashed to earth. So far, it had been a very long night.

He stood outside the shop, pressing his body against the wall in order to conceal himself as well as possible. Bombers droned above his head, while anti-aircraft fire continued to boom from the city's gun sites. From his pocket, he took a large handkerchief before stooping to pick up a sharp stone. If he timed his actions well, he would get into Bell's without attracting attention to his behaviour.

When a missile hit the ground some hundred yards away, he lifted an arm to protect his face from flying glass as he broke the side window of the shop. With the handkerchief wound around his fingers, he removed the glazing and stepped into a display of mops, buckets and scrubbing brushes.

The blackout panel fell away and clattered among ironmongery. Liam strode into the shop, saw her standing next to a counter with a lighted candle in her hand. 'I didn't bother to knock,' he said. 'Because this is my home, you see.' He brushed dust from his sleeves and walked towards her. 'You stole my property, Mrs O'Brien.' He grinned, displaying his teeth in a menacing way. 'Your other daughter is out there, Mrs Bell. Do you prefer to be called Bell? Your daughter, your Cathy. She's in Liverpool waiting for a bomb to hit her. She is on her way to you. So is Maureen Costigan. They'll never get here, because the world is on fire tonight.'

Bridie was terrified. Cathy, Cathy. The waking nightmares had plagued Bridie, had driven her out of the shelter. She needed space, needed air. For what had seemed an endless time, she had stood in one position with the candlestick in one hand, the knife in the other. Mammy's broken rosary was in a pocket of her cardigan.

She stared at him, knew that her feet had solidified. Where was Cathy? Was she really on her way here, or had Liam made up the story to cause further torment? Her breathing quickened when she imagined Cathy out there with all the bombs.

'Are you alone?' he barked.

She nodded jerkily.

'Your younger daughter?'

'In ... in a shelter.' That was the truth. He must not

touch Shauna, must not touch Tildy. Cathy, Cathy. Where was Cathy?

Anthony, too, was in the area, though Liam had made no mention of him. Had Anthony followed the girls? she wondered. He had talked about missing children ... Her breathing quickened when she thought about Cathy wandering the city streets during this heavy raid.

'Are you really alone?' he asked.

She was not alone, but she did not want to lead him to Shauna and Tildy. 'Yes,' she lied, opting once again for the smaller offence.

He looked around the shop. 'I need to go into the storeroom – the one in the living room.' The letter from Sam to Bridie, the letter he had intercepted and concealed in his cell, had revealed the hiding place. That stole was in a box behind a heavy cabinet. She would not have discovered it, he felt sure. Some of dad's secret caches had been almost impossible to penetrate. 'There is something of mine in there,' he said.

There was something of Bridie's in the living room, too. Bridie's something was a living, breathing child in a Morrison. 'You can't go in there,' she said. 'The storeroom was ... was hit. It has been declared unsafe.' Did several small sins build up to become mortal?

'Nevertheless, I intend to take what is mine.'

With panic pounding in her breast, Bridie backed away until she stood at the bottom of the stairs. 'No,' she said.

A temporary silence was broken by shells from a gun site. 'I shall do exactly as I please,' he snarled. Anger rushed into his temples, made him hot and uncertain. Martin was talking to him, was telling him to leave well alone. 'Shut up,' snapped Liam.

Bridie, who had not spoken, felt the hairs on her arms standing up. If she retreated any further, she would be in the living room where Shauna and Tildy lay in their cage.

Screaming was not an option, as that would either alert the girls or be drowned by the noises outside. She should have told the warden, should have sent for help.

'No more, Liam,' begged Martin.

Liam shrugged off his alter ego and advanced on his prey. 'You must be punished,' he said. 'You were having lovers' quarrels with my brother long before Dad's death. Now, you are no more than a harlot, no better than a street whore.'

Bridie tried to swallow the panic. 'Stay away from me,' she whispered.

He looked at her. The candlelight made her young, waif-like and almost ethereal. 'You look like a dead child,' he said, his tone softer, gentler.

Bridie ran a dry tongue over her lower lip. 'I am no child, Liam.'

The man frowned. 'I am Brother Martin Waring,' he told her. 'I am one of the *Frères de la Croix de St Pierre*.' He shook himself, literally forced his body into a series of spasms. 'No, no, I am Liam. This is Liverpool, so it's my turn.'

She tried to smile, failed abysmally. The mother had to win, had to protect her innocent child. Bridie forced herself to speak. 'Tell me what you want and I shall get it for you. A priest or a brother should not go into an unsafe room. Describe whatever you need, then I can fetch it.'

Liam Bell was not going to be confused or confounded by this small and unimportant female. He silenced Martin by stepping forward and grabbing the candlestick. She struggled, seemed quite strong for a person of such small stature. The candle tumbled and was snuffed out, but the fallen blackout allowed in light from the side window. Flames cast eerie shadows, made monsters of items stacked all round the room.

As if in a dream, Bridie felt her arm lifting itself from

her side. Slowly, slowly, the knife in her hand slid through fabric, pierced skin, sliced its way into the man's shoulder. Blood poured, splashed, hit her face.

Feeling no pain, he used the candlestick to smash the knife from her grip. He licked his lips, smiled, ripped the clothes from her upper body, tugged at her hair until it tumbled free of its grips. The familiar excitement was back, the thrill of half-remembered pleasures from long, long ago. Power was pleasure and pleasure was power and Martin was silent. He lifted her effortlessly, seemed not to notice when she rained blows on his face. When she lay across the counter, he smashed a fist into her face and made her quiet.

Like a lover, he peeled away the rest of Bridie's clothing, was almost tender towards her. Unconscious, she was a thing of beauty, an item he needed to possess. While owning her for a short time, he would cleanse her body and pray over her misguided soul. The punishment must fit the crime; he must not be gentle, must not linger in order to prolong his own physical enjoyment.

He ran his hands the length of her body, felt the satin smoothness of her skin, the warmth that emanated from the whore. They had all been warm, had all oozed an earthy heat that needed to be quenched and driven out. God had sent him here to purify, to make whole this poor sinner.

Stepping back and fumbling with his own clothing, Liam made contact with another human. As he swung round, a terrible pain coursed through his head, causing flashes of coloured light to appear all round the shop. As he sank to the floor, he sighed sadly, because he had failed to punish the woman.

Bridie moaned and stirred, felt the soreness in her jaw, was immediately aware of her nakedness.

'He didn't do it, Mammy. He didn't. He was getting

ready, so I hit him with this.' Shauna waved the poker. 'I think I've killed him.' All through the war, Shauna had stayed with her mother, had waited for something terrible. This was the something. This was why she had remained in Scotland Road. Shauna felt sick, inhaled through her mouth to stop the nausea.

Bridie sat up, stared at her daughter. She tried to speak, failed. Her body trembled and her face was sore. Breathing slowly, she waited for a modicum of calmness to return. 'Give me the poker,' she said finally. She took the weapon from Shauna, gripped it hard, stood over the man's body. 'Find some clothes, Shauna,' she said. 'A coat – anything for me to wear.'

Shauna was riveted to the spot. She had just clouted a man hard enough to kill him. It was as if she had blocks of ice rather than feet attached to her legs, and a cold sweat was pouring down her forehead and into her eyes. 'Mammy, I can't move.'

Bridie drank in the shadowy sight of her beautiful daughter. She had been so wrong about each of her children, had worried too much, had judged them prematurely. Cathy had been a thief because she had stolen in order to provide for the truly wretched. Shauna was dubbed a madam because she spoke her mind and shamed the devil himself. Shauna O'Brien had the makings of a brave and powerful woman. While the creature lay motionless on the floor, Bridie spoke to her daughter. 'I love you, Shauna,' she said. 'I really do love you very much.'

'I love you, Mammy. But I'd be a lot more use if I could walk.'

'You'll walk,' said Bridie thickly. 'In a minute, you will go and find my clothes. Thank you, Shauna. I shall never forget what you did for me tonight.'

Galvanized by her mother's naked vulnerability, Shauna

pointed to the poker. 'Belt him with that if he moves,' she ordered. 'I'll find you something to wear, then I'll wake Tildy.' She staggered out towards the living quarters.

Bridie leaned against the counter, watched the man closely, knew that he continued to breathe. Where was Cathy? Had Liam been lying, had he been Liam, had he been Martin?

'Bridie? Is that you now?'

She did not turn when she heard the familiar voice. Her job was to guard the man on the floor. The fact that she was naked did not matter. Nothing mattered, nothing beyond the watching of Liam Bell. 'Yes, Father Brennan,' she answered automatically . . .

'Bridie?'

Her mouth was sore, the lips swelling after that cruel blow from Liam. 'I have no clothes on,' she mentioned almost casually.

The priest tut-tutted his way into the shop, causing a clatter of buckets to travel across oilcloth. 'This is no way to go visiting,' he pretended to grumble. 'I'm not used to coming in through windows. It's all a bit much for a man of my years.'

'Father, please . . .'

He removed his cape and spread the dark garment across her shoulders. 'What has happened here, child?'

She sobbed, bit back the pain. 'I've been attacked. It's Liam.'

'What?'

'Here on the floor. That's Father Liam Bell.'

Michael Brennan looked down at the bearded man. A shiver passed through him as he recalled how he had shared a home with Liam Bell, how he had broken bread with a lunatic. 'Are you sure?' he asked.

She nodded and continued to fight the tears.

The priest prodded Liam with the toe of his shoe. 'Tell me now, were you raped?'

'No,' answered Bridie, her eyes still fixed to the shadowy figure on the floor.

'Thank God for that. You managed to save yourself.'

Bridie placed a hand on Michael's arm. 'Shauna saved me,' she said. 'She belted him with the poker. He probably has a broken skull.'

'That's a good girl. You have two daughters to be proud of.'

'I know.' Bridie continued to watch the motionless figure on the floor. 'He says that Cathy and Maureen are here. Is that true?'

'Yes, they're here.'

'But why? Weren't they safer back in Astleigh Fold?'

'Of course. But Anthony came to find the girls. It seems that Maureen went to mass with Cathy. In the church, Maureen finally realized the identity of the attacker. In spite of Cathy's pleading, Maureen insisted on coming home to see the police.'

Shauna appeared in the doorway. 'Your clothes, Mammy.' She placed a bundle on the counter. 'Hello, Father.' She turned to Bridie. 'Tildy's getting dressed. We can't stay here, not after what's happened.'

Bridie took the clothing and dressed herself in relative privacy at the foot of the stairs. Waking Muth would be a waste of time, she decided. Muth would not leave the house, no matter what the Germans threw at her. All fingers and thumbs, Bridie struggled with buttons and stockings.

Tildy joined her. 'What's going on?' she asked.

Bridie could not bring herself to tell her. 'Go through to the shop. Someone has broken in. Father Brennan and Shauna are there.'

Tildy, Shauna, Bridie and Father Brennan stood round the inert body in the shop. 'Who is it?' asked Tildy.

'Father Bell,' replied the priest.

'What's he doing here?'

Bridie looked into Michael Brennan's eyes. 'We're not sure,' she replied carefully.

Shauna took charge, unlocked and opened the front door. 'Mammy, get hold of one of his feet – Tildy, take the other one.' With Michael Brennan and Shauna O'Brien at the heavy end, the four of them dragged Liam outside.

Father Brennan took a whistle and sent a long blast along Scotland Road. After several seconds, a warden and a policeman put in an appearance. 'Take him, lock him up,' said the priest. He glanced skyward, saw a lone bomber making its weary way home. As it faltered its way over Liverpool, the guns fired and finished it off. In a blaze of flame, the plane dived into the Mersey.

The priest took aside the warden and the policeman, told them to guard Liam well. 'I shall be along to the station in the morning,' he said. 'Just keep him safe.' He tugged at Bridie's arm. 'Come along now. We'll go to the school. Anthony is there taking care of Cathy and Maureen.'

'Our Maureen?' asked Tildy, her voice shrill. 'What's she doing here?'

'You'll know soon enough,' replied Bridie.

They left Liam with his guards, then began the walk towards St Aloysius Gonzaga.

For a reason she would never be able to explain in a million years, Bridie suddenly stopped, turned and retraced her steps. Shauna made to follow her mother, but Michael held her back. 'The bombing seems to be over,' he said. 'Let her go. She'll be back in a few minutes.'

Bridie gave Liam and his companions a wide berth, ran

through the shop and into the living room. From the mantelpiece, she took a small green tin, opened it, sniffed at its contents. The scent of tobacco still lingered, though the box contained little more than dried dust. 'Sam,' she said, 'thanks for looking after us. Wherever you are, I know you are keeping an eye on me and mine.' She slipped the tin into her pocket and returned to the shop.

She heard a vehicle stopping outside, knew that Sam's son was being taken away. Oh, Sam. Always, always, she would keep the tobacco tin.

Bridie looked at the counter on which she had almost been raped, took in the broken window and the scattered ironmongery. The feeling that she would never come back here was strong. She gazed on the piles of books, the mangles and dolly tubs, the sewing machine in a corner, a violin on a shelf.

Prodded by an invisible hand, she left Bell's Pledges and ran towards the church. When the small group had reached Newsham Street, the temporary silence was broken once more by the sound of engines overhead. A crippled Heinkel stumbled across the sky. It seemed so low that anyone might have reached up and touched it.

'He's going home,' said Tildy wearily.

The plane seemed to be dropping by the second. To ease its journey, it released the rest of its load onto Scotland Road. Bridie stood open-mouthed while Sam's shop disappeared in the space of two seconds. She held the tobacco tin tightly in her hand. 'I'm sorry, Sam,' she said inwardly. 'All your hard work gone.' Dirty air rushed at them, caused everyone but Shauna to turn away.

Shauna ran screaming down the road. 'Muth!' she cried. 'Muth, I'm coming.'

Bridie spat out the dust and chased her daughter. 'Shauna! You can't do anything, you can't, you can't!'

The two of them stood at the edge of smouldering ruins. Through clouds of smoke and dirt, they looked into a hole that was once their home.

'There's still the staircase, Mammy,' sobbed Shauna. 'Look at that. Stairs that go nowhere. And Muth is dead, Mammy. Poor Muth.'

Bridie clung to her child. Three brass balls, still attached to their moulded moorings, lay at her feet. The mangle nearest the door remained intact, as did the sewing machine. She shuddered, passed a handkerchief to Shauna, who was weeping softly. Death had been inches and seconds away when she had returned for Sam's tin. Between her shoulder blades, she still felt the strange touch that had propelled her to safety. 'It could be my imagination,' she said. 'But it was as if Sam had pushed me out of there.'

'No, Mammy,' sobbed Shauna. 'It wasn't your imagination. It was Sam. He saved us. He loved us, just as Anthony does.'

Bridie, who had worried herself to the verge of illness about how her children would accept Anthony, knew that she was forgiven. God was the architect, no doubt. But Sam had surely contributed something towards the plan.

Twenty-three

Bridie looked through the small window, saw a bed with a motionless figure lying beneath a white coverlet. Liam had been sedated and the stab wound was stitched and healing. After recovering from the blow to his head, he had become agitated, had screamed at someone called Martin, who, in turn, had given Liam a few tellings-off. His skull was not fractured, though a sizeable bump had appeared on the side of his head. Even now, days after the event, a large, purple bruise sat over one eye.

'He's still asleep,' said Bridie. She looked at the rest of the company, each one of them sitting in a chair against the wall of a green-painted corridor. The floor was brown linoleum, and a nasty mêlée of scents fought in the air – disinfectant challenging polish, overcooked cabbage warring with the sad odour of sick flesh.

Brother Nicholas had been summoned to the prison hospital. Bridie had remembered, eventually, most of what Liam had said, had passed on as much information as possible. Brother Martin Waring really was a *Frère de la Croix de St Pierre*. 'An odd sort of chap,' Brother Nicholas had said earlier. 'Yet so very diligent.' The good brother sat now with a rosary in his hands. He prayed for the man who had been arrested, prayed for Liam Bell's victims and for world peace. The monk he had known for many years was twice ordained and was two people. Father Liam Bell had been arrested, but Brother Martin Waring would also be paying the price.

Anthony Bell drew the woman he loved into a chair next to his. 'Stop punishing yourself, Bridie,' he told her. 'None of us knew where he was; Brother Nicholas did not know Liam's true identity. There is no blame.'

The monk stopped praying for a few moments. 'Martin Waring is the predominant persona,' he told the group. 'I do not know Father Liam Bell. None of the brothers knew him.' He fiddled with the rosary, frowned with the effort of remembering. 'On a few occasions, he has been heard talking to himself, but that sort of behaviour is not rare in a community such as ours. Many of us pray aloud while working, as it concentrates the mind. But we are a friendly lot, and Martin was close to nobody. He is a very unusual man. After talking to the doctors here, I think Liam and Martin were communicating with one another for much of the time at Tithebarn. Such a pity.'

Diddy Costigan blew her nose loudly on a snow-white handkerchief. She had come here to kill a man who no longer existed. Billy kept scratching his head as if confused, and Diddy understood his feelings perfectly. Liam Bell, that bloody awful priest, had raped Maureen. There was still no real proof, yet Diddy knew in her bones that the man behind the nearby door was the guilty party. But he wasn't guilty, because he wasn't Liam; he wasn't Father Liam because he was crackers. 'Did he know who he was when he did it?' she asked of anyone who might be listening.

Anthony answered as best he could. 'He probably did, though he had no control. He invented Martin Waring as a means of hiding from his past. But Martin became real. If my brother has a better side, then he has invested it in Martin.'

'What's going to happen?' asked Father Michael Brennan.

Richard Spencer rose from his chair and walked to the door of Liam's room. 'He's unfit for trial,' he said. 'No court on earth will manage to get sensible answers out of him.' He dropped his chin, stared at the floor for a few seconds. 'He'll be locked away,' he concluded.

Bridie clung to Anthony. 'He was asking about the store-room,' she said. 'He wanted to get in there.' There was no storeroom now. Everything had been destroyed in the Blitz. Muth was dead. She must try not to think about Sam's mother, not yet. Muth had been a difficult, wily, mischievous and totally lovable woman and Bridie would miss her terribly. But there was Liam to deal with first, so Bridie would grieve later and in private. 'The firemen are looking through the debris today. I doubt they'll find much.'

Michael Brennan joined Dr Richard Spencer at the door to Liam's room. 'Will he never get right?' asked the priest.

'No.'

'So he'll not be coming out of here?'

The doctor shrugged. 'He'll be moved from the prison infirmary to an asylum, I suppose. But he'll be restricted for the rest of his life.'

Michael Brennan sighed, turned round and faced the rest of the gathering. 'Bridie,' he began, 'the firemen managed to save a few pieces from your house and shop. One of them was a box containing a green stole. It was Liam's. It was given to me at the presbytery this morning. I recognized it right away as a part of the set made for Liam's ordination. It's been used as a weapon, so the proof we have lacked is with the police.' Sam had left a note in the tin. Surely the police would sit up and take notice now, because Liam's father had, on the day of his own death, taken the trouble to condemn one of his children.

Diddy began to cry. The proof existed. 'My poor Maureen,' she sobbed. 'My poor little girl. She had a big future, you know. She was going to be a singer, or a dancer, or both. And a priest did this to her. You're supposed to be able to trust priests, aren't you?' She carried on, but the rest of her words were drowned.

Brother Nicholas walked down the line and placed a hand on Diddy's head. 'Mrs Costigan, Father Bell's, or Brother Martin's illness is beyond all understanding. You see, he carried on quite nicely for much of the time. In fact, we have not had a better solo vocalist or a more talented carver of wood in many years. Sadly, genius and madness are separated by a hair so fine that only the Almighty can see it.'

'Then why doesn't the so-called Almighty do something about it?' snapped Diddy. 'If He can see it, He can stop it. Can't He?'

Nicholas inclined his head. 'God saw the plague and He sees the war. Mankind makes its own way towards the hereafter. God is not there to make our path easy.'

'Maureen's lesson was on the sharp side,' said Billy. 'What good will come of rape? Did you know he left her pregnant, Brother Nicholas? She tried to kill herself. She went out of her mind and had to be put away. Is that what God planned for her?'

'She'll get her reward,' replied the monk.

Diddy jumped to her feet. 'Her reward would be his head on a plate with an apple stuck in the gob. Her reward would be him swinging at the end of a rope. He finished my Maureen off as if he'd taken a gun to her. She's never been right since. An eye for an eye. Isn't that in the Bible somewhere?'

'It is,' replied the brother.

'Then I want to see him. I want to talk to him.' Diddy

574

wiped her face and stood with her feet wide apart, as if steadying herself. 'I'm not leaving this hospital till I've seen him,' she declared.

Michael Brennan glanced through the glass panel. 'He's still asleep. And if we carry on making all this noise, we'll be thrown out.'

Dr Spencer drew Father Brennan aside and began a whispered conference. Diddy, whose hackles were truly up, tackled the two men. 'What are you hiding and whispering about?'

Richard said nothing. He turned on his heel and walked off down the corridor.

Diddy chose Anthony as her next target. 'You must have known,' she accused. 'You can't have gone through life not realizing that your brother was mad.'

Anthony nodded, made no reply.

'Then why didn't you tell us?'

Michael Brennan stepped into the arena. 'Don't blame Anthony, Diddy. Don't you dare get on your high horse to him. He screamed blue murder at the police fifteen years ago, just after Val was murdered. Anthony was treated like a fool, and the law, which really is a total fool, hanged another man for the crime.'

Diddy dropped back into the chair, fixed her gimlet eye on Anthony. 'Val? He killed Val?'

'Yes.' Anthony chose not to elaborate.

'Is there anything else?' asked Big Diddy Costigan.

'Lots,' said Anthony wearily.

'What do you mean by lots?' Diddy persisted. 'Lots of what?'

'Lots of stuff the police should have looked into years ago,' answered Father Brennan. 'Now, we can't stay here all day. We've all been interviewed by police and doctors, so we've done what we came to do.'

Diddy was not prepared to budge. 'I'll go when I've seen him,' she said. 'And not before.' She folded her arms as a gesture of defiance.

Richard Spencer returned with a man in a white coat. 'Diddy, this is Dr Moss. He'll take us into Liam's room for a couple of minutes. Any nonsense and you'll be out of there quick smart.'

Diddy took Billy's arm and dragged him across the corridor.

Dr Moss, a small man with bad skin and spectacles, looked uncertainly at Richard.

'It will be all right,' said Richard Spencer.

Dr Moss led the party into Liam Bell's room. Anthony and Bridie hovered in the doorway, while Richard, Dr Moss, Diddy and Billy approached the bed. Diddy stopped in her tracks. 'He's strapped in,' she said.

Lengths of leather with buckle fastenings kept the patient from leaving his bed. The upper half of his face was almost as white as the pillow, while the chin remained hidden behind a beard whose glossy black was streaked with grey. 'He's tied up,' she said.

Dr Moss nodded, then pushed the glasses along the bridge of his short nose. 'He came in raving, Mrs ... er ...'

'Costigan,' whispered Diddy. She had not expected this, had not believed that she would find Liam so silent and vulnerable. His forehead, which had always been brown, was pale, waxy, almost unreal, the only colour provided by the bruising. She searched inside herself for a spark of the anger she had nursed since the attack on Maureen, found nothing at all. There was no temper, no hysteria, no forgiveness. Like Maureen, Diddy felt nothing.

Anthony left Bridie, walked into the room and stared down at his brother. When Liam's eyes opened, Anthony forced himself to remain where he was.

'Liam's brother,' said the man in the bed.

Anthony was riveted to the spot. Had he tried to move, he would have failed. The man was looking at him, was even trying to smile, though that coldness was still in his face. 'Hello, Liam,' Anthony managed with great difficulty.

'I am...' The drugs slowed Martin's words. 'I am Brother Martin,' he finally managed. 'Of *Frères ... de la ... Croix de St Pierre.*'

In the doorway, Bridie turned and grabbed Father Brennan's hand. Father Brennan was weeping softly, his lips moving in prayer. 'Pray for him, Father,' begged Bridie. 'And for Anthony, too.' With the priest's warm hand in hers, she felt stronger.

Anthony continued to stand by the bed. 'Martin?' he asked.

'Yes?' The eyes rolled in an effort to remain open.

'Where is Liam?'

There was a short pause. 'Scotland Road. The stole. Punishing the Irishwoman. Stop him.'

Anthony took a deep breath. 'Will he come back to you?'

'I don't know. Can ... can never tell what ... Liam might do.'

Diddy stumbled to the door, grabbed Bridie and Father Brennan, her large fingers digging into their arms. 'I want to go home,' she said. 'You were right, he is crackers. It would be like belting a sick dog.'

'A pound of flesh is not always the answer, Diddy,' said Michael Brennan. 'Revenge is often less than sweet.'

'There is no revenge,' answered Diddy. 'It would be like putting a bullet through a ghost.'

Bridie walked along Scotland Road for what she thought might be the last time for some months, at least. She was to be married for a second time in the Church of St

Aloysius Gonzaga, would be joined to Anthony in just a few short days. Deliberately alone for now, she gazed upon the place she had come to love over the years, a place that seemed to be diminishing by the day.

Striding over a fireman's hose, Bridie studied what was left of the Rotunda, the famous theatre known locally as Old Roundy. Here, she had sat with her daughters to watch pantomimes and variety shows, had joined in with the singing, had seen Shauna and Cathy bright-eyed with pleasure at the exploits of some deliberately inept magician. It was dead now.

Hitler knew where to kick, all right. The Port of Liverpool had taken a hammering for almost six months, though May had been the worst. With Liverpool and London disabled, the Germans thought they would be walking through England within weeks. 'But they won't,' she whispered to herself. 'Never in a million years.'

'Hello, Mrs Bell,' called Flash Flanagan. 'I see you've come to wave the old place goodbye.' He parked his cart and pointed to the ruins. 'We've had some fun in there.'

'I know.'

Flash sniffed back a tear. 'Me and little Maureen Costigan used to entertain the queues. She had a lovely voice.' He coughed. 'They found the stole, then.'

'Yes.'

'Where is he?'

'In the mental hospital near St Helens.'

Flash nodded, lit a cigarette. 'He finished Maureen off, that bad bugger. She's not the same, is she? I hear she's back with her mam and dad, though. If I shut my eyes, I can see her now with her little dance frock and tap shoes. Everybody loved her. I think they got as much pleasure out of her as they got inside the Rotunda.' He spat out a flake of tobacco. 'They'll not bother rebuilding,' he said sadly. 'Like everything else, it'll just get left. Diddy Costigan's right, you know. It'll all look like this in twenty years.'

Bridie agreed with him, though she made no reply. The area was devastated. There had been a mass burial at Anfield Cemetery just days earlier, some 500 people whose injuries had rendered them unrecognizable. Regardless of creed, the remains had been placed in one huge grave over which representatives of many faiths had prayed. Sometimes, it seemed hopeless.

'You all right, queen?' asked the old tramp.

'I'm fine.' She wasn't. She was about to abandon the old neighbourhood to set up home with Anthony and the girls in Astleigh Fold. She felt like a traitor.

Flash said goodbye, then trundled onward with his old cart. As Bridie watched him, she felt that he somehow embodied a way of life that was doomed to extinction. In a tidier Britain, there would be little room for eccentricities like his.

As she surveyed the road, Bridie found herself smiling in spite of her sadness. Razor Sharpe's shop was still standing, though the window had been boarded up. He had pinned a notice to the timber, 'NO LECKY, NO GAS, NO WINDOWS. IF YOU WANT A HAIRCUT, BRING YOUR OWN CANDLE. IF YOU WANT A SHAVE, BRING BANDAGES. IODINE PROVIDED FREE OF CHARGE'. Dolly Hanson was still in business, though the upper storey no longer existed. A butcher displayed a poster of Hitler bending down. On the Fuhrer's backside sat the words 'BEST RUMP ON ORDER, DELIVERY PENDING'. No matter what was thrown at them, the Scottie Roaders remained unbowed.

Bridie looked up at the barrage balloons pulling fruitlessly at their steel anchorage. They resembled huge, legless insects. In the side streets, some houses stood, others had been removed like bad teeth. There were craters and fire-hoses everywhere, and the air smelled dirty, tasted terrible.

She reached the undertaker's, saw a coffin lid propped casually next to the door. This piece bore the legend ADOLF HITLER crudely painted in runny whitewash. How on earth would the Germans have coped with people like these? They were un-put-downable, cheeky, resilient and very powerful.

Lord Haw-Haw was doing his best, of course. He had been on the wireless again talking about Mary Blunn, a very famous little woman who sold fruit outside the cinemas. The 'Gairmany calling' messages were a source of great amusement to the locals. 'Mary Ellens?' they would say. 'He's the biggest bloody Mary of all, a right little mammy's boy. Wait till we get hold of him. We'll set Mary Blunn and all her mates on him – they'll soon wipe the haw-haw out of him.'

Bridie leaned against Razor Sharpe's boarded-up window. Razor himself put in an appearance. 'Want a tidy up, love?' he asked, scissors waving in the air.

Bridie grinned at him. Good old Razor carried on with his job in the shop, only to spend his nights running round with buckets of sand and water. Rumour had it that he kept a specially sharpened open razor in his back pocket, an item religiously honed to perfection in case he caught a Jerry. 'I'll peel his onions for him, all right,' Razor was heard to boast when in his cups.

'Bloody mess, eh?' he asked.

'It is,' agreed Bridie.

He stepped onto the pavement. 'Listen, love. You get yourself gone out of here. It's soft stopping here when there's no need. Think of your girls. Think what you can do for all the children who've been shunted out of their homes.'

Bridie turned to him and threw her arms around his neck. 'I'll miss you all, Razor,' she told him. 'Flash and the Mary Ellens and the market. It got hit again, I'm told. And there they all are again with their bits of wood and corrugated iron.'

Razor blushed. He wasn't used to holding a woman in broad daylight, especially a woman as pretty as this one. 'They'll not do us down, Bridie. They're only a load of bloody foreigners.'

She smiled at him, planted a kiss on his cheek, then carried on walking. He was right – she had to go. Shauna was already living in Anthony's cottage. Edith was seeking a bigger house for Bridie so that all four of them could live together. Fortunately, Bridie could withstand the loss of her business, because the Cathshaw Stables provided the bulk of her not inconsiderable income.

At last, she reached her 'new' shop. It had taken a bit of a blast, but it was steady enough. Diddy and Billy Costigan had refused to accept charity. The business would continue to be Bell's, and the Costigans intended to take their weekly pay, no more than that. There were few antiques, as most had perished with Muth, but Billy had scraped together some bits and pieces for the window.

Maureen emerged. 'It'll be mostly chandlery,' she informed her boss. 'And I'm helping on Paddy's, too. Our Nicky's busy down at Littlewood's, so the stall will be my responsibility.'

'Thanks for all you did for Muth's funeral,' said Bridie. 'Anthony and I really appreciate your efforts.'

Maureen picked up a broom and began to sweep the cluttered pavement. 'I'll stop at home till the war's over,' she told Bridie. 'Then, I'm going to . . .' Cathy knew. And Mam and Dad. But for the most part, Maureen kept her dream to herself.

Bridie was pleased. Maureen was still a lovely young

woman. Maureen had always intended to go into the theatre, and she would probably do quite well. 'How's your mother now?' she asked.

Maureen stopped sweeping. 'Well, she's accepted it. I mean, she couldn't clobber Father Bell, could she? Because he isn't who he was when he did it. And she's pleased because I'm feeling better.' She paused, looked hard at Bridie. 'It's no fault of yours or Anthony's,' she said. 'Or Father Brennan's. That po-faced policeman would never listen to anyone who wasn't a Mason or an Orange Lodger. Still, at least he's lost his job over it.'

Bridie sighed heavily. When would the Catholic versus Protestant match be over? The game was well into extra time, had gone on for centuries. She wished with all her heart that the antagonism would cease. Still, the war had brought the factions together, though only when strictly necessary.

'I'll miss you,' said Maureen. 'And I'll miss Cathy, too.' She grieved also for the countryside, for the smell of new-mown hay and the whinny of horses.

'You can visit after the war,' suggested Bridie.

'We'll see,' replied Maureen. She picked up the broom and attacked the dust of war. 'Yes, we'll see.'

She wore a bit of dyed silk that had been intended for a parachute. It occurred to Bridie that she might be depriving the occupant of some crippled plane a chance to jump out safely, but Edith reassured her. 'It has a couple of flaws,' she explained. 'It will hold together for a wedding, but not for hundreds of feet.' She arranged Bridie's bouquet of roses and gypsy grass.

Bridie gazed at herself in the mirror over Diddy's mantelpiece. She had lived here for a couple of weeks, had sheltered in a Morrison under the stairs. Public shelters continued to be one of Bridie's nightmares.

Tildy, Maureen, Shauna and Cathy were bridesmaids, but Nicky had gone to work as usual. The noise from the gaggle of female attendants drifted down the stairs. Bridie remembered her last wedding, the one she had attended with great reluctance and two unhappy children. There had been an over-large wedding ring and an unknown groom.

'That shade of blue suits you,' declared Edith. The material had turned out a bit streaky, and the dye would not survive washing, but the overall effect was pleasing. 'I'm pleased that you and Anthony are to be legal at last,' she said. Edith had tolerated the relationship eventually, though her discomfort had sometimes been obvious.

Bridie grinned ruefully. 'Sam knew, Edith. He left me to Anthony like a bequest.' And Father Michael Brennan had almost lost his parish because of Bridie. He was an unusual priest, she thought, very human, very gentle and understanding.

'And I'm glad you're leaving this place,' said Edith. 'It is far too dangerous.'

Bridie swivelled round and faced her companion. 'That's not why I'm going,' she answered quietly. 'I'm leaving because my husband lives elsewhere.' There was a void in her heart, an emptiness created by the imminent loss of her dearest friends. 'I love Scotland Road,' she said firmly.

Edith tightened her lips. Had it not been for the intervention of Lord Derby, many more would be dying in the raids. Whole families travelled each evening to Lord Derby's estate. They slept in his property, then returned to their work and schools every morning.

Bridie took something from her shopping bag and

pushed it into a pocket. 'I'm ready,' she said. Anthony would be waiting at the church. This time, he would not be sitting with a crying Shauna, would not be watching his twin brother officiating at the altar.

The bridesmaids, also in dyed silks, clattered down the stairway. Bridie looked at her beautiful daughters, thought about Cathy's success at school, about Shauna's undeniable courage. Tildy was grinning from ear to ear, while Maureen simply stood looking elegant and composed. 'You are all lovely,' said Bridie.

Tildy stuck out her tongue. 'Come on, then,' she said. 'Let's get it over with. I'm expected at what's left of the library in a couple of hours.'

Diddy came in with Billy. She wore a typically dreadful hat, with the same murderous hatpin skewering the less than lovely creation to her tightly curled hair. She was going to miss Bridie. Holidays had been offered, yet it would never be the same. Bridie was part of the neighbourhood. Would she have stayed if the shop had survived the bombing? Yes, she would have remained until Sam's mother's death, Diddy answered herself.

Bridie held out her arms and pulled Diddy close. 'Don't let them take it all away,' she whispered. 'After the war, they'll start moving you out.'

Diddy laughed grimly. 'They'll need a battering ram for my house, love. Come on, this is your happy day.' She pulled away, straightened her collar. 'Onward Christian soldiers,' she cried. 'Billy? Have you cleaned them shoes?'

Bridie left the house and took the arm of Dr Richard Spencer. He was a splendid man, so much nicer than the one who had given her away last time. They stepped over holes in the pavement, avoided stretches of hose, picked their way carefully to the church.

The organ played triumphantly. Bridie looked at the packed church, wondered where they had all come from.

In the middle of a very cruel war, the folk of Scotland Road had made time for her and for Anthony. No matter what Liam had done, these people forgave unreservedly.

She stood next to her lover, made her promises happily, then signed the register in the presence of Michael Brennan. Looking a bit wet around the eyes, the priest laughed and joked about how much he loved a happy ending.

Outside, a few Brownie cameras took snaps, while Richard Spencer used his better camera to mark the occasion. Bridie kissed her husband, kissed her children and everyone else within reach, then walked back to Diddy's on Anthony's arm.

'What is that in your pocket?' asked Anthony. 'Your mother's rosary?' He had noticed how his bride had kept plunging her hand into the pocket of her skirt.

Bridie took out the item and showed it to Anthony. 'It's all we have left of Sam,' she said.

Anthony opened the lid, saw the bits of dried-up Virginia and a wedding band. 'Oh, Bridie,' he said, 'how did I manage to get through life this far without you?'

They dried their tears on a shared handkerchief, then strode on towards their wedding breakfast.

1984

Dr Caitlin O'Brien, a woman in her early sixties and of average height and build, rose from her desk and picked up a pile of books. She placed them in a carton with the photographs she had removed from the walls. Today, she would retire.

How many years had she been at this hospital? She knew every crack in the walls, every corridor, every ward. Thirty, almost exactly, she told herself. Thirty years spent digging her way into the minds of others. Psychiatrists, she often told herself, were probably the sickest of all people, because they had chosen to spend their lives investigating human behaviour. There was a dent in her door where an agitated man had tried to smash a chair, and an odd section of glass had taken up residence in one of the windows. The original piece had been removed by an unhappy woman bent on suicide.

Cait dragged a packet of Benson's from her bottomless bag and rummaged for a lighter. Inhaling deeply, she pulled out all the photographs again and lined them up along her desk. The largest was a black-and-white print of the Costigan family, Billy, Diddy, Charlie, Nicky with her Graham Pile, Maureen and Tildy. Jimmy did not feature, because Jimmy had never returned after the war. This picture had been taken on a very special day, the day when the church bells had rung again after a long silence.

The bells of Scotland Road had pealed, but Bell's shop was no more.

'You saw his grave,' Cait whispered to Diddy. Diddy had been drunk to the point of unconsciousness when she had finally agreed to be poured onto the aeroplane. Of course, with two airborne journeys under her belt, Diddy had extolled very loudly the virtues of flying, though she had been no further than Blackpool since.

Cait closed her eyes, pushed herself backwards in time to the fateful day when Diddy had moved to Kirkby. The house was boarded up like a fortress. Mammy and Anthony were there, trying to shout words of wisdom through a letterbox that no longer existed. Diggers and lorries were backed all the way down Scotland Road, the workforce standing by idly while waiting to demolish the street.

'I'll come out in a coffin,' screamed Diddy from somewhere within the citadel.

Tildy and Maureen stood on the pavement with Cait. Nicky and her Graham had emigrated to Canada, had taken Charlie with them. Shauna, too, was in Canada. She had married her Canadian sailor, had set up in business with Nicky and Graham. The cakes and pies from Pile's English Bakeries were sold all over the New World.

'Mam?' shouted Tildy. She had left her children at home with their dad, a nice, quiet chap with a string of fish and chip shops. Tildy lived in Waterloo, had managed to avoid the exodus to Kirkby. 'Mam? What about food?'

'I've got a fridge full,' came the snappy reply. 'And a load of tinned stuff.'

'It'll run out,' replied the ever sensible Tildy. 'What happens when you run out?' She glanced at her watch and frowned. Tildy was supposed to be ordering new stock at the Picton Library. 'Mam? Do you want to starve?'

No answer was forthcoming.

Father Brennan arrived. 'Bring yourselves out of that house this minute,' he ordered. 'Billy Costigan? Wasn't enough harm done the day you marched on the council offices and got yourselves arrested? You'll be in trouble again, Diddy,' he continued. 'You've made your point.' Reporters and cameramen were arriving. 'When you built your bonfire on the steps of the civic buildings, you expressed how you felt, right enough.'

Cait tried again. 'You can't stay,' she told her imprisoned friends. 'The house comes down today.'

'Then we come down with it,' screamed Big Diddy.

Cait turned to the priest. He was well into his eighties, yet he remained sprightly for a man so large. 'What do we do?' she asked helplessly.

Michael Brennan grinned. 'What did we ever do with them, Cathy?' He always used Cait's baby name when he saw her. 'Wasn't that the most glorious family you ever met?' He sighed heavily. 'Scotland Road was all about family. They survived because they had one another. If a child returned to an empty house, sure he had a dozen aunties and uncles who would give him shelter and a bite.'

Cait bit her lip, thought about what was happening here. The houses were being destroyed along with a whole way of life. 'Will they keep them together in Kirkby and Huyton?' she asked.

Father Brennan had a theory, but he kept it to himself. The words 'divide and rule' had sat at the forefront of his mind for several years. He had seen some of the earlier letters, had wondered over possible ambiguities. Some of the Scottie Roaders had been overjoyed to move away. Promises of bathrooms and inside toilets had been dangled like carrots before donkeys. There would be green fields, space, newly built council flats and houses. But many had moved to Kirkby in the mistaken belief that their old homes would be demolished and rebuilt.

'Father?'

'Yes, Cathy?'

'Will they keep the extended families together, within reach of one another?'

'No. They'll be put where they fit and they'll fit where they're put and to hell with what they might be wanting.'

'God,' breathed Cait.

'I've said a word or two to Him myself,' replied the priest. 'We've women coming back here two and three times a week to shop. They stand where their houses used to be, and the sadness in their faces would break the hardest heart. They've few shops out there, you know. And a boy I met told me about his dad walking to work every day with the other dockers. The lad would stand at his window and watch a river of ants making its way homeward each evening. Those ants were working men travelling home after a day's toil. Let's hope they get some more buses soon.'

Tildy was becoming upset. The bailiffs had arrived with large hammers and tin helmets. 'Stand back,' roared one of them. He swung his hammer while Tildy ran at him. She clouted him across his back with her shopping bag. 'My mam's nearly seventy,' she roared at him. Cameras clicked. A BBC outside broadcast crew filmed the action.

Anthony grabbed Tildy's arm. 'Leave them to it,' he said quietly.

'They're pulling my bloody house down,' cried Tildy. Huge tears ran down her face while newsmen moved in on their prey. 'Bugger off,' yelled Tildy. 'You're like Dracula, always drinking in other folks' lifeblood and misery.' Since becoming a qualified librarian, Tildy had adopted a colourful turn of phrase.

The hardened crews remained unmoved, kept their film rolling.

Bridie pushed aside the man with the hammer. 'Diddy?' she called.

'What?'

'You can't stop it. You can't stop what's happening. And you've a good man in there who's recovering from a heart attack. This will do him no good at all. Diddy, it's like trying to hold back an erupting volcano. No matter what you do, the house is coming down.'

A reporter approached Bridie. 'Is there anything you would like to say to our readers?'

Bridie stared into the dispassionate eye of a television camera. 'Oh, yes,' she replied sweetly. 'I've plenty to say.' She eyed the newspaper man, smiled over-sweetly at the television crew. 'This is euthanasia,' she said. 'Many of the younger folk have moved on voluntarily – not all to Kirkby, I might say – to better themselves, yet here's the hero of the piece,' she waved a hand at the man with the hammer, 'come to throw out the older people. They don't need to go yet. Why drag them screaming all the way to those little cardboard houses with no shops, no cinema, insufficient buses? Why? Can't they have their last years in peace in the place they love?'

The hammer-wielder spoke up. 'Only doing me job,' he grumbled.

'As were Herod and Pontius Pilate,' she answered smartly. 'And they won no medals. The schools here have been excellent. They have bred a generation of successful people.' She dragged her elder daughter into the frame. 'See this one of mine? She's a doctor. She started off here at Father Brennan's school. My other daughter spent most of her school years at St Aloysius Gonzaga, and she now runs her own business with other Scotland Road people out in Canada. There is no better grounding anywhere. So they're destroying it.'

'There will be new schools,' said the BBC man.

'Not like these,' replied Cait. 'Schooling here has been strict and old-fashioned, none of your Maria Montessori learn-if-you-feel-like-it and never mind the spelling. And the streets have a soul of their own.' She pushed past her mother and grabbed the arm of a reporter. 'Write this down,' she insisted. 'Those who have gone ahead are not happy. You can give them all the bathrooms in the world, gold-plated taps and tiled walls. But they'll still miss their homes.'

The door opened. Billy Costigan stepped into the street. 'My wife will be just a minute,' he said.

Reporters gathered round him, threatened to swallow him up. Since his illness, Billy had shrunk in stature, was stooped and tired.

Father Brennan raised his voice. 'Get away from that man,' he shouted.

'Billy! We're here, Billy!'

Everyone swivelled round to see an army marching up the street. They had come from council estates all over Liverpool to watch Diddy and Billy's last stand. The news people backed off hurriedly to save their precious equipment from the advancing troops. Billy mopped his face with a hanky, then turned to watch his wife closing the door.

'What about your furniture?' asked Anthony.

'They can have it and welcome,' snapped Big Diddy. 'We might as well have everything new while we're at it.' She smiled at her dark-clad daughter. Maureen looked so pretty in black. 'You're quiet, girl.'

Maureen hugged her mother. 'You'll be fine.'

'Will I?' asked Diddy.

While the crowd jeered and cheered, Diddy's suitcases were loaded into a waiting car. As she left the street for the last time, Diddy did not look back.

The phone rang. Cait, forced back into the present day, answered. She replied to questions, replaced the receiver, sat with elbows on the desk, chin in her hands. Diddy Costigan had died suddenly within weeks of leaving the house in which she had been born. Billy, older and frailer than his years, had lasted a further six months.

Cait looked at the images of Edith and Richard Spencer who had left her all their worldly goods. She lived at Cherry Hinton, kept the stables going, drove daily to her work. How good the Spencers had been, how kind and loving.

Sam stared out of the next frame, watch-chain pulled across his chest, a trilby hiding the threatening baldness. Cait did not remember him in great detail, yet she always smiled when she saw his picture. It was like greeting an old friend after a long separation. Sam had given her Noel, that grand, mixed-up dog who had lived to be almost fifteen.

She picked up a tiny snap of Grandmuth, the wonderful lady who had died in the Blitz. 'Get yerself outside of a bowl of porridge every morning, love. It'll stick ter yer ribs and keep you well-lined for winter.' Grandmuth had been full of advice, full of a gentle sort of wickedness.

Last of all, there was Mammy and Anthony. A love such as theirs was a rare specimen. During their marriage, there had been few cross words and buckets of laughter. Cait closed her eyes, saw Mammy running through the fields with sixty-odd evacuees on her heels. She saw Anthony watching Mammy, as if he would die without the sight of her.

Dr Cait O'Brien sniffed back a drop of moisture. Mammy had died just weeks earlier, and Cait's grief had been weighted down beneath mounds of work. Tomorrow, she would visit the graveyard where the lovers shared their final rest. Since Anthony's death, Mammy had been fading away, had breathed her last while sleeping. 'I bet you were dreaming of him the night you died,' Cait told the photograph. 'I miss you, Mammy.'

She walked to the window and looked down on the lawn where voluntary patients strolled, played ball games, sat reading or knitting. Another part of Cait's life was over. The future promised to be different, though her love of animals and the urge to travel would keep her active, no doubt. Cait had never married, had never found her Anthony. Perhaps living in the shadow of so blissful a relationship had encouraged her to higher her standards. Mr Right had not appeared. 'I'm an old maid,' she told herself aloud. 'And talking to myself. Perhaps I should stay on here and book a bed.'

In the centre of the desk stood the clock that was her farewell gift from the staff. It ticked away the seconds of its new owner's life, chimed when it touched five o'clock. 'That's it,' she said. 'One more little job, and I'm out of here.'

Her step was light as she made her way along the corridor. Retirement was going to be an adventure, a test of her ingenuity. Twenty-four hours in each day, and she intended to fill them. There was her sister in Canada, there were nieces and nephews, places she had longed to see. She intended to 'do' America and Canada next year. Then there was Europe, Asia, Africa. She would see New Zealand, Australia, the five oceans and every sea on earth. Life was just beginning, she reminded herself.

Cait pushed open the door of a single room. 'Brother Martin?'

He was at his prie-dieu, the hood of his blue-grey habit hanging down his back. The rosary clicked between gnarled fingers, while his lips moved in prayer. 'A moment,

Doctor,' he replied. At the grand age of eighty-four, Martin Waring continued to work and pray daily.

Cait turned, nodded and smiled at the nun in the corner. Brother Martin allowed just two visitors – Cait and Sister Margaret Mary. The latter was polishing some fine wood carvings while she waited for the brother to finish his prayers.

He rose eventually, smiled at Cait. 'So we are losing you today,' he said. 'You will be missed.' He went to a shelf and picked up a wooden figure. 'I made this for you,' he said. 'Enjoy it in good health.'

Cait took the gift. It was an owl with its wings wide-spread as it landed on a branch. 'It's beautiful,' she said.

Martin picked up a knife and carried on working. In all his years as a patient, he had given little trouble. Liam did not visit him any more; Liam had disappeared beneath layers of drugs and treatments. Brother Martin was allowed tools for five hours each day, and he handed them back in good order each afternoon.

Sister Margaret Mary stood up and placed the finished work on the shelf. She took Cait's hand in hers. 'God bless you for all the good work you have done, Cait.'

Cait knew that she was going to cry. 'Sister, I'll be in touch with you and with Brother Martin.'

'You'll be in our prayers,' said Margaret Mary.

The two women said their goodbyes to the patient, then went out into the corridor. Cait stroked the smooth wings of an owl which had been carved by a murderer.

'I'll see you soon,' said the nun.

Cait rubbed away the tears with a cuff of her cardigan. In the face of Sister Margaret Mary, the doctor saw all that she had loved and lost. 'Keep well,' she said.

The woman who had been raped by Liam Bell, who was Martin Waring's only visitor, swished her black-clad way towards the hospital exit.

'They had guts and they had love,' murmured Cait.

Margaret Mary turned in the doorway. 'Ta-ra, queen,' she said, laughter in the words.

'Ta-ra, Maureen. I'll be seeing yer!'

THE END